THE END OF IT ALL

She sat there, trying to take it all in, trying to fathom what her husband was telling her. A world without daylight . . . a place where their children might never snatch at a dust mote floating within a sunbeam. She wanted to say something, *anything,* but she couldn't get her mouth to work. Next to her, Frank was silent for a long time while thunder rumbled across the gale-flattened cornfields. Eventually he gathered her in his arms and held her tight, and his words were the most frightening of any she'd heard so far.

"It's all so *fragile,* Crystal, thousands of years of evolution wiped out in the space of a single week. And civilization? By the time Millennium is through, I don't think there'll be such a thing."

Bantam Books by
Yvonne Navarro

AfterAge
Species
deadrush
Aliens: Music of the Spears

FINAL IMPACT

YVONNE NAVARRO

BANTAM BOOKS
NEW YORK TORONTO LONDON SYDNEY AUCKLAND

FINAL IMPACT
A Bantam Book

PUBLISHING HISTORY
Bantam edition / February 1997

ISBN 0-553-56360-2

Published simultaneously in the United States and Canada

Bantam Books are published by Bantam Books, a division of Bantam Doubleday
Dell Publishing Group, Inc. Its trademark, consisting of the words "Bantam Books"
and the portrayal of a rooster, is Registered in U.S. Patent and Trademark Office
and in other countries. Marca Registrada. Bantam Books, 1540 Broadway, New
York, New York 10036.

PRINTED IN THE UNITED STATES OF AMERICA

OPM   10   9   8   7   6   5   4   3   2   1

This novel is dedicated
to three friends:

JEFFREY OSIER
For years of confidence, support and
friendship, pep talks,
don't-give-ups,
and a mind of gold.

TAMMY THOMPSON
You'll never laugh
or cry alone
as long as you
have me.

WAYNE ALLEN SALLEE
Who jumpstarted everything.
A person so special that God knew the world
could handle only one of him.
For ten-plus years of wild and wonderful friendship
that will endure into the Millennium and longer.

Endless thanks to . . .

Don VanderSluis and Richard A. Marasas, Jr., M.S., for helping plot the end of civilization as we all know it, and to Peter Kenter for checking to see that it worked. Who else could have done it so well?

Howard Morhaim, who is sharp, enthusiastic, and always debonair;

Anne Lesley Groell, for amazing patience, humor, and insight;

Paula Guran, Kurt and Amy Wimberger, Brian Hodge and Dolly Nickel, Tammy Thompson, Tina Jens, Jay Bonansinga, Barrett McGivney, John Platt, Steven Spruill, Beth Massie, Alexa deMonterice, Eric Secker, Marty Cochran, Sean and Jessica Doolittle, Kathleen Jurgens, Harry Fassl and Diana Gallardo, and Augie Wiedemann, each of whom has given a smidgen of themselves in enthusiasm or encouragement to keep me going on this seemingly endless project;

Cathy Van Patten, Jeffrey Osier, Peter Kenter, Don Kinney, Fred Hirt and a number of folks on the J. Pournelle roundtable on Genie who answered questions and offered information;

And Kevin Greggain, who has the patience of a saint.

I wonder if this one is long enough for Ed.

Come visit:

http://www.para-net.com/nynavarro

***

PROLOGUE
MOLDING THE FUTURE

STEPLAND, TEXAS
1971...

"You are part Mexican, and part Papago Indian, child—a red-skin. Always remember that, and always be proud of it."

I am a redskin.

My skin is red.

What is ... red?

It was October, her father said they were in Stepland, Texas, and that Stepland was a small, dusty town somewhere at the bottom of God's left foot.

Water must have been scarce, too precious to spare for the bushes that lined the parking lot of the Zayre store into which Magena Casilde's parents turned the family car, a 1957 DeSoto so rusted out that Gena could smell the decaying metal every time she climbed in or out of the back door. She didn't know how many bushes had been planted along the curbs and in the centers of the small concrete islands that occasionally divided the parking lot into orderly driving lanes. There couldn't have been many. As the car eased past each one, Gena could hear the bare branches rubbing against each other, a dry rustling that sounded like someone shaking a bag of toothpicks.

In the front seat, her mother and father were silent. Usually they fought, rocking the inside of the never-stopping car and Gena's overdeveloped hearing with their shouts and curses, slamming hands and whatever else was within reach against the cracked dashboard for emphasis. Old containers from the cheapest fast-food places, empty beer cans, or crumpled road maps were all fair game. Their raging made her head hurt and her ears ring but she would have preferred it to the ominous sound of nothing that now oozed through the interior. At least it would have meant that things were *normal*, that they weren't going to—

Gena bit down hard on her bottom lip, worrying at the soft flesh with her small top teeth, not trying to break the skin but hoping the pain would turn her attention away from what she had come to call The Black Future. The Black Future was relatively new, born of her parents' unspoken decision five days ago in a different town, a different state, and she didn't care enough about the place, now far away and like a thousand others in her short life, to try to remember its name or location. She was not supposed to know The Black Future but she did, though she didn't know *how* she knew. That was just the way it was.

Her small hands, road dirt etched into the fine, babyish creases between the fingers, clenched into fists and rested on the seat on either side of her. The fabric of the seat should have been comforting, its worn wrinkles and small tears filled with the familiar smells of her parents' cigarette smoke and the little-girl sweat of her skin from nearly a thousand days of traveling, of exploring every inch of the nubby material with her roughened fingertips and finding every secret lost among the folds between the seat and its back. But she found no comfort there now, only black dread.

"Here," her father said as Gena felt the DeSoto slow, then stop. He was trying to sound normal so she wouldn't be scared, but his heavily accented voice, so rich and melodious even in anger, was stiff and unnaturally formal. "*Aquí*—this is a good spot."

Gena's left fist unclenched and her fingers brushed the surface of the seat until they found Sunshine, the worn little rag doll that had been her only companion in the back seat of this car. She had named the doll Sunshine because holding it made her feel warm, the way the sun's rays did when they bathed her face through the car windows. Now, in the ninety-five-degree heat and the stuffy back seat of the DeSoto, Gena felt cold, the doll felt cold, the car felt cold, her *parents* felt cold. Sunshine could do nothing to warm her in the face of The Black Future. Still, Gena was loath to leave the doll behind and her small fingertips caressed the frayed yarn hair longingly for a moment before curling next to her leg again.

"Here, Gena," her mother said. Usually her voice was husky and comforting, but today it was tired and thin, too many arguments, too many tears, such a huge thing she was about to do. "We're going to let you out here by the door while we go park the car. Don't forget to take Sunshine with you."

"I'm going to leave Sunshine here," Gena said softly. She slid reluctantly to the passenger side and waited for her mother to open the door, trying to burn into her mind the way the car had felt and smelled in happier times, before The Black Future had come to her parents' minds and then, in the way that things did, had passed to Gena.

"Leave her here?" her mother repeated, bewildered. "Are—are you sure you want to do that, honey?"

"Yes." Her mother hadn't counted on that. Normally Gena took the doll everywhere with her, but she'd had almost a week to decide about today.

Silence as her mother and father thought about this, then her mother opened the door and got out. Her steps on the gravel-strewn concrete faltered a bit, then she opened the back passenger door and Gena turned on the seat and carefully climbed down. Her mother's cold hand wrapped around her small forearm to steady her; Gena remembered when that touch had been warm and full of love. Things would change a lot in the next couple of hours.

"Okay," her mother said as she walked Gena the short distance to the sidewalk in front of the store. "You stand right here. We'll be back in a minute." Now her mother sounded as though someone had encircled her throat with a drawstring and pulled it tight.

Gena did as she'd been told and said nothing. The Black Future came full force then, as unstoppable in her own mind as the idea had apparently been in the minds of her parents. Felt for the first time nearly a week ago, The Black Future had been a series of impressions rather than true thoughts of the present, some too adult for her child's mind to understand, but the overall meaning was still clear—

Next month is my birthday, and I'll be four. In another year, I'll have to go to school and what will they do then? A regular school won't work, and who has the money for special schools? They would have to stop traveling and stay somewhere, the same place for a very long time, and they would hate that so much. And they would have to get jobs, but Papá has no green card— whatever that means. It's so hard to take care of me now, and it will be even worse next year—

"Are you sure you don't want Sunshine?" her mother asked shakily.

Gena shook her head and stayed where she was as her mother walked away, worn loafers scuffing across the concrete. Her mother opened the door on the passenger side of the DeSoto and climbed in. "Back in a minute," she repeated as she pulled the door shut. The words were hollow and dull-sounding, overpracticed.

"Good-bye, Mamá," Gena said clearly. "Good-bye, Papá." For a moment the silence returned and Gena thought they would change their minds.

Then they drove away.

Standing there as the people went in and out of the department store, nothing more to her than laughing and chattering breezes passing at uneven intervals, Gena thought about Sunshine and wished she hadn't been so stupid about leaving her on the seat. She'd had an idea that seeing the doll there would make them feel bad, maybe even make them come back for her, but now Gena didn't even have Sunshine to keep her company.

The first hour turned into two, then inched toward three. She was tired and hungry, and when she began to need a bathroom, Gena put her smudgy little hands to her face and started to cry. Someone passing her stopped immediately, then someone else, and suddenly there were a dozen breezes—people—around her and the questions were flying, fast and furious—

"Where's your mother, little girl?"

"She was out here when I went inside forty-five minutes ago!"

"How long have you been here?"

And the funniest one, of course—

"What do your parents look like?"

Gena didn't know; she'd never seen them. She'd never seen *anything.*

Stupid, stupid, *stupid*, she realized as someone took charge, someone who said he was a policeman and knew what to do about her. She should have kept little Sunshine with her, should never have let her mother and father drive away with her best friend.

Now she would never have Sunshine again, and the tears flowed harder, hot and stingy against her thin redskin cheeks. Her mother and father would not think about Sunshine as Gena had, or take care of her, or *love* her. At the first place they stopped, some road-side market or gas station far enough away from Stepland, Texas, and its Zayre store to be safe, they would do the same thing to Sunshine that they had done to Gena.

They would throw her away.

CHICAGO, ILLINOIS

"Mom," Simon said softly, "don't you think you'd better turn off the television? Dad'll be home any minute, and you know he don't like to see you watching it all the time."

Lila Chanowitz's eyes were dull as they stared at the image on the screen. It was color—the only color TV in this section of the building—and she didn't want to know where the money'd come from to buy it. It was what . . . four, five o'clock? Closer to five, probably; Simon had been home from school for a while and she'd heard him cleaning this morning's dishes in the kitchen and making the beds. She thought he might've wiped down the bathroom and picked up the dirty clothes, too. Such a good boy.

Such a shame.

"Mom," Simon said again. "Come on. I'll help you get dressed, okay? That way Dad won't be mad when he gets here."

Like he always is, was the unfinished line in her six-year-old son's head, and Lila heard it as clear as if he'd spoken it out loud. She couldn't seem to stop her whispered response any more than he could help his thoughts. "Don't make no difference, Channy. Today he's gonna be mad anyway." Simon had put his hand on her arm and she felt him flinch when she said the words. *I should've taken him away from all this,* she thought miserably. *After Zeke, I should have taken the boy and just got the hell out.* She'd been going to, oh sure, had once even packed up a bag for herself. But the timing'd been wrong, Zeke had still been a fresh and bleeding wound in her heart, and her mind was constantly fogged from the Bad Shit, the stuff that Searle had kept her pumped up on all the time to fuck up her head and blast away her memories of their tiny, dead son. The years had gone by, almost three of them, and now here was Channy—Searle hated it when she called him that, but sometimes it seemed so right—looking at his seventh birthday just three days away, a Christmas Eve baby. They didn't have a Christmas tree—Searle claimed they had no money—and little Channy thought his birthday was just another day, just another statement in the way the world worked. The sky is blue, today is my birthday, gym class is my favorite; nothing special there. This was their last year together, and she hadn't even gotten Channy a birthday card—

"You listen to me, Channy." She sat up suddenly, her voice fierce although it never rose above a whisper. Her hands where they gripped his little-boy arms were long-fingered and bony; already she could see that if he made it Simon would be shaped like her, with a long, lanky body and those prominent cheekbones that Searle always unkindly called "horsey." "When you grow up, don't be weak like me. Make your decisions and don't wait on someone else to do things for you—they never come through. Do things for yourself—don't let no one take control of your life like I done with your daddy. It ain't good, Channy. It ain't *healthy*." Her son looked confused, and despairing, Lila knew it was to much for him to understand, he was too young. She needed to explain things some more, needed him to *know* somehow. How do you explain money and drugs and gambling debts to a six-year-old? Or power, plain and simple? "Your dad—"

"How come you always know when Dad's gonna be pissed off when he gets home?" Simon suddenly interrupted.

Lila knew she should say something about his language, but she didn't bother. Things were going to happen tonight that would rip them apart, and a few dirty words from the mouth of a first-grader meant nothing in the huge, horrible face of the next few hours. But the boy had asked her a question, and it was an important one, wasn't it? The answer could reveal a lot—her black and white mood swings through the years, why she'd spent so much time escaping in the oblivion of the heroin that had left its scars on her arms and mind and life.

Scars. . . . Hers were nothing compared to the boy's. He had them everywhere—from cigarette burns for making too much noise during Searle's Sunday football game to the inch-long pale line that went through his soft bottom lip and faded into his chin, his daddy's gift for being too slow in taking out the garbage one night. A dozen more, but they were nothing, *nothing*, compared to the monstrous thing coming in a little while. And Lila knew already that she couldn't stop it.

But she hadn't answered Simon's question, had she?

"Because I . . . see things," she said slowly, "in my head. Stuff that people don't think can be seen, stuff that makes your daddy mad when I tell him about it."

"Then why do you *tell* him? Why don't you keep it a secret?"

She frowned and the blurred shadows under her eyes seemed to darken and spread until they fanned out at the ends and met the sunken hollows below her cheekbones. "I guess because telling is a part of how it has to be," she answered finally. "I always figured what's coming was the way it is and I've never tried to change it."

Simon's eyes, so large and blue in his thin face, met hers steadily. "But if you know that something bad's going to happen," he said, "why don't you try to run away?"

Child logic, straightforward and too heartbreakingly simple for his cruel surroundings. Lila pulled Simon close and hugged him, inhaling the scents that made up her son. He smelled like the Chicago Housing Authority project in which they lived, cooking grease, dirty clothes, stale air . . . but underneath all that, the good part was still there, the perfect smell of an innocent little boy. Nothing could hide that, or take it away.

Well, almost nothing.

Zeke . . .

Simon let her hug him, his nose cold and a little runny from the drafts that crept through the warped windowsills. "Sometimes I have to run away at school," he admitted shyly, his face pressed against the fabric of her dress. "And sometimes, even though I'm scared, I have to . . . you know. Fight."

Lila rocked him and nodded, remembering the swollen spot on his mouth last week from a skirmish on the street. The punch of a fist not much larger than his and Simon had waved it off—*"It didn't even hurt, Mom."* Of course it didn't; at six years old, the boy was already used to blows from a much stronger source. "Sometimes you have to fight," she repeated in a strained whisper.

Simon glanced at her, ashamed. "I'm sorry."

"No," she said, her voice evening out. "Don't be sorry for standing up for yourself, Channy. That's exactly what I'm telling you to do. Okay?" Searle had buzzed Simon's hair into a crew cut barely a quarter-inch long and she hated the way it made her son look. His hair was too pale for such a short haircut, too fine; all you saw was his scalp . . . and more scars. To Lila's eyes, the faded white nicks might as well have been splashed on Simon's skull with scarlet paint. She ran her hand thoughtfully over the soft hairs, turning Simon's questions over in her mind, wondering what would happen if . . .

Everything Lila'd seen in her head about tonight shifted then, melting away at the edges of her mental vision like butter burning in a cast-iron skillet. The outcome relating to her didn't change, and she hadn't expected it would; the important part was that for the first time, she felt she could really *do* something about the rest of it. The visions in her head fogged over everything except for the feeling of her small son in her arms, but she might as well have been on the moon for anything else. She didn't even hear Searle's key in the dead bolt.

It was Simon's frantic tugging on her arm that brought her back. "Mama, come *on*. Please—you've got to get up!"

Lila stood automatically, then herded Simon toward the kitchen before her husband got the door open. Her legs were stiff—how long had she sat on the couch in front of that damned television? Too long, while the world moved around her and her six-year-old son got home from school and did the things she should have been doing. She blinked and tried to clear her hazy vision, then pinched herself sharply on the soft underside of one arm to make sure she'd shaken the last of the daydream. She'd known for maybe the last three days that tonight was going to be bad; now it was the here and now and it was time to deal with it.

Something crashed in the other room—the front door, slamming open against the wall. "Lila!" Searle Chanowitz bellowed. "Lila, where the *fuck* are you?"

"I'm right here," she called. She grabbed Simon's jacket off the doorknob and threw it over his shoulders, turned the boy toward the back door and pushed him forward. "I want you to go out on the back porch," she said calmly. "And I don't want you to come back in the house unless I open the door and tell you to. No matter what happens, you hear? If your daddy comes after you, you run off the porch and hide somewhere for a while."

"But—"

"Lila, get out here!"

"I mean it," his mother said. "Now go. Can you unlock the bolts by yourself? Good." She bent swiftly and kissed him on the cheek. "I love you, Channy." She ran a gentle hand over his hair again, then turned and hurried into the living room.

Shrugging on his jacket, Simon watched her go and shivered as he went over to the back door and reached for the bolt locks, his heart already starting to thud heavily in his narrow chest. He didn't know why, but he had the feeling that things tonight were going to be worse than usual, worse than *worse*. The look on his mother's face, the way she'd told him to get out of the apartment . . . there was even a strange, faraway tickle in his own head, something he couldn't identify or understand and that scared him almost as much as his father. It was like something struggling to break free in there, something weird that ought to just stay where it was and be still. Maybe like whatever was in his mom's mind that made her see things.

He got two of the three locks opened, but the last one was too high and Simon couldn't reach it. His dad was still shouting at his mom in the other room—something about not ironing his shirt and a scratchy tag—when Simon started to drag one of the beat-up kitchen chairs over to the door; the little boy winced as he heard the thud of Searle's fist hitting flesh and his mother's cry, then realized too late that the sudden stomping footsteps meant his father was headed toward the kitchen. Lila had pulled the door shut behind her and that only served to enrage Searle Chanowitz more; he opened it with a vicious kick that pulled it off the top hinges and left it tilted at an unstable angle in front of the stove.

"What the hell do you think you're doing, kid?" Searle charged across the room and plucked Simon off the chair by the back of his jacket. "Going somewhere? I bet your mom told you to leave, didn't she? *Didn't she?*"

"N-n-no," Simon lied. He didn't want to, but common sense told him the truth would be worse right now and he tried desperately to think of something to add to his story. "I w-was—"

"Shut up," Searle snarled. "You little *liar*. You know what they do to liars in some places, Simon? Huh?" He laughed, a sound more like a growl than anything else. "They cut out their *tongues*!"

"Leave him alone, Searle." Lila was standing in the kitchen door and Simon felt himself swing dizzyingly as his father spun and faced her. "He's just a little boy. I told him to go."

"So he *was* lying," Searle said wonderingly. He made no move to release his son. "I'll be damned."

"I told him to," Lila said dully. "Now put him down." Her cheekbone—the same one Simon's father always seemed to go for—was swollen and purple again and she was having trouble keeping her balance.

"Gonna teach him a lesson first. Boy's a troublemaker, just like his brother was." Simon felt his position undergo a rough midair change; now he was tucked under his dad's arm like a crumpled version of the Sunday paper. He tried to squirm free and got a halfhearted crack across the face for his trouble and a "Be still, Simon."

Lila's overly thin frame was no match for Searle and he pushed her aside with barely a glance as he headed toward their tiny bathroom. She tried to grab his arm but missed, then followed unsteadily, ricocheting from spot to spot as she looked for something to keep her upright. "Searle, stop—"

"Lookee here, Simon my boy, what do you see?" Hoisted up and balanced on the rim of the bathroom sink, without warning Searle slammed Simon face-first into the medicine cabinet. There was a blast of pain and the mirror cracked, but Simon didn't know if the sound was the glass or his nose breaking. He screamed as blood sprayed the jagged-edged triangles in the mirror and the painted door of the cabinet, then screamed again as his dad began to pound his head against the remnants of the mirror. "I—see— a—lying—little—bastard!" His father punctuated each blow with a chanted word and above it all his mother's shrieks rose like an out-of-control siren.

Searle pulled Simon back in preparation for another impact, but it never came. Instead, his father released him abruptly and Simon fell hard to the ceramic-tiled floor, while above him Searle roared in pain as something big and heavy—the iron—smacked into the side of his head. Lila drew back and tried to swing the iron again but her grip was tenuous at best; by the time Simon clawed his way to his feet, Searle had lunged through the bathroom door and seized his wife. Her screams faded fast under the onslaught of his fight-scarred fists, and it made no difference to Searle that the neighbors and the CHA Police were pounding on the door. Wailing as loudly as his lungs would allow, Simon threw himself at his father over and over, hoping to at least slow the punches, but Searle brushed him away as though he were no more than another annoying cockroach. When the CHA Police finally broke down the door, it took two neighbors, two cops, and eight whacks from their billy clubs before Searle finally stopped hitting his wife.

Lila Chanowitz was dead long before anyone could call for an ambulance.

MT. VERNON, ILLINOIS
1972 . . .

She'd followed the dog into the woods and cornered it in the small cave that bordered the creek bed, now dry and full of dust and little round pebbles at the height of the hot month of August. The dog was thirsty and had gone to the creek in search of water that had dried to nothing but a memory more than a week ago. The dog was also rabid.

Mercy Ammon could sense its sickness and its fear of the water it so desperately needed, imagine the way the mutt's tongue was swollen and cracked, sympathize with the drawn-in throat trying uselessly to swallow the mass of foamy saliva leaking constantly from its gaping jaws. Rawboned and starving, big for a stray, it must've had a lick or two of the Hoeboggons' male Great Dane in it plus some of that silver-coated German hound, the kind with a name she couldn't pronounce and that was always winning prizes at the county dog shows. Mercy could see the silver shine underneath the dried mud and crusted foam along its muzzle where no one else could, all that beauty driven away by the disease blasting the life out of what could have been one fine, fine animal.

And would be again.

"Here puppy-puppy, come here now, that's it, it's all right, I won't hurt you, that's a good boy—" One long chant, a singsong cooing in her little-girl's voice as the mutt snarled and snapped and backed its hind end right into the rock wall of the cave. Trapped, it crouched, eyes wild and seeing something that surely no seven-year-old farm girl had ever imagined. Discolored lips pulled back as far as they could to show its fangs, bright white and sharp, teeth of a pup not even a year old.

"It's okay, I won't hurt you, poor thing, you're so skinny and hungry, aren't you, so thirsty—"

Touching the dog now, too late to heed the oft-repeated warnings of avoiding animals gone mad in the woods, she stroked its shuddering, pain-racked body, the filthy, matted fur of its feverish skull above the wildly rolling eyes. Mouth open to bite her, to attack, but it *couldn't*, something inside wouldn't let it as the charge began to flow from Mercy into the dog. Never tried it with something this big, never anything larger than that baby rabbit the plow horse stepped on, didn't even know if it would *work* or just leave her to face the frenzied jaws of the sickened animal—

—still learning how to *use* it, couldn't even control it yet, but maybe someday—

—and her hand spasmed and dug into the fur around the animal's neck. A quiet yelp in response to her grip and Mercy realized she was kneeling next to the mutt, and he was licking her face with big, happy slurps as the mud-encrusted tail wagged two-forty on his back end and he gazed at her with clear, adoring eyes.

"Hey," she said softly, and scratched his head. "How's it going, pooch? Good dog." The dog licked her again and sat, then offered one paw in a companionly handshake. A few feet away a sound suddenly rippled through the birdsong and hum of the late spring crickets in the bushes. Mercy and the dog looked over at the same time, and the little girl gasped as she saw her grandfather finish priming his old double-barrel and raise it to his shoulder.

"No!" Mercy shouted. She tackled the dog, her skinny, under-sized body knocking the canine on his side only because he allowed her. She draped herself over him, feeling the smooth, strong breathing that made the sharpness of the dog's ribs seem absurd, knowing in her soul that the dog was no longer sick and worse, that now he trusted her to take care of him. She just *couldn't* let him down. "He's fine, Grandpa! He's ain't sick, he's ain't—don't shoot him! Please!"

"Move aside, Leah," the elderly man said evenly. "I seen for myself that the dog's rabid. Get away from him a'fore you get bit."

"No," Mercy said stubbornly. "He's *ain't* rabid—not any-more." She hugged the animal fiercely, wrapping her bony arms around his jutting collarbones. "Look at him, Grandpa, look real *close*—if he was sick, he'd have already bit me."

"Leah—"

"Come on, boy," she interrupted. She jumped to her feet, being sure to position herself between the barrel of her grandfather's shotgun and the dog. "You show Grandpa what you can do. Sit now, come on—*sit*." Obediently the dog pulled himself up and sat, hesitating enough to make Mercy think he'd still been learning the familiar command when whatever animal had bitten him—rac-coon maybe, or skunk—had given him the sickness. "Good dog," Mercy said as she shot a pleading glance at her grandfather. On that note, the dog offered his paw again, thumping his straggly tail against the grass. "See, Grandpa? See?"

Reluctantly, the old man lowered the shotgun, staring hard at the thin dog. His sharp gaze cut to Mercy, then softened. She breathed easier as she saw him thumb the safety into place on the gun's stock before lowering the well-worn butt to the ground. "You take that dirty mutt back to the barn and give it a bath," he said finally. "And mind you keep it out of your parents' sight until you do. I think you know why."

Mercy nodded solemnly and raised herself off her knees. The dog came to his feet when she did, gazing up at her adoringly. "Thanks, Grandpa." She dug her fingers firmly into the tangled fur around the dog's neck and turned back in the direction of the farmhouse. The big young mutt came with her without resistance.

"Don't thank me yet, child," she heard her grandpa say softly. "When your new dog's cleaned up, you come and get me. It's time for us to have a serious talk, Leah Merari."

There was no use pretending she hadn't heard.

Grandpa was waiting for her later, after she'd finished bathing Lincoln—she'd named him that after the president they'd learned about in school on Friday—and brushing the tangles out of his thick, ginger-colored fur. Cleaned up, Mercy could definitely see the Great Dane in him. She'd been right, about the hound part, too, because now that strange silver undertone was more visible than ever, especially when the dog bounded joyfully across the sun-filled front pasture to meet Grandpa Ammon. This time the old man had left his battered Winchester double-barrel at the house and when Lincoln pranced at his feet and begged for attention, he patted the dog's head thoughtfully as Mercy ran to join them.

"See, Grandpa?" she said breathlessly. "He ain't sick, not anymore."

"He *isn't* sick, Leah. Not 'ain't.' "

"He *isn't* sick," she repeated. Then again for emphasis, "See?" Her face, so thin and small-boned, was pinched with worry and the need for his approval.

"Yes, honey. I can see that, all right. He isn't a bit sick." Mercy's relieved grin almost faltered when the look on her grandpa's face seemed unaccountably sad, but she slipped her tiny hand into his and the elderly man's frown softened. His fingers were warm and rough around her palm, her softer skin scrubbed clean from the soap she'd used on the dog and still lightly speckled with feed dust from tending the chickens on her way here.

Still holding tight to his work-hardened hand, Mercy skipped along beside him as they took the path that skirted the back pasture and into the small wooded part of the family farm. Mercy thought it was a great place to be on a lovely Sunday afternoon, with dinnertime and Mama's fine fried chicken only a couple of hours away. Mercy might look like a twig, but she had a hearty appetite fueled by the fresh farm air and her chores. Around them some of the trees were still sprouting pale green buds, while others had branches already crowded to the limit. Ivy—the good and bad kind—grew everywhere amid the tree trunks, but she and Grandpa stayed on the well-worn path with Lincoln trotting respectfully behind. With a bath and bellyful of food, Mercy thought he was on his way to being one of the best-looking farm dogs in the area.

"Where're we going, Grandpa?" She tilted her face up to look at him, squinting under the sunbeams leaking through the gaps in the leafy canopy overhead. "If we go too far, we'll be late for supper and Pa'll be mad."

"Not much farther," he promised. "Right . . . over there. That's good." He stepped off the footpath and went a little ways into the trees where an oak had fallen years before Mercy was born. Now the stump was black and green with age—black where the wood had both softened and hardened from the elements, greenish where soft moss grew like swaths of a child's paintbrush. He peered at the stump and brushed away a daddy longlegs, then settled onto the wood and invited Mercy to join him. "You remember I said I wanted to talk to you?" he asked seriously.

Mercy nodded, her small face solemn. "Sure, Grandpa. It's about Lincoln, isn't it?"

"Yes . . . and no." He looked away for a moment, and Mercy had the impression that he wasn't really there anymore. Then his gaze refocused on her. "It's more about you than your new dog." He studied her carefully. "It's more about what you *did* to him."

"Oh." Frightened but unable to understand why, Mercy tilted her face down until she no longer had to meet her grandfather's eyes, staring at the scuffed soil instead. There were a hundred unvoiced questions hanging in the air between them, and when he didn't say anything, eventually Mercy decided she was expected to offer some sort of . . . *explanation* for what she'd done. She opened her mouth to try, but what came out was a question instead. "Was it wrong, Grandpa? What I did today?"

For some reason beyond her grasp, everything in her world

hinged on the old man's answer, and it was a long time in coming. He finally sighed. "Not in and of itself, child, no."

Mercy frowned. "'In and of itself'? What does that mean?"

"I guess it means that you can't let anyone see you do what you did," he said. "It—"

"So, it *was* wrong!" Mercy exclaimed. At the increased pitch of her voice, Lincoln turned from his nosy forays into the brush and came to her side. "Why else would I have to hide it?"

"Because people won't understand, Mercy." It was the first time the little girl had ever heard her grandfather call her by the nickname. "And what people don't understand, they condemn."

She cocked her head, not following. "'Condemn'—what's that mean? How can it be wrong to make something well again when it was sick?"

"I . . . I don't know, child." For an instant he looked sick himself, and Mercy felt her heart jump in alarm. He seemed so full of life and energy that sometimes she forgot that her grandpa was *old,* her father claimed nearly as old as some of the trees on the farm. "I don't have the answer for that. I only know that it happens, maybe because people are afraid of what they can't explain. Can you explain to me how you did what you did? *Can* you?"

She looked at him earnestly and spread her hands. They were small and pink-palmed, with little round work calluses rubbed into the edges of the forefingers and thumbs. "I don't guess so. Lincoln was sick, and then he wasn't. I just sort of . . . *charged* him, I think."

Her grandfather nodded. "See what I mean? Now think about trying to explain that to a down-to-earth man like your papa. Or maybe your teacher at school. Do you think they would believe you? I don't suppose they would. Or if they did, maybe"—he gave her a sidelong look—"they'd end up being a little afraid of you."

Mercy's mouth dropped open. *"Me?"* she squeaked.

"I'm going to tell you a story about your grandmother," Grandfather Ammon said, "that even your papa doesn't know. Oh, he knows lots of pretty stories about his mother, but not this one. If I pressed him, he might remember a good bit of it on his own, but I don't think, given the way your papa's mind works, that he'd ever admit it."

"My grandmother?" Mercy said wonderingly. She knew the woman only as a face in the single, age-damaged photograph

Grandpa kept on his nightstand. The picture showed an exotic-looking woman with dark, haunted oriental eyes.

"You take after her, you know. Your grandmother was Chinese and her name was Shoi Lin." He grinned, something he rarely did, showing a sturdy set of teeth that were still all his own. "She was a beauty, tall and thin as a cattail stalk, black hair and those lovely tilted eyes. I can tell already that you're going to look a lot like her when you grow up." He was silent for a moment and Mercy waited patiently, holding in another hundred questions. "Anyway," he finally said, "we were an odd pair, all right, a Chinese woman and a Jewish man, not something you saw a lot of in the Adirondacks in the 1930s. But that's where we were, all right. Shoi Lin came through Europe and into Ellis Island all by herself—another oddity, since most folks traveled with their families. I was working with Immigration then, processing paperwork on the thousands of folks coming over to this country. She had all the right papers and knew all the right words, but beyond the memorized lessons she was utterly *lost*. She asked me where to get a room, and a job—said she'd take anything—and I knew she'd get eaten alive once she stepped outside. Even back then there were sharks on the streets."

"Sharks?" Mercy repeated, puzzled.

"Never mind, pumpkin. You'll understand that part someday on your own." He glanced up, tracking the sun's path across the late afternoon sky. "Don't have time to give you our life story, Leah Merari, at least not before dinner. To keep it short, obviously I courted her for a while, then we got married. We moved out of New York as soon as we could, and got us a little scrap of land in a small but growing town in the mountains. Times weren't easy but we made do; Shoi Lin took in fine tailoring and special washing, and I managed to keep us fed by doing the books for most of the folks in the town, sort of the town accountant. Numbers were simpler back then and it didn't take a college degree just to figure up a profit-and-loss statement." He glanced at her and saw that same baffled look on her face.

"Never mind," he said again. "I'm getting off track anyway." Grandpa Ammon reached down and picked up a long twig, scratching aimlessly at the ground with it as he talked. "So we had your pa, but he was the only child God saw fit to give us. Still, we were content. We had a healthy boychild, we had food, and if we didn't exactly have luxuries, we always had enough for the next round of supplies. We were real happy for a couple of years, at least until the Jensens decided they needed a barn and got the town involved in a barn raising one Saturday afternoon in August."

Mercy drew her knees up and hugged them, her backside teetering on the log as she unconsciously maintained her balance. "What's a barn raising, Grandpa?"

"It's just what it sounds like, pumpkin. A whole bunch of townsfolk get together on someone's land and they all pitch in to help, and they raise up a barn. Most of it gets built in one day, the frame anyway, but a handy bunch of men can usually slap the roof and sides up while they're at it. At the end of the day a family's got a brand-new barn where the day before they had only a few loads of two-by-sixes and some sheathing."

"Sounds like it would cost a lot of money," Mercy said doubtfully. She was comparing it to the only thing she could: a picture in the Sears Roebuck catalog Mama'd got in the mail last week had shown a kit to make a doll house almost as tall as Mercy herself. With her eighth birthday coming less than three months away, she'd promptly announced that the dollhouse was what she wanted; what followed was a disappointing lesson in family finances.

"It would cost a lot more—too much—if a fellow had to hire someone to do it for him," Grandpa said, nodding his head. "So if a man needed a barn and could afford the wood, everybody pitched in and helped build it. Then a while down the line, if his neighbor needed a new barn or a fence built—"

"The first man came and helped him make it!" Mercy exclaimed. "I get it!"

"Exactly." Instead of looking pleased that she understood, her grandfather continued to stare at the end of the branch he'd positioned between the toes of his worn work boots. "Everybody . . . *helps*."

"So you helped build him a barn," Mercy prompted. "And then what?"

"The Jensens had a pile of kids, and one of them was a four-year-old boy named Cain. The older ones weren't watching him like they were supposed to, and he was playing where he shouldn't have been, by one of the wagons stacked high with the two-by-sixes waiting to be used for the inside framing. Must've been two or three hundred of them still there, and not balanced right at all—men'd been sliding timbers out the end all day, at whatever height they could get their hands on. To Cain it must've looked like a great thing to climb, but when he tried it, half a wagonful of wood came down on his head."

Mercy's hands flew to her mouth and she almost lost her balance before dropping her sneakered feet to the ground to stop herself. "Oh, no!"

"Boy was almost completely crushed," her grandpa said bluntly. "He was still breathing when we got the wood pulled off, but not much else. Anybody with a brain could see the child wasn't going to make it to the doctor." Something seemed to catch in Grandpa Ammon's throat and he stopped for a moment, then kept going, his voice a little hoarser. "Then along came your grandma."

Grandpa didn't say anything right away, but Mercy could fill in the blanks for herself. She might be only seven but she wasn't stupid. "She healed him, didn't she? Right in front of all those people?" Mercy grinned, pleased at her guess, thrilled by the wonderful deed performed by her ancestor so many decades earlier. "What did it look like when she did it?" she asked excitedly. She was practically hopping up and down. "What—"

Her grandfather cut off her babbled questions. "She came out of the crowd of townsfolk and walked over to that poor boy's mangled body like she was in a trance and just couldn't stop herself. She *looked* like she was hypnotized, although that's not the word people used later on. And yes, she healed him, she sure did. Wasn't much to see of the whole thing except a little flash of light that might or might not have been real and the faintest smell of something nobody could recognize. Suddenly there was Cain, all fresh and healthy, and crying to beat the dickens."

"Wow," Mercy breathed. "I bet she was a hero, right? Did they give her a present? Or a big party?"

"No, Leah Merari. See, it was a small place, and the people weren't very accepting or open-minded about things they didn't know. They didn't give her a party." Grandfather Ammon looked her full in the face and Mercy was stunned to see tears sliding down his weathered skin. His next words made the bottom drop out of her small world.

"They all betrayed her, Mercy. Our friends, the people she washed for—even the Jensens. They called her a witch and turned her into an outcast. She was so ashamed she couldn't eat or think right anymore, and I guess my shoulders weren't strong enough to help her bear the burden. She gave up and turned sickly—didn't bother trying to heal herself, and I don't know if she could've anyway.

"My Shoi Lin died of shame the following spring."

GARY, INDIANA

"Get your jacket on, Lamont. We're going out."

From his sprawled position on the bed, the boy looked up in surprise as his father stopped in the doorway. Banned to his room three hours ago except for bathroom necessities, Lamont had pulled out his small comic book collection to help pass the evening and was reading his favorite—*Superman*, of course. It wasn't until his father had spoken that Lamont realized he was nearly nodding off; it was ten o'clock at night, and tomorrow was a school day.

But arguing would only get him grounded longer, so Lamont said, "Yes, sir," rolled off the bed, and hastily swept his comics into a neat stack. When he went to the closet and pulled out his navy canvas coat, his father's deep but quiet voice stopped him. "Not that one. I want you to wear the red flannel one your mother and I got you for Christmas last year."

Lamont started to protest, then wisely snapped his mouth shut. He was itching to ask why his dad wanted him to wear that particular coat, but he was in too much hot water over that refrigerator thing earlier in the kitchen—

"Isaac! Isaac—come quickly! You need to see what your son is doing!" The shrillness of his mother's voice should have warned him that something was wrong, that she didn't find it nearly as cool as Lamont did that he could pick up the refrigerator—the whole thing—far enough off the floor so she could sweep under it. He'd thought his mom and dad would be proud of him and happy to know that he was far stronger than other kids and getting stronger every day. In fact, it was getting to where he almost didn't have to touch something to make it move, and that had been the next thing Lamont had planned to show his mom . . . until she went into hysterics.

—to make matters worse by questioning his father's instructions. He put the canvas coat back on its hook and dug farther into the closet to where the bright plaid jacket had been pushed when he had outgrown it by the end of spring. Now, in September, he was by far the stockiest boy in his third-grade class, and when he shrugged on the jacket, the back was stretched tight and the sleeves were too short. But his father had eyes and could see that for himself.

"May I use the bathroom first, Dad?" For a strange moment Lamont thought his father was going to refuse, and now the young boy was completely confused. His dad wasn't a mean man—why would he want him to be uncomfortable like that? Then his father gave a curt nod. Lamont hurried out of his room and down the hall, glancing automatically into his younger brothers' room as he passed. Joey was sleeping soundly, his smooth, chubby-cheeked face in dark contrast to the white pillowcase. His thumb was in his mouth and Lamont wished his father wasn't watching from the doorway so he could zip into Joey's room and pull it out—if Dad saw it, he'd scold him tomorrow. In the three steps it took for Lamont to pass the door, Joey stirred and pulled his hand away from his face, tucking it securely beneath his pillow as though he'd read his older brother's thoughts. The youngest, Isaac, Jr., was only a year old and had been sound asleep in the crib across from Joey's bed for hours.

Lamont took care of things in the bathroom as quickly as he could, unable to escape the impression that his dad was standing just outside the closed bathroom door and waiting. He wouldn't be, of course; his father was much too polite for that. Lamont flushed the toilet and rinsed his hands, stopping only for a quick check of his reflection in the mirror above the sink. Nothing special there—an ebony-skinned eight-year-old with nearly black eyes and close-cropped hair, nothing that would distinguish him from any other kid.

"Let's go, Lamont. I haven't got all night." His father's voice was the same as always, quiet and modulated, although tonight it was cut with the "Do it because I said so" tone that was reserved for when he was really angry or disappointed with one of his sons. If it weren't for that and the fact that the two of them were going somewhere in the middle of the night, Lamont would have thought his father sounded much as he always did.

"Coming," he called softly. When Lamont came out of the bathroom, his father *was* waiting, but at the top of the narrow flight of stairs that descended to the first floor of their small home. Curiosity finally got the best of him as his dad led the way downstairs and through the kitchen until he got to the door that opened into the garage. Lamont's mother was nowhere in sight. "Where are we going, Dad?" he ventured.

"To see some people," was the only answer his dad would give him. Lamont climbed into the back of his parents' blue Impala without being told, sitting and staring out the back window for most of nearly an hour's drive. He still didn't understand why he'd gotten into so much trouble or why both of his parents had looked so terrified to see him proudly and very easily hefting the two-hundred-pound appliance. What *was* clear, however, was that he'd doggone well better never do it again in front of them.

Lamont was a good reader and when his dad finally pulled the car over, the signs they'd passed just a few miles earlier on the highway had said JOLIET. There'd been another sign announcing a turnoff coming up for a different highway leading to Aurora—didn't Mom's sister live there with her husband? It was kind of late to go visiting—

But Lamont was delighted to see a tiny carnival set up in the parking lot of what looked like one of the city's schools. At a little past eleven at night, the fair was still going strong: lights blazed, hawkers shouted, games rolled on at frantic paces. Color, sight and sound, a riot for the senses as his father led the way through the hundreds of people milling throughout the grounds. Lamont wanted to ask if they could go on some of the rides, but didn't dare. His father's wide face was grim and he showed no signs of stopping at any of the ticket or game booths as he led the way through the fair; besides, if the senior London had come to meet with some people, going on the rides didn't make sense. But why would he meet them at a carnival, and why would he take Lamont with him?

A dozen questions and no answers.

The fair was a magical place, full of lights, riotous noise, and people of all ages, though at this time of night few were Lamont's age. Some adults, but mostly teenagers wearing open denim jackets or baggy, brightly colored knitted sweaters that looked handmade. The girls had long, ruler-straight hair and wore short blouses above hip-hugger jeans that showed their belly buttons, the boys all had hair hanging past the shoulders of screamingly loud tie-dyed T-shirts. Laughing among themselves and surreptitiously smoking grass, they watched with interest as Lamont and his father, the only Negroes Lamont had seen so far on the carnival grounds, hurried past.

In a few more minutes they had left behind the nicer part of the fair, and dark tents and the small hulks of rusty travel trailers surrounded them, some with weak lights flickering through slits in the musty canvas fabric or dirty windows. No cheerful strings of multicolored lights hung here; black shadows were everywhere, broken only by the pallid glow of the parking lot's occasional streetlights. Lamont could still hear the screams and laughter of the people on the rides—the Octopus, especially—but they were tinny and faraway, as though the noise couldn't quite make it through the distance and the difference in the atmosphere surrounding them. Lamont was starting to feel scared, and despite the excitement of coming to the fair, he was sleepy, too. It must have been eleven-thirty, or later, and he was sure that he'd seen a sign when they'd come in that said the carnival closed at midnight. The only thing familiar here was his father's warm hand clasped around his own. Did Mom know where they were?

"Dad—"

"Be quiet, Lamont. We're here."

They stopped abruptly and Lamont barely missed colliding with the backs of his father's sturdy legs. In front of them was a medium-sized tent, its canvas cracked with age and dirt, mended in a dozen places with silver duct tape or wide, crudely sewn stitches. His father slapped an open palm against the tent's entrance flap a couple of times, dull thuds that sounded overly loud in the darkness and easily drowned out what little remained of the noise of the carnival. Lamont glanced uneasily behind him and was startled to see that they'd gone only to the far corner of the parking lot—the heart of the carnival was only about two or three blocks away. It was so hushed and dark back here that it seemed like they'd walked for miles.

Something rustled inside the tent and Lamont's head whipped back toward the flap. His father stood impassively as a dark hand, joints knarled with age and exposure, drew the flap aside. Someone peered out and Lamont got the impression of *eyes*, ones that saw everything and everyone in a way that wasn't really right somehow. His father exchanged a few words with the man inside in a voice too low for Lamont to catch, then the flap was pulled wider. To Lamont's horror his father tugged him forward and steered him through the black maw of the tent's opening.

At first Lamont could see nothing. It was nearly as shadowed inside the tent as it had been outside, except for the glow of a small, old-fashioned lamp that looked like the antique one his mother had on the sideboard at home. Its feeble glow made a soft circle around itself and did nothing to cut the rest of the darkness.

"Come 'ere, boy. Let's see what you look like."

The raspy, ancient voice made Lamont jump; his father's hand tightened around his briefly, then was inexplicably gone. Lamont started to turn, but something grabbed his wrist and jerked him forward, a touch so dry and rough it felt like a cluster of living tree branches had wrapped around his forearm. He gave a frightened squeak as he found himself face-to-face with a man like no one else he'd ever seen.

Old beyond Lamont's understanding, the man's face and body were hung with layer after layer of withered, discolored flaps of wrinkled skin, a living skeleton wrapped in bands of mummified flesh. Hunched atop a child's wooden stool and barely distinguishable from his murky surroundings, dressed only in a filthy muscle-man T-shirt and baggy pants, he looked like a petrified praying mantis waiting to pounce on this small, unwelcome visitor. Pulling away was impossible; the grip on Lamont's arm might as well have been a circlet of steel chain.

"What's yer name?" The voice was still as harsh but at least Lamont could see where it was coming from. He tossed a furtive glance over his shoulder and inhaled with relief when he saw his father still standing by the entrance to the tent; for a few moments he'd thought . . . never mind.

"L-Lamont," he managed.

The hand on his arm let go and swung to grip Lamont's small face before he could lean out of reach; dry nails dug into his jaw and turned his face in one direction, then another as the boy's pulse pounded in his ears. "Well, you a fine-lookin' kid, ain'tcha. Fine-lookin', indeed." The old man moved his spindly fingers away and wrapped them around Lamont's hand, swallowing the shorter fingers in his. Lamont thought of how his father had held his hand only moments ago and he wanted desperately to pull away.

Suddenly his captor threw back his head and whooped with laughter. Gaps showed in his mouth where teeth were missing and the remaining ones were long and yellowed. "Come on, boy," he wheezed, then cackled again. "You come with me. Gonna show you something—gonna show you what it'll be like if'n you have to come live with *us*." The old man stood abruptly and Lamont realized he was too tall for the low-ceilinged tent. He turned and began dragging Lamont toward the darker rear area, shoulders hunched to keep his head from smacking into the support ropes running near the ceiling, skull bobbing hideously on the end of his neck.

Live with *us*? "No—Dad!" Lamont cried. "Daddy, *please!*" He turned his head, but his dad was still standing by the tent's flap. In the undependable light, his father's expression looked as though he wanted desperately to rush to Lamont's side . . . yet he said nothing and didn't lift a hand as Lamont was pulled farther away. Left on his own, the child began to fight and kick, knowing he could get away if he absolutely *had* to, he could *always*—

Lamont shrieked in terror and forgot what he was thinking as arms the texture of hard, cracked leather swept him off his feet and lifted him up, cried out again when one of those huge tree-branch hands spread across the back of his head like a spider and pulled his face to within an inch of the man's grisly mouth. "Don't you try no *funny* business on me, boy," he growled into Lamont's face. He gave Lamont a single brutal shake and the boy thought he felt his brains rattle inside his skull. From far away, Lamont thought he heard his father draw a sharp breath, but he must have imagined it because no one stepped forward to save him from this horror. The old man's breath smelled like rotting pork. "Your daddy tol' me about you and that shit you done by your mama t'day," he continued. "How you thought it was funny an' scairt her so bad by pickin' up that icebox when you shoulda left things alone. Shit like that makes you a freak, boy—didja know that? Yeah, jus' like me and the others." His chuckle sounded sinister. "Your daddy's gonna save your baby ass by letting me show you how normal folk treat people like you once they find out about 'em, and I guess I— *we*—can well oblige. So, you jus' mind you'self for the next few minutes and things'll come out aw'right. You get funny on me, and I promise you'll regret it, you hear?"

Lamont whimpered and the man must've taken that as a yes, because he set the boy on his feet and pulled him along without another word. A few more steps into the darkness and he began to talk, his words sounding like the scrape of a rusty metal file on steel.

"Your pa and I go back a ways, to when we was both not much older than you. We went different ways in our lives—" He laughed again, high and sharp, and Lamont wished he could slap his hands over his ears to shut out the sound; his stomach felt unsettled and . . . *green,* and Lamont was sure he was going to vomit any minute. "I guess I don't need to tell you how it ended up with your pa. But I mean to teach you a little somethin' tonight 'bout how it ended up on *my* side." He spun and lifted Lamont again, settling him on his hip as though the eight-year-old weighed no more than a toddler; Lamont squirmed but the old man's hold only tightened and he gave Lamont a ghastly smile. "Like you, I'm a little different from most folks, boy. Can you see that?" Another slight shake. "Huh? Can you?"

"Y-yes," Lamont gasped. "Yes, sir!"

"That's *good*, boy. Real good." The old man reached out a dried thumb and rubbed Lamont's cheek, the movement just short of painful against the child's soft skin. He chuckled. "You feel so *fine,* boy. Can't hardly see nothin' of you in this here tent but yer eyes and yer teeth. All that sweet, dark meat . . . carny'd eat you alive, kid." Lamont almost wept with relief when the hand moved away. Where was his father, and why had he left Lamont with this terrifying stranger?

"Yeah, I'm different, all right," his captor continued. With Lamont still riding stiffly on one sharp hipbone like a stuffed doll, the man lifted a flap at the rear of the tent and stepped outside. The chilly night air smelled of oil and overused food grease; it took Lamont only a second to recognize the scents that were so preferable to the vague smell of decay that had permeated the tent. He gasped when the old man's spittle-flecked lips suddenly brushed his ear. "Your pa tells me you really is different, too—that you's a little stronger than you oughta be, and that you's *proud* of it besides." In the low gleam of the faraway carnival lights, the man's eyes were hard, black rocks, flat and filled with as much kindness as a rattlesnake's. "What'd you say about that, *Lamont*?"

Lamont hadn't expected this man to remember his name or know anything else about him; hearing it from the mouth of the crazy guy holding him was a little like having his mother and father push him into the middle of a traffic-filled highway. He couldn't breathe, he didn't know what to say or how to escape the onrush of doom. "I—I—"

"You fancy yourself strong, so I'm gonna show you what a strong man's life is like, Mr. *Lamont*. Gonna show you what it's like and how folks treat you when they find how you're different from them—oh, they jus' love their strong men, the normal folk do. Gonna give you something to think about tonight and for a long time to come, something to roll around in that comic book-filled head of yours." He'd been moving the whole time he'd been talking, carrying Lamont through the passageways that wound between the back tents of the carnival and farther away from his father and familiarity. Now he stopped outside another tent, Lamont's small, stocky body still clutched in a one-armed embrace. This one was larger and bordered the main walkway of the carnival; the final attraction, people still seemed to be seeking it out as a hawker bellowed promises from an ancient wooden podium out front.

"Freak show, here! Get your tickets now a'fore they all go out to roost and you miss yer chance! Last night, folks, last night! Come one, come all, get your tickets, on sale right 'ere! Show starts in only ten minutes, come one, come all!"

"So you think you're strong, do you, boy?" The old man's warm-meat breath washed over Lamont's face again and the child fought the urge to gag, afraid of the consequences if he did. "Well, strong is more than just being able to pick up stuff and toss it around. Strong's *inside,* as well as out. Use your eyes in here, kid, and learn what strong'll getcha in the way of the *real* world."

Before Lamont had a chance to process the man's words, they stepped inside the larger tent. Eyes glittering with fascination and mouths hanging open, people crowded around a center-lit circle of cages positioned on a dirt floor. The occupants of the cages were the most bizarre things that Lamont had ever seen, their faces mean and tortured in the wildly flickering light cast by the harsh glow of a dozen bare bulbs strung across the tent's ceiling. A bearded lady, a fat man, a person so full of tattoos that Lamont couldn't tell if it was a male or female. Another cage held what Lamont thought at first was a dog boy, then he realized it was a wizened old man who'd let the hair on his face grow long and silky, then colored it with hair dye so its shade would stay a rich, deep auburn. But the occupant of the last cage made him draw in his breath, made the sharp-fingered hand on his right hip fade to a faraway annoyance, the way Joey was when he sat outside the closed door to Lamont's room and whined to be let inside.

The strong man.

Lamont felt his eyes widen and his gaze locked with the man in the cage. Surprisingly, the strong man wasn't all that large—not much bigger than Lamont's father, in fact—and not nearly as tall as the strange, fleshy man who'd carried Lamont in here. He did have muscles, though, and lots of them, but they were . . . *wrong* somehow, too round and close together, too *many*. Lamont thought it looked like God had decided to make this man strong not by giving him muscles that were better than the muscles of a normal man, but by cramming a whole bunch extra into the same tight skin space. Lamont felt his own skin crawl at the sight of the lumps and bulges that crowded together everywhere on the man's body, even opened his mouth to say *Okay, now I've seen him—can I go back to my dad now?* Then the old man stepped over the coarse rope separating the group of cages in the center from the battered rows of folding chairs grouped close to it and carried him right up to the grimy iron bars of the strong man's cage.

"Wantcha to meet Yultaro the Strong Man, boy," the man holding him said cheerfully. He gave Lamont a little bounce in the direction of the cage, like he was settling that toddler more comfortably on his hip. "Yultaro, this here's Lamont."

Yultaro gave them both a dark scowl that made Lamont want, absurdly, to stick his thumb in his mouth the way that Joey did when he slept. "So?" Yultaro rumbled.

The old man grinned, the extra folds of flesh around his eyes rippling. "Boy's father wants me to show 'im around, as it were." He gave Yultaro a wink that grotesquely twisted the side of his face closest to Lamont and the child flinched. "Seems the boy fancies himself kinda strong or something, kinda *special*. His old man thought he ought to know what life'd be like if'n he kept on thinkin' that way. How folks'll treat 'im when they notice 'im and find out he's so *strong* and all. Maybe you could pass on a little of your ex-per-teese."

If the look on Yultaro's face a second ago had been unfriendly, now his expression was downright *black* as his lips pulled themselves into a sneer and he shoved his face against the bars of the cage so hard that Lamont saw the iron press into the man's cheeks. "Oh *yeah*? Well, ain't you just a prize now?"

Without warning Yultaro reached through the bars with one hand and snatched the front of Lamont's flannel jacket in his knotty fist; before Lamont could cry out he felt himself lifted out of the old man's grasp and pulled tight against the strong man's cage. As it had against Yultaro's, cold metal pressed against Lamont's cheekbone and mouth, and the smells of rust, dirty straw, and unwashed skin crawled up his nose. Tears started to form in his eyes and he tried desperately to hold them back.

"What's the matter, boy? I'm the strong man—don't you like me? Don't you wanna *be* like me?" The old man's breath had been bad but Yultaro's was much worse, filled with the smell of tooth rot and something indefinable that Lamont could associate only with bad meat. He gagged and tried to twist out of Yultaro's grip, but he felt like a rag doll dangling in midair as the man easily hefted his ninety-pound frame higher against the cage, until he was level with Yultaro and the strong man was staring at him eye to eye. On the verge of panic, Lamont knew suddenly that as strong as the bars of the cage were, they were *nothing* to the man who held him. "Does it look good in here, kid? Does it *smell* good? Suck it in real deep, 'cause this is what I smell like every day. This is how I *live*."

Lamont was crying outright now, bawling like little Isaac did when he was wet and hungry in the middle of the night. Yultaro paid him no mind as he thrust his arm all the way out, Lamont hanging on the end like a sack of damp laundry, and began to move around the cage, passing the boy from hand to hand as he went. He stopped by the back corner and lowered Lamont slightly, until the child could see a dirty plastic bowl with something that looked like old oatmeal with chunks of bloody meat in it. Again Yultaro pulled Lamont's face against the bars, forcing him to look as a fly crawled sluggishly along the bowl's rim. "Lookie here, yum-yum!" Yultaro said gleefully. "Dinner!"

The fly barely escaped the knarled hand Yultaro thrust into the gray mush. Goo dripped from the fingertips he brought up and wiped across Lamont's face; Lamont wailed in protest but no one paid him any mind. "Ain't it *good*, kid? That's what I eat every night during the show, and you know why? 'Cause that's what the crowd expects a *strong man* like me to eat." Abruptly he yanked Lamont upward, scraping the child's soft, salt-stained cheeks against the rough bars. "That's what *you'll* eat, too—when you come and live with me. I bet you're lookin' forward to it, ain'tcha?" He grinned maliciously. "Well, you just keep on being strong, little pal. And I'll be waiting for ya." He gave Lamont a final bruising tug against the bars, then tossed him backward as if he weighed nothing.

Lamont landed hard but he was young and flexible, and back on his feet in barely more than a second. He spun, sobbing, running and searching wildly for an exit, somewhere—*anywhere* to run, then screamed when he was again lifted into the air.

"Hush, Lamont." His father's voice was quiet in his ear. The arms holding him trembled slightly, then steadied. "It's okay, son. We're going home now."

Lamont buried his mush-smeared face against the shoulder of his daddy's jacket and cried with relief as he was carried out of the tent and away from the carnival, the sound of Yultaro's ugly laughter still echoing in his ears.

1.
DARKNESS DESCENDING

CHICAGO
JUNE, 1998...

"Gena? *Mi querida,* wake up. The alarm went off fifteen minutes ago. It's time to get up."

Luís's lips were warm against her ear, tickling and erotic. His breath was lousy, as it always was in the morning, but that was easy to ignore as Gena rolled over and smiled, snuggling against him. It was Friday; it would be so nice if she could convince him to stay home from work—

Noise filled her head, a scream, the sound of gunfire. Absurdly, the warmth of a summer morning sun washed over it all. He'd seen something he wasn't supposed to, a woman with a gun who'd done something to someone else, and now Luís was falling—

"No!" Gena sat upright without warning, the top of her head catching Luís under the chin and making him bite his lip where he'd been leaning over her.

"Jesus, Gena!" he cried. "What's the matter? Were you having a nightmare?" The bed bounced as he jerked away.

"Luís, listen to me." Her hands searched through the blankets and sheets until she found him and pulled him close. He came willingly but she could smell the blood from the nick in his lip, not much, but enough to make him wipe it away with the back of his hand before he pressed his mouth against her hair. "Stay home from work today," she said urgently. "We'll make love, then take a long shower and go to the park—no, the zoo. We'll go to the zoo, okay?" Luís loved the zoo and it was free, but they hardly went because of her; the animals fascinated him but she couldn't see them and he didn't think it was fair to make her walk for a couple of hours for nothing. She couldn't make him understand that she didn't care, as long as she was with him. Besides, she could smell them better than most people, link right in there with the wildness in their hearts that other folks missed. It would be a fine way to spend the day—

"No," he said and kissed her hair. "The shop's got appointments lined up until six tonight. All the usual stuff, plus two valve jobs. Too busy." He slipped a rough-skinned hand inside the loose armhole of her nightgown and found her breast. She inhaled as he stroked the nipple, then he pulled away. "We'll make love when I get home tonight." She heard the smile work its way into his voice. "We could take a shower together then. But right now, I have to get dressed." He gave her a quick, warm kiss on the nose and started to climb out of bed.

"Wait—"

—to the ground. The noise built inside her head until it was unbearable, like the world's loudest static blasting through a radio. Then gunshots ripped easily through it, guided by quick and professional aim, one, two, and her finely built husband crumpled into a ball from a massive pain in the center of his chest. The cool, rough surface of the concrete sidewalk came up to slide against the tender skin of his face—

"Gena, cut it out. I *mean* it. You do this all the time—where did you get the idea we could afford for me to take a day off work anytime you feel horny?"

"This is *different*, Luís!" She tried to grab at him but missed, almost slid off the bed before she could right herself.

Luís started to reach for her—damn it, she *heard* his intake of breath and sensed him leaning toward her—then he backed away. They'd been through this enough times, and Gena knew he was thinking that she didn't need his help and if she got hold of him again, she *would* make him late. For a precious three seconds she lost track of him; he took advantage of her disorientation to slip across the room and step into their small bathroom before he answered. It made Gena want to punch the wall in frustration—

now he could shut the door if he had to. He wasn't a cruel man, but as far as he was concerned, sometimes she just flipped out.

"It's no different," he insisted from inside the bathroom. She heard him pick up his comb. "You just want company. You should make your job into full-time, be around people more. And the money wouldn't hurt either."

"I don't *like* people," Gena said as she climbed out of bed and walked carefully to the bathroom doorway. "Besides, this isn't about other people. This is about you. And you should stay home today."

"Gena," he said patiently, "you don't *own* me. I'm not a favorite doll you can keep with you all the time. This is real life, baby—"

"I know that!" The sharpness in her voice escalated. "And I'm not fucking around this time, Luís. I've got a bad . . . *feeling* about you going out, that something terrible will happen today. Please, just for today, okay? Stay home?"

"You always have bad feelings about something or another," he retorted. She knew he'd hung his uniform and a clean pair of briefs on the bathroom wall hook last night; fabric rustled as Luís shrugged off the boxer shorts he'd slept in and draped them over the side of the bathtub. "Pj's are on the tub," he said automatically.

"And my feelings always come true!" Her voice was too loud in the tiny room and Luís winced.

"I don't have time to argue with you this morning, Gena. I'm going to work and that's all there is to it." By now he would be climbing into the fresh underwear and trousers, then reaching for his shirt.

"I told Mrs. Pangelli that her purse was going to be snatched and it was," Gena said as if he hadn't spoken. "And remember the Nazanyo boy?" Her voice was moving uncomfortably toward begging. "I knew he was going to die before he—"

"I said, *stop it*." Luís yanked so hard on the shirt that she heard the plaster crack around the hook on the old wall. "You don't know what you're talking about. Things happen, that's all."

"Don't you ever say that! You don't know—"

"What?" Luís yelled at her. "That shit happens, Gena? Well, it *does*." He pushed past her, ignoring her grasping hands. "You—hell, *I* could sit here and say somebody's going to get hurt today, or somebody's going to die. Well, of *course* they are. It's a big city loaded with people! We have a lot of neighbors and live in a shitty neighborhood. What do you expect?" Punctuating his words, a bus rumbled to a stop at the corner below the apartment's open second-floor window, filling the living room with engine noise and the hissing of air brakes. "Now I'm gonna be late again, and Carlos is going to be a dickhead about it. Are you happy?"

—scraping it raw and splitting his soft upper lip, scouring the smooth skin along his right eyebrow, all inconsequential and blotted out by the sense of suffocation as he tried to breathe around the agony and couldn't—

"You have to stay *here* today, Luís!" She reached out, trying to find him, hating herself and her blindness more at this moment than at any other time. *Never* in the twenty-nine years of her life had she wanted so badly to be able to see so she could stop her husband from walking out. And it was so unfairly *easy* for him to elude her, just duck around her flailing fingers and be gone. Gena wanted to screech in fear and frustration the next time she heard his voice, because it came from across the room as he opened the front door.

"We'll talk about this when I get home tonight, Gena," he said tightly. "I'll call you on my break."

"*Luís*—" She stumbled toward him as the door closed, panic disorienting her and making her smack the side of her hip on the rickety buffet in the dining room in her futile attempt to get to him. She righted herself quickly but hadn't even covered half the distance to the door before she felt the vibrations in the floor from his sprint down the steps, then heard the downstairs entry open and shut. In the space of time it took her to try to hear him, he was out of earshot forever. Then, as much as it could ever be to her heightened senses, the building was silent.

—and the darkness simply swept him away.

Gena crumpled to the floor and wailed for as long as her breath held out, then kicked and pounded the floorboards with her fists and sobbed, shaking the floor, shaking the building, shaking the *world* if she only *could*, if it would only bring him *back* to the apartment—

"*No! Oh, no, God—please! Please don't take him, too—*"

—and screamed again. By the time the two policemen knocked on her door forty minutes later, she had cried herself into exhaustion and curled into a shuddering fetal position on the dining-room floor. Although they could hear her weeping inside the apartment,

Gena wouldn't answer their banging, so the officers were forced to hunt down the building super to let them inside.

When they came in and found her, Gena clapped her hands over her ears and fought them when they tried to talk.

She already knew what they were going to tell her.

JULY...

The only reason Lamont decided to check on his parents' condo was because he was in the neighborhood. His mom and dad were on vacation, their first one in over a decade, and since there had been a break-in while the elder Londons were at Sunday services two months ago, the kids had come up with a plan for keeping an eye on the place. A good thing, too—there was a shaky period for about a week and a half after the burglary when the seven-day trip to Alabama for Dad's high school reunion almost got canned completely. Finally, though, the parents had relented and gone on the holiday they'd planned for nearly eight months. Lamont, Isaac, Jr., and Roanna each agreed to check on the condo twice, while Joey, who lived the closest, volunteered to double that number and drop by four times; that way, someone would be in the condo once a day for the duration of their parents' ten-day absence.

Personally, Lamont had his doubts that any of this mattered. He was a workman's compensation lawyer, not a cop, but it wasn't hard to look at the last theft and think it was someone within striking distance of the condo, someone who knew when the occupants were home and when they weren't. His mom and dad were totally predictable—they went out for breakfast, then attended services at the Morning Star Baptist Church on Martin Luther King Drive at the same time as they had every Sunday for the last twenty years. Every child in the family had gone through his or her time with it; how many people in their Hyde Park building also knew the London family's routine? Too many to think about. Privately Lamont was convinced that whoever had robbed the condo wouldn't hit it again; after all, they already thought they'd taken everything of value. That they hadn't found the wall safe in the oversized pantry was a lucky break.

Isaac had already run by the condo at about three that afternoon. That was the beauty of Isaac's job as an interior design consultant for one of the downtown architectural firms—he was out and about all the time and his drop-ins at the condo couldn't be pegged to a predictable time. Unfortunately, Isaac, Jr. was also swamped with work and client appointments; apparently his firm started pushing Thanksgiving and Christmas layouts in the summer—something that always made Lamont shake his head—and the warm season was Isaac's busiest time. Now it was nearly midnight on Monday and the area just to the south of downtown Chicago was all but deserted, especially the part through which Lamont was driving. Known for cop bars, most of the area's undesirables avoided the near south section of State Street in favor of the neighborhoods farther west.

The idea of stopping by had occurred to Lamont a little while ago, after meeting a client who got off shift at one of the larger printing plants just outside the Loop. The guy's hours were odd and he was working two jobs to try to support his family, so Lamont had agreed to meet the man for coffee at the Marquette Restaurant on Madison Street at 11:15 and get him to sign the forms needed to file his case on Wednesday. The case had come in late, just under the statute for filing and far too late to trust the mail, but Lamont enjoyed his work and it was no big deal to put in some extra time at the office. It was a short meeting: a half cup of restaurant coffee for each, a few signatures, and both men went on their way.

The ride to his parents' building was as uneventful as the empty streets. He used his electronic card to open the door to the parking garage and pulled inside, marveling as he always did at the difference between the ornate old-world style of the building's exterior and the stark concrete blandness of the parking garage. The garage ran two levels underground, but as he negotiated the last of the tight turns, he discovered he couldn't pull into the reserved spot that went with the condo because someone had already parked in it. He braked and stared at the vehicle, rubbing his fingers on his chin in irritation. He didn't recognize the car, a pale blue 1995 Lexus sedan with temporary tags on it, and the vehicle seemed a little expensive for anyone in the building, which was populated mostly by middle-income retirees. Someone's visitor? Maybe, but if they had a key to the garage, they should also know that it was full and there were no visitor spaces inside.

Unless this person knew no one was home in unit 8E.

Still, it could be as innocent as someone figuring that the Londons were on vacation anyway, and why not let their girlfriend park in the 8E spot?

Or it could be something else.

His mom and dad's spot was the last one next to the elevator wall and there was just enough room to put the back end of his white Grand Am along the wall and leave the front parked solidly in front of the Lexus; they'd be blocked in and have to wait for him to come back down, but Lamont figured that if they had to wait, they deserved it for parking in someone else's spot.

The back elevator lobby was deserted and dim, and Lamont thought that the building was slipping as the years went by—a lot of the elegant old Hyde Park residences were, not stepping up lighting and safety measures despite the ages of the unit owners and renters. At least the elevator still moved smoothly and stopped at each floor with a muted ding that didn't annoy the people in the condos on either side of it.

The eighth floor was like all the rest—softly lit with a carefully polished mahogany chair railing running down both sides to each door and small, half-oval shelves between every fourth door on which groceries and packages could be placed. Mahogany-framed mirrors with beveled edges above the shelves reflected the muted glow of the miniature candelabra chandeliers evenly spaced along the high ceiling. In the hallways, the building still showed its antique beauty, although Lamont and his siblings hadn't appreciated it when they'd been growing up.

The Londons had bought their unit two decades ago when the building had first been converted to condominiums, something unheard of at the time in the Hyde Park area. It was a calculated risk that had paid off well, and one of the most obvious advantages to being among the first to purchase was a choice unit at the end of the floor with a living- and dining-room view that looked east over the park and Lake Michigan, as well as a generous number of southern windows. The building was deeper than it was wide and had only three apartments at each end; down here the hallway split into a T-shape and dimmed, illuminated by a lone overhead light fixture. Lamont had always thought it was too dark and hearing the noises inside his parents' condo as he went to slip his key into the lock made him freeze for an instant and remember all those childhood fears.

He slid the key the rest of the way in, turned it, and pushed open the door in a single silent motion. Stepping inside put him into a small foyer tiled in deep red ceramic and Lamont automatically stayed on the balls of his feet. In front of him was the darkened living room, its windows joining with those of the dining room to the left and giving a panoramic view of Lake Michigan, like a moonlit expanse of black oil beneath the night sky. To his left was the kitchen, clean and empty, while on his right was the hallway leading to the rest of the condo's four bedrooms and two baths, tiny laundry area and a sort of walk-in combination pantry and linen closet. Bleeding down its length from the open pantry door was the faintest of glows, flicking and weaving . . . a flashlight. Although Lamont strained to hear, now not a sound accompanied the beam's quick movements.

At five-ten and a hundred eighty pounds, Lamont was a sturdy man. But he was not a "lumberer," as his mother teasingly called his father. Planning for a late night, at about seven o'clock he'd switched his suit and tie for the pullover and jeans he'd stuffed into his workout bag this morning. Likewise, the office wingtips had been traded for Reeboks, so his swift stride down the hall was soundless. At the last second, common sense made him halt outside the pantry when he would've stormed through the doorway—what if the guy had a knife, or a gun? In fact, the burglar *would* have a weapon if he'd managed to get the wall safe open, because his dad kept a nickel-plated Smith & Wesson .38 inside. That someone had found the safe in the pantry to begin with was another indication that Lamont was facing a professional. Most people installed their safes in bedroom closets or, ridiculously, behind wall paintings; theirs was built right next to the circuit breaker box and was cleverly disguised to look like part of it.

Lamont peeked cautiously around the doorjamb. Predictably, the burglar was dressed entirely in black, including black gloves and a black ski mask. The guy's back was to him as he dug a hand into the open wall safe and pulled out the last of Lamont's mother's jewelry; on one of the linen shelves a few feet away was the pistol, easily within the man's reach. Two steps inside the door, Lamont estimated, and he would have the guy by the back of his shirt—this was just *so* personal that he had to put his hands on this man. The open safe bothered him a lot—all his parents' most personal things were inside and were being carelessly perused by this bottom-of-the-gutter criminal. It was a sacred, private place and this man had no right to go through its contents. He'd grab the guy, all right, but first Lamont decided to close that damned safe.

The intruder was about eight feet away and Lamont could see the opened safe in the wall just over the man's right shoulder. The heavy steel door had been swung wide to allow easy access, and now the safe's interior gleamed emptily when the thief ran the flashlight over it a final time. From his position just outside the pantry, Lamont focused on the door and concentrated, just a flash thought of what he wanted. There was a slight, instantaneous ripple in the air in front of him as though something invisible shifted—

—and the safe's door slammed shut with a clang.

A heartbeat later, the flashlight's beam snapped off.

The burglar tackled him, and without the light to see by, Lamont was as helpless as anyone else. Something hard—the flashlight case—hit him on the side of his face and brought a shock of pain; he grappled with the other man, felt a stocky body like his own but more muscular and in better shape—here was a man who had nothing inhibiting his workouts like Lamont's forced self-control. The pantry was small and windowless; with no place to hide and thoughts of the gun lying somewhere on the counter, Lamont swung his right arm in a tight arc and connected, a lucky punch but one that sent his attacker crashing against the opposite wall of shelves. When Lamont backpedaled, his hip bumped the doorjamb and he turned and swatted at the wall—wrong side. He leaned to his left and tried again, was rewarded with a bright wash of light from the overhead bulb.

"Don't move—no, no. Don't turn around."

Lamont froze as the voice sunk into his head. Ahead of him was the hallway wall—no pictures visible on it at this point—and behind him, a gunman. But that voice—

He whirled without thinking. *"Joey?"*

A flash of fire and thunder blotted out the rest of the night.

AUGUST...

"I'm asking you to voluntarily resign, Dr. Ammon."

"What?"

The woman behind the desk didn't move. Her hands were folded calmly on the uncluttered surface and her voice was emotionless and even, the verbal equivalent of a flat-lined EKG. "I dislike repeating myself. I believe you heard me the first time."

With both hands, Mercy gripped the back of one of the two leather wing chairs set carefully in front of Erica Richmond's desk. For a second her pulse slammed triple time and she felt like fainting; thank God for the chair in front of her. She had once considered this woman a friend. "Erica, I-I don't think—"

"Let me rephrase my words. I'm *requiring* that you voluntarily resign. If you don't, you will be summoned before the board of directors for review. The charges will be misdiagnosis and negligence. Appearing before the board in and of itself will expose this hospital to further charges of malpractice and slander. I can guarantee that you will be dismissed and your medical license suspended."

"The boy was beaten! You were there when he was brought in—you saw him with your own eyes!"

"I saw nothing." Dr. Richmond stood unhurriedly, stepped to the side, and pushed her chair under the desk, as if the most troublesome thing she must deal with in the world today was the precise placement of the chair's wheels on the thick, steel-gray carpeting.

Mercy gaped at the older woman and dug her fingers deeper into the hard leather of the chair back. "You're *lying*," she whispered. "Why? What's in this for you?"

"You're babbling," Dr. Richmond said with finality. "There's no point in wasting further time, as I don't plan to reconsider."

"There's nothing to be gained from my leaving," Mercy said desperately. "I'm no threat to you or your position here. I just want to heal—to practice medicine. You're using your power to eliminate me from the hospital as if I'm after your job, when my ambitions are a million miles away from anything remotely like it! Hospital administration is the last—"

Dr. Richmond cut off Mercy's words with an impatient flick of her hand. "My career is not the focus here, nor is it your concern. If you choose to remain and face the charges, it will be my recommendation to the board of directors that your trauma medical license be revoked. The Zimmermann family has also indicated that they plan to check with their attorney regarding criminal charges of malicious mischief and slander." Despite her age, or perhaps because of it, Erica Richmond was an attractive woman and the low, decidedly unofficelike lighting of the room made her soft blond hair glow and her pale blue eyes glitter. She took a small step toward Mercy and for the first time her voice was tight when she spoke. "Because of what happened in the emergency room this morning, Dr. Ammon, your ties with this hospital are detrimental and I plan to see that they are severed immediately. Surely you can understand that." She tilted her head slightly, waiting.

"But I—I didn't do anything *wrong*." With her life crashing around her, Mercy's voice had dropped to a whisper again but she knew Dr. Richmond could hear her.

"But you did *something,* Dr. Ammon, and it is that *something* that cannot be tolerated within the walls of this building."

"No," Mercy said weakly, "that can't be it. That isn't enough." She wanted nothing more than to sink onto the hard leather chair and curl herself into a ball, hide from this whole scene—Dr. Richmond's cold office filled with Early American furniture and stiff brown leather, the four-year-old boy in the ER six hours ago, his parents, the police.

Erica Richmond, the hospital administrator.

"I'm asking you to voluntarily resign, Dr. Ammon."

"I disagree." Dr. Richmond glided past Mercy and stepped to the door on the far wall. She paused with her hand on the doorknob. "This meeting is over, Dr. Ammon. Shall I tell my secretary that you will be dictating your resignation to her, or shall I tell her to telephone the Zimmermanns and advise them that you will be pursuing the charges of child abuse in spite of the fact that the boy has no injuries? I'm afraid that in making your decision, you do not have the luxury of time . . . *Doctor.*"

Mercy hung her head, defeated. "I'll . . . resign."

"Good," Dr. Richmond said with satisfaction. "I'm glad to see we've come to terms on this." She started to pull open the door.

"Terms?" Mercy lifted her face and stared at the other woman; she'd be damned if she'd cry in front of the person who was destroying her life. "Don't insult me. These are not *terms*. This is blackmail."

Erica Richmond ignored her and pulled the door open the rest of the way. "Your resignation shall be effective as of, say, four o'clock today. As you will not be allowed to return, all personal property must be removed with you tonight, and all patient records remain the property of the hospital. You may not take any originals or photocopies with you. Please dictate your resignation and gather your personal items as quickly as possible; my secretary is on overtime." She looked pointedly at the diamond-studded timepiece on her wrist, then purposely turned her back on Mercy and walked out without another word.

Damn her, Mercy thought helplessly as she watched her go. The woman was actually *whistling.*

. . .

"Well, well," Mercy said hoarsely. "Here we are."

The parking lot of Althaia Hospital at eleven forty-five at night was dimly lit and not particularly safe. Sitting in her car, a Dodge Shadow less than a year old, Mercy knew she should leave and head home before she called unwanted attention to herself—and in this neighborhood, that was easy to do—yet she couldn't bring herself to go, not yet. The car was running, her seat belt was fastened; she had only to shift into first gear and go. But when she did, she would never see this place again the same way. In the scheme of this terrible time in her life, having to change the way she viewed the old brick building should have been the least of her problems, the smallest of inconveniences. After all, it was the way in which the world—or at least the part of it that comprised the medical profession—viewed *her* that was the most problematic here. It was that viewpoint that had taken a devastating turn.

Fear settled into her mind, a smoky shroud of terror insinuating itself in every cell and cerebral impulse. She had dreamed of nothing but becoming a doctor all her life, and it had taken everything she could give to attain it. Her family was not rich, and while she worked and studied hard, scholarships were few and the students vying for them many. She had gone to both college and medical school on partial scholarships, working part-time jobs and taking out long-term student loans to pay the rest of her tuition. Her choice within the profession, ER work, didn't offer the higher salaries and private partnerships that specialty work did; her student loans were still there, being slowly paid along with a host of other financial obligations—rent on the town house, car payment, a hundred other little luxuries. All those things might not look like a lot to a physician with a private practice, but with no job and bleak prospects, now they loomed over Mercy like a suffocating cloud. That she'd kept the bills in the reasonable range while she whittled away at the student loans wasn't much comfort; now she wished she'd lived in a studio, kept her old 1980 Monte Carlo until it fell apart under her, and poured money into those loans to pay them off.

The idea of searching for another position brought with it an entirely different set of difficulties. How would she explain her sudden departure from Althaia, her lack of references? Even if Erica hadn't been such a threat, no one in their right mind would vouch for her, not after today's farce. A doctor without a work history was nothing but a walking question mark, and in this age of lawsuits and gargantuan malpractice premiums, references were seldom left unchecked, personal referrals preferred. Stupid, *stupid*—she'd had such iron control since that nasty business in the third grade the September after she'd gotten Lincoln, such resolve. But she'd lost it today, felt her willpower just . . . slip away behind the curtain in the ER when the little boy lying on the blood-spotted sheets had opened his eyes and whispered, *"Please make it stop hurting . . ."* around a mouthful of blood.

Someone stirred under the streetlight about ten cars down and began to move her way, making Mercy press her lips together. Experience had taught her it was safer to back into the parking spaces out here and now she put the car in gear and pulled out, leaving whoever was sneaking around the parking lot—one of countless creeps every night—to deal with the security guards. Mercy's last look at Althaia was a glimpse in the rearview mirror as she guided the car out of the lot and onto LaSalle Street; when she dropped her gaze to the dashboard, Mercy saw the LED display of the clock on the dash blink from 11:59 to 12:00.

For a brief moment, she wondered if Dr. Richmond knew about today, then realized what a ridiculous question that was. Of course she had—the woman would have reviewed her file carefully before their meeting. Whether or not the administrator had noted the minuscule piece of personal trivia was anyone's guess, though Mercy was betting Erica had taken particular delight in the timing of demanding Mercy's forced resignation.

She made the light at North Avenue—something that almost never happened—and drove woodenly toward Clark Street, getting a brief reflection of her face every time she checked her rearview mirror. The dull shock she saw in her eyes didn't surprise her; the bitterness did, but she couldn't help that right now. With an ongoing habit of thinking out loud, Mercy had driven roommates in both college and med school crazy until they learned to block it out; tonight, however, she said only one quiet sentence within the stillness of the car on her way home.

"Happy birthday . . . *Doctor."*

SEPTEMBER . . .

Rats and cockroaches; Simon Chanowitz could hear one and see the other, but it was a toss-up as to which infested this building in greater numbers. He drew in a breath and was immediately sorry he hadn't closed off his nostrils; the air in this apartment smelled of dog crap, human feces, rotting garbage, and something else he couldn't identify. The two cops beside him coughed and looked at each other meaningfully before the older one, a burly man in his mid-forties with prematurely gray hair and a name tag that said PACIEN, met Simon's eyes. His words were matter-of-fact.

"There's a dead one in here somewhere."

When the cops had pounded on the door a few minutes ago, all the noise inside—crying, barking, babbling—had stopped abruptly, no doubt due to a long-standing warning from Mom. Even kicking in the door hadn't been enough to break the silence; now everyone in here just stared at them and waited. Simon scrubbed at his cheeks with his hands and shoved the hair out of his eyes, then took two steps and bent his knees, lowering himself until he was eye to eye with the cowering form in the corner. He peered over the rim of his glasses. "Hi," he said softly. "My name's Simon. What's yours?"

Wide eyes the color of semi-sweet chocolate stared at him. The boy could be three; he could be six. In malnutrition this far advanced, it would take a doctor to find out. "Jamill," the child finally answered. He stuck a dirty thumb in his mouth and glanced quickly around, as if he were waiting for the hand of doom to descend; his voice was raspy from a cold and his nose was runny. The apartment was cool, maybe sixty degrees, but all the boy wore was a filthy pair of loose shorts.

"That's a very nice name," Simon said. He tilted his head confidentially. "Nicer than mine," he whispered and smiled a little. The boy blinked without smiling in return, but that was okay. "Where's your mother, Jamill? Is she here?" As her partner moved cautiously to inspect the rest of the apartment, Officer Miru, the younger of the two cops, joined Simon and tried to smile reassuringly at the child. She didn't succeed and Simon couldn't blame her; there wasn't much going on here to smile about. When Jamill didn't answer, Simon tried a different question, nodding his head at the six other children who had backed against the walls and so far refused to speak. Hiding behind the legs of the oldest was a small dog so thin that it looked like a skeletal caricature. "Are these your brothers and sisters, Jamill? Are they family?" Jamill's answer was a noncommittal shrug. A quick, elusive touch on the surface of the boy's mind,

—*flash*—

nothing more than the brush of a feather, and Simon realized the boy really *didn't* know. Jamill's life was a black hole of hunger, fear, and cold, highlighted by occasional visits from several women who sometimes brought food but more often arrived with men and liquor, and slapped the kids around if they got in the way. The child's thoughts were so confused that he wasn't even sure anymore which of the women was his mother.

A muttered curse from Officer Pacien made him glance at the doorway to one of the apartment's other rooms; the sturdy man stepped back into the front room cradling an emaciated baby in his arms. Above the delicate hold on the unconscious child, the policeman's face was pale and scowling. "This is one of twins," he said through grinding teeth. "The other one's been de—" His gaze flicked around the children pressing themselves against the wall and staring at him. "Gone," he amended, "for a day and a half, maybe two."

"Call it in," Simon said wearily. "Maybe Columbus-Maryville Youth Center can help us out again, if they've got room." Knowing that the boy and the rest of the kids in here found him scary, he showed the child his hand, palm up to prove it was empty, before he lightly touched the boy's shoulder. At the gesture, Jamill's eyes flicked nervously back to Simon. "I'm from the Department of Children and Family Services," he said carefully and loudly enough for all the kids to hear. The children probably wouldn't understand, but he refused to just march into their apartment and hustle them out like kidnappers. "The police officers and I are going to take you guys somewhere and get you something to eat and some warm clothes. Won't that be nice?"

"We're not supposed to go with strangers." Finally, a few words from one of the other children, the oldest girl. She looked like she might be eight or nine, but again, it was hard to tell. These kids weren't exactly well fed.

"That's a pretty good rule," Simon agreed. "But it would be okay if you went with the police, wouldn't it? That's different from regular strangers."

The girl hadn't moved from her position against the wall and Simon's stomach churned as he saw a cockroach scuttle down the wall and onto her shoulder. He wanted to knock it away, but didn't dare make a quick movement. "I—I don't know," the child said finally. "We're not even supposed to go to school. I don't want to get in no trouble."

"Trinetta, you got a roach crawling on you," the boy standing next to her said suddenly.

She glanced sideways at the insect on her shoulder and smacked at it with an open hand; stunned, it fell to the floor. Instead of stepping on it—she had no shoes—Trinetta turned her mistrustful gaze back to Simon, ignoring the policewoman standing next to him. "You don't look like no cop."

"Well, I'm not really a cop," Simon admitted. A gentle pressure on Jamill's shoulder brought him with Simon when he moved to stand in front of Trinetta. The other children, their thin faces curious and cautious, had clustered into a little group next to her now, fronted by the oddly silent mutt. He'd never seen six kids together in the same room be this quiet. "I'm from Family Services, but you wouldn't be going with me. You'd be going with Officer Miru here and her partner, Officer Pacien, who will take you somewhere and get you something to eat. Then we'll take it from there."

"I don't want to go," the girl said sullenly. "Mama will be really mad." Her skin was gray with dirt, little hands clenched into bony fists at the sides of a worn-out, stained jumper that was too small.

"I'm sorry your mother will be angry," Simon said softly. He reached to touch a strand of her tangled hair and she flinched; he paused, then finished the movement to prove he wasn't going to hit her. "But I think this time she's going to have to accept it." He glanced at the other kids and saw a wild play of emotions: rebellion, fear, desperation, *hope*. He leaned a little closer. "I'm going to have to go back to work and do some things, so I need someone to kind of be in charge of the other kids, Trinetta. To tell the officers what their names are and how old they are, where their moms and dads are, stuff like that. Can you do that for me, Trinetta? Can you be in charge?"

"I—I don't want to."

Her voice had dropped involuntarily to a whisper and Simon had to lean forward to hear her. Trinetta's hollow-cheeked face was fearful and her eyes were filling with tears, and when Simon brushed over her thoughts,

—*flash*—

he almost recoiled. She was remembering something from a while ago and he could catch only fragments, her little girl's mind bringing back only the worst; a hand, large and dark, swoop-

ing down and cracking her brutally across the face for going outside the apartment, other punishments too appalling for Simon to
dwell upon.

"It's hard to be in charge all the time, isn't it?" Simon's voice
was sympathetic and the child's moist gaze cut to the small bunch
of children, then returned to Simon. She opened her arms and
Jamill went to her, curling into the crook of her elbow with his
thumb still tightly in his mouth. When she didn't say anything,
Simon slowly stood. He glanced at Officer Miru and she came
over to stand beside him, this time successfully smiling down at
Trinetta and Jamill. "But this will be the last time you have to do
it, and Officer Miru will help you. Okay?"

Finally, Trinetta nodded. "What happened to your face?" she
asked with childish bluntness.

Simon answered truthfully, eyes steady behind the lenses of his
glasses. "Someone bad did this to me when I was about your age."

"Who?"

"My father." It was a sad and bitter thing *not* to see any surprise on the faces of the children listening to him.

"Did it hurt?" The timid question came from one of the other
children who hadn't spoken until now, a light-skinned child who
stood out among his darker companions.

Simon nodded somberly. "Yes, it hurt a lot. But some people
like these policeman came and helped me, so that the man who did
it went away and it never happened again." Time, he decided, to
get back to the business at hand. "Trinetta, are you ready to talk to
the officer?"

"Uh-huh." Her voice was small and slightly shaky; still, she
looked expectantly at Officer Miru.

"Good girl," he said gently. "Things'll be better by tomorrow, I
promise." She nodded again and Miru bent and began talking
softly to her, asking questions as she made notes on her clipboard.

Simon felt the gazes of the others as he shuffled through the
incredible amount of debris on the floor and joined Officer Pacien
out in the hallway. A young, shocked-looking DCFS worker
named Meredith had taken the gaunt baby from the policeman and
wrapped it in her sweater while they waited for the ambulance and
the coroner to arrive. "Any clue where the parents are?" Simon
asked, his eyes on the infant's still form within the rocking circle
of the woman's arms.

Pacien shook his head. "Not yet. There's no one home

downstairs, but the woman next door fed us a few details. She says that *if* anyone shows up, and there's a good chance no one will because one of the women was here with a boyfriend last night, they'll go in the first-floor apartment. She says it's rented by two or three women who come and go with too many men to count."

Simon's eyebrows raised. "Prostitution?"

Pacien shrugged. "Maybe—probably. It's pretty common. Anyway, the woman wants to remain anonymous. Says she's afraid of everyone in here."

"Why doesn't that surprise me," Simon muttered.

"So what happened here? Can you tell me that?" Pacien's eyes were hard, and Simon knew exactly what he meant.

"I wish I could give you a good answer," he said. "I went through the social worker's files this morning while I was waiting for our lawyer to get the motion heard at court and the order signed. There's a solid paper trail that says he was here twice a week for the last six months and everything was all happy-crappy every damned time. Last visit was yesterday afternoon."

"Maybe he was getting a little . . . you know"—Pacien made a crude gesture with his hands—"on the side."

Simon's mouth twisted momentarily. "Maybe he was getting a lot of things on the side," he retorted. "What he *won't* get is another paycheck from the city, *ever*."

"How'd you find out about it?"

"Somebody called it in," Simon said vaguely. He couldn't very well say that the social worker, who'd just been reassigned to work under Simon's supervision, had sat across the desk from Simon at their introductory meeting and spilled the mental beans. *"All my cases are current, Mr. Chanowitz,"* he'd said with a lying smile on his face. *"In fact, I've seen significant improvement in several family situations."* Fresh from a visit to the building in which Simon now stood, the truth had rushed into Simon's head without him have to fish for it.

"Here comes an ambulance and the meat wagon," Pacien noted as he glanced out a glassless window in the hall. "We'll run the rest over to the DCFS in the squad. Hell"—the big man dug at the bare floorboards with his shoe as his partner joined them—"it could be worse. The M.E. could be bringing eight little bags instead of just one."

Relieved of the child by one of the paramedics, Trinetta, Jamill, and the other four were being patiently herded out by the two remaining social workers from Simon's staff. The other paramedic waited downstairs to check each child and decide who went to Cook County Hospital and who went to the DCFS. Simon opened his mouth to reply to Pacien, but his words were cut off by a tap on the shoulder from Meredith. She held up a portable phone. "Mr. Chanowitz, you've got a call."

Simon seldom got calls in the field, unless it was a serious emergency. "Who is it?"

"I have no idea, but he said the receptionist at the office gave him this number and that it was important he find you." Meredith looked puzzled. "They wouldn't give your field number out to just anyone, would they?"

Simon shook his head and took the telephone from her hand. He didn't waste words. "Chanowitz here," he said into the receiver.

"Channy, my boy," said a distantly familiar voice. "It's been a long time, hasn't it?"

If Pacien hadn't reached out and snagged his arm, Simon knew he would have fallen as the portable phone slipped from his suddenly numb fingers and his knees buckled.

2.
ALL THE LITTLE PIECES

CHICAGO
NOVEMBER, 1998 . . .

"Wake up, sleepyhead. This is your last day to enjoy being lazy before you go back to the factory, and here you are, wasting it in bed."

Lamont opened his eyes to find his sister Roanna standing next to his bed. He smiled at her but made no move to get out from under the comforter. Inside his chest, his heart was thudding lightly, a mini-anxiety attack that didn't show on the smooth, seemingly drowsy features of his face. Her coat was off and the smell of coffee and bacon permeated the town house. Both were certainly welcome, and he didn't mind her using her key—that's why he'd given it to her—but how long had she been downstairs, moving around without trying to be quiet while she set up breakfast for him? How long had he so blissfully slept while another person wandered freely around his home?

Family, he told himself sternly, *that's why you didn't wake up. She's family.*

But so was someone else.

"Come on, silly." Roanna found the lump of his foot under the comforter and tugged on his big toe. "I don't have much time before I have to take off. I've got plans to meet friends and go shopping, so today you do your own dishes."

"Shopping?" Lamont sat up, ignoring the faint pain that still slipped through his chest, a shadow in the morning when he was stiff from lying down all night. "You shop more than any person I know. What the heck are you going to buy—more baby stuff?"

"Is there anything else in the world right now?" Roanna laced her hands under the smooth circle of her stomach, pulling the fabric of her aqua-colored maternity top snugly around it.

"You look like you're going to give birth to a basketball," he teased as he eased his feet over the side of the bed. He was still so slow-moving that it drove him crazy sometimes, but experience had taught him that moving quickly was best avoided, especially the twisting motions of getting out of bed.

"And you look like a movie star," Roanna retorted. "Especially the face part."

Lamont laughed. He was an oddly *hard* sleeper, and he always got patterns in his skin from the creases in the pillowcase—he greeted each day looking like a wrinkled rag doll. The cuffs of his flannel pj's were bunched around his knees and elbows and would be stuck in those positions when he stood. "Which one? Eddie Murphy?"

Roanna snorted lightly. "Only if you lose fifty pounds, chunky boy. At least *I* have an excuse."

"My weight fits my frame," he protested as he followed her somewhat wobbily into the hall and down the stairs to the kitchen. "All the health club charts say so."

She threw a skeptical glance over her shoulder as he slipped onto a kitchen chair. "Maybe they did before you got hurt, but things have . . . ah . . . settled a bit. Besides, Eddie Murphy's got a space between his teeth." A kinder-than-expected choice of words but Lamont couldn't think of a reply; they might be joking around, but the truth was that being confined to the town house for nearly three months had taken a real toll on his overall fitness. He felt like his muscles had gone to mush, and a soft roll of belly spilled over the elastic waistband of his pajama bottoms. He was eating more—boredom—and not exercising at all. He'd gotten so far out of the loop that he'd had to force himself to start the mile walks his doctor had ordered two weeks ago.

"Here you go," Roanna said cheerfully. She set a plate of bacon and three eggs in front of Lamont at the table in the kitchen's eating nook, then added a glass of guava juice and double biscuits. There was another reason he'd put on the pounds—Roanna's cooking. It wasn't that he didn't appreciate all the assistance his little sister had given; he just wished she didn't cook such huge, old-fashioned southern meals. At this rate, he'd die of hardening of the arteries before the last of the gunshot wound healed.

"Roanna," he began. "This is too much—"

She shook her head, a gesture that reminded Lamont uncomfortably of their mother. "I don't want to hear it, Lamont. I know all about cholesterol levels, fat intake, and eating healthy. That was the first in a never-ending series of educational lectures my doctor is still pounding into me. You just need this extra rich stuff while you're recuperating, that's all. Tomorrow you go back to work and your regular life, and you can eat however you want." She waved at the spread of jams and butter on the table. "You think I cook like this normally? I don't think so—unless I'm up for a case of prenatal diabetes mellitus. Just eat up, bro."

Lamont reached for the butter for the last time, resolving to throw it out with the trash tomorrow night and go back to no-fat spread. "You've been a tremendous help. I don't know what I would have done."

"You were always the most independent," she replied. "You'd have figured it out." Her voice was a bit on the sharp side—shades of his mother's disapproval—but Lamont said nothing. Now was not the time for an argument, and what would be accomplished by it anyway? More bitter, useless words.

He cleared his throat a little, trying to swallow the bite of biscuit that had unaccountably dried out. "So it's back to the daily routine tomorrow," he said. "I wonder what's going on with my cases."

"They'll be waiting, I'm sure. At least the ones that haven't gone to hearing." Roanna sat delicately on the chair across from him, an odd movement that made it seem as if she held a baby in her arms instead of in her womb and was being careful not to wake it. "Lamont, I'm not trying to be a nag, but . . ." She raised her eyes to his, doe-brown and wide below a halo of shining black curls. "Don't you think that it's kind of dangerous? Going back to work while whoever shot you is still out there?"

Lamont shook his head and pushed cut-up pieces of egg around his plate, feeling his stomach sour at the turn the conversation had taken. Still, Roanna would have her say and he might as well answer. "That had nothing to do with work, remember? I surprised a burglar in the act, and got shot for my trouble."

"And you still don't remember anything about the man who shot you?" Her eyes narrowed slightly as she waited for his answer. Sometimes he wondered about her and just how much she seemed to . . . *guess* about other people.

"Man or woman," he corrected. "It could've been either. I got shot as I turned around, before I saw anything." He was trying to enjoy this last homemade breakfast—his normal morning meal was fat-free yogurt and coffee—but it was getting more difficult with each moment. He felt fixed in Roanna's dark stare, trapped under that disapproving gaze that reminded him so much of his mom's. He loved his sister, but right now he wished she'd just leave for her shopping trip. He was looking forward to having some privacy again, to family *not* dropping in at all hours to check on him.

"But you always say *he* when you talk about it."

"A figure of speech, that's all," he said patiently. "Masculine, feminine—who cares? I'm talking, not writing a politically correct court brief."

She ignored his sarcasm and stood, glancing at her watch. "Time for me to run. I've got to be at the Century Mall in a half hour. I think you ought to see someone about this memory thing, a psychologist or a hypnotist, someone like that. Maybe it would help."

Lamont got up and walked with her to the front door, then held her oversized coat while she slipped into it and pulled it across her stomach. "What's the use?" he asked. "It was a burglar, a sleazy thief with a gun who I'll never see again. It's not like I have something permanently wrong with my head other than typical trauma memory loss."

Roanna pressed her lips together in irritation. "I can't believe you don't *want* to know who did it. You—"

"Are going to be late if you don't get going," he reminded her gently. He leaned over and kissed her on the cheek, then gave her belly a friendly pat. "Take good care of my nephew."

"I could have a girl," she said, exasperated.

"No way. I want another boy to play ball with." Lamont grinned.

"You really don't remember?" Her eyes searched his. *"Really?"*

"Really. Now go." Another peck on the cheek, this time from

her, and the door closed. For the first time in months, Lamont felt like the town house was truly his again, could nearly feel it trying to shift back to its normal ambience. The carefully neutral expression on his face dissolved and he found himself standing in front of the closed door and scowling, fighting the ugly jabs of his conscience as he recalled Roanna's acceptance of his words.

God, he hated lying.

DECEMBER ...

The work at McDerwin Animal Clinic was good for the heart, if not for the pocketbook.

The best that Mercy had been able to dream up as the reason for her sudden departure from Althaia Hospital was a conflict in personalities. She'd occasionally tried something more elaborate, such as a dispute involving medical treatment procedures, but wound up pressed for details and trapped in a verbal corner every time. In this age of instant lawsuits, work histories were checked carefully and the heavily connected Erica Richmond had done well in her subtle and untraceable character assassination. After months of trying to set up interviews, Mercy was forced to accept that for the time being she simply could not get another position in Chicago. Always at the back of her mind was the possibility of *never,* but she couldn't think about that, didn't dare dwell on that black, hopeless possibility. There was still the option of relocating to a smaller town with a retiring doctor who would be happy to pass along his practice to an experienced physician, albeit one with a slightly tarnished past. After all, she'd never had a malpractice suit filed against her, and as far as she knew, the Zimmermanns had let the thoughts of malicious slander slide into the woodwork. Fear, Mercy believed, had been the deciding factor with the Zimmermanns—fear that bringing such charges against their accuser would expose other things they didn't want revealed. Mercy knew what she had seen, and what she had done. So did Erica Richmond, and so did the Zimmermanns.

But to leave Chicago ...

How could she? All those years of college and medical school, on to an internship at Cook County Hospital, then the coveted trauma residency at Althaia. Chicago had given her everything she needed, that supremely important outlet for the constantly churning energy inside her for which she had no medical explanation but that would not be denied. She needed to heal or she would *explode,* fry her brain on the inside and end up a babbling schizo-phrenic. So many years of moving among the sick, one of the best recovery rates in the history of Althaia's ER, and so what if she did it by cheating? No one knew, she reaped no benefit other than a sort of psychic relief, and the men, women, and children who came across her examining tables gained everything. Besides, how could it be cheating when she simply did what came naturally? Mostly little things, a healed broken bone, a halted asthma attack, a deeper cut suddenly nothing more than a scratch. Bigger prob-lems, too, but always unseen—a ruptured aneurysm that suddenly stopped hemorrhaging, advanced leukemia that went into inex-plicable remission, an unborn baby with a fading heartbeat that suddenly strengthened and stabilized.

Until the Zimmermanns' little boy, of course. She'd thought he was comatose, but then he'd opened his eyes and whispered the one thing she could not refuse.

"Please make it stop hurting . . ."

How ironic that she couldn't remember his first name now, after letting the power flow from her fingers and into his battered face and fractured skull, through the deep soft tissue damage in his abdomen to the internal bleeding, all the result of a terrible beating by one or both of his parents. It had happened without conscious will or thought and had been far too strong to stop once it was started; too late she'd remembered telling the desk nurse to call and report the case to the DCFS, and she had blatantly for-gotten about Erica Richmond's unexplained presence in the ER. By the time a social worker got there, the boy was sitting up and smiling . . .

And Mercy had no proof anyone had ever touched the boy.

His parents and the hospital administration were enraged by the charges, the rest of the ER staff was confused and cautious, the DCFS was suspicious of the parents, Erica had lied, and Mercy's career was ruined.

Desperate, facing loans that she couldn't pay and unwilling to add the humiliation of bankruptcy to the mess her life had become, Mercy had walked into McDerwin Animal Clinic off the street to answer a help wanted notice taped on the window of the small north side vet's office. It was close to "home," a few short blocks from the studio apartment into which she'd moved in October, right after she'd sold her Dodge Shadow. The money from the sale of the car had gone for the first two months' rent and security on the new apartment, several months of loan payments, plus the cost of her new car, a ridiculously rusted green Plymouth Duster that reminded her of the sixties and happier times. There was enough left for a month of groceries, but nothing else—not even utilities. She'd stepped inside the door to McDerwin Animal Clinic a woman without a past and with nothing to show for her life but the lie she'd told them on the job application—

"I've worked mostly in nursing homes and hospitals as an aide, but I've worked with animals off and on. The elderly are so sad . . . I think I'd prefer to go full-time with animals. I've got a pretty good knowledge of the ropes, but the last place I worked was a small-town vet's office that went out of business. I don't really have any references."

Besides, who needed references to clean up animal examining rooms?

LATE JANUARY, 1999 . . .

Gena didn't want to go to work this morning.

Nothing new there, Monday morning blahs . . . just like the ones that came Tuesday, Wednesday, et cetera. Of course, if she didn't go to work, then she would sit in the empty apartment and think all day about Luís and how much she missed him, about the way his fine muscular body used to fit with hers each night, the way his hair smelled, the way his skin had tasted.

No, not a good idea. If she sat on the couch all day with nothing but her rambling thoughts to keep her company, she would want to die. She wouldn't turn on the television because she couldn't stand its anonymous chattering, the endless sob stories of make-believe people who in reality lived in multimillion-dollar mansions that Gena couldn't imagine. What was a multimillion-dollar home *like*? Her world was based on touch, smell, sound . . . and darkness. Would the couch in an expensive home feel more comfortable than hers? Would the bread on the counter in her kitchen smell more enticing if it were offered on a cherrywood cutting board rather than in the plastic bag from the grocery store?

Two more hours before it was time to leave. She never slept late anymore; the bed was too big and too cold without Luís, the sheets like a crinkling expanse of ice in the cold January mornings. It was January, wasn't it? Of course it was—she knew that because a few weeks ago it had been Christmas, and after that New Year's, more days off work to simply sit.

Christmas morning was still a bitter recollection. She'd decided on the spur of the moment to go to church, and armed with her hateful cane and CTA pass, she'd walked the four blocks east to Broadway and taken the bus to St. Ita's at the 5500 block. She'd stood on the front steps indecisively while people filed around her to go inside for the nine o'clock Mass, feeling the cold bite through her mittens and inexpensive boots, not caring that her wool coat was too thin and no match for the wind and light snow. So much effort to get here—everything was an effort—but she didn't know if she wanted to go in now that she'd made it. What did she think she would find? Comfort? *God?*

"May I help you inside, miss?"

Gena whirled and almost fell, felt a strong hand grab hers, warm through her mitten as it guided her fingers to the metal banister that followed the line of steps to the church's entry doors. "Who is it?" She felt immediately foolish for panicking—she was on the steps of a church, for crying out loud, on Christmas Day. It stood to reason that someone would feel like playing good Samaritan. Of all the days to do it, this was the day to rack up those heavenly brownie points.

"I'm sorry for startling you. I'm Father Barrett. Mass is about to start. Would you like to go in?"

Her derision was replaced by shame and she nodded wordlessly. He let her left hand stay on the banister and took her cane, then placed her right hand on top of his shoulder. Of course; as a priest he would be used to dealing with handicapped—sorry, visually *challenged*—people of all kinds. She followed him carefully up the remaining steps and felt the warm air of the vestibule wash over her face and leave her skin tingling in response. He paused just inside and she remembered she was expected to genuflect; after she did, Father Barrett repositioned her hand and led her inside.

"Where would you like to sit?" he asked in a low voice. "Closer to the front?"

"I don't care."

She felt his shoulder twitch at her bleak answer, then he kept walking, forcing her to follow him or be left floundering in the aisle. She could feel the people around her, smell their hair, the wet wool scent of their coats and hats cut by the occasional richer smells of leather gloves and cologne; St. Ita's probably wasn't a huge church compared to some, but it was Christmas and they had a full house. Gena could hear hundreds of people whispering and moving in the pews as she passed. She didn't know why, but Father Barrett continued to a pew almost all the way at the front and steered her gently into it as the people there shuffled their belongings to make room, more brownie points for being willing to let the priest seat his little blind mouse next to them. At least there was another pew in front of her to hold when she had to stand or kneel.

Five more minutes and Mass started, and after the processional had come up the center aisle and taken positions at the altar, Gena recognized the voice of the priest who had helped her as he began the service. She left her dark glasses on beneath the jagged ends of her overlong bangs, not caring if it seemed disrespectful. The sisters at the Catholic Charities orphanage had insisted she wear them practically from the moment she'd become their responsibility. Sitting in this church, surrounded by the trappings of familiar religion, it was easy to recall their stern voices as they implanted the seed of a lifetime: *"Except for sleeping, you must wear your dark glasses all the time, Magena. People find the way your eyes look unnerving."* As a child, it had taken her a long time to understand the lesson, although she'd obeyed the simple rule. How could her eyes *look* at anything when she was blind?

She found no comfort in the Christmas Mass. For every statement the priest uttered her mind formed a question, for every question, a bitter answer. Still, she felt calmer being surrounded by the practiced words of the crowd, a smooth noise that blotted out her mind and its terrible ability, and the only bad moment was during the Sign of Peace, when she had to shake the hand of the people on either side of her in the pew. She disliked touching strangers anyway, but the black depression that had settled over her since Luís's death had made her vulnerable, an easy mental target. The man on her left gave nothing but a quick, impersonal shake that made her think she would do okay, then the woman on her right clasped Gena's cold fingers in both her warmer hands and squeezed, giving Gena a brief flash of real emotion—

In her head was a scream of metal striking metal—car versus something huge, a truck—and shattering glass, the sensation of motion at a speed far too great for the woman to survive—

Gena swallowed and pulled her hand away too quickly, knowing the woman would be confused but helpless to do anything about it. Her mind had supplied her with another piece of brutal, useless foreknowledge. *We all die,* Gena told herself grimly. *I can't help her because I don't know when.* It was the *when* that counted the most, and that was sometimes—most often with strangers—so infuriatingly left out. Like now: the woman with the warm hands and who smelled like Jontue cologne was going to die, but it could be tomorrow, or it could be next year, although that far ahead was probably stretching Gena's time limit. Opening her mouth would label her a nutcase and probably get her humiliated by a public screaming scene.

Gena shoved her right hand deep into her pocket and turned back in the direction of the altar, wishing she could leave now and knowing the woman was watching her in bewilderment.

Finally, communion and the danger of others brushing past her, *touching* her, was over and the priest said his final words.

"God be with you."

"And also with you," the people murmured.

"The Mass is ended," Father Barrett said. To Gena's ears, he sounded as if he regretted the thought of letting all those parishioners leave. "Go in peace."

"Thanks be to God."

Gena hadn't said any of the words, despite their indelible imprint into her memory. Muted chatter filled the small church as all around her people stood and pulled on their coats and hats, talking all the while about their plans for the day. The noise was good, filling her ears and head like white static on the radio or the deafening noise at the factory where Gena earned the money that kept her from becoming a ward of the state. Not quite enough, though, to block out *every* conversation. The woman-beside-her-who-was-going-to-die was driving to her brother's home in downstate Illinois for Christmas dinner; she couldn't wait to see her niece and nephews and watch them open the gifts she was bringing.

Gradually the drone lessened as Gena waited patiently for most of the crowd to clear out, especially those with whom she shared the pew. The sounds on her left took on an air of finality as a pocketbook scraped along the well-worn wood of the pew and keys jingled. Without warning, the woman turned and touched Gena's arm. "Do you need someone to take you outside?"

Gena shrank away, terrified that another grim prophecy would blossom in her mind. The woman's fingers had brushed her for only a second, but it was enough to give Gena a rare flash impression of the past. Instead of future disaster she got a sensation of love and delirious happiness, a strong memory passed to Gena only because today was Christmas and also the woman's anniversary—

Her Christmas wedding a decade ago, a hundred fifty people come to share that special time—

"D-don't touch me!" Gena blurted without thinking. She whirled and stumbled down the length of the pew in the opposite direction, going as fast as she could, barely hearing the woman's stuttered apology. Too late, she realized she'd left her cane and would have to go back and get it, say something to the woman because of her behavior—

"Miss?"

She paused at the more familiar voice. "Yes?" Her voice barely made it above a whisper.

"I'm Father Barrett, remember? Here—I picked up your cane. May I walk with you outside?"

"Outside?" Gena scowled. All the way outside was a very long time to have to endure the company of a stranger . . . but how could she refuse? He *was* the senior priest, after all. As reclusive and gruff as she'd become, even she couldn't refuse him. Her upbringing demanded respect and courtesy to holy vestments.

"Forgive me," said the priest. "I thought you were ready to leave. Why don't we stay here for a few minutes instead? That will give the congregation time to thin out."

"Don't you have to talk to the people who're leaving?" Gena asked. "Shake hands with everyone or something?"

Father Barrett chuckled. "There are others who can easily say farewells for me, and I would rather talk with you before you leave." He paused, waiting for her to say something, but she didn't. The silence stretched between them for almost thirty seconds—Gena counted—before he cleared his throat. "I haven't seen you here before. Are you Catholic, or do you normally attend another church, Miss . . . ."

"Gena. And I'm Catholic," Gena said shortly. She wished he would go away and leave her to find her own way out. It wouldn't be that hard to do, and then she could go home.

Big fucking deal.

"What are you going to do today?" Father Barrett asked, as if reading her thoughts.

"I don't think that's any of your business." Gena's voice was harsher than she'd intended, but she couldn't bear the thought of telling this man, kind as he was, that she was going to do nothing at all. In return for this information he would give her pity, and she didn't need or want that. Pitying her would not make her feel better, would change nothing in her life.

"Ah." He didn't seem offended, but it was a moment or two before he spoke again. "Were you comforted by the Mass?" he asked finally. "You seem very troubled. Perhaps I can help."

Gena opened her mouth to tell him to go to hell, then remembered where she was. "God gives me no comfort, Father Barrett."

"God is there for everyone, child. Sometimes you just have to search harder."

Gena gave a laugh that sounded as if something were caught in her thought. "I didn't say I couldn't *find* God. I've never doubted He was there—I'm reminded every morning when I open my eyes and see *nothing*."

"Bitterness is a state of mind that can destroy a good person," the priest said. "It's best to accept what God has given and make the best of it, work at making a difference—"

"Let me tell you something, Father." Gena leaned toward him on the pew, close enough to smell soap and hair—he had a beard. "I can deal with the blind part. I'm *used* to it, okay? My parents dumped me on the side of the road when I was a kid and I was raised in a Catholic orphanage, so I was even used to being alone. Then I met a man, and I got married, and for the first time in the miserable thing called my life, I was *happy*. God didn't do that— he didn't marry me or hold me in his arms at night, or call me from the shop at break time. What God *did* do was take my husband *out*, Father Barrett, let him get murdered on the street when he went to work one morning."

Father Barrett cleared his throat again. "If you can attribute your sorrows to God, Gena, why can't you attribute your joys?"

That short, choking laugh again, coming unbidden to her lips. "Because sorrow is pretty much all He ever gave me, Father. Luís and I were married less than six months. The rest of my life has been spent like . . . *this*." She waved a hand at herself. "Besides"— Gena's mouth worked itself into a sneer that she couldn't stop— "people like you made a point of telling me at the funeral that it was the will of *God*."

"God's will is sometimes difficult to understand," the priest reminded her patiently. "But He loves us all. He gave His only son—"

"If you believe what the Catholic religion teaches," Gena interrupted coldly, "then He gave nothing He didn't expect to get back right away. I have to go—no, no, don't get up. I'd rather find my own way out." She stood, balancing awkwardly in the small space between the pew and the kneeling cushion. When she reached for her cane, Father Barrett placed it in her hand.

"Gena, please." The priest's voice was quiet but insistent. "Sometimes people enduring the blackest times of their life turn against God and they don't believe. I don't know what to say to convince you otherwise, but I do know you'll feel a whole lot better if you turn *to* Him rather than away from Him."

"After the wonderful life I've had, I suppose I should wave a cross and root for Him," she said caustically.

"Please don't go. Let's talk some more." He touched her hand briefly, flesh against flesh, and she knew him suddenly, knew that much later tonight he would sit alone in his room and drink too much wine while he thought about her and wished he could have done better by her. She had ruined his Christmas, and for that she was deeply sorry. She hadn't meant for that to happen, but she still couldn't let him think what he would later tonight.

"Don't mistake my feelings for self-pity, Father Barrett, or worry about anything I might do because of the things that I've gone through. I haven't turned away from God." Gena's expression was stony. "I'll keep going until I'm beaten into the ground, if for no other reason than to defy Him. God is still the same to me as He always was." She turned and moved into the aisle, then turned left and let her cane lead the way with a series of soft, sweeping taps. She spoke her final words over her shoulder.

"He's my *adversary*."

So much for Christmas memories, 1998.

The New Year's holiday hadn't been any better. Alone, floating within her perpetual cocoon of darkness, Gena kept the television off intentionally, wanting to avoid anything to do with welcoming the next, bleak year. She bought a six-pack of Blackberry Jack Country Cocktails early in the evening, planning nothing more than to bring in the new year with an alcohol-induced sleep. It did no good; at least three other apartments in the building had their tubes turned so loud at the magical hour that, drunk as she was, Gena woke at 12:01 to the sound of merrymaking. All the booze had gained her was a nasty headache in the morning and nausea for most of New Year's Day.

She didn't know why she was remembering those two holidays on this particular morning as she found a pair of blue jeans and slipped them on, then pulled a loose sweatshirt over her head. Maybe because those two holidays were the landmarks by which she had set her life and goals: if she could get through those without Luís, she would pass the test. She would be able to go on.

Feeling the bitterly cold air of winter on her face as she shoved one hand in her pocket and walked slowly east to the bus that would take her to the factory, she could imagine nothing in her future that held any more promise than the barren twenty-four hours stretching in front of her right now. Shivering mostly from the cold deep inside and paying little mind to the twenty-mile-an-hour wind scouring at her cheeks, Gena wondered if she had finally given up.

MARCH . . .

"Simon, it's him again."

Simon looked away from the report on his desk to see his secretary, Felicity, standing in the doorway to his small office. She looked profoundly sorry to interrupt him with the one piece of information she knew he detested hearing. He glanced at her and was immediately sorry—

—*flash*—

—when he suddenly knew she had a crush on him and all she wanted in the world was to make the man on the other end of the telephone go away forever. Felicity knew only the caller's name— and thus his connection to Simon—and that Simon wanted nothing to do with him. Each time she had to come in with this same announcement, she got more shamefaced about it, as if having to pass along an unwanted message meant she was doing a shoddy job. It put her in the middle of affairs that were best left out of the workplace, yet there was nothing Simon could do to stop it.

"Tell him I'm in a meeting." He bent his head back to his paperwork, then lifted it again when she made no move to leave. He raised an eyebrow.

"He says he knows you're here and if you don't take the call he'll come down to the building," she said, unable to look him in the eye. "I don't know how he found out you were in the office. I never said a word." She was only twenty, but her gray business suit, flat shoes, and the angry expression on her pretty face made her look twenty years older. Simon knew she was trying to act more mature—she'd even yanked her hair into a tight knot on the back of her head—but he wished she'd lighten up a little. *Trying to look older because of me,* he thought sadly, *thinking that will make the difference.*

"Okay." Simon kept his voice even. "Put him on hold. I'll get to him in a minute."

"If he comes down here, we could have security stop him at reception," she offered. "Or call the police."

"That won't be necessary. I'll handle it." He gave her a charming smile that he hoped looked genuine. "Don't worry." Finally she nodded and withdrew, pulling the door closed behind her.

A small room with a window and a few absently tended plants, a little piece of the city in which Simon had managed to find solace and, hopefully, work a little good over the years. A quiet, solitary home life with a cranky white cat to keep him company because while women were attracted to him, it was impossible to date someone when you knew that even though they liked you, they thought you were about as attractive as an actor in monster makeup. If he asked Felicity for a date, he would be taking advantage of their work connection—and she would probably end up regretting their relationship and wishing it had never happened; that was unthinkable. But Simon was all right emotionally, even if he had given up on dating; he had friends, that stupid cat, and an edge over other people that he tried to use constructively. Lonely sometimes, but some people were stuck with being alone, and he was probably going to stay that way. Beyond his work and the people involved in his caseload, he bothered nobody, but now, after twenty-seven years—

Stop it, he told himself. *Get it over with and put it behind you.* Before he could chicken out, he jammed in the telephone button that was blinking and snatched up the receiver.

"Chanowitz," he snapped.

"That's not a very friendly greeting for your father, Simon." The voice sound amused and smooth, far too relaxed for someone released from the penitentiary only six months ago.

"I thought you were dead," Simon said flatly.

"Only in your dreams, my boy."

That, Simon thought, sounded much more at home coming from the mouth of the man who had murdered his mother. "What do you want?"

"You never came to visit me. I don't even know what you look like. Let's meet somewhere."

"Why? So you can finish the job?"

"Simon, Simon—all that was a long time ago. Let's put it behind us and start fresh. I made a mistake and lost my temper, that's all. We—"

"Is that what you've called it all these years?" Simon asked incredulously. "A *mistake*? You call murdering my mother and maiming me losing your *temper*?"

There was a pause on the other end of the line and Simon could imagine the devious gears of Searle Chanowitz's mind shifting, trying to find a way to recover ground. He didn't know why the man wanted to see him, but he doubted it was out of love. There was no way for him to find out over a telephone line; to do that they'd have to come face-to-face and Simon had no intention of doing that.

"An . . . unfortunate choice of words. Forgive me."

"I haven't forgiven you for anything, and I never will."

"Meet me somewhere and we'll talk, Simon. If you don't, I'll come to your office."

"If you come here, I'll call your parole officer, who will call the police. I had quite a lengthy conversation with him yesterday, and he's pretty uncomfortable about the fact that you keep calling despite the fact that I've told you to get lost. In case you've forgotten, the terms of your parole were that you were to make no effort to contact me. You've already violated it, and a complaint could get you put back in prison, Searle. Would you like that?" Simon's voice was uncharacteristically nasty but it was impossible for him to be otherwise. "Maybe I should go on and complain. I'd be doing the world a favor."

There was no sound on the other end for a full ten seconds, and Simon was starting to hope Searle had hung up. No such luck—when he started to pull the receiver away from his ear, he heard the man speak again. "I'm disappointed in you, son." His father's voice had changed in a way that Simon couldn't quite grasp, but he didn't pause to think about it.

"Don't call me son!"

"I had hoped we could get together for coffee and talk this out, but it doesn't seem like that's going to be possible. That's very unfortunate."

"Frankly, I don't see how it makes any difference," Simon cut in. "I've certainly been able to live happily without you in my life."

"No, no, Simon. That's not the way a father and son relationship is supposed to work." Searle was making a valiant effort to sound soothing, but Simon finally put his finger on the difference between now and the start of their conversation. Searle's end of the conversation now sounded remote . . . *rehearsed.* As if he'd known it would come to this all along. "You see, I learned quite a lot in prison. I'm sorry for what I did to your mother, and to you. I didn't come home that night intending to do those things. Being in prison has shown me a different way. A different *light.* I've accepted God into my heart and learned to face my actions and atone for my mistakes. Won't you let me do that?"

"No," Simon said flatly. "I know you too well. And I don't believe you anyway."

"You know the man I *used* to be."

"You listen real hard here, Searle. This is the last time I'm going to talk to you, and I'm going to hang up when I'm finished because I don't want to hear anything else you have to say. *Stay out of my life.* In my profession, I've learned that people like you who have a taste for violence don't change that drastically. Sometimes they manage to get a handle on it, but mostly they just get too fucking *old* to keep beating on people. You say you've changed? Maybe, but it doesn't make a damned bit of difference. I don't care about what you did to me—I've even learned to live with it.

"But I'll curse you for the rest of my life for killing my mother . . . *Dad.*"

NEW ORLEANS
APRIL . . .

Eddie Cuerlacroix just woke up with it one day.

It didn't start with a headache, or a bump on the noggin, or even something as exciting and sympathy-generating as a mugging in the French Quarter. No, his life had been the same last night as it had the night before, and the night before that—a midweek nine-hour shift at Jackson Brewery, where he'd made a decent amount of money but certainly nothing to write in the record books. When he finally finished college (he was currently on a self-imposed hiatus), he was going to be an elementary school teacher—he liked kids—but Eddie still needed to figure out how to pay for the thirty-four credit hours that remained before he could get his degree.

The room faced east and was sun-filled and eye-blistering bright. The dusty, closed miniblinds might as well have been clear for all the light they blocked when, at about eleven in the morning, the sun found the perfect angle to throw its rays through the front window of the apartment. Naomi, Eddie's girlfriend, was lying next to him, her face crosshatched by the stripes of sunlight leaking through the blinds. She was a dancer in one of the more respectable bars on Bourbon Street, the word *respectable* applying only because she wasn't required to drop her G-string within reach of the customers. One of ten or twelve strippers in the joint, Naomi danced safely enclosed within a box of unbreakable Plexiglas while the visiting voyeurs slipped dollar bills through a paper-thin slot as they tried to get her to peel away that final layer of lace and satin privacy. So far as he knew, she never had. Then again, what did he *really* know about Naomi Lauren beyond the physical side of her randy, round-at-the-edges body?

Eddie looked at her, and he knew she was going to die.

He shook her by one shoulder. "Naomi, wake up." The air in the apartment felt cool and clammy, as it always did on spring mornings. It had been an unusually cool season for New Orleans and it was still taking until about one in the afternoon for his sprawling, century-old apartment above Kaldi's coffee shop to soak in the day's warmth. That would change, of course; Eddie did not have an air conditioner, and summer would bring sweltering heat and enough humidity to make a man think he could drown in the sheets of his own bed at night. Right now, he and Naomi, who stayed over two or three nights a week, were enjoying the unseasonable temperatures and cool night breezes. His girlfriend's skin was dry and soft, the color of eggshells against the much-washed but graying sheets. She smiled without opening her eyes and tried to burrow deeper into the king-sized mattress that served as a bed, shrugging off his hand.

"Come on, I mean it. Wake up."

His tone of voice was enough to cut through the fog and she opened her eyes, then squinted at the brightness. "What the hell," she said crabbily. Her gaze followed the end of the mattress to the

LED display of the alarm clock. "For Christ's sake, Eddie, go back to sleep. It's not even noon."

"I can't." His ginger-colored hair was a rat's nest of tangles hanging in his face and Eddie flipped his head back. He was starting to feel a little sick to his stomach, and it had nothing to do with the three bottles of Blackened Voodoo Lager he'd tossed back after work last night. Every time he looked at Naomi, his gut twisted and his mind filled with dread. "Sit up, would you? I want to talk to you."

Naomi said something into her pillow that might have been *"Fuck off,"* but Eddie wasn't sure. It certainly wouldn't surprise him. "I've got a feeling that you're going to die."

Eddie had been sure that would do it, but he might as well have said *My nose itches*, for all the attention she paid him. God, she could be so *infuriating*. He stood abruptly, yanking both the sheet and cheap comforter with him; Naomi got a smart half spin when the part she'd wrapped around her thighs pulled out from under her. "Shit!" she cried. She tried to grab for the covers but Eddie jerked them out of reach and backstepped on the mattress. "What the hell are you doing?" Madder than a rabid fox maybe, but at least she was awake and listening.

"Did you hear what I told you a second ago?" he demanded. "I said I've got a feeling you're going to *die*."

She stared up at him, her small, heart-shaped face twisted into a scowl. "What are you talking about? What happened—nightmares or something? I bet it's from that crap you call beer."

"It has nothing to do with beer or anything else." He reached down and grabbed her hand, pulled on it until she finally stood. "I just got this . . . I don't know what it is. Premonition."

"Yeah, well, I don't believe in premonitions," she said sulkily. "You can sit on it and spin, boyfriend. I was up till past six and I want to get some more sleep."

Naomi tried to pull free of his grasp, but he wouldn't let her. "I'm not fucking around here, Naomi. I'm *serious*. It's like I'm seeing the future or something."

Without warning, she balled her free hand into a fist and punched him in the shoulder. Eddie wasn't a big man—a hundred fifty pounds at his heaviest in the middle of winter—and Naomi was only five feet two, but she still managed to make him rock back on his heels and release her. "Hey!" he yelled. "That hurt!"

"If you can see the future and shit, then how come you didn't see that coming, funny boy?" She stomped off the bed and started grabbing for her clothes. Her hair, ramrod straight, shoulder length, and dyed deep blue-black, swung wildly as she yanked up her underwear, then wadded her jeans and T-sheet into a ball. "You know what, Eddie? You're just too weird sometimes. Call me when you get a grip."

"Naomi, wait—" But she was gone, striding out the door at eleven in the morning in nothing but a pair of panties like it was the most natural thing in the world. Eddie scrambled to the window in time to see her storm out of the door on the first floor—at least now she had her shirt on. The window was a monstrosity of rotting, warped wood but Eddie fought with it anyway, managed to force it up enough to stick his head and shoulders through. "Naomi!" he bellowed. "Come back!"

His girlfriend threw him a look so completely disgusted that he recoiled and whacked the back of his skull against the windowsill, then had to pull his face inside and shake his head to get out the fragments of wood and paint chips that had fallen into his hair. Now what? He didn't know whether to be furious or frightened. Going back to sleep was out of the question—he felt like he'd swallowed a half-dozen hits of speed. Standing in the middle of the apartment and looking around, he wondered if Naomi was right. She had good reason to be pissed, Eddie decided. He'd be ticked off too if someone woke him up in the middle of his beauty sleep and told him he was going to die—especially when there was no logical evidence to support the announcement. It wasn't like he had details or anythi—

And suddenly he did. He saw Naomi stand up and drop some change on a small table next to an empty coffee cup and a half-eaten beignet, then saw her walk along Decatur in front of the Café du Monde. It was still daylight but not for much longer, and she had that very Naomi-like walk about her, purse swinging, hair blowing in the wet spring wind, an "I don't give a shit about anything" look on her face as she headed back toward her place to shower before going to work. But Eddie knew more than most that the sneer on her face was a charade, and when the hood in the dirty sailor's T-shirt and wrinkled painter's pants sped by and tried to grab her purse, the thief found out fast that his mark was a natural hellcat. Snarling and kicking, moving on instinctive adrenaline, Naomi spun so that the strap of her purse wrapped around her shoulder and jerked the robber up short. Then, so very foolishly, Naomi waded into the guy. Trying vainly to pull her purse from his grip, she threw more of her quick, round-knuckled punches and added a kick at his shin when she should have just let him take it and run. So many people on the French Quarter's streets, and no one giving a glance to the feisty babe and the sailor, no one noticing until the guy was long gone and Naomi sank to her knees, still holding that oh-so-fucking-precious purse as the side of her favorite puke yellow BONGO *T-shirt suddenly grew a huge crimson blossom. All those people, tourists mostly, gaping and circling around, too stupid to do anything until one of the waiters at the café ran inside and called an ambulance, then sprinted back with wads of napkins and tried to push them against the puncture wound that went upward through her intestines and damned near halved her pancreas. So many people with so many good intentions, and may they all rot in hell as they let his bitchy, sharp-witted and beautiful Naomi bleed to death on the sidewalk.*

It was a long time later, but when Eddie could finally see his apartment again, he discovered he was crying.

His shift at the restaurant started at four, so he called in sick. Eddie knew the night manager would bitch him out—Thursday nights were nearly as heavy as Fridays—but he didn't care; he could get another job if he had to. It wasn't like he was building a pension or anything, and he had more important things on his mind than a gig waiting tables. He and Naomi had been dating for eight months; in all honesty, he didn't think he loved her . . . but he liked her a helluva lot and keeping her alive and kicking made the world—*his* world—a lot more entertaining. It seemed really shitty that she was set to die before her twenty-second birthday next month. Eddie didn't know if he could change things, but it was worth a day's pay to try.

He went to the Café du Monde early in the afternoon, ordered a round of café au lait and an order of beignets to nibble as he waited. Around him people laughed and talked, unconcerned, unknowing; he was afraid to look at them too closely, afraid that he would see something personal and deadly about each and every one, as he had with Naomi. Then what would he do? Chase them down and tell them about it, or follow them like some self-imposed bodyguard or superhero until he could save them from whatever horrible fate awaited? *If* he could change anything.

Eddie was thinking too hard, suffocating in his thoughts and concentrating so hard on *not* connecting with anyone around him that he damned near missed seeing Naomi when she stood and paid her check at a table on the other side of the café. He choked on the bite of beignet in his mouth and spat it out as he scrambled out of the chair, never registering the look of disgust from the woman sitting a few feet away. Naomi was moving onto the sidewalk already, and it was no use screaming her name because she'd never hear him over the babble of voices between them. Fighting his way across the expanse of the Café du Monde, dodging tables and overturning chairs and ignoring a dozen protests, he felt absurdly like one of those tiny metal balls in a child's water puzzle, sweeping through the corridors only to lose ground as someone else suddenly stood. He'd never make it in time, she was already nearing that crucial spot on the sidewalk where the park's steps became fully visible at the end of the retaining wall. There, too, was the guy in the painter's pants and T-shirt with his roaming, hungry gaze finding and fastening on her purse, assessing her and throwing some dark mental ON switch. Eddie had made it to the front but was still tangled amid the customers and tables when the man who would kill Naomi shifted into a run and went for her purse.

Fuck the exit! Eddie thought wildly. He shoved somebody out of the way and grabbed the railing of the fence that separated the café area from the sidewalk. He was no gymnast and his attempt to vault it landed him on his hands and knees on the other side—but at least he was over. A dozen feet away Naomi's back was to him and Eddie hauled himself up and sprinted for her, saw the killer-to-be running from the other side, closer than Eddie and no way could he reach her before the man with the knife.

"Naomi!" She didn't hear him, and in the time it took him to propel his body eight more feet she and the hood were already doing a dance on the sidewalk. Eddie saw the gleam of silver in the guy's hand, got a much better view of Naomi's face this time. Close enough to hear her gasp and realize she knew it was coming, dear God, *she was actually leaning TOWARD the point of the blade—*

Eddie body-slammed her to the sidewalk, felt the *snick!* of a razored edge catch on the fabric of his shirt as it stabbed at the air where Naomi had been only a moment before. At the same time that Eddie hit hard enough to make his vision shimmy, Naomi cried out as the skin along her forearms was burned raw by a street-level ride along the concrete. Still running on instinct, Eddie jockeyed himself in front of her and pushed to his feet, but Naomi's attacker was already running, a quarter block away amid the crowd and moving too fast to catch.

Eddie turned back to his girlfriend and saw her sitting on the sidewalk, dazed. The backs of both of her forearms were bleeding. "Hey," he said. "You okay?"

He reached a hand out, but with that swiftness that was so characteristic of her firecracker personality, Naomi jerked herself out of any shock that had tried to settle over her. "So what the hell was *that*, Eddie?" she demanded. She slapped his hand away. "Now what did you do?"

"What?" Eddie stared at her, bewildered. "That guy had a knife, Naomi. He was going to kill you."

She smoothed her shirt, then stood and grimaced at the raw flesh on her arms. No one passing on the sidewalk paid any attention to them or the blood. "No shit."

"I told you this morning—"

"Yeah, and I think I told you to fuck off," she snapped. "Now you've gone and messed up everything."

Naomi turned and started down the sidewalk in the direction her attacker had fled, and Eddie followed. His shoulders were beginning a slow, dull ache, remnants of his poor attempt at tackling. "Wait a minute—what are you talking about? Are you saying you *believed* me this morning but didn't care?"

"I believed you just fine, you moron."

He snatched at her shoulder to slow her down. "Then what's the problem? Did you *want* to die, is that it? Hell, pick a roof!"

Naomi tossed her head, her brown eyes glittering in the lights thrown by the shop windows. "No, I didn't want to die. But I was supposed to, get it? This wasn't like a disease or something—people can always come back from the edge of that with medicine and shit, and it wasn't like a—I don't know—bomb or something. Stuff like that, where a bunch of people bite the big one all at once is all numbers—*random*. What was supposed to happen to me today was fate, *destiny*. And you fucked it up, changed everything." As she glared at him, Eddie saw something flicker in her eyes, then they widened. "God, Eddie—don't you know what you've done?" She balled up her fist and he couldn't keep from flinching; he'd taken enough hard knocks today. But she only smacked it against her own chest, in the bony spot above where her breasts began; the gesture gave an unexpectedly hollow sound that made Naomi gasp. "Hear that? There's nothing there—*he* took it."

They had stopped in front of one of the shops, some tourist trap filled with imported junk that all said "New Orleans." Eddie reached out a hand to the wall and steadied himself. "You lost me, Naomi."

Before he could jerk out of reach, Naomi grabbed a handful of his hair and pulled his face close to hers. "He took my *soul,* Eddie. I'm not supposed to be here, walking around, talking, breathing." She stared at him, her gaze cold and dark. "Kiss me."

"What?"

She didn't bother to ask again, just yanked him the rest of the way and crushed her face against his. Her mouth was un-account-ably cold, the lips dry; when her tongue tried to probe into his mouth, Eddie couldn't stop himself from shoving her away. "Stop it!"

Naomi laughed. "What's the matter, boyfriend? Did you taste the *difference?*" She laughed again and a chill ran up Eddie's spine and crawled beneath the hair along his scalp line. Suddenly Naomi's voice dropped to a whisper and he had to lean forward to hear her, mentally bitching himself out for the flash of cowardice that washed over him when she looked up and pinned his gaze. "It was so . . . *fast,* Eddie. He took it and then ran off, just like—" She snapped her fingers for emphasis. "*That.* Don't you see?"

"I see you overreacting," he replied. Eddie made his fingers reach for her wrist and close around it. "Come on," he said gently. "Your head's just a little messed up over this. Let's go to my place."

Naomi didn't pull away this time, but she made no move to follow him. "And then what?" she sneered. "Fuck? You up for necrophilia now?"

"Damn it, Naomi," Eddie said furiously as a passing couple scowled at them. He tugged on her wrist, but she still seemed frozen to the sidewalk. "You're acting like an idiot. Besides, you never even believed in God. How can you start spouting about souls now?"

"It doesn't matter what you used to believe when something is suddenly gone," she told him. "When your convictions have been altered. I don't feel like I . . . belong here. There's no place for me to exist in the world anymore, no plans for me to do anything. I'm like a—a ghost or something, a walking dead person."

Eddie released her before anger made him squeeze her wrist too hard, found he went right into clenching his fists. "Bull*shit*. You're not dead any more than I am. You've been watching too many Coffin Joe movies."

She gave him a smile that made him involuntarily step back. Between the blue-black hair and the night-darkness of her eyes, her pale skin seemed whiter than normal, ghoulish. "You're wrong about that, funny boy. I'm dead, you're dead." She turned her back, a gesture that Eddie had learned the hard way meant whatever conversation they were having was over. Before she strolled away, Naomi tossed one last comment over her shoulder.

"We're *all* dead now."

CHICAGO
MAY...

He'd had Kiwi The Cat for fourteen years and Simon still didn't know if he liked her. He *did* know that he was used to having the animal around—she was his sole source of company while he was at home—and that something about her had changed. Through the years, Kiwi had been a lot of things to him—aggravating, indifferent, and arrogant came most readily to mind—and while affection wasn't something the cat often displayed, occasionally she honored him by sitting on his lap while he watched the wildlife programs or *The Next Step* on the Discovery Channel, purring as she allowed him to stroke the soft, white fur of her back for a few minutes. Those days had stopped, and now that Simon thought about it, he realized it had happened with startling abruptness. One day she was fine; the next she wasn't.

It took a full fifteen minutes and a hunt behind and underneath nearly every piece of furniture in his four-room apartment before he found her, saying "Here, Kiwi-Kiwi-Kiwi," like some stupid cartoon bird calling out in a wheedling, ridiculous voice that the cat completely ignored. This time her hiding place was behind his old Zenith console television set, perfectly centered on the floor behind it so that when he looked the first time, Simon's view behind the set was blocked by the cover over the end of the picture tube. He saw her only because he caught a flash of white when the cat's tail flicked involuntarily.

She didn't run when Simon lifted one edge of the walnut console and pulled it away from the wall. The movement angled the other end of the set closer in and effectively blocked any retreat anyway. She barely glanced at him as he reached down and swept her into his arms, then began to talk to her. He always did; after all, she was the only thing around.

"Where've you been?" he chided. "You didn't eat your food, so I . . ." Simon's words faded and he frowned at the small, furry bundle in his arms. Something was definitely wrong with this picture—Kiwi was just . . . *hanging* there, not a shred of resistance as she let him carry her where he would. She *hated* being carried, always had, and the last time—

Simon shifted her in his arms, then gasped and held the cat up to face level, his big hands wrapped around her rib cage with the thumbs hooking together beneath her forelegs. She blinked once, pale green eyes dull and oblivious to Simon's surprise.

The last time he had picked her up, Kiwi had been at least three pounds heavier.

McDerwin Animal Clinic on Clark and Rascher was one of those places that looked small from the outside but hid an interior that sprawled for a quarter of a block beyond a waiting room the size of a small kitchen. A half-dozen clean vinyl chairs the startling color of ripe oranges faced each other below a four-foot wall and counter that separated the reception desk from a waiting area that was always full of people and animals. As usual, Simon's timing was impeccable: today was Saturday, they didn't take appointments, and the place was a mob scene.

Simon stood patiently off to the side—all the seats were taken—holding the limp-bodied Kiwi and staring blankly over the heads of the other men, women, and children seated around the room. Vague thoughts filtered in once in a while,

—*flash*—

like the cranky-looking woman who was in front of him on the list but couldn't make herself believe that the receptionist would call the names in order. As always, there was that blurry undercurrent of curiosity.

—*flash*—

about his face that immediately materialized in every crowd when Simon joined it. Resigned to a wait of at least forty-five minutes, Simon leaned against the wall and let his eyes close, feeling the skeletal ribs of the cat swell softly against his forearm as she breathed. Time passed, people left him alone; just the way he liked it.

"Kiwi?"

He opened his eyes and looked toward the counter, where one of the assistants was looking questioningly around the room. "Here," Simon said. His voice was hoarse and the little stab of fear that went through his gut caught him by surprise. A solemn, slightly cantankerous feline, Kiwi had been in and out of the cute kitten phase in record time, and he'd never thought of Kiwi The Cat as a real . . . *pet*. She'd just always *been* there, like the plant you watered once in a while, then realized that ten years later it was touching the ceiling of your apartment. Part of his apartment; part of his *life*.

Simon followed the receptionist through the door that led to the back rooms, hearing the whines and barks of dogs echo through the hallways from the boarding area in the back, bits and pieces of conversation from the examining rooms undercut by a range of emotions running from near hysteria to celebratory relief. "In here," she pointed through an open door. "Hold him on the table and—"

"Her."

"Sorry, *her*. The doctor'll be right in." It was only a few minutes more but it felt like another hour. The aluminum surface of the table was cold and Kiwi was uncharacteristically trying to crawl back into his arms when the door opened at last. A middle-aged man with reddish hair and a Mormon-style beard walked in, holding Kiwi's chart in his hands—Simon had been bringing the cat here for years—and frowning at the latest data recorded by the receptionist.

For an instant, Simon felt like something had sucked all the air out of the room. Although he could still feel his feet firmly planted on the industrial vinyl floor, the room tilted slightly, giving him a brief sensation of what a bug must feel like sliding down the side of a glass jar. The doctor's voice shattered the illusion, bringing Simon back to the suddenly less preferable reality. "Hi, Mr. Chanowitz. I'm Dr. Moyerson."

"Sure," Simon replied. "We've met before."

The veterinarian smiled slightly, then his gaze landed on Simon's cat and his humor faded. "Let's take a look." He held out his hands and Simon nodded and gave Kiwi a little scratch on the head before handing her over.

It was the last time he ever touched her.

Standing in the reception area an hour later, Simon thought that half of him was numb and half of him was feeling like the world's biggest coward. *"Based on what you've told me about the change in her behavior and the blood tests, the most probable cause is cancer,"* Dr. Moyerson had said after a few too-short tests and a physical examination. *"I can run more tests, even open her up, but at her age and physical condition it's unlikely she'll survive the surgery. I've seen this too many times, Mr. Chanowitz. I'm sorry, but the kindest thing you could do for her is put her down."*

The doctor hadn't seemed surprised when Simon declined to be with the cat, just nodded in understanding and again said how sorry he was. Simon himself was unnerved at the sense of loss that blasted through him—he'd always felt that he and Kiwi had at best tolerated each other through the last decade and a half. Looking back now, he realized that for a man whose mind wouldn't let him enjoy the company of his own kind, an animal's tolerance wasn't such a bad thing. He was going to miss the white cat's presence in his life, the way she sometimes slept on the foot of his bed without touching him, the way she slipped into the kitchen and watched when he ran fresh water into her bowl and refilled her food. A thousand memories taken for granted until only this morning, and now what? He was *truly* alone.

Simon blinked furiously when unexpected moisture blurred his vision as he wrote out the last check to McDerwin Animal Clinic. A woman softly cleared her throat and Simon looked up to see an assistant in a white coat standing next to the receptionist. She was holding Kiwi's gray-and-silver collar—Simon had bought it three years ago, thinking it was hilarious to put a studded collar on such a small ball of fluff—and looking at him with sympathy in her dark, Oriental-shaped eyes. "Mr. Chanowitz," she asked quietly, "would you like to have this?"

Simon nodded mutely and glanced back at his checkbook, crossing the final *t* on his name before setting the pen back on the counter and holding out his hand. She placed the collar on his palm without smiling as the receptionist took Simon's check and paper-clipped it to a folder, then headed into the back. Shame bled through him as he stared at the empty piece of leather—he had made Kiwi go through her final minutes alone, abandoned her after all these years. In the last moments of her life, he had thought only of himself and his fear of being with the cat as she died and of picking up on things he didn't want to know. His fingers folded around the small collar and for the first time in his life, he actually loathed himself.

When Simon looked up, the woman was still watching him. He started to turn in the direction of the exit and nearly tripped over his own feet

—*flash*—

when he caught the full impact of what was in her mind. It was another first time for him when he was unable to stop himself from turning and gaping at her across the width of the reception counter.

"I know what you are," he said in a low voice.

Her eyes widened, then narrowed. "I beg your pardon?"

"Have dinner with me," he suggested impulsively. "My name is Simon Chanowitz, but, you know that, don't you? You get off at eight o'clock—I'll pick you up here."

"Thanks for the offer, but I have plans."

She was trying to act casual, but Simon knew he was scaring her badly. Thoughts of stalkers and other weirdos were banging around her mind and he cursed himself; that's not what he wanted to do. "Your name is Mercy, right?" He leaned over the counter, keeping his voice too low to be heard by the thinning crowd in the waiting area.

"How did you know that?"

"It's on your coat," he said easily. "I—"

"No," she said a little too harshly. "It's not on my coat."

Simon's gazed dropped to her left shoulder and his pulse skipped. Major blunder—Mercy was her nickname and the one everyone used; the name stenciled on the coat was her given name, Leah. He'd just made things worse.

"I'm sorry," Simon said quickly. "I must have heard someone else call you that and it stuck."

She didn't say anything for a moment, just stared at him with dark, suspicious eyes. "What did you mean when you said 'I know what you are'?" she finally asked.

"Nothing, really," he said awkwardly. "You know, just that—"

"I hate liars."

"—you could have healed my cat," Simon finished abruptly. What the hell, he thought. Go for it all the way.

They stared at each other in silence. The wash of emotions coming out of her was too much for Simon to sort through in the fraction of time available. Fear, anger, curiosity, even relief were blasting like liquid from a shattered water balloon, and all he could do was wait it out and see if he got wet—or drowned. He might be able to read minds, but he couldn't predict the future.

Suddenly she looked very tired. "You're not going to go away, are you?"

Simon shook his head, bluffing. She had no way of knowing that if it came to down and dirty, he wasn't the blackmailing type. If Mercy stuck to saying no, he would never force her.

"All right. Eight o'clock." She looked defeated, and for the second time in a few short minutes, Simon felt deeply ashamed. He forced himself to ignore the feeling and instead looked Mercy steadily in the eye. "But don't be late," she added. "I hate people who are late almost as much as I hate liars."

Simon nodded and almost said *I knew that*. Sucking in a quick breath, he turned on his heel and walked out before his mouth could get him in further trouble.

"So what exactly do you want?"

Simon whirled beside the driver's side door of his Blazer, almost using the hot cup of coffee he was holding to redecorate the front of his jacket. He yelped as some of it sloshed over the side and onto his fingers. "Christ! Did you have to sneak up on me like that!"

"Sorry. Did you get burned?"

"Nothing worth mentioning." He set the dribbling Styrofoam cup on the Blazer's beat-up hood and wiped his hand on his blue jeans, then impulsively thrust it toward her. "Simon Chanowitz," he said. "I'm . . ." He was lost for a moment, then he rushed on. "I'm pleased to meet you." He tried to smile and regretted it immediately, knowing what it would do to the appearance of his face. Her return gaze was steady and

—flash—

frank, and beneath the overlay of common courtesy she had a curiosity about his disfigurement that was refreshingly clinical rather than morbid. As she shook his hand, he also knew that she was angry at him for backing her into a corner, and still a little afraid.

"Mercy Ammon," she said and dropped her hand back to her side. "But you already seem to know everything about me, Mr. Chanowitz. What do you want?"

"Look," he said imploringly. He was botching this terribly. "I guess I don't really know *why* I wanted to talk with you. I—can we start over?"

"You've got a strange way of introducing yourself."

She wasn't warming up, but at least she wasn't as furious as before, and Simon grabbed at the chance. "Simon Chanowitz," he repeated. "I'm thirty-five and I live a few blocks from here." He felt like he was spreading a verbal résumé at her feet. "I've worked for the DCFS for about thirteen years—"

"Is that what this is about?" she interrupted. He was startled by the fury in her voice. "Why are you here, Chanowitz? What are you—some kind of private investigator?" her eyes were fierce and the side of her fist thunked hard against the fender of the Blazer every time she fired another question at him. "Did Erica send you?"

"No, not at all," Simon said, taken aback. "I—"

—*flash*—

"Christ," he said softly, "you got yourself in one helluva mess over that, didn't you?"

"I don't know what you're talking about." Her face was rigid. Tall and overly thin, stress was vibrating from her like tones from a tuning fork.

"Now who's lying?" Staring at her, Simon saw tears of frustration form in her eyes.

—*flash*—

saw her blink them away just as fast. The truth was

—*flash*—

—*flash*—

pouring into his head now, her unstoppable memories rushing into him to satisfy the mental voyeur that had always been embedded there.

—*flash*—

He shook his head, hard, not caring if he looked like a crazy fool for a moment as he tried to slow the flow of details. "No one sent me, Mercy. I'm just a guy who walked in off the street with a cat you could've healed but didn't because you never had a chance to be alone with her in the examining room."

Mercy's mouth opened, then closed. "How on earth could you know that?" she asked softly. Her eyes said she already knew the answer.

Simon shrugged helplessly. He wanted to blurt it out—*You heal, I read minds*—on the theory that a woman who could do the things she could ought to accept that he could read minds at face value. On the other hand, he knew she wouldn't; healing was something she did in the physical world, not the mental. Results were immediate and recognizable, and there were too many deviants in the world who could have easily obtained most of the information he knew about her. Instead of answering her question, he said simply, "You're a healer."

Her return laugh was short and bordered on shrill as she rolled her eyes. "Not anymore. That was taken away from me." Her hands, long-fingered and scrupulously clean, reached to tug nervously at the heavy braid of black hair that hung over her shoulder and swung nearly to her waist. The movement was a distraction, something a person did to pull their own attention away from the feeling that they wanted to cry.

"The title was taken, but not the ability." Simon watched her carefully. "You know what I'm talking about."

Mercy said nothing for a moment, then she eyed his beat-up brown-and-white Ford skeptically. Simon knew what she was thinking but kept his mouth shut and tried to block the input. He didn't want to know everything in her head so quickly, but turning it off was like trying to look at the word *stop* and not know what it said. If he anticipated everything she said, why would she bother talking to him at all?

Eventually, she turned back toward him. "You want to take a walk?"

"Sure. Anywhere in particular?"

It was her turn to shrug. The glow from the streetlights, store windows, and passing cars made Clark Street quite well lit, though the constantly changing shadows lent a gauntness to her features that at times made it look skeletal. He motioned for her to lead and she turned south, moving along the sidewalk at a brisk pace that barely let them scan the storefront windows as they passed, though neither had any real interest in what they saw. Simon didn't know what to say to the woman he was following down the sidewalk, didn't really know *why* he'd insisted she talk to him to begin with. She

—*flash*—

was testing him, he realized, right now. He'd heard the thought *Are you going to get another cat?* as clearly as if she'd spoken it out loud. If he answered it, she'd know that another person's privacy was a rare thing around Simon, an elusive treasure he could never seem to give. If he didn't, he would be lying to her by letting her think his gift was a sometime thing instead of something he lived with day and night. If she didn't walk away from him on a truthful answer, he'd deserve it if she did for a lie.

"No," he said as casually as he could. "No more pets. Kiwi was a cool cat and I'm going to miss her, probably more than I feel right now, but she never gave me what I needed. And she can't be replaced so easily anyway."

To her credit, Mercy didn't gape. She was scared to death of him—it was impossible for Simon not to pick up on her fear—but she refused to run or let her feelings show on her finely boned face. That wasn't the way she'd been raised, and it wasn't the way she was trained now. When she spoke this time, it was aloud, an oral confirmation that she accepted that he'd answered the question she'd never vocalized. "What about a dog?"

Simon shook his head. "I spend too much time at work and my hours aren't predictable. Sometimes my job takes me out of the apartment at crazy hours. It wouldn't be fair to the animal."

"Ah." Mercy had slowed her stride to let him catch up. "That must be hard on the social life."

"I have my work." His comment was shorter than he'd intended and she glanced at him, but there was no turning back. Visions of his clean but now empty apartment came unbidden to his head; now there would be no soft ball of white fur waiting patiently by the nearly empty food bowl at the end of the day. "What about you?"

"I thought you knew everything," Mercy said. The light tone of her voice was false.

"I try to block as much as I can," Simon answered honestly. "It's too much like prying, and overloads my head with stuff I can't do anything about. I guess I'm successful at it about eighty percent of the time, more when I know something strong's coming and I have a second or two to prepare. Lots of things—too much—still get through."

Her gaze flicked to him, then dropped back to the sidewalk. They were passing an old Scandinavian food store, a mom-and-pop operation that had survived all these years in the neighborhood by catering to the Germans and Swedes. Mercy paused to look in the window, smiling slightly. "Look at those," she said, pointing at the window. "See the little nut-shaped wafers? They're filled with a sort of fluffy dried chocolate filling. I used to eat them by the dozens when I was a child. I didn't know they had them here—I'll have to come back sometime."

—flash—

She wouldn't come back, Simon realized. He fought to keep a scowl off his face. Mercy had no money to spare; even the four dollars she had in her wallet right now had to last her until Friday. She packed her lunch every day, had sold her car, her furniture, and most of her clothes, all to keep paying on student loans and credit card bills that were nothing but remnants of a former physician's dreams. "You were telling me if there was anyone special in your life." He tried to keep his voice light when what he really felt was a starburst of anger at the way Mercy's life had upended itself.

"I was?" Mercy's small smile was surprisingly mischievous, his first flash of the impish nature she concealed. "I don't remember answering. I thought I was changing the subject."

"You were *trying* to."

She smiled again, more subdued. "You win. I go out sometimes, but no one special right now."

—flash—

Simon stumbled and found his footing before Mercy could comment. She was watching him carefully and he fought to keep his expression unruffled. She went out, all right, but the nights on the town weren't dates; they were more like excursions into hell. He cleared his throat. "Maybe I could take you to dinner tonight?"

—flash—

Shock that he would ask her, indecision. Somewhere in his mind Simon found a metal door and slammed it shut; he didn't want to know ahead of time what words she would use. Women didn't generally accept when he asked for a date because they couldn't help finding the way he looked repulsive; he supposed he couldn't blame them. If they were around him enough, Simon knew he sort of grew on them, like a homely dog, and having a gentle, caring personality was certainly an asset that went a long way to making up for his appearance. But he seldom asked again; he could forgive but not forget their initial judgment.

"Okay."

He blinked. For a moment he literally lost his command of the English language, then autopilot kicked in. "Uh, great. Where would you like to go?"

She shrugged, fingers again digging nervously at the heavy braid of her hair. "I don't know, anywhere. We don't have to get dressed up, do we?"

—fla—

Simon cut the flow in midstream; he could guess on his own that she no longer had much to wear beyond more of the same used denim jeans, sweatshirt, and wool coat she now wore. He didn't want to *automatically* know all of the daily details of Mercy Ammon's life. He wanted to learn them like anyone else. In a detached way, Simon was still reeling from her acceptance and felt vaguely proud of the speed at which he'd closed his mind. Maybe that meant he was finally gaining a measure of control over his ravenous inquisitive ability. "How about Ann Sather's?" he asked. Nothing elaborate, just good Swedish food and plenty of it. "We could have cinnamon rolls for dessert."

"Sounds yummy."

"How much time do you need to get ready?" Simon was going in exactly what he was wearing—which wasn't that different from Mercy's outfit—clean jeans and a lightweight blue-and-green flannel shirt under a sturdy, oversized black denim jacket, but guessed she'd want to get out of the clothes she'd worn all day at work.

Mercy glanced at the braid in her fingers as if checking to see if it was dirty and Simon almost laughed. "Is an hour all right?"

"Sure," he said easily. "Should I pick you up or—"

"I'll meet you there,"

—flash—

she cut in quickly, "so you don't have to go out of your way or anything."

"Sure," he said again. She was ashamed of her apartment and didn't want him to see it, but Simon could deal with that later. He was well acquainted with embarrassment and the myriad ways of handling it. "I have a few things to do in the meantime, so that'll work out perfectly."

Simon could have set his watch by Mercy's promptness. She walked through the door at precisely nine-thirty, looking uncertainly at the crowd of people shuffling around the restaurant's small foyer near the cashier. As it always was on a Saturday night, Ann Sather's was packed and the hostess was taking names from people who came in and adding them to the bottom of a two-columned list that was fast approaching a second page. She stopped Mercy, then motioned her through when Mercy nodded toward Simon, positioned near the front of the group.

"Hi," she said. "Wow—big crowd. How long will we have to wait?"

"I think we're three down from the top."

Mercy looked at him and raised an eyebrow. "Really? I could have sworn I heard the hostess tell someone in front of me that there was an hour wait." Although she still wore the same black-and-gray wool coat, it was open and Simon could see that she had changed into a fresh pair of jeans and a dull gold sweater. Her hair was loose and he was surprised at the unbroken length—no bangs—that spilled over her shoulders in dark waves all the way to her waist. Behind her round glasses, her slightly tilted eyes regarded him frankly. "Have you been standing here all that time?"

"No," Simon answered truthfully. "I did stop by and put our names in, though. Then I slipped out of line and did my errands." He didn't add that the biggest part of his errands had been nothing more than finding the men's room and washing his face and glasses, then fighting with the mop of wispy hair that in honor of his "date" wanted to stand out from his head in every direction. "And I picked up something to make a good impression." He slipped his hand inside the front of his jacket and pulled out a small, pale yellow rose he'd bought from a street vendor down the block. He had the sudden urge to offer it to her with a flourish but resisted, suddenly feeling a little foolish. He knew people were staring at him and then at her, and thinking snide thoughts like *Beauty and the Beast*. He wondered if she liked flowers

—*flash*—

and regretted it when his hungry mind dived into hers and came back with the answer: yes, she did . . . but she never bought them. Prying involuntarily again, did she feel awkward because of the way people were looking at them?

—*flash*—

Not a bit; she simply didn't pay attention, focusing only on Simon and herself with a doctor's trained concentration. Simon's mouth turned up in relief at the same time she broke into a genuine smile—the first full one he'd seen—and accepted the offered rose. "Thank you," she said. "It's lovely." Most of what she'd done and said in the short time he'd known her was unpredictable, but this wasn't; she lowered her nose to the bloom and breathed in, eyes closed.

"I didn't—" he began, but she stopped him with a soft touch on his hand.

"Wait," she said. "Did you register under your first name? I think she just called it."

"Yeah," he answered. He glanced toward the front and saw a different hostess use a pencil to run a line through a name on the list.

"Simon?" the hostess said again, scanning the crowd. "Simon for two?"

"Right here," Simon managed as he stepped back and let Mercy go ahead. Her fingers had been like a hot feather on his skin and his mouth was dry; he felt like a schoolboy on his first date, listening to the drumming of his heartbeat in his ears as they threaded their way through the tables scattered across the dining room to one in the back. Even the new hostess's double take when she saw him didn't register.

After they were seated and the waitress had given them water and menus, Simon finally felt like he could speak again. He was starting to worry that a coherent conversation might be more of a challenge than he'd anticipated. He couldn't imagine why he'd reacted the way he had—after all, they'd met only a couple of hours before. Maybe it was because he'd refused, at least for the most part, to let her thoughts flow freely into his. Was he so used to knowing everything about the people he met that the slightest mystery fascinated him?

"You've been here before," Mercy said, breaking into his reverie. "What do you recommend?"

He said the first thing that came to mind. "Swedish meatballs." Simon picked up his own menu, glad for the need to focus on something else. But the words on the page seemed to swim in front of his eyes, and after a few moments of trying unsuccessfully to concentrate, he decided to order the same thing. Despite the crowded dining room, the waitress took their orders and brought them soft drinks in less than five minutes.

"So," Mercy said, "you know all about me and I know next to nothing about you except your name and where you work." She overlapped her hands on the tabletop; her hair, parted in the middle and so dark brown that it was nearly black, cascaded over both shoulders and down the front of the gold sweater. The sweater had a V-neck and suited her skin tone perfectly; a small, upturned nose and a wide, full mouth completed the picture. The whole ensemble—the essential *her*—looked vaguely like an artist's painted portrait of a girl from the 1960s. She could have been a teenager except for the faint frown lines between her eyebrows.

"Well, I—" Simon cleared his throat. "What do you want to know?"

"Anything," Mercy said promptly. "Everything. I want back on equal ground, so I suppose you'll have to spill it all." She sent him an engaging grin. "Family, friends . . . girlfriends."

"None, some, and none."

Mercy laughed. "You can do better than that, Simon. I just know you have articulation hiding inside you somewhere."

He couldn't help chuckling. "That was kind of skimpy, wasn't it?" He took a deep breath. "Okay, the family part." *What the hell,* he told himself, *dive right in.* "My father is . . . around, but I haven't seen him since I was little. I was raised by my uncle, and we parted company when I graduated high school. It wasn't exactly the ideal family situation."

"What about your mother?"

Such an innocent question, and filled with the pain of a lifetime. Still, he had to answer. "My mother's dead," he said quietly. "I have my father to thank for that, as well as a number of other things."

—flash—

A slip, not his fault, the intensity of Mercy's emotions too strong for his mental blocks to resist. In a way it was a relief, because it told him that he wouldn't have to give her the gory details unless or until he was ready; she *knew* it all instinctively—too many cases of child abuse had passed through her hands as a doctor, too many mental tap dances around traumatized patients to not be able to comprehend words that were never said. The sick throbbing that had started in his temples when she'd asked about his mother subsided and he reached for his glass of water and sipped it, feeling the cool liquid slip down his throat and momentarily wash away the taste of old grief. Without warning, Mercy reached across the table and deftly plucked something off his shoulder. "What was that?" he asked.

She held it up. "A cat hair." Her hand slipped to her side and she flicked it away, then studied him. "You're going to be very lonely now, aren't you?"

He shrugged, ignoring the sudden lump in his throat. "I'll get by. Maybe I'll change my mind and get another cat." But his voice was too light and the only thing that saved him was the waitress arriving with the food. A man crying in public over a cat? Not quite, but Mercy's question had brought it all home that everything Kiwi had represented was now gone. He would be okay, of course. Eventually.

An excellent, filling meal

—flash—

and the first time Mercy'd eaten meat in months, no wonder she was so thin. Cinnamon rolls still warm from the oven to wind it all up, and no doggie bags for either of them—they'd practically swabbed their plates clean. The conversation took on a lighter tone as Mercy told funny stories from work, purposely steering clear of the hundreds of times the ending had not been so happy. Time to pay the check and Simon's guard was down again, lulled by the effortless dialogue and a feeling of growing harmony with the calm-natured woman sitting across the table from him. He reached for his wallet at the same time she picked up her purse

—flash—

and he couldn't let her do that, because the money she'd picked up at her apartment was slotted for something else, a necessity—groceries, the ComEd bill, he didn't catch what—and she would surely regret the pride that made her want to pull her own weight. Careful here, or he would hurt her feelings, a tricky balancing act of emotions and knowing what to say between not wanting her to be ashamed of herself, topped with being blatantly stunned that she didn't care if she had to pay her own way, she would do without to spend some time with him. No one had ever wanted to do that.

"My treat," he said with a grin. Another inward grimace; he

always forgot that smiling made him look his worse, pulled on the mass of scar tissue along the left side of his face until it started to drag the corner of his eye downward. Mercy hadn't been around him enough to get used to it; he should remember that.

"I'll leave the tip, then," she said.

"Don't bother," Simon said. "Then I'll have to get change. There's still people waiting for a table—let's just get out of here."

"Okay . . . thanks." Mercy took a final sip of ice water as Simon waited, then he followed her out of Ann Sather's. She moved quickly around the crowd waiting for tables, slipping easily between people but never touching, emergency-room training incorporated into everyday life. Simon found her movements intriguing and graceful, like the quick, swooping dance of a strangely elongated hummingbird.

Outside the temperature had dropped and Mercy shivered despite her wool coat. She turned north and Simon stayed by her side, not talking, just enjoying her company and nearness, the easy way she'd seemed to accept him without judging or prying too deeply. A couple of blocks down Clark was a Baskin-Robbins ice cream shop that was still open and Simon touched her arm and motioned at it. "How about a second dessert?" Anything to prolong the evening; he couldn't remember the last time he'd felt so comfortable with anyone.

But Mercy shook her head. "Thanks anyway. A tempting thought, but I'm already freezing. Ice cream would really do me in."

"It is kind of chilly," Simon agreed. He pushed his disappointment aside. What had he expected anyway—that the evening would go on forever? He might want it to, but the real world was bound to poke itself back in. "I'll walk you home."

Mercy smiled,

—*flash*—

pleased, and tucked her hand into the bend of his elbow as if it were the most natural thing to do in the world. The move sent a flash of warmth down his arm and into his chest, then beyond, and Simon fought the rush of desire, dismayed at the way he was responding. "I'd like that," she said simply.

He didn't know what to say and didn't bother trying to make awkward conversation as they kept going. A few more blocks and they turned right on Rascher, practically across the street from the animal clinic. Her building was a brick two-flat about a quarter of the way down the block, her part of it the illegally rented basement with only a back entrance. Simon stayed with her on the walkway through the dark, silent yard at the side of the building and around to the back, where she pushed a key into the lock on the outer door of what he thought was a not very sturdy-looking enclosed back porch. The *snick* of tumblers seemed very loud, competition for the slamdance that Simon's pulse had begun again. He felt as if he were walking on a tightwire: he wanted to ask if he could see her again, but was afraid of her answer; he could find out what she thought, but was afraid of that answer, too.

Mercy pulled the door open, then glanced back at him. The backyard was unlit and her face was a heavily shadowed oval in the night, framed by the inky wash of her hair. "Can you come in for a while?"

—flash—

Simon couldn't help it, sometimes his mind stretched out on its own, pure instinct that hurt its eternal quest for self-protection. No injury this time, though; the only thing he found was the innocence of her question, the genuine hope that he would accept tempered by that same background worry about the way her place would look to him. He started to speak and couldn't find his voice, had to clear his throat—he seemed to be doing a lot of that tonight—before he could force out the answer. "Sure."

Mercy pushed open the door and led the way, pulling a light string and descending a narrow set of steps to a small storage area cluttered with old furniture and water-stained boxes, used tires and God knew what else. There was barely a path on the concrete floor for them to follow to the apartment door, itself hardly more than a rickety wood panel covered in peeling gray paint and showing gouge marks around the lock. Funny, Simon thought sourly, how people were so good at disguising things; from the outside, this looked like an above-average building. He was too much an idealist; after the things he saw in the course of his work, he shouldn't have been surprised.

Mercy's apartment was dark, damp, and shabby. The walls hadn't seen a new coat of paint in at least twenty years, and Simon thought it was almost a given that the faded pink and black tiles on the floor were asbestos-based. But first impressions were deceiving, and under the dampness floated the scent of pine cleaner, ammonia, and furniture polish, and Simon didn't doubt for a minute that the floors and walls were hospital-clean. The furniture was a mix-and-match assortment of leftovers that probably came from the alley or friends, the coffee table and single end table from different sets and bereft of knickknacks or decoration. The whole place had only two windows, but despite the dimness there was a blurry sort of shine to everything—walls, floor, the tiny kitchen appliances—that told the eye it was spotlessly maintained. Mercy was watching him anxiously; Simon's hands were folded behind his back and he dug the nails of one hand into the back of his other hard, letting the temporary streak of pain distract his devious mind before it could poke into her thoughts. He had no business there, he reminded himself sternly. Consciously trying to maintain someone else's privacy was a new and nearly bewildering concept: he'd never cared enough about a woman to try.

"I'm sorry," Mercy said. Her cheeks were reddening. "It's not much. If you're uncomfortable—"

"It's fine," Simon assured her. He wasn't lying; he found it sad that someone as special as Mercy had to live like this, in an under-heated room that was never meant to house anything but forgotten family artifacts, but she didn't need a spacious apartment to make a good impression on him. He needed to turn her thoughts away from the embarrassment she felt or it would build and bring a sad and clumsy end to the evening. "Do you have anything to drink?"

"Uh—sure." Mercy shrugged off her coat and hung it on a hook on the wall next to the front door. "Do you want me to hang up your jacket?"

"This'll do fine," he said. Simon slipped off the denim jacket and dropped it on the hook over Mercy's.

"Let's see what's in the fridge," she said. The kitchenette was only as far away as the width of the single large room that served as the combination living, dining, and bedroom, and she was there practically before she finished her own sentence. A quick puttering at the tiny counter and she'd slipped the rose into a glass filled with water. Then she pulled open the refrigerator door and peered inside. "I've got . . . Diet Pepsi, lemonade, and water. Nothing strong, I'm afraid—but I can make some coffee. Would you like that?"

"Lemonade sounds good."

"Okay. Make yourself comfortable."

Too nervous to sit, Simon drifted to the rickety bookcase under the front window and found mostly medical-based textbooks and used trade magazines. Interspersed here and there were a couple of well-thumbed older romances and he picked one up and looked at it, wondering about this woman who read both *The Trauma Patient: Care-Giving for Violent Crime Victims* and *The Flame and the Flower* by someone named Kathleen Woodiwiss. "Not a big selection," Mercy said from behind him. He turned and accepted the glass of lemonade she offered. "I don't read much fiction."

Simon held up the romance novel. "But when you do . . ." He smiled. "This looks like a happily-ever-after book."

"Happily ever after doesn't happen in real life," she said sharply.

—fla—

Stop it, Simon told himself. He set the glass down so he could put the book back where he'd found it, concentrating so hard on keeping his mind to himself that he almost missed her next words. Her hand on his arm, however, was impossible to overlook. "I'm sorry," she said quietly. "I didn't mean to snap at you. That was rude."

"Forget it. You've got a lot of reasons to be pessimistic." His brain—or was it his heart?—made him do something rash; powerless to stop himself and praying that he wasn't stepping over an invisible line, he clasped the hand on his arm, then raised it to his lips and brushed the clean-scrubbed knuckles. "Don't waste your time living in the past, Mercy," he said softly. "Just deal with today and right now, and let tomorrow work itself out."

Mercy stared at him but didn't pull her hand away. "All right, Simon. I will." He released her reluctantly and watched as she reached past him and placed her own glass on the table next to his. When she straightened, she slipped her arms around his back and kissed him fully and deeply on the mouth. The taste of her tongue and the pressure of her lips made the room spin and Simon held on to her gratefully, as if she were the only stable thing he could reach in a hurricane-strength storm. Heat surged through him, a hit of sexual electricity that nearly made his knees buckle; in his arms, Mercy trembled, and he didn't have to pry to believe her response was real. When she tilted her head, her hair swept over his arms like a dark, silken sheet and he felt himself pull her closer. She came willingly, shocking him again as her warm fingers tugged the back of his shirt from the waist of his jeans and slid underneath the fabric, her palms slightly rough as they moved across his skin.

Simon pulled back. "Maybe I should go," he managed. "I don't want to do something wrong, push too far or something." He sounded like a terrified schoolboy, but it was the best he could manage. This whole evening had a sense of unreality about it, as if at any moment he would wake in a hospital bed and be told these fine and wondrous moments were nothing but morphine-induced sweet dreams.

"Nonsense." Mercy leaned forward to speak, her voice velvety and low, her breath tickling and incredibly erotic against his ear. "Maybe you should stay." She raised one hand and dipped it into the mass of his hair, combing it back from his face with her fingers. "Don't you want to?"

"You don't know me," was all Simon could think of to say. His scalp was tingling, the rest of his body going into overload. Of *course* he wanted to stay—but he wanted more than just tonight, more than the few disappointing one-nighters he'd experienced in the past. It had nothing to do with the gift that she had and everything to do with . . . what? Karma, maybe. Destiny. He couldn't bear it if she was just another one of the women he'd dated who'd slept with him for no other reason than to prove to themselves how liberated they were, how appearances meant nothing to today's compassionate, modern woman. Appearances could be *everything*.

Key words: *could be*.

"But I'd like to." Holding his hands, Mercy backed away, pulling him with her to an old, overstuffed couch covered by an ancient-looking but clean couch throw in an impossibly dated red-and-green pattern. She reversed their positions until his back was to the couch and gave him a gentle push to make him sit—then pushed him again, until his gangly six-foot-four frame was sprawled gracelessly across the couch covering. Certain he must look like a giant Gumby doll, he was still searching for the words to make a rational protest when she said, "We'll start with the couch, just like high school kids," and squeezed lengthwise next to him onto the cushions. Facing him, touching the length of his body with her own, how on earth could he ignore the urge to kiss her again?

Another moment of hesitation and she met his questioning gaze steadily. "Let go, Simon. I won't hurt you."

—*flash*—

Unavoidable as his mouth met hers, but there were no fantasies or memories of someone else's face in her mind to help her make it through the sex, no self-righteous, sacrificial bullshit or visions of martyrdom. Simon found everything Mercy felt and reveled in it: need, desire, simple gratitude that he hadn't rejected her advances. The strangeness of her happiness to be with him, the sensation of someone who enjoyed touching him as much as he was immersing himself in her was something so completely foreign he could have been staring at hieroglyphics. Most of all, as they moved from the couch to the lumpy double bed in the far corner and explored the essence of each other, Simon was drowned in Mercy's mysterious sense of simply belonging with him.

JUNE . . .

Blue bubble lights split the darkness with sudden, shocking brightness, and Joey London could have sworn they'd dropped out of the sky. No one had been behind him a few seconds ago; again, he would've sworn to it. His gut did a slam dunk, then recovered out of the need for self-preservation. He couldn't afford to look nervous or guilty. The way he truly felt still came out in a single, muttered sentence.

"Now I'm fucked."

Not necessarily.

Joey didn't know where the thought came from or why, but it gave him a stronger sense of self-confidence than he'd felt a few moments before. He pulled the Lexus smoothly to the curb and shut off the engine, then got out of the car with his wallet already in his hand. He'd learned a long time ago that it was better to meet the cop halfway than make him come to you; this worked especially well in the rain. This one was already climbing out of the squad car—a woman. Shit, he thought irritably; sometimes they could be the worst of all. He took a surreptitious glance at the uniform and realized it was a beat sergeant, someone who could cruise from district to district if he or she so pleased—his luck really was running low tonight.

Not necessarily.

Joey resisted the frown that wanted to slide over his features. What the hell?

Aloud, he said, "Evening, Officer. Is there a problem?" He didn't take out his driver's license yet; as far as he knew, he hadn't blown any traffic law. She would want to see it, of course, but only for identification. She'd want to check the registration on the Lexus, too, but that was to be expected.

The policewoman who faced him had light gray eyes and short blond hair with platinum streaks in it. Her face was professionally neutral, the narrow set of her eyes perpetually suspicious. "No problem, sir," she said in a clipped voice. "May I see your license and registration, please?"

"Of course." He pulled his license from his wallet and held it out. When she accepted it, he nodded toward the car. "Hang on a moment and I'll get you the registration." She nodded and Joey opened the driver's door and bent inside, knowing that she was watching every move he made. God, he hated being put in this position.

After scanning the registration Joey pulled from the glove compartment, she nodded. "Would you mind waiting, Mr. er— London, while I do a routine check?"

"Not at all," he answered. Calm on the surface, inside Joey was furious. *Sure lady,* he thought, *you do your fucking routine check while the biggest deal of my life gets tired of waiting for me to show up.* But wait, he did; it was either that or shoot her, and he didn't think the general public would take kindly to that. Damn— he and his associates had argued about the timing on this deal. They were still stuck in the old routine of running around at night, but Joey had wanted to do it during the day, right at the heart of the morning rush hour. Where else would the cops be but snarled up with the traffic flow and tending to those stupid fender benders? Oh no, no one would notice a pearlized white Lexus—he'd traded in the blue one he'd damaged by forcing Lamont's car out of the way in the parking garage—slinking around this neighborhood at night. Fucking idiots.

Joey watched the cop walk back to the squad car, his mind spinning. Everything would check out in the computer, but it was all too easy to guess her next question. He had a story ready, a babe dressed to the nines and waiting in the neighborhood for him to pick her up, a couple of late jazz theater tickets good only for tonight carefully tucked in the breast pocket of his four-hundred-dollar sports coat. It wasn't the best backup he'd ever put together, but it would have to serve. Lana, Leena—hell, he couldn't remember her name—was going to be pissed as hell when he didn't show up, but she was what Joey considered disposable; when she called to give him a piece of her mind, she'd never get past the answering machine in his rented one-room "office" on Milwaukee Avenue. Of course, if he ended up with a cop on his tail all night, Lana-Leena might get to see that jazz performance after all.

Another moment or two and the squad car door opened and she stepped out. Joey thought she looked sort of like a walking pear—all hips and no waist, although her face was pretty enough. Her eyes were her best feature, but they were damned cold. She was short, too; whatever the minimum CPD height requirements were for women, she'd barely made it. When she was close enough, he saw her name tag flash: MARTEN. "Okay, Mr. London," she said as she handed him back his license. "Everything checks out."

"Great," Joey said heartily. "Will there be anything else?"

Officer Marten's gaze swept him up and down. "Actually, yes. Would you mind opening the trunk of your vehicle, please?"

He minded extremely, but he wasn't in a position to say so. Her squad car was parked about six feet from the back of the Lexus bumper, and the video camera in the car was pointing accusingly from behind the windshield. Had she called for backup? Maybe. Probably. Even if she hadn't, it was now a part of the CPD's data history that this particular cop had checked his registration. If anything happened to her, he'd be a prime suspect.

Outwardly calm, Joey's hand was shaking as he activated the remote signal on the control module dangling from his key chain. In response, the trunk lock released with a barely noticeable thump. "There you go," he said as calmly as could.

"Step to the side, please."

He nodded, watching as she panned the beam of her flashlight inside the carpeted trunk, the strong light washing out the weak illumination of the trunk's bulb. Nothing much to see: an open but full CD tote, his sports bag and a pair of Rollerblades, the flap of carpet that covered the compartment where the spare tire and jack were stored.

"I'd like to look in the bag. Any objection?"

Plenty and he opened his mouth to tell her to fuck off, get a search warrant. Another thought from nowhere stopped him—*Let her.* It strangled whatever protest had been on its way out of his mouth and left him able to only shrug. He'd never been this close to getting busted before and now some stupid voice in his head was going to put him in the slammer for the next ten years. *Shit,* he thought with unaccustomed carelessness, *if I'm hearing voices in my head, maybe that's where I ought to be anyway.* There was an odd sensation of slowness about her movements as she positioned the flashlight inside the trunk so that its beam gave her the best visibility, then unzipped the heavy-duty Nike bag. The expression on her face went from efficient curiosity to surprise as she shoved aside a thick, white terry-cloth towel and saw what was underneath. There was a pistol in the pocket of Joey's summer jacket that she didn't know about, a beautiful, silver-handled .38. He could shoot her if he had to, then blow apart the video camera. He didn't know if it would work, but it was the best he could come up with.

Officer Marten's eyes were glittering as she looked from the neat row of heavy plastic bags and back to Joey's face. "Don't tell me, Mr. London. It's baby powder, right?" Her hand dropped to the butt of the gun in her holster. "I think you'd better turn around and place your hands against the roof of the vehicle."

Now.

Now <u>what</u>? Joey opened his mouth, but the words that came out were as much a shock to him as they were to her.

"I don't think so. Why don't we meet for coffee in an hour and talk about this?" Something insane inside him screamed with laughter while another part stood frozen, amazed that he would say such a stupid thing, horrified at the idea that he was going crazy, splitting into multiple personalities over which he had no control while he rode along and watched.

She looked at him incredulously. "You think I'm *nuts*? You've got at least twenty pounds of cocaine or heroin—"

"Cocaine."

"—and you expect me to just let you drive away? You're under arrest, asshole—get your hands on the roof of the car *now*."

Her hand had been hovering around it, and this time she did unsnap the strap across the holster of her service pistol, intent on drawing out the weapon. The craziest idea sank into Joey's head then, sharp and hard like something in his eye, enough to make him blink spastically for a second.

Do it.

"I'll be at Max's at the corner of Belden and Clark in an hour and a half. Meet me there. I'll buy the coffee, plus I'll have something I think you'll appreciate."

Nothing Joey had ever done in his life had been this foolhardy, but now something flickered across her eyes, a kind of sly shadow that darkened the fine gray irises to the color of storm clouds. Joey was unprepared for the way the deepening of her gaze hit him, and suddenly he was overheated, warmer than the cool night temperature called for, hot for *her*. His face felt thick and he could feel rivulets of sudden perspiration following the well-defined lines of his chest and back muscles; pretty soon it would be obvious that he was sweating, and the last thing in the world a guy like him wanted was for a cop to see him drip. What the hell was going on? He needed to wrap this mess up, bring it under control for at least the amount of time it would take him to get the coke over to his buyers; instead, Joey found himself staring into those steel-gray pools and so filled with sexual desire that he had to shift on his feet to get comfortable. Whatever had gotten him wasn't lost on her, either. He heard a faint *click* and saw her finger push the snap back down, then her hand dropped away from the gun. Amazingly, she smiled.

"All right, Mr. Lon—Joey." The pitch of her voice had lowered and he had to strain to hear her; the breathy sound her words made only increased the energy rushing through him. "You do that. And mind you don't stand me up."

"I wouldn't think of it," he managed.

But she was already walking away.

By the time she walked into Max's, Joey was beginning to think he'd hallucinated the entire episode. Occasionally he dipped into the blow himself, at parties where it had to be known that he could be a generous provider and his stuff was prime enough to use himself. Not much, though—he'd seen too many promising dealers turn into cokeheads who eventually ended up in the joint when they started ripping off customers or got so desperate and careless they sold to an undercover dick. There was also the danger of getting your face blown away on a deal where the buyer hadn't been checked thoroughly and turned out to be a pro thief.

Sitting in the booth at the far back with a cup of coffee cooling in front of him, it was hard to bring back the feelings that had seemed so suffocatingly *huge* an hour earlier. Had he really been stopped by a female cop who'd then let him walk despite all that snow in his trunk? That alone was enough to make him think somebody'd slipped a happy pill into the veal marsala he'd eaten earlier at Manzo's. But the rest of it, that *attraction* . . . Everything was against it, and right now Joey could tick off a mental list of strikes against the idea. He could start with the fact that she was white, and Joey had never been attracted to white women. As far as he was concerned they were prissy and spoiled and far too bland in the passion department. Thin lips and pale skin that reminded him of frozen fish didn't help, either. He liked his women sleek and as dark as possible, and there was nothing at all trim about the spread of hips on that cop. And there it was, of course, that final, inescapable strike-you're-dead detail: she was a *cop*. Her position in the world gave her a forever hand of power over him, and he could never tolerate that. No, something weird had gotten into his mind for a minute there, heat, panic, whatever; he should—

And it all came back when he saw her walk in the door of the coffee shop.

Joey hadn't been paying attention to the time and somewhere between now and meeting her on the street she'd gone off shift. The Chicago Police Department uniform was gone, replaced by a pair of blue jeans and a mint-green sleeveless tank top that showed strong arms and hung long enough to minimize the hippiness—not that her hips mattered anymore. Whatever objections he had broke apart like a smoke ring when her eyes met his. By the time she walked the length of the restaurant and seated herself across from him, Joey felt as if he were drowning.

"So?" Officer Marten tilted her head and the move made her look vaguely girlish. "You said you had something for me?"

Joey cleared his throat and brought up the package from its place on the seat next to him. He'd stopped at Walgreen's and bought wrapping paper to make it look like a present, bright but considerably less obvious than a brown paper bag. "Here," he said. "Happy birthday."

She laughed and reached for it. "And how old am I supposed to be?"

Joey couldn't help smiling. "Forget it. A guy could get in trouble answering a question like that." He waited a few beats, but she didn't open the box. "What's your first name?"

"Alva."

"What is that, German?"

She nodded, then gave him a grin that he couldn't have described as anything but dirty. "The master race."

Joey scowled at her, wondering if there was a purpose behind the insult. Probably not; Alva seemed very much like a woman who said shit like that just to goad people, and right now she reminded him of a razor blade attached to a coiled spring; if he took the bait, he might just get his head sheared off. Besides, if that was the way she really felt, he didn't give a damn. "I didn't think you'd show," he finally said. She laughed again, the sound rubbing along his ears like something warm and slightly rough, the feel of carpeting warmed by the heat from a fireplace. A drop of perspiration at the base of his throat suddenly grew into a delicate line of moisture that followed the curve of his collarbone and down, until his body hair soaked it up. He hoped to God she didn't see him shudder.

"What?" Alva said mockingly. She inclined her head toward the gaily wrapped box. "And miss this? What exactly is in here, anyway?"

Joey raised one eyebrow. "Jellybeans." Relief clamored faintly in his head; smitten, yes—but not stupid.

"I don't think so."

"Yeah, well. That's what I'm stating. For the *record*."

She sat back against the booth and nodded. "I get it. You think I'm wired, don't you?" When he didn't answer, she grinned again. "Nothing like trust to start a relationship off on the best foot, right Joey?"

"Who said we had a relationship?" he retorted. But his heart had begun hammering in his chest and his palms had gone damp. He had a sudden vision of the two of them, crashing together amid a pile of tangled sheets. Jesus.

Alva glanced around the coffee shop, as if making sure that no one else was paying attention to them, before giving him a sidelong glance. "Oh, I think we do, Joey London. We do, indeed."

His rented condominium overlooked Lake Shore Drive, Lincoln Park and the lake, and gave him moist, cool breezes filled with the scent of green from the grass and abundant trees. "The balcony," she'd whispered when he'd opened the door and ushered her inside. "Oh, God, yes. Let's do it on the *balcony*." He'd been living here for a year, but the idea had never occurred to him, for obvious reasons. Neighbors with telescopes, for one thing; it was a common, snidely accepted pastime of the high-rise class to window cruise, and it wasn't that hard to get infrared attachments that would let the voyeur pick his own hours. For the most part, Joey kept his blinds drawn if he wasn't dressed.

Alva waved his objections aside and gave him a smoky glance, then stepped to the sliding-glass doors and slid them open. "So what? You ashamed of what's under your clothes, black boy?"

Fuck this, he thought. Maybe he *would* simply kill this bitch and be done with it. He grabbed her by the wrist and yanked her around to face him. "Don't call me that," he growled. "I've had enough of your bullshit." Without warning, she dug into his shirtfront with her free hand and pulled his face to hers, then bit him, *hard*. Pain flashed across his lip and he yelped and let go, backstepping unwillingly. "What the hell!"

She laughed—she was *always* laughing—and literally rushed him. For an endless moment Joey didn't know what to do, fight or flight instincts jumbled together into a third reaction that accomplished nothing in the way of saving his ass. Turning and twisting in confusion as her hands went everywhere, then he heard fabric tear and realized his two-hundred-dollar shirt was gaping in the front, buttons falling to the floor like pearlized pebbles. "Hey," he said stupidly, then Alva's arms were around him and he gasped as she half dragged, half pushed him toward the balcony door, grateful at least for the reflex that let him snatch at the switch on the wall that killed the lights in the condo. Not absolute darkness but enough to let him blend into the night a little. Alva's colorless skin was still shockingly visible, and there he stood with his mouth hanging open like a fool as she bunched both hands around the collar of her green top and tore it wide open, stripped off the pieces, then tossed them gleefully over the railing. The breeze up here was substantial and the air current instantly whipped them away; shoes and jeans were next, thankfully wadded into a corner rather than thrown over. Less than sixty seconds after they'd walked into his condo, this crazy white stranger was standing naked twenty-five floors above the Outer Drive and staring at him expectantly.

Joey felt . . . timelocked, somebody's movie character separated from reality by the screenplay and witness to things that were never meant to happen in the ordinary world. Whoever was writing the lines had left him hanging, though; the sting across his mouth was forgotten and the best he could manage was a breathy "Well."

Alva looked at him from beneath half-closed eyelids. Her hair was mussed and she was panting lightly. "Aren't you . . . hot?"

Hot? Why, yes—he hadn't noticed it before now but suddenly he *was*, fire blasting through him with an intensity that rivaled anything he'd ever felt. The shreds of his shirt and the fabric of his slacks and socks felt like metal armor on a cloudless hundred-degree afternoon, his shoes like the ones made of cement the old mafia movies were so fond of referring to. Joey's entire body seemed to be made of wet lead: dark, heavy, and glistening with unanticipated sweat. He tried to lift a hand to pull off his shirt and found he couldn't; he was trapped by his own body and Alva's stormy gray eyes. All he could do was whisper helplessly, *"Yeah, I'm . . . hot."*

She grinned and reached for him. "Well, then. Let me help you get . . . *hotter.*"

Joey had done a lot of things in his life, none of which—except maybe having to shoot Lamont—he'd regretted, but this was the first time he'd met someone who made him think he ought to just lie down and bare his throat, as though he were nothing more than a feast for a night creature too powerful to escape.

Bruised.

Joey lay on his back and stared at the ceiling, tracing the roller pattern of paint and trying to make his mind work again. Every part of his anatomy ached, from the bite mark on his mouth to the concrete burns on his knees from the time they'd spent on the balcony—and those were made worse by carpet burns from when they'd moved inside. Dawn was creeping into the condo now and he turned his head and looked at the woman sleeping next to him. With her eyes closed and her face relaxed, Alva looked innocent and peaceful, but Joey wasn't foolish enough to believe the illusion. He had an idea that when he got out of bed, even to use the bathroom, those eyes would snap wide and alert, a sleek, dangerous jungle cat roused from a nap by the noise of prey.

He thought of last night and trembled, then was ashamed of himself. What the hell had she done to him, to his body, to his *head*? Something about her attracted him on a level he couldn't identify, fucked around with his sense of self-confidence, called to him like heroin lured an addict. The power trip part was tricky but not impossible to deal with—he'd certainly handled shit like that before. The sex end didn't matter; fucking was an integral part of life but not a controlling one, and he wasn't a high school mope who let his dick tell his brain he was in love. Last night had been wild and unlike anything he'd ever done, Alva Marten was unlike anyone he'd ever been with . . .

But he'd still be able to kill her if the need arose.

NEW YORK
JULY . . .

[fade to Marti Nunciata]

From the closing segment of the seven o'clock Cable News Network broadcast:

"Astronomers at the University of Arizona have discovered a rogue planet entering the far reaches of our solar system. Called a rogue planet because it is so much larger than any known asteroid and because of its spherical shape, this object is hurtling through space at a hundred twenty thousand miles per hour. While information at the moment is sketchy, experts estimate that the rogue planet is roughly the size of Earth's moon, or about two thousand miles across, and is headed toward the general vicinity of Jupiter. Astronomers say this will be the first astronomical object to come within striking distance of Jupiter since Shoemaker-Levy in 1994. While insisting that it is still too early to project, experts have nonetheless christened the rogue planet 'Millennium' because of preliminary calculations which indicate it will pass close to Jupiter early in the new year."

[fade out]

AUGUST . . .

"The noise in this place is deafening," Lamont shouted to the foreman guiding him through the stamping area of the dishwasher plant to the superintendent's office at the rear of the building.

The other man, who had a work shirt on with the name RUSSELL stenciled across the pocket, shrugged. "The workers all wear ear protection," he yelled back. "Even the folks who work in the fringe areas. In here—Caligraro is the guy in the white shirt." Lamont nodded as Russell opened a gray door with a window in it and motioned him in.

"Mr. Caligraro?" Lamont realized immediately that his voice was too loud; when the door closed behind him, it had blocked at least ninety percent of the racket. But no one here seemed to be bothered by either the noise from the plant or the volume of his voice. The man he was addressing was fiftyish and about twenty pounds too heavy for his medium frame; when he looked up to meet Lamont's gaze, his eyes were small and close-set in a round face. Thick gray and white curls started from the crown of a high forehead. He already looked annoyed.

"You must be the lawyer Sowa hired." Caligraro looked ready to spit. "Can we make this quick? I gotta desk full of things to do, Mr. . . . ."

"London."

"Yeah, right. London." He folded his arms and his mouth turned down. "I thought this was all wrapped up. The insurance company looked into it and gave the go-ahead to pay the maximum on Sowa's workman's comp. What's the problem? To be honest, I don't understand what you're doing here." Caligraro's words were so heavy with a clipped south side Chicago inflection that a good number of his *d*'s sounded like *t*'s, his *o*'s like *a*'s. *I taut dis wuz all wrapped up. Da ensurance company looked inta it.*

"Your insurance company's investigator interviewed a number of the plant's employees, Mr. Caligraro," Lamont explained. "Although they've approved Mr. Sowa's claim, they are undecided as to whether or not management at the plant knew the safety switch had been compromised on the machine which caused the injury."

Caligraro's eyes narrowed. "You're telling me they think I'm running an unsafe shop here?"

Lamont shook his head. "Not at all. Sometimes in the day-to-day business of managing a plant, things get overlooked, reports get lost or misfiled. Mr. Sowa indicated that one of the workers in the back office warned him about working on the press the morning he lost his hand. The insurance investigator interviewed her, but his report was inconclusive. Therefore, I've been asked to conduct a final interview."

"Somebody from in here warned Sowa?" Caligraro looked completely befuddled. "I don't remember seeing him in the office that day."

Lamont had left his briefcase in his car in favor of a small leather notebook. He flipped through it quickly to verify something before continuing. "According to the report, that conversation took place during the nine-thirty break in the coffee room."

"Well, I don't know who he could've been talking to. I didn't think anybody in the plant ever paid attention to the shirts in the office other than to complain about a payroll deduction. I must've been out the day the investigator was here." The superintendent scratched one eye as if it suddenly pained him. "I gotta tell you, Mr. London. Lots of weird shit's been going on in this place—hell, *everywhere,* since it was on the news about that asteroid."

"Asteroid?" Now it was Lamont's turn to look puzzled.

"You know," Caligraro explained, "*Millennium*—that planet thing they think is gonna come real close to Jupiter at the start of the new year. People getting hurt, getting sick, just acting *different*." He looked at Lamont suspiciously. "I can't believe you haven't heard of it," he said, shoving his hands into his pockets. "Don't you watch television?"

"I've heard about it," Lamont replied, flipping back through the folder, "and to answer your question, no. I don't watch much television at all. I guess I just hadn't made the connection."

"Well, there you go," Caligraro said, as if that somehow explained it all.

Lamont found the copy of the investigator's report and scanned it. "The person I need to talk to is Magena Savanna."

An expression of impatient disgust flowed over the other man's face. "Well, I should've known. If you'd have told me that right off, I could've saved you a bunch of trouble." Caligraro reached into the breast pocket of his shirt and pulled out a pack of cigarettes, then shook one out of the pack and shoved it in his mouth despite the prominent NO SMOKING sign on the wall behind him.

"Why is that?"

" 'Cause she's a freak, that's why. I wouldn't even have her on except the law requires I hire a certain percentage of—nothing personal, you understand—minorities and cripples. Worse than that, she's one of the bitchiest women I've ever met, and ever so often she goes off her rocker and starts yanking somebody's chain about how something bad's gonna happen to them." Caligraro scowled. "She's lucky. It's too late to do it now, but if I'd have heard her spouting off back then I would've suspended her without pay for a week. She's been warned about that crap already."

Lamont drew a deep breath, hoping he could maintain a neutral face. Cripples and freaks? This guy was really starting to get on his nerves. "Let me see if I understand you. Ms. Savanna—"

"We call her Madge here in the office," Caligraro interrupted. He gave Lamont an odd, vaguely insincere smile.

"Ms. Savanna," Lamont repeated, "may have told Mr. Sowa in advance that he shouldn't work on this particular machine on the basis of some kind of . . . premonition?"

The superintendent grinned unpleasantly. "Still wanna talk to her?"

"Yes, I do," Lamont said. He wasn't put off in the least by the idea. "Very much."

Magena Savanna was sitting at a data entry terminal with a headphone set over her ears when Caligraro showed Lamont into the tiny room in the back. Any notion of being introduced went out the window when Caligraro turned on his heel and left, pulling the door shut behind him. The room was large enough to hold only a couple of chairs and two gray Steelcase desks on which were two terminals covered in grimy fingerprints. One desk was cluttered with stacks of precariously balanced papers among which were shoved used Styrofoam cups, pens, and other desk paraphernalia. The other desk was bare of everything but the terminal and a can of Diet Pepsi. A young woman wearing dark glasses below shaggily cut hair the color of coal sat before the terminal, head bent slightly down as she keyed in information she was apparently getting from the earphones.

"Who are you?" she asked without looking up or missing a keystroke.

"My name is Lamont London. I'm an attorney with the law firm of McGuire & Day." The two desks faced each other and Lamont pulled the chair away from the messier one and rolled it over to where he could face the woman. "We're handling Pavel Sowa's injury claim. The superintendent says you're Madge Savanna."

The woman's head snapped up. "My name is *Magena*," she snarled. "That dickhead told you to call me Madge because he knew it would piss me off." She slapped at a key on the keyboard hard enough to make Lamont wince, then gave the keyboard extender an angry shove that sent it sliding backward under the desktop with a bang as the screen, too dim for Lamont to read to begin with, went totally dark. "If three syllables are too much to handle," she said sarcastically, "try *Gena*."

"I'm sorry," Lamont said simply, but she didn't respond. She sat and waited instead, staring down at her hands. Between the choppy ends of the black bangs reaching to the midpoint of her nose and the black-lensed glasses, Lamont had caught only a glimpse of her face, which was a little on the broad side with high cheekbones and a long, straight nose above a full mouth. The shabby thrift-store clothes, haircut, and glasses made her look very much into the gothic night scene, and he guessed that when she stood, she was only about five-two and slightly chunky. Her night-black hair and dusky, reddish skin made her unmistakably American Indian. Her eyes, he imagined, would probably be as black as her hair. A silver wedding ring gleamed on her left hand.

"What do you want?" she asked finally. Some of the fight had gone out of her voice, but Lamont was sure it hadn't entirely disappeared.

"I just need to ask you a few questions about the accident. It shouldn't take long, a few minutes at the most. Then you can get back to work."

"I can't wait."

The sarcasm again, but Lamont didn't know if she was talking about having to answer his queries or getting back to work. He cleared his throat and decided to keep going. "Mr. Pavel told the insurance investigator that you went up to him during the coffee break the morning of his accident and warned him that he shouldn't use the press when he went back on shift," Lamont said. "According to the insurance report, you told the investigating claims representative that you'd had a bad feeling about it." He sat forward, his face earnest. "I can tell you now, Ms. Savanna, that Mr. Pavel's claims have already been approved so his settlement is in no jeopardy if you answer my questions with honesty. Did you see someone modifying the safety switches on the machine? Alternatively, did you hear anyone talking about doing such a thing?"

Incredibly, the woman laughed. "Mr. London, no one talks to me in this place unless it's absolutely necessary, and they all shut up and move the other way when I'm within earshot. I caught that fool Pavel by surprise and he just wasn't smart enough to leave before I opened my mouth. As for seeing, Mr. Hot-Shot Lawyer, you tell me. What do *you* think I see?" She tossed her hair back out of her face and pulled off the black sunglasses.

Her eyes were as white and empty as large, shining pearls.

• • •

It was the fifth of August, and Lamont had no business being at this woman's door.

The weather was all wrong. Yesterday the meteorologists had promised a bright summer morning and temperatures in the eighties, good hot weather that made the thought of another damp Chicago fall as far away as China. Instead an overnight cool front had swept down from Canada and a steady rain had started yesterday afternoon and soaked the city through. Now everything was an ugly, shiny gray, as though the world had been encased in a dirty sheath of that protective plastic that had been so popular on furniture in the sixties. Lamont had beaten the traffic simply because he couldn't sleep that night and he'd given up trying at four A.M. By five o'clock he was already on his way, and a trip that should have taken twenty minutes had stretched to almost an hour, his Grand Am crawling along the rain-slick streets like a small white sailboat.

She'll slam the door in my face, he thought. *I certainly would if some lawyer banged on my door at this hour of the morning.* He couldn't wait any longer, though; he'd thought he seen somewhere in the reports that Magena Savanna was a part-timer. If today was a workday for her and her hours ran with the shop's, she might be getting ready for a seven-to-three shift. If that was true, she'd be walking out the door in about forty-five minutes, and Lamont wanted to talk some more with her first.

Lamont had planned to ring the bell like anyone else but the lobby door was open, propped by a wet newspaper someone had wedged between the door and the woodwork to stop the latchlock from engaging. He knew he should ring anyway so she would have some warning, but he skipped it and went on up instead, kicking the newspaper out of the way as an afterthought; he detested people who made buildings unsafe for other residents because they were too lazy to take their keys. The doors were marked with painted-over raised numbers and letters, the kind that homeowners usually nailed over garages. It made finding the right apartment easy, but when he got there and raised his hand to knock, he suddenly lost his nerve. What the hell was he *doing*? Bewilderment hit him, and sheepishness, too. He'd never be able to explain his presence or the sense of . . . necessity that had kept him awake all night and pushed him out of the town house in the middle of a predawn summer storm.

Before he could turn to leave, someone began unlocking the bolts on the inside of the apartment door.

Lamont stepped back, intent on hurrying down the stairs before he was caught, but he wasn't as familiar with the dim stairway as Magena Savanna was with her front door. Familiarity be damned, it was completely unnerving for him to hear her say, *"Mr. London, wait. Don't leave,"* before she had the final lock disengaged.

The door swung wide and she was standing there, framed by the dark, worn wood of the hallway. Nothing in the apartment behind her was lit and Lamont could barely see her. Still dressed in an inexpensive cotton nightgown, her spiky black hair was even wilder than it had seemed yesterday at the plant. "Come in," she said in a low voice. "I've been expecting you."

The apartment was still filled with darkness after Lamont turned on one of the living-room lamps. The used furniture was upholstered in a mishmash of somber colors—worn navy, faded forest-green, an assortment of unmatched shades of brown. Nothing went with anything else but, of course, that didn't matter to Gena. Here and there he saw unexpected dashes of color—a brilliantly colored Mexican serape, a bloodred vase holding dusty yellow silk flowers on the tiny kitchen table centered beneath a wide window. The glass was covered by a tightly drawn shade gone gray with age that belittled the attempt to dispel the gloominess of an apartment over ten decades old. Perhaps the missing husband had brought these touches of brightness into Gena's life. If that was so, the man's influence was slowly bleeding away.

"Coffee," Magena Savanna said. "You take it with cream."

Standing at the window in the living room where he had shoved the curtain aside to see the street below, Lamont turned to stare at her as she stepped out of the doorway to the kitchen. Two steps forward, a precise left turn, and she walked confidently across the bare wooden floor and offered him a mug. Lamont took it from her, his hand brushing her slightly shaky fingers. "Perfect," he said.

She moved carefully backward, then did a half turn and lowered herself to the couch, one hand sweeping the cushion absently to make sure she was positioned correctly. "Please, sit down."

"I . . . " He looked around, suddenly uncertain. What was he doing here? As he stepped over to an old rocking chair facing the couch, he couldn't answer that. He chose instead to stare into the coffee mug, a promo from some fast-food restaurant, watching the way the swirls of powdered creamer still whirlpooled in the center of the coffee. His life felt like that right now. She wasn't saying anything either, so Lamont finally asked the most obvious question.

"How did you know it was me?"

Magena Savanna laughed lightly, a sound full of unhappiness but not at all cruel. There was a noise outside the closed window, traffic already building, and her head tilted in that direction momentarily before her attention returned to him. She shrugged. "The same way I knew Pavel Sowa was going to get his hand cut off by the punch press," she said matter-of-factly.

Lamont frowned. "You had a feeling? That's all?"

She jerked and he saw her fingers momentarily dig into the fabric of the couch. "You take this too lightly, Mr. London." When she had invited him inside a little while ago, her voice had been calm and reasonable, nothing like the caustic front she wore at her job; Lamont was sorry to see the hard facade return but her next words made him forget about that. "This isn't some back-woods superstition that says a fucking crow flying into your house means someone's going to die. This is the kind of thing that made me know that the day my husband walked out of this apartment on his way to work, he'd never come back."

"Lots of people have premonitions," Lamont began. "I don't disbelieve—"

"No," she interrupted. "You don't. And I know why."

Lamont blinked. "I beg your pardon?" He wished he could see her eyes, but she wore the dark glasses even inside her apartment and it was impossible to tell if they were fixed on him or on the ceiling. She was blind and he supposed it shouldn't have mattered, but it did.

"You shouldn't have touched me when I gave you the coffee cup," she said softly. "When people do that, sometimes, because of the way they'll be thinking about something later on, touching gives me bits and pieces of their past. Worst, sometimes I know their future."

"Really." There was no mockery in Lamont's tone, only genuine curiosity. "And what did you learn about me, Ms. Savanna?"

"You might as well call me Gena." She twined her fingers on her lap, bunching the washed-out flowers of the calf-length nightgown she still wore beneath the open front of a hastily thrown-on robe. When she spoke again, Lamont had to lean forward to hear. "I know that it was your brother Joey who shot you in your parents' condominium, Lamont. And I know that tomorrow, or next week, you still won't have figured out a way of telling them the truth without tearing your family apart."

His shock was a physical thing, like a punch in the gut, and he almost dropped his coffee cup. "How—how could you know that?" he sputtered. "Who—"

"And I know about the other things that you can do."

Silence between them then, the hot sides of the ceramic mug stinging against his palms as her words sunk in. *I know about the other things that you can do.* "This is . . . incredible," was all he could think of to say.

She shrugged again. "Why? You move things with your mind, I see—sort of—with mine. When you really think about it, why is one more incredible than the other?"

Another question for which he had no answer—she seemed to have hit them all on the head. "You must know a lot of things."

This time her laugh was harsh. "You don't know the half of it."

Lamont set his cup down on the coffee table. "That's a lot for one person to shoulder," he commented.

"Like I said," she snapped. "You don't know the half—"

"Stop it."

Gena's head snapped in his direction. "What?"

Lamont stood and strode to where she sat on the couch. Without warning, he reached out and slipped off the dark glasses. Her eyes, so pale and large, gleamed in the low light of the room. She pulled back, but it was too late.

"What did you think you'd find?" she asked mockingly.

"The real you," he shot back as he wrapped a hand around one of her wrists and pulled her to a standing position in front of him. "The person who's hiding behind the glasses and the bitchiness."

"I wear the glasses because my eyes make people nervous," she said sullenly.

Her face was aimed toward the floor and Lamont put one finger of his other hand under her chin and lifted it. "Who cares?" he demanded. "You can't run or hide from the world, Gena. It's always around you."

"You don't know what you're talking about—you've been hiding from your own abilities for years!"

"I've learned that sometimes it's impossible to fight," Lamont retorted. "Sometimes a person just has to do their best to fit in."

"I'm not the only one who can't see sometimes." She sounded disgusted. "Fitting in is a matter of having a place to fit in *to*. It's a luxury, not a right, and you have it. I don't."

He stopped her from pulling away. "Are you going to spend the rest of your life wallowing in self-pity?"

"You're full of shit, London. Why don't you just leave?" Her jaw was rigid.

"If this isn't self-pity, what is it?"

"I don't need your fucking lectures, okay?" This time Gena did pull free of his grasp, and she gave him a little shove that made him dance backward to keep his balance. "I didn't ask you to come here!"

"But you knew I was coming."

"You think that's a *revelation*?" She sounded ready to cry. "Stuff like that's the *smallest* of what I see, you idiot. In here"— she slapped an open palm against her forehead hard enough to make Lamont recoil—"I saw and *felt* Luís die before he left the apartment, but he didn't believe me. I told Pavel Sowa not to work on that damned machine, but he didn't believe me either. Thousands of things like that, but no one ever *listens*." Lamont drew in breath to speak but she held up a hand. Her mouth worked for a moment before she continued in a low voice. "And what the hell do I do about the bigger things, the stuff I'm only *lucky* enough to see every now and then?"

He stared at her, afraid to ask. Afraid not to. Finally, "What . . . things?"

It took her a long time to answer, long enough that he thought she might have decided against it. When she eventually spoke, her voice was tired and full of pain. "I know that the rogue planet my dickhead boss rants about all the time is the one thing in his whole, miserable life that he's right about.

"It's going to destroy the whole fucking world."

It took Lamont a while to take in Gena's news. It wasn't a matter of believing or disbelieving—any doubt he'd had about what she could do had vanished the moment she'd said his brother's name. Now they were sitting in Gena's tiny kitchen, at a table barely large enough to hold their coffee cups and two small plates on which she'd placed hot pieces of toast. She moved smoothly within her space, never bumping into anything or stumbling, but Lamont wasn't surprised. He thought there was a stronger woman inside Gena than she would acknowledge. He felt ludicrous sitting here with toast and coffee ten minutes after the news that life as they knew it would cease to exist inside of a year, but as Gena had pointed out with a wry twist of her mouth, "That's quite a while away, Lamont. You do have to eat in the meantime."

He tried, but the toast was like a lump of paste and sawdust in his mouth, forced down only with the aid of the coffee. "You're certain?" he finally asked, not because he doubted, but because he had to hear it.

"No, I'm not," she said, surprising him. "Nothing's written in stone, I suppose. If Luís had listened to me the day he died, would he still be alive? Maybe—I don't know."

"So we at least have hope." Lamont pushed his plate of half-chewed toast aside and leaned toward her over the top of the table. "What do you see, Gena?"

"I . . ." Her voice cracked abruptly. "Terrible things," she ended up whispering. "But how do I describe them to you when I don't know what they *look* like?" The dark glasses were still off and lying on the couch in the other room; now she let her head fall forward onto her open palms. "But I can *feel* it," she said thickly. "Pain, misery, despair. Terrible destruction and darkness. Death . . . and worse."

Worse? He reached for her hand without hesitating and she let him pull it back to the tabletop. Clasped in his larger, darker one, her fingers looked small but sturdy, quite capable despite her handicap. "There's no place to go, nothing that can be done?" he asked. "Of all people, you would know that."

She blinked as tears spilled down the ruddy skin of her cheeks. The neckline of her blue-and-black plaid robe was wet with them. "Some things are inescapable," she said quietly. "And besides, you're wrong about me. I don't hide, and I don't give up." Gena stood and her hands found his broad shoulders and tugged insistently at his shirt until he rose from the chair and faced her. Now it was Lamont's turn to be startled when she stepped closer, then lifted her face and kissed him on the mouth. Her lips were soft and deliberate against his, unexpectedly enjoyable.

"Wait a minute," he said uncertainly. "What are we doing here?" He felt flushed and warm, downright dizzy, but he had no desire to pull away. When they'd moved to the kitchen a little while ago, Gena had let him raise the shade covering its small window and now something outside glittered and caught his eye. The sun—breaking through the layer of clouds to shine on the waterlogged trees on the corner, making the leaves suddenly sparkle like bunches of crinkled metallic Christmas paper. With doom hanging over the world, sometimes beauty could be found in the most unlikely places.

Gena pulled his attention back to the here and now by slipping her hands around his waist before kissing him again. Tears forgotten for the moment, her voice was a warm, breathless murmur as she pressed close to his chest.

"Saving time."

SEPTEMBER . . .

"So," Jim Kaiser looked at Searle Chanowitz from across his desk. "How's it going? You got a job?"

Searle shifted on his seat and fought the urge to rub his damp palms along the legs of his pants. "Not yet, but I've got a few leads." At least his voice sounded okay; God, how he *hated* these twice-monthly meetings with his parole officer. The tether of prison, still fastened tight.

"Yeah?" Kaiser studied him. "What sort of things are you looking into?"

It was time for twenty questions, but Searle kept his cool. The last visit had been downright nerve-racking, with Kaiser letting him have it good for the calls he'd been making to Simon. This time Searle was clean, but the memory was still an ugly scab. "I'd prefer something to do with charity or the church. I was sort of, you know, getting into that stuff in the joi—in prison." There, that ought to sound good on the verbal résumé. Frankly, Searle didn't give a rat's ass what he did, so long as he had money. He'd had some jobs working for Manpower, but the last one had ended almost a week ago. Funds were getting thin, and you didn't get much unemployment when your work history for the last thirteen months consisted of temporary minimum-wage gigs that made you push a broom or a mop all day. Hell, people on welfare didn't do shit and made almost was much money as he did—but going on the public titty was a no-no for a parolee. After spending nearly twenty-seven years in the pen, he felt a lot like a suckling pig pulled from a sow and tossed into the river.

"Charity work, huh? Well, I got a lead you can look into." Kaiser's buzz-saw voice cut into Searle's reverie. His parole officer was digging a rumpled, overstuffed file out of one of the desk drawers; written across the top in Kaiser's heavy scrawl was RELIGIOUS/NON-PROFIT ORGANIZATIONS. "There's a new one here that came in a couple of days ago. I dunno much about the place, except that they're looking for affordable labor."

Searle nodded. Translation: *cheap.* "And?"

The interruption earned him a scowl, but Kaiser pulled out a two-page information sheet. "I'll make you a copy of this. The company's called After Help, Inc. It's come out of Althaia Hospital. It says the company"—here Kaiser peered at the paper as if not quite believing what he saw—" 'sprang out of what we perceived as a need evolving from the anxiety caused by the announcement regarding the rogue planet Millennium presently headed for Jupiter.' " When Searle looked at him blankly, Kaiser shrugged. "Who's to say who needs the help and who doesn't, right? A crock of shit, but it's a job."

That it was. "Where do I go and who do I talk to?"

Kaiser scanned the info sheet more thoroughly, and Searle wanted to ask him why the hell he hadn't read it through when it'd first come in. Not a good idea, though; Kaiser was a burly man who'd been a cop before a bullet in the ankle had slotted him to permanent desk work. It had been the temper thing with Lila that had landed Searle in the joint to begin with, and he had gotten a handle on that bad habit right quick due to the fast and efficient tutoring of the prison guards and cell-block kings. Released and enjoying a measure of freedom he hadn't known in over a quarter century, Searle had made the mistake of mouthing off to Kaiser on his second visit, then spent the two weeks until his next meeting nursing a nose that missed being broken only by a tweak of lady luck.

"Well," Kaiser finally said, "I was going to send you to Human Resources, but apparently this After Help thing isn't really associated with the hospital. It's the private baby of the hospital administrator." He tapped the papers smartly on the desktop before setting them aside and picking up a pen to scribble out the address. "I think you go right to the person at the top. Sit tight while I make the setup call."

· · ·

There wasn't much fancy about Althaia Hospital. The LaSalle Street address had made Searle think it would be something special, headed as he was into the heart of Old Town, a neighborhood that had come full circle from the bad reputation it'd had around the time his marriage had been . . . terminated. Now Old Town was full of yuppies and BMWs, swank new condos and hundred-year-old buildings renovated to ten times their original value—none of which had apparently rubbed off on this aging and worn-out hospital. The reason was obvious: too close to the Cabrini Green housing projects for comfort, the area's six-figure residents preferred to take their illnesses and accidents to the more prestigious lakeside Northwestern Memorial.

The floor of the foyer was covered in linoleum that had once been an industrial off-white; now it was gray with age and gouged by a hundred thousand heel marks. The piece of paper from Kaiser instructed Searle to check in at reception for a visitor's pass, then ride the elevator to the administration floor where a secretary would greet him. Nothing tough about that, but as he stepped to the reception desk and waited for the woman seated there to write him out a pass, he didn't know whether to smile or scowl. Jesus, but this place—the sullen-looking people, the mixed antiseptic and urine smell, the muted sounds—reminded him of the penitentiary.

The administration floor, however, was a world apart from the gray and tan realms of the rest of the hospital. The receptionist was a perky little thing who would've lasted about two minutes inside the walls of a prison, so Searle's earlier comparison quickly dissolved. Long strawberry-blond hair swayed above a nice, tight ass, perfectly manicured red nails, and a miniskirt—what the hell was this babe doing in this dreary place? Youth and inexperience probably, that same song and bullshit about having to starve somewhere to get experience before you could make a decent buck. Just thinking about it pissed Searle off; hell, he'd probably end up pushing a broom here, or worse. What was it Kaiser had said about this job coming about because folks were scared about that stupid asteroid? Could be that he'd end up wiping old folks' back ends after they shit themselves in fright.

The receptionist led him to a closed door beside which was a wall plate that said E. RICHMOND, then tapped softly. *Knock it off,* Searle reminded himself. *Like Kaiser had said, it's a job.* After a few seconds, someone called out and the sweet-smelling thing beside him turned the knob and pushed open the door. "Go on in," she said. She smiled at him, but it didn't reach her eyes—*those* were hard and judgmental, too flat and emotionless for Searle to register their color. *Bitch,* he thought, but he nodded agreeably and stepped far enough across the threshold so the young woman could pull the door shut behind him. The room in which he now stood had plush, steel-gray carpeting and was lit more like a showroom than an office, the better, Searle supposed, to show off the attractive woman seated behind the expanse of wood desk that dominated the room.

When she finally looked up, for a single maddened moment, Searle thought he was looking at Lila.

"You must be Searle Chanowitz," she said. "I'm Dr. Richmond, the hospital administrator." She rose and came around to the front of the desk, offering her hand.

"H-hello," Searle croaked as he shook it. Her grip was firm and all business, and he cleared his throat awkwardly and hoped he sounded like nothing more than a nervous guy on a job interview. Now that she was standing in front of him, the resemblance—most of it, anyway—had dissolved. Her face wasn't nearly as long-featured—he'd never seen a woman with features so drawn down as Lila's—and her eyes weren't quite the right shade of blue. The hair was short and stylishly, *expensively* cut. The last time he'd seen Lila's hair, the long, dull blond strands had been matted with blood and—

"Mr. Chanowitz?"

He blinked. "I—excuse me, I didn't hear." Flustered now, Searle could feel his face redden and anger trying to step in to defend him from the humiliation of being caught daydreaming.

Dr. Richmond tilted her head to one side, eyes matching the receptionist's in their complete lack of emotion as she studied him. "Do I . . . remind you of someone, Searle? May I call you that?"

Searle blinked again, then caught himself and willed his twitching eyelids to be still. He must look like he had grit in his eyes or something. "Sure, Searle is fine. And yeah, I guess you do remind me of someone."

"Really." She circled him slowly, bringing back other, uglier memories of the prison's exercise yard at Joliet. "Is it a bad memory, or a good one?"

Shit, he thought. *What the fuck is Kaiser trying to pull?* This had to be some kind of psych evaluation. Old recollections blasted into his head without warning and he barely held himself in place. Lila, with that same secret smirk on her face—*There's something about me that's better than you, Searle!*—that he'd tried to beat out of her so many times; Lila when she shot up, who could fuck as fast and furious as a rabbit until he thought his balls would fall off from exhaustion. He suddenly realized he had a raging boner and folded his hands casually in front of his zipper to hide it. "Both," he said carefully. They stared at each other for a few moments, then she smiled. In it, Searle saw a lot of things that *were* just like Lila, but a lot more that generated feelings he abruptly realized he was going to have to fight to control.

"Why don't you call me Erica," she suggested. "I think we'll be spending a lot of time together." She stepped to the desk and hit the intercom button on her telephone; when someone answered on the other end—the receptionist or maybe a personal secretary— she said simply, "I don't want to be disturbed for *any* reason for the next hour." Then she walked behind him again and he heard a noise—

The click of the lock on her office door.

"After Help, Inc.," Erica told him much later, "exists solely for all the people who have taken the news of the coming Millennium/Jupiter impact to the . . . ah . . . extreme. You'd be surprised at the numbers we're talking about here, Searle."

Searle was seated on one of the leather chairs that faced her desk, his hands resting lightly on the arms, ankles casually crossed as if nothing out of the ordinary had happened. The door to Erica's office was again unlocked and if the nameless receptionist or some secretary walked in now, the only thing to greet her would be this seemingly innocuous job interview—although Erica would no doubt choose her words more prudently. He tried to concentrate on what she was saying because he knew it was important, but under his clothes Searle's skin was still tingling and lightly slicked with moisture. It'd been a long time since he'd had anything but the cheapest, dirtiest hooker, and he could still feel a ghost of sensation at all the places Erica Richmond's mouth had touched. He hoped to God that today wasn't a fluke, the one-of-a-kind instance of a moneyed woman acting out a crude fantasy, but how could it be otherwise?

Forcing the thought aside, Searle leaned forward on his chair and focused on her words. "I'm not sure I understand," he admitted. "What exactly are people freaking out *about*?"

Erica tilted her head and let her gaze wander around the room. "Coincidence, I suppose. Just as the calendar rolls into a new millennium, suddenly there's this planet-sized rock barreling through space toward another—the biggest—planet in our solar system. It didn't help matters that when they first spotted it, the astronomers didn't mention it was going to actually *hit* Jupiter. They dropped that news bomb nearly three weeks later, remember? So now—"

"A lot of folks don't trust them," Searle finished for her.

"Exactly. There's a massive panic under the surface of this country and I plan to be there to capitalize on it when it comes to a boil."

"Capitalize in what way?"

Erica grinned, showing small, pearly teeth that had to have cost as much as a midsized sedan. "In the same way that religion does, organized or otherwise. By offering comfort to the fearful, counseling to the needy, planning for the future to the paranoid. And by accepting donations to pay for all that comfort, counseling, and planning."

Searle raised one eyebrow. "Sounds pretty fishy to me, and I'm not a nosy bureaucrat trying to stay voted into office. Besides, what happens when this rock hits and the show's all over?"

Erica's smile widened. "That's exactly the beauty of it, Searle. *Nothing* happens. The world goes on, just as it is now, just as it has for the last millennium while it's waited for Christ to reappear. Mankind and civilization go on, the world doesn't crumble, and the sun still shines tomorrow. After Help's function is not to dissuade anyone from their beliefs, whatever they may be—our position will remain safely neutral. If you're Jewish, believe it'll hit and want to protect your family, we can help you set up the survival retreat. If you're a lapsed Catholic who's terrified but doesn't believe the Church's prophecy that everything will turn out fine, we can counsel you as to the proper prayers to say in front of the Virgin's statue. If you're just alone and afraid, we'll find someone to hold your hand."

"For a price."

"Wrong. For a *donation*." Erica sat back and stared at the ceiling dreamily. "It's taken six weeks and a half-dozen very expensive lawyers to get the paperwork in place, but it's all ready.

I've got advertising coming out and the permission of the hospital to say that After Help is affiliated with it."

Searle whistled. "That's a coup. How'd—"

"A percentage, of course. As the old saying goes, money talks. The first full-page newspaper ad comes out next week, followed in October by a black-tie costume charity ball at Bloomingdale's on Michigan Avenue. The invitations go out tomorrow afternoon. Then—" She frowned at him suddenly. "What? What's the matter?"

Searle shrugged. "Nothing's the *matter,* though it seems to me like you're skipping a big part of your potential market here, all the middle- and lower-class people. They're the ones who're going to need the comfort and shit that you're selling the most. Hell, the rich folks can *buy* all the happy crappy they need."

Erica nodded. "You're right, of course. All these Bible-thumping preachers get the majority of their income from people just like that who sit at home and watch the holy rollers on cable. Trust me—I haven't forgotten or neglected that area. But I need the hard money as the jump start. It's the connections I make at that ball that will hold up if pressures build later on. The mayor, the aldermen, our senators—hell, every politician and lawyer and doctor and entrepreneur and lottery winner we could find is on that invitation list. It reads like a damned who's who of seven-figure bank accounts."

Searle nodded. His skin had finally dried and his head was clear; it was time to ask The Question. "And what's my position in all of this?"

Erica's expression turned thoughtful. "I need someone on the—how shall I say this?—other *side* of things." When Searle said nothing, she continued. "I've got carloads of lawyers and socialites and politicians. If I want to, I know just who to hire to have someone . . . *persuaded* to do or say something they might otherwise not be inclined to. The problem is, they all wear a suit and tie—whether they're wearing it or not." The drapes were closed in her office and Erica's eyes glittered ferally in the low interior lighting. "Do you understand what I'm saying?"

Searle nodded. "You can spot 'em anywhere."

"Exactly." Erica looked pleased.

"And you think I'll blend in."

"Among the everyday people, yes. As you pointed out, *those* are the source that will provide the largest share of this company's revenues. When we have meetings, I want you in there with the crowd, looking, listening, *feeling* everything out. If there's a problem with the way we're perceived by the common masses, I want you at the heart of resolving it because I think you'll understand them." Erica looked at him, her eyes narrow, and for a moment Searle felt like he was one of a circling pair of wolves. "I don't know what you came in here thinking you'd be offered, but this isn't a janitor's job. Does it sound like something in which you'd be interested?"

No broom, no mop, no dirty dishes to wash or tables to bus. He didn't give a shit about the responsibility part, but this was something challenging and different, and maybe even offered him an occasional ritzy piece of ass. Searle's smile was wide and genuine, and a damned good match for the one that had been on his mug when they pushed him out the doors of the pen.

"You'd better believe it, lady."

3.
LIFE AS THE WORLD NOW
KNOWS IT

NEW YORK
EARLY OCTOBER . . .
[fade to Marti Nunciata]

From the middle segment of the seven o'clock Cable News
Network broadcast:

"Excitement continues to build as astronomers around the
world prepare to record the impact of the rogue planet Millennium
on the far side of Jupiter in late November. The rogue planet was
dubbed Millennium because when discovered by the Kitt Peak
National Observatory in Arizona, it was originally estimated to
strike Jupiter early in the year 2000. Now, however, astronomers
estimate the impact will occur on November twenty-sixth, the
Friday after Thanksgiving. This is what Professor Frank Gelasias
had to say when asked about the more than one-month discrep-
ancy between the originally projected date of impact and when
scientists now believe the rogue planet will actually strike the gas
giant."

[cut to window and expand to fill, Professor Frank Gelasias]

"There are many factors which can affect the date we calculate
that a body in space will strike another one, or pass close by, so

much changing information on an object of this size and speed, that exact projections early on are chancy at best. But we're fairly certain that this one will strike the day after Thanksgiving, and when it does, the impact on Jupiter will dwarf what Shoemaker-Levy did to the planet in 1994. Millennium is *huge* by comparison, and the resulting damage to Jupiter's atmosphere could change the way we see the planet—its gas atmosphere—for decades."

[fade out]

LATE OCTOBER . . .

A personal night in hell.

That's what Mercy called her weekly visits to places like Neo, or the Club 950, or the seedy bars she could no longer name. No one, including Simon, had ever been with her on a . . . Nights Out, not that anyone but Simon had that right, anyway. *Nights Out* was a term that had taken root in her mind for no reason other than the singular form simply wasn't big enough to cover the impending sense of overload. She never told Simon that she was going for a "night out on the town." Her explanation, if it could be called that, was a short "I need a Nights Out." He didn't pry, verbally or mentally—at least as best he could avoid it—because he trusted her. If he knew that there were things she did on those Nights Out that she shouldn't, he also knew they were done only as a means to accomplish goals that had nothing to do with betraying his trust or love.

I love him, and he loves me.

Walking south on Lincoln Avenue at nearly midnight on Friday, the vibrations from the elevated train roaring past made the bones in her feet and knees jitter—like Simon did when he held her and ran his big hands over her bare back. Mercy giggled out loud, then looked around guiltily, embarrassed at the idea that she was walking down the street and acting like a schoolgirl. Every day with Simon was more of an amazement than the last, and every morning she still got a small shock when she opened her eyes and saw him lying beside her and snoring softly, the sound small and comforting, running lightly along her mind like the far-away, slow rumble of train wheels on a track. Never would Mercy have thought someone like him existed, and his mind-reading abilities had nothing to do with the qualities that amazed her. Patience, understanding, trust—how many lovers had stormed away from her over the years, fed up with the mysterious Nights

Out or furious that they had seen her somewhere with hands or arms entwined around another man or woman? Simon had never seen such a thing, of course—because he'd never stooped low enough to follow her. If he ever did see her with someone else, somehow she believed he would understand.

The streets were dark and cool, deceptively quiet. People were out, but this was far enough from Fullerton to thin things down to two or three stragglers per block, and the closer she moved to the Club 950, the less appealing the people on the street became. Mercy hadn't been to this particular club in nearly six months, since before she and Simon had . . . what? Exactly what *had* they done? Started dating, become lovers, moved in together? All of the above, she thought with a smile. Their lives were intertwined irrevocably now; his was the first face she saw each morning and the last every night, and that realization made her smile widen. To her, everything about Simon Chanowitz was beautiful, from his fine blond hair to the feet that were oversized for his slender frame—all those scars in the middle diminished nothing.

The sidewalk outside the Club 950 was already littered with trash and blowing papers, a day's buildup from the fall street fair the neighborhood association had put on earlier in the day. Music pounded from the open door, and the bored-looking bouncer swaying to the beat in the doorway made it seem like something alive, invisible hands pushing him back and forth along the sidewalk. His skull was shaved clean to just above his ears, the remaining hair pulled into a tight ponytail that had been dyed blue. A dozen or more tiny silver rings encircled the rim of one ear, while a lone one danced at the outer arch of his right eyebrow. "Ten bucks," he told her. He had to shout to be heard over the clamor of the music, but he still managed to sound bored.

Mercy nodded and pulled the money from the pocket of her jeans without reservation. The cover charge, she remembered— that was probably the reason she hadn't been back. Now that she was living with Simon, money was no longer as much of an issue. Her budget was still tight and the student loans still hovered, but Simon refused to let her share the rent or utilities. "This isn't a motel, Mercy," he'd told her stubbornly. "The rent didn't go up because of double occupancy, and the utilities are pretty much the same as they were before." Sometimes his black-and-white logic was hard to challenge; now she pitched in for groceries but that was about it.

Her ten-dollar bill disappeared into the bouncer's money belt and he moved aside without ever looking at her face. Going through the doors was like wading into a shadow-and-laser-light-filled chaos. The place was jammed to the seams with dancers and cruisers and people on the make. Mercy headed straight for the dance floor without bothering to stop for a drink; she didn't want beer or wine, and she didn't want to sit. She wanted, *needed* to get out there and touch, to *heal*.

If she couldn't do it in a hospital, then she'd do it in hell itself.

Mercy was nearly exhausted. The music, relentless in volume and beat and too industrial for her tastes, wore her down. Was it just her, or did the club seem hotter than it should be on a cool October evening? Too many bodies and not enough ceiling fans elevated the temperature, kicking it into the low eighties and making the hellish faces of the dancers shine with sweat and running makeup, streaks of kohl liner leaking from the corners of their eyes like black tears. All that din and movement was nothing compared to the energy pounding inside her for release, making her head and belly feel like a pressure cooker forgotten on the stove two hours ago.

overload-overload-over-over-over—

Mercy blinked and shook her head, trying to get the screeching litany out of her mind. She staggered toward the ladies' room, dizzy and sick with the realization that coming here had been a misjudgment. While the decision had been an innocent one—she could've gone anywhere—she needed to get out now, while there was still time to find someplace else with a late license. It was almost three, and her options were disappearing fast. Who would've believed that in a club this size she could find no one ill enough to give her the power drain she needed to stay sane for another few weeks? Little jabs, that's all, mere sparks of healing that teased with the promise of release but in the end only maddened.

The rest room was empty and Mercy nearly knocked herself senseless on the side of one of the stalls as she fell inside, yanked down her jeans, and went to the bathroom. In contrast to the main room, this one was as cold as a meat locker; between the sudden drop in the temperature and her frustration she was almost physically sick, could hardly fasten the snap at her waist. At the sink finally, staring at her own wild face in the water-splattered mirror, she saw her dark hair sticking to her skin in perspiration-soaked tangles and tried uselessly to smooth it back. Her slightly tiled eyes seemed huge tonight, twice as large as normal behind her glasses; the flesh of one cheek was smudged with dirt from somewhere and her lips were swollen from the heat and from chewing at them for the last two and a half hours.

overload-overload-over-over-over—

"Shut up!" she whispered fiercely. "Just shut up!"

The door to the rest room slammed open behind her and Mercy spun with a small, surprised scream. The young woman who careened into the room and fell against the far wall looked nearly as crazed as Mercy felt. Multicolored hair—shock white, bright orange, and lime-green—stuck out in hatchet-cut tufts from her scalp. Her face was streaming with sweat and heavy eyeliner ran down it in black streaks to mingle with the blood leaking from one nostril. Mercy was rightfully called thin, but this girl was emaciated, with prominent cheekbones and huge, muddled blue eyes. Mouth twisted in an exaggerated sneer, she reminded Mercy of a movie star ... Lance Henriksen in female form, swathed in a decrepit leather jacket that looked like a bundle of dull black rags. Below the jacket was more black: spandex leggings ripped off above the knees and oversized army boots on sockless feet.

Those eyes, scarcely focused, tracked around the small room and trained on Mercy. "What're you looking at?" the girl snarled.

"Your nose is bleeding," Mercy said calmly. The overload song in her head had retreated, content to sit back for the moment; she felt absurdly like a vampire as she watched another surge of blood coat the young woman's lip before it fell to a spot on her collarbone in a splatter of painted red, small but telltale evidence that something so much larger was wrong. Mercy reached automatically for the towel dispenser and pumped the lever until she got a handful of brown paper. A quick pass under the faucet and she held it out.

"Fuck you." The back of a hand that looked like it hadn't seen water in a month swiped across the girl's face, turning the red and black streaks into a horrible smudge that looked like movie makeup. Mercy tossed the wet towels into the sink without comment but didn't move or look away. When that vaguely savage gaze found hers again, this time it turned crafty, the glare of a rabid fox trapped in a cave. "What, you see something you like? Maybe you're some kind of lesbo cruisin' for action."

"Maybe," Mercy said carefully. "My name's Mercy."

"Yeah? That's real pretty." The other woman threw back her head and laughed, the sound more a shriek than anything else. Her teeth were dirty and traced with blood, and it was hard to tell if it had come from her own nose or if she'd bitten someone. "Well, mine's Lily, like a flower, lily of the valley, don't I look like that?"

"Sure."

Lily's mouth, grotesquely rimmed in red and black, twisted. "Keep staring at me, bitch. Maybe you'll get what you're lookin' for." She closed her eyes for a second and her hands reached up and dug into her hair, then yanked for no reason, harder than anyone should have been able to tolerate. "Oooh, that's feels so *good*." Her eyelids lifted again, gaze raking Mercy up and down with no trace of sanity or cognizance. "I like a bitch with long hair," Lily said in a voice that had turned guttural. One hand disappeared into her jacket pocket and the other fumbled at the zipper on its front and started to pull it down; as the worn fabric began to open, bare skin showed underneath. "Come 'ere and let me show you what I got."

Because there were only two stalls, an old-fashioned lever lock was still embedded in the heavy door to the bathroom; Mercy reached past Lily and slid the bolt into place. "Take your jacket off," she said. Her voice was shaking, but she didn't care. "I need to touch skin, not leather."

Lily gave her a leer, then shrugged. Her head jerked a couple of times, as if something inside it had slammed against the inside of her skull in an attempt to escape, then she blinked and squirmed most of the way out of her jacket, leaving it to dangle off one wrist. "I'm ready if you are. Name your pleasure, honey." She trailed a filthy hand across nearly nonexistent breasts, then down her rib cage; the bones were so pronounced that her fingertips made tiny thunking noises. Her skin was vaguely gray.

Mercy took a cautious step forward, then pointedly looked at the floor on the far side of the woman's foot. When Lily involuntarily followed her motion, Mercy sprang forward and grabbed the wrist hidden beneath the folds of the jacket, slamming it backward against the wall as she nimbly slipped her other arm around Lily's back and yanked her forward. Somewhere within that leather-covered grip was a knife, or a switchblade, or a razor, *something,* and Mercy's only advantage here was surprise; she outweighed Lily, but lunacy would give her captive more strength. Caught in Mercy's embrace, Lily screeched in rage and began bucking against her. Starving and covered with sweat, it was like trying to hold on to a slick bundle of jerking twigs, but Mercy had no choice. If she released her now, Lily would kill her.

"Let me go, damn you!"

Lily's other hand began tearing at Mercy's hair, and God knows there was plenty of that. Pain rippled through her head, but she ignored it; as long as the woman didn't grab near the scalp, she wouldn't be able to pull Mercy away. "Stop *fighting* me, Lily! Stop—" All she got for her gasping plea was a vicious bite on the corner of her mouth that brought tears to her eyes; thank God Lily let go and began yelling again.

Then Mercy's air was gone and her vision went with it as everything in the bathroom dissolved into a swimming mist of black and yellow sparkles, precursors to unconsciousness. A sudden surge of power vaulted between the desperate grip of her fingers and the soiled skin of Lily's back and made Mercy dig in with her fingernails to keep the contact. Only Mercy's hearing remained, a trickle of perception that let her hear Lily's furious screams change to a garbled yelp of surprise. They went down as the strength left Lily's legs, tangled and each still fighting, as another rush of power pulsed through Mercy and into Lily; by the time the third and final one hit amid their screaming, Lily had started clinging to Mercy instead of pushing her away.

Someone was beating on the bathroom door.

Mercy sat up and shook her head to clear her eyes of sweat and hair, immediately regretted it when everything about her began to hurt; nestled against her chest like a child, Lily made a small, contented sound but didn't open her eyes. How long had they been out? A minute? Or ten? "Just a second," she called in response to the angry but indecipherable words coming from the other side of the locked door. "Lily, wake up," she said urgently. "Someone needs to get in here. It's time go to."

Lily opened her eyes and stared at her. All traces of confusion were gone, and in her sunken face, the young woman's clear blue-gray irises reminded Mercy of a storm-filled sky. "You did something to me," she whispered. At their backs, a fist hammered on the door again and Lily glanced at it fearfully, then untangled herself from Mercy and stood; after a second's hesitation, she reached for Mercy's elbow and helped her stand, surprising strength showing in her skeletal arms.

Mercy struggled up, grateful for the help. She'd never felt so bruised or drained; her scalp burned, her mouth hurt, and bouncing against the walls and floor had made the bones in her spine feel like someone had taken a baseball bat to them. She caught a glimpse of her reflection in the mirror and saw smeared blood from the bite on her face; blurred black lines from Lily's kohl makeup crossed her skin as though she'd drawn on herself with a Magic Marker. She started toward the sink but Lily's hand on her shoulder stopped her. "I just want to rinse my face—"

Lily shook her head, matted hair looking like a moving beach ball as she pulled her jacket back on. "There's no time. Just keep your face low and follow me. I'll take you somewhere you can get cleaned up."

Mercy nodded reluctantly and cast a final longing glance at the sink, then staggered after Lily as the younger woman slipped back the bolt. Five or six women stood waiting, looking angry enough to kill.

"What the fuck were you two doing in there?" one of them spat. "We've been standing out here for twenty fucking minutes!"

"You two are out of here." The bouncer's voice came from just behind the group, and they parted to let him through. "Take your party somewhere else."

"No problem," Lily said smoothly. "Sorry about the wait. My friend wasn't feeling good, that's all."

"Yeah, but I bet she is now," sneered someone else in the line.

Mercy glanced at Lily nervously, but the other woman only lifted an eyebrow as she shouldered her way through the crowd. They were almost past the last one who'd tossed out the insult when Lily guided Mercy around her and pushed her a few feet ahead. Almost out of earshot, she nearly missed Lily's silken words. "What's the matter, honey? Are you jealous . . . or just hot for me?"

"Bitch," someone else muttered, but Lily laughed in reply. Then they were free of the women crowded around the rest room and headed toward the door, the bouncer watching them with a scowl.

The temperature outside had dropped and the air, still

city-soiled but fresher than the smoke- and booze-filled haze cir-
culating inside the club, felt damp and chilly, refreshing.
"Where're we going?" Mercy asked. She was feeling better as
each minute passed, but there was still blood rimming the side of
her mouth; she didn't look like anyone who should be riding a city
bus home and she didn't have enough spare cash for a cab. The
two of them must be a sight, both with matted hair and blood and
dirt crusting their faces and hands.

"My place," Lily said crisply. "It's right up here, just off Racine.
We'll get you cleaned up and then we'll talk." She sounded lively,
downright *sharp,* while Mercy felt like someone had shaken her
awake after only two hours of sleep. Lily might look like hell, but
her even, polite voice was a testament to not judging someone on
appearances alone.

Only a half block to go, and Mercy sensed someone watching
them, turned her head to see a Chicago Police car slipping silently
alongside them on the street beyond the cars parked end to end at
the curb. She felt an unexplained moment of panic when her eyes
met those of the woman driving, pieces of gray ice, the watchful
gaze of a beast pacing its prey in the bushes. Then Lily was
steering her into a dark gangway and up a flight of narrow, gray-
painted back porch steps much like the ones from her old apartment. She could sense the police car at their backs as it paused for
a moment, then moved on; more victims to find in the chilly night.

At her side, Lily began searching uselessly through the pockets
of her leather jacket for a key; after a moment she swore under
her breath. "Fuck it. I probably didn't lock it anyway." She opened
a rickety screen door and tried the doorknob. The door swung
open and she stepped inside, pulling Mercy after her. "Watch
your feet," Lily said. "I haven't been up to housecleaning in a long
time."

Watch my feet? Mercy thought. *How?* The apartment was in
total blackness. Not a sliver of light leaked into it except for the
wan glow of the low wattage bulb high on the ceiling of the porch
outside; its weak light seemed to stop at the doorstep and retreat,
afraid of entering this sightless realm. She knew Lily was going
for a light switch, but the waiting felt like forever; smells of rotting garbage and sweat and grease, and yes, there were things
brushing against her shoes as she tried to move a few feet farther
inside. Light then, exploding and harsh, and Mercy was unprepared for it and scrunched her eyes shut. When she opened them

again, the squalor before her was beyond anything she'd ever imagined. Maybe Simon had seen it in his fieldwork with the DCFS, but this, Mercy realized, was a firsthand look at the other side of the lives of some of the psychotics she used to treat for physical injuries in the emergency room.

They were in the kitchen where garbage, unemptied for months and left to rot in the humid heat of summer, littered the floor. The walls surrounding the stove were so black with grease that it was difficult to connect that area with the expanse of dirtied white tile by the sink counter. Tattered curtains gray with grease hung at the windows, and suddenly Mercy knew why it was so dark. The kitchen window—and no doubt every other one in the apartment—was painted flat black; even in the daytime the place would be like a rank cave. A card table with dented legs served the small kitchen and the remains of countless old meals could be seen in the folds of its ripped vinyl top.

"I told you," Lily said flatly from the other room. She glanced around the kitchen from the doorway and frowned. "Come in the living room. It's pretty seedy, but at least it's not like this."

Mercy nodded and stumbled along a narrow path through the trash. The place had only two rooms, and the other one served as both living room and bedroom. With more black paint on the windows, this room was drowning in ripped newspapers and old, stained magazines obviously pulled from Dumpsters and trash cans outside. In the center of the largest wall was a rough tweed couch that had been folded out into a bed, and Mercy didn't want to know what things might be crawling amid sheets that had probably never seen a laundromat. God knew what the bathroom looked like.

She stood uncertainly in the center of the room, swaying slightly. She felt completely empty, like a sponge wrung out and left to harden on the sink. Soul-deep exhaustion teased at her and the idea of closing her eyes had never seemed so desirous, but she couldn't stay here; late was one thing, but Simon would worry if she didn't come home at all. Cockroaches scuttled along the baseboards and she swallowed, wanting desperately to sit but unable to make her knees unlock.

"Sit here," Lily said at her side. "Stay away from the couch."

Mercy glanced down and saw Lily sweep aside a leaning stack of newspapers to expose a beat-up wooden rocking chair, then gasped with relief when she felt the cool, curved wood of the seat against the back of her jeans. "May I—I have a glass of water?" she asked after a few moments. Getting off her feet had made a huge difference; a minute ago she doubted she'd have been able to ask.

"Sure," Lily said. "I'll be a minute, okay? I'll have to wash something out."

Mercy nodded, leaning back and closing her eyes, shutting out the sight of the wretched room. Her senses were coming back and she could hear Lily moving around in the kitchen, the clank of the forgotten dishes piled into the sink, the scrape of paper and other things being shoved aside punctuated by mutters of disgust. Soon afterward came the sound of running water, a ping as the side of the glass bumped against the faucet.

"Here you go."

Deep into her own thoughts, Mercy blinked at the glass that suddenly waved in front of her face, then folded her fingers around it. The outside was still wet and dripping; now that her head was clear, Lily had probably shied away from the idea of drying it with any towel that might be lying around that abominable kitchen. The water that flowed past her parched lips tasted of nothing it shouldn't have and Mercy berated herself mentally. What had she expected— dishwashing liquid? She'd known Lily such a short time before their encounter in the rest room, yet she had already decided unfairly that she was incapable of dealing with mundane tasks. Not anymore; the young woman who declined the pulled-out sofa bed in favor of sitting on the edge of an old console stereo cabinet was someone entirely different, healed, with a new future and a new outlook.

"So," Lily said after Mercy had nearly drained her glass. "What happened back there?"

Mercy opened her mouth to answer, but could find no words to explain it. She'd never been in this situation before, where she had to stand and face the person she'd healed and try to explain, and while she'd saved uncountable lives over her years as a doctor, never, *ever,* had her abilities stretched themselves to mending someone's mind. When she'd seen Lily with blood leaking from her nose, Mercy had assumed a tumor, something big and malignant eating away at the frontal lobe and undiagnosed by some overworked mental health provider who juggled eighty-five cases a week and treated all his patients with Prozac. Erratic behavior, paranoia, hallucinations—these could all be symptoms of schizophrenia; in a teenager who was wild and did drugs and lived hard, the early pain might never have been talked about. Later, when the pain had begun to reach its fingers beyond a person's normal threshold, the Prozac would have dulled her senses and made her accepting, and who knew what other kinds of drugs they'd thrown her way—Valium, Librium . . . the possibilities were endless. Perhaps, and this was most dangerous of all, they'd even pumped her full of prescribed painkillers when she started complaining that her head hurt. After all, didn't all mental patients say that at one time or another?

"Mercy?"

"What—I'm sorry. I was thinking."

Lily looked at the floor and one of her booted feet kicked forward with admirable speed to crush a cockroach, probably the first one that had been killed in here in years. It wasn't hard to imagine the girl that Lily had once been sitting on the floor and *playing* with the things. "You can't answer me, can you?" Lily's gaze left the floor and found Mercy again. Her face had been rinsed and now her hands, soaped clean from washing Mercy's glass, went up and dug through her hair. Mercy had a fleeting, horrible moment where she thought there would be an inexplicable repeat of the hair-pulling scene back at the Club 950, but all Lily did was massage her scalp and wince a little. "You fixed my head," Lily said at last. She looked around the apartment in part horror, part wonder. "Christ on a stick, I didn't even realize I was living like this."

"I should be going," Mercy said. She set the glass carefully on a dilapidated bookcase jammed with half-destroyed paperbacks, then rose. Her footing was steady, her head mostly clear. "I have someone at home who'll worry if I'm not back soon, and it's a long way."

"I'll go with you," Lily said promptly. "And I cleared out some of the crap in the kitchen sink so you can get the blood off your face." Then her cheeks reddened, something Mercy would have never foreseen. "I did that, didn't I? I can't remember, but I'm sure it was me. I'm sorry."

Mercy shrugged and began picking her way toward the kitchen with Lily at her heels. "It's okay." She grinned suddenly. "I work in an animal hospital; I've been bitten before."

"God," was all Lily said, her color deepening. "I can't believe I've been *biting* people. I mean, what kind of a person does a thing like that?"

"Usually someone who's really ill," Mercy told her earnestly. The sink was still a nightmare, but at least the knobs and faucet had been wiped and there was enough space to cup her hands and lower her face. She came up dripping but feeling refreshed, her teeth grinding together from the water sting that ate into the wound. "Someone who needs help and isn't getting it."

Lily watched Mercy shake out her hands over the sink. "I don't have a clean towel to give you."

"Forget it. I won't rust." She dried her eyes on the back of a forearm. "You don't have to go with me. I'll be fine."

"I want to." Lily's face was hopeful. "I don't think you have a clue what you've given me, Mercy. I don't have much of a memory about the last fifteen years, but the pieces I do have aren't the kind of shit I'd want to share with anyone."

Mercy's mouth dropped open. *Fifteen years?* "God, Lily. Why didn't you get help?"

The whip-thin woman shrugged. "I thought I had, and no one could have told me any better anyway. I wouldn't have listened." Her boot shot out and another cockroach was dispatched; Mercy had a feeling there would be a lot of that in the coming days. "I'd really like to make sure you get home all right. That's not too much to let me give you after what you've done, is it?"

"But it's so far—you must be tired."

Lily chuckled. "The way things have been, the hours blend into one another. You, on the other hand, look completely blasted out." She spread her hands. "C'mon, Mercy. It's no big deal, okay?"

"Well . . . all right." She'd lost the rest of her money somewhere in the club and Mercy had to admit that the thought of the long walk home had been appalling; now it didn't seem as bad. But Jesus, it was far—they had to be less than twenty-eight hundred north and Simon's apartment was nearly to Bryn Mawr. If Lily went with her, at least they could talk on the way and the time would pass faster. At the other end, Lily could, if she wanted, take a shower in a clean bathroom with clean towels; when Simon got up—assuming he would still be sleeping when they finally arrived—she'd ask him to drive Lily back. Aloud, she said, "I wonder what time it is?"

Lily grinned; her teeth still needed a solid brushing, but the smile was bright and gave a hint at a prettiness Mercy hadn't noticed before. "No idea. I don't think I've ever had a watch. We'll find out eventually, there'll be a bank clock or whatever along the way. Hey—I just remembered something." Lily scanned the kitchen and frowned, then shoved aside some of the junk and scraps on the table. Reaching brazenly under another pile, she pulled out a couple of bus tokens. "Ta da!"

Mercy's spirits lifted. "Oh, Lily, that's wonderful!"

The younger woman stepped past Mercy and pushed open the back door. "What do you say? You ready to face the day?"

Mercy squared her shoulders and forced back the exhaustion that was trying to make her feet drag, ignoring the dizziness that lack of sleep always brought her. "Let's go for it."

Simon was awake when Mercy finally made it back to the apartment and led Lily inside. The walk to the bus stop and ride had taken only about an hour, and Mercy shuddered to think of the walk it might have been without those precious bus tokens. Had that been the case, she would have been a fool not to call Simon to come and pick them up, yet she wouldn't have. Nights Out were her responsibility; she would not burden him with cleanup if she was late, or lost, or beaten up in the process.

Sunday morning sunshine was pouring through the two windows at the rear of the apartment, bathing the kitchen in a heated glow that reminded Mercy of the southern Illinois farm of her childhood; added to that were the smells of frying bacon and old-fashioned fried potatoes, a high-cholesterol double treat that Simon allowed himself—and now her—only once or twice a month.

"Hi," Simon said mildly as they walked into the kitchen. His gaze slid to her injured face and he frowned, then glanced over at Lily. God bless him, though, he wasn't the kind of person to launch into a tirade. "Rough night?" was all he asked as he went back to prodding at the bacon with a pair of tongs.

"Simon, this is Lily," Mercy began. "She—"

"I did it," Lily blurted. Her face went scarlet as both Mercy and Simon looked at her in surprise. "I'm sorry. All I can say is that I didn't know what I was doing at the time."

Silence ticked around them for a long count of five as Simon stared at Lily, his jaw tight, the scar tissue across his face gone a deep, rich pink. Mercy didn't speak; the next move was Simon's and she had no right to steer him one way or the other. She wondered offhandedly if Simon was reading the younger woman's mind, but she didn't think so. By now she'd come to know his expressions and mannerisms well, and it was getting absurdly easy for her to pick up on when he was using, voluntarily or otherwise, the gift he so hated—hence the reason she knew he tried his best to respect her privacy. At last Simon's expression relaxed somewhat. "If it's all settled with Mercy, then I guess that's it. We should get antiseptic on it, though. I've seen bite marks before, and they can cause a terrible infection."

"I'm sorry," Lily said again.

She looked so miserable that Mercy would have gone to her had she been able to get off the chair she'd homed in on the moment they'd stepped across the threshold. "It's okay, Lily. Really." Mercy did manage a tired smile. "I'm a doctor"—she panicked for a second, not intending to say so much, then found an out—"of sorts, right? I'll take care of it." Simon said nothing but she could feel him watching them both from the corner of his eye as he gathered eggshells from the counter and dumped them into the trash.

Looking slightly mollified, Lily tilted her head. "Can you, you know, heal yourself?" Suddenly she glanced at Simon in horror, realizing she might have also divulged something she shouldn't have.

"It's all right," he said. He began pulling dishes and silverware out, his movements quick and sure. Mercy loved to watch him work like this, on home ground where he felt safe and his defenses—most of them—were down. He hadn't a clue just how jittery he was in public when he dealt with other people. Or was it just her, being nervous *for* him? It wasn't such a farfetched conclusion. "I know what's going on, Lily." He glanced at Mercy and for a second she saw a glint of amusement in his eyes; she almost grinned back when he said, "We don't have many secrets around here." The amusement in his gaze flitted away and for a second he looked troubled. "Lily—that's a nice name. My mother's name was Lila."

Simon *never* talked about his family and Mercy was surprised into silence for a few moments. "To answer the question—no, I can't heal myself," she said, recovering. She chewed at her lip for a moment, then stopped when she realized it made her face hurt. "I don't know why, maybe because I'm the source rather than the end. I just know that nothing happens when I try it." She blew upward, ruffling the sticky strands of hair across her forehead. "Guess I'll have to do this one like everyone else."

"Almost everyone else," Lily corrected. She glanced at Simon thoughtfully and Mercy, who'd never read anyone's mind in her life, could easily guess her thoughts.

"Breakfast is ready." Simon lifted one of the skillets from the stove and began ladling scrambled eggs and potatoes onto the plates. "Have a seat, Lily. You're not going anywhere until you eat some real food. When was the last time you had meat—April, right?"

Lily gaped at him and Simon's cheeks flushed guiltily. A slip, Mercy knew, one of those unintentional thought-leaks that he simply couldn't stop. She almost smiled; being around him so much had made her learn to live with them and she hardly noticed it anymore, but to a stranger they must be truly disconcerting. Lily's recovery, though, was admirably quick, her grin easy and accepting. "Yeah," she admitted. "I think I might have been in a hospital for a week or something." She settled onto a chair and eyed the plate, then unexpectedly licked her lips. As Simon filled Mercy's plate, then his, Lily's eyes took on a mischievous shine. "Gee," she said nonchalantly, "I guess now that I'm fixed, people will actually expect me to *use* these."

Mercy saw Simon duck his head and his shoulders shake a little, then she glanced over at Lily and laughed.

Lily was holding up the knife and fork.

NOVEMBER...

Lamont had dreaded doing this from the moment he'd opened his eyes in the hospital almost a year and a half ago. Some people could keep a secret, no matter what; they didn't care if it ate them up inside or who it might or might not hurt in the process. Lamont wasn't like that, and his was a tale that had finally come to its time, though he would have certainly preferred anything but the week before the Thanksgiving holiday.

Roanna had unwittingly started it, tossed out the snowball that eventually built itself into a boulder that had to be faced. His nephew Robert had been born only a couple of weeks after Lamont had returned to work. With Robert's first birthday coming up, their other three-year-old boy, Louis, and thoughts of again trying for that elusive girl, Roanna and her husband, Douglas, had started looking for a larger place to live. The parents had come up with the idea of selling their sprawling Hyde Park condominium to Roanna and Doug, then buying something smaller and easier to maintain. The condo was in a better location than where Roanna and her family now lived, and with all the kids long gone, the parents no longer needed or wanted all that extra space—and, of course, they would sell it to their daughter and her husband at a price considerably reduced from current market value.

That was where the problem had arisen.

Joey was bitterly opposed to the sale. As far as he was concerned, Roanna and Doug should pay the same price as anyone else would. The proceeds should then go into their parents' bank account or be rolled into the purchase of a new residence of equal or greater value. Roanna and their parents had been stunned into silence for all of thirty seconds, then everybody in the room had started yelling at once—Isaac, Sr., at Joey, Joey at his mother, Roanna and Doug at everyone else. The bottom line for Joey was money, as it had always been; he wanted nothing less than full market value for the property because frankly, he figured to get his share of it when his parents died. To sell it to Roanna and Doug at a reduced price was not only showing favoritism, but was giving her a gift that would take out of his pocket as well as the till that belonged to Lamont and the younger Isaac as well—not that he really cared about anyone but himself.

"Jesus, if you want their money so badly, why don't you just push them out the window right now?" Roanna demanded in a shrill voice. "What on earth is the matter with you?"

"Just shut up, okay?" snapped Joey. "Of course you'd go along with the idea—it was probably yours to begin with. You'll be getting a two-hundred-thousand-dollar condo for half that, then you'll sell it in two years and pocket the profit."

"You watch your tone of voice, buddy," Doug said hotly. A big man who'd played football in college and still kept his skills sharp on a weekend rugby team, he was scowling so deeply his eyes nearly disappeared under his eyebrows. "I don't care if you *are* her brother, there's no call to talk to my wife like that."

"You just stay out of this," Joey shot right back. "This is a family matter that's none of your business." Joey shoved his hands into the pockets of his jacket. "It doesn't make any difference, anyway. I'll never agree to let you do it."

Another round of babbling, until Lamont stopped the whole

thing by using the only method he could think of: banging an aluminum pot on the stove until everyone else shut up. He wished Gena were here to tell him what to do next; hell, she'd probably already known this was going to happen today but hadn't told him, since it probably would have happened anyway.

Joey stared at him. "What the fuck are you doing?"

Frieda gasped and the elder Isaac's face darkened. "Joseph, you mind your mouth in the presence of your mother."

"I won't have—"

Lamont cut Joey off with another whack of the pot on the stove top, this one loud enough to make his mother give a small cry of surprise. *"Stop it!"* he barked. When they were finally silent, he set the pot aside and folded his arms. "I have something to say here," Lamont said firmly. The emotion on the faces around the room ranged from exasperation, shock, and anger to outright fear—that from Joey, and Lamont knew why. "And I'm going to say my piece *without* being interrupted." He took a deep breath to try to calm the sinking sensation in the pit of his stomach, but it did no good; whatever tenuous threads had held this family together had finally been frayed to the width of spider silk by Joey's greed. The last of the gossamer strands would never bear the weight of this final confrontation.

"Mom, Dad," he said carefully, "the condo is *your* property, to do with what *you* want." Joey's mouth twisted and he started to speak, but Lamont held up a hand. "Forget it, Joey. You have no claim on it or right to tell them what they can do with it. If they want to give it to Roanna and Doug, or sell it and dump the proceeds into the Elgin riverboat gambling slots, that's the breaks."

"I'm not going to listen to this," Joey snarled. "You don't know what you're talking about. This is our inheritance—"

"No," Lamont cut it. "It's *not*. You can fight over a will or an estate until the moon turns red after someone passes away, although it doesn't say much about someone who ignores a person's last wishes. While someone's alive, their property is their property, and that's the way it is."

"Then I'll get a *real* lawyer instead of a hack like you and I'll have them declared incompetent."

"What!" Isaac, Sr. made a choking sound, then grabbed for his wife's arm when she swayed.

"I've never heard such a ridiculous thing in my life," Roanna cried. "What's gotten into you?"

"Forget it," Lamont said icily. "Obviously the rest of the family *won't* back you up." Something shifted suddenly in his head and he felt a tickle in his hands. *Oh, shit,* he thought offhandedly. *Hold on. Don't lose your cool—this is not the time.* Despite the mental command he found himself almost nose to nose with his younger brother.

Joey's expression was ugly as he glared at Lamont. "Isaac, Jr.—"

"Will tell you you're crazy and you know it."

"I think you'd better leave, Joey." His mother's voice slipped between the two of them like a soft scarf. "I—we've got some thinking to do."

"Not until we get this straightened out," Joey said stubbornly.

"I think Mom's right. You should leave now." In everyday life, keeping a grip on things was nothing, as unconscious and natural as breathing. But the grip slickened under the pressure of heavy emotion—fear, excitement, anger . . . especially that, fueled by things about which his parent knew nothing. *Yet.* Propelling his younger brother's stocky body across the room was trivial in the way of a mental stretch, the brushing aside of an annoying mosquito, Keeping him upright and stopping short of hurling him— now *that* took willpower. Of all the people in the room, only Joey didn't seem surprised when he stumbled across the carpet and fell against the door; the fear was back on his brother's face, this time coupled with a dangerous mix of resentment and hatred. Joey's teeth were grinding together so tightly he could barely speak.

"Thanks, Lamont. I guess I was going *anyway.*" He had the presence of mind to grab at the umbrella he'd left in the stand, then fumbled with the doorknob; Lamont gave him a little help there, too. The door pulled open hard enough to smack his brother in the shoulder, but Joey only grunted and shot a final, murderous glance in Lamont's direction before he stormed out and slammed the door shut behind him.

No one said anything for a long time.

Roanna and Doug had gone home. For once Lamont's sister seemed to have no fight left in her; this last bitter argument had sapped her strength and silenced her, but Lamont knew she would bounce back. Fighting among siblings was one thing, but between parents and a child was something else; his mother and father would not recover so easily. Now they sat across the table from him in the dimly lit dining room, their hands folded, their faces shadowed with hurt. Outside the row of windows another rainstorm blew, one of a seemingly endless series that had started earlier in the month; every time lightning flashed over the lake, Lamont saw the betrayal reflected in his parents' dark eyes.

"Incompetent," Isaac, Sr. said wonderingly. "He said that, didn't he?"

Lamont didn't know what to say. Well, he *did,* but not how to say it—was it really wise to deliver another blow so quickly? He couldn't answer that; he knew only that the time had finally come to own up and the truth was a huge, coiled spring inside him that had finally stretched to the breaking point. "Listen," he began hoarsely, "there's something else you . . . you should know. About Joey."

"Oh, I think we learned a lot about Joey tonight." His father's deep voice had regained its calmness and now the older man slipped his arm around Lamont's mother and hugged her. "I don't know what's got into him, Frieda."

She nodded, then looked at Lamont. "You said there was something else we should know?"

Lamont swallowed, then gave a small nod. "Yes." His voice seemed very small to him, although he knew he was speaking normally. "I—I wasn't exactly telling the truth when I said I didn't . . . know who shot me."

His parents were smart people, and it hadn't taken much more for them to get the picture. Listening to them had been like watching a dying person go through the standard phases after being told they had only two months to live, but within a ten-minute time frame: disbelief, denial, belligerence, resignation—it all blasted through and moved on, fueled by the memory of Joey's ugly words still hanging in their minds. The only thing missing was a sense of enjoying what was left to the fullest in the time still available; Lamont had stayed only another hour, but by the time he'd walked out the door Isaac, Sr. had called his personal lawyer, a friend from childhood, and told him to start the paperwork on selling the condominium to Roanna and Doug. The next telephone call had been to a friend in Florida with instructions to find them an apartment to rent for a few months while they looked for something small to buy. His mother had opened the telephone directory to LOCKSMITHS and selected one to call in the morning; by nine A.M., Joey's key to the Hyde Park condominium would be useless. Both parents were in shock and neither wanted to ever see Joey again.

Christmas was a month away, his family was in ruins, and Lamont wished to God he'd never walked in and caught his brother robbing that damned safe a year and a half ago.

NOVEMBER 26 . . .

"Can we turn on the television?"

Lamont looked up in surprise. Gena was standing at the bottom of the steps leading into the family room, one hand clutching the banister to give herself a sense of location within the oversized room. She preferred the formal living room and hardly ever came downstairs; the family room was too spacious, its furnishings too spread out to let her make her way down its length with any ease. "Sure," he said as he rose. "Any particular channel?"

"I . . ." Gena hesitated, then shrugged. "CNN is as good as any, I suppose. Something that shows . . . everything." Above a pale rose-colored sweater he'd bought her, her reddish skin looked dusky and soft, her hair startlingly black. Her face was carefully expressionless.

Lamont raised an eyebrow as he picked up the remote control, then went over to take Gena's hand. Her skin was cold and clean, slightly damp; he knew she'd been upstairs washing the dishes from yesterday's Thanksgiving meal—their first with each other—and this morning's breakfast. He'd wanted to help but she'd insisted on doing it by herself, although she'd allowed him to run a sinkful of water and soak the mess overnight. Skipping the annoyance of the usual morning alarm clock routine, they'd slept late, then made love. Hunger had finally driven them to the kitchen and an odd meal of seasoned potato pancakes made from last night's leftovers.

Settled on the couch now, Lamont found the right channel, then handed the remote to Gena. Her hearing was more sensitive than his and he tended to have the volume too loud for no reason. The broadcaster was already talking about Millennium and Gena was listening with rapt attention. "What are you listening for, Gena?" Lamont asked softly. "You already know what's going to happen."

She turned her head slightly in his direction. "Hope, I suppose."

"Hope?"

"That something's changed what's coming, or maybe that something *will* change it. I don't know."

Lamont watched her in silence for a moment, then slipped his arm around her shoulders. She leaned against him willingly, then let her head drop back against his shoulder, as though she were tired of all the weight she carried around in her mind. He couldn't blame her. "The scientists say the asteroid's going to hit Jupiter."

Gena's head lifted and she turned her face back toward the television, the moving lights from its image flickering on the lenses of the dark glasses she still insisted on wearing all the time. "I know what they said," Gena said quietly, "but they're wrong. I don't know why their calculations won't hold up or what's throwing them off, but this thing wasn't meant for Jupiter, Lamont. It was meant for Earth, and it's going to get here one way or another."

"Then why bother listening?" Lamont asked pointedly. "You always say that no one believes you, now you seem to be showing that same disbelief in yourself."

Gena was silent for a few moments while in the background some mindless television star nattered on about deodorants. "I *have* to hear it, I suppose. This time it's so . . . so awful that even I have to confirm it."

And so they watched and listened to the special broadcast, something called "Fire on the Gas Giant," and followed along with the excited astronomers and scientists as they counted down the time to impact and waited for the satellites to send back images that they thought would dwarf those born from the Shoemaker-Levy comet of 1994.

An hour passed, then two, and Lamont remembered a program from more than a decade earlier, where a Chicago talk show host named Geraldo Rivera had assembled a huge press conference to film a construction crew breaking through a concrete wall below a downtown Chicago hotel, entering what he'd claimed was an undiscovered hideaway of the legendary Al Capone. Several hours and thousands of pounds of concrete rubble later, Rivera and his viewers had nothing but empty basement rooms and a warning from the city engineers that further drilling could break through the retaining wall and into the Chicago River. Tonight, as the computers were programmed with new information, the viewers waited, and the newscasters demanded answers, the scientists began pointing out how difficult it was to make accurate calculations regarding an object of this size and speed when it was traveling around the far side of Jupiter. Then the tone changed again, and the feverish undercurrent returned as the people on the screen began to talk about something unexpected and exciting, an area around the planet that most people never knew about called the Roche limit.

"Roche limit?" Lamont said. "Sounds familiar. What is it?"

"An area of gravitational pull around a planet—in this case, Jupiter," Gena said.

"Really?"

Gena must have felt his surprise because it was the first time he'd seen a ghost of a smile from her all day. "I've been listening to a lot of the specials they've been putting together."

Lamont frowned. "You've been doing this all along? But—"

"If we can't hope, then we have nothing left."

Whatever Lamont was going to say about Gena not immersing herself in what was coming dropped out of his mind. She was right, of course. What was left if you could only look to the past? Aloud he asked, "So what does this Roche limit have to do with anything?"

"Depending on the size and strength of this object and its distance from the planet, something that passes through it could break apart because of the gravitational pull. All the planets have a Roche limit." She hesitated. "It's sort of like undersea diving—the pressure would kill a person without the proper equipment, but a metal diving suit could easily take the same depth. I don't understand it well enough myself to explain it any better."

"Well, that's pretty clear." And when he thought about it, a favorable thing. "That's good, then. No more rogue planet, right?"

"Wrong." Gena's voice was low, a strained whisper that brought darkness to the deceptively cheerful afternoon sunlight streaming through the high French windows of the family room. "It means that instead of one moon-sized planet headed our way, there are several hundred smaller ones."

NEW YORK
DECEMBER 5 . . .

[fade to Marti Nunciata]

From the opening segment of the seven o'clock Cable News Network broadcast after two hours of quarterly-hour bulletin interruptions:

"The world is in shock tonight as professional and amateur astronomers alike have stepped forward with claims regarding a newly charted course for the remains of Millennium. Millennium was the moon-sized rogue planet that for months was predicted to strike Jupiter on its far side the day after Thanksgiving, but which was torn apart by an intense gravitational field around the planet called the Roche limit. Some astronomers and astrophysicists are now saying that the shattered remains of the rogue planet—asteroids—number well over a hundred and are on a collision course with the Earth. In addition, these same scientists insist that any one of these pieces is large enough to cause a repeat of the events which most paleontologists believe directly resulted in the extinction of the dinosaurs one hundred sixty-five million years ago. An impact of this magnitude, they theorize, could cause the extinction of mankind."

[reduce to window next to *Special Bulletin* logo]

"Agreeing to speak with us tonight is Professor Frank Gelasias, head of the Kitt Peak National Observatory in Arizona, which first discovered Millennium last summer and predicted its impact—which never occurred—with Jupiter on November twenty-sixth. Professor Gelasias, what do you have to say about the predictions that are being made which say that this asteroid is now on an collision course with the Earth?"

[cut to window, Professor Frank Gelasias]

"First of all, Millennium doesn't exist as a single object anymore. The moon-sized rogue planet broke apart as it passed Jupiter and is now nowhere near its original size."

[cut to Marti Nunciata]

"Well, then, what about the reports that those *pieces* are headed for Earth?"

[cut to window, Professor Frank Gelasias]

"Oh, they are. But they pose absolutely no danger."

[cut to Marti Nunciata]

"I beg your pardon, Professor, but the reports from astronomers and astrophysicists around the world clearly say—"

[cut to window, Professor Frank Gelasias]

"Hype, Ms. Nunciata, pure and simple. Every facility in the world wants to be the one to predict the end of it all. Given the current trajectory of the remains of the rogue planet, there are undoubtedly a couple of large pieces that could conceivably endanger our planet. I assure you, however, that these will be dealt with swiftly and efficiently before they present any real threat."

[cut to Marti Nunciata]

"I see. How large are these 'pieces,' and how would they be dealt with?"

[cut to window, Professor Frank Gelasias]

"It's far too early to make determinative calculations on exact size because right now the pieces are clustered very closely together; as they string apart in the coming weeks, we'll be able to make more accurate projections. As for dealing with them, given our current proficiency in space, it will not be that technologically difficult to launch intercept missiles at the appropriate time and change the path of any of the larger pieces that may pose a danger."

[cut to Marti Nunciata]

"Our sources say that the University of Arizona has been working closely with NASA and the Department of Defense since the first reports came out that Millennium—or rather its remains—are on a collision course with our planet. Is this true, and if so, is your facility already working on something which will alter the trajectory of the larger pieces that endanger us?"

[cut to window, Professor Frank Gelasias]

"While it's true that the general direction of Millennium is toward the Earth, no one said that any of the pieces are actually going to hit—"

[cut to Marti Nunciata]

"I don't mean to be argumentative, Professor, but reports have been pouring in from hundreds of sources which contradict that statement."

[cut to window, Professor Frank Gelasias]

"As I said, hype and nothing more. However, as a precautionary measure, the White House has issued a mandate which allows our facility to work closely with NASA and various other military divisions in the event human intervention becomes necessary."

[cut to Marti Nunciata]

"Would you clarify that for our viewers, please?"

[cut to window, Professor Frank Gelasias]

"Certainly. If we need to fire a missile or two to redirect pieces of Millennium, we will be ready to do so when it becomes appropriate."

[cut to Marti Nunciata]
"Thank you for speaking with us, Professor."
[fade out]

PHOENIX, ARIZONA ...

"I watched the broadcast from the home last night. You lied."

Facing her husband, Crystal Gelasias could feel her fingers twitch inside the pockets of her jacket. Soft sun poured through the window of their Fountain Hills town house; Crystal called it that because at this time of year the sunlight lacked the blistering heat so typical to an Arizona summer. The light washed everything in golden yellow, made it seem clear and bright and ... false. Not Frank's fault, of course, but he had contributed to the feeling nonetheless.

He'd been sitting at the table and staring into the cooling coffee inside his mug; now he lifted his gaze to hers, then shrugged. In ten years, this was the first time Crystal had come home from her shift as head night nurse at Saguaro Acres Retirement Center and seen him sitting at the kitchen table before work without a morning paper. The reasons why Frank might no longer bother with it terrified her. "What else could I do?" he asked.

She opened her mouth, then closed it and poured herself a cup of decaf from the second coffee maker. It was a small thing, but the idea that he'd still gone through the routine of making a pot of decaffeinated coffee for her to drink when she got home in the morning gave her a little comfort. Mug in hand, she went over to the table and sat, cold, nervous fingers now wrapped around the porcelain in search of warmth. To be cold in here was ridiculous; the air-conditioning was off—they both hated it—and the tiny thermometer stuck to the fridge door said eighty-one; still Crystal felt chilled to the pit of her stomach. "I don't know," she finally said. "You could have ... I don't know." Still, her voice wasn't accusing.

"I had my *orders*," her husband said bitterly. Dressed in a striped cotton shirt and navy Dockers, he gestured at his arm and his voice roughened. "Maybe they should have given me a swastika armband." For a moment Frank looked like he actually *loathed* himself and she felt her stomach tighten in sympathy. So young—at forty he was the youngest professor in the astrophysics department—and so smart, but it was amazing how intelligence was simply bowled over by governmental bureaucracy at a time when it was most needed.

A swastika? Crystal didn't know how to respond to that, so she just sat quietly with him until he left for the University. When he was gone and she was ready to lie down and try to sleep, she rinsed his cup and put it in the dishwasher, then looked at her own mug as she poured the cold remains of her coffee down the sink. The cup had some awful abstract fish design on it, and her neighbor had given it to her a year ago. She hated it, but kept it out of politeness because the woman occasionally dropped by in the late afternoons and Crystal had wanted her to feel like the gift was appreciated. The way things were headed, she decided it didn't really matter anymore.

She threw it in the trash.

DECEMBER 25 . . .

Christmas morning at six-thirty, and Simon knelt in front of the entertainment cabinet in his living room. "Which one?" he muttered. His fingers traveled along the old LPs, arranged in meticulous alphabetical order. The first thing he found was something called "The Pat Boone Family Christmas," and he made a face and pushed it back in—still in the shrink wrap after more than three decades, he had no idea why he'd bought it back then. When he got to the *H*'s, he finally found something he thought Mercy could deal with, a Christmas album by Emmy Lou Harris. He wasn't worried about the words—Mercy was agnostic and would pay no attention—but he wanted a holiday atmosphere; a rock and roll lover from childhood, too much country twang would make her shudder. Emmy Lou's sweet soprano voice, however, would probably be okay.

He wished it were snowing outside, no heavy white Christmas but a scattering of fluffy snowflakes would have done just fine to finish off the morning. Instead the streets were clear and dry, the temperature disturbingly high for the end of December. He couldn't remember the last time Chicago had had a winter like this one, too warm to really kick up the heat, too chilly and damp to do without it—the dryness today had been the exception rather than the rule since the beginning of October. Thanksgiving had brought a torrential downpour that had actually flooded the courtyard in front of the entry door downstairs; if Mercy had still been living in that garden apartment on Rascher Street, she'd have undoubtedly been standing shin-deep in dirty water.

Simon pulled out the old vinyl disc and set it carefully on the turntable, made sure the volume was on low before he moved the slide to REPEAT and lowered the needle. Muted bells eased out of the double speakers and Simon smiled, pleased with his choice. They had no tree or religious mementos—he, too, had started wondering about the reality of God after a few years of DCFS field service in the projects—but he had candles and mistletoe tucked here and there around the apartment, and a tacky, sparkling snowman with a comical face presided over everything from the top of the mantel above the disconnected gas fireplace. Religious beliefs aside, the Christmas and Hanukkah season were still supposed to stand for a time of giving and love, joy and peace. This year, for the first time in his life, he felt all of those things.

"Hi."

Mercy's sleepy voice made him turn and he grinned. Barefoot, she was dressed in the flannel sleep shirt he'd given her a couple of days ago, a ridiculously red thing that hung to her knees and was covered in a pattern of flying Christmas mice. She'd left her glasses on the nightstand and stood squinting at him in the hallway entrance with her hair rumpled on one side and pillow creases on her cheek. God, she was beautiful.

He walked over and pulled her into his arms, breathing in the sweet smell of her hair and the Cactus Flower lotion she'd started rubbing on her chapped hands when she was home. She snuggled close without hesitation. "Morning. Did I wake you?"

"Nun-uh. I felt you get out of bed." Mercy raised her head from his shoulder and smiled. "I was hoping you'd come back."

Simon kissed her nose. "Later. It's Christmas Day, remember? We have stuff to do."

She blinked, visibly trying to clear the sleep from her mind. "We do?"

"Come on," he said smoothly. "I'll make coffee. Starbuck's Christmas Blend. Then I'll give you my gift."

"Simon, we talked about this and agreed that this year we'd skip your birthday and Christmas. You weren't supposed—"

—flash—

"Don't worry," he said quickly, more to stop his own nosy prying than her words, "it's just a little thing. I know we talked about not blowing a bunch of money." Mercy said nothing and he forced himself to concentrate on measuring the coffee, three generous scoops to make it strong, into the brown paper filter. He didn't need to delve into her head to know she was upset, but surely she had to realize that he couldn't let the holiday pass without giving her *something*. Getting something in return wasn't the point. Nothing on the face of this earth had filled his heart and satisfied him more than these last eight months with her.

When the coffee was brewed and poured, Simon took their mugs in and set them on the coffee table. She sat next to him on the couch, then turned sideways and tucked one ankle under the other knee until she was sitting in a sort of half-Indian style. He slipped his hand in his pocket and closed his fingers around a small, foil-wrapped box, then had a sudden, frigid moment of fear. Such a small thing inside, yet it meant so much that was absolutely *huge* . . . What if he was wrong about her, them, the whole thing? Of all the chances he'd taken in his life, this one had the most potential to devastate him. Their life together was, at least to his mind, almost perfect, and if Mercy's dreams were to go back to medicine, then he'd do whatever he could to help her along, even if it meant moving—something he wasn't sure why she hadn't already considered. But if her feelings didn't match his, how would they continue? Could he sleep next to her tonight knowing that he was good enough for now, but not for forever?

He should check first, just slip in—

—*fla*—

Stop it!

Simon pulled the box out and offered it to her, wishing he'd been able to stick a bow on it for good measure, or at least tied a ribbon around it. It looked so plain in the palm of his hand, so small and vaguely incomplete in its festive red paper. A little plastic heart, now that would have been nice, or—

Mercy's fingers, long and surprisingly delicate, lifted it carefully and turned it over. Gone was his chance to back out, to say *I've changed my mind, maybe the timing isn't exactly great on this, why don't we go out to a fancy dinner at Stefani's instead?* The tip of one of her fingernails eased under the tape at one end and parted it cleanly from the paper in a movement so careful it might have belonged to a surgeon; for a second Simon's breath caught, and he didn't know if it was seeing a hint of all Mercy's lost opportunities or terror at what the next sixty seconds would bring. Then she was slipping the paper off and opening the petite, pale blue velvet box, and looking at the twinkle of gold inside.

"It's a Claddagh," Simon said. His voice sounded absurdly loud and gravelly to his ears, like one of those annoying water sticks that were supposed to simulate rain when you turned them upside down. "An Irish wedding band."

"I know," Mercy replied softly. She pulled it from the layer of cotton with two fingers and held it up to the light. "It's beautiful."

—*flash*—

Impossible to ignore, not his fault. "I think you know what it— it—" He simply couldn't get the rest of the sentence to come out.

"Simon, I can't read minds like you." Her eyes were big and dark behind the magnification of her glasses, her voice solemn. "I can only guess. And if I'm wrong . . ." She tilted her head questioningly.

He swallowed. "I guess I thought—I mean, I wondered if you might, *we* might . . . get married." There, it was out, and as much as he wanted to just lose himself in her, he couldn't. One slip of his control and his traitorous mind, already fighting for freedom, would leap into her head and search out the answer he wasn't sure he wanted to know. With his hands folded in his lap, outwardly serene, he hoped she couldn't see the way he was pushing his nails deep into his skin, the sting giving him something on which to focus other than the enormous words still hanging on the air between them.

"You don't know me."

Surprised, Simon forgot about the small pain in his hands, felt in an abstract way the temporary derailment of the hungry part of his mind as he tried to process what Mercy had said. "What?"

"I said you don't know me. Not really." Her gaze slipped away from his and flicked around the room like a trapped animal. "And you don't know what I do on those Nights Out, or what I've done in the past in order to . . . to *get* to people I wanted to help." Her face turned back toward his and he saw panic in her eyes; he knew without looking that she was afraid of losing him, and God forgive him, he felt gratified. "I know how hard you work all the time *not* to find out what goes on in my head, and I know that you truly do honor my privacy, because if you hadn't there's no way you'd ever let me stay here."

"Mercy—"

She held up a hand. "Let me finish." She placed the ring on the cushion between them, then looked down at her hands and turned them over, front to back, as if certain she could find something there that would tell her the whys and hows of the wonderful and terrifying ability locked inside them. "Simon," she said in a low voice, "what I do can't be done in public most of the time. A finger touch, a hand on an arm—that just isn't enough contact to—to make a difference. Sometimes even a . . . even holding someone on the dance floor isn't enough c-contact." Mercy choked a little, then raised her face; Simon saw that her cheeks were wet with tears and white, the skin as smooth and fragile as the petals of a pale daisy in a rainstorm. "Do I have to spell it out for you?"

Simon ran his fingers absently across the mass of scars on his face and winced; sometimes, when emotions ran high and hard like they were now, if his thoughts turned back to that awful night in the 1969 Christmas season—and how could they not: Christmas then, Christmas now—he got a streak of phantom pain across his face. Like the scars, it was something he'd learned to live with. Man: the most adaptable creature on Earth and Simon more than most. "No," he answered. "I get the picture." For a moment he said nothing, then he reached over and took her hands, that mental fist holding fast in his head. "We all do what we have to do, Mercy, to fill ourselves up inside. No one ever said that the methods are a hundred percent right all the time, or that meeting or loving someone would be enough for whatever's inside that needs to be satisfied." His fingers squeezed hers and he felt tentative pressure in return. "I can deal with whatever you do because I know *why*. I'm not asking you to change for me, Mercy, or to stop. I'm just asking you to let me love you for the rest of my life."

"And for me to love you in return."

He stared at her. He'd been on such a roll, the words flowing as naturally as if he'd planned them all a week or a month ago. Now he felt like someone had pulled the typed speech from the podium and asked him to explain in scientific detail the reason the Earth was held in its orbit around the sun. "Well, I—"

"I can do that."

Simon let go of her hands and sat back, fumbling for a response. His tongue was thick and numb in his mouth. "I—I'm sorry, I guess I shouldn't have asked. You never said—"

Mercy reached over and tugged on the sleeve of his shirt. "That's just it, Simon. Listen to what I *said,* not what you expected to hear."

"What?"

"I said I could do that. I could love you for the rest of your life, and mine. I'll marry you."

"You said that?"

She grinned, those almond-shaped eyes crinkling at the corners. "Doofus."

Simon's mouth spread in a smile that he tried to stop, his face again, stretching into that familiar caricature of ruined flesh. In twenty or thirty years, he didn't want her to remember him looking that way after she'd accepted his proposal. "Well I . . . that's wonderful."

"Hey," Mercy said softly, "it's okay to smile at me." Her fingers, so capable and filled with a concentration of power that he'd never felt or understood, came up and traveled lightly over his cheekbone and temple, then slipped into his hair. "I love you, you know?"

—flash—

He couldn't stop it and in retrospect wouldn't have wanted to. Warmth blasted through him, the closest thing possible to a physical manifestation of the emotions running riot through Mercy's mind and heart, so strong that he nearly arched his back in instinctive reaction. He tried to say something in return but lost it when Mercy leaned forward and kissed him, forgot everything and let the heat just take him away.

"I almost got you another cat," Mercy admitted later. "Along with all the other weird stuff, fertility seems to have tripled and it would have been easy to pick up a free kitten from someone at the clinic. Ultimately I wasn't sure whether you really wanted one or not."

Simon chuckled and tugged on one of the strands of her long dark hair that was tangled over his shoulder. The rest lay fanned across the pillow behind her, a blanket of wavy mahogany on the pastel linens. "I don't. I don't think Kiwi and I ever really liked each other."

"We could get a dog."

He caught a hopeful note in her voice that made him glance up in surprise. "We'd have to move," he said simply. "But if you really want one, that's what we'll do."

Mercy was silent for a moment. "Let me think about it," she

said eventually. "Neither of us are home much. Simon, do you think we're all going to die?"

He gaped at her. "What?"

She gestured vaguely, her gaze focused on something he couldn't see. "Everyone's saying those asteroid pieces are going to hit the Earth next summer. Right now it seems like a long way off, but it's only . . . what? Seven or eight months? That's not such a long time left if it's all you have."

Simon was silent for a few minutes. "I guess," he said finally, "that I can't believe they won't *do* something about it."

"Yeah, but who's *they*? And just what can they really do?"

Simon rubbed at the light growth of beard across his chin. "Well, I suppose we're talking about NASA. The space program—" The ringing of the telephone on the end table, its volume set loud so that Simon would hear it in the middle of the night if need be, cut off the rest of his words. His eyebrows raised. "Your family?" he asked as she reached for it.

Mercy shook her head. "No, I always call them on holidays, not the other way around." She lifted the receiver. "Hello?"

Simon watched her listen for a moment, until he felt his mind shift and start to gather strength, the way it always did when his curiosity was building high enough to try to override his common sense. He pulled his gaze away from Mercy's attractive, slightly exotic appearance and swung one leg over the side of the bed, intent on getting up for the second time. Before his toes could do more than brush the floor, Mercy covered the mouthpiece with her hand. "Simon, it's for you."

He stopped with one foot still under the blanket and twisted sideways to look at her. "Who is it, did they say?" Jesus, surely he wouldn't have to go into the field today—it was Christmas, for God's sake, and far too early for people to start beating on their kids. *Let it be a mistake,* he thought. *Please this one time, let it be a mistake.* When she shook her head no, he held out his hand reluctantly. "Chanowitz here," he said.

"Merry Christmas, son. What do you say I drop by and have a holiday dinner with you and the girlfriend?"

That voice again—unwanted and hated, spilling its ugliness and agonizing memories into what should have been the happiest day of his life. On his feet without remember having risen, Simon ripped the telephone from its plug and threw it against the wall.

Then stood over the fragments of plastic and plaster, horrified at his own explosion of temper and staring helplessly into Mercy's shocked eyes.

DECEMBER 31 . . .

"Damn it!"

Something hit the floor and broke, the crash of glass and impact one of the first sounds in her life that Gena had come to associate with disaster—this time doubled because she didn't know what it was that she'd knocked off the ledge or how much it meant to its owner. For a second her orientation in the town house deserted her and she felt like she was falling in midair; instinct made her drop into a crouch but common sense stopped her fingers when she would have reached for the remains of her accident.

"Hey, Gena," Lamont called from somewhere upstairs. "You okay? What broke?"

"How the fuck should I know what *broke*?" she snarled, then immediately regretted it. Lamont was so good to her, meant so much and tried so hard—what was the matter with her that she would lash out like that? She opened her mouth to say she was sorry, she didn't mean it, but what came out was a sob instead. What good was her so-called second "sight"—and that was a fucking laugh, wasn't it?—when it couldn't clue her not to put her hand somewhere so she wouldn't break something?

Footsteps in front of her but hard to judge the distance; Lamont already hurrying down the lushly carpeted stairs, the warm thumps of his feet disappearing under the stupid snuffling sounds that were starting to spill from her drippy nose and mouth now that the tear storm had started in earnest.

"Hey, what's the matter?"

Alarm radiated in Lamont's voice, the kind of concern that had nothing to do with pity or obligation but with affection. Her thoughts, insidious and perpetually black, immediately reminded her that only two other people had ever felt that way about her, her mother and Luís—and both, after a fashion, had abandoned her. Gena went all the way to her knees then, ignoring the sting of glass fragments as her shoulders shook and she fought not to wail out loud like a terrified toddler. "Nu-nu-nothing," she managed, and hearing herself voice such a ridiculous lie almost changed the tears to hysterical laughter.

Gena felt Lamont lift her completely clear of the floor but there was no fear of falling as he effortlessly swung her past whatever destruction she had caused and carried her to the couch. Her sense of placement within the town house was completely lost until she felt the soft, ribbed fabric beneath her hands and her memory automatically righted her within the scope of her small, lightless world.

Settling next to her, Lamont pulled her close and his lips brushed her wet cheek. "Want to talk about it?" he asked softly.

"I—I broke something," she stuttered. "I'm sorry. This place is so big, it has so many l-ledges—"

"This is not about breaking a vase," Lamont said. His hand, warm and comforting, stroked back the shaggy bangs that covered her eyes. "What's bothering you? Is it really the move to the town house? Do you regret coming here?"

Gena opened her mouth to say *Yeah, I really hate it,* but the words wouldn't come out. They weren't true; she hated being in *unfamiliar* surroundings and bumping into stuff when she wasn't outright breaking something. Lamont still wasn't used to no longer being able to habitually pick something up and put it down in a different spot. But unfamiliar surroundings and physical objects that never stayed in the same place were the way Gena's world had always worked. They were annoyances and inconveniences that had to be adapted to, not something to make her sit down and weep like *this.* "No," she said aloud, "I guess it's not that bad." Her voice was gaining a measure of control; now she only sounded like she had a wad of cotton stuffed up each nostril.

"Then what?" Lamont's fingers were still rubbing against her shoulder, a smooth, reassuring touch that had anchored her since the first time she'd felt it in her old apartment.

"I'm . . . *afraid.*" Her voice dropped to a whisper.

"Of what?"

God bless him; for the first time in her life here was someone who would actually believe her if she told him something bad was going to happen. And it was—there was plenty of that coming, but not yet, not for another two seasons, and not just to them. In the meantime, they had each other and this town house, and the small world that they had built from each other. If she was terrified of something, all she had to do was tell him—no argument, no convincing, no being told "You always have bad feelings about something or another." How well she remembered Luís saying that on the morning he'd walked out of her life forever.

"Of what, Gena?" Lamont's voice pulled her back from the painful memories. "Don't hold it in—tell me."

"Of now, of the future. I—I don't know," she finally had to admit. "I swear to God, Lamont. I just don't *know*."

It was New Year's Eve and Gena was doing the dishes when her mother-in-law called. Thinking about it later, she wondered if she should consider Lupe to be her *ex*-mother-in-law, but somehow that didn't seem right. She and Luís hadn't gotten a divorce— he had *died,* but she knew of at least one woman who'd gone to the reunion held by her dead husband's family two years after he'd passed away, only to be told by her stepson that she had no right to be there because she wasn't a part of the family.

Perhaps it was the coming new year, her second since Luís's death, that had made Lupe think of Gena. Luís had always taken her out to dinner, and while their budget had generally precluded anything fancy, there were fine neighborhood restaurants that served excellent Mexican food—Gena's favorite. She and Lamont had spent yesterday snuggled in front of the fireplace, basking in front of its warmth while outside the weather had once again turned disappointingly gray and nasty, this time with the threat of a snowstorm hanging over the city like the mailman coming up the walkway with bad news. At first this winter had been wet, but right after Christmas that had changed to a deep, biting cold punctuated by a storm that had left six inches of snow in its wake. Inside the town house, however, the snow and minus-fifteen-degree temperatures seemed as far away as Fairbanks. Lamont had conned her into listening to the movies he watched, and for the first time in her life, Gena was enjoying films. Of course, it might've had something to do with the fact that he always picked movies full of uproarious sound effects—screaming lizards and people with bad Japanese accents. He told her they were Godzilla movies and she sat with him, listened, and laughed while he watched, her small hand secure in his larger one, at peace—most of the time—with her life. One of the more amazing things was that it didn't seem to annoy or distract him to keep up a low, running description to let her know what was happening to the characters. His voice, a steady, dark velvet, circled around her like the sheltering folds of a cherished afghan.

Gena's hands were wrist-deep in the hot, sudsy water, methodically searching out the plates and cups, wiping and rinsing, running her super-sensitive fingers along the surface of the plates to check for missed spots. On her lower right was a dishwasher, but it seemed to take her twice as long to rinse and stack the dishes—every time she tried to put a new one in, she had to search the rack all over again to find the next empty slot. When the telephone rang, she thought nothing of it; Lamont was a popular guy at work, he had family in the area, and he got calls all the time. He wasn't above giving his home number to a client if he thought the person needed to reach him, holiday or otherwise. The music from the triple set of Mozart CDs in the player stopped abruptly as Lamont hit the PAUSE button before going for the telephone.

"Gena, it's for you," he called from the living room. "Wall phone's to the right of the refrigerator, about shoulder height."

She froze. Who knew she was here? She'd quit her job at year end right before moving in with Lamont, picked up her W-4 form and final paycheck, and not bothered to leave a forwarding address. How . . . the old telephone number, of course. Lamont must have had the phone company run a recording referring any calls to here. But who . . . ?

"Gena?"

"On my way," she yelled back. "Give me a second." The town house wasn't big, but it felt like it took forever to find her way down the length of counter and past the refrigerator; when her hand touched the plastic of the phone, it felt cold and not at all welcoming as she picked up the receiver and pressed it to her ear. "Hello?"

"Gena, it's Lupe, Luís's mamá. I was thinking about you, and then I called and was so surprised to find out that you moved. Why didn't you call me? When did you move? I would've had the boys come to your place and help." Gena, whose childhood knowledge of Spanish had been completely obliterated through the succession of orphanages in which she'd spent mini-lifetimes, had always found Luís's accent sultry and fascinating. Her mother-in-law's whine sounded like an aging Rosie Perez.

"I . . . I managed fine." Gena gripped the edge of the refrigerator, wishing it were Lamont instead of the cold metal. But he'd hung up the phone at his end and gone back to whatever he was doing upstairs; she dimly remembered hearing the click on the line in the midst of Lupe's words. "I moved not so long ago." Her lips

wanted to make her words stutter and she bit her tongue intentionally, reaching for the sensation.

"Who was that man who answered the phone? He sounds like a
Negro."

"H-his name is Lamont." So much for being in control of her
voice. "This is his p-place."

There was a momentary silence on the other end and Gena
could imagine Lupe standing by the stove in her small kitchen, surrounded by the smell of homemade tamales and *chille rellenos*. For
Gena her in-laws' house had always been a horrifying thing; filled
with clutter that always changed location, pieces of furniture set
too close together and which might be shoved across the floor at
any time. Going there had made her feel like a pinball in a game
with a dozen flippers.

Silence. Then, "Gena, you're *living* with someone already? My
sweet son is not a year and a half in his grave and you've done
such a thing?" There was a quiet sense of marvel in the older
woman's voice.

"I needed someone to help me," Gena heard her own words
from far away, hated them as they came out. They weren't true,
but she had to say them, *had* to, for so many complicated reasons.
To punish this woman, who had so much family to furnish support
and who had abandoned Gena like everyone else had, to stab at
her for leaving her widowed daughter-in-law to drown in loneliness and grief, to make her *go away*.

"You could have called me," Lupe said sharply. "I would have
been glad to come by. I kept in touch."

"No." The stutter was gone and her voice had dropped to a
whisper again, the most telltale sign of emotional pain. "No, Lupe.
You called twice in a year and a half and forgot about me the rest
of the time. You should forget about me now." Gena didn't want
to be talking to this woman; nowadays there was a blackness
always licking at the outside of her mind, bleak promises of a
future so very, very close. The fewer people she knew when it got
there, the better. Was it so much to ask not to go insane?

"You should be ashamed of yourself for saying such a thing,"
Lupe said coldly. "We tried very hard to get to know you when
Luís first brought you into the family, but you never wanted to be
included."

That tone—how well Gena remembered hearing it. Always
before it had been directed at one of the other family members for

some household infraction, but hearing it transported Gena momentarily back to that crowded and not especially pleasant-smelling house. Lupe always smelled like the food she cooked—

The world outside was a changed place, colorless and stifling, lawless . . . brutal; the feel of the sun's rays was gone, missing for weeks now beneath a suffocating cold cloud cover. The wind wouldn't stop blowing, the rain wouldn't stop falling, the people wouldn't stop killing. At the height of its chaos, Chicago was dead center in the Grayzone, the only place left that fostered survival. But it might as well have been called a battleground as the people who were left looted and pillaged whatever they could and fought to hoard scraps and supplies. She could see the remains of Lupe's home, but only in that oddly subjective way she'd ever seen anything, and she knew, knew, *that the front and rear doors were busted open and the hallways were dark and cold and filled with the rank smells of decomposing flesh. She knew, too, that these people, who had been so cherished by her dead husband, were themselves days dead and there was nothing she could do to save them . . .*

She tried anyway.

"You should get out of that house," Gena said suddenly. "I have a feeling that something . . . that it's not a safe place to stay. There's still plenty of time, though—sell it now and move, come to the north side of the city. We could put you and the rest of the family up here. It's not that big and it would be crowded, but we could manage." She was babbling, making no sense at all; she'd never felt that much love for her in-laws to begin with, yet she couldn't bear to think of them as she knew they would be, lifeless and ignored, left to decay in a ransacked house without so much as a few last words said in memory. "You'll come, right?"

There was another of the heavy pauses that Lupe had fine-tuned over time. "So you're still having those 'feelings' of yours."

"I—It's the asteroids . . ." Gena's words faded out. Nothing had changed here, she realized in despair. She still saw the same things, the darknesses, large and small, in the future of everyone's lives, and they all still disbelieved.

"Did you know my son was going to die?"

Gena whimpered; she couldn't help it. She had never told her husband's family the truth of what had happened in the apartment that morning, the final argument between her and Luís. Even if they didn't believe her, they would hate her. Somewhere in the center of their minds would be that doubt—*Could she have saved him? Why didn't she?*—that would condemn her in their eyes for the rest of eternity. But to be asked outright . . . could she lie about this? Deny the nucleus of herself? But she despised liars and so often she knew when they lied, yet she *had* to do so now, to protect herself. If she didn't—

"Yes," she whispered unwillingly. "I knew."

"So you could have stopped it." Lupe's voice was flat and cold, smooth steel coming over the phone lines.

"No, he—"

"Murdering *bitch,*" Lupe hissed and slammed down the receiver.

Lamont found her sitting numbly on the floor of the kitchen and had to pry the telephone from her hands.

4.
MILLENNIUM'S DARK EMBRACE

NEW YORK
JANUARY 1, 2000 . . .

[fade to Marti Nunciata]

From the opening segment of the seven o'clock Cable News Network broadcast:

"Tonight New York rests uneasily under a citywide four o'clock curfew as tanks manned by armed militiamen patrol its main streets. Those New Yorkers who witnessed and were lucky enough to escape the riot which started last night at the stroke of midnight in Times Square weren't the only ones exposed to violence and injuries as the world bid a brutal farewell to the twentieth century and the second millennium. As the new year passed from time zone to time zone around the globe, would-be revelers worldwide were beaten, injured, and even killed in what were supposed to be new year celebrations. Public gatherings turned hostile, erupting in urban battlegrounds as people vocalized their fears and anger over the predicted impact of the remains of Millennium. One hundred fifty-six people were killed in Times Square last night, and the number of injuries has not yet been calculated. Moreover, the death and injury toll continues to rise as reports come in and tell of similar situations from private parties across the city. At the scene in Times Square and supervising the cleanup under the watchful eyes of the National Guard is Police Chief Talbot Enzi, coming to us via equipment we set up before today's curfew went into effect. Tell us, Chief Enzi, what do you believe sparked last night's riot, and will this type of behavior continue in the months ahead?"

[cut to window and expand to fill, Talbot Enzi]

"I don't have an answer to your first question, miss. If it was just here in Times Square, I might try saying it was a bunch of fools with too much liquor who managed to start a chain reaction— except I've never seen so many people die at once because someone drank too hard. I think people are scared about the future and what's going to happen, and they're taking it out on each other. Do I think it's going to continue in the future? You're damned right I do, and let me tell you that the police are not going to be able—"

[voice-over stops abruptly; cut to technical interruption display; fade to Marti Nunciata]

"Chief Enzi?"

[cut to upper right window, unidentified man]

"I'm sorry, but—"

[Talbot Enzi, off screen]

"Who the hell are you?"

"—Chief Enzi's duties require his presence elsewhere. I'm from the City Office of Information, and the mayor has asked that all future news information and interviews be channeled through this office. As the schedule here is rather hectic tonight, please have your network contact us at another time. Good evening."

[window flickers to black; abrupt cut to Marti Nunciata]

"Uh—as you can see, the situation in Times Square remains tense. We will continue to bring you further updates as soon as we have them, but right now our news stations around the globe report rising instances of rioting. Cities across the United States— Boston, Atlanta, Chicago, Denver, Phoenix, Los Angeles, even Honolulu—have instituted curfews and sought help from the National Guard to stop the escalating violence and destruction."

[fade out]

JANUARY 3 . . .

"Frank."

He heard Crystal's voice but ignored it, then felt suddenly

guilty. In a moment of startling clarity, he saw himself as she must: surly, unshaven and unshowered, hunched in front of his computer for hours on end next to an ashtray overflowing with half-smoked cigarette butts. He'd given up the habit in high school and knew his wife detested the smell, but they were going to die anyway, so why not? He raised his head and saw her standing in the doorway, her sleek figure silhouetted by the brighter light of the living room behind her. Good God, he was sitting here working in the dark. When had the sun gone down?

Frank started to speak, then had to clear his throat before the words would come out. "Yeah, hi." He damned himself when he heard the "Go away, you're interrupting me" tone in his voice, tried again, softer this time. "What . . . what's up?"

"I've fixed dinner. Do you want to eat with me or shall I bring you a tray?"

He frowned; her voice was dull, as if she barely had the energy to speak. "What time is it? Are you going to work?"

Crystal shifted slightly, a half step sideways that made her able to lean her weight against the doorjamb. "Eight," she said wearily. "My shift starts at eleven."

Frank glanced at the calculations on the computer screen, then pushed his chair away from the desk and stood, wincing at the stiffness in his knees. As he walked to the door, the hopeful look that crossed Crystal's face made him feel about as worthy as a dirty rag. "Hey," he said gently. "Are you okay?"

She shook her head, not bothering to lie. "Just overly tired, I guess." She gave a short, hollow laugh. "Like you're not."

"Come on," he said, steering her toward the kitchen. "I'll serve the food—are you at least hungry?" There was no question she'd go in tonight, so he didn't bother to ask. Forty percent of the staff at the retirement home had quit since the Millennium announcement a month earlier. Crystal nodded reluctantly and he walked with her to the kitchen, squinting at the bright lights as he pulled out a couple of plates and napkins, then dished out the food. Nothing fancy—a couple of seasoned chicken breasts, baked potatoes, and steamed broccoli—but suddenly his mouth was watering and he was thinking about the people who'd quit the retirement center and everywhere else. Did they have other ways of finding money for food and rent? Or had they disregarded day-to-day things like rent and started throwing all their purchases on charge cards they never expected to have to pay? A short-lived method, though; one of his colleagues at the University had mentioned that American Express had revoked any account that was past due and was routinely canceling the account of any customer making more than a hundred dollars a day in purchases. Some of the other companies—Discover and Diners Club among them—had simply frozen all the accounts "temporarily," while none of the smaller department and local stores extended credit at all anymore. The Visa and MasterCard accounts were still holding out, but Frank doubted it would be for long.

"So," he finally said. Crystal hadn't uttered a word since following him from the office to here; beneath the long cap of strawberry-blond curls, her face was drawn and slightly puffy, more pale than her normal fairness and with blue shadows under her normally clear eyes. *I'm an idiot,* Frank thought. *My wife is buckling from exhaustion right under my nose and I haven't noticed.* "I know you're shorthanded at the home," he said hesitantly, "but you really don't look up to going in."

She shrugged. "Not much choice, but I can probably cut my shift short—*if* no one else has quit." Crystal shook her head and pushed a piece of potato around the plate. "Christ, they aren't even bothering to call anymore." She paused for a moment, then looked at him without raising her head. Below the faint arch of her brows, her china-blue eyes were large and troubled. "Frank, is this really it? Everyone's acting so crazy, like no one believes there's any hope left. Isn't there anything we can do? I know you said NASA and Russia were working on a missile project but—"

"The optimal date for launch was yesterday." Frank had dreaded this question for the past week and his voice was hoarse as he tried to answer.

"Yesterday?"

He nodded, glad that they had finished most of their meal before starting this conversation. Otherwise, neither of them would have eaten. "But it was too soon—they simply couldn't get the project pulled together in time."

Crystal set her fork carefully on the rim of her plate. "And what does this mean to we the world?"

Frank rubbed absently at his temples, wishing he could massage away the stress headache that always seemed to be there. "We haven't given up, if that's what you're asking. There are more governments involved in this than the U.S. and Russia. The

U.K. and Japan are pumping in funds and research, not to mention Sweden, France, Spain—a lot of others."

"If everyone in the world is pitching in on this, I don't understand how it can't be done in time," Crystal said. Her voice had an edge of stridency to it that made Frank wonder uncomfortably how close to panicking his wife was.

"Unfortunately some of the more religious nations either don't believe it's really going to happen or insist that it's destiny and we should simply accept it." Frank tried to choose his words carefully. "But we're still making progress."

"But you said that yesterday was the best—"

"The optimal launch date," he said quickly. "But not the *only* date."

"What exactly are they launching?"

Frank opened his mouth to remind her that she knew he couldn't repeat top-secret information, then thought *Screw it,* instead. This was his wife, and anything he said was going to eventually be released to the public anyway in an effort to stem the rising violence. The White House felt that if the public regained hope, perhaps it would regain its collective mind. Personally, Frank doubted it; he thought the people who were going haywire already were acting that way because they *wanted* to—that insidious, whacked-out survivalist faction that thought it would be *fun* to go back to the stone age. Well, they were all going back somewhere, all right. Aloud he said, "We've sent a Titan IV to Russia. They've modified the Energiya so it can carry the Titan up to the Mir space station, where it'll rendezvous with another Titan waiting with two multimegaton nuclear warheads as its payload. The warheads will be mated to the fueled Titan from the Energiya, then launched. The *Salvation* will already be docked at Mir and a combined American and Russian crew will be waiting. They're calling it 'Project Valentine' because they've set a target date of February fourteenth for the final launches. Cute, huh?" He gave her a sickly smile.

But Crystal wasn't about to be sidetracked, and now her mouth dropped open. "Two warheads? But everyone knows there are over a hundred pieces, Frank!"

And now, he thought, for the part the feds *think* they can downplay in this final deadly drama. "We're going to take out the two largest ones. The shuttle *Atlantis* is still being retiled and we've got more boosters in production, but this is the best we can do right now."

"I can't believe that," Crystal said brusquely. "There are plenty of rockets available besides ours and Russia's. Why can't—"

"But only a few that can take a loaded Titan to geo-transfer orbit. We have to use something to get the fully fueled rocket to the space station where it can be loaded with the warheads, then launched toward Millennium," Frank explained. "Right now only the Russian Energiya can do it. Ariane 4 can't carry the payload, and the last three attempted launches of an Ariane 5 were aborted due to dangerous malfunctions in the liftoff sequence. The cause is being researched—stepped up now, of course—but they haven't found the problem and are refusing to attempt another launch until they do. They're projecting April as their earliest possible launch date, and that's far too late. Manufacturing facilities both here and in Russia are being run around the clock, but time is a serious problem. We're close to completion on a couple more Titans and Russia claims the same on another Energiya, but we've got to get something up right *now*. In the meantime, we aim for the two largest pieces first, the ones that are likely to hit and do the most damage."

"And what about the rest?" she demanded.

He could tell by her eyes that she already knew the answer.

JANUARY 9 . . .

"Well, if it isn't wonder boy himself."

Alva looked up as Joey half snarled at a man who'd just walked into the restaurant. The family resemblance was unmistakable in the ebony skin and broad features of the other's face, and Alva knew this must be Lamont, the brother that Joey despised. While her lover was clearly startled by the arrival of Lamont and his companion, Lamont looked oddly . . . resigned.

"Hello, Joey."

Alva stepped closer to Joey and watched the two new arrivals narrowly. The woman on Lamont's arm was obviously blind; if the dark glasses she still wore after sunset weren't enough of a giveaway, any peek at her eyes was obscured by a dated but well-done shag hairstyle that dropped bangs all the way to the bridge of her nose. Short and sturdily built, the black hair and reddish skin made her unmistakably American Indian, and she turned her entire body toward whoever was speaking rather than just her head. Saturday night and packed despite its new cash-only policy, The Gale Street Inn was a popular steakhouse on Milwaukee Avenue; there was a triple pause of awkward silence before Joey, his voice too loud for the knot of people waiting around the hostess's desk at the front, continued. "So this must be the girlfriend you told Mom and Dad about." Joey's brother nodded but didn't say anything and Alva finally shot Joey a disgusted look—he could be such a prick sometimes—and stuck out her hand in Lamont's direction. "Hi," she said as sweetly as she could muster. "My name's Alva Marten. It's nice to meet you." She offered her hand to Lamont and he took it automatically, gave it a gentle, controlled pump, then released it. That done, she turned to the woman beside him and offered her hand again, knowing Lamont would have to tell her to take it. "And this is?" Alva prompted.

Lamont looked at her hand as if he wanted to tell her to drop it back to her side but couldn't think of a way to do it without insulting both Alva and Joey. "This is . . . Gena. Gena, this is Alva." He looked even more uncomfortable. "She's, uh, offering her hand."

As Joey stood sullenly next to her, Alva saw the woman flinch visibly and press her lips together as Alva lifted an eyebrow and waited. The police force was a handshake world, and while the gesture wasn't always offered in peace or friendliness, *not* accepting it was a clear insult. If this woman was that stupid and rude, she was going to deserve the sharp words that Alva would send her way. Finally, though, Gena reached out a hand, although it was intensely obvious that the last thing she wanted to do was touch Alva. "How . . . how are you," Gena ground out.

Their fingertips would have only brushed, but Alva was too quick; she'd be damned if she'd let this bitch treat her as though she hadn't washed her hands in a month. Trained reflexes took over and before Lamont's girlfriend could pull back, Alva wrapped Gena's small, dark hand in her own and squeezed firmly—well, more than firmly, then held on, looking for all the world as though she were simply extending an intimate greeting to someone she knew. She'd teach this babe to embarrass her or anyone else.

She wasn't quite sure what happened next. Gena's mouth formed an "O" of shock and her hand convulsed within Alva's grip. The policewoman felt . . . *something,* but she wasn't sure what, a double pulse of energy running through the flesh, then

Gena choked back a cry and her knees gave out. From her left she heard Joey's sharp intake of breath, but Lamont was right on the money; with his arm still slipped around Gena's waist, he seemed to be effortlessly holding her up despite the fact that her feet were clearly limp on the floor. Alva released her hand and saw Gena do an almost instant recovery, small feet finding purchase on the decorative flagstones. "What's the matter, Gena? Are you all right?"

"Luís," Gena breathed, "oh, my *God*. It was you, wasn't it?"

Alva scowled and took an involuntary step backward. This time it was Joey who offered his strength to her as his warm hand sought her suddenly cold one. She forgot about the restaurant and the other patrons casting furtive, curious glances at them, forgot about the wisdom of asking questions that would continue the conversation rather than stop it clean. "I don't know what you're talking about," she said instinctively. "Who's Luís?"

"Gena?" Lamont's voice sounded frightened, ludicrous coming from such a sturdily built man—and especially so if he had the unnatural abilities that Joey had claimed.

"He was my husband." Gena's voice could barely be heard, and it was a damned good thing because her next statement would have insured an openly captivated audience. "It wasn't the drug dealer who did it, it was you. *You* shot him!"

Alva felt her stomach do a bungee-cord drop as she flung out her other hand for balance in a room that was suddenly rocking like a motorboat; Joey was there, his compact frame steady and anchoring.

"How—"

"I think we should go," Joey interrupted wisely. He turned her toward the door and guided her through the crowd, shooting a last, malicious glance over his shoulder. "Dinner's ruined anyway—for *both* of us."

Then she and Joey were outside, where the cold, damp air seemed to use the chill in her veins to its own advantage and seep all the way to her spine before settling. Alva kept hearing Gena's words in her mind—*"It wasn't the drug dealer who did it, it was you. You shot him!"*—and each time they repeated came that same gut-dropping sensation of leaping off a hundred-foot tower.

"You want to fill me in?" Joey's low voice cut through the roller-coaster ride of her stomach and pulled her back to Milwaukee Avenue and the traffic and people filtering past, the real world versus the one she'd thought was done with and safely behind her. "What was she talking about?"

"I—I shot a man not quite two years ago." Alva was still too shocked to contemplate the wisdom of confessing the crime to Joey. "He was a civilian, a bystander, but he saw something he shouldn't have—a meeting, if that's what you want to call it, that went bad between me and an associate. I thought it'd be okay—for Christ's sake, I set the meet up for quarter to seven in the morning. How was I supposed to know some Puerto Rican grease monkey was going to cut through the gangway on his way to work? I knew I was going to have to kill the dealer, but then I had to kill the guy who saw me do it, too." Joey said nothing, and the past half a year had taught her to read between the lines. The question in his mind might as well have been floating on a blinking banner in front of her face: *So, what's your point, Alva?* "The thing is," Alva continued, "*no one* saw it. It was my word all the way, and there were no questions raised. You know cops, Joey—we *always* carry two guns. I'd whacked the dealer with my service revolver, but when that spic showed up, I blew a hole in his chest with the .44 that was in my jacket pocket. The thing was stolen and all I had to do was plant the piece on the dealer. I lost a little blow out of the deal because the .44 was loud enough to bring half the neighborhood out and I had to plant that on the dealer as well, but that was the end of it. How the *hell* does that woman in there know about it? She was in her apartment alone when it happened—I know the uniforms who went to her place to give her the news. I remember, because they said she was already crying when they got there—"

"She has to be psychic."

"Don't fuck with me, Joey!" Alva cried. "This is serious shit I'm talking about here!"

"I *know* that," he snapped. "But is it really so hard to believe, considering what your pals told you about her and what I've told you about Lamont?"

"I don't know that I believe you about that," she said. As they finally arrived at the parked Lexus, Alva's irritation with the whole contemptible situation was starting to surface. "It sounds like carnival crap to me."

Joey glanced around the sidewalk cautiously before keying off the car alarm, then he shrugged and opened the door for her; things had calmed down somewhat since the feds had released the word about the upcoming missile launch, but there were still plenty of weirdos on the streets. "I don't give a shit if you believe me or not. You saw what happened—she should've hit the floor when she realized who you were, but Lamont was holding her with one arm and not even breathing hard. Did you see the look on Lamont's face when he saw us? He wasn't a bit surprised—I'd put up double odds that she told him we would be there. Which is not the point anyway."

"And what is?"

"The point," Joey explained patiently, "is that if she really does know the stuff about you that she claims, can you afford to let her run around the city telling everyone you killed her husband?"

"No one's going to believe her."

"I don't think that matters." He stood on the other side of the car, staring across the roof. The halogen streetlights made his eyes look like shining, oiled stones, cold and emotionless as a rattlesnake's. "Letting her mouth off is going to draw all kinds of unwanted attention. So you have to take her out."

"Why? According to everything I'm hearing, the end of the world is coming anyway."

Joey snorted. "Yeah, sure it is. But just in case it doesn't, you better think about dealing with this."

"And?" Alva's hands were freezing and her teeth were chattering, and neither had anything to do with the ugly late-winter weather.

"And that's going to be pretty fucking tricky with Lamont around."

JANUARY 15 . . .

" 'Rica, look at this. Ain't it amazing?" Nearly asleep, Erica Richmond opened her eyes as Searle gazed at the bedroom's portable television with rapt attention. "Since they started talking about that asteroid hitting the Earth, the world's gone completely nuts."

"Why?" Erica pulled herself to a sitting position and stretched. She wasn't really sleepy, just warm and satisfied, content. Having Searle around made her feel safe despite the escalating craziness at the hospital and on the streets. "What's going on now?"

"Same as yesterday and the day before, I guess." Searle leaned back, his gaze on the screen. "It's just so strange to *see* people acting like this out in the open. Look." He pointed at the screen and her eyes tracked his finger, then widened at what she saw.

"That's some backwoods town in Wisconsin with a population of a thousand, yet they've had to institute martial law to stop the looting. It's getting like that all across the country."

Erica frowned, fully awake now. "We anticipated that the less populated areas would panic first because they have fewer supplies and facilities. But I didn't think it would happen this fast. It's only been six weeks." She pulled the two pillows on her side of the bed together and stuffed them against the headboard so she could lean back. "We certainly have our work cut out for us." Her anticipation must have shown in her voice, because Searle looked up at her curiously.

"Erica," he said guardedly, "don't you believe the news reports?"

She couldn't help chuckling. "No, I'm afraid I don't."

"But two days ago the government stopped denying that part of it's going to hit—now they're talking about launching missiles. Everyone knows the thing's got more than two pieces and this is just a smoke screen—they don't know what the hell to do about the rest. If—*when* this thing hits us, that's it." He snapped his fingers for emphasis. "End of the world, or most of life on it. Mankind goes the way of the dinosaurs. Kaput."

Erica sat forward. "That's just *it,* Searle. I shouldn't have said I don't believe the rocks are headed for Earth. What I don't accept is that NASA and the Department of Defense will sit idly by and let anything hit the planet that will do that much damage. One way or the other, they'll stop it—probably by sending up more missiles. In the meantime, I intend to set myself and my family up for the rest of my life. And you, too, of course."

Searle's eyes brightened with interest. "I didn't know you have family. I thought you were pretty much by yourself. You got kids?"

"None of my own." Erica glanced around the expensively furnished room—teak furniture with hand-carved inlays—and swallowed the sudden lump in her throat. Amazing how loneliness could come crashing down even when someone else was in the room with you. It was that big picture thing again; after all, was Searle really the rest-of-her-life choice? He was older than her, but not by much; rough, sexy, *dangerous.* A challenge. But forever? Hardly. He was . . . *insurance,* her protection against the nastiness that might be coming. "But I have a brother and sister-in-law, and a nephew. The boy has a hard time of it." She picked at the gold brocade surface of the comforter. "My brother has a . . . heavy hand."

"Boys need a lot of discipline."

She raised her head, unsurprised at his response. After all, what could she expect? He might not realize that she knew the details, but she was familiar with Searle's background and what he'd done; the thing that perplexed her was why she'd had anything to do with him other than hiring him as the security coordinator for After Help. Taking him into her life and bed was so much a mystery that it gave her a headache when she tried to figure it out—which was often. Was she really convinced he was the answer to keeping herself safe in the coming year? "That's what my brother always says," she said shortly. "And he damned near killed his son two summers ago. If you ask me, he missed being thrown in jail by a damned miracle."

Still not used to the remote control, Searle got out of bed and walked over to the television to shut it off, then began filling two of the crystal mugs on the tray beside it with ice cubes from the bucket. That done, he poured them both a generous shot of Chivas Regal. "What happened to stop it?"

Erica studied him carefully. Of course he would ask—she'd practically issued an open invitation. He'd be interested, too, in more ways than he realized right now. First, because he had paid a heavy price for his loss of control all those years ago, and second, she knew something he didn't. Would he believe her? It didn't matter; she paid him to do his job for After Help and, whether he thought of it that way or not, handle her needs physically and emotionally. Listening to her and accepting what she said, whether or not he believed or agreed, was part of that. Searle was a smarter man than he let on, and she was damned sure he knew all the things he did for her—*all* of them—were just part of the job as far as she was concerned. There was no love or support or comfort here; loyalty and protection were more the order of business. "You remember telling me about the woman Simon's living with," she said casually. Searle nodded. "She used to be a doctor at Althaia. An emergency-room physician."

"No kidding." He handed her a glass and took a sip from his own. "Did she have something to do with it?"

Erica gave him a wry look. "Oh, you'd better believe it. I don't know what the hell my brother was thinking when he *disciplined*"—she couldn't stop the sarcasm from hanging off the

word—"Ryan that day, but he and his wife brought my unconscious nephew in with far too many injuries to explain. The most
obvious was a fractured skull, and there was no doubt he had
internal injuries as well. A catheter showed that his bladder was
full of blood, he was bleeding from the rectum . . . the list went on.
Simon's girlfriend was the trauma specialist on call and she was
right on top of it. She'd already had one of the EMT's call both the
police and the Department of Children and Family Services before
my brother's message made it through to me."

"Did she know the kid was your nephew?"

"No. Stan—my brother—was extremely careful *not* to tell
anyone about that. For someone who constantly loses it when it
comes to his emotions, he functions with almost frightening effi-
ciency in the business world."

"So what happened?"

"I ran through the ER and got a quick look at Ryan before
going back out by the nurses' station for a few words with Stan,
and the poor little boy was a mess. He might have survived, he
might not, but Daddy was definitely going to jail over this one.
Then I intentionally went back upstairs, and by the time I came
back down to the ER, it looked like I'd come in response to a sum-
mons from the head trauma nurse. You know the setup down
there—Althaia's a small hospital and it seemed like half of the ER
was taken up by cops, social workers, Stan and his wife, and the
ER staff. Plus Dr. Ammon—that's her name—and my nephew, of
course. Complicating the situation was the fact that Ryan was sitting up on the side of the table and smiling. There wasn't a thing in
the world wrong with him. He didn't even have a skinned knee."

"What!"

Erica smiled. "He was completed *healed,* Searle. Over the
course of that day I spent hours with the staff members, the police,
Stan and Mickee, and those damned DCFS social workers. Dr.
Ammon was the only person who'd had any time alone with the
child, when she'd sent both of the EMTs out of the emergency
room to line up an operating room and rush the bloodwork. She
didn't even have that long, three minutes maximum, before
someone else from the ER would have wrapped up their case and
come over to pitch in. She's the only one who could have done it."

Searle scratched his chin. "You're saying she healed the boy."

"Exactly."

Searle's expression was puzzled. "So she's a doctor and a . . .

'healer.' But my sources say Simon's girlfriend works as a staff assistant in an animal clinic. Are you sure we're talking about the same person here?"

"Definitely. I've kept tabs on her quite closely after her resignation."

Her lover stretched out next to her on the bed. His body was long and hard, and she knew he took pains to keep it in the same shape as it had been when he'd been working out in the prison yard. Scar lines crisscrossed his flesh at irregular intervals beneath a fine layer of hair gone prematurely gray; when she'd asked about them, he'd said tersely that in prison he'd learned the hard way to stay alive. "Why did she resign?"

Hugging her knees, Erica stared at the blank screen on the television without really seeing it. "I forced her to. It was too much of a threat to have her in the hospital knowing what she did about my brother, too much of a chance that she'd make the connection between him and me. Sooner or later she'd dig deeper into Ryan's records and find the connection. It might have been obscure, but it would've turned up—maybe in a 'Notify in Case of Emergency' box on a form somewhere. And she . . . she made me *nervous*." For a moment Erica was silent, and Searle didn't push. "Can you imagine having that kind of power, Searle? A person like that could do anything, *demand* anything and get it."

In the first gesture of genuine comfort she'd ever seen him give, Searle reached over and squeezed her arm. "I could see why something like that would creep you out. What I don't understand is how she ended up cleaning animal cages. I mean, she's a doctor *and* she can heal. Why would she decide not to practice anymore?"

"I forced her out," Erica said simply. "I was angry and I panicked over how close my brother came to getting caught. I thought if I could at least get her out of Chicago, I could stop worrying about Stan's uncontrollable temper. Mercy's just not cut out—"

"Mercy?"

Erica gave him a wry grin. "That's what everyone called her because of her attitude. Anyway, she's never wanted to be anything but an ER physician, and I guess now we know why. After I demanded her resignation from Althaia, I made sure that every time another hospital called for a recommendation, it came through my office. I kept my opinions professional and off the record and she couldn't land a job in this city to save her life."

"But she didn't leave."

Erica frowned momentarily, then the expression melted into a dark smile. "No, but don't you think that's rather . . . fortuitous given this thing with the asteroids? I was surprised, of course, especially when she was stonewalled everywhere. Unfortunately, it doesn't take much of a guess to know that I'm the reason she couldn't get a job."

Searle took another sip of scotch and swirled the cubes in the bottom of his glass. "I don't see how it makes any difference," he commented. "If you stepped back now, she could easily get a job, what with all the riots and shit going on. Emergency rooms are packed to the gills. At this point they're so desperate they probably wouldn't check."

"Maybe," Erica said absently. "It's interesting, but I don't think she's tried since . . . I don't know. Way before the job as a veterinarian's assistant. And it does make a difference, you know." She leaned past him. "I want her back," she said pointedly. "I want her working for me, for After Help."

Searle stared at her. "You're kidding, right? I mean, all joking aside, if I were her I'd sooner spit on you as look at you."

"Such a way with words," Erica said scornfully, but he only shrugged. "And I don't care what she thinks about me. *I want her.* One way or the other." Searle started to say something, but she held up a finger. "In the meantime, the guy heading up the Louisiana chapter says he's found someone who he thinks could pave the way for an entirely different area. He's got an eye toward the future and a good track record, so I'm going to send you down to bring her up here for training. Prices are high now, but I've set up an expense account to cover your costs, plus you can whoop it up for a few days."

Searle's face brightened. "Where am I going?"

Erica smiled serenely. "New Orleans. Clear your schedule from the day after tomorrow until the middle of next week and pick your ticket up from my secretary tomorrow morning."

Searle yawned. "Why the personal escort? You'd save a bundle if you just told her to buy a ticket at the airport and you'd pay for it."

She sighed. "Jesus, Searle. Do you have to question everything I say?"

For a moment a scowl flashed over his face and Erica saw a glimpse of the young man who must've exploded in a tenement apartment more than a quarter of a century earlier. Her pulse quickened, but Searle's expression smoothed out again and his mouth turned up. "Just curious, that's all. It's a natural tendency to want to know."

Sure it is, Erica thought. *And you wouldn't cut my throat the minute you found where I keep the After Help hard cash reserves, either.* Aloud she said, "I'm told she can be difficult, plus she has rather . . . *interesting* nonreligious notions. Apparently she's built up quite a following down there, nearly started her own mini-cult, and we believe she can do the same here. My figures indicate that there's a large gap in the age groups that After Help is pulling in. The company's attraction seems to start at about age twenty-seven, when the general work force starts thinking about and planning for the future. That leaves an entire segment untapped and this young woman and her group fit right into that slot—too young to know what to do and too stubborn or rebellious to go to their parents for assistance. I think she'll be the catalyst we need to draw in younger members and get to the money in that group. I'm planning on using her in advertising to reach the more eclectic of Chicago's youth—after all, they have money, too."

For a change, Searle didn't comment, so she continued. "One of your responsibilities will be to charter as many buses as needed to bring up anybody who wants to go with her—that was the deal. As his part, the New Orleans chapter president has convinced her that After Help is just the thing she and her people are looking for." Erica smiled outright, pleased with the whole idea. Odd, but the concept of After Help had run so smoothly from start to finish that she was actually *bored* with it; it could use someone with a personality to spice it up and give it new goals. "She sounds like quite a character, Searle, with a whole new slant on the asteroids and why she thinks the world's going to come to an end. I can't wait to bring her to Chicago and turn her loose."

JANUARY 17 . . .

New Orleans in January—Searle couldn't have asked for a better place to "whoop it up for a few days," as Erica had so snootily put it. The air in the French Quarter was cold, damp, and smelled like wet concrete, cooking grease, roasted coffee beans, seafood, and beignets. In Chicago winter had a gridlock on the city, burying everything in icicles and dirty snow; here there was a larger variety of greenery that fought the idea of winter at every turn. Trees that still had leaves swayed in the offshore breezes and dripped water on the passersby for hours after the latest thunderstorm, and Searle didn't miss the subzero temperatures a bit. The first thing he did when he got into town was to check into the St. Louis Hotel, then hit Kaldi's coffee shop for the biggest, blackest cup of French roast he could find. All those chain coffee shops were full of shit in thinking they could compete with the real stuff, shipped straight across the Gulf, ground up fine as coal dust and tasting ten times as strong. Price gouging was normal now and Searle shelled out nearly five bucks for the oversized mug without comment; the man behind the register had a Taurus 9mm in a side holster and didn't look in the mood to be fucked with.

After paying, Searle found a table against the far wall that still gave him a clear view of the window, then settled onto an old wooden classroom chair. The place was damp and overheated by the steam radiators, the rattling fans hanging from the fifteen-foot ceilings doing little beyond making long strings of cobwebs dance idly on the humid air. Underneath the aroma of burned coffee was an older smell of decaying brick and slowly rotting timbers, all mingling with the odor of rusty pipes and the sweat of the thousands of people who'd come and gone in this dusty shop over the years. The whole thing—the shop, the dangerous streets outside, the tempting decadence of the city—was mesmerizing, beckoning. Sitting there and sipping the hot brew, Searle smiled and thought that if it weren't for Erica and the asteroid, this was a place he could get lost in, and fuck Kaiser and his twice-a-month meetings and the entire Illinois state correctional program. If Millennium did hit the Earth, the whole idea of government was doomed anyway. This part of New Orleans—and maybe all of it, by now—was like a sleazy whore with shining red lips and a voodoo touch who could take you in and drain you dry, then leave you hooked and helpless to escape. There was nothing wrong with finding your soul city, even if you had already swung past the hard edge of fifty. Too bad he hadn't come here a year ago, before—

Erica. Searle air-rolled another sip of scalding coffee over the rounded edge of the cup and stared blankly out the window. He'd never been to New Orleans before but he'd heard plenty about it in the joint. None of the inmates' stories and braggings could come close to matching the air of blatant menace that hung on the streets now, and each day that passed made it more obvious that Erica had been right on the money. After Help's chapters around the country were doubling in size as each week passed, taking in members like a hungry corporate vampire glutting itself on public fear. Rapes, murders, theft—the numbers had skyrocketed as people around the globe simply let *go*. Others were flocking to After Help on the hope factor alone, that same thing that he and Erica had talked about the night she'd told him he was headed here. He couldn't call Erica's belief that the asteroids would never hit "hope," though, because she spoke with such utter confidence that Searle could've sworn she was able to see the future and had just never admitted it. In the meantime he did what she said, followed her orders, and fucked her good and as often as he could— the only part he liked about their relationship. The rest of it required the kind of iron self-control that a man learns only from being at the mercy of prison guards and "wolves" and wanting above all else to find his freedom again and still have all his body parts intact when he did. If not for Erica Richmond and After Help, Inc., he'd still be in a sleeping room off Belmont and Broadway and busting his ass for minimum wage at some Manpower job. The After Help gig had basically fallen out of the sky, and no one appreciated it—or Erica—more than he did.

Speaking of the job, it was time to get to work. Searle finished the last of his coffee regretfully, then stood. Erica had told him to take a few days for himself before playing chaperon, but he had a hunch most of that would be used on the chore of finding and figuring out how to get the girl and all of her so-called cult followers back to Chicago. What little information they had pointed to a number of about a hundred or so, and that would mean getting together a double crew of buses with dependable drivers who weren't too cowardly to make the trip; according to the news reports, now the open interstates were the worst places for carjackings and murders and there weren't nearly enough troopers to patrol all the highways. It was a good probability Searle would find the kind of men he needed in the strip bars on Bourbon Street well after the weaker ones had gone home; the *real* business had always been conducted at night.

He found what he was looking for in a place with a six A.M. license called The Bare Babe on Bourbon and Toulouse, a sleazy all-nude place that the bartender told him had recently installed the iron-barred cages to protect the dancers from the increasingly rowdy crowd. Searle didn't know how it was going in the other large cities around the country, but New Orleans seemed to have quickly fallen into the routine of arming its shopkeepers; the weapon of choice for both of the bartenders here, sawed-off Mossberg 590 shotguns, swung from their shoulder straps. The four shapely girls in the cages looked tired and wary, dancing with pseudo-enthusiasm in time to too loud music that didn't fit any particular type. Despite the bars, or perhaps because of them, no one in the sparse crowd seemed particularly interested in the strippers.

The first guy Searle tagged was sitting at the far end of the bar and nursing a glass of whiskey. He was shaggy and swarthy-skinned, a Cajun maybe, twice Searle's size and watching the red-headed babe in the enclosure closest to him dance with a sort of lazy interest, generally minding his own business. Searle waited for the man to finish his drink, then slipped onto the stool beside and gave the bartender a two-fingered signal. When he turned to look at the man beside him, a mask of cool suspicion had slipped over his mark's features. "What's with you?" the guy asked. Searle was gratified to note that the voice wasn't surly or drunk, the accent there but understandable.

"Just in town for a few days, that's all." Searle kept his voice pleasant and paused long enough only to pay the bartender when the drinks were delivered. "Looking for a driver, somebody willing to make a run up north, then make his own way back if he doesn't want to stay."

The man pushed his empty glass away but made no move to reach for the complimentary drink. "You a cop or a dope runner?"

Searle pulled out one of the business cards Erica had ordered printed up for him; he'd felt supremely foolish carrying them but now he realized they'd come in handy after all. "Neither," he said mildly, going with the title on the card. "I'm the coordinator for After Help, Inc. It's a division of a Chicago hospital. I'm looking for someone to drive a busload of folks up to the hospital."

"Forget it." The guy turned his shoulder to Searle and leaned his elbows on the bar. "I ain't driving a bunch of sick people anywhere."

Searle chuckled, drawing a sidelong glance from his mark. "I wouldn't either. But they're recruits for the company, not patients. Say, what's your name?"

"Sam."

"Okay, Sam. You look like a guy who's capable of doing the job. If you want it, here's the deal." And Searle spelled it out for him, cold cash under the bar, two hundred tonight, another three hundred when he showed up at Searle's hotel room in two days, and twenty-five hundred more when they got the bus and its load of people safely to Chicago. He made it clear to Sam that the balance of the money waited at the corporate offices of After Help and not in his pocket or room at the St. Louis—no sense getting his throat cut five minutes after he walked out of The Bare Babe. Three grand; not bad for a two-day drive, even on a trip where you might have to dodge a bullet or two and return fire. The way things were going, that kind of money might never be seen again.

Sam's eyes were still skeptical, but starting to shine a little. "I don't want to get to the bus and find a carload of people who're dying or some shit," he rumbled. "I don't cotton to being around those contagious"—he pronounced it *contangious*—"diseases and such."

"You won't," Searle promised. "They're just regular folks, like you and me and anybody else."

Sam was silent for a few moments, then he shrugged. The careless movement didn't fool Searle. "Why the hell not?" he said offhandedly. "I got nothing better to do than make a fast buck." He stroked a hand across a face that hadn't seen a razor in days. "You need someone else? My brother's looking for work."

"The other slot's already been filled," Searle lied smoothly. "Maybe next time." No way was he idiot enough to pull two brothers in on the same high-money job; he wanted strangers—no ties, no friendship, no treachery.

Sam didn't argue, just took the card that Searle offered him with the name of the hotel on it and tucked it carefully into his wallet with the down payment. "I'll be there," he said in a no-bullshit voice. "On time."

Searle left him sitting at the bar and moved on, keeping an eye on his back to make sure he wasn't followed as he wound his way back to the street and over a few blocks, into another dive called The Sassy Kat. This one's nudie show had the girls dancing on a platform behind the bar instead of in suspended cages. Searle had a knack for picking out the kind of man you'd want on your side in a fight, a hard-learned skill picked up in prison and put to good use now. The next guy wasn't as big as Sam but was just as sturdy; tanned, hard-muscled arms showed beneath a gray T-shirt and the green eyes under dark blond brows were clear and distrustful, a good sign, considering the way the world was now. The same deal, nearly the same words, and it was done. This man's name was Wexler and he wasn't averse to telling Searle that he was an out-of-work deckhand, but he could drive anything that had a motor and kept all its wheels on the ground. Searle walked out feeling confident that both would show up when they were supposed to; if not, he really didn't think either would be too difficult to replace. That part of his duties done, he headed back to the hotel for a few hours' sleep.

New Orleans in the early morning was . . . *changed* somehow. Although Searle had never been to this city before a few days ago, he knew instinctively that the undertone, the *heartbeat* was different. Although it had always been a night queen, New Orleans still started the day, as did any other place, in the early hours— deliveries were made and picked up, wares were stocked, restaurants were cleaned and prepared, food was cooked, shops were opened and workers were fed. This morning, however, the place was like a ghost town: empty, damp and cold, with trash blowing across the sweep of Dauphine and no one in sight. Cars were parked but they were shadowed hunks of metal, while people slept within the apartments above the century-old shops behind crumbling windows shuttered against the sea-chilled breezes. The question, Searle wondered as he strolled toward Bienville where Erica's newest recruits stayed, was *Did they sleep peacefully?* He doubted it.

The building the girl lived in was at the worst fringes of the French Quarter and was as much of a pit as the cell block back in Joliet; Searle couldn't help question the lucidity of someone who would stay in a place like this of their own free will. Whatever was going on—or not going on—in the rest of New Orleans, he could hear movement and noise, voices already engaged in soft conversation behind the battered door on the second-floor landing, which smelled like someone had dropped a pound of bacon in it and left it to rot. He rapped on the door only twice before it was thrown open without so much as a "Who is it?"

The girl who stood staring at him was small and round at the edges. Searle found himself marveling that neither she nor anyone else asked him for identification; she just waved him inside and turned her back, and never mind that he could be anyone, a killer, a rapist, one of the thousands of guys who were taking particular delight in what they perceived to be an end-of-the-world free-for-all. That would all change, Searle thought grimly; Erica had said this girl's safety was paramount, something about crazy dreams she'd been having in which the girl was a major player and how getting her away from this coastal city was essential. But when she finally turned to face him, Searle believed every one of Erica's dreamy, half-garbled descriptions of the power this girl had buried inside her.

"You must be Naomi Lauren," he said evenly.

"How'd you guess?" Her voice was a sneer, but oddly emotionless. Searle had the sudden realization that there was something indefinably *black* in her gaze and he knew that had he been one of those men at her door this morning, a hood with a knife or a gun, he would have run rather than face this small woman with hell in her eyes and the promise of damnation in her expression. She turned her face toward the interior of the apartment and her hair swung across her shoulders like strands of straight, exotic black threads. *She used to be a dancer,* Searle thought suddenly. There was no doubt about it; watching her graceful, rounded-hip movement across the floor confirmed it. How on Earth had she gone from stripper to Erica's next prodigy?

A grin suddenly split Searle's face, and he didn't care if anyone in the room—packed with dozens of people—saw it or not. For that matter, how had *he* gone from ex-con to "coordinator"?

He moved farther inside without invitation, drawn by the scent of strong, bitter coffee, stepping over trash and bottles on the floor, purposely stepping on the oversized cockroaches that seemed to be everywhere. In contrast to the filthy walls and floors and the garbage-strewn furniture, the occupants—and he'd been wrong about the number; it looked more like his entire double busload was right here—were spotlessly clean. They milled around, most silent but a few engaged in intense conversations; none were inclined to sit on the floors or furniture, or even lean against the walls. Most just stood, head down, hands folded in front of them as though they were sleeping on their feet. It was eerie to see all these men and women, and a few children, together in one place but so silent, nearly motionless.

"They're a sight, aren't they?" Naomi was at his side again, this time with a mug of steaming coffee that smelled vaguely of burned almonds. He took it without comment; he had learned not to be too critical at Joliet, and it was a lesson that didn't go away. "Just standing there, hardly talking, hardly *breathing*."

"You guys should've cleaned this place up," Searle commented. His gaze raked the piles of unbagged trash; surely there were rats hiding in here with the insects. "It's not very healthy."

Naomi shrugged. "No one cares, Mr. . . . Chanowitz, isn't it?" She cleared her throat and continued. "The physical world is not important, and we don't belong here anyway. It's become an ugly and unwelcoming place and there's no desire to try and make it pretty anymore."

"Call me Searle." He studied her freshly cleansed face. "But if you—and they—believe that," Searle pointed out, "then why bother washing and putting on clean clothes?"

Naomi turned that dark gaze up to his. "Because our bodies are our houses, whether we like it or not—"

Searle couldn't help smirk. "The holy temple thing and all that?"

Naomi laughed, the sound surprisingly harsh. "Not at all. It's just what we're stuck with. We should at least try to keep it upright."

Searle sipped his coffee. People shuffled around, no real purpose in their movements, no interest in their eyes. "I don't get it—all these people, you. What's the deal here—and why is everyone dressed in black?"

"We're dead people," Naomi said flatly. "Everyone in here"—her eyes flicked toward a tall guy standing by the windows with his arms folded and a faraway expression on his face—"well, almost everyone, including me, has cheated death. Been 'rescued' right before the end, so to speak."

Searle registered where her glance had gone and instantly made the connection; that must be the boyfriend over there, Eddie Cuerlacroix. Watching her now, he couldn't help the frown that swept over his features. "Personally I'd sort of think that was a good thing. Why are these people walking around like it's the end of the world?"

"Because for them it *is*," Naomi said heatedly. The sudden spark of anger gave her cheeks a pinkish tint that had been missing before. Above the rounded collar of her black T-shirt, her face and neck were like floating orbs of white chalk; not so much as a trace of lipstick cut the paleness. Her lips were a natural purplish-pink and they reminded Searle of the occasional inmate who had opted for suicide by hanging. Naomi and the rest of the crew were so quiet and indistinctly . . . *fragile,* like little vampires who didn't have the sense to get out of the sun before it destroyed them. They were so thin—did they eat? "The life of each person in here ended on the day he or she *should* have died," she continued. "The day their souls were *taken*."

Searle started to laugh, barely hid it behind the gesture of wiping his mouth with the back of his hand. Beliefs were a funny thing in a person; ridicule them and a man might find himself at the other end of a lot of shit. "Souls?" he managed. "You mean that now they're like zombies?"

This time it was Naomi who laughed. "Nothing quite so Hollywood, I'm afraid. No"—she glanced around, then rubbed her hands across her eyes—"they're just . . . lost. They don't belong here anymore. Some believe they're being punished for something they've done in their lives and must now atone, some just don't care. But we all seem to find one another. They found me, and now I can't seem to shake them. Isn't that funny?"

In reality, Searle thought she sounded anything but amused. "And how do you feel?" Searle asked. "Which category do you fit into?"

When she answered him, her eyes seemed blacker than they had when she'd first answered the door, twin pits of night sky floating within her skull. "I guess, Mr. Chanowitz, you could call me one of the . . . *hungry* ones."

JANUARY 28 . . .

Respite in a false touch of spring.

Mercy turned her face up to the sunlight gratefully. The Januarys that she remembered from her childhood in southern Illinois were like this, cold but not bitterly so with the temperature hovering around thirty and the air peppered with birdsong and breezes bearing the smells of damp soil. While the mercury had finally climbed, the city remained brittle and wet, soggy under an overdose of cold rain that had left everything the same dirty shade of gray and the tree branches like spindly wire sculptures. Sometimes Mercy felt that the only warm spot in her life was Simon, always there for her with a gentle word or comforting touch at the right time. In spite of the ongoing despondency over the loss of her medical career, he had helped her to achieve an uneasy balance in her mind between what her nearly uncontrollable power demanded and what the physical world could tolerate. Even her Nights Out had developed a pattern and, incredibly, a safety net:

Lily, who always talked Mercy into meeting her somewhere first, then followed her silently through the clubs like a protective shadow, invariably there if Mercy needed her but never interfering otherwise. This morning, with the sun finally burning its way through the hazy cloud cover, Mercy felt blessed with the love and companionship of these two strange, strong people, rich in a way she'd never thought possible.

She glanced at Simon and he smiled slightly and squeezed her hand; his face had that faraway look that said he'd managed to leash what he called the "demon in his head," distract himself or block it behind a wall of noise that he sometimes compared to the noise from a television when the station went off the air for the night. The park itself was deserted; it seemed no one could be bothered with something as simple as enjoying a walk on a rare mild day in January. Not quite two months had passed since the news reports started coming in about Millennium striking the Earth, but the effects of the continued barrage of doom-news, as it was being called, were far-reaching and profound. The Andersonville area hadn't been hit that hard by crime—yet—but Simon and she had both agreed it was only a matter of time before the roving gangs and looters worked their way deeper into their quiet Swedish neighborhood. Oddly enough, business at the animal clinic had nearly doubled—people were claiming all sorts of erratic behavior and strange illnesses in their pets and blaming it, of course, on the asteroids. Mercy did what she could—not much, considering the number of people who passed through the small facility, and the notable lack of privacy. The frightening thing was that some of the stuff clearly *wasn't* imagined; sure, Mercy could heal anything given the chance and a minute alone with the animal, but she no longer knew *what* she was healing. Not that the information had ever come to her in a mental flash or anything, but she was a *doctor,* for Christ's sake, and it wasn't hard to make an educated guess based on some of the symptoms. As it was, things were getting weirder every day, and who could explain the fourteen cases last week of cats trying to cannibalize their own front paws?

"I'll be damned," Simon said beside her. "There's a water fountain over there and it's on. You thirsty?"

"I could use a little," she said, happy to have him pulling her bleak thoughts back to the sun-filled path they were following along the lakefront. "And look." She pointed ahead. "People, finally. I was started to think Lincoln Park had turned into a recreational ghost town."

Simon chuckled, but there was a faint sadness to the sound. "At this time of the morning, we're okay. The way things are headed, I'm not sure how long the park will be safe, no matter what time it is."

Mercy was silent as they made their way toward the water fountain. Simon was right, and they probably shouldn't even be here now. In previous years the kids—greasers and gang members—had gathered in groups of several hundred in some areas, usually the beach parking lots, along the expanse of the park that sprawled for more than six miles by Lake Shore Drive. Now most of the people who had used the park during the day were too intimidated or frightened to go in; those swarms of aggressive, sneering teenagers had been replaced by wandering bands of sadistic hoods who robbed and beat—or worse—their hapless targets. To not be able to stroll in Lincoln Park anymore . . . the idea nearly made her cry.

Simon touched her arm. "Mercy, I'm sorry. I didn't mean to bring you down."

She shook her head, fighting against the sudden tears in her eyes. "It's not your fault, Simon." She sighed. "It's the way people have turned—" She broke off and her eyes widened as she got a good look at the two other people making their way down the park path, apparently angling for that same water fountain. One was a solidly built black man; his companion was a short woman with a sturdy frame and the reddish complexion of an American Indian. Clutched in one of her hands was a white cane, stilled as she let her partner guide her forward.

"Mercy, stop it," Simon admonished her suddenly. "You can't just walk up to strangers on the street and grab them." He tugged on her jacket sleeve to make sure he had her attention.

She started to retort, then grinned sheepishly instead. He was right, of course, and she wasn't foolish enough to think he'd had to read her mind to guess what she'd been contemplating. Most likely the woman had been born blind, and Mercy couldn't repair what had never existed. "Well, let's talk to them, anyway. They're the first people we've seen out here."

"Uh-huh." Simon sounded amused. "And it *is* eight A.M. on a Sunday, you know."

"Good morning!" Mercy called out cheerily. "Isn't it nice to finally be able to take a walk?" Bedside manner—Mercy had excelled at it and the skill was seldom lost.

Although the woman stayed quiet, the black man nodded back guardedly. When he spoke, his voice was a quiet rumble, like a train easing along the tracks. "The weather's broken," he agreed, "for a few days, anyway. And the park is . . . quiet."

Mercy smiled pleasantly, but kept her hands in her pockets. "My name's Mercy. This is Simon," she said with a tilt of her head. Beside her, Simon kept his face neutral, and Mercy knew he appreciated that she had positioned herself between the two men and refrained from offering her hand. He didn't like shaking hands with strangers; it was hard enough, he'd told her, to keep his head out of their thoughts without direct contact.

The black man seemed to have no desire to offer his either, but that didn't stop him from returning Mercy's smile. "I'm Lamont," he told her. "This is Magena."

"What a beautiful name," Mercy said immediately.

The other woman seemed to hesitate, then spoke in a voice almost too quiet to be heard. "People call me Gena for short."

Lamont glanced around, his eyes watchful. "You two walked this far by yourselves?"

"It's still pretty early," Simon said, then glanced at his watch. "We figure we have another hour—"

"The rovers are coming out earlier now." Gena's suddenly stronger voice sent a momentary chill skating along the skin of Mercy's arms. "We should really all head out of the park now."

From the corner of her gaze, Mercy saw Simon's eyes widen, then narrow thoughtfully as he glanced first at Gena and Lamont, then thoughtfully at the seemingly deserted park. "You're right, of course."

Of course? Under other circumstances, Mercy might have protested, but Simon's unexpected agreement surprised her. "Hey," she suggested, "we don't really know anyone in the area. I hope it doesn't seem too forward, but . . . would you like to grab a cup of coffee somewhere?" Now it was Simon's turn to look startled. The impulse thing, catching even him off guard.

"No," Gena said, too quickly. "I—I'm sorry. We have to get back."

Lamont gave her a puzzled look but didn't argue. Instead, he shrugged apologetically. "We were just stopping here for a quick drink," he explained. "Sorry."

Mercy nodded amiably, hiding her disappointment as Simon cleared his throat and looked pointedly at the fountain in an attempt to ease the sudden awkwardness. "No problem. Us, too."

Mercy watched in silence as the shorter woman ran her hand lightly around the rim of the stone fountain until she found the stream of water, then lowered her mouth carefully. She couldn't help wonder what Gena's eyes looked like behind the dark glasses and the stylishly cut, overlong bangs that fell to the halfway point against the lenses. *Stop,* she told herself shortly. *Simon's right; you're getting outright pushy.* It was the pressure, she thought resignedly, building, as always, nearly to the point of detonation inside her. She'd put off a Nights Out for longer than usual because the people were getting more and more dangerous, but now she felt like a pot of water approaching the boiling point. What happened when the power inside her actually hit critical temperature?

As Gena finished drinking and straightened, Mercy stepped forward and instinctively put her hand on Gena's arm to steady her. Despite her unacknowledged desire to help this woman, the gesture wasn't connived—Mercy didn't think that way. Because of that, she never expected what happened next.

Her hand pulsed once, *hard,* then gave her a bright flash of pain. Gena gasped at the same time that Mercy yanked back in shock and nearly fell. Nothing like this had ever happened—it was some kind of backlash, something—

"Mercy?" Simon's voice was full of fear.

"What happened?" Lamont demanded. He started to reach for Gena but missed as she suddenly lurched forward and flailed at the air.

"Where are you?" Gena cried. Her voice bordered on hysteria. "Come back—touch me!"

Trancelike, Mercy took a step forward and caught both of Gena's hands in her own, gritting her teeth in expectation. Another strange, hot surge through the skin and muscle, but no pain this time, only a sense of unreality and dizziness, like sitting in the restaurant at the top of the Hancock Building as it revolved with agonizing slowness to give her a total view of the Chicago skyline—slow dancing on the top of the world. "I'm here." She was whispering and she didn't know why.

"You can't help me, Leah," the shorter woman said urgently. Simon's gasp sounded like it came from a lot farther away than her side; still holding Gena's hands tightly, Mercy would have tilted sideways on a sidewalk that felt like it was stealthily turning under her feet. "I am what I am, and you knew that already. But you *mustn't* go out tonight. If you do, Lily will be too late to help you this time. You'll die."

The last thing Mercy heard before the concrete pathway slipped out from under her was Simon's growl of fear.

When Mercy opened her eyes, she thought for a few moments that she was at home, safe in bed and cradled warmly in Simon's strong arms. Two seconds later and she felt the cold from the sidewalk seeping through her blue jeans and registered that she was seeing a blue sky sprinkled with tiny grayish clouds instead of the painted white ceiling. "Oh, boy."

" 'Oh, boy' is right. How do you feel?" Simon's face, tight with worry, filled her vision.

Mercy struggled to sit up, embarrassed. "Fine, really." She ran her fingers over her head quickly. No scrapes or bumps, even on her hands. "Didn't I hit my head when I went down?"

"No. I—we caught you." Lamont and Gena were still there and Simon shot the black man an enigmatic look.

"I—I'm sorry." Mercy fumbled her way to her feet, using Simon's arm for leverage. "I don't know what happened."

"Is your invitation to go for coffee still open?"

Mercy gazed at Gena helplessly. She wanted to say yes but she wanted to say no; for the first time in her life, she found herself afraid of someone for reasons she couldn't explain.

"Mercy?" Simon prompted softly.

"I . . . of course." She could think of a dozen excuses why they shouldn't go, chief among them the half-remembered sensation of having this woman, this *stranger,* inside her head for the briefest of moments. Mercy would have thought she'd be used to that, after living with Simon for all these months. Wasn't she prepared to spend the rest of her life with a man who could read her mind as easily as she could tie her shoe? But what Gena had done was fundamentally *different;* rather than a speed-read of what was happening inside her skull right now, Gena's touch in her mind had been like someone skimming through her life's files—a basic tidbit here, an essential fact there, enough to get the lowdown on the whole picture. But for what purpose? Why, to look ahead, of course.

Of course?

"I think that's a great idea," Lamont said a little too heartily. "Where—"

"There's a place that still serves breakfast at the corner of Sheridan Road and Windsor." Mercy couldn't decide if Simon's scowl was meant for Gena and Lamont—what had happened after she'd fainted?—or because they were pushing the edge of safety by still being in the park. "It's not very big but it's comfortable and the food is decent."

"That's good," Gena said. "We need to leave now, though. Another ten minutes and we'll have . . . unwanted company."

The four of them started walking quickly, with Simon holding Mercy's hand in a grip that was a little too tight, as though he were afraid to let go of her around these two strangers. While Mercy understood they might not have much of a choice, Lamont led Gena along much faster than Mercy would have thought wise or safe considering Gena's handicap. As frazzled as she was about this entire morning, she couldn't help fearing that Gena would fall; the thought finally occurred to her that perhaps Gena wasn't as blind as Mercy had assumed.

The dinky restaurant was in an old building and reminded Mercy of tiny places in her hometown. A hand-lettered sign in the small picture window next to the front door read "Sheridan Diner—Breakfast and Lunch Only. Close at One." Inside it was clean but dim and not much larger than a commuter train car, long and wide enough for only a single row of Formica-topped tables, front to back. Since they were here at Simon's suggestion, he led the way inside and started to stop at the first table up front, but Gena's hoarse request—

"Not by the window, please."

—compelled him to go deeper in the restaurant. Mercy wondered briefly how Gena had known there was a window there, then dismissed it as an assumption on the blind woman's part. Simon kept going and finally stopped at the second table from the back. "Is this okay? Any farther and we'll have to duck the swing of the kitchen door."

"It's fine." Some of the stress had evaporated from Gena's voice and Mercy looked at her narrowly. She had the feeling that she was outside the circle here, missing some vital chunk of information that linked these three together and left her in the cold. A hazy sense of jealousy swept through her and she pushed it aside; she was afraid, that's all. She'd gotten so used to Simon and living a life that was secure and nearly devoid of secrets that she had to learn to deal with the real world all over again. He would fill her in soon enough.

They settled at the table in a sort of awkward silence as a tired-looking woman appeared with single-sheet menus for each of them, then took their order for coffee and, at Simon's insistence, a small plate of homemade biscuits and jam. When the coffee and biscuits came, Mercy realized that Simon had known they were all hungry and ordered for them. He was right, of course, and she felt herself calming as the hot coffee and slightly salty baking powder biscuits settled into her stomach. Gena and Lamont looked as though they felt better, too, although for some reason it was hard for Mercy to imagine the solid, quiet black man across the table as anything but in total control. Gena had lost the terrified-rabbit look and now sat with her hands wrapped carefully around the warm porcelain coffee mug in front of her.

Enough of this. Simon could sit there and read minds all day and she would have no clue about what was going on. "So what . . . are we doing here?" Mercy asked at last. The question wasn't really the one she'd planned, but it was a start.

"We need to talk," Gena said before either of the men could answer. "You're planning on going out tonight, to meet Lily." Gena tilted her head oddly, as thought she were reading from some invisible script. She leaned forward and Lamont automatically swept the plate with the remains of her breakfast out of the way. "Don't go tonight, Leah—"

"Mercy. Everyone calls me Mercy." It was an inane interruption but she couldn't help it.

"I know," Gena said simply. "I'm sorry. Of all people, I should understand a name preference."

"Why can't I go out?" Mercy asked carefully. The two biscuits she'd eaten that had tasted so good now sat in the pit of her stomach like uncooked dough; she thought she could actually *feel* the butter on top of the undigested food as the whole mess floated on a bed of coffee and bile. She'd already passed out once this morning; now she was fighting the urge to vomit. *Get a grip,* she told herself silently. *It's not like you didn't expect something peculiar.*

"Because you . . ." Gena hesitated, struggling, then abruptly turned her face in Lamont's direction. He reached over and squeezed her hand, a silent show of support. "If you do, you won't make it back," she finally finished. "I . . . I'm sorry."

Mercy stared at her in shock. "How could you know something like that?" she whispered. "And why should I believe you? Simon?" She glanced at him, but the expression on his face was anything but comforting.

"I see more than you realize," Gena said urgently. "I know what you can do, and what Simon can do—what he's doing right now. He knows I'm not lying when I tell you that if you don't listen to me, you'll die tonight. And that mustn't happen, because somehow we . . . *need* you. We all need each other."

"Gena, what are you talking about?" Lamont asked. He looked completely perplexed. "You've never mentioned any of this before—we just met these people."

"That's because I didn't *know* any of it before she touched me at the fountain." Gena ran her fingertips idly along the edge of the table, her fingers skimming lightly over the chips and grooves of the old Formica. It was strange to watch her talk to Lamont but never bother to look at him, watch her fingers express the things that would have shown in another person's eyes.

Mercy sat back and thought about this. It wasn't so hard to accept in the face of the things that she and Simon could do. If she could heal and Simon could read minds, the miracle before her was not that Gena could tell the future but that she and Simon had stumbled across her, ostensibly in time to save Mercy from . . . *dying* tonight, a future that was difficult to contemplate. Her eyes scanned Gena's face briefly then went to Lamont, and she wondered how long he'd known, how hard it had been for him to accept. Then again, had it?

"And what do *you* do, Lamont?" Mercy asked suddenly. She waved a hand around the table. "I can account for myself, Simon, and now Gena, but what brings you into this interesting group?"

"Me?" Lamont looked suddenly flustered. "Nothing special."

"He moves things with his mind," Simon said softly. Mercy's eyes widened as Lamont's shoulders jerked, then he looked down at the table as though he were embarrassed. "But he can't stand admitting it because he was brought up to believe it was wrong."

"Jesus Christ," the dark-skinned man muttered. "No secrets around *you*."

Simon shrugged. "Sorry. I just wanted Mercy to know the truth and I knew you wouldn't tell it." He gave them all a rueful smile. "In fact, I spend a lot of time trying *not* to poke into people's heads."

An unexpected grin slipped across Lamont's mouth. "What the hell," he commented with a chuckle. He elbowed Gena lightly. "It's not *that* much different than putting up with her highness here."

"You asshole, you're just using me to avoid traffic jams," Gena said with an amusing mix of bland crudeness.

Mercy couldn't help smiling and Simon joined in with a laugh, but it faded quickly and his expression turned serious. "Gena," Simon said earnestly, "what did you mean when you said we need each other? What"— he glanced apologetically at Mercy—"would have happened to Mercy tonight had we not all met at the park?"

For a moment Gena's mouth went slack, as though the essence of her had slipped out and gone somewhere else for a fast look-see, then she swallowed and visibly refocused her attention on Simon. "Nothing . . . connected to the rest of us." Mercy had no doubt the woman couldn't see a thing in the physical world, but Gena's face turned toward her nonetheless. "Just someone too far gone for you."

"I've never met someone I couldn't heal unless they were born with their problem," Mercy said flatly. Lamont blinked and made her realize that up to now he hadn't grasped exactly what her "skill" was.

Gena's smile was gentle, oddly diplomatic. "I've no doubt about that at all, and your biggest achievement so far is Lily, isn't it? But what neither you nor Lily know is that Lily was always as mentally ill as she was when you saved her—she *was* born with it and you were able to help her anyway."

Mercy's mouth dropped open. "But that's not possible!"

"Yes, it is. I think it depends more on the *person* than you, whether the potential is there for you to work with. As much as you might want to, you can't bring someone back from the dead, right? The capacity for healing, for *life,* isn't there." Gena reached forward and brushed Mercy's fingers, then cocked her head while the three of them watched, again giving them all that discomforting sense that she was daring a glimpse into some secret realm. "The impression in my head is gone, because you've changed your mind. All I can remember of it is a man and a switchblade, and a lot of screaming."

"Where was Lily in all of this?" Simon asked. Mercy glanced at him and their eyes met; like her, he had come to depend upon Lily as Mercy's self-appointed bodyguard.

"She would have died, too," Gena said quietly, never turning her face away from Mercy. "Fighting for you."

Gooseflesh rippled across Mercy's arms and she rubbed them. The heavy pressure that had been building inside her and making her crave a Nights Out was gone, knocked out of her like the wind had been when her father had once hit the softball she'd pitched to him straight back and into her stomach. Today she felt a lot like she had then, except now she was sitting on a chair in a restaurant instead of lying in a field and staring up at the sky in airless surprise. "Well," she said shakily. "I guess I don't feel like going out after all."

"You haven't answered Simon's other question, Gena," Lamont said quietly. "What do the four of us have to do with each other?"

"I can't really tell you," the blind woman admitted after a discomforting moment of silence. "It's just a feeling, a certainty, that as a group we have to make it through the asteroid hits together or we don't make it at all. All for one and all that crap."

"So it *is* going to hit," Simon rasped. "They're not going to be able to stop it." It was a statement rather than question; there was no doubt he believed everything she said.

"Oh, yeah," Gena said, then she frowned. "Nothing can. But something about that's going to be . . . funky, different than what everyone thinks although I can't figure it out enough to explain it." On the tabletop, her fists balled up in frustration. "Sometimes it's all so fucking *muddled* in my mind!"

Mercy stared at her hopefully. "But you're talking about how we have to make it through, and surely you can't mean just us. Other people are going to survive, aren't they? That much you *can* see, right?"

Again Gena was silent long enough to make them all squirm, then she nodded reluctantly. "Yes . . .

"But we're not going to like it."

FEBRUARY 3 . . .

"What the hell are we doing here?"

Eddie's voice caught her just before she could slip into a doze and Naomi sighed. It would be so much nicer to ignore him and burrow into the covers, curl as close to his skin as possible. Chicago in February was cold, but she was always colder. Wishful thinking, unfortunately; Eddie would never let her sleep now that the question was out in the open. "Does it matter?" she asked aloud, knowing that it did.

"Of course it matters," he said irritably. "Back home it's warm enough so that leaves are probably already starting to form on the trees. Here we're freezing our asses off."

"We're going to die anyway."

She regretted her words, but only because they made him angry enough to jerk away from her and climb out of bed. "Always full of good cheer, aren't you, Naomi?" Since coming to the boarding-house rented by After Help, they'd had to adapt to the company's early-riser schedule; it was the only part of this new life that she truly, truly despised. At barely six in the morning, Eddie's face was pale and puffy in the gray dawn light filtering through the slits in the blinds. "Damn you, anyway."

"I'm sorry," she lied. She reached a hand toward him before he could stalk away and he hesitated. "I won't say any more about it. Come back to bed, okay?" For a moment she thought he was going to refuse and she had to bite back the venomous remark that wanted to escape; patience, she told herself. Not everyone jumps when you say so and inwardly she grinned; too bad . . . although the hope she saw in Eddie's eyes when he gazed at her gave her a pang of guilt. She knew he wanted the old Naomi Lauren back, the sultry stripper with hot blood and a hotter temper. How many times did she have to tell him that woman was gone forever?

The cheap mattress settled under his weight as he slipped back under the covers. She pressed herself against him, seeking warmth, and felt him shiver in return; no matter—she knew just the right moves to warm him up. A good thing, since her cold hands had to feel like frigid gloves as they slid up his thighs.

"Jesus, Naomi," Eddie said with a little gasp. "We have to get you an electric blanket. Your whole body is freezing!"

You have no idea, she thought. Aloud she said, "Can't you be my electric blanket, sugar?" It sounded corny, but from his crooked grin she could tell the words were right. Lying snuggled next to him and stroking, her pelvis was pressed against his hip-bone and she could feel him respond in the way his body tempera-ture climbed. It was as though she'd left what little warmth was hers behind after the murder attempt in New Orleans, and now she'd become some sort of magnet for body heat; she craved it like other people craved food when they were hungry—or maybe like Eddie craved her. The thought brought another small stab of guilt but it was washed away by desire, the need for a shot of warmth that she couldn't seem to hold on to anymore. He was kissing her now, his warm, moist mouth easily building her own response, tongue running lightly along her lips and teeth, hot and wonderful. His hands felt like heated mittens as they ran over her skin and Naomi almost purred; she slipped one arm under his back and tugged on him until he came closer, then followed her lead to roll on top of her. Another moment and he was inside her body, filling her, finally, with spreading fire.

"You never used to like being on the bottom," he murmured in her ear.

Eddie's breath was warm and ticklish against her hair and she wrapped her arms around his back and held on, letting him set the pace until he found a good rhythm. She didn't bother to answer, betting that he wouldn't appreciate knowing she liked it now because it sandwiched her between his body and the bed and created the quickest buildup of heat—which was not to say he didn't also please her. He was doing a damned fine job right now, as a matter of fact. As least *that* hadn't been taken away from her.

Naomi felt her pelvic muscles tighten as an orgasm began to build, a sharp, electric pulse of feeling that spread through her abdomen and made her legs want to go weak. Eddie's breathing stepped up along with the tempo and he moaned gently; cheek to cheek, she felt a droplet of his sweat slide from his jaw and onto her upper lip. Gasping for air, she licked it reflexively as she nuzzled against him, her fingernails raking pink, painless furrows along his lean flanks as she rocked with him. The tang of saltwater spread across her tongue, warm and delicious, making her open her mouth and run her teeth and tongue hungrily along the corded muscles of Eddie's shoulder and neck, smearing her face with the taste and texture of him. Climaxing suddenly, bright and feverish, Naomi truly didn't realize it when her small, sharp teeth bit down in earnest.

"Ow!"

She almost lost him and the whole feeling then, saved it only by bucking her hips hard to stay with him when he would have pulled out. "Sorry," she mumbled against his neck. "Here—I'll kiss it and make it better." Quick, small kisses, keeping up the rhythm until Eddie found it again and forgot the pain for the moment. Her orgasm, so intense, the best she'd *ever* had, and all thanks to Eddie and his fine skills as a lover and the hot flavor of his blood dribbling so sweetly into her mouth.

"Damn, Naomi," Eddie complained later. "What were you thinking?"

"I wasn't," Naomi admitted. "Otherwise I wouldn't have bit you." She hoped her voice didn't sound too bland. "Anyway, it's just a nip."

"Easy for you to say. My whole neck's sore."

"It'll get better," she said soothingly, but he didn't know whether she was talking about the soreness of his neck or something else entirely . . .

NEW YORK
FEBRUARY 11 . . .

[fade to Marti Nunciata]

From the opening segment of the seven o'clock Cable News Network broadcast:

"Tonight's top story, of course, is Project Valentine, the U.S./Russian cooperative space launch which NASA informs us will destroy the two largest pieces of the former rogue planet which are hurtling toward the Earth and predicted to strike our planet on July second. Recently appointed by the Department of Defense as their official spokesman on the Valentine Project is Professor Frank Gelasias of Kitt Peak, Arizona, who has spoken often with us regarding Millennium since its discovery by his facility last summer. Professor Gelasias had these responses to our questions earlier today:

[cut to window, Professor Frank Gelasias]

"Project Valentine is the cooperative effort of the U.S. and Russian governments. Essentially the Russians are using their largest rocket, the Energiya, to carry a fully fueled American Titan IV rocket to the Mir space station. The U.S. will have the space shuttle *Salvation* docked and waiting at Mir, where the crew will load the Titan from the Energiya with nuclear warheads from another Titan IV, this one launched from Cape Canaveral and also waiting at the space station. Once loaded with the warheads, the second Titan IV will be launched toward the remnants of Millennium, where ultimately the warheads will separate and neutralize individual portions of it."

[cut to Marti Nunciata]

"Has this sort of operation ever been done before, Professor?"

[cut to Professor Frank Gelasias]

"No, it has not. But we have every confidence that it will be a successful mission. Nothing indicates otherwise."

[cut to Marti Nunciata]

"Professor Gelasias, it's well known that the remains of Millennium comprise upward of one hundred pieces. Why are only two warheads being sent up?"

[cut to Professor Frank Gelasias]

"At this time, NASA has determined that only two of the pieces of Millennium pose any threat to the Earth and thus only two warheads are needed."

[cut to Marti Nunciata]

"But if those two are on a collision course with Earth, why wouldn't the rest of the pieces also strike?"

[cut to Professor Frank Gelasias]

"The remainder of Millennium's pieces are either too small to pose a danger or on trajectories that will cause near misses with our planet. Of the pieces that do place the Earth in their path, only the two which we are targeting pose a threat. The smaller ones which are still headed toward us are expected to burn up once they enter the Earth's atmosphere."

[cut to Marti Nunciata]

"With a four o'clock curfew still being imposed across the United States, I'm sure you realize that professional and amateur astronomers around the world are denouncing the launch as nothing more than a desperate attempt by governmental authorities to quell worldwide panic while misrepresenting the facts and the truth. Many, in fact, claim that nothing short of a one-to-one ratio—that is, a missile for every piece of Millennium—will stop the destruction alleged to be coming. What do you have to say to the assertion that all life on Earth will end when Millennium hits?"

[cut to Professor Frank Gelasias]

"Wild and fallacious speculation, that's all. These claims are designed to foster panic and lawlessness, and their very success is an unfortunate statement about society today and the root of why martial law has had to remain in force nationwide. I assure you that NASA and governments around the globe are giving this matter their full attention, and everything is being handled appropriately."

CHICAGO
FEBRUARY 14 . . .

The address they'd given her was a town house in the yuppie-ritzy area on Seminary about midway between North Avenue and Fullerton, the part filled with three-hundred-thousand-dollar town houses and six-hundred-thousand-dollar rehabs. Despite being at the tail end of a wet, nasty winter, the small front lawns here were carefully manicured, the leafless bushes smartly trimmed; no piles of rotting leaves here, thank you very much. Midway down the block Lily saw a young mother maneuver a stroller onto the sidewalk; the little girl inside looked like she was upward of three years old and should have been walking rather than riding— spoiled by mom and dad already. Lily wondered what it would have been like to grow up in a place like this, where the windows were new and tight against the drafts, the rooms inside the buildings dry and warm, the people—most of them, anyway—clean and soft-spoken. Most of her own childhood memories were fragmented, fragile impressions of a cramped and chilly house trailer and a man and woman whose eyes reflected pain every time they looked at her. While it was true that she was finally sane, even cleaned up and dressed in clothes that were slightly less radical than before, Lily felt like a pimple on the face of this neighborhood as she found the right address and rang the bell.

The door was opened by a stocky black man wearing a brightly colored sweatshirt that read "Babylon 5: Our Last, Best Hope . . . for Victory!" over a space station and swirl of stars. Before she could open her mouth, he gave her an engaging smile and pulled her inside. "Hi, you must be Lily. I'm Lamont, and the others are in the living room. Make yourself comfortable, grab anything in the fridge that you want."

Sudden awkwardness, as he waited and she stood paralyzed: could she, with her still wildly cut, multicolored hair and gothic outfit, really just waltz into this man's kitchen and help herself to his food? No—that had to be impossible, she couldn't—

"Lily? Is that you?"

Mercy's voice calling from another room broke through the fear and Lily felt it drain away, like the chill on the surface of her skin had when the heated air inside the doorway of this place had washed over her. She swallowed and cleared her throat, was finally able to answer. "Yeah."

Soft footsteps on the carpet and there was Mercy, long hair flowing over her shoulders and eyes smiling with welcome behind her glasses as she threw an arm around Lily's shoulders and hugged her. "It's good to see you. You've met Lamont?" At Lily's wordless nod, Mercy tugged on her arm until she followed her down a short hallway and into a living room with a cathedral ceiling, and it was all Lily could do not to gape like a fool at the bright space above her head. "Simon's here, of course, and over there is Gena, Lamont's girlfriend. I'll be right back." She hurried away.

"Hi." Gena nodded in her direction when she spoke and Lily realized the woman was blind. Should she say something else? What? Wait—there *was* something she could do, a whim she'd let take her on the way here that she'd thought might break the ice. She was horrible at meeting new people, seldom got along well enough with anyone to make new friends. "I . . . uh, happy Valentine's Day," she said. Was her voice shaking? She held up a bag, not too rumpled, she'd tried to be careful. "I b-brought cookies."

Simon chuckled and stood; two steps brought him to her side and he took the bag and peered inside. "Good job," he said approvingly. "I love butter cookies, even if they are cut into heart shapes and frosted in pink." He grinned at her, then reached over and rumpled her hair like a kid's.

"Hey, cut that out!"

"I knew the feisty you was hiding in there somewhere," he teased. "Loosen up. No one here's going to bite."

"Coming through," Lamont said from behind them. "Lunchtime." In his hands was a platter of submarine sandwiches and he set them on the coffee table; on his heels was Mercy, cans of Diet Pepsi, Coke, and 7-Up balanced in her arms. "Thanks for bringing dessert."

Lily nodded as Simon put the bag of cookies next to the sandwich platter, then dropped back in his spot on the couch. "Let's eat before we turn on the television," he suggested.

"What time is the final launch?" Lily asked. She let her canvas backpack slide off her shoulder and dropped it on the floor next to the couch, confident for the first time in years that she was among a group of people who wouldn't steal everything she had at the first opportunity.

"Two o'clock." Gena's voice was calm and vaguely melancholy.

"I'd kind of like to see the stuff before it," Lily said. "You know, where they do the coupling or whatever it is at the space station."

Mercy glanced at her, then over at Gena. "All right," the blind woman said.

Now she sounded resigned, and Lily frowned. "If you guys don't want to, that's fine."

"No, it's okay," Mercy said quickly. "Lamont?"

"CNN, here we come," he said. He plucked a remote from one of the end tables and aimed it at the entertainment center; a second later, a twenty-seven-inch Panasonic television blinked on, giving an instant, startlingly colorful shot of the control center at Cape Canaveral. The sound was low but they could still hear a news announcer's voice murmuring about the upcoming launch.

After a moment, Lamont increased the volume and they listened to rehashed descriptions of the two launches that had already taken place, the warhead-loaded Titan from Florida, and the Energiya that had been sent up from Russia carrying another Titan. They ate in silence, picking at the sandwiches and cookies in spite of Simon's earlier enthusiasm, then sat and watched the news special without talking. Now Lily wished she hadn't asked that they turn on the television; she felt as though she'd ruined the lunch, pulled too much reality into something that should have been a small chunk of escape time. The voice of the announcers— they switched from location to location and from one person to the next so fast that Lily couldn't keep track—seemed more intrusive than anything else, but she tried to keep up with the flow of narrative and the constantly changing views from the television cameras.

"As we can see from the photographs which are being sent back by the Mir space station, the coupling of the warheads to the waiting Titan IV has just been successfully completed and the astronauts are now in the process of prepositioning the armed Titan IV. We've seen a lot of new technology employed here today, including what you see now on the screen, a small "space tug" which will tow the missile to a far enough distance away from the space station so that its launch will be considered safe and also enable the astronauts to return to the space station relatively

quickly. The launching of a fueled missile in upper space—that is, a zero gravity environment—has never before been attempted, so the Titan IV will be towed and the final adjustments made as far as possible away from the space station itself. Then the astronauts will—

"Wait! Wait! We've just received word—the newsroom is going crazy here—"

Lily felt her stomach twist as she stared at the television. Nothing showed on the screen except a blue, seamless sky above the Kennedy Space Center in Florida. Then the camera swept the grounds at the outer fence of the space center and showed crowds of people staring up at the sky, as though they could see beyond the Earth's atmosphere and into the black universe that waited. They looked like tiny, frozen ants . . . until they began running in all directions. At the other end of the couch, Gena shook her head and buried her face in her hands while the other three stared at the floor. No one here seemed surprised—what was going on?

"We've just received word that the Titan IV has exploded! Details are sketchy at the moment, but it appears that the three astronauts who were working on the missile have surely been killed. In addition, all communication from the Mir space station and the Salvation has ceased, and NASA and Russian officials fear that the explosion, which apparently took place before the Titan IV could be towed any effective distance away, has caused serious damage to both the space station and the shuttle and may have killed the occupants of both. They are unable to get any response from the four cosmonauts inside the space station or from the two astronauts who remained aboard the space shuttle, and none of the transmissions from Earth are being acknowledged, I repeat—"

Lamont used the remote to snap off the television.

"Well," he said flatly.

"We'll need to leave." Gena uncovered her eyes, then twisted her fingers together, the movement jerky. "Find another place, one that's safe. This won't be good—"

"What the fuck is going on here?" Lily stared around the bright room and was dismayed to see nothing but guilt on the others' faces; even Mercy wouldn't meet her eyes. Whatever was happening in this room was tied inexplicably to the explosion they'd heard about moments ago. But she was new here, effectively isolated from the things these four, including Mercy and Simon, shared among themselves. "Did I, like, miss something really important? Anybody want to clue me in?"

Finally, Mercy spoke. "I . . . well, I don't really know what to tell you, except that we all knew that the launch wouldn't work."

"Then why are we all sitting around here watching it?" Lily demanded. "And how did you know in the first place?"

"I told them."

Lily's head turned toward Gena, who sat quietly on the couch, her fingers still twisted around each other.

"And how did *you* know?"

"She can see the future sometimes," Mercy said softly.

If the claim had come from anyone but Mercy, Lily would have laughed out loud, then left. But this was Mercy, after all, and Mercy—and Simon, too—could do things that other people, *normal* people, couldn't. Was it possible that they'd really found someone who could see those things, someone like Gena? "So this means . . . what?" Lily asked. She was trying to sound nonchalant, but fear, such a strange, new feeling, was creeping into her voice. This wasn't a nightclub where she and Mercy were cruising the crowd for an outlet for what Lily had come to call Mercy's "energy"; this was real life, real *big*, and what the hell could they do about it if what she was thinking was true?

"It means the world is going to get hit by the leftover pieces of that planet," Simon said. His voice was calm and precisely modulated, the practiced tone of a man used to talking to people who were scared and confused. "It means that . . . everything we know is going to change fairly drastically."

"But they—the feds or whatever—they'll try again. I mean, they won't just sit back and let us all get whacked into oblivion, right? *Right?*" No one answered and suddenly Lily understood the truth, the reason they wouldn't have bothered to turn on the television, why they couldn't answer her now. This spacious, cheerful room with its fancy decorating and sweet-smelling air, the soft couch she'd sat on just a few minutes ago, the expensive television that had brought the first news of the impending death of her world—it was all a lie.

"It won't matter what they try, will it?" she asked. Her voice was raspy and she felt a chill work its way up her spine and settle uncomfortably at the base of her skull. "No miracles this time, huh?" She gave an unsteady laugh, then let her bewildered gaze sweep the room until it stopped on Mercy. "Why did you bring me here to watch this if you already knew the outcome?"

"I . . . wanted you to be safe," Mercy admitted. "You've done so much for me, saved me so many times, that I wanted to try and do the same for you."

The blossoming anger melted away and Lily nodded. Of course—now it made sense. *I wanted you to be safe . . .* or as safe as anywhere, she supposed. To live and die among friends; Mercy and Simon were the only ones she had. The other two, Lamont and Gena . . . who knew? Mercy and Simon obviously trusted them, and given time they, too, might have become close. To have four real friends in this world—whoever would have thought such a thing was possible for crazy ol' Lily?

"Thank you," she said simply. She walked to the side of the couch and picked up her backpack. "But I have to go now."

"Lily, wait!" Mercy hurried over and gripped her arm; her fingers, usually so warm, were icy and stiff. "W-where are you going? C-can't you stay w-with us?"

It was odd to hear Mercy, who was so like Simon in her ability to stay calm, try so hard to speak that she began stuttering. Lily patted Mercy's hand with a reassurance that she didn't feel. "Don't worry, I'll be fine. But I have to go home, to my mom and dad."

"Why?" Mercy cried. Her fingers dug into Lily's flesh. "What did they ever do for you but let you down when you needed help? You should stay here, with me. With *us*!"

Lily pried Mercy's hand free. "I *can't*."

Mercy whirled to face the couch. "Gena? Gena, *please*!"

Gena sighed. "Let her go, Mercy. You can't force someone to stay if they don't want to. Life doesn't work that way, remember?" The blind woman stood and made her way expertly around the coffee table to stand next to Mercy. "Do you need money, Lily? Maybe some food to take with you?" She touched Lily's arm. "We could . . . uh . . . pack—"

Lily snatched at Gena's hand, held it for a moment, then pushed it away. "Damn it, I know what you're doing, and don't you tell them anything," she said fiercely. Her cheeks were flushed with indignation. "Not even after I'm gone. You have no *right,* do you hear me? That's *my* choice, not yours."

Gena stumbled backward a half step, then caught herself. A second later Lamont was at her side. "You're right, of course," she said. She sounded ashamed. "I'm sorry—I shouldn't have done that."

"Swear it to me," Lily insisted. "Swear that you won't tell."

"I—"

"Gena!" Mercy cried. "You can't do that!"

"Mercy, I *have* to." Gena's voice was pleading. "What I see isn't meant to be known by everyone, it's . . . it's . . ."

"Private?" Simon came up behind Mercy and she turned and buried her face against his shoulder with a sob. "Don't you understand, Mercy? It's like you and me, and how hard I try not to know what you're thinking, and how much you—or anyone—would despise me if I told someone else those things without your permission." He stroked her hair. "No matter what we can do or see or feel, we have to respect someone else's right to be what they will, without interfering. We can't play God, sweetheart. That was never meant to happen."

"But I just want her to be *safe*!" Mercy wailed against his shoulder.

"We all want to be safe," Lamont said softly. "From a lot of things. But we each have to find our own way of doing it."

Quickly, before she could change her mind about leaving, Lily reached forward and squeezed Mercy's shoulder. "I told you I'd be there for you and I meant it, Mercy," she said quietly. "I'll be back." She nodded at the others, turned and walked quickly down the hall and out the front door. Before it closed, she heard Mercy already demanding an answer from Gena, and the Indian woman's soft, sad answer.

"I'm sorry. I just can't say."

"I think we're screwed," Joey London said.

Alva looked up from where she was working at his kitchen table. Resting on newspapers in front of her were the pieces of her service revolver, each one meticulously cleaned and waiting for reassembly. "Why's that?" she asked as she worked on the last part, carefully polishing.

"Because of the asteroids. Remember that Project Valentine launch? I just watched the special on what was supposed to be the final . . . I don't know. Stage, or whatever they call it. The thing blew up in space. I think we're really going to get hit." She said nothing and he wandered over to the floor-to-ceiling window at the end of the counter and gazed out, drawn by the sight of the afternoon sun on the surface of Lake Michigan. How strange that at times like this it looked like liquid gold, yet at night it could be compared to nothing but black, black oil. Too far down to clearly distinguish, traffic moved along Lake Shore Drive; as Joey watched, one car sideswiped another on the passenger side and nearly forced it into the center guardrail. As the car that had been struck braked sharply, the other one sped away without bothering to stop, disappearing around the curve farther up the Drive. A couple of moments later, the first one began to accelerate rapidly until it, too, whipped around the curve and out of sight. Joey thought it was a good guess he was going to chase the guy who'd hit him; what would happen if the two finally met? "This is going to change everything, you know," he said thoughtfully.

"In what way?" Alva snapped the cylinder into place and spun it experimentally.

Joey turned to stare at her. "Alva," he said in exasperation, "did you listen to what I just said? The damned asteroids are going to *hit*."

She finished what she was doing, then grinned at him. "And I suppose you think it's the end of the world."

He glared at her, then turned back to the window in disgust. Why even bother to answer? The woman was crazier than anyone he'd ever met in his life—except himself, for getting involved with her to begin with. He still couldn't believe he'd let her actually move in here with him. A cop—what the fuck?

"If it is," she said from behind his shoulder, "then we ought to be making plans about what to do."

He didn't turn. "What do you mean, 'what to do'?"

Alva moved into place beside him. "We should be thinking about how we're going to survive. Where we're going to stay, food, weapons—"

"I think we can kiss it all good-bye," Joey said sarcastically. "Remember the dinosaurs, baby?"

"If you want to lie down and turn belly up like a whipped dog, that's your business," Alva said roughly. "I don't cave in so easily. And yeah, I *do* remember about the dinosaurs and all that shit. Maybe *you* should pay a little more attention to crap before you quote it at me. Sure, the scientists all claim that an asteroid or a comet made the dinosaurs extinct, but it didn't kill all life—just the big, stupid things that couldn't adapt. Like *you*." He turned to

watch as she flounced back onto the kitchen chair, crossed her
ankles, and glared at him. "You surrender, Joey-boy, and you do it
by yourself. I plan on being among the survivors and I'd pegged
you for the same . . . but it won't be the first time I mistook an
imbecile for a man."

"Bitch," he said.

She folded her arms and said nothing, waiting.

"Maybe," he said at last, "we should forget about Lamont and
his weird girlfriend and concentrate on other shit.

"Like how to stay alive this summer."

It was strange, Erica Richmond thought, to be sitting comfortably on a six-thousand-dollar Roche Bobois sectional in the den of
her Hinsdale home, wearing a designer silk-and-cotton jumpsuit
and holding a glass of top-shelf cognac while she watched the start
of the end of everything. She had been so *positive* that this asteroid
business would be taken care of by the government and the space
programs, all those bureaucrats working together and in charge of
overseeing that most fundamental of needs for humankind—the
right to peaceably follow an orbit around the sun in a universe that
she could never fully comprehend. She understood that same universe and its odd and unpredictable contents about as much as any
one of those astrophysicists understood how alcohol caused the
process of a human liver to stop working when it was riddled with
sclerosis. One thing she was finally beginning to grasp was that
Searle's doomsaying had been correct all along: no one was going
to be able to do a damned thing to stop Millennium.

"Cool," Naomi said.

Sitting next to her, Eddie Cuerlacroix looked as shocked as
Erica felt, and the doctor wondered for an instant if she and Naomi
weren't paired with the wrong men. Before she could respond to
Naomi's ridiculous statement, Eddie untangled his girlfriend's
legs where they were thrown over his and pushed her away, his
face twisted in anger. "What kind of a thing is that to say?" he
snapped. "Don't you know what this means? We could actually
die here, Naomi—as in the whole world, you know?"

"Well, *duh*," Naomi sneered. "I've got ears and a brain. I heard
the news just like everyone else in this room."

Eddie jumped to his feet and began to pace the distance from
the couch to the big-screen television; images danced across the

screen, silent now that Erica had hit the MUTE button to blot out the senseless station identification break, the frantically jabbering newscasters. "Yeah, that's great, Naomi, just great!" His voice had risen to a shout and his face was red, blood gathering until his cheeks nearly matched the ginger shade of his hair. "Maybe you want to die, but what about the rest of us? What about Erica, and Searle, and *me*, huh? *Huh?*"

"Lower your voice," Erica commanded. The young man spun and looked like he was going to scream at her, too, then changed his mind and stalked to a chair across the room. "Arguing with each other isn't going to change anything or help us figure out what to do in the future."

"There's nothing *to* do," Naomi said blandly. "We just sit back and wait to die." Unexpectedly, she threw back her head and laughed, the sound high but eerily throaty, reminiscent of a coyote's howl. "Finally everyone else gets a chance to catch up with me and my people. You might not be the same as us, but you'll know in a roundabout way what it feels like to be dead. After all, with Millennium on the way, that's what you are."

"You and your people are only 'different' in one way," Eddie snarled from his place across the room. "You're all fucking lunatics."

"And you're not, funny boy," Naomi said, unruffled. "Even though you followed us all the way here from New Orleans."

"I came with you because I care for you!" he said hotly.

"Spare me."

Silent until now, Searle finally spoke. "Why don't you two save the personal arguments for later on, between yourselves. Me and Erica don't want to hear it." Eddie opened his mouth, then snapped it shut when Searle raised a warning finger. "That's not just a *suggestion,* kid."

"Listen, everyone," Erica said quickly, hoping to deflate the escalating tension. "If this thing really *is* going to hit, we've got what . . . about five months to plot the groundwork for some kind of survival plan. We—"

"Assuming you want to survive," Naomi interrupted. Her face, so white and seemingly bloodless within its halo of blue-black hair, was serene. "*We've* been waiting for it. We're going to go outside and lift our arms to the sky in welcome the day it hits."

"If you do, Naomi"—Eddie's voice, barely audible, had lost its anger—"you'll do it alone."

"I never expected otherwise," Naomi said. She was sitting perfectly motionless, like a white marble statue with ink-colored eyes beneath a dark wig. "Each one of my people has been alone since the day he or she died—"

"You didn't die, damn it!"

"—the first time."

Eddie shook his head in defeat but kept silent. "If you like, Eddie, you can work with us," Erica offered. "While Naomi and her group haven't . . . worked out to my expectations, we can always use a good hand."

"Fools, all," Naomi said scornfully. "What did you think we could do for you? I never made any secret of our feelings or beliefs. What exactly did you expect?"

"Certainly more than I got," Erica snapped. All those grand plans to use Naomi to reach out to that segment of the population in Naomi's age group had lurched to a halt; within a week of the arrival of this group of strangely silent young people, it became clear that Naomi would not cooperate with Erica's marketing plans, and she'd laughed outright at the idea of becoming involved in the advertising push. Erica had known little about Naomi Lauren other than that when she'd been recruited, the girl and her group had comprised the single largest group of new enrollees in After Help in the country. The rest was secondhand information, projections made by the man in charge of the New Orleans chapter—who had, by the way, been missing for the last four days and was presumed to have either abandoned his post or been killed. All that talk about how Naomi was a magnet for people like herself . . . only a smoke screen for what Erica now believed was Naomi's clever way of getting After Help to pick up the bed-and-board bill for a group of people too mentally unstable to take care of themselves anymore. Erica almost admired the younger woman for pulling it off.

Perhaps bringing Naomi to Chicago had been a rash and useless decision—maybe boredom had even played a part—but Erica had tried to make it work nonetheless—hence the young girl and her companion's presence in Erica's home for the past week. Ultimately, however, a futile effort. "Never mind," she said briskly. "Whether you want to participate or not, the rest of us are going to look to the future and what it holds."

"The future? The predictions aren't good," Searle said. He rubbed his jaw, his rough fingers grating over the day's growth of stubble. "Of course, everything's garbled up and full of rumors, but they all basically amount to the same thing. There's a reason the whole damned country's under a curfew, and fools're starting to hoard food and supplies, and probably weapons, too. If you ask me, it's going to be kill or be killed—and we're halfway there already."

"There must be something we can do," Erica said. Anxiety slid neatly into her stomach and she felt her pulse start jittering in the hollow of her throat. "I can't believe we take Naomi's suggestion to just sit and wait for this rock to fall out of the sky and destroy us."

Naomi giggled but Searle ignored her and shrugged. "You're the one who always has such an optimistic outlook—maybe they'll still be able to do something about it. Like you said, we've got five months."

"That's not much time when you're talking about asteroids and space," Eddie commented. He rocked absently in the chair. "I remember them saying on the news that the remains of this thing are traveling over fifty-four thousand miles per *hour*. Astronomy might not have been my strong point in school, but it doesn't take a degree in astrophysics to know that there are better times than others to intercept something. Lots of things have to be considered—planet positions and orbits, whether other planets are in the way. It might seem like the closer it is, the easier it is to hit, but I don't think that's the way it works. The more time that passes, the less chance we have of success."

"Then we really *do* need to develop a survival plan."

"Like the rest of the world isn't already," Searle snorted. He looked tired, worn down by the strain of the last three weeks. She knew it hadn't been easy overseeing security while everyone on the staff went wild with panic. "You think you know what's going on, Erica? I bet you find half the supply closets in the hospital have been raided. Don't you realize we have no idea what this thing is going to do? It could cause . . . what? Floods, fires, volcanoes, earthquakes—all the food, guns, and medicine in the world won't help you if part of a building falls on you and breaks your back." He shook his head and stared at the carpet.

They were all silent for a moment. On the couch, Naomi sat and gazed into space, a smug smile twisting one side of her mouth. Eventually, Erica spoke. "There is . . . *something* . . . that's better than all the medicine in the world, Searle."

Eddie and Searle glanced at her in surprise. "What?"

"We talked about her before, remember? Simon's girlfriend. The woman who can heal."

Eddie looked intrigued, but Naomi sat up abruptly and gripped one of the throw pillows. Her dark eyes looked twice their normal size. "What did you say? A healer—is she for real?"

Erica ignored the younger woman. "If we can somehow convince her to become our ally, we won't *need* any medicine," she pointed out.

"Yeah, and you're her favorite person," Searle said derisively. "I don't think so."

"You're serious about this," Eddie said. "You really believe someone can do this?"

"Not someone—*her*. I've seen the results of her handiwork in the form of a boy who should've died but didn't and—"

"She's got to be *stopped*!" This time it was Naomi who was up on her feet and frantically moving across the living room. "Don't you see what she's doing?" she demanded. "She's just like the bastard who should've killed me and didn't. She takes away their right to die and leaves an empty shell behind!"

"Oh, shut *up* about that, already," Eddie said in disgust. "Don't you get it yet? You didn't lose anything but your sanity the day you got mugged—it's all in your head. The only fool in this room is *you*."

"Where is she?" Naomi spun to a stop in front of Erica. "I'll stop her myself." She seized Erica's wrist and pulled on it, hard enough to yank Erica to her feet. "You tell me, you stupid old witch, or I'll beat it out of you!"

"Let go of me!" Erica cried. How dare Naomi threaten her, after all that she'd done for her and her people—

Without warning, Erica's wrist was free and Naomi was walking backward, her feet involuntarily following the movement of her head. Deep within the crown of her hair, Searle's harsh grip at the scalp pulled the young woman to the other side of the room, where he flung her against the wall. "I don't think you're going to do any such thing," he said icily. "In fact, I think you've just become a personal security risk to Erica. It's time for you to leave After Help. Right *now*."

Naomi scowled at him and balled her fists, but Eddie stepped forward and held up a hand. "Hey, wait a second, okay? Maybe you're right and she *should* leave." She snarled from behind him and Eddie's expression was pained as he shot a quick look at her. "But not today, not when there's only about an hour left until curfew. Where will she go? She'll end up shot—or worse—by one of those goons running around out there who think they're the next best thing to God." Searle started to shake his head, then hesitated. "Please," Eddie said beseechingly. He turned to Erica. "Nothing'll be gained by turning her out tonight. Maybe she's stupid enough to want to die, but do you really want that on your conscience? What harm can it do to let her stay one more night and leave in the morning?"

Searle looked over at Erica and she nodded, although reluctantly. Eddie was right; Naomi was clearly insane, delusional—call it what you will, but Erica didn't want her around any longer. Even this final night made her uneasy. "Searle will walk the two of you to your room," she said. "And lock you in. You can stay if you like, Eddie—in fact, we'd love to have you. But Naomi leaves tomorrow morning as soon as she can get her things together."

Eddie looked relieved as Erica walked stiffly to the door. Without being told, Searle's hand slid over Naomi's wrist in a iron-hard hold; Erica knew that during the rest of her time here, the young woman would never again see the inside of any room but her own without Searle as her shadow.

"There's one more thing," Erica said without turning. A note of bitterness had crept into her tone but she didn't care; she *hated* being duped, or used, and Naomi had pulled a good one on her. "All those demented little cultists you brought with you from New Orleans?

"Take every last one of them with you when you leave. You'll need the company when you go out and raise your arms to welcome Millennium."

NEW YORK
FEBRUARY 15 . . .

[fade to Marti Nunciata]

From the opening segment of the five o'clock Cable News Network special broadcast:

"Five U.S. astronauts and four Russian cosmonauts died in yesterday's disastrous explosion of the warhead-loaded Titan IV rocket. The explosion damaged the Mir space station, the U.S. space shuttle *Salvation,* and the Russian shuttle beyond repair, and this morning the U.S., Russian, and British governments have announced a formal alliance and intergovernmental agreement to take whatever steps are necessary to manufacture the space vehicles and rockets needed to divert the pieces of Millennium which are predicted to strike the Earth on July second of this year. The explosion of the Titan IV is being blamed on early ignition of the final stage engine directly beneath the warheads. While the nuclear warheads did not detonate and were flung clear, the premature ignition ruptured the fuel and oxidizer tanks below it in both the other stages of the rocket and caused the massive explosion we reported. The astronauts and cosmonauts who gave their lives in the service of their countries will be honored next Sunday in special memorials from both countries. CNN will bring you a simultaneous broadcast at eleven A.M. Eastern Time.

"In the meantime, the White House, NASA, and the Department of Defense continue to assure the people of the United States that every step is being taken to protect the Earth from any strike whatsoever by the asteroid. NASA and Department of Defense facilities in Utah, Louisiana, Iowa, and Virginia have been put on round-the-clock shifts in order to assure the production of numerous rockets. In addition, completion of the retiling of the other shuttle, *Endeavor,* originally planned for June, has now been rescheduled for February twenty-sixth. This incredibly accelerated date has been targeted in order that the *Endeavor* may be set up at the Kennedy Space Center in time for a planned launch on March first, at which time Russia will have another Energiya waiting at a rendezvous point. The overall strategy of firing a warhead-armed rocket at Millennium remains the same at this point, although officials are still discussing whether another U.S. Titan IV or a Russian Proton should be used as the missile that carries the loaded warheads. We will keep you immediately advised of any new developments.

"On the international front, governments around the world continue to impose marital law as violence rampages out of control. While the U.S., Japan, and most European countries attempt to maintain a four o'clock curfew, other countries such as Russia, China, India, and other third world areas have imposed curfews that allow civilians to leave their homes only a few hours each day. Military fighting and attacks are sweeping across Bosnia, Bulgaria, Turkey, and the Ukraine, where the peace treaties of 1998 now seem like so much wasted ink and paper. Entire villages have been torched and thousands of people have been left dead or dying, countless others homeless as the 'End of the World Syndrome' continues to encircle the globe. One exhausted United Nations official leaving the latest round of emergency meetings and who asked to remain anonymous is quoted as saying 'Even if Millennium never hits, the world may never recover from its impact.' "

[fade out]

5.
THE FALL OF MAN

Eddie woke up to the sting of a razor blade across the bend of his right elbow.

He screamed and someone pressed a pillow over his face, not hard enough to suffocate him—yet—but more than sufficient to muffle his cries. He tried to move and couldn't. He was tied in a crucifixion position on the bed; he could feel the muscles in his arms and legs as they stretched against whatever it was that held him—ropes, sheets, he had no idea. There was enough play in the bindings to show that it hadn't been difficult to gently tie him in his sleep. And it wasn't hard to guess who'd done it. For a moment, all he could do was lie there in disbelief, his mind spinning with thoughts. *Shit. Less than a year ago I saw in my head that someone was going to kill* her. *Why the fuck didn't I know that she was going to kill* me?

"Naomi!" he cried. The cotton pillowcase filled his mouth and he whipped his head from side to side, trying to fling it away. "Naomi, *stop it!*"

"Then quiet down, for Christ's sake—stop fighting me!" Her voice was a hiss in his ear, her breath surprisingly cool. He'd gone to sleep naked and now he registered the feel of her bare thighs against his, the soft feel of the hair between her legs across his groin—she was straddling him. Eddie's arm felt like someone had run a red-hot poker across it, but the surprise was past; he made himself stop bucking and bit back the torrent of curses that wanted to come out. Naomi pulled the pillow off his face and he lifted his head until his arm came into view; he saw the steady flow of blood at the same time he felt its warmth trickle around and soak into the sheet. Relief filled him—she'd cut deep but it wasn't spurting, so she'd missed the artery. He'd bleed but he probably wouldn't die.

"Why did you do that?"

Without bothering to answer, she leaned over and fastened her lips over the inch-long wound.

"Naomi!" He thrashed and nearly threw her off. By the time he opened his mouth to yell again, she was sitting upright across his hips and scowling down at him. Her mouth was hideously smeared with blood—*his* blood—and she held up a roll of silver duct tape, then leaned close to his face.

"I found this under the sink cabinet in the bathroom. Holler again and I'll cover your mouth. Is that what you want?"

He swallowed and cringed away from her. "N-no."

"Then shut *up*."

Helpless, he watched as she placed the roll of tape next to his face—a reminder, no doubt—then leaned over and again began to suck at the wound on his arm. Pain crawled up his arm and he whimpered and pulled involuntarily at his bonds. "Naomi, stop," he pleaded. "It *hurts*. What's the matter with you—why would you do this? It's *sick*."

"Poor Eddie," she murmured without raising her head. "But I can take your mind off it. Here, think about how this feels instead." One hand held his arm above the cut but her other was free and he gasped as he felt her cold fingers find his genitals and begin to stroke. "Time to think warm thoughts, boyfriend."

"This is enough—cut it *out*!" Reflexively he tried to push back into the mattress to escape her touch, but it was useless—tied, bleeding, and with the threat of that stupid tape hanging over him, there was nothing he could do, nowhere he could escape. The harder he tried to pull away, the faster she stroked him and the more frantically she nuzzled at his arm; now she was rubbing herself against him and he was forgetting the horror and the stinging across his arm as heat spread across his groin and made him moan out loud.

Then she was sliding onto him and riding, faster and faster, sitting upright and finally finished slaking her perverted thirst, her left hand clamped firmly across the bend of his elbow to stop the bleeding. For Eddie it was a sensory overload—the fire encircling his arm, the feeling of being inside Naomi for the first time without a condom, the electric feel of her full breasts against his chest as she bent forward and swayed across him. Light-headed, Eddie squeezed his eyes shut and turned his head away from the sight of Naomi's face and her scarlet smile as her body tightened around his and pushed him to a shuddering, reluctant orgasm.

"Untie me, damn you." Eddie demanded. "My arm hurts."

Naomi ignored him and put the final items in a canvas bag. She'd washed the blood off her mouth but Eddie fancied he could still see it there, a smear like the glow of purplish-white beneath the black lights of the seventies. Surely it was deep within the crevices between her teeth; if they kissed now, would he taste it? *Bleh.* He felt ridiculous, lying there still naked and tied, while she was dressed and on her way out of his life—would she leave him humiliated like this, to be found later by Searle or one of his flunkie guards?

At last she straightened and smiled at him. "Well, I guess this is good-bye."

"For Christ's sake, Naomi!" Eddie exploded. "Will you fucking tell me what that was all about? When did you start thinking you were a vampire?"

She tilted her head and looked at him thoughtfully. "I think . . . that's what I'm *becoming*." He started to speak but she held up a hand. "No, really. I know you think I'm crazy or sick or whatever, but right now, I feel warm, *finally,* for the first time since the day I got zinged outside the Café du Monde. I had a hint of it the night I nipped you on the neck, but . . . not enough."

"What are you saying?" Eddie asked incredulously. "That you have to drink blood to survive? That belief isn't new, Naomi. There are entire books written about blood deficiencies—"

"Oh, give it a rest," she said impatiently. "I don't need blood to survive, you fool. I can still eat like anyone else. Haven't you been listening? I think I just need it to be *warm*. Here—feel."

He flinched instinctively when she touched his cheek, then his mouth dropped open. The palm of her hand felt like a furnace against his skin, damned *uncomfortable*. Had she not pulled away, he would have protested.

"See what I mean?" She smiled. "You did a great job of wheedling Erica into letting us stay these extra two days so we could prepare, and for that I'm really grateful, although I'm sure you don't believe me. But it's time for us to move on—did you know the rest of my group is just like me? They're always cold, too . . . and I think I've just found the cure."

Eddie gaped at her, horrified. "You mean you guys are just going to wander around draining people? Even if you don't all get sick and die of God knows what, how long do you think you'll get away with it?"

"Who's going to stop us?" she pointed out. "You? Erica and Searle? Please—everyone has enough to worry about in planning for their own lives. In five months no one's going to care anyway and the world will be a new place, wonderful, dark, and just waiting for the birth of a whole new breed of human."

She walked to the side of the bed and stood over him, then held up the razor that had slashed his arm. Blood had dried along its edge and Eddie's breath caught as she lowered it; a second later, the sheet that was wound around his injured arm slacked and fell away. She tossed the razor on the nightstand, then drew a finger longingly across the bruised flesh around the gash. A brief flash of pain to match the twist of fear in his gut, then Naomi pulled away and he curled his arm protectively across his ribs. "Searle will show up the minute I step out of this room. You ought to be able to get free by the time he escorts me and the rest of the group out of the building.

"So long, Eddie."

NEW YORK
FEBRUARY 23 . . .

[fade to Marti Nunciata]

From the opening segment of an early afternoon emergency Cable News Network special broadcast:

"International plans to launch nuclear warhead–loaded missiles at Millennium in an effort to prevent the Earth from impact suffered a serious setback this morning when terrorist explosions occurred nearly simultaneously at manufacturing facilities in

Utah, Louisiana, Iowa, and Virginia, as well as in manufacturing and launch facilities overseas in Russia, Great Britain, and China. In Florida, two more explosions severely damaged the nearly completed space shuttle *Endeavor,* in addition to the launch support platform and several short-term solid rocket booster storage buildings at the Kennedy Space Center in Cape Canaveral. The Russian government is reporting irreparable damage to all three of their Energiya rockets and says its only hope for a launch of sufficient payload capability within the next four months is to piece together a single Energiya from the remains of the other three. Further explosions occurred in Kourou, French Guiana, and Brazil within hours of the American and Russian destruction, and Great Britain reports the European Space Agency program as being 'effectively crippled' by the damage. Dozens of extremist religious groups around the globe immediately claimed responsibility for the incidents, including Destiny's Children, a loose gathering of about one hundred twenty individuals who have garnered recent national attention by claiming to be the walking dead. Federal investigators have dismissed the statements of the so-called Destiny's Children faction and say the group clearly has neither the resources nor knowledge to accomplish any of these sabotages. However, declarations by other groups such as Muhammad's Tahajjud and the Brazilian Abrazo de Dios are being seriously investigated. Security has been increased but CNN has learned that certain government officials have been overheard saying that the space programs may not be able to recover from these incidents in time to protect the Earth against an impending Millennium impact. Repeated attempts by CNN representatives to contact Professor Frank Gelasias, the Department of Defense's spokesman for the failed Valentine Project, have been unsuccessful, and Professor Gelasias remains unavailable for comment at this time . . ."

[fade out]

CHICAGO
FEBRUARY 28 . . .

"My family doesn't know I'm here, Dr. Richmond. I tried to talk to them about After Help when the organization first began making the news, but they weren't responsive."

Erica nodded sympathetically at the articulate elderly woman sitting on the leather chair across from her desk. "People are often resistant to unfamiliar things, Mrs. Dellaportas. Despite its impeccable reputation, After Help is breaking new ground with its concept of individual support and I'm not surprised when people tell me they've encountered resistance. The important thing is that we can support our members."

Ellen Dellaportas shook her white-curled head. "Well, this *did* surprise me. My children are usually quite receptive. Mine is a large family, Doctor, with more than its share of creative people, including a number of youngsters—by 'youngsters' I mean people in their thirties and forties"—she flashed Erica a smile—"who have ventured out on their own in areas that would have made my grandfather faint." Mrs. Dellaportas folded her hands primly over one knee; her back was straight and her face fairly unlined for a woman in her seventies. "I've always tried to be flexible with my children. You can't fight change, Dr. Richmond. In all its forms, it seeps into everything—the schools, the churches, the home. The family learns to adapt or it fragments and ultimately falls apart." She glanced away for a second and a shadow of hurt passed across her gaze. "I felt that my children seemed almost . . . hostile about this."

Erica nodded again. "So you've encountered opposition instead of support."

Mrs. Dellaportas lifted her chin. "Yes. The crux of the problem seems to be that they have certain . . . doubts about the validity of your organization."

"I see." Erica sat back. "If you like, I can contact them and explain the way the company works. Our records are, of course, open for public inspection at any time during business hours."

"That won't be necessary." Mrs. Dellaportas studied her delicate fingers for a few moments without speaking. "I'm quite capable of managing my own affairs and I do not need anyone's permission to make decisions for myself. The truth," she said at last, "is that I'm quite afraid of this Millennium asteroid. My family, however, remains convinced that the world leaders will solve this little annoyance for them and appears more interested in dictating how I should allot my funds than offering comfort to their widowed matriarch. Once again, they have surprised me."

"That's very unfortunate." *Careful here,* Erica thought. If she pushed too hard, she could drive the old woman away, send her and all the money from this small but wealthy Chicago import firm into the arms of the waiting Greek Orthodox Church. A good point, and Erica decided to face it head-on; this woman would appreciate honesty. "Surely your church offers some support programs or counselors?"

The expression that sped across the fragile, pale face was noticeably withering. "Of course they do. And every one expects you to drop to your knees, accept your fate, and open your bank account to the mother church. Somehow the idea of paying God to save me just doesn't set very well."

No religion? "I see. Then what are you looking for from After Help, Mrs. Dellaportas? You have a fairly religious background and it's my experience that people respond better in that arena to familiarity—while we can offer spiritual support in any denomination, the words of a family priest or rabbi are generally much more comforting than the sermons of a stranger. You don't seem to want us to reach out to your family on your behalf—"

"I'm looking for a way to survive, Dr. Richmond." Mrs. Dellaportas's eyes were small and bright, as the elderly's often were, and Erica thought she could sense the desperation hiding behind the false show of strength. "I've read that After Help has a division that is devoted to installing members in survival centers being constructed in areas where the impacts will have a less devastating effect. In particular, I'm interested in the one in the mountains outside of Colorado Springs. I've always wanted to live in the mountains." For a moment, she looked dreamy, then she tapped a finger sharply on Erica's desktop and the twenty-thousand-dollar ladies' Rolex watch encircling her bony wrist glittered. "I want to be a part of that group, Doctor. You take donations, right? I'm prepared to be quite generous with mine so I can be included."

Erica nodded sagely. "We would be honored to have you join us, Mrs. Dellaportas." She punched a button on the intercom. "Judy, please bring in the information folder on Colorado Springs."

A few minutes later, with her face somber as she carefully went over the pros and cons of the private mountain retreat with Ellen Dellaportas, inside Erica was smiling from ear to ear.

MARCH 7 . . .

Crystal found her husband sitting in the midst of a pile of oddities on the garage floor. It was her first day off in two weeks, and while it felt good not to have to face a shift at the retirement home tonight, physically she'd certainly been in better condition. Thank

God she'd been paying attention when she'd hit the button to the automatic door opener. If not, she might've run right over him with the Lincoln Town Car. Instead, she shut off the engine and got out, then walked to where he sat surrounded by at least a hundred different tools. He did not look up when she stopped in front of him. "Frank," she said finally, "what are you doing?"

"We're leaving," he said, as if that explained everything. Frank continued to look thoughtfully at the selection of scattered tools, then carefully picked out several of them and set them aside.

Suddenly her cream-colored gabardine slacks didn't matter very much and Crystal sank to her knees in front of him, getting a dull stab in one kneecap by a screwdriver before shoving it out of the way. "Where are we going?"

Frank glanced up and gave her a little smile and Crystal felt the tension along her neck lift somewhat; there was nothing at all crazed about that look—it was the same one he always gave her when he had something to share but was confident she would agree with whatever it was. "We'll start by heading east," he said. He unfolded his legs and stood, then offered her a hand to help her rise. "Come into the kitchen and I'll show you on the map. Maybe you'll have some suggestions."

East? She followed him silently, willing her brain not to go on overload. Stretched across the kitchen table was a laminated map of the United States; scrawled across it in black marker were arrows and crosshatches. "What do these mean?"

"Okay," he said. "According to my calculations, when impact occurs it will be down here." He made a motion with one hand that Crystal took to mean some undefined area to the southwest, far off the visible area of the map. "If we're correct, the hits will occur at the equator in the Pacific Ocean, directly south of the Hawaiian Islands."

"If 'we're' correct?" Crystal wished she could feel numb, but that was a luxury that seemed to have deserted her body at about the same time the nausea had settled in, three weeks ago today, to be precise.

Frank's expression was sour. "Oh, I'm not the only one who's made all the projections, Crystal. I'm sure there are hundreds, *thousands,* of others. I'm just not going to sit beneath a telescope, wait for the boom, and watch as it smacks me."

"The Pacific Ocean. It seems . . . so far away," she said softly.

For a second a flash of anger crossed Frank's handsome features, then it disappeared and his dark brown eyes regarded her patiently. With a start, she realized the silver specks in his hair had doubled, no *tripled,* over the last month.

"Far away?" He smiled ruefully. "Yeah, I guess it does. On paper, anyway." He rubbed his eyes, then his big hand wrapped around hers. "I don't know if we can make it, sweetheart," he said earnestly. "I don't know if *anyone* can. But I think the farther inland we move, the better chance we have. They've been theorizing about the big one that killed the dinosaurs for years, but this isn't one—it's more than a hundred. There may not even be a stone age to go back to after Millennium's through with this planet. But if we head east, and maybe north, we could stay away from the fault lines, the coasts, and the tsunamis but keep near fresh water—"

"I'm pregnant," she blurted.

Frank drew in a deep breath and for a moment she thought he was going to keep going on as though she hadn't spoken. She didn't think she could find the air to repeat herself, it had taken such a *huge* amount of courage to say those words—

"How can this be, Crystal?"

His voice was soft, neither believing nor disbelieving. Stunned. Crystal swallowed and made herself speak. "Dr. Tavis says he isn't sure how, but that the scar tissue around my ovaries and fallopian tubes has apparently disintegrated and allowed an egg to pass through to the uterus." *Too clinical,* she thought. *I sound like a recording, spewing the words on fast forward.* Nevertheless, she gripped the side of the table for support and rushed on. "He says a lot of strange things have been happening in his field lately, and my . . . *our* case is actually one of the minor ones. He says the rate of pregnancy has increased by four hundred percent."

Frank jerked and his eyes widened. "That's preposterous."

Crystal shrugged. "He believes that a lot of people simply aren't bothering with birth control anymore, but a lot more—like me—are exhibiting spontaneous regeneration of damaged or—or m-missing tissue—"

"What!"

"Well," she finally ended, "that's what he said."

Frank scowled and looked around the kitchen, as if he might find the answer to this immense puzzle stuffed behind one of the appliances. "The man's been dipping into his own pharmacy," was all he could offer.

Crystal grabbed his shoulder and stared at him. "Is he, Frank? Really? Or is there some other explanation for my being able to conceive after fifteen years, three surgeries, and a clinic full of specialists who told us it would never be possible?"

They stared at each other wordlessly, then she ran her finger over the slick surface of the map. "Here," she said decisively.

Frank followed her finger, then took a deep breath. "That's a long way, Crystal. The way things are now . . . it could be difficult to get there—*if* we make it at all—and even harder once we do make it because it's a densely populated area. People aren't exactly getting more friendly."

Crystal looked at him. "It's inland about as far as we can get away from the oceans without actually going into semi-arctic climates, and there's lots of fresh water. We'll stay away from the city proper, stick to the countryside in the outlying suburbs." Her eyes were wide and full of hope. "We have to at least *try,* Frank. We have to go as far as we can, for ourselves and our child."

He nodded and followed her gaze back down to the map and the clean, manicured tip of her fingernail.

"Here," she repeated. "Just outside . . ."

Chicago.

CHICAGO
MARCH 16 . . .

"I thought we were going to get married."

Standing at the mirror on a Thursday morning and adjusting his tie, Simon blinked in surprise. "I . . . uh . . ."

Mercy couldn't help the quick grin that flashed over her mouth, although it faded fast. She didn't remember there ever being a time when Simon had been so utterly thrown off guard. For a second she imagined being in his place: the world was going to hell but he still tried to work, tried to step in and help whatever kids he could; then his girlfriend turned fiancée suddenly rears up and announces *Hey, Simon says . . . haven't you forgotten something?* She wanted to give him a teasing little push to lessen the sharpness, but she didn't dare; now was not the time to touch him and invite him to read her mind. "What's the matter, smart guy? Cold feet?"

He reached for her automatically, but she ducked out of range and left him standing there with his hand outstretched. He looked at his own fingers, puzzled, then dropped his arm. "No, of course not. I guess the whole idea just got sort of sidetracked—"

"Well, I haven't forgotten about it," she said pointedly. "And if you have, I suggest you bring back the memory." She folded her arms and lifted her chin, fought down the dread that coiled in the pit of her stomach. With her hands pulled into fists, she dug her fingernails into her palms, let the bright flash of pain override anything floating out of her head that Simon might pick up on. "If you've changed your mind or you don't think it's important anymore, just say so. You won't be the first man to have a change of heart."

He stared at her. "We never talked about a date. I always had the impression it wasn't a big deal to you."

"Well, it is now."

"All right." His voice was level. "How about next Saturday? I don't know the details, but that should give us time to figure out stuff like a license and blood test."

"And if they're not doing those anymore, then we find a preacher somewhere and do it anyway, however we can."

"Done."

They stared at each other and Mercy saw his jaw twitch on one side as he crossed his arms, his knuckles going white as he curled his fingers around his upper arms and held on. It came to her how hard this must be for him, to hold back his natural urge to just jump in and find out what was driving her, it would be so easy—

"Would you like to tell me now what brought this on?" he said in a low voice. "Because I'm having a hell of a time right now."

Mercy swallowed and looked at the floor, knew exactly what he meant. "I—I'm scared, Simon," she said. She sensed him step toward her and held up one hand. "No—don't touch me, not . . . yet." He stopped and waited, and she dug her bare toes into the Berber carpeting in the extra bedroom of Lamont's town house. How much longer would they feel the warmth and comfort of a normal house, a normal life? The city, *civilization,* was deteriorating more every day, and already Lamont was suggesting that maybe they should leave. Mercy wanted to stay and wait for Lily's return—*if* Lily ever did—but she was wise enough to know that soon she might be outvoted. She would always have the right to choose for herself, stand her ground and stay put if she so desired, but she had others to consider. If they decided it was the best thing to do, Lamont and Gena would probably go without her, and rightfully so, but Simon would never leave her behind. To stay here would endanger not only him, but—

"Do you remember," she said slowly, still watching her toes rub across the blue-and-white carpeting, "the day you asked me to marry you—"

"Christmas."

"—and how I said I'd nearly gotten you another kitten?" He nodded, bewildered, and she continued, eyes going dreamy as she thought back to when the animal clinic—closed and abandoned by the owners for almost a month now—had been running at full speed. "We had so *many,* Simon. Dozens upon dozens, people bringing in litters born to females they'd sworn were spayed or too young or too old to give birth. Puppies, too—the same circumstances. Animals born all over the freaking place, some normal, a lot not right at all, although we were all so overwhelmed with work and no one we contacted anywhere seemed interested in the mutations or the preemies, or—or *anything.* I told you how it was by the time Dr. Leverett shut it down . . . in six weeks' time we'd gone from more people than we had room for on the sign-in sheet to less than two people a week. With supplies costing through the roof and no patients . . ."

"What does this have to do with us getting married?"

"The *point,*" she said loudly, "is that no one cared about them anymore." She stalked to the window and yanked on the cord for the miniblinds; anemic sunlight dribbled into the room. "All those little things being born and suddenly no one was there for them." I'm doing this wrong, she thought, and the notion made her all the more frantic. He had to understand her feelings before she could tell him, she had to be *sure*—

"Mercy, *please,*" he said desperately.

"Simon," she started, and then it all rushed out. "Simon, don't you see? It's the end of the world and we're going to have a baby. And I need to know that you're going to stand by me and that this is okay even though it wasn't planned, and if it's not all right or if you think you can't or won't be there for me, for *us,* then I need to know that right now, too, so that I can try to do something about it."

"Oh, I'll be there, Mercy. Every second of every day."

Her face split into a smile, the first true bit of joy she'd felt since discovering her pregnancy.

Bless him; Simon never so much as hesitated.

MARCH 25 . . .

"Do you know what Carl Sandburg once said?" Lamont whispered in her ear.

"Wasn't he a writer?" Gena murmured. "I imagine he said a lot of things."

"He said—"

"If you don't shut up, I'm going to kick you in the ankle, Lamont. I have to see with my *ears,* remember? So I can't *see* with you talking."

"I don't think he said he was going to kick me in the ankle," Lamont muttered, and then Gena did kick him, not too hard, but enough to make him know she meant business. Kick or not, she felt his silent chuckle through the vibration in his arm. She smiled in spite of herself and tried to concentrate on the words being said, but they were all muddled up in her head, twisted around some of the things Lamont was going to have to say after the ceremony—

"And do you, Leah Merari Ammon, take this man, Simon Lance Chanowitz—"

Lance? Interesting; she'd never picked up on that. Then again, she seldom touched Simon, too afraid of what might come of the combination of his mind-reading ability and her tendency to see the future. She frowned slightly, realizing she'd lost track of the proceedings.

"What are they doing now?" Gena whispered.

"Facing each other, and holding hands," Lamont murmured. Over the past months they had grown accustomed to one another, and his voice automatically slipped into that neutral but vaguely singsong state that he used to narrate television programs for her. Doing this had become such second nature to him that Gena doubted he realized it happened. "The judge is standing right in front of them and facing us. He has a Bible open in front of him and is reading from it, following the words with his finger—"

"—by the powers vested in me by the State of Illinois—"

"Now Simon is putting the ring on Mercy's finger, and she . . . oh, that's so pretty. She's handing him a yellow rose. I wonder where she got it?"

"—I now pronounce you man—"

"They look so good together. He's wearing a sky-blue shirt and a white tie, and Mercy's dress is red."

"—and wife."

Red, Gena thought. *Like me.*

A bad luck color.

"You may kiss the bride."

"Carl Sandburg," Lamont said smoothly, as though an hour had never passed between the time he'd started this conversation and right now, when they were standing outside and next to the City Hall building on a morning that wasn't quite warm enough to be considered spring, "said that 'A baby is God's opinion that the world should go on.'"

"Lamont, what is your point?"

"You're pregnant."

"I am not."

"You're gaining weight."

"I'm chunky," Gena said, exasperated.

"That's a load of shit."

Her mouth dropped open but she could think of nothing to retort. A load of shit? *She* was the one who said crudities like that, not Lamont. Abruptly she laughed; he'd said it to shock her into silence, and damn it all, he'd succeeded.

"How much longer are you going to deny it?" he demanded.

"Until . . . next week?" She tried to sound hopeful, managed to get an answering chuckle before her spirits did a drop. "Lamont, for Christ's sake. We can't have a baby. I'm *blind,* and a bunch of asteroids are going to destroy everything we can imagine plus a lot we can't. Yet what are we doing? Coming down here, watching Simon and Mercy get married, and clapping our hands at the end of the ceremony like it was just another ordinary day in the universe. We're . . . *insane* or something." She put out her hand and felt the stone facade of the building behind them, its solidness. A truck rolled by on what Lamont had told her was LaSalle Street but the stone beneath her hand never shook; it must be immense beyond her wildest imaginings.

Like the responsibility of caring for a child.

"We're enjoying what's left of our world," Lamont said gently. "Watching two people we treasure take their vows, talking about the future—"

"That's just it. *What* future?" Her voice was getting shrill and Gena made a conscious effort to control it.

"The one you're carrying in your womb," he said clearly. "It's quite obvious, you know. With your height, you look kind of like a little potbellied stove."

"Damn you," she spat. Furious, she swung at him and felt her small fist connect with something soft. Suddenly horrified, her hand fluttered out, trying unsuccessfully to find him. "Lamont?" Always before, he had easily ducked her swings, she'd never meant—

"Ouch," he said mildly from a foot or two away.

"Where—?"

"My elbow."

"Well, you should have gotten the hell out of the way," she said huffily. Thank God; for a frightening moment she'd lost her sense of orientation and been afraid she'd popped him in the nose.

"So, back to this baby business."

Gena sighed. "Yeah, *that*. Why is everyone in the world getting knocked up all of a sudden?"

"I just told you," Lamont said patiently, " ' A baby—' "

" '—is God's opinion that the world should go on.' Great." She tried, really she did, but Gena couldn't keep the bitterness out of her voice. "Maybe this time he'll let the child see the same as everyone else."

APRIL 1...

"Hello, Simon."

Simon stopped guiltily, then thought how ridiculous that was. Of course Gena would know he was coming to talk to her, but . . . when was the last time he had touched her? Maybe she didn't have to touch people anymore . . . perhaps being around them was enough for her to pick up impressions about the future. Things were changing so fast, it stood to reason that she could have changed, too. After all, both she and Mercy were pregnant—who knew what that could be doing to their abilities. Mercy hadn't healed anyone in months, but neither had she felt the urge. There were, thank God, no more Nights Out; it was as if every ounce of energy she had were going into the child she carried.

"Hi, Gena," he said now. She was sitting on the overstuffed chair by the French doors that looked out at the small terrace off the living room, perfectly still with her legs curled comfortably onto the seat cushion. Warm spring sunlight bathed her face and hair and he'd never seen her look more at ease. Simon knew Gena was part American Indian, but he wondered idly what kind—the way she unconsciously gravitated toward the sun and preferred warmer than average temperatures, surely her ancestors were at home in the hot sun of the West.

Gena motioned him closer without turning her head; Simon obeyed, and the feeling that he was like a little boy who ought to be wringing a hat in his hands as he approached made him grin. As always, there was that iron band of control around the surface of his mind, and he liked to think that it had grown stronger since he and Mercy had been spending so much time here. Hell, for all practical purposes they were *living* in the guest bedroom, with their apartment visited—well, raided—irregularly for personal items. It made him sad to think that all those things that meant so much to him would probably be the last things in the world he and Mercy worried about in a couple of months. With nothing to be done to change it, he shook the thought away and brought himself back to why he'd come to talk to Gena, but when he opened his mouth to speak, she suddenly giggled low in her throat.

"What's so funny?" Simon asked, thrown off guard.

"Me," Gena said promptly. Her smile was dark. "Sitting here like some ancient, wise . . . *witch* or something, waiting for you to come close with your request. Did you ever see the movie *Pumpkinhead*?"

Simon shook his head, then remembered to speak. "No."

"Lamont narrated it to me, though he was afraid I might get frightened—not likely, at least by a movie." She paused for a second, then continued somberly. "Anyway, he told me there was a blind old witch in it that just sat there and didn't turn when the star of the movie, I can't remember his name, came up behind her. She knew who he was and what he was going to ask. Just like I do." Finally, Gena's head turned toward him. "Of course, her price was much higher."

"Well, I—"

"Me, I'm thinking about collecting . . . earlobes."

Simon burst out laughing. "Gena, for God's sake—you really had me going!"

She grinned then, the mischievous side of her that they seldom saw surfacing for a moment. Then she sighed. "Oh, Simon . . . you're going to tell me that Mercy wants to know about her parents, why they don't answer the phone when she calls to tell them she got married. This is so *hard* for me, don't you understand? I don't know the world right *now,* only tomorrow. Do you realize that I haven't touched her since the day we met in the park? If I hold her hand today, maybe I'll be able to tell her they still won't answer her call tomorrow, but not necessarily *why.*"

Standing next to the chair, towering over her small figure, Simon suddenly felt absurd. He lowered himself to the floor, then pulled off his glasses and rubbed his eyes. "I'm not sure I follow."

"If I tell her I don't know what's going on with her mom and dad," Gena explained patiently, "she'll decide to go to them and find out what's wrong. When she makes that decision, and truly intends to *do* it, tomorrow as it exists for her . . . changes. Then I can probably tell her what she'll find when she gets there or . . ." Gena swallowed and her voice dropped into a troubled whisper. "If she'll get there at all."

Simon stared at her. "I see."

Her head jerked toward him. "No, you don't see at all, Simon. You may be the mind reader among us, but it's easy for me to guess what you think you can do about this problem, how you believe the foresight can be manipulated." Gena shook her head vehemently. "Whatever's in here"—she smacked herself in the forehead—"can't be fooled. It will know if she's truly going to downstate Illinois, or if she's just trying to think she is because you told her that will make me be able to see. Maybe the future can be changed, Simon, but what I see can't be orchestrated."

"I'm sorry," he said, deeply ashamed. "I shouldn't have considered it."

Gena laughed lightly. "Sorry for what? You think I haven't spent countless hours trying to dream up ways of tricking myself? You bet I have." She fell silent for a few moments, then folded her hands together briefly, a vaguely prayerlike movement. "Bring Mercy in, but don't tell her anything we've talked about. Remember that whatever happens has to come naturally. You know that the way things are now you would never suggest a trip to her hometown, so don't say it just to plant the idea in her head."

Simon stood, feeling his knees shake with tension. Suggest a trip, with the shootings and riots increasing every day? Not a chance. "All right. I'll go get her." Gena said nothing as he walked to the hallway. He looked back over his shoulder and wanted to say *Good luck,* but the idea was absurd.

Wasn't it?

"Gena, I—I wouldn't ask, but . . . they won't answer the *phone.* I know this is a terrible thing for you, and I know how much you hate it—"

"Stop," Gena said. "You don't have to apologize. Just give me your hand."

If someone had asked him to describe how he felt right now, Simon didn't think he would have been able. Watching Mercy walk hesitantly over to Gena as Lamont sat on the couch nearby, his dark face as still and hard as granite—it was like viewing an act onstage, something idiotic about zany séances, spiritualists, and tables rising on invisible wires. After all, it was April first—maybe this entire day was some sort of great cosmic joke.

Yeah, just like the asteroids.

He saw Gena stretch out her hand, saw Mercy reach over and take it. Dread filled him and he wanted to run over and snatch the two of them apart before

—*flash*—

Gena held on for a second, then broke the grip. "I'm sorry," she said.

"What?" Mercy looked over at him, confused, then back to Gena. Simon felt his shoulders tense and knew that Gena had been right all along, not only about what he might have tried to do had she not caught him, but about how Mercy would instinctively respond.

"I didn't get anything at all." Gena folded her hands

—*flash*—

placidly, but Simon knew that inside she was twisting, agonized; she might not know about Mercy's parents, but

—*flash*—

Jesus, she knew what was coming from Mercy.

—*flash*—

Simon nearly moaned out loud. He wanted to move, to stop what he saw from Gena's thoughts was going to happen, but he was paralyzed.

"You're lying," Mercy said coldly. "I *despise* people who lie to me."

"I'm not lying to you, Mercy."

Faster than he would have thought she could move, Mercy's palm lashed out and connected sharply with one side of Gena's cheek. The other woman didn't bother trying to avoid the blow.

"Lamont, don't," Gena said evenly. Out of the corner of his eye, Simon saw Lamont start to stand, his expression furious; at Gena's words, the stocky man sank back onto the couch, a spring waiting for release. With a sort of detached horror, Simon found himself admiring Gena, normally such a vocal hothead, for keeping her voice level, for not striking back at Mercy in return.

"It's just like with Lily, isn't it? You're not going to tell me because you don't *want* to." Mercy's mouth was a rigid line. "Who was it this time who convinced you to shut me out? Simon?" She darted an enraged glance at him.

"Mercy, wait. I didn't—"

"Shut up, Simon. I don't want to hear it." Impulsively, she bent close to Gena until their noses were only inches away. "Damn you, this is my *family* I'm asking about, not some stranger on the street you'll never see again. You won't tell me? Fine—I'll go to Mt. Vernon and find out for myself."

"Mercy!" Simon protested. "That's not feasible—"

She straightened and glared at him. "Feasible, Simon? This is not a DCFS case where you can waltz in, take charge, and fix everything. This is me, and my parents, and my *life*." She turned to stride away. "I'll get there somehow, even if I have to—hey, let *go*!"

Gena lunged forward and grabbed Mercy by the arm with both her hands, then hung on as Mercy tried to shake free. Simon's paralysis broke and both he and Lamont sprang toward the two women,

—flash—

then Simon clapped a hand to his head and cried out. Lamont stumbled and gaped at him in surprise as Mercy's gaze jerked to his. "Oh, Gena, no!" he said miserably; his legs gave out and he sank to his knees.

"Simon?" Angry thoughts forgotten, Mercy tried to go to him and found her arm still in Gena's grip. The blind woman was pulling on Mercy with all her weight, fighting to keep her hold. "What the hell—"

"Mercy, don't go," Gena said urgently. Perspiration had broken out on her face and was running down her jawline. "You'll get there all right, and you might even get back—but I'm not sure. I can't . . . quite . . . see that—"

Mercy stopped trying to pull away but her expression was anything but convinced. "Really. And what will I find when I get there?"

—*flash*—

Simon gagged and shoved his fist in his mouth—*damn* this involuntary connection to Gena! As Lamont crouched next to him and put a comforting hand on his shoulder, Mercy's head whipped in his direction again and realization crashed over her. She started to stagger but Gena's hold was firm.

"How long?" Mercy asked hoarsely. "How long have they been dead?"

"I . . . don't know exactly," Gena said in a hushed voice. "For some time, I think, and I d-don't know how. Forgive me, Mercy— I swear I wasn't lying to you. I couldn't see it until you made the decision to go. Now I can only tell you what you'll find." Her hands slid down Mercy's arm until they found her fingers, squeezed briefly, then she released her.

Simon saw Mercy cover her face as her shoulders began to shake, then abruptly she looked up. "I—oh, *God,* Gena." One hand, so capable of gentleness, reached and touched Gena's cheek. "I *hit* you . . . I'm so *sorry.*"

Gena's laugh was strained. "It doesn't matter, Mercy. There'll be worse things to come."

Simon and Lamont watched without comment as Mercy surprised Gena by reaching over and hugging her fiercely.

"But not from me, Gena. Not ever again."

"How did you know, too?"

It was dark and quiet in the town house, hours after the terrible scene downstairs. Lamont and Gena had gone to bed, or maybe they'd just felt the need to get the hell away from the two people who'd caused them so much anguish today. Simon was exhausted from the unwilling look into Gena's head this afternoon and was glad they'd all retired earlier than usual.

Mercy was warm within the circle of his arms, her crying finally stopped, at least for now. "I couldn't stop her thoughts from blasting into my head," he admitted. "They were just . . . I don't know how to explain it. Overwhelming." The room was dim, its only light a diffused shadow from the sheer curtains covering the big window on the east wall, the one that would send dawn blazing in if there wasn't cloud cover. The soft bed in the nicely wallpapered guest room, the warm down comforter, the full refrigerator downstairs. It was all so deceptively peaceful, a big . . . *lie*. Just the thing that Mercy hated so much. "I found out other stuff, too," he said slowly.

Simon felt the pillow move as Mercy turned her face toward him. "Not good?"

"No." He squeezed his eyes shut, searching for a way to tell her without evoking the pictures that had screamed through his mind. Show, don't tell—an old writing rule he remembered from college. He wanted to do the opposite here, to spare her the things that Gena couldn't escape. "They were all jumbled up with each other, it must have been because of the connection."

Mercy's hand found his and her thumb rubbed across the skin, the movement slow and reassuring. Anchoring. "What connection, Simon?"

"Between the . . . I don't know. Subject matter, I guess. Your parents, and . . . Lamont's. His family." Simon blinked in the dark, forcing his eyes to focus and refocus on the dim objects in the room rather than glaze over and fix on the images still in his memory. "He's got a big one, you know. A sister, another brother besides the infamous Joey, a bunch of nephews and a niece."

"Ah."

A single syllable, but Simon could hear the trepidation in it. He didn't say anything for a long time, then Mercy sighed. He knew without trying that she had to ask. "Will any of them . . . make it?"

"It was hard to tell," he confided, "but I don't think so. Maybe one of the boys. I don't think Gena herself is sure."

Mercy said nothing, but it wasn't long before the mattress began to shake as she quietly cried. All Simon could do was hold her and mourn with her in the dark.

NEW YORK
APRIL 10 . . .

[fade to Marti Nunciata]

From the opening segment of the seven o'clock Cable News Network broadcast:

"More riots and violence plague our country as NASA and the Department of Defense remain unsuccessful in putting together another launch sequence to stop the oncoming asteroid. Reports of the ESA's failure to repair its space facilities and trace the launch problems of Ariane 5 and their subsequent refusal to attempt another launch, and also of both Russia's and China's failure to thus far complete repairs from the previous sabotage bombings have added fuel to the unrest. Here in the United States, our military reports that many smaller towns in rural areas have been completely destroyed, with armed residents looting burned-out stores for supplies and food before retreating into the woods where it is believed some have banded together and set up heavily reinforced and guarded survival camps. This is what Harvey Thayer, Director of the Federal Emergency Management Agency, had to say this morning."

[cut to window and expand to fill, Harvey Thayer]

"These groups are comprised of paranoid survivalists. They're dangerous, plain and simple, and my advice is to stay as far away from them as you can. People in the cities haven't got it as bad, because supplies are there and residents aren't panicking—yet. Do outside shopping only if you have to, don't hoard supplies—there's no quicker way than that to get you in an argument with someone else—and report any price gouging, looting, or violence to your local police station by dialing 9-1-1. If the local law enforcement agency can't address the problem immediately, they'll turn it over to one of the many military units patrolling the area. If I may take this opportunity to remind everyone, price gouging is *illegal* and violators will be arrested. On a more serious note, looters will be *shot*—the soldiers are going to shoot first and not bother about asking questions. I'm here to tell you that there isn't much you find through the broken window of a store that's worth losing your life over. The best thing to do until this mess is past is to lock yourselves in your homes, ration your food, and don't come out. Don't worry about your jobs—you can sort all that mess out after this asteroid crap is behind us and people regain their senses. We are in one helluva mess here."

[cut to Marti Nunciata]

"Clearly Director Thayer ranks among those government spokesmen who believe that the predicted Millennium asteroid strike is incorrect. Others, however, are not so convinced. With us for a brief interview is Dr. Trent Zuriel from the Kitt Peak National Observatory in Arizona. Dr. Zuriel, you've just heard Director Harvey Thayer's advice that the public should simply stay inside their homes and ride out the general hysteria until the impact date passes. What do you have to say about Director Thayer's point of view?"

[cut to upper right window, Dr. Trent Zuriel]

"I'd say it doesn't matter."

[cut to Marti Nunciata]

"Excuse me?"

[cut to Dr. Trent Zuriel]

"I said it doesn't *matter*. Stay in your houses, go out on the streets. We're doomed anyway. You can listen to the government gloss-over if you want, but the fact is, Millennium *is* going to hit this planet on July second, and this strike is going to make the dinosaur extinction at the end of the Cretaceous look like recess at a day-care center."

[cut to Marti Nunciata]

"Uh . . . is this your personal opinion?"

[cut to Dr. Trent Zuriel]

"You wanted to know."

[cut to Marti Nunciata]

"I see. If you don't mind my asking, Dr. Zuriel, CNN has been trying to speak with Professor Frank Gelasias for some time, but we've not been successful at contacting him. As you know, he is the spokesman for—"

[abrupt cut to Dr. Trent Zuriel]

"He's gone. He and his wife packed up and took off. No one saw them go and they didn't leave a forwarding address. But they're both fools, you know. There's no place to hide—no one's going to survive this."

[cut to Marti Nunciata]

"Surely you must be exaggerating your predictions, Dr. Zuriel. Neither the army nor the Department of Defense has stated anything to support the idea that nothing would be left if we were to actually be hit—"

[cut to Dr. Trent Zuriel]

"Hey, do I look like I'm joking to you?"

[fade out]

CHICAGO . . .
APRIL 15

The telephone's midnight ringing coincided with the wail of a siren a few blocks off, another screaming note in the ongoing death song as the city thrashed around them.

Erica fumbled for it, cursing the too loud bell, cursing Searle as he snarled something in his sleep, cursing her own idiotic idea about moving into a private suite here at Althaia until this Millennium business was over. Flailing stupidly in the dark, the windows covered with light-blocking shades to keep out the nasty glow of the streetlights, she finally brushed the lamp and found the switch. There was the telephone, blaring out an intrusion into her most private of places, and Christ, couldn't these people give her one night of uninterrupted sleep?

And yet . . . that old professional mode, snapping into place when what she really wanted to do was shriek at whoever had done this to her *again,* and by God, she had a very good idea just who that was.

"Dr. Richmond here," she said smoothly.

"D-doctor?"

Ellen Dellaportas's voice was shaking and Erica pressed her lips together. She had thought it would be a good business move to give the woman the number to her private line, but it had turned into a grappling hook straight into Erica's life. Now what?

"Yes, Mrs. Dellaportas. What can I do for you?"

"I'm sorry to call you again, but this is the only time I could get to the telephone without someone interfering."

The only time? Somehow Erica seriously doubted that; instead of being soothed by her reservation at the Colorado Springs camp, as the weeks passed Ellen Dellaportas had became more and more paranoid. Erica glanced at the clock and scowled. "It *is* nearly three-thirty in the morning."

"I know. I'm—I'm sorry." At least she sounded contrite. *"Listen,"* the elderly woman's hushed, breathy voice sped up, as though she were afraid someone would snatch the phone from her at any moment. *"My daughter might wake up and catch me, so I have to make this short. They're sending me away tomorrow—"*

Erica sat up. "What?"

"—to stay with my other daughter in Indiana. She lives in Lafayette, where she and her husband renovate houses—"

"I see," Erica said, before Mrs. Dellaportas could launch into a detailed history of that branch of her family. "How long will you be gone?"

"That's just it! Melinda—that's my daughter—says they'll bring me back in mid-July, after the asteroid 'hit' is over. The thing is, they don't think it's going to hit at all, so they've decided

to handle my affairs for me." Mrs. Dellaportas's voice went bitter. *"They've also decided I no longer have the right to decide what to do with my own future. Please, Doctor—you've got to stop them! I don't want to go to Lafayette. I'm supposed to go to Colorado Springs, remember?"*

"Mrs. Dellaportas, I have no legal right to—"

"Melinda's husband is an accountant with First Chicago Bank—my bank—and he works with computers. I thought a person's money was their own business, but somehow he got into my records without my permission and he told my daughter about the three-hundred-thousand-dollar donation I made toward building the retreat in Colorado Springs." The voice on the telephone was rising toward stridency and Erica knew the other woman's notion of a secret conversation was going to be short-lived. *"I never did like that young man. Now the children are telling me that they'll reconsider making me go to Lafayette if After Help refunds the money I donated."*

"Mrs. Dellaportas," Erica said carefully, "you must know that's impossible. Those funds have already been used. After Help is a nonprofit organization—we have no cash reserves set aside for anything resembling a 'refund.' " She paused. "The money you donated was of your own will—we never asked for a cent."

"Then I won't go," Ellen Dellaportas said with finality. She suddenly sounded like a petulant child. *"And you'll have to give me my money back. If I can't go to Colorado Springs, I'll take my chances in Chicago. At least I'll be in my own home."*

"Mrs. Dellaportas—Ellen—I'm afraid you've misunderstood the concept of a donation," Erica said. She kept her voice even and tried to sound empathetic. "You did not *pay* for a place in the Colorado Springs facility. After Help set aside a room for you at the Colorado Springs survival location free of charge because you *wanted* it. Your donation—and it was very generous—was spent to help build the facility, a task which is not yet complete, but we would have offered a place to you whether or not you contributed to the construction fund. That's what we do. We are a *charity*-based organization. You wouldn't give money to the American Cancer Society and then ask for it back, would you?"

For a moment there was silence. Then, *"You're going to let them take me away, aren't you? You were so supportive before, and I was going to donate even more, but you don't really care. You—"*

"Ellen, I'm *sorry*, but there's absolutely nothing After Help can do to intervene in your family affairs. We simply don't have the legal right to do so—difficulties with your family *must* be worked out among yourselves. I'll be happy to speak with them and see if I can make them understand the nature of After Help's purpose, but beyond that I'm completely paralyzed." Erica took a deep breath, trying frantically to think of a way to save the situation. Until the last comment about being willing to donate more, she hadn't cared a bit about where this elderly woman spent the next three months; now that she knew the donations could continue, she had to find a way to keep them rolling in. "I'll come by the house tomorrow—"

"You'll do no such thing, Doctor—stop it, Mother! Let go of the phone!"

A clang on the phone line made Erica blink. Damn, she thought as the muted sounds of scuffling and the old woman's faint protests came over the handset. "Mrs. Dellaportas?" she asked, although she already knew what had happened. "Who is this?"

"This is Melinda Janisopoulos," an icy voice answered. *"I know who you are—that doctor from After Help. You are not to contact my mother again, do you understand? You've screwed her out of enough money already, and you can bet you won't see another dime."*

"Ms. Janisopoulos, I assure you that we asked for nothing from your mother—"

"Oh, I'm sure," the young woman on the phone sneered. *"Mom may trust you to save the world—or at least her—but the rest of us can see right through your scam. You prey on these poor, frightened people, feeding off their fears and soaking them for every dollar you can until you run their bank accounts dry. Well, your time with this victim just ended, lady. Maybe we can't do anything about the money my mother already gave you, but if you contact her again, I'll start by getting a lawyer and then I'll move on to the newspapers. Am I making myself clear?"*

"Crystal," Erica said grimly.

"Excellent," Melinda Janisopoulos snapped. *"Go suck on someone else, you fucking parasite."*

Erica winced as the phone on the other end was slammed down, then replaced her own receiver carefully. Damn, she thought again. How much would Mrs. Dellaportas have donated had her family not intervened? She pulled her feet back under the comforter, then reached over and shut off the lamp.

No sense worrying about what she couldn't change.

APRIL 18 . . .

"Joey," Alva said, "come here and tell me what you think."

Finally, something that pulled his attention away from the window and his obsessive surveillance of Lake Shore Drive. He turned and glanced at the array of guns on the table, then brightened and headed over. Good old Joey—you could always count on a good gun to lighten his mood. "Nice," he said appreciatively. His fingers skimmed over the inventory, pausing here and there, then moving on—too many good things to play with all at once. "This is one hell of an inventory, babe."

Alva grinned and flipped her hair back impatiently. Her last haircut had been . . . when? December, that was it. The next one should've been in February but by then the salon was closed, her fairy hairdresser packed up and no doubt deep in some hidey-hole. She hadn't bothered to find someone else; soon no one would care anyway. But damn, this stuff hanging in her face annoyed her constantly. "Check this out." She reached for something leaning against the table leg and held it up. Joey's eyes practically bulged.

"Where the hell did you get *that*?" he gasped. He reached for the 9mm Spectre M-4 and she handed it over willingly. "Jesus!"

"The box holds fifty shots," she told him. "Besides what's on the table, we've got six boxes, loaded up and ready to go. Pretty heavy, huh?" Her smile widened.

Joey hefted the submachine gun thoughtfully. "So when do we leave?"

"Monday at the latest. Anything past that and we might not get out without fighting, weapons or not. Right now shooting at anything will only draw attention to us, and that's the last thing we need."

Joey's eyes went back to the window and he handed the Spectre back to her. "Maybe we should stay here," he suggested. "There's food, water—hell, the lake is our backyard." His deep brown eyes were troubled as he scanned the neat row of pistols, revolvers and ammunition on the tabletop, all small things easily concealed. "I've been watching outside and it's pretty brutal. If we get stuck outside after curfew . . . " His voice trailed off.

"We won't," she assured him. "And that lake in our backyard is more of a problem than anything else. What if there's a tidal wave—"

"From the *lake*?"

"Why not?" she demanded. "It's water, it's big—where's it going to go? Or maybe the lake water just rises, okay, and there it is again—right into this ritzy-snitzy building on the edge of Lincoln Park. I say we get out while we can. We move in the early hours, start hunting for the next place to sleep no later than noon each day. I'm telling you, Joey. I've been seeing for years how people can be when they freak out; we don't want to be around for this. Out of Chicago, out of the city . . . hell, let's head southwest, where the weather'll be easier to take when there's no electricity and ninety percent of the buildings in the world are nothing but crushed wood."

"But why now, so soon? There's more than two months to go—"

Alva joined Joey at the window and draped an arm over his shoulder. "C'mon, look down there." She pointed below at something she'd never thought she'd see: a U.S. Army tank loaded with soldiers, cruising slowly down Lake Shore Drive. Cars, a pitiful few, dodged around it, and farther south, she could see two more tanks. "You've said yourself how brutal it is now—what'll they be doing in two weeks? Or four? By then the army won't be thinking about whether to shoot, they'll be wondering where to put the bodies before they rot . . . or maybe where to duck from the civilians shooting at *them*."

Joey said nothing and she studied him for a while. Finally, she massaged the bridge of her nose, trying to work away some of the tension. This was more of a problem than she'd considered; she didn't want to go alone—she didn't dare, but she couldn't tell him why. Knocked up . . . her, of all women! So much for birth control pills. Joey would find out in good time, but if she told him now she had a feeling she'd never be able to get his ass out of this place. She didn't care a whit about some damned kid, but Joey's upbringing was different—he had brothers, a sister, small children in his family. He might think only of himself, but he could be very possessive of his stuff, too; she didn't want to get caught in some mental crossfire over "his" baby versus "her" safety. She was a heavy-hipped woman who didn't exercise much; it wouldn't be that hard to hide a few pounds for a couple of months, provided she didn't start puking every hour. And there were more problems to deal with.

"You don't really think it's going to happen, do you?" she asked.

"I . . . just can't believe it," he admitted at last. "I look around and see all the shit going down, and it just floors me. So much has changed, but so much of it is the same, you know?" He gestured at the condo's living room. "I mean, we still get HBO and The Disney Channel on the tube, the mail still comes through—most of the time, anyway—we can still go to a grocery store and buy a *TV Guide*. If the world's coming to an end, Alva, how come we can still do all those things?"

"Because so many people have hope, Joey. It may be false, but it's the one thing that keeps everyone from killing each other right now and getting it over with—that and the military, of course." She balled her fists in frustration. "There are those who believe our goose is cooked, like me, and those who don't. Are you with the bunch who don't, Joey? If so, that's great—I say more fucking power to you. That's what America and freedom of choice is all about. But why not play it safe in the meantime? If nothing happens, if the feds aren't lying out their asses and Millennium does miss the Earth, then . . . all this stuff will still be here, right? So we can just load up from wherever we are and drive back, and the world will be a sane place again. You can go back to hating Lamont and I can worry about not getting thrown in jail for walking off the force six weeks ago, or maybe that your brother's girlfriend will someday find a way to convince people I whacked her husband. If I'm wrong, *it'll all still be here.*"

Joey turned to stare to her. "And if you're right . . . "

"Hopefully we'll be as far away from other people as possible, and maybe we'll have a chance to live."

GUTHRIE CENTER, IOWA
MAY 3 . . .

"What're you lookin' at, mental case?"

Lily opened her mouth to retort—*Nothing much besides a plow girl*—then sighed and turned away. What good would it do? If she started an argument with her cousin Georgene—they'd always despised each other—the two of them would end up whaling it out in the middle of the floor. Then the whole damned family would get in on it, start taking sides, her father would start bellowing, her mother would screech at first, then cry—what a fucking night-mare. Thinking back, Lily wished she'd pulled Mercy's friend Gena aside and had a serious talk with her; would Gena have been able to tell her that nothing on the face of this Earth—and certainly nothing crazy ol' Lily had to say—would convince her family that (a) Lily was now as sane as any of them (and couldn't *that* be the argument of the month?), and (b) wouldn't they like to consider what Guthrie Center, Iowa, might be like on July third? Hell, she wouldn't have wasted her time and risked her neck coming out here. She'd much rather have stayed with Mercy and Simon, and even Gena and Lamont were probably okay. That Mercy and Simon trusted them enough to stay at their place said a lot.

Mercy and Gena . . . Jesus. Had she caused a big rift between the two women? Ignoring Georgene for the moment, Lily got up and wandered to the big window that looked out from the living room of the double-wide trailer. It was pretty outside today, warm and sunny, a real indication that spring was here. There were buds along the trees surrounding the clearing, big old blackbirds darting through the branches as they searched for muddy twigs and trash to make their nests. Just behind the porch, one of the old hounds, a bitch, slept peacefully in a patch of sunlight; as Lily watched, another one padded over and nosed the ground around the sleeping dog's muzzle. One wrong touch, and a *snap!* and suddenly the two dogs were snarling and biting; the skirmish was over as quickly as it had begun and the two dogs settled on opposite sides of the scrubby yard with uneasy growls. Had Lily done that to Mercy and Gena—made them argue and mistrust each other? Standing here and staring out the window, all she could think about was how she'd left Chicago and the last time she'd heard Mercy as she was going down the town house steps, demanding that Gena tell her if Lily would be safe. Now she was here, *home,* and Lily's shoulders slumped. Well, she thought, she sure hadn't missed much.

Georgene's voice shrilled from behind Lily, making her wince, unintentionally echoing her thoughts. "If you don't like it here, Miss Hotshot, why'n't you go on and leave?"

"Shut up, Georgene." Lily's father came into the living room, using his overalls as a towel to dry his wet hands. "Why're you always trying to pick a fight?" He glowered at Georgene and she looked away sulkily. He was a big man, his face scoured by the weather and already tanned from working outside though it was only May. "Your ma's still waiting on you to eat, Lily. You could at least try—you're skinny as a pitchfork." The smells of fried chicken and potatoes hung thick in his clothes from the midday meal; in his pocket was a double lump wrapped carefully in a clean cotton napkin—homemade biscuits and butter for an afternoon snack while he was out in the fields. Cholesterol junction, but did it matter anymore? No.

Lily glanced at him but didn't move from her stance at the window. "Sorry, Pa. I'm not hungry. I—I don't each much."

"Well," was all he said, then he shoved his hands in his pockets and looked at the floor. So big and imposing over the rest of the family, he'd never had a clue how to deal with her. "Your ma and I was talking about you last night," he finally said. "We're real happy to have you back, you know. And seeing as how you got so much better, Tom Kramer said he's willing to make a spot for you at Jerky's as a bagger. You could work your way up to cashier after a couple of months."

Lily would've smiled if there hadn't been so much hope in her father's voice. She tried to picture herself as cashier working in a small-town grocery store for the rest of her life, and couldn't; she tried to picture the rest of her life . . . and couldn't do that either. Then again, a year ago a job offer like that would have been unthinkable—for as long as she or anyone could remember, she'd been as controllable as a jackhammer from whatever awful thing had been bouncing around in her head. How much courage had it taken for stodgy Tom Kramer to offer this? A lot. Now she was calm, coherent—but Lily still looked the same, just cleaner. She had to give the conservative old grocer credit for ignoring the outside view and searching to see what was inside her—not a lot of folks around here were willing to do that.

Lily turned from the window, refusing to be too cowardly to look her father in the eye when she made her announcement. "I'm not staying, Pa," she said softly. Her father's expression sagged; from the corner of her eye she saw a flash of relief cross Georgene's face and suddenly Lily understood. There wasn't much here for her cousin—Lily's mother and father had taken in the girl at age six, when her parents had died trying to stop a barn fire on their rented property. Now that Lily was healed, she was . . . *competition* for everything that Georgene had and treasured: life on this small farm, her aunt's and uncle's affection, the few still-available men within their small circle of acquaintances. She and

Georgene were almost the same age, but Georgene was plain and kind of . . . "farmy"-looking. Lily's hair was still orange and white and green, but the colors were growing out and she hadn't bothered to redye the streaks; the underlying white was natural, a smooth, shining platinum that complemented her pale complexion. Before she'd shown up in the middle of March—the damned curfew had made the journey into over a month's trek—no one around here had seen her since she was fifteen and a total, filthy head trip, before she'd taken off one night for parts unknown. Lily might still dress kind of strange, but now she was clean and sane and maybe a little pretty, a threat that had fallen out of the sky and into Georgene's life.

"This thing that's coming," Lily continued reluctantly, "these asteroids . . . there are people I have to make sure are all right."

Her father's broad face hardened and Lily saw an array of emotions cross it—resentment, stubbornness, jealousy. "If you really believe them rocks are gonna hit," he said, "your duty is here, with your family. We're the ones who ought to be standing by one another."

Uh-oh, touchy ground. To tell him that they weren't *family* to her, just strangers who shared the same blood, was unthinkable. They'd never protected or done much to help her . . . but could they be blamed for that? Ignorance is no excuse, she reminded herself . . . but what if they *had* tried harder to find relief for her, and still failed? Never mind; no one would ever know the answer to all the what-ifs. She stretched out a hand toward her father pleadingly, but he only gave her a stony look and started to turn away. "Wait." He paused and she drew a breath and tried again. "There's someone I owe," she said and tapped the side of her head, "for this, for giving me a life."

Her father frowned. "A doctor?"

"Not . . . really." Yes, Mercy had been a doctor at one time. The healing, however, had nothing to do with the medical profession, so it wasn't really a lie. "She did something no one else was able to," Lily said. "She fixed me, Pa. Without her I'd be dead."

He swallowed and looked away, his gaze sliding blindly across the window and around the room before coming back to her. "What about us?" he asked finally.

"You'll be . . ." Lily hesitated. "As good as you can be. Like you've always been." She looked over to Georgene, who Lily knew sat silently hoping against hope that she really *was* leaving. "I don't belong here, I don't fit. I—"

"You'll always be welcome in my home."

"That's not the same as belonging, Pa. I have to go back to Chicago." Lily reached beneath the beat-up coffee table and picked up her backpack; she'd packed her few belongings in it this morning. She looked toward the kitchen, but this time she did chicken out. Her mother was a fine, hardworking woman, but someone Lily had never really known. To be honest, she didn't think she could handle the way the woman would wail.

"Tell Ma good-bye for me."

CHICAGO
MAY 8 . . .

Searle studied Erica from across the room, wondering what she was working at so diligently. She had papers strewn all over her desk, charts, books, more crap that he didn't have a clue about. On the credenza behind her the computer was humming quietly, a small yellow light in the front blinking every so often while its insides made a noise like an injured cricket. *She thinks it's not going to hit,* he thought. After all this time and all her big talk about survival plans and socking away supplies, she still can't bring herself to accept that Millennium's going to smash the shit out of the wealthy world she's built for herself. Forty-five years old, a pampered princess with a brain too big for her own good and not a clue how to use those smarts to save her ass.

"Erica."

She looked up and smiled; Searle's sight was good enough to see that it didn't reach her eyes. "Hmm—what is it?"

"I've done my part. You've got as many armed guards around the supply rooms as I could hire, more patrolling the emergency room to weed out the idiots who think they need help but could go home and bandage themselves. All the side entrances, first- and second-floor windows are sealed, and the doctors and nurses who weren't smart enough to get out before the guards moved in have been 'convinced' that Althaia needs them on staff twenty-four hours a day until after the crisis is over. Now what?" With a jerk, Searle realized he was standing and his voice had escalated into a shout. Tension, that was it, building to a cracking point. "How am I supposed to keep these people in here for *two more fucking months?*"

Erica put her pen down carefully, as if it might explode in her hand. Her face was pale, cheeks sunken; he supposed the pressure had been working on her, too. For the last week she'd thrown up everything she ate. "I don't *know,* Searle," she said irritably. "Pay them, I suppose. Give them money, liquor—drugs, if you like. Don't you have connections on the street somewhere to get the stuff?"

Searle stalked across the room and glowered at her. "No, I don't, Your Bitchiness. While you've been sitting here working at your computer and dreaming about how rich you're going to be in August, I've been trying to deal with the real world. And in the real world, you can't get the good shit anymore. The people who deal it are keeping it for themselves and they don't care how much money you offer because unlike you, they plan on trading it for the things that are really going to matter this summer—like food and water. Money isn't worth much to Joe American anymore, because anyone with a quarter brain knows that pretty soon its only good use will be for kindling."

"I don't care!" Erica suddenly shouted into his face. He drew back, startled, as she leaped to her feet and stomped around the desk. "That's your job, your responsibility—that's why you're *here* instead of back in prison where the cops have been throwing all the parolees just to get them off the street." She was punctuating her words with sharp jabs of her index finger into his shoulder. "So damn it, Searle, you just handle it and stop whining. If you can't, then get the hell *out*—but leave me *alone!*"

"You poke me one more time and I'm gonna break your hand."

Her next jab stopped in midair. Face red with fury, Erica drew a breath and turned her back. "The first time you hit me will be the last," she said coldly. "You think the armed men walking around here work for you? They don't—every one of them knows who really controls this place."

He stared at her, feeling a hard pulse in his temple, dimly aware that his hands had folded into fists. One good punch—

"Searle—I'm sorry." She turned back to him, and this time her hands on his shoulders were soft. "I don't want to fight with you. It's just all so hard, so . . . frightening." Her shoulders drooped. "I've felt so lousy, I can hardly drag myself around anymore."

"Forget it." He stepped away and went back to the couch, feeling the pressure of his pounding blood slow, forcing his stomach to unclench. The guards were nothing, former bank security weenies, night-shift johns—he could take any one of them out before they figured out how to unholster the gun on their hip. But the other . . . she was right on the head about that. It was all over the city news about how the governor had signed a temporary law allowing the local cop shops to round up the ex-cons who couldn't prove they'd worked steady for the last two months. All those stupid, lazy saps had been tossed back in the joint for "safe-keeping." She hadn't said as much, but the fucking bitch had him by the balls. *Blackmailed*—it almost made him snarl out loud.

"Please don't be angry. I didn't mean it." Erica sat down beside him and stroked his thigh, let her fingers move higher, then higher still. "Here," she cooed, "let me help you relax."

He wanted to slap her hand away . . . but he didn't. She was droning on about something . . . what? Oh yeah, that girlfriend of Simon's, and how she'd been doing a lot of thinking about her and maybe it was time for Searle to just go and get her. "Go and get her?" Searle said hoarsely. He was starting to feel really warm, but when he looked over Erica's shoulder he could see that the door to her office was wide open. That didn't seem to matter to Erica, though, and he sucked in his breath as she reached up and undid the clasp on his belt buckle. The sudden notion that he might get caught with the hospital administrator fondling him just excited him further, and he licked his lips.

"Sure," Erica said lightly. "Like you said, we've got all these men and guns."

At her glibness, Searle tried and failed to recapture the rage that had so thoroughly taken him a few minutes before. Erica had pulled his shirt out of his waistband and unclasped his slacks; now she was wriggling her fingernails beneath the elastic of his briefs. Her fingers were very, very hot. It didn't matter how pissed off he was, he always forgot about it if he got sexually excited. If only Lila had figured that out, she might still be alive. "They've moved," he managed. He was gripping the cushions of the couch, involuntarily stretching his legs out straight. "They're not . . . they're not there any—"

"You can find her." Erica's voice was encouraging—*You can do anything, Searle.* "Didn't you tell me that Simon still goes to work? Just follow him." Her searing fingers closed around him and Searle gasped and arched his hips, barely heard her final words before she pulled him free and her mouth closed over his flesh.

"He'll lead you right to home base."

NEW YORK
MAY 17...

[fade to Peter Hoshi]

From the opening segment of an early evening emergency Cable News Network special broadcast:

"Coming to you from New York City, I'm Peter Hoshi sitting in for Marti Nunciata, who has taken a . . . leave of absence.

"Yesterday CNN was the first to bring our viewers the official announcement that due to ongoing sabotage bombings, the hoped-for Russian and American launches of multiple warhead–loaded missiles toward the Millennium asteroids will not be possible in time to intercept the pieces of the asteroid that experts around the world are saying will strike the Earth on July second.

"Tonight, in the wake of the terrible admission, is the following live news conference direct from the Department of Defense. Speaking to the country from Washington, D.C., is Harvey Thayer, Director of the Federal Emergency Management Agency."

[cut to window and expand to fill, Harvey Thayer]

"It is with great reluctance that I advise the American people that a national state of emergency has been declared by the President of the United States. The White House acknowledges that there is a possibility, and I stress the word *possibility,* that a very few pieces of what was once the rogue planet Millennium may strike the Earth. Despite our repeated assurances that there is no cause for alarm, civil violence has continued to mount. The death toll is unconscionable; theft, murder, rape—if this frightens those who are listening to this broadcast, *good.* Never in the history of this country have we faced times like these. Attempts at quelling the wave of unacceptable behavior using local police forces and state-empowered National Guard units have failed. As of three o'clock today, the whole of the United States had been placed under twenty-four-hour full military rule. No civilian will be allowed on the street before eight o'clock in the morning or after four o'clock in the afternoon, and those time limits may be shortened at any time in the future without prior notice if and when it is deemed necessary. By presidential decree, the work week is shortened to four days per week and the work hours will be nine until three until further notice. If you are one of the smart ones and still have a job, your employers can advise you as to which four days you should report to work. If you are no longer employed, we strongly recommend that you stay in your homes unless absolutely necessary.

"Armed civilians unable to immediately produce a valid firearm permit will be placed under arrest and transported to holding facilities. Civilians violating the curfew at any time will likewise be placed under arrest. Anyone resisting arrest for any reason will be shot. Looters, rapists, and muggers will be shot on sight. Anyone apprehended during the commission of a murder will be summarily executed. There will be no age distinctions or concessions given during this state of military rule, that is to say that a ten-year-old looter will be shot as quickly as a fifty-year-old. All soldiers have been instructed to shoot to kill, and all corpses will be deposited in mass graves. No next of kin will be notified.

"Folks, if you really think the planet's going to be smacked by an asteroid, then this is a time when people should be sticking together to help one another. Instead, our country—the *world*— has gone mad. It's a sad, sad thing that we have to respond to this terrible behavior with such drastic military retaliation. These are the worst times I've ever seen, and I hope I never live to see them again."

[fade out]

BLACKWELL, OKLAHOMA
MAY 23 . . .

"Frank—Frank, wake up. No-no, stay quiet!" Crystal's lips brushed his ear, her voice barely audible. He was awake instantly, grateful to feel her hand on his chest. If not for that, he might have popped from the driver's seat like a jack-in-the-box. "Someone's outside the car." She moved away from him, sliding carefully away so he would have room to—what? He could start the engine and get the hell out of here, that's what. A dangerous option, though; whoever was out there was surely armed. Did he really want to go screeching into the night with bullets smashing through the back window? There was the military law thing to think about, too. So far they'd been able to get around the curfew by parking the Town Car, which no longer resembled anything that had ever had the word *luxury* attached to it, in secluded spots and staying inside it. First light always woke them, but the darkness seemed to be no problem to whoever was outside now. If that person had a flashlight . . .

His hand moved toward the ignition.

"Don't," Crystal whispered. "Just be really, really still. We'll be all right."

Frank wanted to tell her she was crazy, but he didn't dare. Okay, no flashlight—they'd be using it already. He knew all four doors were locked but he had a terrible, ridiculous urge to turn his head and check, like suddenly being convinced you'd forgotten to turn off the iron. Where were they? He heard the crunch of a heavy step outside and guessed the person was wearing boots . . . Oklahoma, that's right. He'd put the car in reverse and eased it down a footpath he'd found at the rear of a rest area off Interstate 35, had barely gotten the thing to fit. Outside it was a cold country night with puffy clouds scurrying across a sky heavy with stars and a half-moon—way too bright for comfort. If the clouds split, the area would light up like a city park with streetlights. It had been a hard, hard trip; Crystal had been sick a lot for the first four weeks, enough so that he nearly turned back. People were hostile and suspicious, and more often than not he got the impression that Crystal's condition was the only reason they weren't shot when they carefully asked about buying supplies in these small, dusty western towns.

Everything about Frank's body seemed heightened. Beyond the thunderous sound of his heartbeat, the intruder's steps outside felt and sounded like the impact tremors from the T-Rex in that movie *Jurassic Park*. The scent of his skin and Crystal's, both unwashed but familiar and not unpleasant, filled his nostrils so heavily that he became absurdly convinced it was their scent that had drawn the unwanted company to the car to begin with. The air currents in the interior bathed him gently, but that was ridiculous because the only part of the surrounding air that moved was the in- and exhalations from him and his wife. Surely he couldn't be feeling those—

A scream locked in his throat as the door handle on the driver's side vibrated once, then again as the visitor tested it. *Why is it that people always have to try the handle twice to make sure?* Frank wondered numbly. He heard another step in the blackness outside as the person started to leave and he drew a ragged breath—

—as the clouds moved away from the bright moon.

Frank could see his own hand in the moonlight, resting on the bottom of the steering wheel in roughly the seven o'clock position. The grinding step outside hesitated, then returned.

"Don't move," Crystal warned again. Even with his increased sense of hearing, Frank almost missed the instructions. The words were slurred; she was speaking without moving her lips, panting lightly, her breath like the brush of butterfly wings in the dark. "Just pretend you're . . . fading into . . . the car and . . . he can't . . . see you, as long as . . . you don't look . . . at him or . . . meet . . . his eyes."

Frank did what she said because he couldn't think of anything else. The door handle jiggled again, then a face leaned close to the driver's side window, white skin heavy with an untrimmed beard, small eyes above a pudgy, overly wide nose. Any other details were lost because Frank dared not to look to the side to see—

Don't look . . . at him or. . . meet . . . his eyes.

—as the man tilted his head first one way, then the other to get a better look through the window. *Dear God,* Frank thought hysterically, *what is he seeing?*

The face disappeared and Frank tensed, certain that the door window would explode at any second, pulverized by a bullet or a boot, it didn't matter which. The crash never came, perhaps because of the noise it would make; instead Frank's hearing followed the man around the car as he tried all the doors, ending at the passenger side by Crystal. Straining to see without moving his head, he could easily discern the mound of his wife's stomach two feet away, her hands placidly linked just beneath her belly button and clearly highlighted by the stream of moonlight through the windshield. Something shimmered and Frank fought a nearly irrepressible urge to rub his eyes—had he just seen what he thought he had? The skin of his wife's hands and the dark denim of her blue jeans *shifting* to resemble the smooth leather pattern of the front seat?

A minute, an hour later—he didn't know how long—then Crystal was squeezing his leg reassuringly. "We're okay, Frank. He's gone."

Frank blinked and shook his head vigorously. "What did we just do here, Crystal?" he asked. His throat was so dry he could barely speak.

The smooth skin between his wife's eyebrows furrowed in concentration. "I'm not sure, but . . . I think we *camouflaged* ourselves somehow." She turned her head and stared out at the moonlight. "Isn't it amazing? He looked right at both of us but never saw a thing."

"That's preposterous."

"It is," Crystal agreed. "As preposterous as me being five months pregnant, and as preposterous as Dr. Zuriel walking right past us in the driveway the day we left. Remember that, Frank? We never talked about it, but you can't deny it happened."

Frank took a deep breath, held it, then let it out slowly. His wife was right, of course. The same thing *had* happened in Arizona, but neither had brought it up out of fear, disbelief, whatever. He could still remember that morning, the back seat clear for sleeping but the trunk loaded and ready, and he hadn't bothered to call in at the observatory that morning because he didn't care enough about the government bullshit to bother with it anymore. Standing at the front of the car with Crystal, trip checklist in hand, and then there'd been Trent Zuriel, pulling into the driveway, big as you please. Only he hadn't seen them right away because of that big, gangly saguaro by the mailbox, and by the time Zuriel stopped the observatory's van a few feet behind the Lincoln, Crystal and he had been damned near paralyzed with fear. What had kept them that way as Zuriel got out of the van and marched blithely past them to pound on the door to the house was a mystery—amazement, suspicion . . . *instinct*. Although they hadn't left yet, the small stucco house already had that empty feel to it, and Zuriel had picked up on it immediately; ninety seconds later the astronomer was driving away with a furious expression on his pinched face. A minute after that and Frank and Crystal were speeding in the opposite direction toward Interstate 10. And she was right: they'd never once talked about it.

Until now.

"Preposterous," he said again.

"For a scientist, you sure use that word a lot."

"As a scientist, I generally require proof of something out of the ordinary," he said rigidly.

"Okay." He felt her hand close over his and pull his arm toward her. A second later, she pressed his palm against her stomach and he felt something flutter. *Our child,* he thought, and a lump rose in his throat. They'd given up hope over a decade and a half ago, decided that if they couldn't have their own son or daughter, they didn't care to raise someone else's . . . yet here it was.

"Preposterous," Frank whispered into the dark.

CHICAGO, ILLINOIS
MAY 29 . . .

Lamont heard it first.

He'd always assumed that if anyone sounded an alarm in the

middle of the night it would be Gena. Regardless of whatever ability she had to see the future—and damned if that "specialty" didn't fail her when she most needed it—Gena was the blind one among them, the one whose remaining senses were developed far beyond what his or Mercy's or Simon's would ever be. Yet here she was at two in the morning, sleeping soundly on her side of the bed, the warmth of the early spring night having oddly separated them. Gena was always cold, Lamont was always hot; he had pulled the sheet from under the light comforter and draped it carelessly over himself, left the heavier bedcovers to her searching fingers. There was a streetlight not far from the window and he could see her figure in the wan glow that leaked through the split in the curtains, the cold blue light that never failed to look warm against the superb reddish hue of her skin. Gena lay on her side and the comforter was drawn up and over one shoulder; at first Lamont thought that the muffled *thump* he'd heard was her accidentally knocking something off the nightstand as she dragged on the covers—she was always saying there were too many trinkets lying around this place. Then it came again—

—thump—

—and deep within the logic part of his brain it registered that what he was hearing was the sound of a booted foot on the yard-wide strip of soft oak flooring that circled the carpeted part of the living room. The French doors—someone must have jimmied them. Who the hell was in his house?

Something fell to the carpet downstairs, another thud, then a muffled curse. No one ran around after dark anymore without being armed—hell, whether you knew it or not, most people on the street during the day had weapons, military threats or not. Another mishap and the burglars would give up all pretense of being quiet; if it came to that, they'd probably shoot anyone who walked in on them—

"Who's down there?"

Mercy!

Lamont twisted out of bed and found his footing, no longer worrying whether he'd wake Gena. He felt the mattress bounce against the back of one leg as she sat up, then snatched at his pajamas; the material slipped out of her fingers and he couldn't stop to reassure her.

"Lamont—wait!" Gena cried. "I couldn't see—"

"Mercy, don't go downstairs!" he bellowed, charging out of his

bedroom. From the other end of the hallway, Lamont heard
Simon's voice rise in alarm, saw the taller man skid onto the
landing, then barrel toward the stairs at the same time he did.

"Mercy . . . what the heck are you doing?" Both of them
stopped at the top, and Simon looked like he was about to leap
over Lamont.

Mercy was two steps away from the first floor, and she looked
up at them innocently, then managed a lame smile. Below her, the
living room spread into a pool of darkness. "Jeez, guys. I guess I
woke up the whole house just because I thought I heard a noise.
I'm sor—*owww!*"

A hand, sheathed in black leather, seized her by the hair and
hauled her off the stairs.

Lamont and Simon both headed down, then froze at the cold
words that floated from below.

"Hold it right there, or I'll shoot her."

Behind him, Lamont barely heard the door to the master bedroom open as Gena slipped into the hall with them, her steps as
silent as a shadow spilling across the bed. Regardless of her blindness, he wanted instinctively to motion her back, but he wasn't
certain if the gunman—or was there more than one?—would see
him and misinterpret the move. Damn it—if only he could see, he
could do something!

But the only thing visible from the night-light halfway down
the staircase was the hem of Mercy's robe and her slippers. As
they halted, Mercy struggled instinctively against the unseen hold,
then made a choking sound. "Be still, you silly bitch," the voice
snarled.

"Fuck this," Simon growled unexpectedly. He shouldered past
Lamont and gripped the banister. "I know that voice, you bastard.
Why don't you just give it up, Searle? Let her go—didn't you
come for me? Just can't stay away, can you?"

"Ah ah ah—you stop right there, Channy. Don't go doing anything stupid. I brought a couple pals with me for support."

"Who the hell are you?" Lamont demanded. More than one—
he could still deal with it. He couldn't chance taking his gaze off
the area below, but he needed to keep watch on Gena, too. What
was she doing, creeping toward him like that?

"Oh, please. Let *me* do the honors," Simon said sarcastically
from his spot on the stairs. "Lamont, meet my father, Searle
Chanowitz."

Simon's father? For a second, Lamont's brain did a trick on him, twining the past with the present. First he was here and then he was in his parents' condominium, facing off with a man in black who had his brother's voice and a killer's gun. He floundered, mentally and physically—*this man is white and I don't know him*—and when Gena's small brown hand found what she'd been seeking all along and flipped the light switch, he was way too slow in his reaction time.

The man with a neckhold on Mercy yelled in surprise at the same time he jerked his pistol in Lamont's direction and fired. But he had no way of knowing what he was dealing with, or what the faint gray shimmer that swept through the air in front of them meant; the shot went wild and the gun was wrenched from his hand at the same time that Simon scrambled down the remaining steps and grabbed for Mercy. Even with a silencer, the pistol's report still made Gena cry out from behind him, but Lamont didn't have to move a muscle as he disengaged Searle Chanowitz from his son's wife and dragged him backward. When two accomplices lunged forward from the foyer to help their boss, the elder Chanowitz's feet jerked uselessly as he was yanked into midair with his hired help while more weapons seemingly danced away from their owners. A moment later all three guns were unrecognizable lumps on the floor and the burglars were wailing in fear.

Lamont gave them a dark grimace. "How do you like being the victims?"

"Shut up, you stupid fools," Simon snapped at his father and the prowlers. He gripped Mercy's shoulders protectively and Lamont thought he'd never seen so much hatred in Simon's face. "Or do you *want* to draw the soldiers? Remember what they do to burglars nowadays? If you ask me, they'd be doing us all a favor."

Mercy pulled away from Simon, then darted forward with a balled fist and punched Searle sharply in one knee. He yelped and tried to pull away, but there was nowhere for him to escape. "That's for pulling my hair, you—you *animal*." She waved her fist at him and for a second Lamont thought Mercy was going to crack him again, but she turned in a huff and stalked back to Simon. "If you weren't so high up, I'd pull *yours* so you'd know how it felt!"

"What were you doing here, Searle? How did you know where to find me, and what did you want with Mercy?"

"Stuff it, *son*." Searle Chanowitz looked ready to spit. "You want to call the soldiers and have us shot . . . *do it*."

Searle's hired help looked stricken at the suggestion, but Lamont knew Simon would never do such a thing. Simon started to say something in response but Mercy's voice overrode his.

"Where's Gena? I can't believe she'd sleep through all this."

Lamont turned. "She's right here—*Gena!*" His concentration shattered, the older Chanowitz and his companions hit the floor with a crash and a tangle of legs. Weaponless, all three dove for the still-open French doors as Mercy clawed her way past Simon and headed up the stairs toward Gena's crumpled body.

"Hey," Simon bellowed, "you three stop!" But Lamont was helpless, his mind filled with what he'd seen only a second ago.

"Let them go!" Mercy shouted at him. She shoved Lamont out of the way and he fell back against the wall, glimpsed the fleeing backs of the men as they rushed for freedom.

Bastards, he thought. *Let them go? I'll* help *them.* A second later and all three were flung out of sight, as far as he could do it without being able to see. Howls of pain drifted back before Simon darted forward and slammed shut the French doors, then hastily dragged one end of the sofa in front of them as a blockade.

Lamont turned and found enough space to kneel between Mercy and the wall. He moaned at what he saw, and knew it was a good thing that he hadn't gotten a full view of this before he'd decided to toss Searle Chanowitz into the night. Gena, *his* Gena of the feisty temperament and always colorful vocabulary, was silent and unmoving across the hallway floor beneath a bowl-sized hole in the wall that was splattered with red. The right side of her head was a gaping, bloody slash; beneath the scarlet moisture, Lamont thought he saw shards of bone, and dear God, was that gray tissue he was seeing, was that her *brain*—

"She's still breathing," Mercy said. Her fingers, soaked with blood, had found the pulse point on the carotid artery. "But not for long." Her voice was faraway and clinical, oddly distorted. Lamont blinked at her and saw she was chewing viciously at her lower lip.

"Oh, Gena," Lamont murmured. He leaned over to take her in his arms but Mercy's outflung arm stopped him.

"Simon," she said in that same even tone, "would you . . . take Lamont downstairs for a minute, please?"

"What?" Lamont looked frantically from Mercy to Gena's

motionless figure, then up at Simon. The other man bent, put a hand under Lamont's arm, and pulled him to his feet; his face was as white as cotton and his terrified gaze kept darting to Gena. "I can't leave now!" Lamont protested. "I have to stay with her!"

Simon's arm settled casually over his shoulder and steered him away. "I know you're frightened for her," Simon's voice was low, his best attempt at being soothing, "but right now Mercy needs to spend a few minutes with her, just the two of them. Do you understand?"

"No, I—"

"Don't you remember what we talked about that day we all met in the park? When we were in the restaurant having coffee?"

They were all the way down the stairs now and when he looked back up, all Lamont could see was the back of Mercy's bathrobe as she bent over Gena. He couldn't believe he'd let Simon take him into the living room and away from Gena's side when she was so badly hurt, but as his muddled thoughts finally sorted out the memories and began dropping them in place, Lamont understood exactly why he'd instinctively allowed it.

"Wait," Lamont said slowly, "I *do* remember—"

Gazing back over his shoulder despite Simon's efforts to distract him, Lamont thought he saw something flash in front of Mercy, a small thing really, as though the woman had unstopped the tiniest bottle of blue-white lightning. Then it was gone, and he forgot about it forever because the next thing he heard was—

"How do you feel, Gena?"

"Okay, I suppose. I—Mercy, what—what's that all over your lower lip? It looks very . . . bright."

"Why, it's blood. I must've chewed . . . *Gena, can you see me?*"

The silence stretched on and on while he and Simon stared up in shock and heard Gena's voice at last.

"Is this it, Mercy? Is this . . . *red?*"

SAVANNA, IOWA
JUNE 4 . . .

Day by day.

Lily never imagined it would be this hard to get back to Chicago. Guthrie Center and her family were a month and a day behind her and fading fast from her head. She knew the date only because she had a pocket calendar and she'd been X-ing out the days as they passed, careful not to miss one; she didn't think she was going to make it back to the town house before the big hit, but at least she would know when it was due and be as far out in the open as she could get when it happened.

Getting the pocket calendar a few days ago had been a trip in itself, a lot harder than coming up with the small, used motorcycle that had choked and sputtered her toward the Illinois state line. For that she'd only had to blank out her mind and let the dealer and his son use her body for a couple of nights. They hadn't hurt her—much, anyway—and she'd insisted on wearing her jacket the whole time, never forgetting the reassuring feel of the switchblades strapped to each wrist. On the third day, she'd gotten up, dressed, and walked outside; waiting in front of the building was the battered blue Suzuki, its tank full, the engine running like a grumpy old cat. A compact lesson in how to work the clutch—she learned fast and it wasn't that different from farm equipment—and she climbed aboard. The younger guy's hand on her wrist had stopped her; when she met his eyes, he shoved a fistful of cash at her. "For gas," he said tersely. She'd nodded her thanks and sped away, thinking that maybe he wasn't such a bad guy after all. Sometimes the good guys were dressed up like the bad guys, and vice versa.

And sometimes you couldn't tell the difference.

"Hold it right there."

Lily was standing in front of the busted-out picture window of a drugstore in the remains of some tiny no-name town. There wasn't much left of either the store or the town, not even a metal sign announcing what it had been called. There, just inside the windowsill, was what had caught her eye—the silver shine of a plasticized booklet the size of a playing card. She could see the year *2000* printed in white across the top with the words *Calendar and Planner* centered beneath it. And suddenly she wanted that calendar, had to have it so she could figure out how much time she and all the rest of the world had left.

All she had to do was step over the glass-encrusted metal sill and pluck it from the ruins of the display.

Looters will be shot on sight.

For some reason, her mouth went dry. The drugstore was already trashed, the town was empty . . . if she took this tiny booklet, would it make her a looter? She didn't think so . . . but what if someone else did? Someone she couldn't see?

"Hold it right there."

Lily blocked the urge to whirl and stayed where she was, staring at the pocket planner in the debris a few feet away. Its silver coating expanded and filled her vision momentarily: did she want this thing so badly that she would die for it?

She let her head turn in the direction of the voice and saw the soldier. His eyes were dead and cold, the eyes of someone who liked to kill and only needed a reason to make it legal. He didn't wear a name tag and his gun was leveled casually at her waist, as if it were the most natural thing in the world to do. It dawned on her that it *was* natural for him; he'd probably done the same thing a thousand or more times over the past month. "Hi," she said.

"What're you doing there?" He was good-looking and young, maybe twenty-five, a National Guardsman pulled into service for his country from some job at a record store or gardening center. He punctuated his words with little jerks of his rifle. What was it called? M-40? M-80? *Don't be stupid,* Lily thought. *That's a firecracker.* The old Lily would have given this guy the finger, then rushed him; the old Lily would have died. The new Lily wanted very much to live for whatever time was left in the world. Wait— he'd asked her a question. If she didn't answer, he would get pissed. "Just . . . looking." She glanced back into the drugstore and spoke again in a voice that was so much calmer than she felt, beating his next words. "Do you know what the date is?"

"June first." His voice had a flat, trained quality that was dimly terrifying. His eyes narrowed as he studied her. "What're you looking *at?*"

Lily raised one hand and carefully pointed. "That. The little calendar in the right corner."

"That's all?"

She nodded. Her heartbeat was thudding in her ears. Careful, careful . . . but it was such a *small* thing. "Do you think I could have it?"

He was too smart to ask why. "Take your coat off," he said harshly. "I want to see your arms."

He thinks I want to go inside for drugs, Lily thought. If she took off her leather jacket, she was doomed—the same as if she refused. She swallowed and did what he'd ordered, moving slowly so he wouldn't get spooked. Thirty seconds later there she was with her leather on the ground at her feet; to beat the heat under the daytime sun, she wore a mesh shirt above her ripped leggings and nothing else. It was easy to see everything—her small, bare breasts and rib cage beneath the nylon fabric, the skin of her arms that was free of needle tracks, the switchblades taped to the insides of her wrists. Knowing it was idiocy to try to hide them, instead Lily turned her hands palm up so he could see at a glance how they worked. She was helpless before the rifle, anyway.

"I could shoot you for being armed," he said softly.

Lily nodded. "It's just me, by myself. I don't have a gun or anything else. I'm alone." She couldn't think of a better explanation.

He didn't say anything, but he didn't lower his rifle either. After a few moments he stepped around her; she stayed still, listening to the crunch of his boots through the debris behind her as he stepped through the drugstore's window. A moment later his hand came over her shoulder. She flinched without meaning to, but all she saw was the small calendar. "Take it," he said in her ear.

She didn't need to be told again. Her fingers closed eagerly around it and she couldn't stop herself from opening it, flipping backward through September and August—months that might never be—through July to June. There, June first; Thursday, just like he'd said. "Thanks."

He stepped in front of her again, then glanced over at the cycle. "Where'd you find that?"

"I bought it." His eyes fixed on her again, merciless, disbelieving. "I paid for it with my body," she finished. "I did what I had to."

The soldier looked away again, strangely appeased. "We all do. You can put your jacket back on."

Lily wordlessly gathered up the leather and slipped into it, then stood waiting. Finally he motioned toward the Suzuki with the barrel of the riffle. She'd left it running—it was a bastard to restart after it heated up—and her hands were trembling with tension as she walked past him and climbed onto the seat. He stepped close and peered at the odometer for no reason, then plucked the calendar from her hand. She had to bite her lip to keep from protesting, but he only flipped it open to May and drew a big "X" across the whole month with a pencil he pulled from his shirt pocket. After a second, he paged over and drew a shaky circle around July 2.

"The end of the world," Lily whispered. The words slipped out before she could stop them.

The soldier closed the calendar and gave it back to her, then handed her the pencil. "You'll need this."

Nodding, she slipped both into her jacket's breast pocket. She could smell the dirt and perspiration on his skin, the oil along a scalp nearly shaven under the fatigue green hat, all scents of fear and desperation. "Thanks again." Lily revved the engine lightly, but before she could slip it into gear he shouldered the rifle and pulled her close, closing his mouth over hers in a kiss that stopped just short of being painful. Too surprised to fight, she felt his tongue press against her lips; an instant later she opened her mouth and let him probe. It wasn't long before he pulled away, but she never closed her eyes. In the days to come, she would remember the look of pained concentration on his face and wonder if he'd been trying not to cry. When he let her go and backstepped, Lily felt his saliva on her lips but didn't wipe it away.

"You taste like chocolate," she said impulsively.

His mouth stretched into a genuine smile, startling her. Beautiful, clean teeth, and his eyes crinkled at the corners. He shoved a hand into one of the thigh pockets on his pants and came up with two candy bars. Lily caught both automatically when he tossed them. "Enjoy," he said. "Now go on and take off."

She tucked away the candy and raised the kickstand as he started to walk away. "Wait," she called. "What's your name?"

He stopped and turned back, and Lily's heartbeat jittered when she saw that his eyes had gone dark again, twin black holes in his rugged, handsome face. "My name?" The soldier laughed hoarsely. "I don't have one anymore. It's been blasted out of me— just like this town."

I was right, Lily thought. *No-Name, U.S.A.* He stared at her and she felt as if she were sliding back in time. Was it really ten minutes ago and would she have to convince this dangerous man all over again not to kill her?

"I—I think I'll leave now," Lily said.

"That's a good idea. I'm walking my rounds and I don't think you should be here when I get back, because I don't know who I am from one minute to the next anymore. You won't, either."

She nodded and took a shuddering breath, then eased the Suzuki into gear and slowly rode away. Too petrified to look back, her mind was filled with the image of him bringing the rifle to bear and taking careful aim at the center of her back—

Then Lily was on the four-lane that led to the interstate and opening the throttle as wide as it would go, wanting desperately to put as much distance as she could between the soldier and herself. Not much time left before curfew, and something stupid would probably stall her anyway—there were wrecks and homemade roadblocks to go around, more idiots to hide from who weren't, thank God, as dangerous as the man she'd left behind in No-Name.

The end of everything was on its way, and the country was filled with men who had dead eyes and the desire to help speed it along.

Lily thought about the soldier a lot over the next few days, especially each morning when she carefully X-ed out another day. The thought crossed her mind once or twice that maybe she should go back, talk to him, keep him company. And then what? Lily Randolph, Saver of Soldiers' Souls? She sneered at the notion and kept going. Leave the saving to Mercy.

By the time she reached Savanna, Iowa, Lily was wrung dry. The thing with the soldier had cost her more than she'd realized— an erosion of confidence, a double shot of unexpected fear. Who would have thought that crossing the farm country of Iowa could be so difficult? She'd been shot at twice by genuine American good ol' boys, and one of the bullets had gouged her a good one across her upper back, leaving her bruised and stiff. The only thing that'd saved her was the heavy jacket, and she'd still lost a few ounces of flesh. Dressed like a punk, riding a whining motorcycle like a small, skinny hellion, no weapons but two trusty-rusty old switchblades, and never stopping—shit, why *bother* to waste ammunition on her? Target practice, she thought grimly. Something that moved fast enough to be a challenge and was a sight more interesting than a chittering squirrel or terrorized rabbit.

Savanna reminded her of Guthrie Center in a roundabout way. Small, close-knit, it hadn't quite deteriorated into a shooting gallery and seemed a few months away from becoming a ghost town like No-Name. There were soldiers, of course—they were everywhere—and they watched her constantly, but she stayed away from the stores with carelessly boarded windows and made a point of openly going to the only still-functioning grocery and filling station, a sad-looking mom 'n' pop outfit dead center in the town. She used the rest of her money to fill the Suzuki's tank, emptying every pocket she had to find the last nickel. The elderly woman behind the counter nodded and swept it away without comment, then studied her as Lily shuffled her feet nervously in front of the counter.

Lily knew she was a mess—her face and hands were streaked with road dirt and mud, the shoulder of her jacket was crusted with dried blood from the skim wound across her back. On top of everything else, she had a head cold—who could've believed that such normal things like that would still pester people at a time like this? She sniffed and wiped her nose on the back of her hand, then cleared her throat and tried to remember how to talk politely. "Uh . . . ex-excuse me, ma'am." Her voice was hoarse from disuse—she hadn't talked to anyone since that nightmarish soldier. "I—I guess I'm, uh, out of money." She glanced around the store and saw that the shelves were almost bare; she'd get no charity here. She hesitated, then kept going. "Is there anything—I mean, any*where* to get something to eat? I could work for it . . . sweep up, or wash dishes . . . " Lily looked at her fingernails, rimmed with black dirt, and felt like a fool; the old woman was cleaner than she was, but not by much. Who cared anymore?

"The army," the woman rasped, surprising her. "They got a tent with a soup kitchen on the east edge of town." Lily nodded her thanks and noted that the shopwoman's small, watery eyes were still bright blue, sharp with intelligence. "But they'll only feed you once," she warned. "I've heard they get a mite . . . nasty to roadie civilians if'n they don't move along after the meal."

"I'll keep that in mind."

Under a canvas tent erected to hold back the hot noon sun, Lily shared a table with a half-dozen soldiers and one other roadie, a jumpy little man with skin that sagged under his jawline and along his arms, evidence of a lifelong plumpness quickly depleted by his new existence. She didn't talk to him and he didn't try to talk to her. Lily made herself eat slowly and concentrate on her meal, determined to savor the feel if not the taste of the food in her mouth. Her bowl was filled with a sort of soup-stew made up mostly of potatoes and onions; a few chunks of unidentified meat floated in it and she ate those, too. It might be pork, it might be horse or dog; as long as it wasn't human and it was cooked, she didn't care.

Curfew was a problem. Pushing the cycle to the tent to ration her gasoline, standing patiently in line, and then eating had taken nearly three hours, and somehow Lily thought it might be a bad idea to ask the soldiers at the table with her where she could go for the night. There were just as many female soldiers, but they seemed worse than the men, more suspicious and sly, better at disguising the viciousness inside. No, she would have to find someplace to go on her own, without making it any more obvious to the military around her that she was a stray, a roadie without shelter for the coming curfew.

Lily finished her food and obediently carried the metal bowl and spoon back up front, where some flunkie in a stained apron took both, dunked them a few times in a bucket of soapy gray water, then tossed them back at the front of the food line. She walked back to the Suzuki, her gut uneasy about the coming evening. Usually she was on the open road when curfew hit, where it was easy to hide herself and the cycle amid the overgrown thickets and bushes that edged the farms along the interstate—all she had to do was be careful she didn't encroach on someone else who was doing the same. Today, however, hunger and the need for gasoline had driven her close to too many people; if she rode out of town now, a couple of the soldiers would probably follow her, just for the fun of bringing her down when four o'clock hit.

Lily steered the bike back toward town without starting the engine, knowing she was being watched and that her choice of direction would make it seem like she had a place to go. Heading up the main street, she turned off as soon as she was out of sight of the soup tent, pushing the cycle and putting as much purpose into her step as she could. With her stomach filled for the first time in days, the roadwear was finally weighing her down; right now all Lily wanted to do was sleep. A great concept—but first she needed a safe place to do it.

Four blocks off the main drag put her in a mini-industrial area, blocky single-story buildings that in better times had housed machine shops and small businesses. Lily turned the Suzuki down an alley and trudged along for another third of a block, then veered into the back parking and loading area of one of the bigger buildings. A car, a dirty white Ford, was already parked there, but no one was inside and the doors were all locked. When she walked around the beat-up vehicle and placed her palm on the hood, she found it was warm—the engine had been running not so long ago. She peered through the driver's window again and considered breaking into it. Risky, but this time she was sure no one was around . . . then again, maybe this Ford was someone's home. She could see nothing on the front seat, no clothes or food wrappers, the kind of travel shit that travelers always ended up with, yet Lily had the oddest feeling there were people inside, and that she just couldn't see them . . .

She shrugged and let it be. Who was she to break into someone's car, anyway? If she was caught, they'd probably shoot her and she couldn't blame them. She'd worn a watch, a cheap generic thing, since the curfews had gone into effect, and checking it showed there was only twenty minutes left. The patrols would start at four sharp, and she needed to be inside somewhere by then. Scanning the small parking area, Lily stopped when she saw a couple of the big trash bins by the corner of the building. She hurried over and threw the lid back on the one closest to the wall; the dry, stale smell of old paper and dust filled her nostrils and made her sneeze—bingo! No rotting food garbage, just old packing materials like cardboard, crumpled paper, and foam nuggets. As far as she was concerned in was in, and what did it matter if her "in" was a Dumpster or a building? A couple more minutes to rearrange both bins so that they'd have to be moved before they could be picked up by a loader, then she stashed her cycle behind one where it couldn't be seen from the street and climbed inside.

Lily woke in the morning feeling like a baked potato. Her sinuses were thoroughly plugged and the air inside the bin was heated and stifling—apparently the back of the building faced east and the sun had crested the roof across the alley. She lifted the heavy metal lid and peered out cautiously, thinking she finally knew what a rat felt like as it nosed its way out of a garbage can, always watching for a prowling tomcat. The Ford still sat twenty feet away—

But now there were people in it.

An entire family, man, woman, two quiet kids. Lily watched them narrowly, wondering how the hell they could've gotten out of wherever they'd been hiding and into that car without her hearing them. She'd slept well, but not deeply—sound sleep was a luxury she'd lost and doubted would ever be regained. Something would have roused her—a soft footstep, a cough, the quiet sound of a car door latching. Unless . . . they'd never gotten out of the car in the first place.

The alarm nerves were singing in her head, but they were

tinged with a deep, uncontrollable curiosity. She *had* to know how these people had eluded her, had virtually passed right under her nose. Damn it, if she couldn't find out any other way, she'd go right up and ask them.

Without taking her eyes from the Ford, Lily raised the metal lid on her trash bin. If she could get it most of the way open before they saw it or before she had to let it drop back against the wall, she could cover the distance from here to the Ford before the man could start the car and take off. There were four of them and one of her . . . she was clearly outnumbered, so maybe they'd be willing to talk for a minute. An inch, then two, while the man and the woman talked animatedly in the front seat; to Lily, their words were vague murmurs floating across the small lot. When she tried to bring the lid up another few inches, Lily was dismayed to hear the metal hinge behind her *screech* in response. In the car, all four occupants froze.

Then, in front of Lily's disbelieving eyes, they simply . . . faded from sight.

"What?!" She pushed the lid all the way back and clambered out, not caring when it crashed against the wall behind her. Never losing sight of the now-empty car, she jumped down and sprinted to the driver's door. *Empty.*

"This is crazy," she said out loud. She circled the car, then did it again. "I know what I saw." But did she?

Frustration made Lily yank futilely on the driver's handle, which was as locked as it had been last night. "Damn you, I *know* you're in there!" She leaned forward and gazed through the window again, but there was nothing—only the unbroken expanse of the stained white vinyl seats. Backing up, Lily spied a fist-sized rock next to the loading dock and picked it up. Returning to the Ford's driver-side window, she hefted the rock thoughtfully. Should she break the window? She had no real compulsion to do so except—

Something moved beyond the glass, the faintest shadow. Lily caught a glimpse of a man's face, staring forward, deep in concentration—the only giveaway was a tiny, scared movement of his eye as it followed the up-and-down movement of the rock in her hand. She stared, fascinated, and spied the outline of his body; then it filled in with the background of the car's interior, like seeing a tide roll in on a beach using faint time-lapse photography. "Oh!" she said in surprise. She dropped the rock and put a hand to her mouth. Jesus—they were like . . . chameleons or something, lizards that could take on the colors of their surroundings! She stood there indecisively for a few minutes, wondering if they'd realize she posed no further threat, wondering if they cared. On her cheek and arm, the sun's heat quickly built. It had to be hot in the car . . . surely they wanted to get out, walk around, stretch, pee, *something*. Were they so afraid that they'd risk heatstroke rather than face her?

Lily shook her head and turned away. It didn't have to come to that—she had no use for the information, but she'd found out what she wanted to know. The ability to camouflage themselves—certainly an amazing, useful talent. She forced the trash bins aside and rolled out the Suzuki, her gaze going back to the car time and time again without conscious will. Once she thought she saw something shift in the back seat—it must be harder for kids to stay motionless. Within five minutes of her discovery, she was comfortably astride the motorcycle and headed east and out of Savanna forever.

LITCHFIELD, ILLINOIS
JUNE 10 . . .

Well, it wasn't Texas, but it was as far southwest as they were going to get tonight.

At least they were out of the city. The more he thought about it, the more Joey decided that Alva had been right to push them away from there. The closer they came to July second, the crazier everyone was getting; Litchfield wasn't exactly paradise, but the people seemed okay and nobody had shot at their car when they'd guided it down the dusty driveway next to the spray-painted sign that declared WELCOME TO STAY THE NIGHT. Alva hadn't wanted to stop, but Joey had insisted. It was good to be suspicious, but it was a half hour from curfew with an army barracks only two miles behind them. They could take their chances here or with the trigger-happy servicemen.

Joey drove in and pulled over not too far from where the driveway ended in a huge clearing that looked like it had once been a county fairgrounds. Getting out of the car, he and Alva discovered a place that was the nearest thing to a commune either of them had ever seen. Children ran everywhere with barking dogs, adults milled around makeshift tents, cars and ridiculously painted vans were parked haphazardly around a hand-operated water pump.

Everyone seemed happy and carefree and Joey found himself scowling as he stood next to his woman and watched all these fools. Did they think it was some kind of big back-to-fucking-nature adventure or what?

"Relax," Alva murmured. "You wanted to stop here so bad, now you look ready to kill someone."

He opened his mouth to retort, then realized she was right—again. Incredibly, no one paid any attention to them, and they stood and watched as the people in the clearing—there had to be close to a hundred—ran around in a sort of organized chaos until their numbers began to thin. A pregnant woman with shining, strawberry-blond hair hurried by them with a squalling baby in her arms, then paused and looked back over her shoulder. "You're new here," she said as she bounced the toddler on her hip, trying unsuccessfully to quiet him. "You'll need to be in a tent or inside your car by curfew. The army sends a jeep around a couple of times every night to check." She shifted the baby again, then went on her way.

Joey watched her speculatively for a few seconds, then he and Alva wordlessly went to the trunk and pulled out their tent, sleeping bags, and a few supplies. Over the last six weeks they'd gotten proficient at setting up for the night; in less than fifteen minutes everything was assembled and they'd each had a chance to duck into the bushes before being stuck inside until tomorrow morning.

"What do you think of this place?" Alva asked when they were safely inside and watching the quickly emptying clearing from behind the tent's screening. Like them, many of the other folks had gone inside their tents but left the main flaps open to the fresh air. It was strange to hear to much noise—the canvas and nylon tents did nothing to muffle sound—but see not a soul or animal outside. And the dogs—the last time he'd seen one of those had been on the side of the highway with its head missing and a bunch of crows pecking at the remains. Living on the road had inexplicably quieted his companion; while the new Alva was calmer, Joey wasn't sure he liked her as much as the foulmouthed but always interesting Chicago Police sergeant. At least she was still a good lay.

"Let's see how it goes," Joey said thoughtfully. "The people seem to mind their own business, so I suppose that's a vote in their favor. But I thought you wanted to get away from others entirely."

"I'm not sure total isolation is a good idea." Next to him, Alva rolled onto her back, then shifted to get away from a pebble somewhere underneath the thin floor of the tent and her sleeping bag. "What if one of us gets sick? Or hurt? We should be close to somewhere we can ask for help if we need to." Her mouth turned down. "I'd thought it would be better to find a farmhouse and hole up in it, but all the owners seem to have the same idea and I'd rather not get my head blown off trying to move in on someone's property. There's a good source of water, we've got a trunk with enough food to get us through the next month and a half. No one came up and demanded anything from us—they seem to have their own supplies and shit. If they'll let us stay here, why not?"

Joey shrugged and didn't answer. Peering through the mesh covering the doorway, he could see dozens of other tents spread around the water pump like spokes on a wheel. More people than he'd seen since they'd left the city, more . . . *supplies*. He hadn't had much of a chance to study everything, but it seemed so happy and homey and . . . out of *place,* like something set up by a 1960s peace-and-love hippie dope grower.

He wondered how many of them had guns.

"I want to move on," Crystal said. Joshua, the eight-month-old she'd watched for a couple of hours in return for a two-ounce bottle of shampoo, had been returned to his mother; now dusk was falling and the army jeep had already been around twice to make sure no one was wandering on the campgrounds. The newcomers, a black man and hard-eyed blond woman, had set up their tent about a hundred feet away, but Crystal imagined she could still feel the guy's stare assessing her. Something about him and the way his eyes had tracked her really creeped her out.

Now Frank looked at her in surprise. "But I thought you liked it here," he said. "All the stories coming in say that Chicago is a hellhole now—everyone's killing everyone else, bodies piled in the streets, armed guards at every corner. Don't tell me you still want to go there!"

"For heaven's sake, Frank—lower your voice." Crystal shook her head. "No, of course I don't want to head into the city. It's just that I have a—a feeling about . . ." Her words faded away.

"About what?"

She chewed at a fingernail, then realized what she was doing—

unsanitary. "It's that couple that came in toward the end of the afternoon. The black guy and the white woman."

Frank raised an eyebrow. "I've never known you to have a problem with that."

She sighed impatiently, then rubbed the oversized swell of her stomach to calm herself. "My problem is not with them together, it's with them being here at *all*. There's something wrong about them that I can't identify."

Frank snorted and she wanted to smack him. "That's pretty ambiguous, honey. There's something wrong about nearly everyone around us—we're homeless, verging on hysteria, and paranoid—which is exactly how you're acting, by the way."

"Exactly." She stared at him, trying valiantly to keep her voice from shaking. Her terror must have bled through, though, because Frank's tolerant expression melted into alarm and he reached for her.

"Hey," he said, trying to be soothing. "Take it easy. We'll be okay—look how well we're doing. We never expected to make it this far, remember?"

"Then why am I acting this way now when this morning I was fine?" Crystal hugged herself, chilled in spite of the overwarm interior of the tent. "It's *instinct,* Frank, a self-preservation reaction because of that couple and the way they—*he*—looked at me when I warned them about the jeep that the army sends around. His eyes when he stared at me, the way he stood there and watched me walk past, all without saying a single word . . .

"He made me feel like . . . *prey*."

CHICAGO
JUNE 15 . . .

"We're going to have to be really careful," Gena said nervously. "Really, *really* careful. I can't tell—"

"We'll be fine," Lamont said from the passenger seat. His voice was calm, but Gena thought she could detect the undercurrent of tension. "It's early, the streets are filled with military personnel, and we're going for what's probably going to be our final shopping trip."

"Remember what the news reports said about hoarding," Mercy said.

"I do. But no one can deny that we're shopping for four people, and lots of folks are sharing rides. We should be okay as long as we don't overdo it. I know we decided this was a trip for milk and eggs, bread, vegetables, and whatnot, but don't just get the perishables. Buy dry stuff, too. There's plenty of food in the pantry, as many nonperishables as I've been able to pack in there since Gena first told me about Millennium, but we don't want anyone to look in our carts and suspect we've got a good supply of stuff already, maybe follow us back. We're well stocked, thanks to Gena. She knew we wouldn't be able to get supplies that close to the . . . uh, beginning of the month."

End, Gena thought. He'd been about to say *end.* It didn't take a psychic to figure that out, though . . . which was a damned good thing, since every ability she'd ever had to see the future had disappeared with the gunshot wound two weeks ago and the return— or the *birth*—of her eyesight.

It was all so . . . strange. The clarity of her real world vision flipped in and out; sometimes everything was sharp and crystalline, sometimes things were so fuzzy at the edges it strained her eyes and gave Gena a headache. She still got flashes of intuition, teasers, though nothing at all resembling the full view of the future that she was used to. She had nothing to compare it with, so she couldn't answer Mercy's urgent questions—

Do you think you're seeing fifty percent? Or seventy-five?
Can you see far away?
Is everything close in focus?
Gena had no idea.

"How about here?" Simon's voice pulled her back to the present and she gazed out the window as he steered the Blazer into a crowded parking lot. A grocery store, of course, although she had no idea what the sign said—it had shocked her to realize that while she could read braille with her fingertips, she couldn't read the signs on a street or building. And buildings were another thing— she'd had the definition of big taught to her as a child, but never truly understood the concept until now. All those lessons— how completely ridiculous to think you could explain a ten-story building to a person who'd never been able to see! Plus she'd had no idea that things actually got bigger as they got closer—*perspective.*

"What . . . what does the sign say?" Gena asked.

"Treasure Island," Lamont answered promptly. "I think they call it that because they stock—or used to, anyway—a lot of exotic things that grocery stores like Jewel and Dominick's don't carry." He pointed at something out the window. "Can you see the yellow flowers planted around the edges of the curbs down there? Those are tulips."

Tulips, yellow, islands and treasures—so much to take in so soon. Sighted people never realized how much they took for granted. Colors, shapes, what things *were*. When she'd finally gotten her bearings after the injury, Gena had run from item to item in the town house and gotten herself disoriented all over again. The thing that had most overwhelmed her had been the bookcase, all those volumes of tiny scribblings that she couldn't decipher, bright photographs of hundreds, no thousands of things she couldn't identify because she simply didn't know what they *looked like*. What's this? And this? Abstract concepts like downstairs and upstairs—how could she ever again climb the stairs with her eyes closed and feel safe now that she truly knew what being *up* meant?

Her gaze skimmed the tulips and went back to the front of the store. Today her vision was soft around the edges, what Mercy called "blurry," but she could easily make out the line of people waiting to go inside, the rigid stance of the soldiers stationed outside each entrance. Lamont had told her that the things in the soldiers' hands were army-issued rifles called M-16s, and also that he thought the bullet that had tried to chew away part of her head had been fired from something called a 9mm pistol; he'd shown her a drawing in a book, but it hadn't meant anything to her, just flat lines on paper.

"It's as good as anywhere else," Mercy said. "And we haven't been here before." More unspoken tension; Gena hadn't lost the ability to read voices . . . yet.

Simon got lucky and found a parking space when someone in front of him started backing out; within three minutes the four of them were standing at the back of the line. "I think it'll go fairly fast," he said optimistically. He craned his head and tried to see past the row of people in front of them. "It's hard to read from here, but I think the signs say no more than six of any one item."

"Then we all get no more than four of whatever items you pick out." Lamont kept his voice low. "We should split up—"

"I'll go with Gena," Mercy said quickly. "Women always shop together."

Lamont and Simon cast worried looks at each other, but in the end there was nothing else they could do.

• • •

The inside of the grocery store was like the inside of one of the picture books at the town house.

Row upon row of cans, bottles, boxes, but with lots of gaps in the shelves that Mercy told Gena weren't there before Millennium had come onto the scene. But there were so *many* things in there now that it was difficult for Gena to grasp that there had been more, boxes stacked up the ceiling, cases and cases of soda, crates of spaghetti sauce and stacked risers of plastic-wrapped bread. Unable to read and with her sight so blurred, Gena had to hold each item a few inches from her nose, wondering if she seemed like an idiot not for doing that—poor eyesight excused a lot of things—but because of her selections. With nothing else to go by, she was obviously drawn to the things with the most colorful pictures on them. Mercy stayed close and when the pictures failed Gena, her friend was always ready with an answer.

"That's lychee fruit," Mercy said from behind her. "It's Chinese, very sweet. Personally, I don't care for it—it has a strange texture that's unlike any other food."

Gena didn't know if it was the comment about the fruit's texture—now there was something she could appreciate—or a tinge of rebellion that made her pull four cans of the stuff from the shelf. She'd try it herself, make an independent decision. If she hated it, well . . . with hard times to come, they might eat it anyway; if she loved it, these might be the last four times she ever had it.

It took another hour to finish and go through the line. They all paid cash—something else Lamont had made sure he had available. A wise move, considering the sharp increase in prices; the stores insisted it was because demand was high and shipments were expensive, but everyone knew the retailers were hovering just below the line of price gouging. They'd agreed in advance not to overfill their carts and Gena's groceries barely filled hers to the top, yet the bill came to nearly three hundred dollars. *Oh no,* Gena thought sourly as she carefully counted out the bills, *you guys aren't taking advantage of anyone. I'm used to paying two bucks for a can of green beans.*

Gena felt an immense relief when everything was loaded into the back of the Blazer, covered with a dark blanket, and they were finally pulling out of the store's parking lot. Despite the newly acquired sight and armed soldiers in and outside the building, she hadn't felt safe in there; all those people—the soldiers, the cashiers and baggers, the shoppers—reminded her of people creeping along the edge of a crevice who were convinced that someone was going to push them over at any moment. Muscles tense, gazes darting everywhere—she'd accidentally bumped one woman's cart and apologized, then heard the lady muttering epithets under her breath for a full five minutes afterward.

Back in the Blazer, she could try to relax at last, despite being convinced that the curiously empty Chicago streets were secretly very much alive—Gena could sense eyes on them from a thousand angles, assessing the Blazer and wondering about what was inside. Her vision had sharpened again and she wondered if the blurriness had to do with the stress of the shopping expedition. Overhead, the sun had disappeared behind a sluggishly gathering layer of gray-bottomed storm clouds, and she never tired of watching the fluffy formations as the wind changed their shapes. This time Lamont had put her in the front seat and she found the release lever and let the seatback tilt so she could see the sky better. So pretty—

"Simon," Lamont said, "I think we're being followed. No, don't anyone turn around and look. Just keep looking straight ahead."

Gena jerked upright as Simon's eyes narrowed and began flicking to the rearview and side mirrors. He drove straight on Broadway for a couple more blocks, then flicked on the right turn signal and turned at random down a side street.

"Did they follow?" Mercy asked nervously.

"Yes." Simon's voice was grim.

Gena's hands gripped her knees through her blue jeans. *Damn it!* If she hadn't lost her second sight, she would have known this was coming, been able to tell Lamont that they shouldn't go shopping today, or perhaps to choose a different grocery store. Now she was as helpless as anyone else, at the mercy of . . . what? God? The idea was anything but comforting to her.

"Turn again," Lamont said.

Simon obeyed. "They're right with us."

"They must have watched us load up," Mercy said. "We can't let them follow us back to the town house."

Simon's hands were tight on the steering wheel. "I hate to bring this up, but this Chevy is six years old. It'll go a lot of places a regular car won't, but I can guarantee we won't win in a high-speed chase. I'm a social worker, not a NASCAR driver."

Gena opened her mouth to ask what such a thing was, then closed it again. She felt absurdly like a child, along for a scary ride with no responsibility or say about her destiny. Faced with the prospect of life after Millennium, she thought she'd rather have her second sight back than try to survive without it in the coming months; until now, seeing the strain on her friends' faces and feeling her own fear pulsing through her body, she had never considered how much she had depended upon that hateful gift. Not knowing if what they were about to do would succeed in saving themselves was devastating.

"We can deal with it." Lamont's voice was calm, but Gena thought she heard a note of reluctance in it. Even now he hated using his gift, feared being discovered by someone he couldn't trust, dreaded being singled out as some kind of freak. Poor man; common sense would let anyone in the truck predict how dependent upon him they would all soon be. He scooted to the center of the back seat and leaned forward until he had an unobstructed view out of the back windshield. "Go down the next alley you see, but make sure it's empty and that there's a way out the other end."

Simon nodded and slowed, then chose an alley between a row of large apartment buildings facing north and a street of two- and three-flats that faced south. Narrow and quiet, the alleyway was riddled with trash because garbage collections had fallen off. "The car's full—two men in the front seat, three in the back."

"Then they're probably planning on taking the truck itself," Mercy said.

"And us?" It was the first thing Gena had said since leaving Treasure Island's parking lot. Her question was met with silence—how shocked they must be to hear her ask about the future!

When it became apparent that neither Lamont nor Mercy were going to answer, Simon cleared his throat as he slowly guided the Blazer down the alley. The car behind them was three buildings away and closing. "We'd be . . . disposable."

"Pick a gangway and pull over next to it like we're going to park and unload," Lamont instructed. "That's what they're waiting for."

"You don't actually want them to get out of the car, do you?" Mercy asked, alarmed. Simon was already angling the Blazer to the right, making it look as though they were leaving room on the left for the other car to drive around. "They might have guns."

"They probably do. But I have no intention of letting them get any of the doors open. I do need to see everything up close, though."

"They're stopping," Simon said quietly. His gaze was locked on the side mirror. "They seem awfully far back."

"Gena, open your door—but don't get out."

Lamont had kept his position in the middle of the back seat, using the rearview mirror as his "eyes" behind the Blazer. There was no question that she would do what he said, but her hand was shaking so violently it took three tries to grab the door handle. It seemed that another "benefit" of eyesight for her was anxiety; she could no longer take chances that would have been mundane a month ago. She ground her teeth, raging at herself inside. *Do it, you fucking coward!* Finally she grasped the metal and pulled; Simon had parked close and the door swung open and banged against the bricks of the building.

"Here they come," Simon said suddenly.

"Show time." Startled to hear him sound so bitter, Gena glanced at Lamont as he turned ninety degrees on his seat and stared openly out the back window.

The car pulled up noiselessly behind them—no screaming acceleration or screech of brakes to alert them. Did they really believe the Blazer's occupants hadn't seen them? Or did they merely not care? The latter was obviously the case, because as the rest of them followed Lamont's lead, they could clearly see the man on the passenger side of the car, a blocky-looking Dodge with rust holes in the front fenders, hold up a shotgun. Gena could tell by the way the men inside the Dodge were leaning that they were reaching for the door handles. A quick look at Lamont and she saw him frown, then the view across the back window vibrated, as though something had sent a shimmy of heat waves between the two vehicles. Her hearing remained more sensitive than the others' and she could detect the shouts of surprise as the men inside the other car began to pound on the windows. Then the driver gave them a murderous glare and the Dodge jerked as he put it in DRIVE.

"I don't think so, mister." Lamont sounded like he was talking to himself. "Let's make sure you *and* your car stay there awhile, shall we?"

The air filled suddenly with the harsh noise of metal bending as the driver's side of the automobile behind them began to rise. Two feet, three, until the entire car shifted and moved over and there was the Dodge, its pocked copper paint glinting dully as it settled heavily on the passenger side in the center of the alley, all of four seconds later. No one had to struggle to hear that the angry words of the men inside the Dodge had changed to hoarse screams of fright.

"Time to split," Simon said matter-of-factly. "Before they untangle themselves and break out a window. Gena, you can close your door now." He'd never taken the Blazer out of gear and now he pressed the accelerator and spun away at the same time as Gena yanked her door shut and pressed down on the lock. As they cleared the opposite end of the alley and left it behind, he let a small, relieved smile spread across his face. "That's it—we're clear."

"Home free, guys!" Beside Lamont in the back seat, Mercy was grinning. "Before they pull the car down, they'll have to figure out a way to move it over. Otherwise it's just going to fall through the garage next to it. That was *stunning,* Lamont. To be able to do things like that is going to be so useful—"

The others babbled on while Gena stared out the window. *Useful* . . . now there was a word. What was she doing here with all these people who still had the most marvelous and *useful* gifts? She no longer had anything to contribute to their safety or well-being. In a fraction of a second—the time it had taken for that bullet to carve a path through the side of her head—Gena had become the opposite of everyone else in the car: she was use*less.* She had no experience in the sighted world, no judgment—she couldn't even *read,* for Christ's sake. She was a twenty-nine-year-old toddler who had to be looked after, guarded and protected, *baby-sat* all the time. She had gained the ability to see, but become the worst of all possible things in payment—

A liability.

"You okay, sweetheart?" Lamont reached forward and rubbed her shoulder.

"Fine," she said. "I'm fine." Gena thought she saw Simon glance sharply in her direction, but her vision was starting to blur again and she couldn't be sure.

She couldn't be sure of *anything* anymore.

JUNE 19 . . .

Doomsday was twelve days away.

"Do you remember me telling you about my nephew, Ryan?"

For a moment Searle looked at her uncomprehendingly, then the memory clicked home. "Yeah, sure—the kid that Simon's girlfriend did the miracle patch job on in the emergency room."

Erica nodded.

"What about him?"

She looked down at her desk, then ran a finger over the wood. It came away dusty; most of her cleaning staff had quit, and she had let them go without protesting. Fewer mouths to feed; if she had to expend supplies on people, better it should be medical personnel. "I would like to . . . have him brought here," she said slowly. She raised her gaze to Searle's but kept it neutral. "I've convinced my brother that the boy would be better off here at the hospital if something happens with this asteroid thing. That he would be less of a problem . . . safer." She knew Searle thought she was an idiot for not succumbing to the Millennium panic, but what did he think about her wanting to bring Ryan to Althaia? She found out immediately.

"What the hell do you want a kid running underfoot for?" Searle scowled. "He'll be into everything, jabbering all the time—"

"I want him with me," Erica said stiffly, "because he's the only family I have that I care about."

Searle made a face, but at least he shut up. He pulled a toothpick from the pocket of his shirt and slipped it between his lips. "All right."

"Here's the address." She'd already printed it on a plain sheet of paper, and now Erica pushed it across the desktop. "His mother is less than thrilled about this arrangement. If she's home when you get to their house, it would be best if you didn't linger."

Searle nodded and picked up the paper. "And the father? Any special *skills* you haven't told me about?"

She shook her head and ignored the sarcasm. It was unfortunate that he still blamed her for the fiasco that had happened at Lamont London's home at the end of last month. Nothing she had said could convince him to go back, so after a while Erica stopped trying; he would believe what he wanted and in all frankness, Mercy Ammon probably despised her. "He will be expecting you," Erica assured him. "He's more than happy to have Ryan staying elsewhere for the remainder of the summer. I tried to assure Mickee that Ryan would be back home in plenty of time for the start of his school year at the end of August, but she's being rather uncooperative about the summer plans."

Searle arched one eyebrow. "I wouldn't think she'd have to agree to it if she didn't want to," he commented.

"My brother . . . insisted." Searle was a smart man, sometimes smarter than he let the average person know; Erica saw by the flicker in his eyes that he understood the implications of what she'd said. She was truly sorry to have exposed Mickee to her brother's methods of persuasion, but . . . better her than the boy. Brother or not, if things did get bad, Stan's behavior would deteriorate rapidly. Soon he'd blame Ryan for everything short of the asteroid itself; no doubt he'd start by claiming his son was the reason that the family was unable to go to a safe haven—as fabricated an excuse as ever existed, but where was the logic in the mind of a person like that in dealing with a child? For years Mickee had insisted Stan was "getting help"; now that the pummeling had expanded to include their son, she was a petrified ghost of the bright-eyed bride she'd been a decade ago. Occasionally Erica wondered what the outcome would have been if Mercy hadn't come along in the emergency room slightly under two years ago. Since then, the Zimmermanns' family life had improved, but only marginally. "Stan mentioned that Ryan would be ready right after lunch," Erica said. "His suitcase is supposed to be waiting." She didn't add that Stan was already complaining about the boy being underfoot now that schools were closed for the summer. When she'd called the house, she could hear the tension in Stan's voice; somewhere in the background, Ryan had been crying. It would be best if she could get him out of there as soon as possible. "Maybe you could—"

"I'll have him back here at one-thirty."

Due to After Help and the workload it generated, it had been nearly a year since she'd seen Ryan. Erica was uncomfortable around her brother and his wife, and she seldom visited. The hospital consistently provided her with the best excuse for holidays—everyone knew those were the busiest times in emergency rooms—and she'd learned to skirt other invitations so efficiently that they were seldom extended anymore. Looking now at the pale, thin child standing so quietly next to Searle, Erica damned herself for not thinking of her nephew instead of herself.

She went around her desk and walked over to him. It was impossible not to see the way his eyes tracked her, the gaze of prey measuring the danger of a possible predator. "Hello, Ryan," she said gently. "How are you?"

"Okay."

Erica glanced at Searle and he shrugged. "He don't say much."

She had little experience with children. The pediatrics ward in the hospital was like a foreign land to her, visited only when public relations or political intervention was required. Time for a crash course. The small dark-haired boy standing in front of her was a stranger, but he was six years old and she had paid help; how hard could it be? "We're going to have a fun summer. Would you like that?"

"This is a hospital," Ryan said. "How much fun can it be?"

"Watch your mouth, kid," Searle snapped. "Don't get smart with your aunt."

Erica bit back the urge to tell Searle to stay out of it and made a mental note to say something later. Searle hadn't been there and wouldn't understand that Ryan's last memory of this place was anything but pleasant. Right now she said nothing; it wouldn't be good for the boy to think he could manipulate either one of them. She'd heard tales of how children played adults against each other, going to the other for permission to do something the first had denied. Behavior like that was the basis for shelves of psychology books. Erica was surprised at how much older than six Ryan seemed; then again, a child grew up fast in a family like Stan's.

"It won't be so bad," she said. "You'll have your own room, and there's lots to see and do. It's not only sick people here, you know."

Ryan cast a furtive glance at Searle but said nothing, and Erica sighed inwardly. Already off to bad start. She put her hand on his shoulder and was gratified that he didn't flinch. "I've got a room ready for him next to ours in the private quarters," she told Searle. "Take him down there and see that he gets settled in, please."

Searle looked like he wanted to protest, then decided against it and picked up the child's suitcase. Still silent, he put a hand on Ryan's elbow and turned him toward the door. "Once you're unpacked, I'll stop by and see if you need anything," Erica called. "We'll have dinner together and talk about what you can do while you're here." Her nephew nodded without speaking and Erica watched them go, then frowned as they crossed the threshold of the door and went out of sight. Had she imagined seeing Searle give Ryan a little push to make him walk faster? Distressed, she went back to her chair and sat, letting the smooth, cool feel of the leather soothe her. Silence settled over the room, then was broken by the faraway wail of a siren, then another. She barely registered the noise.

Searle and Ryan. Would this be a problem? Searle's background with children was undeniably vicious, but that was a long time ago. While his son might refuse to see him now, there was no evidence that said he would continue the type of physical violence that had led to his wife's death and prison. Now if she put him in charge of a project, it generally got done without excuses or mishaps. That thing at Lamont London's home was unforeseeable and thus unavoidable; Searle was rehabilitated, a model of dependability, a stickler for details. All good qualities.

But were they *enough* to guarantee that he could spend so much unsupervised time with Ryan? With or without Millennium, there were difficult times ahead. The day after, when all these fools found out it had all been media baloney, was going to produce thousands of calls to After Help; some of these Erica could reasonably predict, most she couldn't. And on the minutest chance it did hit . . . then they'd all be meat loaf and no one would care. But in the meantime . . .

The meantime could last forever for a six-old-boy at the mercy of a child abuser.

JUNE 23 . . .

It's not fair, Ryan Zimmermann thought. *I don't want to be here.*

True—but where did he want to go? Home? Sort of . . . but sort of not. Home meant his dad and his mom, and while he loved his mom a lot, his dad didn't like him very much. No matter how hard he tried, he was always doing something wrong and making his dad angry. That made it seem like it would be better if he *did* stay at this smelly hospital for the rest of the summer; then again, that meant his mom was alone with Dad all the time. Ryan had learned from experience that no matter how bad things with Dad were when his mom was there, they were *always* worse when he was alone with the man. From the bruises that appeared on his mom, Ryan knew it was the same for her. So even though being at

Althaia meant getting away from his dad for a while, it wasn't as good as it seemed.

And this hospital wasn't such a great place either. Everyone believed he didn't remember the night he'd been brought here, but he did. If anything, he didn't recall the pain that went with it, although the cause—Dad, again—was still as bright and fresh in his head as it had been two years ago. Things just after the beating were a little fuzzy, but Ryan remembered knocking over a can of paint in the garage while his dad was working out there. Funny thing was, he was sure the can hadn't been open, and it was the idea of what if it *had* been that had sent his dad into such a fit. And the man who spent a lot of time with Aunt Erica . . . Ryan knew instinctively that Searle was just like his dad. It was in his eyes, cold and sharp, like icicles. Ryan had left his mom by herself with Dad and gotten stuck in this awful place of white rooms, screaming sick people, and guards with guns—only to have somebody who was just as mean and scary following him around all the time.

Staring out the window through a bend in the miniblinds, Ryan could see one man fighting with another at the far end of the parking lot, swinging at him with something that sparkled when he raised it—a bottle? As he watched, an army soldier ran over to the two and swung his rifle into position threateningly. The man on the ground began to crawl away, but the other one turned and raised his weapon toward the soldier. Although the window was closed and locked, Ryan still heard the gunshot, like the muffled popping of a cork; the man with the bottle convulsed and went down, then the soldier leaned forward and shot him again, this time in the head. After shouldering his rifle, the army guy grabbed the dead man by the legs and pulled him off to the side of the parking lot.

The horrible sight made Ryan want to cry, but he struggled against the urge. Every time he cried at home, his dad only belted him harder, and now he was afraid Searle would sneak up behind him and catch him with tears running down his face like a baby. Would Searle hit him?

Sooner or later.

He wondered what Aunt Erica would say when it happened. She was a lot different than his mom; Aunt Erica had a job and money of her own and didn't have to go to someone like Dad or Searle when she needed something, like permission to use the car or go do stuff. In fact, Ryan was pretty sure that Aunt Erica was the one who told Searle what to do—he still remembered her instructing the older man to take Ryan to his room the first day he was brought here. He also remembered the expression on Searle's face when he'd had to do it. Like everything else, Ryan knew he would pay for that.

Sooner or later.

JUNE 25 . . .

"Hi."

Eddie Cuerlacroix looked up as he loaded the last box of canned peaches onto the gurney and tossed a folded sheet on top of it. Ryan was standing there, and Eddie felt a smile creep across his face in spite of himself. He'd met the kid only yesterday, but he'd liked him instantly. "Hey," he said. "How's it going?"

"Okay."

The little guy looked lost in the way that children do when they're stuck in a situation that scares them but they can do nothing about. *Yeah,* Eddie thought wryly. *Join the rest of the world.* "Where're you going?" he asked out loud.

Ryan shrugged, thin shoulders jerking as though an invisible puppeteer had pulled on an overhead string. "Aunt Erica told me I could explore as long as I didn't get in anyone's way or go outside. She said to stay away from the patients and Se—er, *Uncle* Searle."

The way the boy choked over the word *uncle* wasn't lost on Eddie—another of Erica's fabled failed attempts at personal relations. The woman never seemed to learn that you could tell someone what to do in the boardroom but not in their living room. "I see," Eddie said. He tried to put some cheerfulness into his voice for the kid's sake, but it was difficult. He'd had a decent plan all set up, and then in pops this kid, like a brick hurled into a small, quiet pond. But . . . shit. He always *had* been a sucker for kids, and while he might've given up on it, he had never forgotten a long-ago dream of teaching elementary school. He pointed to the laden gurney. "I have to take these downstairs and unload them. You want to help?"

Ryan's glum expression brightened. "Sure." As Eddie began pushing the cart, Ryan fell into step on the other side, his small legs easily keeping up with Eddie's longer stride. "Where are we taking them?"

The "we" wasn't lost on Eddie and he glanced quickly around, made his decision, then grinned at the boy. "To a secret place," he said in a low voice, "but you can't tell *anyone*. Okay?"

The boy nodded, his eyes wide. "I won't, not even Aunt Erica."

They stopped at the back freight elevator and Eddie pushed the button, hoping that the jumbled piles of sheets and towels he'd tossed on top of the boxes did the trick. When the elevator door opened and they pushed the cart inside, he drew an easier breath; so far, so good. "Yeah," he said, picking up the conversation as he pushed the DOWN button, "leave telling Aunt Erica to me."

"What about Uncle Searle?"

Eddie's face darkened. "I'm not so sure about him," he finally said. "Let me think about that for a while."

Ryan nodded solemnly. "Okay." The elevator doors opened and Ryan followed him off, then stopped in confusion. "Wow— where *are* we?"

Eddie chuckled and the sound echoed down the dim corridor. "It's not as scary as it looks. We're only down one level, but this area was closed off some time ago. I think it used to be a radiation lab or something."

"Radiation?"

"They used radiation to treat people with cancer," Eddie explained as he pushed the cart down the hallway, "but I don't think they do that here anymore. It's an old building and I suppose they just never remodeled this part."

"What are we doing down here?"

"Inside the office at the end of the corridor is something called a bomb shelter," Eddie told the boy. "We're going to put all this stuff inside."

Understanding lit Ryan's features. "I get it—that's where you're going to hide when the comet hits!"

Eddie nodded and didn't bother correcting the child. "Exactly. And you can hide with me, if you want to."

Ryan frowned. "But why do we have to keep it a secret? Can't everyone go there?"

A child's logic, Eddie thought as they stopped at the last door and he pulled a key from his pocket and unlocked it. Straightforward and totally unbiased; if only the world could be like that. He put the key back into his pocket and patted the side of his pants to make sure it was there; he'd come across it, labeled simply SHELTER, almost two months ago in the desk drawer of one of the supply rooms and it'd taken another four weeks to locate the shelter itself. The first thing he'd done was carefully peel away the identification label on the door. "Look inside," he said by way of explanation as he swung the door wide. "And you tell me."

It pinched Eddie's heart to see the fearful glance the little boy shot him before hesitantly stepping past. Eddie had left the steel door to the shelter open—there was no way to lock it from the outside anyway—and now Ryan edged to the threshold and peered inside. There wasn't much to see; a ten-by-twelve room with a row of four cots going up one wall, a card table and set of chairs, plastic jugs of water and as many boxes of nonperishable canned food as Eddie could safely swipe from the kitchen and cafeteria. In one corner was a small chemical toilet next to extra supplies for it; on the cots were added blankets, flashlights and batteries, a few changes of clothes in generic sizes. A deck of cards and a stack of magazines on the table, although he didn't know if they'd be able to spare the flashlight batteries on entertainment. On the other hand, the thought of lying in the dark for God knew how long made his guts twist up. He'd found an industrial-sized box of matches and a small crate of votive candles in the chapel and those were tucked under the table, but who knew if there would be enough oxygen for them? For that matter, maybe there wouldn't be enough oxygen down here for people. Well, he'd done the best he could.

"It's pretty small."

Eddie started and realized he'd been staring inside the shelter and going over his mental supply list so thoroughly that he'd forgotten about Ryan. He exhaled, then squatted next to the boy. "This is why we have to keep it a secret," he said. "If everyone knows, then everyone will want to come down, too. But there's only enough room and food for four people to live here for maybe . . . I don't know. A month or so."

Ryan nodded solemnly but didn't say anything, and Eddie was surprised. Children were naturally curious and their questions were fairly predictable; why, then, didn't Ryan ask who else was going to be living in the shelter? For a six-year-old, he was unusually reserved. Since Erica was his only family, he probably assumed she would be included; as for "Uncle" Searle . . . well, Eddie was hoping he could dissuade Erica about that. By choice he hadn't spent much time around Searle since Naomi had left in February. There was something about the man he didn't like, an undercurrent of brutality that was so terrifying that Eddie didn't want to acknowledge it. Maybe it had always been there . . . or maybe it was feeding on the violence and fear that was everywhere nowadays, growing fat and healthy and strong, like a big, evil parasite. Thinking about it brought back Eddie's earlier fears about being stuck down here for days or weeks or longer. What if Searle Chanowitz ended up with them in the shelter?

The thought made Eddie want to cry.

NEW YORK
JUNE 26 . . .

[fade to Peter Hoshi]

From the hourly broadcast interruption tape of an ongoing emergency Cable News Network broadcast:

"In helping to ensure that the American people are kept informed, CNN brings you the following prerecorded tape furnished this morning by the United States Department of Defense."

[cut to window and expand to fill]

"This is Harvey Thayer, Director of the Federal Emergency Management Agency. As of midnight, June 27, 2000, a twenty-four-hour curfew is being imposed upon all jurisdictions within the continental and overseas United States. No civilian is allowed outside of his or her home for any reason until further notice. I repeat, no civilian, local, city, or state civilian worker whatsoever is to report for work at their place of employement today. Those persons already on duty in positions which are considered essential under FEMA standards, such as medical and utility company personnel, will be required to remain in their capacities until further notice and have been so notified. Anyone on the streets other than authorized military personnel will be immediately arrested, and soldiers are authorized to shoot anyone resisting arrest. All jurisdictions are being continually patrolled. *Do not leave your home or property for any reason.* If you need emergency assistance, such as medical attention or water, you may stand in the open front doorway or on the front porch of your residence until seen and acknowledged by military personnel. Do *not* go any farther. If your doorway or front porch cannot be seen from the street, you should dial the operator, state that you need assistance, and provide a detailed explanation. Your request will be responded to by military personnel as quickly as practicable. In this regard, requests for attention that are considered frivolous or unnecessary will be punishable by arrest.

"There will be *no* exceptions to this curfew other than by verifiable law enforcement officers, and such persons are allowed to leave their residences only to report for a previously scheduled work shift. Three forms of identification, two of which contain current photographs, will be required as verification.

"The Department of Defense and the Federal Emergency Management Agency regret the need for such drastic action. However, this curfew is in effect until further notice, and this report will air every thirty minutes until the curfew ends."

[fade out]

CHICAGO
JUNE 27 . . .

"It couldn't have come at a better time," Erica told Searle as they stood in the front lobby of Althaia and watched a maintenance man thread a length of hardened chain through the inside handles of the main doors, then fasten the ends with an oversized padlock. "All these last-minute panic visits were doing was draining emergency supplies we're going to need later." She glanced at him and saw a smirk twist his mouth. "What?" she demanded.

"So you finally admit it's going to hit."

Erica hesitated, then shook her head. "I believe nothing of the sort," she said stubbornly. "There's still time for them to do something about it—"

"A week!"

"—and I think they will." She shot him a irate look for interrupting her. "On our end, who knows what it's going to be like immediately after July second when things try to return to normal? It certainly won't be an instantaneous transition. A lot of people feel they've been treated unfairly by the government, by the military, by their employers—everyone's fighting with everyone else. This full curfew is just the final insult to what the public perceives as bureaucratic bullying. In this instance, I think the recovery is going to be worse than the disease."

"If this is part of it," Searle retorted, "then yeah, I think you're right. Maybe I should remind you that the After Help switchboard is clogged with calls from your so-called patrons." He cocked an eyebrow. "Not to mention the fifteen people you refused to let in who just got hauled away for violating the twenty-four-hour curfew. You think those people aren't going to remember this and spread the word when . . . *if* the time comes?"

Erica ignored the dig, turned and headed back toward her office, assuming Searle would follow. "We can take care of the complaints later on," she said briskly. "This curfew serves us in that respect, too—it will be easy to point out that our hands were as tied as any other civilian's. As for the switchboard, by noon we'll have converted to a 'no message' mode on the voice-mail system," she said briskly. "I've prepared a recorded announcement that will inform callers that due to the curfew, the hospital as well as the support offices of After Help have been temporarily shut down and will reopen on July third."

Searle's laugh was loud enough to be startling. "Oh, that's slick, Erica." She glanced at him but he only laughed harder. "I wish I'd thought of that!"

"I don't think it's funny at all," she snapped. "Nor do I think it's 'slick,' as you so ineptly put it. Shutting down the switchboard is the only answer. Otherwise everybody on staff will do nothing but sit and listen to people whine on the telephones, when they could be accomplishing other tasks."

"No offense, dear, but I thought talking to these people *was* their task." Searle's voice was dry. "I sure hope this shit doesn't backfire on you."

Erica glanced at him sharply, trying to decide if something about his voice had been odd. Nothing about Searle's expression or the way he looked at her hinted at anything out of line . . . still, she never felt she could quite trust him. "Don't worry about it," she finally said. "I'll take care of assigning who does what around here. After Help simply no longer has the time to play . . . baby-sitter."

JUNE 28 . . .

If she heard any more hammering today, Mercy thought she would cover her ears and begin to scream.

It wasn't the sound of the hammering that was making her nuts, but what it represented—the concept that they might not be safe inside a normal house anymore, that the civilized protection of a glass-and-wood window might not be enough to protect them against their own kind. To think that—

"That's not the only reason, Mercy."

She whirled and saw Simon standing a few feet away, his expression sheepish. "I'm sorry," he said. "I couldn't help it. What you're thinking . . . it's sort of *leaking* out."

For the first time since last night, when Lamont had reminded them about the stack of plywood in the town house's garage and suggested that it was time to start covering the windows, she managed a small smile. "It's okay. That part of you came with the package."

Simon looked relieved, then he came over and drew her into his arms for a quick, comforting hug. "If we get hit," he said, "we're going to have a lot of movement in the ground—"

"If? Simon . . . don't you believe Gena?"

"Yes," he answered, but the reluctance in his voice was obvious. "But I don't *want* to. So I keep thinking 'if' instead of 'when,' keep hoping that something will happen to change things. We all know how adamant she is about insisting she's *not* the last word on everything."

"Ah." What could Mercy say to that? She didn't want to argue with Simon about whether he had the right to hope or not—of course he did. Didn't she do the same thing, deep inside? "You were saying something about ground movement," she said. "Are you talking about earthquakes?"

"Exactly. It's hard to tell how bad this could be because no one's been able to get information which can be acknowledged as accurate. The government keeps saying it'll be no big deal, while the astronomical facilities around the world are forecasting cataclysmic results."

"And then there's Gena—"

"—whose predictions are pretty bleak but not exactly detailed," Simon finished. His eyes clouded. "I'd be lying if I said we weren't putting up this plywood partially to keep out other people, but that's not the sole reason. Lamont and I talked about things we could do to make the town house ready, and blocking off sources of flying glass were high on the list. We're going to fix up the doors so they're more secure, take down mirrors and glass-fronted pictures, stuff like that. Move anything heavy to the floor where it won't land on anyone if it falls."

"Really," Mercy said. "And what are you guys planning to do about the ceilings?" She didn't want to be caustic, but the words still came out that way.

"I . . . don't know." Simon sounded so tired all of a sudden that

Mercy was instantly sorry. "We thought about loading up and taking off and at first Gena had suggested that, remember? Then she said no, something about roving bands of men looking specifically for people who did that because it was an easy way to get supplies, killing them and leaving the bodies. Then we worried about Lake Michigan, but decided we're far enough west so that we ought to be okay. Remember that astronomer from Arizona who was the spokesman for the Department of Defense on the Valentine launch? He mentioned on CNN a couple of times that if the Earth got hit, it would be at the equator in the Pacific Ocean; that means tidal waves, and here there's a possibility of flooding because of rising water. Also—"

"You sound like a textbook."

Simon blinked. "I'm sorry?"

"Or a science teacher explaining the basics of Disaster Preparation one-oh-one to his class. Whatever you say, Professor Chanowitz." Pissed but not sure why, Mercy turned her back on him, then brought her fist to her mouth and bit down on it as her other hand gently followed the curve of her belly. Because she missed being six feet tall by a scant two inches, her pregnancy was hardly noticeable beneath a baggy sweatshirt from the now-defunct McDerwin Animal Clinic. But she never, *ever* forgot about it.

Simon's warm, strong hands touched her shoulders, then his arms came forward and crossed along her collarbone. She leaned back, letting him support her weight, drawing strength from his presence as she always did. "I'm sorry," she said quietly. "You don't have all the answers, and it's senseless of me to take out my frustration on you."

Her husband leaned his face into her hair and inhaled; despite the black thing facing them all, Simon sounded contented. "They say you give the worst of yourself to the ones you love the most."

"That's a damned shame," Mercy said flatly. "You should give the best of yourself, not the worst."

"I think that goes along with it," he said. "In the everyday part. We can't see the future anymore, Mercy. But we'll do what we can to survive, and this is where it balances out. *This*"— Simon's arms slid downward over her breasts, then his fingers spread and curved around her stomach—"is where we give the best of ourselves."

GREENS FORK, INDIANA
JUNE 29 . . .

It wasn't Chicago, but it was clean and Frank supposed it would do as well as anywhere else. Depending on what happened three days from now, it might be where their child was born . . . or where they all died. Time and God held the answers.

The new Gelasias home was a clearing along the edge of a small, nameless creek that separated two cornfields about a mile off Interstate 70. They'd been on the run since leaving Litchfield, sprinting each day from one spot in the road to the next, searching for a safe place to stay for the night, praying they'd find someplace permanent. On the outskirts of Greens Fork three days ago, Frank had gotten desperate enough to outright ask the middle-aged woman behind the register of a convenience store if she knew of anyplace. She'd refused to sell them more than five gallons of gasoline, and her answer had been quick and punctuated by a nasty laugh—

"You just head out of here, mister. We got plenty of problems of our own and don't need outsiders on top of 'em."

Defeated, Frank had gone back to where Crystal waited outside by the car and shook his head at her questioning look. Eyeing the highway stretching east, he checked his watch and swallowed. Three-thirty; it looked like it'd be another night sitting motionless in the car. Maybe they could find a used car lot farther in town. They were all abandoned and if they parked on the outskirts of a lot, the beat-up Town Car might blend in—

"That woman always has been a bitch."

He and Crystal started as a teenager paused by the front of the car. There was nothing remarkable about the boy; he was maybe seventeen and dressed in a dusty T-shirt and denim jeans above work boots. He'd have looked like a 1950s farm boy except for the design of triangles and squares carefully shaven into his hair along each temple. Not sure how to respond, Frank shrugged.

The teenager lifted his jaw toward the road that fronted the interstate, then pointed for emphasis. His hands were tanned and callused from hard work. "If you go about two miles past the on-ramp, the road curves to the south and you'll see my grandfather's farm on the right. About a mile past that, there's a rusted gate on the left, kind of hard to see if you're not watching for it. There's a padlock on it but it's just for show—it's open and nobody knows where the key is. Then again"—he glanced back at Frank and his eyes were troubled—"you might want to go on and lock it once you're inside. You can always find a way out along the field edge if you have to."

"Are you saying we can stay there?" Crystal asked.

"For as long as you want." The kid folded his arms across his chest.

"Why?" Frank asked. "I got the impression—"

The young man shot a disgusted glance toward the store. "Why not? Don't pay no attention to her. There's plenty of space and I'll tell my grandfather you're out there so he don't find out by surprise. If you go on down to the end of the trail, there's a creek with fresh water, a little muddy but we don't dump garbage into it." He stared up at the sky. "You might as well kick back for a few days and see what happens. That's what we're doing." He reached behind himself and pulled a cap from his back pocket; unfolded and jammed on his head, Fran saw with amusement that it had a *Marvin the Martian* figure on the front. "You folks take it easy."

"Hey, thanks," Crystal called as the boy strode to a Ford pickup nearby and climbed into the cab. "What's your name?"

The truck's engine started with enough noise to make them wince—no sneaking around here with that muffler-free vehicle. "Tell you what," the teenager yelled. "Ask me next week!" He pulled out of the store's parking lot and was gone, headed east and presumably toward his grandfather's farm.

Frank turned to Crystal. "What do you think?"

She sighed. "What have we got to lose, Frank? At least it sounds like it's far enough off the road to hide us."

Frank squinted against the afternoon sunlight. "I haven't seen any military presence out here."

"No," Crystal agreed, "but we have seen plenty of troopers. My guess is that the local law acts the part."

He glanced at his watch again. "We've got about twenty minutes."

Crystal opened the passenger door and climbed inside. "That ought to give us just enough time to get there."

The night sky was beautiful, even though they weren't that far east of Indianapolis and the air wasn't as clear as back home in Arizona. Once he and Crystal had gone on a rafting trip down the Colorado and slept on its banks at the bottom of the Grand

Canyon; from down there the Milky Way was clearly visible in a great, grand smudge overhead. Not the same here, but at least it was cloudless and they could look up and see the sweep of stars, the faint touch of a celestial paintbrush across the span of their vision. Protected against the mosquitoes and gnats by the netting across the tent's door, the mesh pattern thankfully didn't block the starlight.

"There's so many pieces," Crystal said without warning. "Will we see any of them before they hit?"

"Not from here." Lying on his back, Frank found himself staring at the inside of the tent's ceiling rather than outside. "My calculations said it'll be daylight in the States at impact. Maybe we'll get some afterimages . . . there's really no telling. But we're going to feel it in a big way."

"How long will it last?"

"I . . . I'm not sure." Frank had never lied to Crystal before, and he had no idea if he sounded convincing now that his entire end of the conversation was fabrication. "Without the proper equipment, I can't begin to guess."

Without realizing it, he crossed his fingers and hoped they'd made the right decision in leaving Litchfield. Since they fled the campground, the trip had been spotlighted with arguments over whether populated or unpopulated was better. Troubled by Crystal's size and afraid she had miscalculated her due date, Frank had voted for a more populated area. Better, he contended, to have access to technology and medical supplies and the areas that would be rebuilt the fastest—the cities, of course, as local governments rich in manpower reestablished themselves.

But Crystal was adamant, and as much as he desired what technology could offer, he had to agree with Crystal's reminders about how man treated his own and her prediction that things would only get worse. Before accepting the supervisory position at the retirement center closer to home, she had been an emergency-room nurse in Phoenix's St. Luke's Medical Center. Her career change had made him forget the horror stories she had brought home, and now she wisely reminded him. He didn't need his degree to read the bumper stickers and see an attitude that was different but not better than what was rampant in the crowded urban areas. Popular around here, "Smash 'Em All and Let God Sort 'Em Out!" next to a picture of a falling rock was some enterprising local businessperson's variation on the old standby. Were they any better off in Greens Fork, Indiana than in Litchfield? Or how about Phoenix? Or Chicago?

How long will it last?

Frank wished to God he could just be honest with her.

CHICAGO
JUNE 30 . . .

It's the only way we'll get away with it.

Eddie's words kept ringing in Searle's mind, working at it like a needle stuck in the groove of a scratchy old LP—

It's the only way we'll get away with it.

A fine and valid reason for getting the four of them down here two days before the impact date, and there was no denying that anyone who saw the four of them marching along the hospital corridors the night before the world was scheduled to go to shit would want to know where they were going. So Eddie had brought Ryan down first and instructed Erica and Searle to meet them at the bomb shelter an hour later, with Erica arriving first. Searle had ridden out a half hour of panic before saying fuck it and coming down early after making sure he wasn't being followed. Clawing at the back of his brain had been the suspicion that Eddie and Erica might lock him out of the shelter, trim the herd, so to speak, and leave him to meet his fate with the rest of the gun-toting nitwits prowling around Althaia. But they had been waiting patiently for him, and for the first time Searle understood that if Erica didn't exactly trust him or love him, she still believed in his ability to help keep her alive. Outwardly sedate as they locked themselves inside, Searle had felt a fierce, victorious grin spread along the inside of his skull. *This* was the kind of control he'd been waiting for, and he'd be fucked if she would ever threaten him again once that grand impact day came.

It's the only way we'll get away with it.

The bomb shelter reminded him of prison.

Cramped, stuffy, cool, and dark all the time, the only thing it lacked were the rats. In some respect this room was worse than the pen; Mr. Ingenuity Eddie had said they couldn't waste what candles they had, at least not yet, and the flashlight batteries were even more precious. So here they all were, each lying on a cot made up with a less-than-fancy wool blanket and a small, flat pillow, trapped while they waited for the world to end. At least in the pen the guards had come around to shake things up now and then; in the course of making sure one prisoner wasn't strangling another they kept the silence from getting so huge. Normal conversation would be okay, but the only thing they'd gotten so far had been from the brat, who in the way of a first-grader had start humming something he claimed was the theme from the X-Men cartoon. He'd stopped right quick when Searle had snarled at him.

"Eddie?" Ryan's high-pitched voice cut through the blackness and made Searle wince.

"I'm right here, Ryan."

"How long do we have to stay down here?"

"I think—"

Searle made a fist and punched the bottom of the cot over his head. Below him, Ryan yelped involuntarily. "Shut up, Eddie. I'm not going to listen to stupid questions like that every fucking ten minutes for the next two weeks," Searle said. "We'll be down here for as long as it takes."

"Searle—"

"Keep your mouth shut too, Erica. You wanted me in here with you—well, here I am. But I'm not going to put up with shit the whole time."

"You're more than welcome to leave, Searle." The words from Eddie came quickly enough to override anything Erica said in response. Searle could imagine the hopeful expression on the younger man's face. "For the amount of supplies down here, I really hadn't planned on more than three people being here to begin with."

"Yeah," Searle said calmly. "And I could cut your throat and make it three right now."

"Searle!"

"Didn't I just tell you to shut up, Erica?"

"I—"

"In case you didn't realize it," Searle continued, "things changed a bit when we closed that door behind us. This place feels like old times, like I closed my eyes and opened them again to ten years ago." He smiled in the dark and cracked his knuckles, nice and loud. "You get on my nerves, 'Rica, and I'm just going to climb on down and smack you until you learn not to. Same goes for you, Eddie-boy. About the only smart one in here besides me seems to be the kid. He knows when to shut up, speak when spoken to, all that good shit."

No one said anything and Searle laughed and hooked his fingers into the network of springs above him, then gave enough of a yank to make Eddie bounce on his mattress. The other man didn't dare protest and Searle knew he'd been right—he had total control here, just like in his cell at Joliet.

Just like home.

JULY 1 . . .

The screaming had started last night.

Simon thought a lot about the children for whom the DCFS had been responsible, all those tiny victims that he had come to think of as *his*. The Department of Children and Family Services had been suspended indefinitely slightly more than two weeks ago. Did the people who had comprised his staff still think about the kids? He did, of course, and Mercy being pregnant was like a monumental reminder every day that there were tens of thousands of unprotected children in the city. Not that he had been the personal savior for them all, but at least he'd been able to reach out a hand to a fraction.

Standing at the wood that now sheathed what had been the kitchen window, Simon wished he could be like Lamont and have to see the object of his concentration. If that were the case, he would be safe. Or Gena—raging inside because her ability to see the future was gone, he knew she felt useless and he tried to reassure her whenever he could without being obvious about it, but . . . what would it be like to have the inside of his head *quiet* for a change? He wasn't sure. Part of him was intensely, unstoppably jealous; another told him that the silence would be utterly deafening, a sense upon which he had come to depend suddenly cut off at its heart and leaving a huge void.

He didn't need to touch the wood to hear the screams, but he did anyway, unable to stop his trembling hands from pressing against the rough sheet. The others were downstairs in the family room, gathered around the television although Lamont had reduced the volume to hardly more than a murmur. That's where he should be, but he had come up here on the pretext of . . . what? He didn't remember. Beyond the barrier, the weight of the world pressed against his head.

It wasn't only in his mind. Shuttered inside the town house, he heard that the streets were full of shouts and gunfire, brutal judgment by the soldiers to those brazen or witless souls who continued to disregard the governmental directive about martial law and a twenty-four-hour curfew. The shrieks were bad enough, but some-times they represented anger, frustration, or simply weren't genuine—Simon had lost track of the flashes that told him the hoarse cries for help were dangerous bait for darker intentions. But gunfire . . . God, Simon thought as he leaned against the wood involuntarily. Every time a burst of gunfire came, a life was being thrown away by someone foolish enough to risk it and someone else brutal enough to take it. He didn't know which was worse—though he tended to think it was the idiots who gambled forever against a serviceman's nervous trigger finger.

"Simon?" Behind him, Lamont's voice was low and smooth, his face eerily lit by a small night-light plugged into one of the wall outlets; he'd pulled in a substantial supply of candles but was saving them. "Why don't you come downstairs with us?" he sug-gested. "Up here, it's kind of . . . " He shrugged helplessly. "Harsh."

Simon put his hands in his pocket and didn't answer for a moment. Lamont was right; he should go downstairs and—

They both jerked as a man wailed outside, his cry loud enough to be heard from at least a block away. A second later it was fol-lowed by the *crack!* of a rifle shot. "Why are they doing this?" Simon wondered aloud. "Do they *want* to die?"

Moving to stand beside him, Simon saw lines in Lamont's face that hadn't been there a month ago; he was the oldest of their group, and the events of the last six months had put deep crevices around his mouth and between his eyebrows. "Maybe they're afraid of what God's going to do to them tomorrow," he said softly. "People get a twisted sense of how to save themselves. Some of these religious nuts have been purposely disobeying the curfew so that the military has no choice but to shoot them. They seem to think that a bullet in the head is a lot quicker than having the Earth open up and swallow you whole. They don't want to face tomorrow, but they can't go though with self-imposed sui-cide. So they let the government do it for them."

Simon shook his head, struggling to understand. "I've seen children with more will to survive," he said. "With no idea where their next meal was coming from, daily beatings, and no reason to hope anything will get better, yet they seldom give up."

"The optimism of the young." Lamont ran his fingers over his short-cropped hair. "Or the ignorant. The older ones get tired, I think. Too tired to face something like this, or too tired to believe they can try. Take my parents, for instance. Their position is that God will look out for them, and if they're meant to die, then they will. They're not fanatics, but this is just so . . . *big* that they can't deal with it."

"And your sister and brothers?"

"Roanna and her family are down in Florida with Mom and Dad. Joey and I stopped speaking last November, and Isaac, Jr.—" Here Lamont shook his head. "Isaac is convinced we're all going to die so why bother making the effort? He sits in his apartment and drinks and nothing I say gets through to him. I guess I should count it as a blessing that he isn't somewhere on the street meeting his fate with the rest of the people just like himself."

"But how do we know we can't make it if we don't try?"

"We don't." Lamont reached over and squeezed his shoulder. For once, Simon was grateful for the contact. "I can't speak for the world, Simon. You hear too much of what it says as it is. But as for us . . .

"We'll give it our damnedest."

6.
IMPACT

CHICAGO
JULY 2, 2000: 3:34 A.M.

"We've got to get out of the town house."

"Gena, you know we can't do that." In the dark, Lamont's voice was tense. "One step out the door and we'll end up as target practice for the soldiers. You can hear them going by—they're all over the place."

"I don't *care* if we just get as far as the backyard." Gena wanted to shake him. Next would be Mercy and Simon, both of whom were sitting a few feet away in the darkened family room. "Damn it, I know I can't give you all the gory details I used to, but I still get hits of intuition. We can*not* stay in this building—and most certainly not in the basement."

"There's not much of a backyard—" Simon began.

"That's not the fucking point!" She was almost screeching. "At least there won't be part of a building coming down on our heads. Don't you guys *get* it?"

"So let's get some stuff together and do it," Mercy said matter-of-factly. "We can start by changing into clothes that can't be seen in the dark." She looked at Gena, then at Simon and Lamont, standing so indecisively by the darkened television screen; they'd decided to turn it off hours ago. "I thought you guys were talking about this earlier. Do you want to sneak into the backyard and hide—

"—or stay in here and die?"

THE EARTH
7:17 A.M.

The impacts begin in the Pacific Ocean at the equator where a man named Frank Gelasias once told his wife they would. The first strikes pummel the ocean floor and within milliseconds columns of scalding vapor and flash-boiled sea life are thrown farther into the air than anyone ever imagined. Ground shocks roll through the ocean floor as more impacts occur, a volley of them screaming their way through the Earth's outer atmosphere, destined to feel the grind of her crust beneath their skimming trajectory. The string of impacts open the wounds wider and spread their misery deeply through the globe, down and through the layers of rock and granite, questing for that final hot core of magma to shake it hard and spit it out as hundreds of new volcanoes before the next volley hits, less than a meager day's rest and not nearly enough to give Earth's agonized dwellers a chance for recovery. The pieces swell to their largest number, a celestial strand of deadly pearls, and the sky is filled with lightning and white-hot stars that dive over the horizon and thrust themselves at that same raw place, so careless of the Earth's valiant attempt to maintain its fragile rotation, hammering away at this spinning round obstacle blocking its path. The two largest of Millennium's odd-shaped fragments are each more than three hundred miles across and send a roaring through the sky unlike any other as they charge through the thermosphere and down. For nine and a half days, cycle after cycle, and always that eerie, day-to-day cosmic sequence that offers as its sacrifice to the former rogue planet the same bloody area in the Pacific. The Earth lurches under blow after blow, radial momentum deteriorating and ultimately stopping; ocean waters flee before the molten lava spilling from the Earth's rupturing innards, rush landward in both directions, driving toward the coast of California and the eastern edges of China and Australia. Heat pulses spread in all directions from the impact sites like fiery flowers, annihilating every living thing in their paths. The tsunamis are nearly as high as the vapor columns rising from the impact sites and leave nothing but memories behind as the Hawaiian Islands,

New Zealand, New Guinea, the Philippines, and Japan are swallowed for eternity. As far north as Alaska, the Bering Sea spreads free, over the Bering Strait and the puny land coasts in its way and makes of itself a new northern ocean. At the lower edges of the United States, all of Florida, the dark queen that was once New Orleans, and thousands of other large and small cities and towns from Texas up the length of the New England coast are obliterated and become forgotten history. Caught within Millennium's dark embrace and her offspring of continuing earthquakes and aftershocks, Mexico shrinks to the size of Kansas and its ancient Indian civilizations join the legends of Atlantis.

Mountains rip from the ground along the Pacific and African plates, and the luxuriant West Coast of the United States is no more. Up and up and up, freshly heated rock soars into the stratosphere and beyond, past the ozone layer to lay claim to a full two miles of the mesosphere as its new territory. Matched mile for mile by sister ranges around the world as Millennium's remains continue to ram the Earth and the tectonic plates shit and reshift, each ruthless impact causes more plates to subduct, birthing mountains the altitudes of which mankind has only dreamed. Virgin peaks stretch into the atmosphere from Alaska on down, through thousands of miles of superheated Pacific water to reach Antarctica and west, more ranges bursting from the center of Greenland south to intercept the Scotia plate and blast north again, redefining the western coast of South America and Mexico until it meets, finally, with the oldest by mere days of all of the mountains, at the southernmost tip of a destroyed-forever California.

And between the immense summits of the newborn ranges at their western edge and east in the mid-Atlantic lies the ravaged remains of North and South America as an enormous, newly cloistered valley. Shuddering beneath a trapped but breathable atmosphere spanning some twenty-five thousand miles at its center, the valley is protected from the ink-colored shroud of filth and ground debris that screams across the sky beyond its soaring mountaintops. The still viable atmosphere, swollen with battling streams of cold and warm air, churns with conflicting currents and jet streams and carries its own burden of dusty moisture. The sky boils, a frantic continuing motif of dark cumulonimbus and nimbostratus clouds that spew a never-ending rain onto those who survive in the zones below, isolated by chance on a nearly dead planet . . .

NILES, ILLINOIS
JULY 3: 8:02 A.M.

She couldn't have begun to describe her feelings at that spectacular moment when the ground had started moving for the first time yesterday.

It'd been daylight, of course, for quite some time, yet Lily hadn't left her sleeping blanket. She couldn't go anywhere because of the continuous curfew—signs were posted everywhere—and clocks meant nothing anyway. The drugstore LED watch she'd worn for most of the trip across Iowa and Illinois had given it up last week, the vibrations from the motorcycle and bad roads shaking the life out of it; she hadn't bothered looking for another one. With her destination still the width of a city away, she was alone and had been since three days ago, when she'd wheeled the motorcycle deep into this forest preserve in Niles, a tiny suburb just west of Chicago. At the time, having narrowly escaped getting her head shot off by one of the patrols, she'd felt lucky to be walking upright. She followed the paths inside the preserve as far southeast as she could go, then stopped. There was no choice but to accept that this was it for now; she found running water at a small bathroom facility about ten minutes out of the thicket, but no food—even the trash can's contents had been picked clean. She'd eaten the last of her food, an undersized bag of potato chips, the day before yesterday; all it had done was make her want more, but the vending machine next to the sign that said EDGEBROOK WOODS was smashed and gutted.

As things turned out, the hunger pangs dropped to last on Lily's priority list real quick.

She had some crazy idea about holding on to the motorcycle, then narrowly missed getting one leg crushed when it fell over and began to slide along the dirt. Instead of the miracle machine that had started every morning despite its age and the shitty gasoline she'd kept pumping into it, the Suzuki became a live thing chasing her along the bucking ground as she clawed at the soil and tried to get away from it. Common sense told her that of course it wasn't after her, it was just following the pattern of vibrations in the Earth, but her brain kept screaming until she managed to break the pursuit by putting a knot of trees between her and the cycle. Under the roar building in her ears, there was a *pop!* and the sound of pressurized water from far away as something blew—the pipeline that supplied the rest room station. When the quakes didn't stop,

Lily forgot about the motorcycle and lost all sense of time and herself as she lunged erratically from tree to tree, searching for one that might be stronger, another that was more stable than the one before it as the forest whipped and groaned around her and the bright morning sky began to darken above the churning ground and growing wind.

When the rain started, it did nothing to muffle the sound of splitting concrete and falling trees.

CHICAGO, ILLINOIS
JULY 4: 2:38 P.M.

Quiet was a rare and precious thing, and Simon feared his mind would never find it again.

Around them, the city was still alive and the screams of her children, aloud and otherwise, were nearly constant as the structure of everything collapsed. Simon had spent his entire life avoiding, as best he could, the bedsides of the mortally ill or wounded. Terrified of the things he might read from their minds as they passed from this world to the next or perhaps on to nothingness, he had been remarkably successful at being somewhere— *anywhere*—else at nearly every dying moment that might have crossed his path. Today his head was saturated with the bedlam of Chicago and he wanted to pound his skull against a rock until it split and let some of the terror out. Was this how Mercy felt when her power built too strongly inside, when she surrendered to the urge for one of her infamous Nights Out? Simon didn't know if the unceasing gibberish pouring into his head was better or worse than the rumbling of the Earth that had drowned it out for six- and seven-hour stretches over the last three days. Pleas for help that they couldn't possibly answer, furious curses they wouldn't want to, countless fragments of shock and bewilderment. A hundred thousand people as bruised and battered and dying as they were, all unknowingly reaching out and suffocating him.

Huddled next to Mercy, he felt her head on his shoulder and saw the exhausted rise and fall of her chest as she snatched at a few minutes of sleep now that the worst of their hunger had been eased. Over their protests, last night Lamont had crawled into the rubble that remained of the town house and dug out some food, only as much as they could eat under the cover of darkness. It was a risky thing—if someone saw them, how would they explain his being able to move aside the splintered studs and reach past the caved-in ceilings? But they needed food and water, especially Mercy and Gena, and there was no convincing Lamont otherwise. Now they huddled beneath a plastic tarp pulled from the garage and waited, although they weren't sure for what. No one spoke and Simon found himself envious of the way his wife and each of his friends could turn inward; if only he had that luxury . . . if only he didn't know that Gena strained at every second to see something, *anything,* that would help them survive, and that Lamont wished he could just stand up and fix the entire world starting with this small, devastated backyard, and that Mercy's deepest desire was to simply wander the streets and put an end to all the pain she knew was out there. As for himself—

He was the most selfish. God forgive him, Simon just wished for the return of silence.

NEAR GREEENS FORK, INDIANA
JULY 5: 6:54 P.M.

The end of it all did not come as swiftly and gloriously as Naomi had once prophesied. In fact, the end did not seem likely to come at all, at least not in the way she and her group of ragtag vampire-wannabes had always assumed. A boom, a flash, then a glorious light sweeping them all into the warmth they'd each lost in one way or another—

What a crock of shit.

Around her lay the fruits of all her labor these many months. Some were alive; most weren't. Where had it been said in the news reports that the so-called impact day would go on, and on, and *on*? She'd imagined one big bang and . . . extinction. Join the ranks of the dinosaurs, the dodo bird, and a thousand other creatures wiped out of existence forever by the kiss of God.

Wait—hadn't there been something about more than one strike? Maybe . . . she couldn't remember. Looking around now, it was hard to believe she'd paid so little attention. Eddie, now *he* was a smart guy, always planning and looking ahead, looking out for *her*. Where was he now? Safely holed up with bitchwoman Erica and her goon? Or dead?

"I'll be damned," Naomi croaked out loud. Why should she be thinking about Cuerlacroix after all these months? Who knew— maybe it was a kind of subconscious thing about feeling safe with him, the way he'd always looked out for her—there, she'd thought about it again. Well, she'd certainly switched positions with this bunch of morons.

Fifty feet away and on the other side of a ditch was Interstate 70, and somewhere along the eastern stretch of that, the border of Ohio. If anyone had asked her why last week it had been important to reach that state line, Naomi couldn't have answered them. She hadn't known then, she didn't know now, and she no longer cared to get there anyway. Her followers, as Erica had insisted on calling them, were splayed about the ground like broken, black-garbed dolls. Out of the hundred or so who had made it this far without being sport for the roving companies of soldiers or beaten to death by flying debris from the earthquakes, maybe twenty were still alive. If they bled, it soaked unseen into their dark garments, a secret in the same way that they dressed to blend into this darkness that just wouldn't go away. There had been no shouts of joy as the chosen of them had met their fates; neither was there crying or screaming. Moving as silently as possible beneath the pounding rain, not bothering to dodge the branches and deadly wreckage swirling through the air, they followed her without question, like blind acolytes. They walked when she walked, fed when she fed, and sat when she sat—like now, on the side of this ditch—and never said a word.

Absurdly, Naomi found herself wishing Eddie were here. She was colder than she'd ever been in her life, perhaps only a few heartbeats away from being as cold as the woman in her arms, who had died about three minutes ago. She didn't mind the darkness that had spread over everything by afternoon of the first day, but the ceaseless rain and chilled, storm-strength winds were enough to drive her insane. Thinking about him again, she missed Eddie's sense of humor and zany expressions, although she could do without his lectures and the leftover sense of obligation from his not-so-brilliant lifesaving routine back in New Orleans.

Wherever he was, *if* he was, Naomi hoped he knew she was thinking about him.

There were her "people," sitting along the sodden ditch and staring dully at a four-lane highway that was as lumpy and useless as a twisted piece of aluminum foil. Like her, they had undergone the faintest of transformations during their time on the night roads. Outwardly normal, they had learned to talk with their heads lowered and their mouths nearly closed—self-preservation asserting itself in a world gone crazy. Now their young eyes were strange

and pale, like luminescent moonlight; their probing tongues ran
questioningly along the edges of upper teeth gone unaccountably
sharp enough to split flesh in an instant. There were no padded
belly donut-gluttons here; all were thin ... but not hungry. For
Naomi and her followers, it hadn't been very difficult to find nourishment in a world where people shot each other over a can of
corned beef hash.

Abruptly Naomi pushed herself to her feet, then bent and
slipped deceptively strong hands under the dead woman's arms.
As her mouth began to water, she dragged the cooling corpse
behind the meager barrier offered by a wind-flattened bush a few
feet to her right. Amid all this destruction, warmth could still be
found ...

GREENS FORK, INDIANA
JULY 6: 4:29 A.M.

"Frank, wake up."

"What's the matter?"

He sat up immediately and Crystal could feel his sharp movements as his head jerked in one direction, then another. It was too
dark to see his face, but she could imagine his eyes, wide with
fear, that oh-so-smart brain in his head ready to analyze the next
danger and devise their best course of action. His hand brushed
her arm, then folded around it; his touch was surprisingly warm
and comforting—but not enough to lessen her anger. "It's going to
happen again today, isn't it? Damn you, you *lied* to me when I
asked you how long it would last."

He said nothing.

"Jesus," she whispered. Sheltered from the worst of the wind,
they were huddled on the east side of what was left of the car,
itself crumpled under the weight of several trees. The tears rolling
down her cheeks left a pattern of cold streaks along her skin that
made her shiver. No need to hide her face; the stars and moon
were blotted out by the dense, ugly clouds and the lights along the
highway in the distance had been ripped from the ground during
the first of the earthquakes over four days ago. Since then there
had been only jagged flashes of lightning to give them a view of
the broken lumps of grass and earth that had once been the smooth
patch of clearing around them, not to mention the rushing, limb-
and mud-filled threat that had once been the placid, clean creek.

Four days.

"How much longer?" she asked dully. "Do you think you could tell me the truth this time, Frank? Is it ever going to *end*?" She wanted very much to live, for herself and her husband, and for her unborn child, but this perpetual darkness and cold, the brutal earthquakes and wind strong enough to knock her over . . . How many more days, weeks, or, God save them, *months* would they have to spend searching for something to hold on to and wondering if they'd be alive two minutes in the future?

"Five more days, Crystal." Frank sounded exhausted. "Today is the center of impact." He paused to see if she had a comment, then continued when she didn't speak. "But the hits should start losing strength. When they do the rest of the effects will start to lessen, though it may be . . . a while before everything returns to normal—whatever normal's going to mean."

"A while?"

"I can't tell you how long."

"You—"

"I swear to you—I just don't know."

She gazed into the blackness and wished she could see; for days it had been impossible to tell day from night. Her hand swept the air in front of her, but it was a useless gesture; without a streak of lightning, they might as well be blind. Past days of sunshine and lush green trees seemed like nothing more than a dream now. Without knowing why, Crystal found herself thinking of Arizona, Florida, and California, of groves of citrus trees in the summer sun, the smells of oranges and lemons. In their home city of Phoenix, orange trees were everywhere, by shopping malls and ringing industrial parking lots, planted along the highways; their pungent scent filled the late season air. "What's happening out there?" She wasn't sure she wanted to know; at the same time she needed an idea of what to expect when—*if*—the daylight came back. "Is it as bad everywhere else as it is here?"

Her husband shifted and she heard him suppress a groan. He was hurt but he wouldn't tell her where, claimed it didn't matter because either it healed or it didn't. She thought he might have cracked a rib during one of the quakes but there was nothing she could do to ease his pain; their first aid kit was in the car, but the trunk was crushed shut and they couldn't see enough to find something with which to pry it open. Every part of her body felt battered but at least the baby still seemed to be doing okay.

When he finally spoke, Frank's voice was soft and faraway, as if he were looking at all those other places in his head. "It's probably worse. Harder earthquakes—every fault line in the world has probably been triggered. Tsunamis along the coastlines around the world—the smaller islands will disappear entirely and there'll be drastic changes in the coastal areas of all the continents. A lot of volcanoes and lava caused by the quakes, plus hurricanes; there'll be extreme swings in the weather patterns around the world, heat buildup will probably melt some of the polar ice. I'd expected the thunderstorms, but to be honest, I'm surprised the temperature is as high as it is—everything we've ever speculated about a direct hit indicated otherwise. These shock waves are like nothing I've learned about. I swear to God it feel likes we're on an elevator that's slamming on the brakes. We've got—"

"The people," Crystal interrupted. Her visions of Florida orange tree groves were disintegrating under more horrifying possibilities. "What about them? The cities, other countries—civilization?"

Under the scream of the wind, Crystal heard his faint sigh. "This is so much worse than we estimated. The cities are . . . probably destroyed. Urban areas will be the most devastated—the buildings can't stand up to these earthquakes and the underground lines for natural gas and gasoline will snap, water mains, electrical cables—all of it. Transportation and communication will come to a complete halt—we can already see that not much is going to be left of the roads. God knows when it'll actually be daylight; depending on what's floating in the atmosphere, it could be years before we see the sun again—*if* we ever do. Without sunlight, photosynthesis will stop and what hasn't already been disrupted within the food web will break apart. Mankind may be adaptable, but we've never had to do it this fast."

She sat there, trying to take it all in, trying to fathom what her husband was telling her. A world without daylight . . . a place where their child might never snatch at a dust mote floating within a sunbeam. She wanted to say something, *anything,* but she couldn't get her mouth to work. Next to her, Frank was silent for a long time while thunder rumbled across the gale-flattened cornfields. Eventually he gathered her in his arms and held her tight, and his words were the most frightening of any she'd heard so far.

"It's all so *fragile,* Crystal, thousands of years of evolution wiped out in the space of a single week. And civilization? By the time Millennium is through, I don't think there'll be such a thing."

CHICAGO, ILLINOIS
JULY 7: 11:05 A.M.

On Seminary Street, the southern group of town houses next door to Lamont's home was burning.

No one knew what had started the fire—maybe a ruptured gas line exposed to a spark. In his preparations for the night before impact, the last thing Lamont had done was completely disconnect and cap the People's Gas feed line outside by the back door. As far as Mercy and the others could guess, the only thing that kept the fire next door from spreading to what remained of Lamont's town house—a wet jumble of wood, siding, and soggy plaster—was the gap between the property. The builder had constructed this particular development in blocks of four units with eight-foot spaces between them; rather than use precious backyard areas, it was into these walled-off gangways that the central air-conditioning equipment had been set. The continuous, greasy rain seemed to have no effect on the blaze, and now they could only wait and wonder whether the gangway space would be enough to stop the conflagration. If the fire spread and Lamont's town house was destroyed, their cache of food and drinking water would go with it. Lamont might be able to dig through a mountain, but he needn't bother if everything underneath was made of ash.

"Do you think there's anyone in there?" Simon had to yell at Lamont to be heard over the crackling flames.

The other man turned his hands palm up, his face slick with water and reflected firelight. "I hope not," he shouted in response. "I thought everyone headed outside when the earthquakes started." As if talking about it had awakened something, the ground beneath their feet began a slow, ominous shimmy.

The four of them reacted instantly, their moves rehearsed but hardly routine; dodging away from the crumbling sides of what had been their home only last week, they staggered back toward a spot near the center of the yard. They had talked about it over and over since making it through that first hellish strike, but if there was a safer place to go, they simply didn't know where it was. Muted explosions periodically cut through the air as gas tanks at service stations, cars, oxygen and acetylene setups in the line of body shops along Clybourn, propane tanks for BBQ grills in garages and God knew what else ignited and blew. The people who hadn't run from the buildings during the quakes had undoubtedly been killed, and the numbers of those who had fled into the streets appeared to be thinning each day as the pummeling continued; better to stay where you were than to play explorer.

"Come on, Gena!" Mercy cried. Although Mercy's previous examinations showed that the shorter woman was a month earlier in her pregnancy than Mercy, Gena's balance always seemed to be a little off. It was as though being blind for so long had taught her to walk a certain way and she had yet to master the finer details of judging distance in the visual world. Now that she had been granted sight and the added weight of an unborn child on her stocky frame, Gena had oddly backstepped in her relationship with the laws of gravity, and the erratic rolling motion underfoot didn't help.

Ten feet away, Gena went down on one knee with a grunt. Under other circumstances, Mercy would have laughed at her friend's peculiar curse—"Aw, fuckity!"—but here and now all she could think about was that Gena was far too close to the wreckage of the metal storage shed at the other side of the yard. In the red light of the fire, Mercy could see the dirty sheets of aluminum buckling and twisting, and she didn't know or care if they were really moving like that or if it was just her vision, jouncing up and down in opposition to the jittering ground. Every time the Earth vibrated, she felt like a bar drink shaken over ice.

Gena tried to stand and went down again; as Mercy scrambled forward, she heard Lamont yelling behind her. All that bottled-up strength was useless when he was bouncing around with the rest of the world and couldn't keep anything stable in his line of sight. She was closer to Gena; if she could just grab hold of her wrist, the two of them could use each other for balance and grope their way back to the relative safety of the yard's center. It was there, somewhere between the darkness and the pouring rain; they just couldn't see it.

"Mercy, go on!" Gena screamed. "I'm fine—get back!"

Ignoring her words, Mercy vaulted forward. "Gotcha!" Panting for breath, she pulled Gena to her feet and they began to stagger toward Simon and Lamont, fighting to stay upright with every step. This morning had offered them more than an hour of tremor-free time—Mercy should have known it was only a lull, should never have allowed herself the luxury of thinking the worst of this nightmare was past.

"You should've stayed where you were!" Clinging to each

other didn't stop Gena from raging in her ear. "Are you fucking crazy?"

"Shut up!"

"I will *not*! You don't have to stay by my side every second, you idiot—you have to watch out for yourself!"

The ground buckled beneath the suddenly doubled roaring of the wind and the soft *whump!* of an explosion from an unknown direction; soaked to the skin, both women pitched forward and ended up crawling through mud up to their wrists. Rocks and bits of wood bit into their palms as they worked their way across the yard. Mercy had no time to respond as at their backs one wall of the shed finally tore free; with the rain lashing at her face and Simon's worried cry of *"Mercy—Gena—where are you?"* sounding so very far away—

—she never registered it when a sixty-mile-an-hour gust sent the edge of a heavy aluminum panel slamming into the side of her head.

LITCHFIELD, ILLINOIS
JULY 8: 12:31 P.M.

There wasn't much left that was salvageable amid the ragtag gathering of vehicles that had made up the camp in Litchfield. Joey had told her last month that he thought it was a good place to be, if only because these people didn't appear to take the threat of the asteroid strike very seriously. When they died off, he'd said matter-of-factly, the people who were better prepared would move in and claim what remained. Survival of the strong, and Joey planned to be one of the strongest.

But Alva had had about as much as she could take.

When the vibrations in the ground began again at the brightest part of the day—which wasn't saying much—Alva stayed where she was. When Joey pulled on her hand, she ignored him and closed her eyes. *Fuck it,* she thought. *Let a tree land on me. To die only means to finally get a good night's sleep.*

"What the hell, Alva?"

Joey sounded disbelieving and impatient—*"Come on, come on, let's get moving here!"* How many times had she heard that over the past week? Like a sergeant back at the academy, get your rookie little asses in gear and *work* it, damn it, but he wasn't a sergeant and she wasn't a pupil, and screw everything, she was too drained to move anymore. If she was meant to die she would;

otherwise, just let her be. He yanked on her arm and succeeded in pulling her eight inches across the ground; beneath one arm she felt the questionably dry spot she'd found turn to rain-logged mud. "Let *go*, Joey." She tugged free of his grasp and scuttled back into the alcove between a tree that was still standing and its partially uprooted neighbor—the one that was probably going to kill her. The ground heaved slightly, then quieted; a false lull: they'd been through dozens of them. She shivered and felt the nausea rise again. Should she be grateful she never actually threw up, or should she find a bent piece of metal somewhere in the rubble and try a self-induced abortion? She couldn't decide from hour to hour. "I'm staying here."

"The tree—"

"I don't give a flying fuck."

"Yeah, well I *do*." This time his grip was undeniable and she could either stand and do what he wanted or he was going to drag her.

"Damn you!" Alva screeched. "Let me *go*, you black basta—"

The last thing she expected was the cruel, openhanded slap across her face. She cried out, then found her face inches from his. "We don't have time for your bigoted insults!" he bellowed at her. "I'm going to live through this and so are you, whether you want to or not!"

Alva tried to punch him, but it was a ludicrously weak attempt; most of her strength had been sapped by the constant nausea and anything left got shaken out of her by the ground shocks. To her horror, she began to weep, and she hated herself more at that moment than she hated the asteroids that were pounding her world to bits.

Her tears made no difference to Joey. When she wouldn't cooperate, he gripped the back of her coat in one fist and jerked her away from the cluster of unstable trees; four seconds later the ground began to pitch in earnest. They both fell but Joey wouldn't stay down; still clutching her jacket, he scuttled along like a giant crab, forcing her to stay with him or have her face scraped in the dirt as she was towed.

Alva never knew how long the earthquakes lasted. Each one felt like an eternity, the next always longer than the last, and of all the people in the world she could have died with, she'd chosen an unsympathetic drug dealer. She thought she could feel her sanity stretching more as the days passed, as though each ground shock had an invisible rubber band attached to the logical part of her mind and its sole purpose was to pull as far and thin as it could.

"I hope you're satisfied." Joey's water-streaked face was grim. "You damned near got us killed."

Alva said nothing; she was too fatigued to argue.

"What is it with you?" She flinched when Joey suddenly shouted at her. When she tried to cover her ears with her hands, he slapped them away. "I could use a little fucking teamwork, you know? We're supposed to be a twosome! Or don't you want to stay alive, stupid?"

"I'm tired," she yelled back—she had to, just to be heard above the ongoing storm. "And I'm *sick*."

"With *what*?"

The ground shifted ominously and they both froze, expecting another earthquake. Nothing happened, but Alva's skin crawled. Time to 'fess up; at least it would explain some of her actions. "I'm going to have a baby."

Joey looked like she'd shot him. *"What?"*

"You heard me."

"Shit, Alva!" He waved his arms, but she couldn't tell whether it was for emphasis or balance. "Haven't you ever heard of birth control?"

"Sure, Mr. London." Her voice was a sneer but easily heard. "And would you mind dropping me off at the drugstore on the way to work this morning so I can pick up my pills?"

"Yeah, that's *real* helpful, babe."

"Or maybe you thought I was 'fixed' or something, like a dog."

"That pretty much covers it," he shot back.

"Prick!" she shrieked.

Without warning, the ground jerked under their feet. Alva was already on her knees but Joey landed hard on his ass beside her. A grin still flashed across his face. "I knew the bitch I liked so much was still somewhere inside you."

"Joey—"

His hand snaked out and gripped her arm. "Don't you worry, sugar. I'll take care of everything." Incredibly, he was still smiling. Within the dark circle of his face, the whites of his eyes were strangely almond-shaped. In spite of all the chaos around them, the screaming wind, lashing rain, and the quakes that sent anything and everything tumbling like so much paper, his gaze reminded her of a hunter, like a cat's or a wolf's. Something dark and dangerous that slunk through the night but was seldom seen, and she was damned glad that when his eyes tracked her, he didn't see a target. Or did he?

"I'll see to us just fine."

CHICAGO, ILLINOIS
JULY 9: 9:15 P.M.

Eddie was convinced he had gangrene in his legs.

His father, who had supplemented their family's income by custom grinding tools in the garage, had once told Eddie that the worst infection he'd ever gotten had been caused by concrete dust. While the wound had been courtesy of the grinder, the old man's fabled infection hadn't come from metal shavings or cleaning solvent or grease; rather, he had reopened the gouge while moving a couple of bags of concrete mix. Until now, Eddie had never appreciated the wonders of concrete; having an unknown amount of it layered across everything below his thighs had done a lot to change his point of view. How much weight was down there remained a mystery that a few quick sweeps of the flashlight couldn't solve; neither he nor Searle could move the massive chunks and no amount of wriggling accomplished anything. The pain was excruciating and eventually Eddie stopped trying; he passed the time by staring at his glow-in-the-dark date-watch and feeling the stretched skin and the heated throb of the corruption as it worked its way insidiously up his legs. At times—usually if he tried too hard to free himself—the agony was nearly unbearable and Eddie would jam the side of his hand into his mouth and bite down hard; as the pain exhausted him, the infection faded to a far-off annoyance and it was his cramping muscles that bothered him the most. Since he couldn't move, he was urinating into an empty plastic jug and staying away from solids altogether; after about day three, he was feverish enough not to miss food.

Not designed to withstand hour after hour of earthquakes that measured seven or eight on the Richter scale, the ceiling over the bottom corner of the row of bunk beds had caved in at mid-morning on day two, which would make this the seventh day that Eddie had been stuck on the top berth. He kept wondering if the sagging metal supports of the bed structure would give out, but they never did . . . too bad. He might be killed or maimed when it all came down, but at least he would no longer feel like a puny rat in the world's biggest trap.

Erica had gone a little freaky on day three, but Searle—and oh, wasn't he the understanding man of the hour?—had put a quick end to that. Mr. Chanowitz liked his cellmates quiet, thank you very much, which contributed a lot to Eddie's decision to keep private the ongoing diary of pain running through his mind. Every now and then Erica sniffled, and it pained Eddie almost as much as his leg to think that she and Ryan were crying to themselves somewhere in the dark, forbidden even the dubious comfort of tearful release. Every now and then Eddie would sort of . . . fade out, although it was interesting that he never failed to know it was coming, preceded as it always was by the thought that perhaps this was finally the time that the bomb shelter's salvation would become their tomb. What was going on in the outside world? He dearly hoped he hadn't brought Ryan and his aunt down here simply to die in the blackness at the hands of a madman. He clung to the notion that the impacts or earthquakes or whatever the hell they were had begun to lessen in length and severity, a good thing, considering the up-close and detailed view he had of the cracking ceiling during the rare moments when the flashlight or a candle was used.

His legs . . .

It could be worse, Eddie told himself stoically. Those might be the words spoken by every parental figure in history but . . . yeah. A foot or two higher, and the concrete could've come crashing onto his hips and an area of his body that was substantially more sensitive to pain. Thinking about pain there made him think about pleasure, and that in turn made him think about Naomi. Funny how that stream-of-consciousness thing worked.

If I get out of this alive, Eddie thought, *and assuming I'll someday be able to walk, I'm going to find her.* She'd surprised him with that last bloodsucking thing, but was it truly such a big deal? Naomi was, after all, a Goth child of New Orleans, and while Eddie had never known her to be interested in the vampire culture, maybe it had been there all along and he'd simply never noticed it. Drinking blood couldn't be *that* harmful if it didn't make her sick and she didn't kill anyone to get it. The cut along the bend of his elbow had been sore for a few days but unlike the concrete thing going on with his lower body right now, the expected infection—the human mouth was a pit of contamination—had never come. A week after Naomi had disappeared from his life, so had the razor cut—there was barely a scar to remember her by. He'd never told Erica about the incident; what would the dignified hospital administrator have thought about Eddie and Naomi's last sex-and-blood good-bye?

Finding Naomi . . . that was something else entirely. Yet there was no serious doubt in Eddie's mind that he could do it. He'd always had a sort of homing beacon for her, something that amazed him in light of his belief that he'd didn't really love her. She'd tried her best to drop out of sight after the incident with the sailor at the Café du Monde, but she couldn't shake him—Eddie always knew where she was, day or night. He reasoned that it was logical deduction—if she got paid, she'd stop by the bank, etc.— but after a while they'd both shut up and accepted it. There was no rational analysis that could tell him that on a particular Tuesday night she'd take every piece of clothing she owned that wasn't black to the Salvation Army . . . yet he'd known. Eddie didn't know exactly where Naomi was at this specific minute, but he had a hunch he'd know it immediately if she died . . . and it hadn't happened yet.

Two beds below him, Ryan whimpered and Eddie tensed when he heard the springs of Searle's bunk squeak. Eddie found himself praying—*Please, God, don't let him hit the boy again.* The seconds pulsed by, so slowly, until Eddie felt he could exhale once more. Wasn't it just too bad that he hadn't found a way to persuade Searle that the primo place to be in this little mausoleum was this top bunk? They would have all been better off if Searle Chanowitz had been the one shackled in place by the building. Still, it wasn't hard to imagine Searle chewing through the chunks of concrete to regain his freedom.

More frighteningly, it wasn't hard to imagine Searle chewing through a lot of things.

JULY 10: 4:25 A.M.

She felt like she'd been dropped into a sealed oil barrel with a maddened bear, then rolled downhill.

Come on, Erica told herself. You can keep a grip on it. You *can.*

Her fingers went to the bruise along the line of her right eyebrow—Searle's latest gift—and she grimaced at the jolt of pain she received when she touched it. The headache had finally gone away but the flesh was still puffy and tender, and she could feel the line of dried blood that started at the small lump, followed the curve of her temple, and disappeared into her hairline, little bits of grit that she couldn't see to wash away.

How many times had he hit her now—four? Five? Or more? She couldn't remember. Usually in the face, once in the stomach, and only force of will had kept her from vomiting that time. She was terrified of him, yes, but Searle had no idea that it wasn't his physical violence that scared her so badly, oh, no. It was the sense of dull . . . *acceptance* that had started to take root in some weak spot in the fabric of herself. This, she had finally realized, was how women who were abused and battered year after year became trapped with their tormentors. All Erica's life she had looked down her nose in disgust on those wives and girlfriends who had passed through the social programs in the hospital or, more often, the emergency room like petrified shadows. Fools, she had sneered inwardly as she went over the monthly reports from the department heads and saw the statistics, sometimes recognizing a recurring name. In Erica's view, even her sister-in-law merited no sympathy; why, the stupid woman let her son be used as a punching bag while she stood aside and did nothing. If a man hits you, Erica had always believed, you should get out; stay and you deserve whatever you get.

God, how very wrong she had been. No one could deny that she was trapped more than most in this situation—there was no front door to slam in Searle's jeering face as she walked out forever, no women's shelter to take her in as she reevaluated the influence her lover had gained over her life while she made plans to rebuild. With lots of time in the darkness to think, Erica finally saw the difference between herself and a hundred thousand others: it had been her power and affluence that had given her that sense of superiority, that *confidence* that so many women lacked. Stripped of her right to control and make decisions, her role had become as theirs: terror tempered by dependency, a victim of acceptance based on need, a woman suddenly insecure about the same abilities that had carried her so far in the world and in her life. As so many wives and girlfriends had been primed to believe they could not survive in the outside world without their persecutor, so had she slowly become convinced that Searle remained the only thing standing between her and certain death at the hands of God knew what when they made it out of this underground tomb. She had become vulnerable and fragile, and had begun to believe that without him, she would surely perish.

Brought out in her mind for examination, Erica thought she would prefer to take her chances with the rest of the world.

There were few options here; they would either find an escape route, or they would die. Erica was betting that one way or another, when Searle started to panic about actually *dying* down here, he would find a way to open the door to the bomb shelter, even if he had to clear the debris a pebble at a time to do it. When they were finally up top again, she would be free of this madman. She would *not* accept this mistreatment for the rest of her life, she would *not* give Searle Chanowitz a license to pound on her at will in return for the dubious privilege of his protection. Down here she would hold her tongue and acquiesce to his orders. To do otherwise was unthinkable, if not for her then for Ryan—Searle had already cracked him several times because of an imagined disobedience by Erica.

But once they were free, Searle would see the rebirth of the woman he believed he'd so effectively silenced with his fists.

UNKNOWN BROADCAST
JULY 10 . . .

"Hi, my name is Pax Bailby. I used to be a writer—romances under a pen name, would you believe it?—but I guess that's all over now. I don't think there's anyone around left to publish the books even if I felt like writing them. No one would want to read romance novels anymore. So now I'll just . . . I don't know, write on the air or something, or at least as long as I can find batteries that will keep this thing going or until someone takes it away from me. I don't know much about ham radios, and there's no instruction book, so I'll just be winging it. It's a handheld setup and doesn't look very powerful. Hell, for all I know, I could be talking only to myself.

"Right now I'm in Searcy, which is a small town not too far from Little Rock, Arkansas. I started off in Pine Bluff, but I left when I couldn't f-find my wife. We were convinced that Millennium wasn't a real threat—after all, if it was, wouldn't Washington and the Russians and all those other countries have gotten off their collective butts and done something about it? But

I'm not going to start arguing politics now. It's too late for that. Dora was down in the laundry room of the apartment building where we lived and I was taking out the garbage when the first aftershock rolled through the town. It happened so fast—the whole damned back of the place slid in on itself. I tried to dig her out, but I couldn't do it; everyone else was discovering their own problems and it was only me. Every time I made a little progress we'd have another quake and more of the place would cave in. By day four there wasn't anything left but a pile of wet rubble and I gave up. The whole town was drowning—the Arkansas River feeds off the Mississippi, and there must've been some hellacious waves coming off the Gulf. I'd never seen the Arkansas run so high, swallowing up everything along its banks, sucking up buildings like they were made of tissue paper. Cars, trucks, p-people . . .

"Anyway, I'm not sure how I managed to get this far without something falling on me, or getting shot, but here I am. So if anyone out there is listening, I'm going around and trying to let people know what it's like in the rest of the world, in the places where they aren't. Searcy really took it hard. If there're people left in this town, I don't see them. It's a real small place where the tallest building was maybe three stories high, although it's hard to tell by what's left. A good chunk of the western part is burned out from a fire that looks like it started at some kind of plant. The smoke over there is especially nasty so I'm staying away from that end. I've been checking out the rest of it for about a half day, walking around and listening, but there's not a sound or a soul to be found, not even a dog. It's like everyone just packed up and ran. Or maybe all the bodies are still inside what's left of the buildings.

"I kept telling myself that it couldn't last forever, and the worst of it seems to finally be over. The last earthquake was about three hours ago, sometime around early afternoon, and it was fairly weak compared to earlier stuff, barely a little shake. I wonder how many people are still alive. I'm not positive my watch has kept the best time, but I'm guessing it's after five o'clock right now. The clouds keep it dark enough to be night all the time and there's a lot of rain. Oh, yeah, it's a lot colder than it ought to be for high summer here in Arkansas. There's mountains and desert behind me to the west, colder weather up north, and lots of water straight *south, so I've decided to head east. I'm hoping it'll be a lot easier to travel in that direction.*

"So, uh . . . this is Pax Bailby, signing off for today, which if the calendar thing on my watch is still working, is July tenth. If I'm still alive, look for another broadcast in, say, a week."

7.
THE GRAYZONE

"It's been hours since the last ground shock."

Lamont swallowed, then rubbed his hands together, knowing it betrayed his nervousness but powerless to stop himself. "Yeah," he said. "At least three. But every time we've thought that was it, they started again the next morning. Don't you think we'll get more tomorrow?"

A few feet away, Simon cradled Mercy without moving. Worry was beaten into every line of the younger man's face. "I don't care if we get another quake in five minutes, Lamont. We can't wait any longer. Mercy needs help now, not tomorrow or two days from now."

Between them, Gena shivered and stared at Mercy. The blood from the gash—and there had been so *much* of it—had long since washed away; they had tried to keep the wound clean and dry, but it was impossible. Lamont could dig only so far into the ruins along the edge of the town house; he'd come up with some clean kitchen towels from the wrecked cabinets at the back, but the rain soaked through the makeshift bandages within minutes. Mercy hadn't regained full consciousness for more than twenty-four hours; rather, she'd drifted in and out, mumbling and sometimes crying softly, but never making any sense or recognizing them. "I don't know much about medicine," Gena said now, "but she should have stitches and I'm sure she needs antibiotics. Look at how red the cut is around the edges."

Simon nodded but the rest of his body didn't move. He looked like he wanted to rock his wife as though she were a child but didn't dare make that small, comforting motion. "Stitches," he whispered as he looked down at Mercy. One side of her face was horribly bruised, the eye swollen shut.

Lamont didn't say anything and Gena leaned forward. "Simon, this might sound farfetched, but . . . can you see inside her head? I mean, if she knows what's wrong, maybe she can—"

"No," Simon said hoarsely. "I tried. She's delirious. Nothing she's thinking makes any sense. Fragments and memories, maybe hallucinations. Like fever dreams." He stared hard at Lamont. "She needs antibiotics."

"We don't have any idea what kind. She could be allergic." It was a lame excuse and they all knew it. More than Simon's anger, the bewilderment on Gena's face stung Lamont. Two months ago she would have understood his fear; now she seemed like a stranger.

"One step at a time." Simon began carefully rearranging Mercy until he could slide her from his lap. A few adjustments and her head was propped on a makeshift pillow on the ground. "First we get there."

"Get where?" Gena asked.

"Althaia," Simon said with finality. "It's the closest place where there might be medicine."

Gena glanced at Lamont, but he purposely looked away. "It's probably in ruins." Her dark eyes sought Simon's. "Are you sure it's worth the trip? What if there are no supplies—"

"The only thing I'm sure about is that my wife is going to die if I don't find some help." Simon stood, his hair plastered to his face and making him look like a wet skeleton. "And I'm not going to stand here and watch."

"I think it's a wasted trip—"

"I'm sick and tired of your excuses, Lamont," Simon said coldly. "I won't sacrifice Mercy because you're too afraid to let other people see what you can do."

Lamont sprang to his feet. "Get out of my head, Simon!"

"You think it's some big secret?" Simon yelled back at him. "Even if it wasn't pouring out, we all know how you feel! I can't believe you'd let one of your friends die because of a stupid childhood phobia!" Abruptly Simon bent and slipped his arms under Mercy's back and legs, balanced himself as he positioned her head against his chest, then carefully straightened. "If you won't help me, we'll go by ourselves."

"Don't you understand how dangerous it would be for me to just walk through the streets and toss everything out of the way?" To his own ears, Lamont's voice sounded desperate. "If anyone sees—"

Simon's eyes were unflinching. "Sorry, I don't make the connection. I know you're scared, but who isn't? And I doubt anyone's going to call you a freak if you help them—they'll be too happy to be alive. No matter what frightened you when you were a kid, this is a whole different set of circumstances."

"Simon," Gena broke in, "what will you do for supplies along the way? Water, food . . . on foot, it's so far—"

"We'll make do," Simon said grimly. He shifted Mercy's weight in his arms and she groaned softly. "Maybe I'll see you around." He turned his back and began carefully picking his way across the wrecked backyard, stepping over the heaps of debris that had built up over the past nine days. Paralyzed, Lamont stared after him.

"Wait!" Gena called. "I'm going with you!"

Lamont's pulse did a slam-jump in his throat. *Gena!* He snatched at the sleeve of her coat, but she batted his hand aside.

"You can protect yourself, Lamont. He needs all the help he can get." Clutching an almost full water jug, she scrambled after Simon, who was making slow progress toward a break between the mounds of rubble. Although it should have been daylight, the sky was the color of soot; through the steady rain, Gena and Simon looked like gray, retreating ghosts. "I'll try to get back as soon as I can."

For one horrifying second, Lamont thought about simply *making* her stay—Simon, too. His temporary insanity made him suddenly want to vomit. "We're supposed to stay together!" he called instead. His voice cracked. "You were the one who told us that!"

Gena stopped to regard him, but only for an instant. He barely heard her words over the wind. "The only one keeping you here is *you*."

"But what—" Fear of her answer choked off Lamont's question before he could finish it. He'd been about to ask *What do you think* you *can do to help?* but he could imagine her turning and fixing him with those dark eyes and saying, *More than you.* He didn't think he could stand that. Another ten seconds and they were out of sight.

"You're an asshole and a coward if you let them go," he said out loud. These were his friends and they needed him; of all the people in the world, they had accepted him and never, *ever* condemned him or demanded that he hide what he was. Could he say that for all the people he'd worked with? No—and most painful of all, he couldn't say it for his own family. His parents . . . his *father* had been responsible for instilling this terror of discovery so deeply into his psyche. Hastily Lamont ducked back to the edge of what remained of the town house and gathered a couple of jugs of water, then shifted the chunks of rubbish around until he managed to drag out a relatively dry window curtain that could be used as a covering for Mercy. With him along, they could easily find food on the way, more dry blankets, shelter or whatever. Lamont folded the curtain and tucked it under his arm. Grabbing the water jugs, he sprinted after them. At the edge of the town house's property, he stopped short.

Damn himself to hell, nothing Lamont did would let him step out of the backyard.

NILES, ILLINOIS
JULY 11 . . .

And on the third day she rose again, Lily thought.

Three days—that was how long she'd spent bouncing around that forest preserve like a bug in a jar being shaken by a curious kid. The Suzuki was completely trashed and she didn't know shit about how to fix it; there were parts knocked off that might be ornamental and might be as important as, say, the ignition key. The earthquakes came and went in spells that were fairly easy to track: they woke you up from an exhausted sleep bright and early—*Rise and shine, everyone—WHAM!*—and stopped an eternity later. She guessed each day's version of forever to be about six or seven hours, not counting the smaller aftershocks that rippled through the ground as though the world were a giant round waterbed. After the worst of day three, Lily had clawed her way out of the forest preserve and onto the street; what difference did it make if she stayed in the preserve or hit the streets and tried to make it back to Lamont's town house? There was an equal chance she'd die either way, and hunkering down was a slow, sure way to starvation.

Lily came out of the preserve within the city limits and close to the interchange for Interstate 90, intending to follow the highway until it intersected Webster, where she could cut over and go straight east. As terrible as her time in the forest preserve had been, now she felt as though she'd been encased in a big, tree-laden safety dome. The rest of the world hadn't fared very well at all.

There had been several brick and concrete office buildings at the intersection of the expressway and Caldwell where it turned into Peterson as it headed east. They might as well have been made of paper. Bodies clotted the buckled sidewalks, looking like huge, sodden snails in the gray downpour. Cars and trucks had fallen into the chasms formed when the interstate had ripped apart; now their smashed remains were wedged between the sharp-edged pieces. A few shocked people moved tentatively through the cold rain, going nowhere; like Lily, they resembled bloody, ravaged zombies. She ignored the ones who looked at her as she doggedly pushed deeper into the city and avoided those few who tried to talk—not many, since she looked no better than anyone else, mottled with blood and bruises and filthy from the wet mud that was everywhere.

The soldiers . . .

They were a problem. Lily suspected that while each day sent a new dose of hell, the armed crazies that were the remains of the last bit of authority did quite a bit on their own to thin the number of survivors. Mistrustful by nature and with the imprint of the Savanna soldier burned into her mind like a black shadow, Lily hid whenever the telltale gunfire got too close. Peering from whatever hole in the debris she could find, she lost count of the random, mindless executions she witnessed.

When it was safe and the ground wasn't lurching under her feet, she foraged for food in the storefronts and buildings and found it only because there simply weren't that many people left—competition was scarce and decreasing by the day. Rats were everywhere, and Lily was disgusted by their numbers.

Insects, raccoons, possums, stray cats and dogs skulked amid the demolished buildings, feeding off the rats and the human remains; it'd taken her only an hour to discover that a nail-studded two-by-four was the best weapon against the injured, vicious animals that would sooner attack as get out of her way. An evening's walk showed too many rats to count falling under the teeth of dogs and cats, and Lily imagined a city gone insane with rabies in the not-too-distant future.

The days became a staggering blur of hunger and pain and hiding, and the only thing that kept her going was the thought that somewhere at the end of her trip was Mercy. Were Mercy and Simon still alive? Lily refused to think otherwise. Gena could see the future—she would know what they should and shouldn't do, where they could go to escape the worst of it . . . if there was such a place.

I-90/94 was a severed artery running through Chicago's north-west neighborhoods, and Elston Avenue the crippled, smaller vein following alongside it. Trashed and split, every street surface was a pitted, sunken horror; in the first five days the fires burned almost as continuously as the screams that floated on the grit-filled wind. Eventually both died away, replaced by furtive, soundless silhouettes amid the shaky, skeletal doorways. The cold temperatures did nothing to mask the smell of rotting flesh, sewage, and chemicals.

With nothing to carry and no one to worry about except herself, it still took almost as many days to travel seven and a half miles. Somewhere in the span of time between starting the trek and turning onto Seminary, day and night had blended and the sky was the same dirty color all the time, as if someone had taken a piece of smoke-colored film and tacked it over the eye of the world. The silver calendar in her pocket was spotted with blood and grime but the date was readable amid her careful cross-outs: it was July eleventh, or what the kids always called "Slurpee Day" after the 7-Eleven stores that were everywhere in the city.

The once beautiful row of late-model town houses looked like a house of cards that someone had poured water over then ground into the dirt with a boot heel, but Lily refused to make herself any crazier by standing in front and wondering about her friends. In her past days of insanity she'd never hesitated to take on the frightening things, and there was a fundamental difference between finding out what was inside here and keeping her head with the soldier back in Savanna. Grinding her teeth, she hoisted herself up what was left of the front steps and began climbing through the wreckage.

She'd seen a lot of things on the journey here, but she never, *ever* expected to find the ghost of Lamont sitting quietly in the muck at the back of the property.

"Snap out of it."

Nothing. Lily circled him, but Lamont stared into space as though she didn't exist. What was the matter with him? He looked as though he'd been sitting out here for days . . . surely he'd gotten up to find food, take a pee, *something*. His skin was washed out and ashen beneath a scraggly growth of beard, his dark eyes frighteningly vacant. Soaked, drawn—the last really bad earthquake had been several days ago. He could have easily taken shelter in what was left of the town house and skipped out during the softer groundshocks that had followed. What the hell was he doing sitting in the mud?

"Lamont, what's wrong with you?" Lily demanded. She'd been reluctant to touch him—somewhere she'd heard that you shouldn't treat someone roughly if they were in shock. She didn't know if it was true, but it seemed like a reasonable thing. Still, she wasn't going to wait all day. Squatting in front of him made the neck of her jacket twist and sent a fresh wash of rainwater down the back of her neck. The slowdown in movement had already started cooling her body temperature. The steady, cold rain had become a fact of life, but sitting in the mud? How had Lamont endured it? She tried a different question. "Where are the others?"

Not so much as a blink indicated he'd heard her. *Damn it!* She'd come through the town house but hadn't seen or smelled any bodies, and there were none visible anywhere in the yard. Ten times, twenty times, still no answer and she finally screamed into his face—

"Tell me where the fuck they are!"

—and swung her open palm at his cheek with all her strength. She never touched his skin.

"Don't."

It felt like something unseen had grabbed her by the wrist and stopped her momentum, a lot like the jerking, slam-on-the-brakes feeling she'd gotten from the ground during the worst of the asteroid hits. It didn't hurt and Lily didn't take the time to dwell on what caused it, be it Lamont or something else; she didn't care. The grip disappeared almost instantly and she leaped on Lamont and seized him by the shoulders of his coat. "It's about fucking time you woke up!" she yelled. "Where's Mercy?"

"Gone."

"I can see that, you dumb *shit*." She let go of one shoulder but hung on to the other and pulled. At first, Lamont felt like a block of granite; then she felt him give; thinking she was going to make him stand, Lily succeeded only in tipping him sideways into the sludge. At least he put out a hand to keep himself from landing on his face. "Gone *where*? God, Lamont—you're not a fucking three-year-old. Do I have to play twenty questions?" Her voice was climbing to a screech. She thought she was going to have to pummel him again, then he finally answered in a monotone voice.

"Althaia."

"Why?"

For an instant he looked like he couldn't remember. Then, "Simon and Gena took Mercy there to find help for her."

The whens and what-was-wrongs—none of them mattered. Lily dug her fingers into the sodden fabric of Lamont's coat and pulled; he didn't resist, but he didn't stand either. "Damn you, get *up*," she hissed. "I can't believe you didn't go with them—hell, I can't believe they let *you* stay here!" Across the yard, she spied a break in the mounds of dirt and wood; digging her feet into the ankle-deep mud for leverage, Lily began dragging Lamont toward it. "We're going after them."

"I—I—"

"Shut up," she snarled. "If you've got any useful brain cells left in your head, get off your ass and walk so I don't have to pull you!"

Lamont yanked his arm away and struggled to his feet at last. "Lily, I *can't* go!"

She stopped short and pushed her nose close to his; she had to look up to do it and he was dripping on her, the rain spilling from his close-cropped hair. "Why the fuck not?"

"Because I can't . . . I can't . . ." He looked at her helplessly.

"Well, you *will*." Lily grasped his wrist and began leading him. She had to suppress a shudder; she was freezing, but Lamont's flesh was numbingly cold. How much longer until he would have sat out here and died of hypothermia?

"Lily, I *tried* to follow them," he said desperately. They were almost at the middle point where the yard ended and the alleyway began. In front of them was what was left of a Cyclone fence, smashed flat over the past week and a half. "I couldn't step out of the yard—physically couldn't *do* it."

She paused and looked at him, then glanced at the fence. "You wanna fill me in? I don't see the problem."

"I can *do* things," he tried to explain. He sounded like a child pleading for understanding. "M-move things without touching them. If anybody—*everybody*—finds this out, I'll be a—a—"

"Freak?" Unable to restrain it, Lily threw back her head and laughed. "Jesus, don't you know who you're talking to?" He stared at her uncomprehendingly. "You idiot, I've spent most of my life being pointed to on the street and watching people run the other way when they saw me coming. Not only am I still alive and kicking, I'm actually *sane*. Besides," she said roughly, "you don't have to do anything except go with me. And I'm *not* going without you."

"But people will—"

"People?" Lily laughed again, shrill enough to make Lamont wince. "There are barely any people *left*! The ones that are still around hide most of the time. No one will see you or pay attention, bud. Now your problems are the same as everyone else's—how to keep away from the soldiers and the dog packs and stay alive for one more day." He frowned but didn't say anything and she reached forward in a vaguely motherly gesture and tugged the open collar of his coat together. "Wise up, Lamont. *No one out there gives a shit anymore.* All that's left for you that's worth anything in this world is Gena and your baby, and Mercy and Simon. Stop worrying about yourself and start thinking about them. They could be hurt or"—she stared hard at him—"worse. We know where they went and we've got to find them before someone or something else does. Let's go."

Lamont took a deep breath and nodded, then marched up to where the fence had fallen and stepped on it. It rattled and he put the other foot forward tentatively, as though he were stepping on something alive rather than cold, wet metal. He leaned forward, his face hard with concentration, then his shoulders sagged. "I just can't do it," he whispered. "Oh, *God*."

"Really?" Lily looked around thoughtfully, then her face

brightened as she recalled an old ploy. "Hey," she said and pointed to the ground to the left of where Lamont stood, "what's that?"

"What?" He automatically tracked her movement, and when she shoved him forward Lily put every ounce of weight she had into it.

"Hey!" Lamont's arms pinwheeled as he fought for balance and stumbled, his shoes beating out a clumsy two-step along the fence's slippery surface. While he was still wobbling, Lily pushed him again and he blundered forward to keep from falling. Going for the three-time charm, she risked it once more; in a seven-second span Lamont had left the dubious safety of his yard and was standing in the alley.

"Forward is the only way to go, Lamont," Lily said cheerfully. She grabbed his arm and began pulling him along, getting him into motion and as fast and far away from this place as she could. When he tried to look back, she found the strength to break into a jog that forced him to keep up or trip and fall. "Don't look back. After all—

"What the hell is there to leave behind, anyway?"

CHICAGO, ILLINOIS
JULY 12 . . .

"Do you think this rain will ever end?"

Simon looked over at her. Neither of them had spoken in some time and he seemed surprised to see her struggling along next to him. "I . . . don't know," he said. "I suppose it has to stop sometime." But his mind wasn't really on the question and he lapsed back into silence as they limped along. The clouds above them were as blotchy as oil-stained concrete, but Gena guessed it was close to midday, the best time to travel. The early or late hours brought most of the animals out, as though they followed some newly remembered wild clock, like the deer that could be seen only deep in the woods at hours man seldom kept. Compared to so many previous days and nights, the sky was lightening, bit by bit. She was too afraid of disappointment to hope for a letup in the nonstop thunderstorms and the biting, grit-filled rain, and it didn't take a college degree to know that the downpour was the only thing keeping the fires under control.

What was Lamont doing right now?

A few feet in front of her, Simon stumbled and she moved to help him, still amazed that he was able to carry Mercy for so long.

They were almost there, but it had been a horrifying, never-ending trek, two and a half miles of death and utter destruction. Buildings were caved in or cracked in half, their internal structures revealed like dollhouses hinged at mid-roof and open to the world at the push of a finger. Corpses lay within the crushed remains, easy carrion for the crows and the industrious rats swarming through the debris. The closer the threesome got to Althaia, the more water they saw, floodwater from broken city mains, the dirtier blue of the lake. Simon had speculated that the shock waves had made the lakefront flood, although he'd been surprised to see the damage reach this far. On LaSalle the water was still to the east, although the buckled four-lane street and dipped sidewalks were as wet as anything else. All those dead people . . . every time she stumbled past a cadaver she was afraid it would come to life and clutch at her ankle, beg for help she could not give.

"How much farther?" Gena rasped.

"Four or five blocks, I think." Simon's haunted eyes scanned the street. His breathing was strained and she knew he must be exhausted. "It's hard to tell—everything looks so different."

Gena didn't reply, just moved forward to steady him as he clambered awkwardly over a chunk of sidewalk that had broken off and sunk into the ground at an angle. At first she'd thought she'd made a mistake; what was she to Simon but more of a hindrance, another pregnant woman he had to watch out for as he fought to find a way to save his wife's life? Both quickly learned otherwise; the return of her sight had not negated a skill honed over the course of a lifetime—Gena's hearing remained extremely sensitive. The wraithlike people wandering in the ruins were sometimes dangerous and sometimes not; better that Gena and Simon should know about the others' presence before revealing their own. Those left over from the army and the police were the worst of all, armed killers no longer bound by authority or conscience. Gena and Simon peered in slack-faced horror as those who should have helped the most moved through the streets like insane cowboys armed with machine guns instead of lariats and six-shooters. Unlike the killers' unfortunate prey, Gena's hearing always gave them enough warning to conceal themselves. So she was good for something, anyway.

They pushed on, making painful progress south on LaSalle Street. Was it Gena's imagination, or were there more bodies on the sidewalk in this area?

"There," Simon said suddenly. "I can see it."

Bone-weary, Gena strained to see what he was indicating with a tilt of his chin. It took a moment for her to find what was left of the sign, formerly a long, white plastic tube with black lettering that ran down the corner of the building. Now a good portion of it was shattered and the top had fallen away from its connection; only the letters *haia Hos* were still readable on what was left.

Her heart sank and Gena knew she'd been a fool. She had listened to her heart instead of her head, and apparently, *stupidly,* her heart was still full of hope. As had been, most certainly, the hearts of the people who were scattered across the parking lot and who had died simply trying to get there.

But so *many* . . .

"What is this?" she heard herself rasp. "Why would all these people—"

"After Help," Simon answered dully. "They all thought After Help was going to give them a miracle."

The stench was indescribable but Simon pressed forward and Gena refused to be left behind. She could hear him breathing heavily through his mouth, and it was a good thing she hadn't had to deal with nausea during her pregnancy, because this was enough to make the strongest person retch. So many had perished, hundreds, and now there was nothing to do but to let whatever new nature existed take its course. Who knew what had killed them all—flying debris, shock, cold, bullets—and now no one would bury the dead here, say words over their graves or mourn their passing. The only purpose they would serve was food for the hungry scavengers.

The main entrance to the building, a row of glass and steel-framed doors, was open to the elements, the frame buckled, the glass spread across a front walkway spiderwebbed by two-inch cracks. Standing next to Simon and staring into the shadow-pitted innards of the old building, Gena wished desperately to be able to *see* again—in a heartbeat, she would trade her sight of this gray and death-saturated world for the knowledge about what was going to happen an hour from now and the confidence that such wisdom could bring. Inside this building could be salvation for Mercy or death for all three of them . . . but Gena couldn't see a fucking thing.

"Well," was all Simon said. His voice was soft and thoughtful, barely audible beneath the drum of the rain on everything around them. Gena found herself wondering if it was dry inside and a sense of longing filled her. She felt like a dirty, round bath sponge and she was so tired of being wet. She was so tired of being *tired*—would it never end?

"Oh, Simon." Gena's voice was low, despairing. "I don't know if we should go in there."

His head turned in her direction. "Do you see something, Gena?"

Ashamed, she lowered her gaze. "No. Nothing."

"Then we do the best we can." He was silent for a moment. "Same as anyone else would. Maybe you should stay out here," he suggested. "If the structure isn't stable, it won't be safe." He turned and studied the street. His eyes were sharp but Gena could see the weariness in his shoulders and the way Mercy hung low in his arms. How long had he been carrying her without a break this time? A half hour? Forty minutes? Too long. His gaze moved to his wife's face and softened. "We'll find a place to hide both of you near the front," he said. "You stay with Mercy and I'll look for medical supplies. I—"

Gena's head snapped up. "What was that?" Simon froze, not daring to say anything and mask whatever was making its way into Gena's hearing. "There it is again." Her words were a whisper that only Simon could hear. She could tell by the look on his face that he heard nothing, but he would soon. Something clumsy was blundering through the inside hallway, crawling over and around whatever was in its way. It didn't sound big, but it was certainly energetic—a dog? Twenty more seconds and Simon heard it, too; his grip on Mercy tightened and he began to back out of the doorway, scanning the street for signs of danger.

Gena cocked her head, then touched his arm. "Wait," she said softly. "I . . . think it's a child." Simon looked at her disbelievingly and she nodded.

"Alone?" he murmured.

Gena nodded again, then put her fingers to her lips and pointed behind him. Far back in the shadows where the front reception desk had been ripped free of its anchors and slid into the middle of the hallway, something small pulled itself over the obstacle.

"Hello?" The voice was high and thin, definitely a small boy's. It was followed by a sniffle, but it was hard to tell if it was from crying or because of the cold. "Is anybody out there?"

"Here," Simon said automatically. Gena could have swatted

him; she had thoughts of a trap, the child used as bait to draw in someone soft-hearted like Simon. "Over here," he said again.

Oddly, the boy hesitated after he cleared the last obstruction, as though he were used to being deceived. Gena saw a whole play of emotions run across the child's dirt-and blood-streaked face: fear, hope, yearning. Still a good ten feet away, he stopped and stared at them, his gaze running across Gena and Simon, then stopping on the unconscious Mercy. He swallowed. "M-my n-name's Ry-Ryan." His teeth were chattering from the cold, and Gena saw that all he had was a light jacket, more of a windbreaker than anything else; she didn't know where he'd been, but the outside temperature of forty degrees would be a nasty surprise.

"My name is Simon." Simon tilted his head. "This is Gena."

His gazed fixed on Mercy again, and the boy frowned. "I think I remember her," he said slowly. "Is she . . . is she dead?"

Simon blinked at the boy's words, but didn't pursue it. "No, but she's hurt. We're looking for supplies so we can try and help her get better."

"Are you here by yourself, Ryan?" Gena asked. She had a thousand questions but she tried to keep her voice even so she wouldn't scare him.

Ryan looked over his shoulder, his face pained. "No," he said. "I was with my aunt and two other guys, but they're stuck downstairs." He eyes were big and sunk deep into his face, dark with shock. "One of them is my friend and he's hurt really bad. My aunt and her, uh, boyfriend, they managed to dig a hole so I could crawl through, but there's big rocks and stuff in front of the door and they can't open it." His face brightened. "Hey, I bet they know where there's medicine."

Simon shot Gena a glance and she shrugged: *What other option do we have?* "Okay, Ryan," she said out loud. "You lead the way."

The child scrubbed at his face with his hands; he was so covered in grayish concrete dust it was hard to see what color his hair had been. A purple bruise spread over one edge of his jaw. "There are, uh, rats and bugs and . . . *stuff* in the halls," he said in a low voice. "It might be kind of hard to carry her down there. There's lots of furniture and rocks you have to climb over. And it's kind of wet."

Simon took a deep breath and looked at Gena, but she shook her head. "We'll have to do the best we can," he said in response. A glance behind them showed the unwelcoming expanse of the street; vague spots of darkness moved along the buildings and between the wrecks of cars. "It's not safe to leave her here by herself, and we should really stay together anyway."

Gena nodded. "The more people we have in a group, the safer I think we'll be," she said. Ryan was close enough for her to touch his shoulder; he cringed at the movement and Gena pulled her hand away, wondering what he'd been through. "Okay, Ryan. We're right behind you."

It took nearly an hour to negotiate the piles of rubble and caved-in walls of the hospital, but they were amazed to find that there were still faint working lights. Simon told her about After Help on the way; the company must have prepared the hospital with heavy-duty generators, then given battery backup to its emergency lights. Now they were little beyond soft yellow circles here and there, like the headlights of a car with a draining battery. Not much, but enough to keep them from feeling their way in complete darkness.

With Simon resting often, Ryan led them to and then down a back fire stairway littered with chunks of fallen plaster that showed steel support beams—the only reason the stairwell still existed. Even so, the braces were twisted and bent; cracks spiderwebbed through the metal at high stress points. Gena's senses were overloaded by everything, and part of her couldn't accept the absolute *unfairness* of it—she'd gotten her sight for only four lousy weeks and the world, with all its beautiful pieces and colors, had folded in on itself and gone dark and dead.

"Here," Ryan said suddenly. She'd been working her way after him and Simon without talking for so long that she hadn't realized they'd descended so deeply into the building. Now they were in a corridor and Ryan was indicating a door that was open about eighteen inches. Gena pushed on it experimentally, but nothing happened; at six months pregnant, there was no way she could get through.

Off to the side, Simon squatted and carefully slid Mercy out of his arms, holding her injured head like an infant's until he could rearrange the sodden covering she'd been under into a pillow beneath her hair. She mumbled something and all three of them stopped and stared at her, but her eyes stayed closed and she quieted. Standing again, Simon flexed his shoulders and Gena heard joints pop, saw a grimace of pain cross his scarred features before they smoothed again.

"Okay," he said. "Let's see what we've got." He turned sideways and slipped through the door opening, his angular frame a distinct advantage over Gena's shorter and much rounder build. When Ryan followed him, Gena poked her head through the opening and peered around. The shelter that Ryan had talked about was only a few feet away, its door blocked by several chunks of concrete as large as the boy himself; above them, a wide hole in the ceiling spread into blackness. The door to the shelter had been forced as far as possible, six inches at the most; it was amazing that Ryan had been able to squeeze through. No light came from the opening, but Gena could smell human waste, blood, and fear.

"Is someone out there?" A woman's panicked voice floated through the dark slit. "Help—we're trapped!"

"Hey there," Simon called back. Working together, he and Ryan quickly cleared the door to the hallway so Gena could get through. "Give us some time and we'll find a way to get you out. We've got Ryan with us. Is everyone in there okay?"

There was a heart-stopping five seconds of silence, then a male voice gave a curt answer. "We're still alive."

Gena thought he sounded suspicious, but then who wouldn't be? She glanced at Simon and her eyes widened. The light wasn't good, but it was enough to see his expression of total hatred.

"Fuck," he whispered. He seemed to have forgotten the small, bewildered boy frozen at his side.

Ryan dared a tug on Simon's jacket. "Mr. Simon? What's the matter?"

Simon turned his head and his face softened when his gaze touched on the boy. He drew a deep, shaking breath. "Nothing," he said, but Gena could hear the tension in the way the word vibrated in his throat. *What the hell?* she thought. But he took another breath, then visibly recovered. "Okay," he said briskly as he began to scan the poorly lit area. "Let's see what we can find to use as a lever . . . here." On its side against one wall was a steel bookcase with most of the shelves broken away from the support bars. Simon began kicking at the two that were still attached, trying to break them free. In such an enclosed space, the noise was tremendous and both Gena and Ryan clapped their hands over their ears. The echoing racket seemed not to affect Simon; if anything, he kicked more furiously. Watching him, Gena wondered if he was working out some secret rage.

Finally he had one of the bars free, and a couple of good twists did away with the last shelf still hanging at one corner. Returning to the shelter's door, Simon drove the bar under the first of the concrete chunks and began jostling it aside.

"Thank you for getting the door open," said the woman who'd introduced herself as Erica Richmond. "I was starting to think we were going to die in here." She gave the man beside her an enigmatic look, but he said nothing. All of them were crowded into the bomb shelter, breathing through their mouths to block out the smell. Simon stood next to the row of bunk beds still crookedly hanging from one wall, studying the mass of concrete piled on top of the legs of the man lying quietly on the top rack. Ryan had told them his name was Eddie, and right now Eddie's eyes were closed and he wasn't saying much.

"Son of a bitch," Simon muttered. His hands, the nails scraped and bleeding from fighting with the concrete in front of the shelter, began painstakingly probing the debris, searching out the smaller pieces he could lift away without causing more to fall. "Searle, didn't you even *try* to help him?"

Gena, Erica, and Ryan all jerked in surprise. How had Simon known the other man's name?

"It was too dark to move around." Searle's voice was smooth. "We couldn't risk it."

"We had flashlights," Ryan said.

Searle glared at the boy but Erica's question overrode any comment. "Do you two know each other?"

Simon didn't answer and anything Searle was going to say was cut off when Simon tossed a good-sized hunk of rock in Searle's direction; the older man caught it rather than let it smack him in the chest, then let it drop to the floor. "So what was the problem with the flashlights, huh?" Searle shrugged and didn't answer, his eyes narrow as he watched Simon work.

"He wouldn't let us turn them on," Ryan piped up. "He said we had to stay in our beds and—"

"Shut up, you little bastard," Searle snarled. "What did I tell you about—"

But the hand that lashed out at Ryan was stopped in midair by

Simon. Searle scowled and tried to pull free of the grip the younger man had on his wrist; instead Simon yanked him forward hard enough to nearly pull him off his feet. "I can guess what's been going on down here," he hissed as Gena and Erica gawked. "Touch him again and I'll kill you."

Amazingly, Searle sniggered. "Like father like son, eh?"

Simon shoved him away; Searle stumbled backward and landed heavily against one of the cracked walls. "Not in your life-time or mine, you scum. Why don't you do us all a favor and leave?"

"Oh, my *God*," Erica said suddenly from her spot next to Gena. Her hand flew to her mouth. "I know who you are—you're Searle's son!"

Simon's expression was like granite as he turned to glare at Erica, but Searle looked absurdly pleased. Gena hadn't thought it would be possible to feel colder than they had last night; how very wrong she'd been. "Don't ever call me that again, lady," he said flatly. "As far as I'm concerned, I don't have a father. I became an orphan when this man killed my mother."

Gena saw Ryan hug himself, his eyes blank with terror. Instinc-tively, she reached for him. He looked like he wanted to say some-thing, but when she shook her head, he buried his face against the firm curve of her stomach instead. "Uh . . . Erica," Gena said hur-riedly. "Would you mind coming with me to check on Mercy?"

"Mercy?" The older woman's face lit up briefly, then filled with worry. "Simon's girlfriend—you mean she's here?"

"Don't tell me you know her," Gena said in disbelief.

"She knows her, all right," Simon said with unaccustomed nas-tiness. "In case she doesn't fill you in, Erica is the woman who dismissed Mercy and then kept her from being able to get another job." He lobbed another heavy piece of concrete at Searle, who barely managed to catch it. "By the way, you can thank Searle for the bullet hole you got in your head back at the town house. He was the one who fired the gun."

Erica looked at Searle, startled. "You shot someone?"

Gena grimaced. "Well, doesn't this just suck." Her gaze touched on the child still clinging to her, then on the unconscious man on the top bunk. "Looks like the only two worth saving are Ryan and Eddie. Come on, Ryan." They edged past Searle and out of the shelter, gratefully breathing in the stale air outside the tiny room. Ryan was the first one to go through the outer door and

Gena heard him shout *"Scat!"* When she joined him, the boy had pieces of plaster in his hands and he was hurling them at a dozen rats fleeing down the hallway. Gena gasped. "She didn't get bit, did she?"

"I don't think so." Ryan threw his last piece as hard as he could. "But they were awful close to that bandage."

"Let me take a look."

Gena looked up to see Erica standing a couple of feet away. Her mouth turned down. "Why?"

"Because I'm a doctor," Erica said simply. "Isn't that why you came here—to find help? If you could have helped her, you would have done it already."

Gena felt Ryan's gaze on her and could think of no reasonable protest. "All right."

Erica knelt beside Mercy and untied the strip of grimy fabric around her head, then gingerly peeled off the bloodstained wad of material over the wound. Gena saw her frown but there was no way for her to tell if it was because the wound looked so bad or because Erica was displeased at her own dirty hands; as the last of the bandage pulled away, Mercy moaned.

"Wow." Ryan's eyes were wide. "I bet that hurt."

Erica leaned closer and pushed aside Mercy's hair with a fingertip. "This won't stop bleeding unless we close it up," she said. Her hand moved to Mercy's face and she quickly lifted one eyelid, then the other. "Her pupils are okay, but the injury site is definitely infected. Midrange concussion . . . she needs antibiotics and immobilization." She sighed and sent a bitter glance back toward the bomb shelter. "If Searle will let us use the medical supplies, she'll probably be okay."

Gena's eyes narrowed. "What do you mean, 'if'?"

Erica suddenly looked very old. "I don't think I have to spell it out, do I?"

"Ryan," Gena said, "will you stay out here with Mercy and make sure the rats don't bother her? Your aunt and I are going back in by Simon." The child nodded solemnly and began assembling a small arsenal of snowball-sized items to throw. Gena motioned to Erica and the other woman glanced a final time at Mercy, then followed her back into the room that held the entrance to the bomb shelter.

"Simon, how's it coming?" Gena called when they were at the entry.

"Slow," he answered shortly, trying to inch aside another jagged piece of rock. Searle wasn't doing much beside standing off to one side and watching with his arms folded.

To her surprise, Gena saw that the young man trapped on the bunk bed, Eddie, had opened his eyes. She found one of the chairs and placed it next to Simon, then carefully climbed on it so she could be at eye level with him; without being asked, Erica moved forward and held it steady so that Simon could keep working. The view from up here was bleak—she could see nothing of Eddie's body from mid-thigh down. Simon was in stubborn mode right now, but sooner or later he would have to admit defeat; there were at least three slabs of concrete that he would never be able to move by himself. It was a miracle that the bed hadn't pulled out of the wall. If only Lamont were here—

"Hi," she said as a way of forcing herself to think of what was going on right now. "My name's Gena. Can I get you some water?"

"How about some canned peaches?" Erica asked from below. "We have lots of those, remember? You haven't eaten in days—"

"Not hungry," Eddie croaked. "Or thirsty." His face was streaked and gray with pain; nevertheless, he tried to smile. "But thanks."

Gena didn't say anything for a moment, then she reached up and stroked his forehead. "It might make you feel better," was all she could think of. "Give you some energy for when we get you out."

Eddie lifted his head briefly, then let it drop back to the gritty surface of his pillow. "No," he whispered. "Not getting out."

"Don't say that," Gena chided. "We—"

"—won't leave you," Simon finished in a hard voice. Gena's eyes flicked nervously in his direction; she'd never experienced this side of him before today. Of course, she'd never expected to see him meet his father face-to-face either. "If you don't eat," Simon continued, "I'll force-feed you. And you're not in a position to refuse."

Eddie looked like he was going to do just that, then his face relaxed and he actually smiled slightly. "You don't seem like the bully type," he said. It was amazing to see a sense of humor in this situation, but Gena's small return grin faded when Eddie coughed, then bit back a whimper of pain.

"I'll get the peaches," she said hastily.

"Stay there," Erica ordered. "I'll find—"

"Leave the fucking food alone," Searle said sharply.

Eddie drew a breath and squeezed his eyes closed, but the other three turned to stare at Searle. From the corner of her eye, Gena saw Erica lower her gaze in defeat and abruptly she understood. Food, supplies, medicine—this son of a bitch was lording over it all, wasn't he? Trapped in this shelter with him for a week and a half, they were probably lucky he'd let them have water! She opened her mouth, but Simon was far quicker.

"Why, you slimy, two-bit piece of—"

The sound of a pistol cocking was as loud as the slam of a car door. "Never did like being called names," Searle said acidly. "By anyone, and especially in the joint." Gena saw the barrel of the gun—was it the same one that had so effectively opened her own head?—swing up and stop at the level of Simon's chest. "And this place reminds me of it a real lot. Didn't much appreciate you threatening me, either."

Simon choked off what he'd been planning to say. "Why can't we feed him?" he demanded instead. "It's not that hard to find food in the city."

"Bullshit."

"There aren't that many people *left,*" Gena said. "You can see for yourself if you go outside. Most—"

"I don't want to hear it," Searle said. "And I don't care anyway. This is *my* stash and I'm the one who's gonna use it. Not some guy pinned under a thousand pounds of concrete and who's too stupid to know he's already dead."

If Eddie heard Searle's words, he made no indication of it. "I suppose," Gena said slowly, "the same goes for the medical supplies."

"You bet your sweet ass it does."

Before she could argue about it, Simon lunged for Searle. More experienced and undeniably faster, Searle didn't squeeze the trigger. In a motion too blurred for Gena to follow, he shunted Simon's grabbing fingers to one side and brought the hand holding the gun up hard under his son's jaw. Simon's head snapped up and he yelped and pitched backward; Erica shrieked and Gena's cry of alarm joined in as Simon fell against the precariously placed chair and Gena lost her footing and tumbled off.

To her credit, Erica did try to break the fall, although she succeeded only in pulling Gena to one side. Gena landed heavily on her right hip and arm but never registered the sharp edges of the storage boxes digging into her rib cage; she did, however, feel the exquisite whack of her head against the concrete wall. Inside her skull there was a jolt of light unlike anything she'd ever seen, then everything returned to normal.

"Gena!" Searle forgotten, Simon scrambled on his knees to her side as Erica crouched hastily next to her. When Gena blinked up at everyone, even Eddie was clawing at the side of his mattress, straining to see over the edge.

"Here, let me see," Erica said urgently. Her cold fingers began prodding through Gena's tangled hair.

"Shit, would you stop it?" Gena asked crankily. She pushed Erica away. "It's just a bump on the head, for God's sake. That's a fucking habit in my crowd." She gazed at Simon uncomprehendingly for a moment, then used his outstretched hand to pull herself upright. "I'm fine, I'm sure the baby's fine, but your mouth is bleeding. And *he's* an asshole."

"Careful," Erica murmured in her ear.

"Yeah, okay." Standing again, she stared across the shelter where Searle watched them all with a sneer on his face. "So now what?"

"Looks like you guys made the trip for nothing," Searle said. "You just go and find your medical supplies somewhere else—and *not* anywhere in this building."

"My wife won't survive another trip!" Simon looked ready to jump all over again. "She—"

"—could be useful to you, Searle." Simon stopped and frowned in Erica's direction. "Don't you remember what I told you about her, how she can *heal*? But that's true only if she's alive, of course, and she needs treatment. Think about it," Erica said craftily. "A little disinfectant and surgical thread, a thirty-count dose of antibiotics. There's a full case of penicillin down here and more in the hospital pharmacy—you'll never miss it."

Searle was silent for a few seconds, then his expression relaxed. "All right," he said. "Get what you need out of the boxes. But she"—he swung the pistol toward Gena—"stays here. Simon goes with you to make sure you don't take off." Searle's eyes were cold and hard. "If both of you don't come back, I'll kill her. And what happened to that black guy who was with you?"

"We got separated," Simon said curtly. "And I'm not—"

"It's no problem," Gena said before Simon could argue any further. "I don't have any pressing appointments."

"What do you care if we leave?" Simon challenged. "It makes for fewer mouths to feed and water. I thought you wanted all this stuff for yourself."

Searle's mouth twitched. "That's true. But I want Mercy, too. For that I need insurance, and the more of *that,* the better." He jerked his thumb at Erica. "Now you stitch her up and get her in here. Mind you don't take too long, either. Sometimes I get impatient."

It was the longest half an hour Gena had experienced in years. Earlier today she'd thought there couldn't be more to worry about than staying alive long enough to get here; now they had an entirely new set of problems. Finally she heard the pitch of the conversation in the hallway change and knew that Erica and Simon were getting ready to move the still unconscious Mercy—while her captor couldn't hear anything other than faint murmurs, Gena could almost make out the words. She felt like a mouse in the killing sight of a cat as Searle sat on his lower bunk and stared at her the entire time. Did the idiot think she was going to tackle him and try for the gun? Jesus. When she stood in preparation for the others to return, the ex-convict nearly jumped out of his skin. "They're coming," she said by way of explanation.

Searle started to retort and instead gave her a dirty look when an instant later he heard noise outside the shelter. Positioning himself carefully out of Simon's reach, Searle waved in the trio.

"Gena, clear a spot on the floor next to the boxes," Simon directed.

"Just put her on Erica's bunk," Searle said impatiently. "Stop fucking around."

"No." It was clear that Simon wasn't going to agree. "If the rest of that ceiling comes down or Eddie's bunk gives way, my wife is not going to be underneath it." Gena nodded and quickly pushed aside a few boxes. She found a couple of blankets—dry, how wonderful!—and spread them where the wall and floor met. Her head was pounding with an unexpected headache and her vision was blurring at the edges for the first time since their final shopping expedition to Treasure Island. *Fatigue, stress, hunger—it could be any of those,* she thought. *Nothing more. Nothing.*

A few more minutes and Mercy was arranged on the makeshift sleeping pad, her injured head carefully placed on one of the small surplus pillows. She seemed to be resting comfortably, perhaps sleeping instead of passed out—a definite improvement.

"So what now, Searle?" Simon asked bitterly. "Do you just sit there and watch the rest of us starve?"

Instead of answering, Searle's eyes suddenly widened. "Hey, where the hell is the kid?"

Erica lifted her chin. "I sent him away. I thought he'd be better off taking his chances out there than being held prisoner here."

Surprisingly, Searle laughed. "I'll be damned, babe. You finally did something right."

Erica looked at the floor and said nothing. Gena saw Simon glance at the older woman, then watched something in his expression change—was he reading her mind? Probably, and now he pressed his lips together and said nothing, choosing instead to move to where he could again survey the mess piled on top of Eddie's legs. "Could we have some more light?" he asked.

"Suit yourself." Searle's face was unreadable. "I need it to keep watch on you folks anyway. You can use a few of the candles."

When they'd been lit and a false, soft glow filled the shelter, Simon set about working at the wreckage strewn across the top bunk. Finally, he lowered his hands. "I've gone as far as I can without help," he said. He glanced at Searle but Searle didn't move.

"Searle, we have to eat," Erica said calmly. "Please—there's enough food to feed four people for months."

"Christ," Searle said in disgust. "Just go on and do it and stop your fucking whining. But one can each—no more. Since you like him so much, you can even feed squashed boy up there." He glared at each of them. "But then shut the fuck up for the rest of the night. I like it *quiet* when I sleep, and you can check with Erica if you want to know what happens when I don't get it. And I'm a *very* light sleeper—it comes from spending most of my life in the slammer."

"What are you waiting for, anyway?" Gena snapped from her corner. Damn him, and damn this dark hole in the ground—what a fool she'd been for not appreciating the wet, gray sight of the outside world. Was it the dim light down here or was her sight truly that dark around the edges? How amazing that she had made it through all those earthquakes and falling buildings and everything else, yet a simple bump on the head could jeopardize the magic of her being able to see. Had she known she was that fragile, Gena might still be in that safe backyard haven with Lamont. "If all you wanted was Mercy, why don't you kill us and get it over with?"

Another snide smile flashed across Searle's mouth. "I'm waiting for her to wake up, of course. One of you is how I'm going to control her when she does." His head swiveled and he regarded them each solemnly. "I just haven't decided *which* one."

Gena heard Erica make a small, terrified noise in her throat but neither Searle nor Simon noticed. Of course the woman would be petrified, Gena realized. She'd never expect Mercy to forgive her or cooperate to save her life, not after what she'd done to Mercy's livelihood. Searle was a cold-blooded killer and it didn't take much to guess who he'd eliminate first.

As the candles burned low and they each finished their meager serving of peaches, Searle settled himself between them and the bomb shelter's exit, leaning back against the wall with his legs crossed and the gun in his lap.

Throughout the night, his eyes never fully closed.

JULY 13 . . .

Ryan had never felt so alone.

He wasn't very brave anyway—his dad had knocked away any tendency to stand up for himself some time ago. There had been times when he'd looked at his father's big hand and felt the sting of its judgment that he'd known the world was too big for a quiet boy like himself and he just didn't belong in it. If this was the way the world was now, he'd been right all along.

Never, *ever,* had he imagined something like this. The one thing he'd been allowed to do at home before the world exploded that he'd truly enjoyed was to watch the Saturday afternoon movies; now outside was like what he'd seen on the Japanese monster films after Godzilla had vented his fire-breathing temper all over everything. In fact, since leaving Althaia the child had spent much of his time running from one hiding place to another on LaSalle Street, expecting a scaly green lizard of immense size to come rumbling out from the ruins at any minute—what else could have caused this mess? The asteroid? To Ryan an asteroid meant a big rock, and let's face it: how big could a rock be, anyway?

He'd stumbled over enough bodies to where he'd accepted that the dead people weren't going to grab at him, although they were still *very* scary—a lot more than the ones he'd seen on *Dawn of the Dead,* before his mom had caught him and made him change the channel. Thinking about his mom made him want to cry but he couldn't let himself—whenever he cried, he just wanted to climb in a closet and hide, and while there were plenty of places in the rubble to dig in, there were too many things going on that made him think that would be a stupid thing to do.

Chief among those "things" was the pack of dogs following him right now.

Ryan had never been a big fan of dogs. He liked the puppies he saw on the television commercials as much as the next kid and the cartoon dogs in *101 Dalmatians* were lots of fun, but he hadn't spent much time around the real thing. The few times he had, the dogs were always bigger than he was, always rough, and they jumped a lot. His parents weren't much on animals, and Ryan had petted perhaps two puppies in his lifetime. The dogs that were trailing after him now weren't like any he'd ever seen; they were all about the same size as the leader, which resembled a Labrador like the dog in the movie *Old Yeller,* but was black. That movie had always made Ryan believe Labs were good, friendly animals, but the one shadowing him now reminded him more of the way Old Yeller had been at the end of the movie, when the boy had to shoot him because he'd gone mean and crazy.

Ryan dashed across LaSalle Street again, his goal a delivery truck lying on its side on the curb. It looked to have some good handholds plus it was way too high for the dogs to jump on— maybe he could climb it and rest. He wished Aunt Erica and Mr. Simon had given him something to eat before sending him away, but the only thing Mr. Simon had been able to do was tell him where he and Gena had left a partially filled jug of water hidden outside the hospital door. Ryan had instinctively thrown it at one of the dogs about fifteen minutes ago when it had darted forward and tried to bite his leg; now he wished he had thought to hit the hound with a brick instead. He'd left the hospital three hours ago, although the constant darkness made it impossible to tell the time. Hungry, thirsty, and exhausted, he desperately needed to find someplace out of reach of the pack stalking him. The truck across the street seemed just the thing.

He was three quarters of the way there when the dog pack made its move.

Ryan heard their snarling double and knew he was in trouble— there were seven dogs and only one of him, and the dumb things *never* seemed to get tired like he did. He was scrambling across the rubble and buckled slabs of roadway as quickly as he could, but they were faster and a lot more surefooted. He wasn't about to give up, though, and when he jumped and clutched at part of the metal exhaust pipe on the truck's underside, he was screaming and kicking at the mixed-breed mutt that sailed through the air and fastened its jaws around his ankle.

The pain was too much. Ryan had taken enough hits from his dad to build up his pain threshold, but never had the old man cut him with anything. This felt like someone had wrapped his foot in a vise made of needles and he just couldn't maintain his hold on the greasy pipe. He and the dog went down in a tangle of yelling and yapping, and Ryan knew he was finished—the other six animals would be all over him. From somewhere distant, he thought he heard shouting but it was himself, certainly, voicing his panic as he flailed and punched at the teeth snapping at him.

The world spun crazily and he felt himself yanked forward and up, saw a booted foot flash by his head and connect with the brown, tooth-filled mouth going for his face. For a crazy instant he went rigid and thought he was with his father again, held under one arm like a sack of garbage and on his way to a beating. Then whoever held him turned him upright and set him on his feet, still lashing out at the dogs without loosening the grip on his left arm.

"Get out of here you mangy bastards! Go *on*!" Pulled along as the person did a fine, swift job of disbursing the pack, Ryan didn't have a chance to see his rescuer before he heard someone else's furious voice.

"Are you crazy, damn it? You should've waited for me—what if you'd gotten bitten?"

"Oh, take a pill, Lamont. Everything's fine." A woman, and Ryan looked up to see someone who looked like she'd stepped out of an MTV rock video. Despite being matted with dirt, he could see orange and green streaks in hair that would normally be the color of snow. Her face was thin and hard above a leather bomber jacket and tight, ripped pants, but everything about her seemed to soften when she grinned at him and tugged companionably on his sleeve. "You okay, kid? What's your name?"

"I'm Ryan," he said shyly, proud of the way he kept his voice from shaking. The man with her was a black guy who looked big enough to be a football player. He was frowning, but like this tough, slender woman, there was nothing truly *mean* about his expression.

"Yeah? Well, mine's Lily and this is Lamont." She waved an arm at her traveling partner and steered Ryan in that direction. "He's kinda grouchy right now."

"I am *not*!"

Lily winked at Ryan. "See what I mean? So where're you going?"

"I . . ." Ryan shrugged and looked at his sneakers; his ankle was sore but he didn't see any blood on the cuff of his jeans. "I don't know."

Lamont studied him. "No parents?"

Ryan shook his head, then an idea hit him. "But I have an aunt back at the hospital."

Lily and Lamont exchanged glances. "The hospital?" Lily asked.

"Yeah," Ryan said eagerly. "She and my friend Eddie are in the bomb shelter in the basement there. Searle—he used to be my aunt's friend—won't let her or the other people leave."

Lamont dropped to his knees in front of Ryan, his eyes searching. "Searle, huh? And who are the other people? Do you know?"

Ryan shrugged again. "I don't remember all their names," he admitted. "But one lady's hurt, and I think the other is . . ." He blushed. "You know, going to have a baby or something. Well, I guess they both are."

The two grown-ups didn't say anything right away, then Lily gazed thoughtfully in the direction of Althaia. "The woman who was hurt," she said faintly, "is she . . . alive?"

Ryan lifted his head, surprised. "Oh, sure. My aunt is a doctor, and she put stitches in the lady's head and everything."

"Did she talk to you?" Lamont asked.

"Nah. She was asleep the whole time."

Another minute of silence, then Lily spoke. "Sounds like pay dirt to me. Let's go." Lily tugged on his hand, but Ryan dragged against her. "What's the matter?"

"I don't think I should go back there," he said earnestly. "My aunt told me to run and never come back because Searle has a gun and she said she was afraid he'd shoot me."

"Really." Lily let go of his hand as Lamont stepped forward and lifted Ryan up and over his head, settling him on his shoulders for a piggyback ride as if he weighed no more than a toy truck. "You leave that to me, Ryan. Your aunt's pal and I have met before. His pistol didn't do him much good then."

"And things won't be any different now.

UNKNOWN BROADCAST
JULY 14—MORNING...

"Testing, one-two-three. This is Pax Bailby, broadcasting to anyone listening. Today I'm at Marked Tree, Arkansas, northeast of the last broadcast out of Searcy. Things aren't much different here, although there are a few more people. Hardly anyone will talk to me, though—most folks seem afraid of everyone else, or maybe they just don't want to have to share their supplies.

"The trip here was damned frightening. Like I said before, people will generally leave you be as long as you don't go near where they're holed up—the days of the door-to-door salesman are finally over. The scariest ones are the soldiers left over from the Army and the National Guard. They've gone crazy or something, running around like execution squads and wiping out anything that moves. Yesterday morning I almost walked straight into five of 'em. They'd found a level slab of roadway and were camped out in the open, sitting around a fire and laughing like they were going through nothing more than a training exercise. The only reason they didn't hear me was that they were joking around so much. That fire looked so good and they seemed so ... cheerful—I almost walked up and asked if I could join them. Hell, I can't remember the last time I was warm. Then one of the guys heard a noise behind him and turned around and started shooting, never even looked to see what or who it was. Luckily he was aiming in the other direction, so I got out of there and put as much distance as I could between them and me. Looking back on it, they were eating something they'd cooked over that fire, and I'm afraid of thinking too much about what it was. I guess I really wouldn't have wanted to sit with them anyway.

"The sky around here doesn't seem to be changing much. It's still night all the time and still raining. I think the rain isn't as bad, but that could be my imagination too, unable to face the thought of the rain never stopping. This thing about it being dark twenty-four hours a day bothers me a lot—how long is that going to last? When I was a kid I loved dinosaurs. Remember the theory that an asteroid hit the Earth and raised a huge dust cloud that *blocked out the sunlight and basically starved everything to death? It keeps popping into my thoughts—is that what's going to happen to us? I like to think that people are smarter than that— after all, we have the brain capacity to do something other than prey on each other, the soldiers notwithstanding, so I hope we'd figure out a way not to disappear forever.*

"I'm making better time than I thought I would. There's an incredible amount of water around here, much more than back in Searcy. The Mississippi River is higher than it's ever been; I know I said it was probably being caused by water from the Gulf. I found one guy who actually talked to me and said he was headed north from straight south. He told me that the water in Kansas City is as tall as five-story buildings and that survivors are going through the city in rowboats trying to find food. If the flooding is that bad there, I wonder if places like Florida and New Orleans even exist anymore.

"So, Pax Bailby, signing off. I think it's July fourteenth. I was going to do these broadcasts once a week to save batteries, but I think I'm beginning to figure out this radio thing. The truth is, if I don't feel like I'm talking to someone somewhere, I think I'm going to go crazy from the loneliness."

Wow, Mercy thought as her eyes opened. Inside her skull, something hard and heavy throbbed energetically. Now this is a headache.

Aloud she said, "Where are we?"

Next to her on the floor, Simon sat up immediately, his face so filled with happiness that the sight of it would have made her smile had her head not hurt so badly. They were in some kind of room and it was dry, but cold and nearly pitch-black; only one candle burned on a card table in the corner and she could barely see her husband. Other figures shifted as she spoke, filling the close space with quiet movement, like timid animals confined in a cage. "Hi," Simon said softly. "How do you feel?"

"Awful. Who hit me?"

"*What* hit you was part of the shed's metal roof. Laid your head open pretty good."

She closed her eyes briefly as he reached to touch the side of her face. "Stitches?"

"Yeah. Erica Richmond sewed you up. Shhh!" Mercy stifled

her cry of surprise as his voice dropped so low she had to strain to hear. "We're in a helluva mess here, Mercy. Be real careful about what you say—try to be neutral, no matter what."

"She awake?"

It was difficult to see, but Mercy was sure she'd heard that voice somewhere before. She couldn't quite connect with it, but the recollection seemed anything but pleasant. "Yes," she said, trying to lift her head. She found Simon's hand and gripped it for comfort. "I am."

"Good. I guess using the medical supplies on you is going to pay off after all."

Mercy's mouth dropped open as a memory slid into place. "I remember you!" she exclaimed before Simon could stop her.

"Good." Searle came close enough for her to make out his hard-featured face. "Then you know I'm not going to fuck around. This is my party now."

Mercy was too shocked and ignorant of what was going on to think of a response, so she didn't bother to answer. Instead, she let her head fall back to the pillow; after looking down at her and Simon for a few more moments, Searle went back to whatever corner he had crawled from. "Simon, what's going on?" Mercy whispered. "Where's Lamont and Gena?"

"Gena's here, but Lamont's back at the town house. It's a long story. I'll tell you everything when we get a chance to—"

"Shut up!" Searle barked from the semidarkness.

Searle shook his head at her and raised a finger to his lips. With no other choice, Mercy tried to relax as she waited for the next dark dawn and whatever answers came with it.

Not dawn but several hours later, and Gena's voice made them all jump. Mercy's head throbbed in protest when she strained to find the source of the words. "We can't stay here," Gena said. "The shelter's going to fill with water by tomorrow night—all the basement levels of the hospital will."

"Jesus *Christ*!" Searle exploded from somewhere to Mercy's left. "Where did *that* come from? The crystal ball in your head?"

"Gena, can you see the future again?" Simon asked from his spot next to Mercy.

"What kind of shit is this?" Mercy heard boots scrape along the floor as Searle stood. "I don't have the patie—"

"Yes."

No one said anything for a moment, then Mercy struggled to sit upright, turning until she found her friend's position near a row of bunk beds set in the wall. Gena was no more than a black shadow against a vaguely lighter background. "Your eyes," Mercy managed, "Gena, *can you still see*?"

Rather than answer right away, Gena cleared her throat. When they eventually came, her words were hushed. "It doesn't matter."

Simon sucked in his breath. "Oh, no."

"What are you saying?" Searle's tone was sharp. "That you've gone blind?" For the moment, Gena's prediction of disaster was pushed aside. "Well, isn't *that* just fucking great."

"It doesn't *matter,* damn it! What counts is that we've got to get to street level before the lake water gets here."

"Lake water?" Erica Richmond's voice, so bitterly familiar, floated out of the lightless square that was one of the bunk beds. Next to that godforsaken asteroid, Mercy could think of no worse nightmare than she and Simon being stranded in the dark with the two people they most detested. "Are you saying that we're going to have a tidal wave from Lake Michigan?"

"Not a tidal wave." Gena paused. "Just ... slow flooding, I think. Kind of like what happens when you're carrying a bucket of water. If you stop too quickly, it washes over the edge. I can't think of a better way to describe it."

"You ever been right before?" Searle cut in.

"More than a few times," Gena answered sarcastically. "But you're welcome to stay down here and drown. We won't mind."

"Smart-mouthed bitch." Mercy could see him a few feet away, staring intently at Gena. His face was long and devilish in the wavering candle glow, so much like Simon's but entirely different.

"Searle, a lot of things happen now that didn't before," Erica began. "We all—"

"Great!" Searle threw up his hands and Mercy saw something flash in one of them—another gun. Without Lamont to get it safely out of his hands, that explained why they were trapped in here with this madman. She almost laughed; how on Earth could she have slept through all of this? "Now I've got you on my case, too," Searle continued. "Fine—you all want to leave that bad, we will. In the meantime, get a few hours' rest, you suckers. You're gonna need it to haul out your share of the supplies."

"Listen," Simon began.

"I said shut UP!" Searle was practically screaming. "I'm tired of people telling me what I should do and what I shouldn't!" He swung the gun dangerously around the small room. "If one of you says another single fucking *word* before I tell you it's okay, I'm going to blow little Miss I-Can-See-the-Future's head off! Understand?"

No one answered.

Daylight, at least by the clock in Searle's head. Finally they could move and talk without fear of being pistol-whipped. It wasn't until Searle allowed Simon to step out of the bomb shelter with him so that the women could use the chemical toilet that Mercy realized there was someone else in the shelter with them, another man lying on the top bunk. Before Searle had grudgingly passed out the flashlights, she hadn't known that part of the ceiling had caved in.

Mercy's heart ached for him. She wasn't standing very well on her own and at her insistence, Gena and Erica—and my, wasn't it a strain just to talk to that woman?—helped her stand on one of the chairs so she could get a clear view of him. When she put her hand on the edge of the bunk to steady herself, he opened his eyes and looked at her. "I don't know you," he whispered.

"My name is Mercy. They tell me you're Eddie." He didn't bother to reply and she reached to brush aside the mass of dust-caked hair that had fallen across his face. Under the powder, his hair looked vaguely red in the unreliable glow of the flashlight. Her fingers touched a lump on his right temple but he didn't seem to notice; Mercy was disappointed when nothing flowed from her hands beyond that intangible dose of normal human comfort. She was certain that the thing inside her still existed—was it sleeping until she recovered from her injuries? Another possibility was that the . . . energy, for lack of a better word, simply couldn't *be* if she wasn't up to a hundred percent of herself; perhaps it required too much of a drain and because of her head wound, she simply wasn't able to fuel it. Whatever the reason, she could do nothing for this miserable man right now and couldn't begin to fathom the pain he must be in—under the smells of sickness and waste, her trained nose detected the scent of gangrene. How did he keep from screaming?

"Can you move your legs at all?" she asked now. In the short span of time she had stood on the chair without speaking, he had closed his eyes again. This time he didn't reopen them.

"I . . . stopped trying. It hurts too much."

She didn't know whether to be glad he felt the pain or wish he was paralyzed so he was spared the worst of it. When she turned, Simon was watching her from the doorway. "Searle says he's ready."

Her legs were trembling as she climbed down, and when she was steady again Mercy pulled the chair around and sat. Gena and Erica were silent, waiting, and Searle was thankfully still outside. "I've got to rest." Her head had started pounding again, although this time it wasn't as pronounced. Each hour that went by brought her a little closer to full recovery. If she had only one more day . . .

"Simon," she said in as low a voice as she could. "We can't just *abandon* him."

"I have no intention of doing that." Simon folded his arms. "Once we get everyone to ground level outside, I'm coming back for him. I *will* get him out of that bunk, even if I have to dig the supports out of the walls to do it."

"You could end up killing him if the whole thing comes down," Gena commented. "And end up hurt yourself."

"There's no other way," Simon said stubbornly. "I can't lift those pieces of concrete by myself—hell, two people couldn't do it." He stepped to the row of bunks and studied the underside of the uppermost one. "If I tie him in and then work at the braces at his feet, maybe I can get that end to break free."

"You'd better not be there when it does," Erica pointed out. "You'll have to be *underneath* that end of the bed to get to the junction where the supports go into the wall. That's terribly risky."

"I'm *not* going to leave him."

Mercy nodded; of course he wasn't. Had there ever been a doubt?

"Let's get moving," Searle said from behind them. "According to my watch, it ought to be daylight out by now."

"It hasn't been daylight since Millennium hit," Gena said.

"You already admitted you can't see anything," Searle ground out. "So how the hell would you know?"

"I saw plenty before I got down here," Gena said sharply. "Maybe it was your friendly welcome that made my eyesight jump ship."

"Nice try, babe. I've waited as long as I'm going to. Erica, you get to go first and lead Gena, then Mercy and Simon. I'll be behind you." Searle glanced at Mercy. "I hope you're ready."

Carefully, shooting a tortured look toward Eddie's bunk, Mercy stood. "I'll do the best I can."

Searle motioned them out of the shelter, the pistol held adeptly in one hand. "It better be enough," he said as he followed them out. "I'd hate to have to drag you."

Mercy ignored him and took Simon's outstretched hand. A few feet ahead, Erica began the long and difficult task of guiding Gena back to the world above.

CHICAGO, ILLINOIS
NOON . . .

"What the hell?" It was still dark, of course, and as Searle and Erica gazed around the street outside the hospital, this time Gena wisely kept her comments to herself. "This watch must be screwed up," Searle decided. "Busted during the impacts or something. We've been down there so long we got a whole half day off—"

"No," Simon said. "Gena was telling you the truth. It took us two days to get here and the sky never lightened once." He scanned the murky clouds. "Although there *is* some improvement—I don't think it's as dark as it was."

"It's so *cold,*" Erica said in a small, dazed voice. "I thought it was like that in the shelter because we were underground. This is *awful.*"

Exhausted from the trek through the destroyed hospital, Mercy sat on the ground and stared up at the older woman. When she spoke, there was no softness in her tone, only bitter memories. "Welcome to the rest of your life, Erica. How do you like it?"

"Speaking of the rest of someone's life," Simon cut in smoothly, "I'm going back down to the shelter and see if I can find another way to get Eddie out of there."

"I thought she said it was going to flood," Searle said. His words had a dangerous undertone to them, and Mercy didn't want to think about what he'd do if he thought someone had lied to him. "Now you're saying you're going back in."

"He has enough time." Erica had led Gena to the bent remains of a light pole, and now Gena hung on to it with fierce determination, as though it might disappear if her hands left the cold metal surface. Her fingers were scraped and raw from feeling her way out of the hospital, and everywhere she touched the pole's pitted surface she left faint smears of blood that looked black in the poor light. Mercy couldn't believe how calm Gena was—had she been the one to go blind after being able to see for such a short time, Mercy was sure she'd be a raving lunatic by now. "At least four hours," Gena continued, "before the water starts seeping into the east wing of the hospital."

"I'd go in if I only had an hour," Simon said hotly. "A man's life is at stake!"

"Shit." Searle's lip curled. "That guy's already dead."

"That might not be true," Mercy put in. "If Simon can get him out here, I might be able to help him. I really think all I need is a few hours to recover."

Without warning, Searle turned and spat. "Lots of fancy talk about what everybody *used* to do, and no one's doing anything now."

"I'm surprised you're so skeptical after what you told me happened at that man's house," Erica said. Her voice seemed to be strengthening, perhaps fueled by being out of that awful underground pit. Her eyes, so pale and frightened down in the shelter, had taken on a hard, nearly glassy shine that made Mercy unaccountably nervous. "You said he—"

"Well, he isn't here now, is he?" Searle glowered at her. "Lot of good it apparently did him." His gaze cut to Simon, then he waved one hand at the younger man. "Go, if you want to so bad. Personally, I don't give a shit what you do."

Simon looked like he wanted to say something scathing, then he set his jaw. He bent and gave Mercy a careful kiss on the forehead. "I'll be back as soon as I can," he promised. His gaze flicked to his father. "Listen," he said under his breath, "you be careful around him. Anything can set him off. I know just how easily that can happen, and now that the world's gone to hell there's nothing to stop him."

"Okay," she said quietly and squeezed his hand. "You be careful, too. Listen," Mercy stopped him when he would've pulled away. "Do the best you can, but don't die trying. Understand?"

He nodded wordlessly, then straightened. Mercy shuddered as she watched him walk back and disappear into the inky, shattered entrance to the hospital. But that wasn't the thing that frightened her most.

Far more terrifying was the sight of Gena crying as she clung to her crooked light pole a few feet away.

• • •

"Well, what do you think?"

Secreted behind a couple of smashed cars about half a block from the hospital, Lamont, Lily, and Ryan watched the group argue. Their friends were instantly recognizable as was Simon's father, and Lamont was gratified to see that Mercy seemed to be okay; the other woman was a stranger, and it was the sound of raised voices that had made them think about what they were doing before rushing over to join the larger band. Now he was glad they had waited. "I think he's incredibly dangerous." His fists bunched involuntarily. "He's the one who broke into the town house with a couple of goons and ended up shooting Gena."

Lily's expression darkened and he knew she was recalling the story he'd told her. "I don't get the connection," she complained. "If he only wants Mercy, why keep all the others around, too?"

"So that he can make the others do what he wants," Ryan told her. "Like when he sent Mr. Simon and Aunt Erica out to help the lady who was hurt really bad. He made the other pregnant lady—Gena, right?—stay with him in the bomb shelter until they came back."

"But why doesn't he just let Simon and Gena go?" Lily asked.

"Come on, Lily." Normally patient, Lamont's hushed voice had an edge of exasperation in it. "Do you really think Simon would leave Mercy or Gena with that maniac?" He started to say more, then his voice dropped away. Damn his own phobia anyway—this crap would never have happened if *he* hadn't let Simon and Gena go off without him. And for what? Lily'd been right; no one on the streets noticed or cared about anyone but themselves, and there was barely anyone alive anyway. Most of the city's population seemed to have been crushed by the repeated earthquakes—and who had expected them to keep going day after day? It was easy to imagine tens of thousands at a time seeking shelter in the wreckage, only to perish as the world shook all over again. Those who'd made it through the horror of the quakes then had to fight the dogs, the soldiers, and each other just to see another black dawn. Speaking of which, it was cool now but with each passing day the temperature would probably climb more toward its normal summertime high. The sickly smell of decomposing bodies got stronger all the time; what kind of diseases were going to gain a foothold in a world where the dead were left to rot on the streets?

"Hey," Lily said suddenly. "What's Simon doing?"

Lamont blinked, irritated at himself for letting his thoughts drift. Down the block, Simon had walked away from the rest of the group and was headed for the main entrance of the hospital; as they watched, he disappeared into the doorway and didn't return. "Why would he go back in there?" Lamont asked, bewildered.

Ryan's face brightened. "Hey, I bet he's going back to help Eddie!"

"Shhh—watch your voice, kid." Lily peered worriedly toward Searle and his miserable captives, but no one looked their way. "Who's Eddie?"

"He's my friend from the hospital," Ryan said as quietly as he could. "But he's stuck down there. Part of the ceiling fell on him while he was sleeping and no one can get him out."

"And Searle just left him down there," Lamont marveled. "What a jerk."

"Searle is kind of mean." Ryan looked abruptly nervous for voicing his opinion.

"There are a lot of mean people in the world," Lily said. "Now I think the mean ones outnumber the nice. This guy . . ." she hesitated. "Maybe we should just grab him."

"He has a gun," Ryan said.

"Yeah, Lily." Lamont shot her a disgusted glance. "Remember? So what do we do about that?"

"Whatever we have to."

Lamont shook his head. "I'm sorry. I'm not prepared to go that far. Sure, I can stop him—I can do that all the way from here." Lily raised an eyebrow but said nothing and Ryan looked puzzled. "But that's all I can do. I can't . . ." He looked at Ryan, then took a deep breath. It was a harsh world and unfortunately the child was going to have to adapt. "I can't *kill* him, so we'll be stuck with a dangerous prisoner who has to be watched constantly."

"Then what are we supposed to *do,* Lamont?" Lily hissed.

"I don't know," he admitted. "This is so screwed up I'm completely lost." He stared through the busted windows of the car behind which they were hiding, straining for a better view without revealing himself. What was the matter with Gena? She didn't seem to be hurt, but she didn't look *right*—something about her had changed since she'd left the backyard. Instead of going over by Mercy, she was acting like she was chained to that light pole. Unless—

Ryan pulled on his sleeve. "You could help Mr. Simon," he suggested. "I don't think he can get Eddie out of there by himself. I could show you where they are."

"There's an idea," Lily said.

"I don't want to leave you out here by yourself."

"I won't be by myself," Lily said. She lifted her chin in the direction of the others. "I'll be with them."

"No," Lamont said. "That's out of the question."

Lily smiled sweetly, surprising Lamont. "I don't recall the matter being open for discussion." She dropped to her haunches next to Ryan, then glanced back at Lamont. "Here's how it goes. I'll circle around and pull Searle's attention away from the front of the hospital. You guys grab your chance when you see it, and for God's sake, don't make any noise. Get in there as quickly as you can."

"He'll shoot you." Lamont's face was stony.

"I don't think so. Mercy will never cooperate if he goes around murdering the people she cares about, and I'll make sure she knows it's me before he has a clear shot." She was silent for a moment, as if she were rethinking the idea. "Yeah," she said. "I believe this'll work fine."

"And what about when we come out?" Lamont asked pointedly.

"So you come out the same way you went in," Lily suggested. "Help Simon get this Eddie character to the front door, then let him bring him out by himself. When everyone's attention is focused on those two, you and Ryan make tracks in the other direction."

"And after *that*?"

"Who the hell knows?" Lily pulled her leather jacket tighter around her and flexed her wrists, then began inching away. She shot him a final, small grin. "I'll deal with things when I get there."

Crouching low with his hands shaking, Lamont pulled Ryan close and they watched Lily creep away through the rubble.

Since he already had an idea of what he was going back to, on the way out Simon had kept a lookout for something to use as a pry bar. He'd spotted just the thing and marked its location in his mind—the tapered metal leg of a supply cart—and picked it up on the way back. By the time he got back to the bomb shelter and lit a dozen of the small candles still down there, his heart was thundering not from exertion, but from a deep-seated fear that the young man caught down here had died in the short time Simon had been gone. He tried to tell himself that it meant Eddie would have only died on the way out, but his conscience would have none of it. As a result, Simon almost couldn't speak when he ducked into the shelter and saw only Eddie's arm dangling over the side of the bunk. Swallowing, he dragged the chair back into place and climbed up to where he could see Eddie face-to-face.

He wasn't prepared for the rats.

Simon cried out and jerked back, kept his balance only by grabbing on to the side of the bunk; out of it but still alive, the jarring motion did nothing to bring Eddie around. There were at least half a dozen of the things, filthy and way too healthy and brazen. Industrious little bastards, they were trying to dig beneath the chunks of concrete resting on top of Eddie's thighs to get to the raw flesh below. Up close, Simon could see swells of fresh blood staining the edges of the concrete, the fabric of Eddie's jeans, and—God almighty—the whiskers of the rodents.

"Get *off,* damn you!" Simon swung the pipe wildly and connected with the two that were closest, sending them sailing off the bunk amid the angry squeals of the rest. The other four fled, scrabbling up the concrete to the hole in the ceiling where no doubt a hundred more would have eventually found a way down to where Eddie was waiting, a living feast. Furious, Simon swung again but missed, and this time he *did* tip off the chair and go down; no real damage but enough of a bruising to pull himself together before he completely freaked out.

Christ, he thought as he climbed back up and studied the unconscious man. Bitten by rats, crippled—even if he got him out from under this fucking concrete blanket, would Eddie survive as far as ground level? The injured man's mind was thankfully buried in a self-induced shroud of darkness. Whatever the outcome, Simon had spent his life pulling people out of terrifying situations, and he wasn't about to give up until Eddie was dead or they both drowned. A last look to make sure he was breathing, and Simon stepped down and began working at the supports underneath the bunk.

. . .

Tricky, tricky, Lily thought. *How to do this without getting myself killed?*

"Hey, there!" she called out. She cut a weaving path around the wrecked cars as thirty feet away Searle whirled in the direction of her voice. She felt like she could feel him bringing the gun up to bear in the center of her chest, and bad memories of an Iowa soldier-boy welled inside her head. *Easy does it, girl; just keep moving and make yourself a difficult target until you get recognized.* "Mercy, is that you?"

Lily had been taking a chance in not waiting to be sure that Mercy was fully awake before she crashed the little camp, but time was against her and she had to move now to provide Lamont and Ryan with the cover they needed to get into the hospital without being seen. Her gamble paid off, though; at the sound of her voice, Mercy sat up. "Lily?"

She'd been right about Searle taking aim with his pistol, but she was in the open now, with nowhere to flee. At this point, either she made it or she didn't. With Mercy struggling to sit upright, Searle gave her an unhappy glance, then reluctantly tucked the gun back into the waistband of his jeans. "What is this?" he growled. "A fucking family reunion?"

"Hi," Lily said as she reached the three of them. Gena, she noted, was still over by the light pole. What the hell—was she *tied* there or something? Careful, Lily thought again. She'd been around people like Searle—hell, she'd been *like* Searle—for a good part of her life, at least in the way that made her immediately recognize someone who could drop off the deep side at any second. "My name is Lily." She gave him as inane a grin as she could conjure up, working on his first impression of her. People— foolish, foolish—almost always thought that the way she looked outside was an indication that she wasn't very bright inside. She ran a hand through her hair and fought to keep the image of someone who was easygoing, if not slightly hyper. "Wow," she said brightly. "I can't believe I found this many people alive in one place."

Searle was immediately interested, but it was going to take a bit to put her on his trustworthy list—if anyone ever got that far. "So the destruction really is that bad," he wondered out loud.

"Oh, yeah," Lily told him. "The whole city's trashed." She

looked over at Mercy and felt her pulse jump. Damn, but she looked battered—one side of her face was so badly bruised it was almost black. At least she was sitting up and smiling.

"I'm so glad you're safe," Mercy said. "I thought we'd never see you again."

"How did you find us?" Searle demanded suspiciously. "Out of all the places in this city, how would you know exactly where to go?"

"Lamont told me when I went back to the town house," Lily said promptly. Mercy's eyes widened in alarm and she cast a furtive warning glance at Searle; Lily acted like she didn't see her.

"So where's Lamont now?"

Searle's voice was too casual, but Lily was getting good at this. "He's . . ." This time Lily sent an intentionally distressed look in Gena's direction and lowered her voice. "He, uh, didn't make it," she finished. "It was the soldiers—we tried to get away, but he wasn't quick enough."

Mercy looked horrified. "Oh, *no!*"

Searle seemed unconvinced. "What soldiers?"

"The Army, the National Guard—whoever." Lily swept her arm across their field of view. "They shoot at everything in sight. This is just one big kickass party for them, man. A license to kill anything and everything they see 'cause there's no one around to stop them." Perfect timing—punctuating her words, a faint volley of shots echoed from the west and made them all look up.

Searle folded his arms and gazed at her thoughtfully and Lily knew she'd made a mistake by telling him that part. But the words were out and there was nothing to be done about it now—what a stupid slip up; that kind of information was the last thing a person like him needed to know. "Mercy, what happened to you?" she said to redirect Searle's attention; she already knew, of course, but everyone would expect her to ask. "You look like you got run over by a truck."

Mercy smiled wanly. "Simon tells me it was a piece of a shed roof. Personally, I don't remember." She laughed, a vain attempt to lighten the mood. "What about you?" Mercy asked. "Did you see your family? What happened?"

Lily shrugged. "Yeah, I saw them. They stayed in Iowa, just like I figured they would. Everyone's the same but me." She met Mercy's eyes briefly, then put an exaggerated expression of bewilderment on her face. "So where *is* Simon?"

Mercy nodded toward the crumbled hospital. "In there. We had to leave someone behind and he went back to try and dig him out." Her voice was calm but Lily didn't miss the tension in it. "Gena says the hospital's going to flood. If Simon doesn't get him out, Eddie will drown in there."

"Maybe I should go help," Lily suggested.

Searle looked up. "I don't think so. I think you just stay right here with the rest of us."

In spite of her resolve to remain calm and careful around this jerk-off, Lily felt the blood settle into her cheeks. "Are you telling me I *can't* go down, mister? I don't even know who you and your lady friend are. What's the problem?" She glanced at the female stranger and noticed for the first time the knuckle-sized bruise that colored one temple and part of her cheekbone. More evidence that this guy was seriously bad news.

"No problem," Searle said smoothly. "I just don't think it's wise. You should stay aboveground with us, where it's safe. I insist."

I'll just bet you do, Lily thought derisively. Outwardly she shrugged. "Maybe you're right. Simon's a big boy—he can handle himself." She glanced over at the light pole where Gena still waited. "I'm gonna go say hi to Gena."

"She's fine where she is," Searle said flatly. "Leave her be."

Lily stared at him. She was trying her damnedest to be . . . what would Lamont call it? *Diplomatic* . . . but this guy was a first-class asshole. Her next question came out all on its own. "Who died and left you God?"

Searle's answering sneer was as ugly as anything she'd ever seen. "The rest of the free fucking *world*. So why don't you just put a cork in it?" Lily started to say something else, but Searle held up a finger. "Before you go running your mouth, you give some thought to this: I don't trust you. I don't believe that you walked all the way here from—what was it, Iowa?—for no other reason than to reacquaint yourself with your buddies. I also think you're lying about that Lamont jagoff being dead—a guy like that doesn't go down easily. I'm watching you, honey. One wrong move and I'll shoot your ass about as dead as little Eddie's going to end up." He turned and spat on the ground. "Water or no water, if they're not out of there in an hour, we're leaving."

. . .

Simon had no idea how much time had passed when he started hearing noises. He was hot and cold at the same time, sweating beneath the layers of his clothes as he beat at the bolts sunk deep into the concrete walls, cursing when he realized that somewhere under the masonry they were tied into steel beams. He'd done everything he could think of, including hanging on the foot end of the bunk and bouncing—he was that desperate—in blatant disregard for the possibility that the whole load of rock could come down on his head. Now there were sounds, big ones, coming from the outside hallway and he gripped his stupid, worthless piece of metal and got ready to meet whatever the hell was headed their way. He didn't know what it was, but he could picture thousands of rats, swarming through the hallways in search of fresh victims. *Rats and cockroaches,* Simon thought with more than a touch of hysteria. *They'll be here long after we're nothing but compost.*

"Mr. Simon?" A child's nervous voice. "Are you down here?"

Rats, Simon thought again. His gaze cut back to the hole in the ceiling and he thought he saw the shelter's candlelight reflected from a dozen sets of eyes. He thrust the pipe toward the gap and they disappeared. "Ryan?" he asked out loud.

"I brought someone to help."

Another sixty seconds and Ryan peeked around the shelter's door; at his back, his dark face smudged with plaster dust, was Lamont. He and Lamont stared at each other in awkward silence; around his discomfort, Simon felt relief slide in: here, at last, was Eddie's salvation. "Oh boy, am I glad to see you," Simon said finally.

"I'm sorry," Lamont said.

—flash—

Simon smiled. "I know." He stepped back and gestured at the bunk, with its load of concrete and Eddie, still unconscious. "I can't," he said simply.

"I'll handle it."

"How're you going to do that?" Simon and Lamont had both forgotten about little Ryan, who now looked at them both with wide eyes.

Lamont opened his mouth, then looked at Simon, completely at a loss. Simon grinned and touched Ryan's shoulder, steering him back to the entrance of the shelter. "Ever watch cartoons, Ryan?"

"Sure." Ryan nodded enthusiastically. "My favorite is *The Tick.*"

"Ah. Wasn't he the one that said 'Smack 'em on the nose with the rolled-up newspaper of goodness!' or something like that?"

"I remember that one!" Ryan cried, delighted.

Simon let his face turn serious. "Okay, then. You know how The Tick can lift really heavy stuff that normal people can't?" Ryan nodded. "Well, Lamont can do that, too, just by thinking about it—"

"Cool!"

"—but just like Spiderman or Superman, Lamont has to keep his special powers a secret so that bad people don't find out."

"Bad guys like Searle."

Simon nodded. "Exactly. He—"

—flash—

"—doesn't like Lamont very much," Simon managed to finish. Jesus, Lily was up there alone and headed in to meet Searle? On the other hand, he could imagine how successful Lamont had been at trying to tell her not to go. "So we have to keep it a secret. Promise?"

"I promise." It gave Simon a knot in his stomach to see the sincerity and determination on this child's face. *Dear God,* he thought, *my mind is quieter every day. How many of the children haven't made it through this nightmare?*

"Okay," Lamont said. "Time to get this guy out of this mess." To get a better look, the shorter man hoisted himself onto the chair still positioned next to the rack of bunks. He whistled, then grimaced at the smell of infection. "Man, this has got to hurt big time. It's just as well the poor guy's out of it." He drew in a breath—

—and went to work.

"I don't think so," Lily said hotly.

Mercy's protest came an instant behind hers. "We can't just leave them!"

"Where are we going to go, anyway?" The woman Lily didn't know spoke up, and as angry as Lily was, she heard an edge along the woman's words that had nothing to do with Searle's insistence that they leave. "Until we have a more definitive plan, this is the best place for us. Supplies, food, medicine—it's all right here. Leaving would be extremely foolish."

"I don't recall asking your opinion, Erica." Searle's gaze was ruthless.

"I've had just about enough of you," Erica said right back.

Uh-oh, Lily thought.

Searle's eyebrows lifted. "No shit?"

"Maybe all this"—Erica indicated the ruins around them—"is the final support that signifies you don't work for After Help anymore, or that you don't have any obligation to me." Her expression was steely in her pale face. "That's fine—I can't force you to keep it either way, and it certainly won't do any good to pay you in useless paper now. I'd thought we meant something to each other, but I see that's not the case."

Searle threw back his head and laughed loudly. "That's *rich,*" he said with a gasp. Saliva dribbled into the dirty growth of beard across his face. "First you remind me that I worked for you, then you try and dig some claws into me because we fucked."

Erica's cheeks went scarlet. "You son of a bitch," she said quietly. "I gave you access to everything I had. I gave you a job because I thought you would help me with the business, and you did. I slept with you because . . . well, I don't know *why* I did that." Her mouth took a bitter downward turn. "I've had a lot of time to think on it, but I still can't figure it out. Maybe I had an idea you'd protect me if everything collapsed—clearly a serious misjudgment."

"Erica," Mercy began, "maybe this isn't the time to—"

"Shut up and let her talk," Searle said. "The lady wants to speak her mind so much, hey—who are we to stop her?"

Lily scowled helplessly. There was something unreadable in Searle's voice and this was all wrong, as was her whole feeling about the group. Tension was mounting in the air as though it were a fog coming through the constant, saturating drizzle, swirling in front of them until no one could see what they were dealing with and whether or not it would snap back at them.

On the other side of Mercy, Erica lifted her chin. "We're not trapped anymore, Searle. You can't punch on people to force them to do what you want, and you have no right to make anyone stay here if they want to go—any more than you could claim those supplies down in the bomb shelter. In fact, putting them there wasn't even *your* idea, it was Eddie's. I wanted someone for After Help who was street-smart and tough—the only reason I'd even consider an ex-convict like you—but I also wanted someone with common sense. That's something else I missed the ball on. Maybe you should just move on by yourself and leave the rest of us be."

"So . . . let's see." Searle put on an expression of mock concentration. "According to you, I'm a son of a bitch, I'm stupid, and I should take a hike."

"I didn't say 'stupid.' "

He shrugged. "You might as well have. In my book, a person with no common sense is stupid."

"Look," Mercy said. "Maybe we could just move down the block where we could still see the hospital when Simon and Eddie come out. The flood—"

"One more word and I'll make you wish you hadn't woke up," Searle said harshly.

"Hey, fuck you, old man," Lily cut in. Another statement that came out without conscious forethought and Searle swung around and glared at her. Lily could've sworn he'd forgotten she was there until she spoke. The ball of anger in her gut made her wrists flex again at her sides, back and forth, without her realizing it. "She can talk if she wants, and don't you lay a hand on her."

"I don't know you from the next asshole," he said furiously. "Don't *you* start telling me what to do, too. I'll—"

"What?" Erica demanded, pulling his attention back to her. She'd moved closer to Mercy, and now only about fifteen or twenty feet separated her and Searle. "You're a big man with a gun, aren't you? If not the gun, then . . . your fists? But it's always women and children, right? My God." Erica laughed caustically. "What did you do for entertainment in prison all those years?"

"Ain't it amazing," Searle said conversationally, "how brave you've gotten now that you're out in the daylight? I guess you think that puts you back in charge and now you can push me around like you used to and threaten to run to my parole officer if I don't do the two-step when you say 'dance.' Well, guess what?" He brought the pistol, an oily-looking .38, up until it was level with Erica's chest. "The whole world's changed and I don't have to do shit. Not only that, now I can just get rid of anyone who gives *me* a hard time. Oh, yeah," he said with a dark smile, "I like guns, all right. Up close but damned impersonal."

Everyone froze as the barrel wavered in the air between Searle and Erica. Lily found herself unable to breathe, calculating the distance between her and Searle, knowing, *sensing* that it would be useless to try to reach him before he could squeeze the trigger.

Erica stood straight and tall, looking regal despite the grayish dirt caking her hair and the smudges across her chin and cheeks, her torn and muddied clothing. "I suppose that's your solution," she said icily. "Just 'get rid' of me . . . and the child I'm carrying. *Your* child."

Searle's mouth dropped open, but his recovery and his answer were far too fast to be called anything but malicious. "I'm surprised you didn't do your research first, Erica," he said in a dead voice. "You should have checked with Simon. He would have told you I really hate kids."

And he shot her.

It was hard to tell what happened first after that, although Lily thought that Erica's final cry never had a chance to be heard. It was nothing like in the movies Lily'd seen a thousand times on the boob tube—no graceful, practiced fall to the ground or dramatic gasp. She was so used to seeing the movielike versions that for a second the real thing didn't *look* real: it was too jerky, too *fast*. And there was nothing at all graceful about the way Erica's body got slammed backward and down to the ground, as though the invisible fist of God had swooped out of the sky and smacked her right in the breastbone.

"There," Searle said without missing a beat. His tone of voice was calm, utterly ludicrous after what he'd done. When he looked at Mercy, his expression was full of contempt. "Okay, *Doctor*. Go on and heal her now, you're so fucking great. I always wondered if that was nothing but a crock of shit and I *hate* wasting my time." He swung the gun toward Gena. "And you, you stupid bitch," he continued, "I've lost all my supplies because of some half-assed crap you spouted about flooding. I ought to—"

Who knew where Mercy found the strength to do it, but she hauled herself up and grabbed for Searle's arm; maybe she thought she was going to stop him from shooting again, although Lily doubted it would have mattered. He did squeeze the trigger, but the shot hammered harmlessly into the ground as Gena started screaming and waving one arm wildly in the air in front of her face—

"Mercy, don't!"

—then Searle brought the butt of the pistol down hard on the wounded side of Mercy's head and pushed her away like she was an annoying dog. Mercy's shrieks ended abruptly as she folded and went down, then Lily lost her momentary paralysis and, quick

as a mountain lion, leaped across the space between her and
Searle. The two of them went down to the ground in a madly
thrashing heap.

Except for Eddie, they all heard it: a dull, faraway *thud,* like a
muffled sonic boom. And they all, even Ryan, knew exactly what
it was.

Ryan saw Lamont and Simon exchange alarmed glances.
Between the two men, Eddie hung like a badly weathered scare-
crow, his legs dragging, his head limp against his chest. "We're
almost there," Ryan offered. "Just around the corner."

Lamont started to let Eddie slip down. "We'll come back for
him," he suggested. "We can—"

"No." Simon's voice was sharp. "If we leave him while he's
unconscious, he'll be covered with rats by the time we're out of
sight. That's what happened to him down in the shelter."

Lamont swallowed, then nodded. "All right. Let's pick up the
pace, then." Another gunshot, this one a bit closer because of their
progress. "No more screwing around," Lamont said tightly. "We
are getting out of this hellhole *now.*"

Ryan started to say something but forgot the words as the air in
front of the group kind of . . . *shook.* He'd missed most of what
Lamont had done downstairs because Simon kept having him
check the corridor; now, twenty feet down the hall, the only wall
that remained between them and the hospital's main lobby bulged
as an unseen force pressed against it. A moment of breathless
silence, then it gave way, splitting the quiet with a sound that was
horrifically reminiscent of the ones from the quake days of not so
long ago. If there were more shots from outside, the deafening
noise in here surely drowned them out. Wood, plaster, and the
layer of decorative marble tiles that had topped the wall's surface
shattered into a cloud of flying dust and pieces of debris. A few
more seconds and everything settled; the lobby was finally visible
and beyond it, the shadowy main doors that led outside.

Back in the bomb shelter, Lamont had explained to both Ryan
and Simon that he couldn't carry the unconscious Eddie by himself because he couldn't tell if he was treating him too roughly. He
needed Simon's "touch" for that; thus, Simon would have to help
the whole way, act as a sort of monitor to make sure Eddie was
doing okay in a trip that would probably hurt him a lot to begin

with. Now, with the sounds of gunfire still clear in their minds,
Lamont must have decided that they were close enough so that it
didn't matter anymore. He plucked Eddie from Simon's hold like
a basketball player steals the ball from the hands of another player,
and Simon didn't protest as Lamont clambered through the hole in
the wall and into the lobby area. In only seconds they were all
rushing out of the hospital.

Simon followed as Lamont carried Eddie to just past the crumbling overhang in front of the building and lowered him to the
ground, letting him slide until he lay flat. That done, all three of
them could see everything that had happened, and was *still* happening, in one brutal look:

Erica, lying motionless on the ground.

Mercy the same, not far away.

Gena, apparently uninjured, raging vainly from where she
clung to a nearby light post.

And finally, Lily and Searle, rolling around on the ground, bellowing and beating at each other.

"Oh, *God*!" Simon wailed when he saw Mercy. He sprinted
toward his wife at the same time that Lamont headed for the struggling duo. Ryan didn't know *what* to do—should he follow Simon
or stay with Eddie? And what about Gena, who was stuck over
there by herself and couldn't see a thing?

"Stop it!" Lamont was yelling at Lily and Searle, but Ryan
could see it was way too late for talking. Searle was pummeling
the thinner woman as best he could with Lily as close as she was,
trying in vain to get his gun in a position to shoot her. But Lily was
fast as an alley cat and twice as vicious; to prove it, Searle's
clothes were stained deep, wet crimson in a half-dozen places. It
wasn't until Lily backstepped, then swiped one hand forward with
a snarl that Ryan understood why Searle looked the way he did: all
that time he'd thought Lily was just a cool girl who dressed funny,
she'd had a long, super-sharp knife strapped to each wrist underneath the sleeves of her jacket.

Lily's final strike made the battle hers. Searle looked at her in
surprise, then brought a hand up to his throat and the sudden, spec-
tacularly red fountain it had grown.

"Jesus, Lily!" Lamont cried. "No more!"

Crouched, ready to leap again, something in Lamont's voice
must have gotten through because Lily blinked and at last seemed
to comprehend what was going on around her. Four feet away,

Searle pulled his fingers back and gazed dully at the wash of blood on them.

Then he collapsed.

Lily didn't waste any time on Searle. From the spot where Ryan still stood—things had happened so fast he'd never had the chance to move—the boy heard a muted snap as the twin bloody blades cradled in Lily's palms disappeared from sight. Then she was darting past Searle's body without a sideways glance as she headed for Mercy and Simon.

"Jesus," Lamont said again. He knelt next to Searle as Ryan finally moved forward, but it was hopeless. A few feet away in a puddle was the older man's gun, forgotten, as Searle slowly relaxed across the cold, wet ground. His throat was a raw, open gash, but Ryan thought that wound was only the last one needed to push him over the edge; Searle had another dozen wounds pocking his chest and shoulders. For a moment Searle looked over at Simon . . .

Then he died.

For Gena the blackness had slipped back into her eyes like an old relative come for a visit and decided to stay. That she had lost the marvelous ability to see all that was wondrous and devastated in the world was something she would have to contemplate later, when the thunder of unknown gunfire and the screams that had seemed to go on forever were sorted out. For that, however, she would need someone else's help.

"Will somebody tell me what the hell is going on?" Gena shrieked. *"For Christ's sake, don't just leave me over here!"*

The hands that closed over her shoulders were familiar, the embrace into which she was pulled safe and the only place in the world she really wanted to be.

"She's still unconscious," Simon said, "but she's breathing okay. She doesn't seem feverish like before."

Gena didn't know whether to be relieved or worried. Whatever infection had tried to work its way through Mercy's body had apparently been brought under control by the antibiotics that Erica had prescribed, but none of them knew why or what to do about this latest blow to the already injured area of Mercy's head. And there was Eddie, too, a few feet away and silent, lost in whatever dark realm had also claimed Mercy. Erica was dead, Searle was dead, and the rest of them had no idea how to help their injured. Gena had tried touching them, hoping for a glimpse into the future and afraid of it at the same time. Unlike Simon, however, she'd seen too much death over the years to be afraid of this: she would do it because she must and so they would know what awaited them tomorrow or the next day.

Nothing.

Smooth blackness, but not the same as a warning of death, no vision in her mind of them carrying the bodies off to some niche hidden from the street and covering them with rubble to keep the rats away, as they had done with Searle and Erica. Perhaps her second sight was returning in dribbles as had her vision, temporary as it had turned out to be. She still had a sense of things to come, the good and the bad, and she felt certain that her . . . *skills* would come back as strong as they had been before. Just not as quickly as she might have wished—and wasn't it ironic that not so long ago the only thing she'd desired was to be rid of the capability of foreknowledge?

"We're going to have to get out of here." Lily's voice came from her right and Gena turned automatically so she could listen. "The shots will draw soldiers, sure as shit. If you thought one man with a pistol was bad, wait till you face off with a maniac armed with a submachine gun."

"Where should we go?" asked Lamont. Gena focused on the sound of his voice—how amazing that he could still sound calm after all this—and let it be her anchor. Thank God he had come back; for a while, down in the shelter with Searle, she'd been terrified she would die without ever holding him again.

"East," Lily said decisively, "then south."

"No good." Gena sat up. "It's all flooded, Lily. That's what started this entire mess, what made us had to get out of the hospital to begin with."

"Straight south, then. Maybe it'll be warmer in that direction."

"Warmer sounds good to me," said Simon wearily. His voice sounded faraway and Gena knew he was wondering if he was going to get to wherever they were headed with Mercy, or alone.

"Then let's pack it up and go," Lily suggested. "We have to move as quickly as we can at first. I know it's going to be hard, but we can slow down later. I've seen these army guys in action—

they'll come to where the blood is, but they don't care enough to put any effort into tracking anyone farther." She paused. "At least not yet."

Lamont frowned. "What's that supposed to mean?"

Lily didn't answer immediately. "It means," she said finally, "that I think they'll be more likely to go after us—anyone, for that matter—later on, when they get . . . hungry." Gena's heart did a double beat as the meaning of Lily's words sank in. Beside her, Lamont stiffened.

"Huh?" Ryan's piping voice, filled with curiosity.

"Never mind, kidstuff." He giggled suddenly and Gena could imagine Lily giving him an intentionally goofy smile . . . well, she could *almost* imagine it. She'd never actually *seen* Lily. "You just let me worry about that. Have I let you down yet?"

"Nope."

"Okay," Gena said, trying to pull the conversation away from the soldiers and their unspeakable deeds. "Then let's take Lily's advice and get the hell out of here before we have unwelcome company."

As bruised and exhausted as most of them were, it took only a few short minutes to gather their injured and leave Althaia Hospital behind forever.

JULY 17 . . .

Mercy opened her eyes and said, "I dreamed I was drowning in mud."

Someone beside her jittered, then sat up. "Mercy?"

"It was everywhere," she continued. "The rivers, the oceans, flowing through the buildings in a thousand cities. Poetic, huh?" It took an immense amount of effort, but she turned her head. Lily's bright eyes stared back at her. "Do you think that's the way it is everywhere else, Lily? Nothing but . . . mud?"

Lily hesitated. "I can't begin to guess, Mercy. I suppose there are lots of places that would be like that, yes."

Mercy squeezed her eyes shut, as if Lily had confirmed her fears, then opened them again. "Where's Simon? What happened?" She could hear the panic rising in her own voice, could do nothing to stem it. "I remember—"

"He's fine," Lily said quickly. "Just gone off with Lamont, looking around for supplies and dry wood."

"Lamont's here?" Mercy struggled to pull herself up and Lily's rough-skinned hand closed over her forearm and lifted her to a sitting position. "What about Erica?"

Lily looked away. "She's dead. So is Searle."

Mercy's mouth dropped open. "Simon . . . he didn't . . ."

"No. But I did."

"Oh, Lily," Mercy whispered.

Lily stared down at her hands, as though she could still see a stain of blood. "I never killed anyone before," she said quietly. "And I didn't plan it. He was such an evil scumbag that I thought afterward it wouldn't bother me, but . . ." Lily's blue eyes clouded. "The way Simon looks at me now, I can tell he sees me as a murderer."

Mercy's head gave a sudden throb, as though it were pounding in sympathy. She reached out to squeeze Lily's cold, chapped fingers. "I'm sure he doesn't think that—"

"Of course he does," Lily interrupted. "How can he *not*? It doesn't matter what the man did a lifetime ago or what he might have done to you or anyone else had he lived, or even *why* I did it. Searle was still Simon's father, and I killed him."

Mercy could think of nothing to say in response.

JULY 18 . . .

Mercy's progress was rapid after that. No one could say whether it was the extra "sleep" brought on by Searle's strike to the injured area of her skull or the antibiotics that Simon had dutifully dissolved in water and dribbled down her throat while she was unconscious, but Mercy felt rested and able to walk for short distances within a day after she came to. Eddie, however, was not so fortunate.

"How is he?" Mercy asked when Simon came back from the small pallet a short way from where she sat. They had stopped for the night in Forest View, a small western suburb, and now sat huddled beneath the remains of a lopsided awning in front of what had once been a strip mall. The trip had been arduous and exhausting, with Lamont carrying the heavy load—Eddie—the entire time as they'd followed the distorted pieces of I-55 to the southwest until it stopped just beyond the city's limits.

"I think he's dying," Simon said truthfully. "I'll be surprised if he makes it to morning."

Mercy was silent for a moment. Dying? Damn it—where was that feeling, that *sensation*, that had been her comrade all her life?

Why couldn't she find it as she had so many times in the past? "Well," she said now, "then I can't wait any longer."

Mercy held out her hand and Simon took it doubtfully and steadied her as she levered herself to her feet. "Are you sure you're up to this?" he asked anxiously. "You were hurt so badly—"

"If I don't at least try," she said pointedly, "then everything I am means nothing. I don't believe that I have this . . . talent, or whatever you care to call it, just for my personal convenience. If I can do for you or for Gena, then I can—and should—do for everyone I have to." Briefly she thought of Searle and tried to push the thought away; what would her beloved husband think of her if he chanced to read her mind right now and discovered that she was *glad* she'd been unconscious when Searle died? Or that she was grateful that she hadn't had to face the demand upon herself to help a man she'd considered to be no more than a monster inside human flesh? She looked at Simon gravely. "I'm not entirely sure I'll be successful," she admitted, "but I know if I don't give it the best I can, I'll never be able to live with myself."

Simon seemed as though he wanted to protest but he said nothing, only walked with her over to where Eddie lay motionless. "Mercy," he said quickly, "I know you've seen a lot of things in your career, but you haven't been in a hospital for some time and—"

"I'll be fine," she said firmly. "Thanks for staying with me this far, but you go on back and let me have some time alone with him." Reluctantly, Simon nodded and strode away.

They'd placed Eddie beneath the least collapsed of the over-hanging canvas, at the end where the rain wouldn't be a constant stream onto him. Bending carefully to keep from making her head throb, Mercy eased back the piece of plastic tarp Simon had found and spread across the dirty wool blanket covering the injured man from neck to feet. The smell of infection and gangrene that coursed from beneath the blanket was terrible, far worse than anything Mercy had ever encountered in an ER. The wool material clung to his legs and Mercy tugged it slightly, then winced when she felt something give. Without opening his eyes, Eddie gave a barely audible groan. When Mercy finally got the coverings free, her breath stopped in her throat at what she saw.

"My God," she whispered. Articulating anything beyond that would have been impossible; all she could think of was how much agony this slender young man was in and for how long. On the heels of that was a hearty curse at herself for not getting off her pampered ass and trying to help him far, far sooner. It was almost as if he'd been hanging on all this time and waiting for her, as though he'd *known* she might be able to do something to heal him. Without warning she had an unpleasant flash memory: back in medical school, the forensics portion of her training and the floater that had been her autopsy assignment. There was a disturbing resemblance from that to the mottled purple and blue-black flesh showing below where the others had tried to make Eddie more comfortable by cutting away his pants legs. Red lines of blood poisoning disappeared beneath the ragged material and when Mercy cautiously looked beneath the layers of shirt and jacket, she saw the streaks had already crawled across most of his chest. Simon had been correct in his guess that Eddie wouldn't live until tomorrow; peritonitis had spread throughout his body and by now done massive and irreparable damage to his heart and possibly his brain. This man was meant to die.

But not in Mercy's world.

So afraid a few minutes ago that she would never be able to do what was necessary, Mercy's hands were beginning to tingle, a slow, electrical warmth that seeped from the tips of her fingers and stopped at her wrists. Deep inside herself, the familiar beat had returned, eager for release but not worsening the headache that had been her constant mate since being struck with a chunk of that shed roof. She had no idea whether she was strong enough to take Eddie all the way to recovery, but she was damned well ready to *try*.

She placed her left palm against the hot, ravaged flesh on Eddie's thigh, then slid her other hand beneath his shirt and onto his belly; her fingers found that same feverish temperature below a light coating of hair. What now? For a moment Mercy nearly panicked—shouldn't she perform some kind of ritual? Where was that elusive state of mind that was so vital to her ability to heal, that magical mental incantation she should be thinking? Her shoulder muscles tensed, then she forced them to relax, demanded that her mind let go of the anxiety attack that threatened to paralyze her, and just let it flow, and—

—fire filled her, became unbearable, then desirable. Mercy felt it gather and move inward from the round knobs of her shoulders to the center of her breastbone, condensing until she would have thought, had she been coherent, that she was having a heart attack.

For a second the knot just *hung* there, like a spot of lead the size of a softball. Then the point, the center of herself, exploded, careening through her shoulders and down her arms with enough strength to nearly throw her sideways. Blue-white light flashed in front of her eyes, and Mercy didn't know whether it was in her head or truly visible, then another mini-eruption took her, catapulting from her hands and into Eddie's body. Surely it was someone else who was watching them and seeing Eddie's eyes open wide in shock and disbelief, because Mercy couldn't see a thing past the yellow and red sparkles that were sheeting across her field of vision: there was only the pressure of Eddie's legs and stomach to anchor her to anything that still seemed real in this world.

When the third power charge rocketed out of her, Mercy swore that this time she would *not* lose consciousness.

She was wrong.

ALSIP, ILLINOIS
JULY 20 . . .

"Boy, this is getting to be quite a habit with you." Simon's earnest face beamed down at her.

For the first time in what felt like years, Mercy grinned back. Bone-weary, again, but other than that, she was doing pretty good—no headache, no deep tissue bruises, nothing. A jab of concern made one hand reach to circle the healthy swell of her stomach; in response to its mother's touch, the baby within gave a sturdy kick. "Is it morning yet?" she asked impishly.

Simon laughed and she could hear the relief in his voice. "Well, my watch says so anyway."

"I'm starved," Mercy said. "Do we have anything to eat?"

From his pocket, Simon pulled a can of tuna and a palm-sized can opener, then began prying at the lid. When she wrinkled her nose, he shot her a stern look. "Pretend you're an Eskimo," he told her. "What did you expect—corned beef hash? It's healthy."

Fish or not, Mercy reached for the open can eagerly. "Here," said Simon. From another pocket he produced a plastic spoon that was only slightly grimy. "Never let it be said that I'm married to a savage who eats with her fingers. Besides, it will keep you from cutting yourself on the edge."

Mercy started to lift the first bite to her mouth, then froze. "Where's . . . Eddie?" *Jesus*, she thought, *here I am shoveling food into my mouth and I don't even know if he's alive.* Shame filled her and she lowered the can of tuna.

"He's off with Lily and Ryan," Simon told her with a smile. "They're poking around to see if they can come up with anything useful. Food, water, whatever."

"Ryan . . ." For a moment, Mercy frowned. "I remember him, I think. From a couple of years ago." Then her eyebrows arched and she found herself clutching the can with everything she had. "You said Eddie—you mean he's walking around already?"

"He's *climbing,* for God's sake—and he didn't need nearly as much sleep as you did before he got going."

"How long have I been out?" she asked before digging up a spoon of tuna fish with renewed interest.

"Two days."

She nearly sprayed him. *"What!"*

Simon grinned. "I'd call you Rip Van Winkle, but your hair isn't white."

"Are we . . ." Mercy paused, feeling foolish. Simon must be thoroughly tired of hauling her around like a helpless baby. Jeez, was she ever going to be well again?

"Are we what?"

". . . still in Forest View?" It didn't really matter, but knowing where they were on her mental map gave her a sense of place.

Simon shook his head. "No. With Eddie walking on his own we made great time going farther south. We followed Cicero Avenue straight out; we should be in Alsip now. Another few days and we'll leave the Chicago area altogether."

Leave Chicago? Sadness swept through Mercy. All those memories—college, medical school, the days and nights in the Althaia emergency room before Erica had undermined her career. Misted into those precious moments were her first sweet times with Simon. She looked up and caught him staring at her and had to smile. She would carry those things in her heart forever and leave this place behind if she must—as long as Simon went with her.

"Well," she said lightly, "my headache's gone. I guess all I needed was a good rest."

"You could say that." There was something oddly dry about Simon's tone, as though he were humoring her while he waited for her to finally get the punch line to a private joke. As if to confirm her suspicion, a small grin showed at one corner of his mouth.

"Did I say something funny?" she asked. "Or do you just find it amusing that I slept so damned long?"

Simon's grin widened. "It's not the sleep I think is so funny, Mercy. It's the headache part. Of course, your headache is gone. So is your head *wound*."

She gawked at him. "Excuse me?"

"You healed yourself."

"That's not possible."

"Says who?" he demanded. "Did you ever *really* try it before? I don't recall you ever mentioning that you did. You've always been so convinced that it was outside your abilities that you dismissed it. Well, the surprise is on you, sweetheart." He said the word *sweetheart* in a half-assed Humphrey Bogart impression that made her momentarily giggle. "Eddie wasn't the only person to come out of your little 'meeting' with a fresh new outlook and a renovated body to go with it." He glanced sideways at her and she caught a hint of the old Simon, the one who hadn't been beaten down by the pieces of a rogue planet and the screams of a million dead.

"Hey," he said, "you're lucky. A charge that big, it could've made your hair fall out. Eddie's did."

BLUE ISLAND, ILLINOIS
JULY 22 . . .

"Is it my imagination or does the sky seem to be lighter?"

Lily's inquiry brought Simon out of his reverie. His eyes met hers briefly, then he looked away, unable to hold the contact. Could she really be blamed—

"No," he said out loud, "it's not just wishful thinking. It's hard to catch, but if you think back to how it looked when the last of the earthquakes hit . . . yeah, there's a difference."

Lily didn't say anything for a moment, then, "Simon—"

—*flash*—

He held up a hand. "Don't, please. I know you're sorry it happened, and I know you didn't have any choice because Searle didn't give you one. That's the kind of guy he was." Simon's chuckle was hollow. "He may be dead, but there's no forgiveness in me for him, Lily. Not now, not ever. I think I may have even told him that once."

"And how about for me?" Lily asked softly. "Is there forgiveness in you for *me*?"

She walked away before he could answer.

"How many people do you think are still alive in Chicago?"

What is this? Simon almost snapped. *Question and answer day?* Surprised at his crankiness toward Mercy, he dug his fingers into his palms, then relaxed them. Overload, that's all—as if the damned asteroids weren't enough, it was the threat of losing Mercy—*twice*—that had nearly sent him over the edge. At least the asteroid pieces were impartial, an equal killer. But Searle—that bastard had seemed determined to slaughter everyone Simon had ever loved. Searle's death had been close to everyone and brutal, but the undeniable truth in his own mind was that Simon had wished the man dead for years. The only difference was he'd always expected the deed would come from the authorities in the form of an execution, or perhaps at the hands of another convict. Never had he dreamed he would see it done by someone who walked at his side every day.

"Simon?"

"Huh? Oh—sorry. I was thinking." He scanned the line of houses around them and thought back to the last of the buildings and the cityscape they'd seen as they'd trudged the final length of I-294 to where it crossed I-57 southbound. They couldn't walk on the roadways proper; all those were completely smashed and the long concrete pathways that had been the veins in the country's transportation system had been severed. Transportation from point A to point B had effectively ceased. So many empty houses and buildings—they were all amazed at how few people seemed to have survived. Lamont said it was the repeated quakes that had gotten most of them, and Simon supposed that made sense, but still . . .

"I have no idea," he said now. Lily, Ryan and Eddie followed ten feet behind Simon and Mercy, picking their way carefully along the buckled earthen shoulder of the highway. In front of them, Lamont and Gena set the pace for the group. "I wouldn't know how to estimate it." He fingered his jaw thoughtfully. "There doesn't seem to be many, does there?"

Mercy lowered her voice so that only he could hear. "No, and it's good that we left Chicago when we did."

He raised and eyebrow. "I thought you didn't want to go."

Mercy shrugged. "I didn't, but I don't want to do a lot of

things—and don't get me started on the list because I may never stop." She looked distastefully at her own wet and dirty clothes. "Most of them start with what I'm wearing." She smiled ruefully. "It'll be better for us all to be away from where it was so crowded. All those bodies—God. It's wet and cold now, but the darkness is lifting and I think it's showing a slow warming trend, perhaps a degree a day. All those corpses were already decomposing. Can you imagine how it's going to be if and when the temperature makes it back into the sixties or seventies?"

Simon shook his head. "No," he said honestly. "I can't."

"With little to control it," Mercy continued, "the rat population will explode—"

"It already has."

"—as will the numbers of other small mammals like squirrels, raccoons . . . and let's not forget all those fertile cats and dogs running free. And yes, the rats are up in number, but nothing like it'll be in another four or five months." She ran a hand through her hair and rebalanced her eyeglasses. Simon's had managed to come through unscathed, but Mercy's, whether from the repeated falls or just life in general, had ended up taped at the right side with silver duct tape he'd found in the bomb shelter. It made her look like a grammar school tomboy. Her next words, however, destroyed any thoughts of things like kids and schools filled with laughter. "Rabies," she said grimly. "Plague, cholera, smallpox— all those deadly things mankind had such a handle on. Who knows what kinds of diseases, old *and* new, will spring out of the areas overflowing with millions of decaying cadavers. Everyone always said that living in the country was healthier; this time, they hit it right in the heart."

"Well," Simon said, "I have to say that I think a lot more people survived than we think."

Mercy looked at him in surprise. "Really?"

He nodded. "Remember how you talked about the cats and dogs reproducing like crazy at the clinic before it shut down?" At her acknowledgment, he spread his hands. "Look at yourself and Gena. I've never asked her, but don't you think she was probably using some form of birth control? And Erica—Gena told me she said she was going to have a baby right before Searle did his dirty work. I could've sworn she was in her mid-forties."

"She was, but I don't see—"

"Oh, sure you do," he said with a shrewd look. "It's just so farfetched you don't want to admit it." He laughed unexpectedly. "We're all a bunch of hypocrites," he said, amused. "Here are the four of us with these rare abilities, yet we simply can't believe the rest of the weird stuff the world's throwing at us. Christ—Lamont can pick up a car just by looking at it, yet you can't accept that mankind is reproducing more frequently now?"

"I never said I couldn't accept it," Mercy said sharply.

"Then what's the problem?"

"The problem, Mr. Smartass, is that it won't be *enough* to make a difference to us *or* to the future of mankind in any discernible way. All the woman left in the world can give birth to quadruplets and it still won't stop a plague from wiping us out."

"True." Simon's mouth was a hard slash. "We've gotten tossed into a world we have only the vaguest idea of how to survive in. Everything's different, even the weather." He fell silent for a few minutes, letting her walk along beside him without speaking, holding out a hand to steady her now and then as she struggled over the uneven ground. "And at the end of it all," he said quietly, "we're still our own worst enemy."

Mercy glanced at him. "What do you mean?"

"I mean you can bet that for every one of us who survived, there are three or four more who also made it through but don't think nearly as rationally. Chicago must be depopulated, but out here—" He waved at the countryside, still dotted with occasional buildings, little but unidentifiable rubble amid a sodden, gray-brown landscape. "I'll bet plenty of people lived to tell about it. Some of these old country farmhouses still have root cellars and storm cellars; they're also the most likely places to find stores of food, protected by zealots with wonderful inventions like rifles and pitchforks."

Mercy chewed her lower lip. "Yes, but they *also* have farming equipment and the means to—"

"Do not much of anything unless the sun comes out," Simon interrupted. "I don't know much about growing things, but I'm pretty sure that for most of what's edible you need photosynthesis."

Mercy stopped short. "So you're saying we're headed to parts unknown for no good reason, because we're all dead anyway, right? That we have no hope?"

"Not at all." His voice was almost too cheerful as he gripped her elbow and urged her to resume walking. To his ears, his words sounded vaguely false, but by God he'd put everything he had into it. "I'm saying hope is the only thing we have left."

BEECHER, ILLINOIS
JULY 24 . . .

"Hey," Lily said, "how're you doing?"

The man who looked up at her from studiously building the evening's fire was a world removed from the living corpse that Lamont and Simon had carried out of the basement of Althaia Hospital ten days ago. This, she thought, was how he must've looked when he'd lived in his beloved hometown of New Orleans—except for the missing hair, of course. Eddie had told her his hair had been thick and well past his shoulders, and Simon and Lamont had mentioned finding clumps of it lying around the pallet on which he'd been when Mercy had paid him *the* visit. It was still hard to picture him with the style he described, since all of the handfuls left were charred and nearly black. But Eddie himself—well, he was a fine-looking guy: not much taller than Lily but nicely built, with sincere brown eyes, good features, and a scalp sporting a ginger-colored coating of fuzz that was a double shade darker than the new and rather thin growth of beard across his chin. A little too slender from his ordeal, but what kept him from resembling a concentration camp escapee was the sunny, glad-to-be-alive smile that broke out at any time and for the smallest reason. Perhaps the rest of them had lost appreciation for the hell that their lives had become, but Eddie's experience had made him treasure it.

"Great," he said now. He reached forward and plucked a small piece of wood out of the pile, then held it up for her inspection. "Check this out. Right here—doesn't it look like a guitar if you hold it upside down?"

Lily grinned and nodded, though she would never have thought to turn the gnarled chunk in that direction to see. "Sure." She went and sat next to him, huddling inside her jacket and watching, anticipating, while he arranged the fire setup, then put a match to it. The dry matches were the one good thing that had come out of the shelter in Althaia, and now they, like Eddie's outlook on life, were cherished possessions. To his left, Ryan was already bundled into a bag and sleeping soundly. "He sleeps an awful lot," Lily observed as she listened to the child's quiet, steady breathing. "Is that normal?"

"Probably not, but what is?" Eddie used another stick to poke at the slowly growing fire and a shower of sparks sent a brief flash of light across his cheeks. In front of them, welcome warmth was building. "Then again, lots of people sleep their way through traumatic events in their lives. And remember, he's the smallest one here. With the kind of mileage we're racking up, he's bound to be exhausted—because of his size, he's walking twice the distance we are."

"Poor kid," Lily said softly. "This must be so hard on him—no parents, no friends. Everything he knew is gone."

"He'll be all right," Eddie said firmly. "He has us, and he's the youngest and most adaptable among us. Plus I'll watch out for him." Without warning, he gave her that light-filled smile again. "And what about you, Miss Lily-of-the-Valley? How are *you* doing?"

She had to laugh—if he only knew what had been going on in her life the last time she'd called herself that! "I'm still kicking." She paused, then added, "Always."

Eddie nodded and studied her. His frank gaze made her feel warm and nervous all at once, and she damned herself for this teenager's reaction. How stupid coming from her and directed toward this guy—this *younger* guy, at that. The cause wasn't a big mystery: accompanied by Mercy and Simon, then Gena and Lamont, Lily felt like an outsider because she was alone. Alone was okay—when you *were;* alone was not a good thing when you were with other people. It fucked up your head too badly. Eddie was sort of the same way, and sort of not—he had Ryan to look after and a new outlook on life. But Lily wasn't blind and she saw and felt his warm stare nearly all the time. He wanted her, and she wanted him; it was as simple as that.

Not.

Gena's hand, so warm over her own in the darkness, reluctant psychic while everyone but she and Lily slept. Never again would Lily make the mistake of not letting Gena tell her what lay ahead, not after the misery of her Iowa trip home and her failure to convince her backwoods family to prepare for the disaster ahead.

"What do you see?"

Gena's sigh was like a shadow breath from the infant to which she would someday give birth. "Oh, Lily, do you really want to know?"

"Yes."

Swollen silence, then another of those ghostly sighs. "The two of you," Gena admitted, "and the boy. Eddie is a good man, and he will treat you as well as he can. But he is . . . bound to another woman, although right now he doesn't know it."

"Will that ever make a difference?"

Gena's fingers squeezed hers briefly, more for comfort than vision. "I'm sorry," she said quietly.

Undecided, Lily stayed where she was, crouched beside Gena and the sleeping—or so it seemed—Lamont. "He'll leave me then," she said at last. "Do you know when?"

"I'm not a calendar, Lily." Despite the words, her tone was not harsh. "Just a woman with a constant run of crap going through my head."

"Sorry," Lily said automatically. She let go of Gena's hand and rocked back on her heels. "Then I won't go," she decided. "I may be crazy, but I'm not stupid enough to set myself up for a hurt. It won't be the end of the world; that already came."

"You've made up your mind?"

"Yeah," Lily said. "Thanks for taking the time to—"

Not expecting it, Lily yelped when Gena's hand snatched at hers again. "All right," the other woman said. "Now let's see what happens."

Frozen, her heart pounding madly in her chest, Lily peered into the darkness, trying to see Gena's face. After a moment, Gena's hand dropped away. "Well?"

"If you don't go with them, Lily, the boy will die."

So, she told herself as she watched Eddie across the small glow of the fire, it will be a temporary thing only. Her own dismal little secret.

So be it.

"I wish it'd warm up," she said to break the quiet that had built. "It's freaky to have it so cold and dark and know it's supposed to be the middle of summer." As usual, she and Eddie were the only ones awake; they routinely functioned on three quarters of the sleep the others needed. She held her palms out to the flames, enjoying the way the heated air tingled against the surface of her cold skin.

"Here," Eddie said. He rose and came toward her, then draped a blanket—as damp and dirty as any of the others they had, but at least it was another layer—across her shoulders.

"What about you?" she asked.

One corner of his mouth turned up. "Oh, I'm fine. I'm . . . thinking warm thoughts."

She rolled her eyes and started to retort, then he startled her by leaning forward and kissing her gently on the lips. Whatever those warm thoughts were, they felt like they ran right from him into her; the blush she felt sweep across her face and belly abruptly brought more intense yearnings.

"What—what was that for?" was all she could think of to say after he pulled away.

"To help you think warm thoughts, too?"

It was more a question than statement, and Lily grinned. "Kinda like striking a match in a windstorm, don't you think?" At his quizzical look, her smile turned into an outright chuckle. "If you don't find cover and light the whole book, it just blows out and goes away."

He scratched thoughtfully at the soft fuzz on his scalp. "I'm not much on riddles, but I could swear that sounded like a well-disguised invitation."

This time when he leaned over to kiss her, she didn't hesitate to wrap her arms around him and urge him down beside her.

MOMENCE, ILLINOIS
JULY 26 . . .

"It's got a good source of fresh water, plenty of supplies and not that many dead people lying around," Lamont said. "What do you think?"

Momence, Illinois, had been a small town. They weren't sure what the population had been before the asteroid hit, since the sign at the main entrance to the town had been lost in the impacts; the group knew they had crossed the town limits only because of the first metal sign a few miles behind them that had announced, obviously, MOMENCE: 2 MI. Small brick houses with spacious front yards had stood next to what had been stately Victorians probably a hundred or more years old, lost to history in the events of this past month. Above, the sky was indeed showing signs of lightening although it was just as likely to pelt them with hail from a sudden storm as it was to give them a momentary glimpse of sullen, lighter gray between the constantly roiling clouds. Today, at what Simon estimated to be about three in the afternoon, the darkness had lifted enough for them to see the shards of glass sparkling amid the ruins, spots of unexpected color evidencing the remains of stained-glass windows that mankind would doubtlessly not see again for a century or more . . . if ever.

It was Mercy who answered first. "Let's see if we can find a hospital or a medical clinic before we make a final decision," she suggested. "At the very least, a doctor's office that still has some supplies lying under the rumble."

"What do you need that stuff for?" Lily asked. "You can fix anything that goes wrong, right?"

Mercy smiled. "I think so—but what if something happens to me?" At her side, Simon frowned but said nothing. "After all," she continued, "it has—twice. Everyone needs a backup plan, Lily."

"Good idea," Eddie said. "Let's go find a phone book."

For a second, no one moved. Then Gena burst out laughing.

"Whew." Eddie grinned. "For a minute I thought no one was going to get the joke!"

There was, indeed, a small medical clinic in what they presumed was the downtown area. It was pretty ravaged and most of the supplies were picked over, but with Lamont shifting some of the heavier chunks of concrete, they managed to find a few items. Despite his assistance, digging through the rubble for the small items was tedious and it was deceptively easy to lose track of time as they moved through the ruins and explored the remains of closets and shelves buried under collapsed walls.

It was also dangerously distracting.

"You folks just hold it right there."

The voice was slightly southern and all business. Lamont's first thought was that it couldn't belong to a soldier; according to Lily, that kind would have opened fire and not bothered to talk first. He started to turn and got a curt order to stay right where he was and "Don't you be moving without my telling you to, son." *Son?* The word almost made him snicker—not a good idea, under the circumstances. "Now," said the mystery person, "my name is Howard Tanton and I'm kind of the acting law since our sheriff's department got wiped out. There aren't many of us left here in Momence, and we don't cotton much to outsiders inviting themselves in and raiding what little is left before they move on. So why don't you all just step—real carefully—away from that stuff there and be on your way."

"Actually," Mercy said calmly, "we were going to stay."

Oh, shit, Lamont thought. Was it really wise for her to say that? Simon had told him, and they had all seen evidence of it in the panic before the impacts, that people tended to hoard supplies in and after a catastrophe. Mankind being the generous souls they had always been, it was a given that most would kill newcomers to protect their own stash.

"Well, I don't reckon maybe that's such a good idea," Tanton said. There was a hard edge to his voice that confirmed Lamont's fears. "I don't reckon we *need* a bunch o' strangers settling here—it'd just be more mouths to feed."

"Could you use a doctor?" Mercy's words still had that same implacable professional tone.

Tanton said nothing, the hush stretching out and out. When their captor finally did speak, he sounded more curious than rigid, vaguely hopeful. "Why don't you turn around, young lady."

From the corner of his eye, Lamont saw Mercy turn; in her hands were a couple boxes of gauze that weren't too badly soaked and somehow the sight lent credence to her question. She didn't say anything more, just waited for Tanton to decide.

"And would that doctor be you, missy?"

"Yes. My name is Leah," she said. "Dr. Leah Ammon." She gestured around her. "That's my husband Simon, and these are my friends."

"What kind of medicine do you practice, Miss—er—Dr. Ammon?"

Mercy's mouth lifted at one side. "I'm a trauma specialist, Mr. Tanton. My field is emergency medicine."

More silence, and finally Tanton spoke. "And you're saying you all were thinking of staying on here." He didn't quite look convinced. "Why's that?"

"Yes, we were." Mercy glanced around the wreck of the small clinic, her eyes speculative. "It's small and fairly clear. We passed the Kankakee River on our way; fresh water is always a plus when there's no government agency to supply it."

"Well," Tanton said, "if . . . if you're telling the truth—and I guess it'll show up right quick if you're not—there's a lot of people who're going to be real glad to welcome you." Mercy nodded and glanced pointedly at something Lamont couldn't see. "Oh," Tanton sounded flustered. "Say, I'm sorry. You all can move now, of course. We're just a little nervous, you understand.

Some of the ones coming off the highway haven't exactly been wholesome and good-hearted."

Lamont drew an easier breath and turned with the others to face the man who'd introduced himself as the local law. Of average height, Tanton was in his mid-fifties and slightly overweight; he looked as bedraggled and wet as any of them, though his clothes lacked the filthy stains that time and road travel had pasted on the rest of them. Loose skin under his chin showed where he'd once weighed considerably more. The gun he'd held on them, a no-bullshit double-barrel pump shotgun, was enough to make Lamont break out in a cold sweat all over again. Still easily within firing position, at least the barrels were making a slow but steady progress toward the sky.

Ever the social worker, it was Simon who spoke first. "Hello," he said without fanfare. "Simon Chanowitz." He extended his hand first, then took two unhurried steps to where he could shake with Howard Tanton. The older man's expression was still tense, but he accepted the handshake nonetheless. Simon decided to do the rest of the introductions. "Over there is Gena and Lamont, then Lily and Eddie. The little guy is Ryan."

Through the fine mist coating his face, Tanton blinked at Ryan, as if noticing for the first time that they had a child with them. The maw of the gun crept higher. "Uh, pleased to meetcha."

Following Simon's example, Lamont stepped leisurely forward. "Lamont London," he said, keeping his voice level. "This is my girlfriend, Gena."

"Hi," Gena said. Her glasses were long gone but the hair, grown another half inch, effectively hid her eyes. She didn't move to offer her hand and Tanton didn't push it.

"Howdy," he said. He peered at Lamont. "What is it you do, Mr. London?"

"I was a lawyer," Lamont said with utter seriousness. "Now I think I'm going to have to find a new career."

Tanton laughed and in the sound Lamont heard the shadow of a man who'd once had a fine sense of humor. "How about you two?" he asked of Lily and Eddie.

"Well," Eddie responded brightly, "I used to be a food waiter in New Orleans."

Lily arched an eyebrow. "Ryan here is a kid right now, but we expect he'll grow out of that. I used to be crazy."

Tanton's mouth dropped open, then he laughed again, louder.

"Well, I'll be damned," he said. "Ain't you just a wild bunch!" The shotgun went point up, no longer aimed at anything. "I'm going to feel like a teenaged boy bringing a slew of peculiar pals home to meet my pa."

Mercy grinned, then her face turned serious. "How many people have you got in town now?"

Tanton's smile faded and he looked troubled. "I'd guess there's around fifty or so. That's all that's left out of more than three thousand." He shook his head, then glanced away, slightly embarrassed. "It's strange, but like you all, most of our ladies are . . . uh . . . expecting."

"I'm not surprised," Mercy said. "It seems to be a phenomena caused by the situation. The increased frequency may have started as early as January of this year, and it's not limited to humans—animals are breeding at a startling rate, as well."

"Which explains why a doctor would be especially valuable," said Lamont.

Tanton shrugged self-consciously. "Well, sure. And we've got a few folks who were injured in the earthquakes and such; they could use some looking after that's a little more skilled than what we've been able to provide. Our own doc and his staff," he added, "didn't make it through. We—"

"Just a minute," Lily interrupted sharply. The rest of the group looked her way in surprise. "If all those people got killed—most of your town—why aren't there any bodies?"

Tanton didn't answer for a moment and Lamont felt unease rise in his throat. Lily was right, and hadn't that been one of the things that had drawn them to this small central Illinois town to begin with? Now that she had voiced the question, Lamont realized that Lily had hit on something that could be very, *very* important. She had mentioned before, without going into lurid detail, what more than a few of the army battalions were using as food . . . dear God, surely these people weren't eating their dead?

"A mass grave," Tanton finally said. His voice was heavy and left no doubt as to it sincerity. "At the south edge of town where the wind is least likely to carry the smell back." His gaze swept the piles of brick and wood that stretched down what was apparently the main street of Momence. "We got one of the township bull-dozers running using parts from the other two, and we were damned lucky that the underground tanks at one of the service station didn't blow. We used the dozer to move the corpses." The stocky man rubbed a hand over his mouth as if trying to wipe away a bad taste, and his face suddenly looked on the edge of exhaustion. "The job isn't over yet," he said. His voice was resigned. "We've collected the ones we could find, but God knows how many might still be buried in all these houses. Our biggest fear is that we're missing somebody who's still alive. I have nightmares about people starving to death in basements and such."

Lamont looked at him narrowly, then glanced at Simon to see his reaction, knowing his friend would read a lie as if it were written in the air in front of him. Simon's nod said it all; everything Tanton had said was true.

Tanton squared his shoulders. "But we're trying to get it cleaned up and we got a lot of good people, and never you mind a cranky old bastard like me waving a shotgun." Tanton sounded rushed, as if Mercy and the rest of them would suddenly decide to keep going. "We got a little problem with rats—I won't lie to you about that—but we've got a kind of mandatory rat patrol. Everyone who's able takes a turn, but we worked it out so the duty only comes around about every three weeks. It's not real pleasant, but it's only once in a while."

"Nothing a good ol' American combat boot to the head won't take care of," Lily said blandly.

Ryan sent her a horrified look. "Yuck!"

"Oh, I'm just kidding, dippy." She gave the little boy a friendly push and he made a comical face at her in return. "You think I'd get my boots dirty for *that*?"

"So, how about it?" Tanton asked. He seemed to have forgotten that they'd already made their decision. "You think you might want to try it out here? If you don't like it, you can leave anytime, of course. We'd never force you to stay."

Lamont couldn't help smiling; if the man only knew how true that was, at least as long as Lamont was alive. He found the others looking at him and wondered how on Earth he'd gone from a man cowering in his own backyard to leader, but that was something he could think about another time. Right now, Tanton was waiting for an answer, his saggy face as homely and hopeful as a sad, wet old hound.

"I think it sounds like a fine place to try to build a new life, Mr. Tanton," he said solidly. The others nodded and only Lily looked like she was pretending; she had a enigmatic expression that made Lamont speculate whether she was thinking of moving out on her own one day soon. Eddie, too, seemed as though he were just following along with the rest of them, and the idea blossomed in Lamont's mind that the two of them might look for something else together.

In front of them, Tanton's face had crinkled into a beaming smile. "Hot damned," he said heartily. "Welcome to Momence!"

JULY 29 . . .

"What would you say," Eddie said, "if I suggested the two of us hit the road?"

Facing him across a small table in a cafeterialike area the townspeople had set up under a canvas tent the size of the ones found at carnivals, Lily's face was unreadable. *She thinks I'm nuts,* he thought. *And maybe she's right. We're dry and well fed for the first time since Millennium hit, and here's me wanting to take off. I'm an idiot.*

"Why?"

Oh, boy, the sixty-million-dollar question. He'd known she'd ask it, of course, and had counted on himself to come up with an appropriate answer when it happened. A foolishly presumptuous thing, because now his mind was as blank as a blackboard erased by a teacher. "I don't know," he finally had to admit. "It's an urge, something I can't seem to ignore. Insane, ridiculous, you name it—but it's there." He looked down at his hands, amazed to see fresh, pink skin where the grime had been washed away. Did he really want to leave all this for a life like the one they'd had a week ago?

God help him, he did.

Lily stared at him, her eyes filled with misery. "This is a great place to be, Eddie. We've got food, water, safety. It's hard to imagine giving it up for a case of wandering feet. Can't you just ride out the urge for a few months and see what happens? Maybe it'll go away."

"I don't think it will." People moved around them, already accepting. When they'd first come in the day before yesterday, Lily had drawn the most suspicious looks; now no one paid any attention to her. "But you're right that this *is* the place to be," he added. "That's why we'd leave Ryan here with Simon and Mercy. He'll be a lot better off."

"I thought you said you'd take care of him," she said resentfully. There was something else in her voice that sounded like surprise, and Eddie could understand that, too; like the answer to her *Why?* question, he hadn't planned to say that. The words had just spilled instinctively from his mind and mouth.

"And I am. He's much safer here than out on the road."

"Where would we go?" Lily swallowed the last of her meatless chili and put down her spoon; he knew she ate it only because wasting food was unthinkable. "New Orleans? It's on the Gulf, Eddie. It'll be nothing but water."

"I know that. I wasn't even considering there." Eddie linked his fingers together and rested his chin on them. "I'd like to go east," he said dreamily. "Into the sun."

"No," Ryan said.

Eddie looked at Lily and she shrugged helplessly. Why did he get the feeling that she'd known all along that this would happen?

"I don't want to stay," the boy repeated. "I'm going with you guys."

"But Mercy and Simon are wonderful people," Eddie argued. "Don't you like them? Mercy told me that you and her met before, that she once helped you out the same way she helped me."

"Sure I like them," Ryan answered. He folded his arms in a move that seemed far too adult for a child of six. "But I like you more. And I like Lily." His nose was red, his eyes starting to glisten; he was going to cry at any moment but for now he was fighting valiantly against it.

"Lily, help me out here," Eddie said desperately, but she only shrugged again. There was an "I told you so" expression on her face that made him want to stomp on her toe. Damn her—she was sexy, wild and intriguing; she was also fucking infuriating at times. "Ryan, look around you. It's *nice* here. There's food all the time, you don't have to sleep in the rain—there're even a few kids your own age."

"Dorks."

Eddie groaned and, for the first time since that bullshit in New Orleans with Naomi, wished he hadn't lost that see-the-future touch he'd had. It was long gone, apparently existing only to save bloodsucking little Naomi from an early, useless death. If he'd still had it, maybe he would've seen this coming and he and Lily could've snuck out without telling Ryan—

"If you leave me here, I'll run away and come after you," Ryan said. Shit, Eddie thought; maybe the kid could read minds now. He wouldn't be surprised.

"It's *dangerous*," Eddie pointed out. He knew he was wasting air before he said it; what did a six-year-old know of danger? Sure, Ryan had seen more than his share, but children had such a marvelous bounce-back ability. With Searle and Erica dead, Ryan would feel as safe in the world as he had before that asshole had held them all prisoner; the closest the boy had come to a gun since then had been Tanton, and look how that had turned out.

"Tell you what," Lily said. She ran her fingers through the boy's fine, dark hair, grown overly long like everyone else's. "Let's all hit the sack and think on it overnight. We'll get up bright and early in the morning and deal with it then."

"You're going to leave me!" Now the tears did come; his thin shoulders hitched and the sobs came hot and heavy. Eddie's resolve disintegrated; here Ryan was, like Lily had said, with everything he cared about and knew in the world gone, and what were he and Lily, the only two anchors in his life, about to do? Run out on him.

"No, we won't," Eddie said as he bent down to look his little friend in the eye. When Ryan gulped and sobbed again, he pulled the child into his arms and hugged him tightly. "I promise. We'll be here in the morning, and if you really want to go with us, then you can."

When he met Lily's gaze, he could have sworn it was full of anger.

"You're leaving?" Mercy asked. Her face was bewildered and hurt. "For God's sake, Lily, *why*?"

Lily drew a breath, then let it out slowly. Here in the makeshift office that Tanton and his cronies had put together for Mercy, everything seemed clean and bright, despite not being exactly as sterile as in the old days. It was even in a real building, albeit open on one side with a tarp tacked in place until they could rebuild the wall; the idea of a solid, dry place to stay forever filled her with longing and memories of her apartment as it had been after she'd cleaned up the scum of her years of insanity. Someday, this small town would have real homes for its residents again.

But for her it simply wasn't meant to be.

"Eddie wants to go," she told Mercy. She would not lie to this woman who had given her back her life.

"Then let *him* go, damn it." Mercy turned and slammed a plastic bottle of alcohol down on the table that served as a combination desk and counter. "Why do you have to go with him? He's a nice guy and all, but there are more of those in the world. The ranks may have thinned a little, but they're not empty yet."

"I know that."

Mercy's hands reached forward and grabbed the lapels of her jacket; for a moment, Lily was certain the other woman was going to shake her like a rag doll. She let herself sway there, ready to take the punishment. "You're holding out on me," Mercy said grimly. Her fingers dug into the cracked leather until the knuckles were white and purple. "I've held you in my arms and turned you inside out, and I know, I *know,* when you're not telling me everything."

Lily hung her head and didn't try to pull away. "It's Gena," she said finally. "Ryan refuses to stay behind—says he'll run away and find Eddie if he goes without him. Gena told me that if I let the two of them go without me, Ryan'll end up dead. If I go with them, she says he'll be okay."

Mercy made a strangled sound and pushed her away, then spun and gripped the edge of the table. "*Damn* it," she hissed. "How many times are you supposed to be the savior?"

"As many as you," Lily said softly. She stepped forward and touched her friend's shoulder, felt her gut twist when Mercy stiffened. "Oh, Mercy—don't you understand?" she pleaded. "Even Ryan isn't all of it. I'd have to go anyway, eventually."

Mercy whirled. "What are you talking about? You never had any urge to fucking see the world when we were in Chicago!"

Lily spread her hands. "It's *Simon.* I can't look him in the eye and he can't bear to be around me. He tries so hard, and I know I didn't do wrong, but it's still *there,* always, like a big, ugly zit."

"Can't the two of you learn to live with it?" Mercy whispered. Her eyes filled with tears.

Lily shook her head. "You know that's not possible."

"You're never coming back, are you?" Mercy stared at her. "Not even when whatever happens with Eddie and Ryan is over and done with, because of Simon—"

"Because of *life,*" Lily cut in. "Don't ever blame Simon for me leaving. I'd go anyway because of Ryan. And . . . no." She made herself look Mercy straight on. "I'm never coming back."

   Loaded with supplies, the three of them left the next morning, the farewell cries of their friends penetrating the gray rain and darkness and following them until they were out of hearing range. Behind them lay the promise of a new life with all the warmth and security that could have gone with it, cherished people, treasured memories; stretching ahead was the unknown and all its danger for which they had traded everything.

   With her heart in her mouth and Ryan's warm hand tucked in her own as they began the trek eastward, Lily was so damned heartsick she couldn't talk for hours.

8.
THE BIRTH OF THE DARKZONE

GREENS FORK, INDIANA
AUGUST 2 . . .

Crystal's screaming cut through the constant fog like a shard of glass through skin.

Damn it, Frank thought as he knelt between his wife's legs and tried to see. *It should be* me *having the baby and Crystal doing this*—she's *the nurse, she'd know what to do while I sit here with my finger in my ear.* Clean towels and hot water—ha ha—those were the only things he could remember now. Oh yeah, and that no-big-deal detail about the baby coming a few months early.

"Keep breathing," he said automatically. "You can do it. Come on, one-two-three-four—" A strained, singsong chant was coming out of his mouth and the words sounded like a stranger's; he had no idea what they meant and if he were Crystal, he'd probably say "Shut the fuck up, you're driving me crazy!"

"God—Frank—it h-hurts," she gasped. "Too—much. It's not normal—" Her voice dissolved into a wail and he swore that even with only the feeble glow of the fire and the dubious light from the dark gray sky, he could see her stomach convulse.

"Wait—I think I see the head!" Her response was unintelligible as she shoved a rolled-up towel into her mouth and bit down on it. Fifty degrees, and sweat was rolling off both of them like they were back in Phoenix at the height of July. "Come on, honey— *push*!"

She did as he commanded and her stomach convulsed again, then continued its muscular twisting as she strained to push the painful thing out of her body. A growing knob of bloody scalp protruded from her and Frank ground his teeth; until now he'd never fully appreciated what it meant for a woman to give birth. At the same time as Crystal finally bore down as hard as she could and he reached forward to catch his child as it slid into the world, he felt a fierce, proud joy—

Until, God help them, he turned to place the baby onto the waiting blanket and the fire's soft light washed over its body.

"God," he choked out. The child opened its mouth but nothing happened—no cry, no sound of air rushing into freshly waiting lungs. He saw its chest hitch as it tried to breathe and thought briefly of letting it suffocate; instead he quickly wiped his forefinger on his shirtsleeve, then used it to clean out the mucus filling the tiny mouth. When nothing happened, he did the only thing he could think of: he swept the infant up and held it upside down, then gave its backside a not-too-hard slap. He heard a small gurgle as liquid spewed from the baby's throat, then its cries joined Crystal's in their small camp.

Crystal—

"Frank!"

"What?" He turned, still stupidly holding the child upside down, then had the presence of mind to thrust it onto the blanket and swaddle it. "Aren't you supposed to—"

"Frank, I think there's another one coming!"

Numbly, he sank back onto his knees and prayed to God that if the coming infant resembled its sibling, both their children would die before the morning.

AUGUST 3 . . .

"You're lying to me," Crystal said dully. "Why are you doing this?"

Frank squeezed his eyes shut and wished to God he had some aspirin, luxuries of a world long gone. "Crystal," he said pleadingly, "I'm sorry. This is just as hard for me—"

"Let me see them."

He swallowed hard and pressed his lips together against the argument that wanted to burst out—useless words, useless emotions, useless, useless, useless. These were her children; how long had he expected to be able to hide them? He rose unsteadily and crawled to the opposite end of the small tent, where he had blocked off a corner for the babies. They were still there, of course, silent but alive, their tiny bodies living evidence that yes, things *could* get worse. In fact, they could get so much worse that all a person could do was stand and gape in horror. At least when the asteroids had hit, they'd had the strength to fight for survival; Frank felt no such impulse now, nothing beyond the urge to succumb to absolute surrender.

What had caused this? The impacts? Perhaps it had been him and Crystal, drinking the polluted water left in puddles by the constant rain, poisoned by God knew what as the gritty stuff ran down Crystal's throat and soaked into the growing fetus and her secret twin. What would his wife, so fragile after the extended labor, say when she saw what she had pushed into the world?

"Frank?"

No more stalling. They were wrapped in separate blankets and he picked up the firstborn, a girl, and cradled her in the bend of his elbow, balancing carefully so the head on its weak, fragile neck wouldn't jerk; the second was the boy, a little heavier at what Frank estimated to be four, maybe four and a half pounds. He fit nicely next to his sister and Frank thought it wasn't any harder than carrying an undersized sack of potatoes. Looking down, he felt an unexpected rush of tenderness at his children; what were they besides helpless, completely dependent for life upon their unsuspecting parents? It was a miracle they had lived through the night.

"Here," he said hoarsely. Frank crawled back to his wife using one arm to balance himself. "The . . . bigger one is the boy." Crystal held out her arms without hesitation and he carefully passed the infants over into their mother's care.

His wife peeled back the flap over the girl's face and studied the child, her face expressionless. He waited for the explosion, the wails of denial, a scream of disgust, the fury against who or whatever had visited this unjust thing upon the child—or children—they had waited for so long.

Nothing happened. Crystal left the girl's face uncovered as she meticulously inspected the rest of her, counting fingers and toes, running her hands carefully up the rib cage and down the spine. When she was finished, she rewrapped her, then gently pushed aside the coverings on the boy; although he had grown larger in vitro, her inspection of the male twin brought the same results. Instead of the wailing Frank had prepared for, Crystal slipped a hand inside the wrappings and found the boychild's hand; when she nudged her fingertip against his palm, the baby's fist immediately curled around it.

She lifted the child's hairless head to her lips and kissed his forehead, then opened her shirt and shifted both in a position to feed at each breast. Watching her, Frank had to marvel at the way she had accepted the mottled gray-and-greenish tint to their children's skin and the slightly webbed, six-digit hands and feet.

"Adaptation," she told him calmly. "You're a scientist. If you use the right frame of mind, it's easy to see how they could turn out like they did."

"That's bullshit," Frank said. "Adaptation is nothing but natural selection, and that's a process that takes thousands of years. The babies didn't adapt, Crystal. They *mutated*."

"I don't ever want to hear that word spoken in relation to our children again," she said sharply. "You can think what you want, but if you'd stop using the logical part of that too smart brain and start using the intuitive part, you'd understand. Are *we* mutants, Frank? Or have you forgotten that lovely little camouflage ability we picked up out west?"

"That's different—"

"Oh, stop it already!" She slammed her metal coffee cup down hard enough to make Frank glance automatically toward the sleeping babies; Schuyler and Calypso. He sort of liked the name Schuyler, but . . . *Calypso*? Where on earth had she come up with that? But arguing about it had been as effective as NASA against Millennium. "I get a little tired of the scientific double standard, you know? If it happens and you can explain it, then it must be true; if it happens but you *can't* explain it, it can't be so and you don't particularly care if you've got the damned truth right in front of your eyes!"

"You're way off track," he said heatedly. "All those things I can *explain* are backed up by years of research, hundreds of tests—"

"Well, guess what, smart guy?" He scowled at her and could've sworn she was looking down her nose at him. "The world's a brand-new place with a new set of rules. Instead of trying to explain what your children *aren't,* why don't you try figuring out why the days are getting gradually lighter but we don't have a nighttime anymore?"

"Actually," he said, "I've thought a lot about that and I have a theory." Great; he'd been excited about this when he'd worked it out in his mind, but now he just felt . . . *embarrassed* talking about it. He'd never talked down to her in his life . . . had he?

"I'd like to hear it."

Well . . . she *did* sound genuinely interested. "I don't think the Earth is rotating anymore," he said without preamble. "I think it's stopped in a fixed position on its axis."

Score one for him; Crystal's mouth was a round "O" of surprise. "But . . . *how?*" There was no disbelief in her voice, just amazement. "I didn't know that could happen!"

Frank smiled ruefully. "It's not exactly the kind of thing the government ever felt it needed to conceive an emergency plan for," he said. "But the impacts, the way the earthquakes kept coming and coming, the way the ground seemed to *lurch* under us—I didn't realize it until I started deliberating on it, but the impacts always occurred during the same time span each day—remember how we got to where we knew exactly when *not* to be around anything that could collapse on top of us?"

She nodded. "Yeah, I do. Especially toward the end—"

"Exactly," he interrupted. He couldn't help it; he'd spent so much time mulling this over in his head that finally voicing his speculations was making him excited. "Because of the way the remains of Millennium were strung out, Earth was struck in basically the same area every day. It was impossible to tell at the time because of the darkness, but now that it's starting to lighten up—"

"Why is it so dark?" Crystal interrupted. "Is that dust in the air?"

Frank nodded. "Sure. Do you realize how hard we were hit? Even with the impacts occurring in the Pacific Ocean, millions of tons of dust and sea-floor debris hit the air. The impacts would have triggered the earthquakes, which in turn would have caused volcanic eruptions that probably made Mount St. Helen's look as severe as a home furnace explosion—speaking of which, God knows how many manufacturing, chemical, and refinery plants around the world blew sky-high." Frank glanced involuntarily at the babies, then bypassed the subject and continued. "The impacts must have done what we'd never thought was possible—hammered the Earth in a sequence regular enough to slow and eventually stop its rotation." He tilted his head up as though he could see the sky through the muddied canvas of the tent. "It's a little bit lighter each day," he marveled. "That means the debris in the atmosphere is settling."

"So if I understand this correctly," Crystal said, "this means we're on the light side?"

Frank nodded. "Yes, but I don't know how far in we are, and ultimately we could have to move—the trick being to know in what direction to go."

"Move?"

One of the babies gurgled and they both looked over. Both were still sleeping soundly and they couldn't tell which had made the sound. It was such a normal little noise that for a moment Frank nearly forgot that his delicate infant twins were almost the same color as the tent that sheltered them. "We don't want to be too far into either the light or the dark side," he explained when he had her attention again. "The climate will go from relentless heat to subzero cold between the two. It seems to me that the best place to be would be the terminus, the center point where the light and dark sides meet." He started to say something else, then looked at his hands; flesh and blood, dirty and thinner than months before but still in fine, serviceable condition, thank you very much, still full of oxygen-rich blood pumped by a strong, undamaged heart. Crystal, too, and his children, no matter what they looked like; they were alive, breathing, functioning, *living,* when they and the rest of the world—

"What is it, Frank?"

He sighed and lifted his gaze to hers. "What I can't figure out," he said slowly, "is why we're alive at all."

She stared at him. "What's that supposed to mean?"

"We should all be dead." Frank rubbed his shoulders, tried to massage out the knots of tension and wondered if they would ever go away. "With the kinds of hits we sustained, there shouldn't be a cubic foot of oxygen fit to breathe on this planet for a hundred years or more. The Earth's atmosphere has got to be loaded with rock particles, soot from heat pulses, nitric oxides, corrosive rainwater—but something is keeping the air in this part of the world breathable enough to sustain us and anyone else who's still left. How widespread is it?" Frustration filled his voice. *"Why is it?"*

"God," Crystal said softly. "It's His will that we survive."

"Oh, please—"

"Always the skeptic, right?" She smiled but there was no hint of the anger that had been there a few minutes before. "If you don't have proof, you don't believe it."

"You know I'm agnostic."

"That's fine, if that's what *you* want to be." She sat back, closed her eyes, and folded her hands, and for a moment Frank thought she was really praying.

"You never believed in God either."

Her eyes opened. "No, I didn't. But what's the harm if I choose to believe now? What difference does it make if it brings me a little comfort?"

Frank shook his head and she closed her eyes again; after a while, he heard her breathing deepen as she slipped into sleep. Unable to do the same, he watched her from across the tent and thought of his strange new children, and felt very, very alone.

AUGUST 4 . . .

Naomi could smell the blood in the air.

Fresh blood—not the blood of the corpses on which she and the others had been living. All this wandering had given her endless hours in which to contemplate just what made her and the group that followed her different from anyone else—were they true vampires? Would they drink blood for the rest of existence and live forever because of it?

The notion made her laugh, and the answer to that question was sprawled and decaying in the dirt around her. Occasionally they had come across other survivors, and while they seldom got close enough to talk—most were decidedly territorial—it was easy to see that those people weren't at all like Naomi and her brethren. But were they not all survivors? Had they not all been snatched from the brink of death's grip just as Naomi had been saved by Eddie, and each of her followers had been saved by someone in their own lives? Yet there was no denying the difference between Naomi's group and other people—in appearance, in what they ate, in what they *believed*.

That, Naomi decided, had to be the key. *Belief,* the final, sometimes incomprehensible thing that explained why she and the others were as they were, pale creatures with teeth that had gone inexplicably long and sharp, constantly hungry for warmth and able to find it only in the blood of another. The world might be full of survivors now, but they were all people who believed they were *destined* to survive and who had wanted to do just that. Naomi and every one of her clan believed they were supposed to have *died* at some point before the impacts; it was always the meddling of someone else that had snatched away their final rest, postponed it for another time and left behind an empty shell to flounder for heat in a cold, cold world.

Desperate, starving, many of the others had gone back to regular food because the cadavers were rotting and the blood was tainted with disease now. Too many were getting ill time after time, the nausea and runs a close approximation of food poisoning— although trying to switch back to so-called regular food didn't leave them much better off. Gaunt and soft-footed, the others still followed her without question; did they expect her to feed them all, for Christ's sake? She was one woman, alone despite the company of her own kind, suffocating in their expectations.

But now ... there was this ... *possibility* of hunger satisfied, the trace of rich crimson carried to their noses on the night breeze. Beckoning them, *taunting* them.

They had exhausted all the highway area had to offer. For a time, they'd fed on the bodies lying in and around the cars—not many, considering what would have probably occurred had there not been a martial law in effect. She'd even found a camp of soldiers not far away and slipped into the foul-smelling barracks they used as a holding place for their dead bodies—the freshly deceased were still there, placed among the older ones yet to be buried. In time they learned that the bodies never *did* get interred; the soldiers simply left them in the tent and let them decompose. It didn't take long before the tent smelled like a compost heap into which some large and unknown animal had crawled and died. But Naomi shut her nostrils and blanked her mind and went in anyway, satisfying her own thirst first, then using a small tube to siphon and take back what she could from those bodies in which the blood had settled in livid blotches. New bodies were fewer, too; the soldiers had eventually moved on, perhaps to torment others, perhaps to simply survive.

Tonight, however, the smell was fresh enough to be maddening.

We will not kill, she reminded herself. *Not that, not ever.* We are not murderers or parasites. We are *scavengers.*

The others—had she forgotten their names or never cared enough to know them to begin with?—did not need to be told. When she rose and began drifting east, they followed, silent silhouettes against the constant iron-gray light. With the wind from the east weak and sporadic, it took hours for Naomi to pinpoint the source, but there were no complaints. God help them all, only she seemed to have enough strength left to talk.

She had no idea what time it was when they climbed the twisted ruins of the post and barbed-wire fence separating the pasture from the roadway. Naomi had cared little for time since that day in New Orleans when the sailor who would have killed her had run off with some elusive, essential thing from inside her. Her soul? Perhaps—she couldn't recall if she had ever actually called it that to Eddie in the times of his angry interrogations, but in view of what she and those like her had become, it didn't seem like such an outlandish idea. Another ten minutes to move through the battered grove of trees that acted as a windbreak for the interstate and they stood at the edge of a clearing of buckled sod and soggy brown grass. Across it, they could see a tent lit from within by something small, a camper's lantern perhaps—such a rare thing to find nowadays with the supply of fuel dwindling. But there it was, the soft glow highlighting the shadows of two people within, a man and a woman. As she and her group stared, the woman picked up something and held it close—a baby. There, Naomi knew, was the source of the bloodsmell: *childbirth.* Instinctively her hands went to her own rounded stomach and she thought of Eddie. What would he say if he knew she carried his child, born of that final, bloody coupling in Althaia?

"What to do, what to do," she whispered. She had no answer—
We will not kill.

—but to wait until the man and woman came out of their tent and take it from there.

"Good morning," Naomi called. She had instructed the others, eleven men and eight woman—all that were left out of more than a hundred—to sit and stay out of sight at the far end of the field;

they obeyed her like obedient dogs. She didn't want this couple to
take one look at them and come out swinging a rifle into position.

Both the man and the woman froze, their faces stricken, and
Naomi could see that she'd made the right decision in leaving the
others behind. Naomi could understand; it was eerie the way she
and the rest of the cult had developed the ability to unwittingly
creep up on people, and though they never meant any harm, it was
truly unnerving. Keeping her hands visible, she picked her way
across the uneven ground until she was about ten feet away, then
stopped.

For a moment, no one said anything. Carefully keeping her lips
closed, Naomi gave them the closest thing to a smile that she
remembered how to do—it had been so long since she'd had to
try, she wasn't sure what it looked like. Neither smiled back, and
the woman's eyes were narrow and mistrusting, the eyes of a new
mother set on protecting her young. Eventually, the man cleared
his throat. "H-hello," he managed. He peered over her shoulder.
"How did you, uh, get in? There was a fence . . ."

"Not anymore," Naomi said smoothly. "We just wanted to
get away from the highway, so—" A slip of the tongue, and now
the man's expression turned hard, his eyes mirroring his wife's
suspicion.

"We?"

"How many are with you?" asked the woman. Her eyes
were rimmed with tired shadows and her skin was covered in
bloodsmell.

"Quite a few," Naomi answered vaguely. "My name is
Naomi." She folded her hands. "Please—don't worry. We don't
mean you any harm." She glanced around the clearing and tried to
look dejected. "We're just looking for other people, that's all. A
place to stay."

"There's a town not far from here," the man said. "Why don't
you go there? It's probably got supplies."

"Not many," Naomi answered truthfully. "And we've been
there—the residents are almost vicious. To be honest, we're tired
of being shot at. And we have some supplies of our own left." She
tilted her head. "What's your name?"

"I'm Frank," he said reluctantly. "This is my wife, Crystal."
The woman nodded, never taking her eyes from Naomi's face.

"Naomi," she said again. Now that they had exchanged names,
it would be harder for them to turn her away; some people were

born to be polite, a foolish, age-old weakness. "So," she started to say, "can we—"

A baby's cry, faint and clearly from a newborn, came from inside the couple's tent and cut off Naomi's words. She'd been wondering how she was going to ask about it, but the infant had settled it for her. "A baby!" Naomi exclaimed with as much feeling as she could. "How wonderful!"

"We think so." The woman's voice softened slightly.

"How old is he . . . or she?"

Oddly, Crystal glanced at her husband before answering. "Two days," she answered at last. "His name is Schuyler."

"Ah," was all Naomi could think of to say. Two days old . . . but very much alive. Damn—she'd been hoping for something more promising, a small fresh corpse. The part of her mind that still had a conscience gave her a brief stab of shame, but she pushed it aside; really, she'd done nothing to feel guilty about. Was it guilty to want food? There was little difference between her and the condor who investigated a still form on the desert sands. Another question came to mind and she slid her hands over her own small abdomen to draw attention to it. "And he's doing okay?"

Crystal's expression didn't change but Naomi could tell she'd made points with Frank. After all, how dangerous could she be if she were pregnant? *And I'm not dangerous,* Naomi told herself firmly. *We will not kill.* Why did that statement keep running through her head?

"He's fine," Frank said. "A little underweight, but that's to be expected after everything Crystal had to go through during her pregnancy." He frowned at Naomi. "And what about you—you're terribly thin. Are you and your friends low on food? We could spare a little—"

"That's okay," Naomi said quickly. "We've got enough." She glanced in the direction of town. "This town might not be the best place to restock, but it wasn't far from the last one."

Crystal watched her carefully. "So you're moving on?"

Naomi shrugged, and this time when she spoke she didn't have to playact—at least about most of it. "We wanted to rest," she told them. "Everyone's tired and I've . . ." She paused for effect. "I've been having some pains. I don't think it's labor or anything but I don't want to push it." When she looked at them again, she gave them a wry smile. "After all, it's up to us to repopulate the Earth, right?"

"Only if there are a helluva lot more people out there who made it through than I've been estimating," Frank replied. He pondered something for a moment. "Why don't you and your friends stay in the field here," he asked. "That way you'd get a place to rest up that's fairly isolated from the highway, and we get company but still stay secluded."

Crystal's eyes widened, but of course it was way too late to renege on the invitation . . .

Naomi wasn't really sure why she wanted to stay. Perhaps she was waiting for the infant to die, that fresh corpse for which she had so hoped, but as the days went by, the bloodsmell faded; at the end of three days it was gone entirely. Crystal had been less than pleased when the rest of Naomi's "friends" filed silently into one corner of the field and set up camp, their frayed tents suddenly making this isolated pasture seem much more crowded. On the other hand, Naomi knew the woman wondered just what the hell she and her husband were dealing with here—among the twenty new people suddenly in their lives, only Naomi spoke to them, and then not that much. Crystal never brought the child outside the tent, and sometimes Naomi would lie on her back and stare up at the cloud-filled sky, marveling at the way the baby's cries seemed to echo and multiply, until they sounded as though they were overlapping. The others went about their limited duties and kept to themselves; no one but Naomi dared to wander near the lone tent on the other side of the field.

But they all waited.

UNKNOWN BROADCAST
AUGUST 7 . . .

"Pax Bailby here, broadcasting from what my map tells me is central Illinois. It's been three weeks since my last broadcast. I said back then that I was going to do this more often but the way things've worked out, that just hasn't been possible. Lots of battery problems, finding new ones, and . . . well, some other things I'll tell you about in a minute. I did try a couple of times but couldn't seem to get a clear channel—I guess the atmosphere was just too loaded with crap in that part of the country. The

farther east I move, though, the clearer the signal seems to be getting. At times it's almost like I'm on a real radio rather than a handheld ham.

"The sky here is a lot lighter than in the west. One thing I've noticed is that the Earth doesn't seem to have day and night anymore. Out west it was dark all the time; here it seems lighter and stays that way. That's pretty hard to believe, isn't it? I mean, obviously the asteroid hits did this, but . . . wow!

"The soldiers seem to be calming down—God help us, but maybe they just had to get all that out of their systems. Or maybe, like in the last town I was at—I can't remember the name—the citizens fought back and they started realizing that people were pulling themselves together. That last place wasn't much open to outsiders, but they let me restock on water from their creek and even gave me enough canned goods for a couple of days before asking me to move on. They must've felt guilty about that, because later I found a can of deviled ham in the bag they gave me. Folks just don't give up meat that easily anymore.

"Like the darkness, the rain seems to be gradually letting up. I don't know what it's like for anyone listening, but where I've been it never stopped raining. The ground hit saturation point weeks ago and every window got busted in the quakes; the winds blowing the water around made sure everything inside is just as wet as outside. I don't think there's an unbroken piece of glass left in the world—at least I haven't seen one, although I'm staying away from the larger cities. I've heard horror stories from a few folks coming out of them about the huge piles of bodies in the streets and how everyone who's still living there is sick. I've made it through the worst of it—I like to think so, anyway—and I'd rather not get taken out by some virus or bacteria I can't even see.

"What I really wanted to talk about today is the vigilantes. Remember what I said about townspeople fighting back against the army and National Guard platoons that were on the roadways? It's like these little groups of armed men have sprung up and appointed themselves jury and executioners. And who's around to stop them? That's right, no one. It's hard for me to say that it's okay to do what they do when in a way they're just like the soldiers—they shoot first and ask questions later. Sure, they defend themselves and their own from these marauding murderers, but what happens when they run into someone who's, say, wearing an army jacket he took off a dead soldier? The way these groups operate, it's easy to see they could end up just like the ones they're fighting. Maybe they're just getting together to hunt or to have power—or both. People are returning to the caveman life, hunter-gatherers, and these, I think, are our future hunters. I could be wrong, and maybe there are even worse things out there—and boy, have I heard some stuff—but it scares me to know I'll be one of the gatherer types. Or the hunted. Matter-of-fact, I don't guess they'd even like me saying stuff like this about them, which is another reason I haven't been broadcasting much.

"See, on the way here I got stopped by three different groups for passing through what they called their 'territory.' Yeah, I'm still alive but I have to tell you that I looked into the eyes of some of those men and now I wonder how I made it—you could see that there might not be too much left in the way of compassion or tolerance. If you're out there and hearing this story, you folks watch out for yourselves around these guys. At first glance they might seem like a good solution to the killers the country's militiamen have become, but walk softly around them because they're real close to the edge.

"Another thing I wanted to talk about is . . . well, I don't know quite how to put this. There are people out there that don't seem quite . . . right. To survive, I think these folks are changing in ways that aren't normal. I know it sounds crazy and life-forms are supposed to evolve over millions of years, so maybe I should call it mutating instead of evolving. More than once I've run across people I saw from a distance, then couldn't find once I got up close. It's like they saw me and disappeared or something. No big deal about them—they don't attack or anything; I guess they just hide somehow.

"But there are others who aren't so harmless. About a week back I picked up this feeling like I was being watched. It was scary, the way that I knew there was someone out there, especially because of the tales I've been hearing, ranging from cannibals to vampires to werewolves. I'm sure these are nothing but hysteria and superstition—after all, when you take civilization and dump it back into the dark ages, what else does mankind have to fall back on? Religion and superstition, the same things that have always been used to account for what people can't explain. I believe the cannibal stories, because I've seen some pretty awful things, and I think I talked about that the last time and how I nearly walked into that soldier camp where they were . . . ah, roasting something over

*their fire that was never meant for the human mouth. But were-
wolves and vampires? Somehow I don't feel compelled to start
carrying crosses, stakes, and silver bullets.*

*"But there are some creepy things out there, all right, and it's
a lot more frightening now that we can't see them. Whatever was
following me finally gave up and disappeared yesterday evening. I
hope to God it's because they got tired and not because I'm
coming up on someone—or some*thing—*else's territory.*

*"I've been staying inside as much as I can when I'm not trav-
eling, at least as much as these buildings can be considered
'inside.' Most are pretty pulverized, but you can find some decent
shelter in the ones where a couple of walls are still standing, a
place to get out of the wind. Out west the wind was always
blowing toward the east, and damned hard, too. Sometimes it'd
get so bad I had to hole up—strong enough from behind to push
me down. Once it caught me going downhill and rolled me like
tumbleweed for a good sixty feet. As I crossed the border into Illinois, though, the gusts started easing up; now they seem to be a
constant ten to fifteen miles an hour coming from all directions,
meeting in the middle, so to speak. The sky here is always filled
with clouds that look like dark gray whipping cream being beaten
in a bowl.*

*"Well, that's about it for now. This is Pax Bailby signing off,
coming to you with your cross-country info report—ha ha. I'll
broadcast again when there's something interesting to tell."*

LITCHFIELD, ILLINOIS
AUGUST 15 . . .

"Shhhhh," Joey hissed. "I've got his trail."

"I'm going with you," Alva whispered back. "We'll catch him
on both sides—"

"Forget it. You're wiped out—get back to the camp and wait
for me there."

"But—"

"Just *do* it!" His voice was louder than he'd intended and he
cursed under his breath; he was positive they were too far away for
the man up the roadway to hear—for Christ's sake, he was almost
out of sight—but he couldn't be sure. He and Alva had *smelled*
him as he went by, despite the heavy scent their tent had acquired
over the past two months and the fact that the roadway was on the
other side of the beat-to-shit grove of trees. Their hearing was

more acute, too; from here the sounds of twigs snapping under the other man's boots was sharp and clear.

"Jagoff," she muttered under her breath. Nevertheless, she turned clumsily and disappeared back into the trees, her belly and its five-month cargo leading the way. She was too ungainly to go with him, too likely to trip and fall on her face—or her stomach. Joey might be sick to death of her, but by God, he wanted that child, *his* child, to be born big and healthy.

Returning his attention to the man up the road, he eased through the jumble of boulders, brush and tree stumps littering the ditch and the highway surface. On the ground, most of his noise was lost in the spongy soil. The guy he was following had it a lot easier; with no need for silence, he simply clambered over whatever was in his way and strode on. Joey, however, had to try to close the distance between them silently, do it without losing his footing and gutting himself with the hunting knife hanging from his belt loop. There was no sheath to screw around with; when he needed to get to the knife, it was *there*.

He ground his teeth as a hardened branch scraped along his ankle and drew blood. It would be so much easier to just take his quarry down with the pistol he still carried in the shoulder holster. That would be a bad move, however; they hadn't fired a shot in weeks, not since the last time that had nearly landed a group of five well-armed men on top of them. Alva's aim had been true and the gal they'd shot, a scrawny teenager who hadn't lasted a week, had been easy to drag into the forest with them and hide until the nosy sons-a-bitches decided the camp was deserted and took off. Joey had thought about simply cutting them all down with the Spectre submachine gun, but who knew how many others that would draw. Besides, it would be too much of a waste. A lesson well learned, however, and the guns were kept loaded and as clean and dry as could be managed, but they would no longer be used except in a defense emergency.

The man up ahead might not have Joey's and Alva's sense of smell and night sight, but you couldn't miss his nervousness. Loaded heavily with a backpack and what looked like some kind of radio getup, he kept to the center of rippled concrete that served as a highway as much as he was able and watched both sides of the road all the time, turning often to check his back. He didn't neglect the black-shadowed trees either, peering suspiciously into them at irregular intervals as he heard or imagined some small sound—although Joey had no problem knowing which was real or imagined. Rushing him was not an option; just because they no longer used firearms didn't mean other people didn't. Getting shot didn't fit into Joey's plans for the future.

Too far behind for the guy's normal eyesight to pick him out, Joey grinned as he climbed soundlessly over another felled tree, rather enjoying the game. It felt good to have the guy in his sights, and it *was* more of a challenge than getting a bead on someone with a revolver. He'd always felt sorry for the deer in the sights of the hunter's rifle; it really wasn't fair. The deer, Joey figured, ought to at least have fangs and be able to sneak up on the guy with the firearm. Where was the sport if you had the advantage and your target never saw it coming?

But this was cat and mouse—or maybe wolf and rabbit.

The guy was the perfect prey.

GREENS FORK, INDIANA
AUGUST 18 . . .

After nearly three weeks, Eddie knew immediately.

"This is it!" he said excitedly. "We made it!" Exhilaration coursed through him and he whirled in place, a kid's gesture of spinning glee.

"This?" Lily was silent, but Ryan looked around doubtfully. "What's so great about here?"

"I'm not sure how to explain it," Eddie responded. "But it's right—I can *feel* it."

"I'll just bet you can," Lily murmured.

Eddie frowned but didn't know how to answer that—was he even expected to? He couldn't for the life of him figure out what had happened between him and Lily, but something had gone . . . *bitter*. That was the only word he could think of to describe it. She wasn't nasty or argumentative—in fact, she was just the opposite. Loving, passionate, attentive—she was reveling in all these emotions and soaking them up like a cactus takes in water and holds it for later. Underneath, however, was a current of sadness that Eddie couldn't understand. He knew she was upset at leaving Mercy and the others, but it had been her choice and her reasons for choosing to go with him were sound. If not for him, sooner or later she would have gone anyway, and at least she had a couple of people who cared about her at her side. Better that than heading into this godforsaken country alone.

"Let's get off the main highway," he suggested. "There's nothing around here but busted-up cars and stuff." And *stuff*— bodies, of course, although they looked strangely desiccated. For these corpses, decomposition had been . . . off-kilter somehow, as though they were dried out and left as little more then shells before nature moved in to claim the empties. On the way here, they had seen cadavers like this on and off, amid the bodies that were decaying normally, but the ratio of normal versus virtually *mummified* had increased until the remains they saw now had become the rule rather than the exception. Maybe it had something to do with the climate—the sky in general had been gradually lightening over the duration of the journey. There was a marked difference in the temperature and amount of light here. Eddie thought they must be heading toward what had now become the warmer part of the United States.

"I'm hungry," Ryan said.

Eddie glanced at Ryan in surprise and got a sharp look from Lily. "We ran out of food yesterday," she said pointedly. "Remember?"

Eddie felt his cheeks redden. Christ—how could he have been so careless? She had asked him several times since then to detour so they could try to find supplies, and each time he had said, "In a little while," or "Over that next hill." Pushing, pushing, and he didn't even know why or what it was he was looking for. He had promised both her and Ryan that he would take care of the boy, and look at the fucked-up job he'd done. The thought that he had made this child go hungry because he was too preoccupied to stop was horrifying.

"I'm sorry," he said. "I guess I got caught up in getting here."

Lily said nothing—she was doing a lot of that these days—and somehow that made him feel worse, as if she knew exactly what the reason was, whether he did or not. *Damn,* he thought sourly, *if she does, I wish to hell she'd share it with* me. "We'll veer off here," he said, pointing to a crumbling strip of asphalt that had once been an exit ramp. Something in the back of his mind reminded him snidely that this had been his intention all along, and who was he to act like a white knight now?

"All right," Lily said. Any trace of edginess was gone and her voice was neutral. She looked at Ryan and her face softened. "How's that sound to you, short stuff?"

Ryan nodded. "Okay." End of conversation and Eddie felt

worse for having had it; where was the boy's usual spark and banter? As their travel time had lengthened, he'd watched with amusement as Ryan took on more and more of Lily's rough-and-tumble characteristics and, even funnier, her dry sense of humor. It was a marvelous thing to see, especially considering Lily somehow managed to keep any hints of her sarcasm from carrying over into Ryan's "education."

They followed as Eddie led them carefully around the jagged pieces of concrete and the rusted spikes of rebar poking in all directions. Of all the things that might happen to them, Eddie's worst fear was centered on the rust-coated metal that seemed to fill the world around them—the exposed edges of automobiles, the rebar that was everywhere, countless other twisted hunks that couldn't be identified. One scrape that broke the skin, and *wham*—lockjaw, and no Mercy alongside to run the miracle mile for them. When the ramp ended in another road just as smashed up as the main one, he stopped in indecision. There wasn't much to see—just another battered country road in either direction.

"Crap," he complained under his breath.

"That way," Ryan said suddenly. When Eddie and Lily followed the child's pointing finger, they saw what had caught Ryan's attention. In the sky to their left was a faint curl of smoke—a sure sign of a campfire. Either they had hiked right past it, or the fire had just been started for the night.

Eddie grinned. "Good eye, Ryan. Let's go."

"There's no guarantee we'll be welcome," Lily said. "We could end up being shot at."

Was that a touch of desperation in her voice? Or fear? "I've got a feeling we'll be fine," he said honestly.

Lily stared at him. "Are you back to seeing things the way you were able to in New Orleans?"

The question startled him. Was that it? "I . . . I don't think so," he said uncertainly. "I just know that we'll be okay, that's all. I don't know *how* I know, but I do."

"Then let's *go* already," Ryan said impatiently. "I'm *hungry*."

Whatever Lily's reservations were, that was enough to shake her into moving again, though it was clear she was less than enthusiastic about the idea. "We'll be fine," Eddie said again and reached out to touch her arm. He caught her by the sleeve and hung on until she finally turned her head and looked at him. "If it looks no good for any reason, we'll find somewhere else. I promise."

"Yeah," she said. "Sure, Eddie. Whatever you say."

Damn, he thought. *I've made us go way too long without food—now I'm seeing things.*

Had Lily's eyes been filling with tears?

They followed the smoke in the sky. It took longer than Eddie anticipated to find where it was coming from, a small pasture that was separated from the road by a grove of broken trees clinging to the soil with exposed roots like black, wasted fingers. The only thing that stood out to mark the entrance was a single, skewed fence post; up close they saw that strands of barbed wire still clung to it and disappeared into the muddy gravel-strewn ditch. Eddie went in without hesitation, so sure was he that this was the right place. At the point where the barely discernible path that had once been a driveway expanded into the field beyond, he finally slowed. What if he was wrong? Lily had brought up a valid point: this time was *not* like what had happened to him in New Orleans. He'd had no visions or clear notion of what to do, and he couldn't risk endangering Lily and Ryan on a whim.

"You guys stay here," he said as they crowded behind him. "Just in case, I'll check it out, make sure we're not likely to get shot."

Lily didn't argue as she pulled Ryan closer to her. "Be careful of what you find," she said. When he smiled reassuringly, she reached over and kissed him softly on the mouth. He kissed her back, then squeezed her shoulder. Ryan's eyes were wide with concern and he gave the boy a backward salute and a grin to ease the tension.

He'd learned a lot of things about foraging for food and life on the road, how to be sharp and quick while at the same time stay light on your feet and whisper-quiet. But he flubbed it badly as he peered around a damp tree trunk and across the mushy brown expanse of the clearing. Without thinking, he opened his mouth and said *"Oh!"* well within the hearing range of the two groups of people there.

Jesus Christ—was that Naomi standing over there and staring back at him? *Pregnant* Naomi?

Be careful of what you find . . .

"I never thought I'd see *you* again."

Eddie grimaced; the way Naomi had emphasized her statement, he had to wonder if she thought that fate would intervene or he was too stupid to survive. "Well, I guess you thought wrong."

She smiled a little. "Considering everything that's happened, you're looking awfully good, Eddie. How . . . *amazing* that you came through everything—the asteroid hits, the traveling, all of it—without a single scar."

He shrugged and fought to keep his eyes locked on hers, afraid if he looked away she'd know he was lying. "Good luck, I guess."

"I'm sure."

This time her remark bordered on a sneer and he decided to turn the conversation away from areas where it might lead to Mercy. He didn't want to fight about that, and about Naomi's whacked-out beliefs that because she should have died in front of the Café du Monde, someone had taken her soul. He'd nearly died, too, but he didn't feel any different than before that ceiling had fallen on him. In fact, he felt damned good, and happy to still be breathing. "So where'd you go when you left Althaia?" he asked.

She looked away, her head turning in the direction of the main highway beyond the tree line. "We just . . . wandered. Never stayed anywhere very long . . . until now, that is."

Eddie thought he detected a note of longing in her voice and his gaze strayed to her stomach. Was this his child? He wanted to ask but couldn't get the words out, wasn't sure he wanted to know the answer. "So you're staying here."

Naomi turned back to him. "For a while, anyway." For some reason, Naomi glanced over to where Lily and Ryan talked with Frank and Crystal. "This is their place. We just sort of . . . joined in."

"Ah." Naomi's camp had been set up on the far side of the field, across the widest expanse of it. "How come you're all the way over there?" he asked.

"Just different, I guess. The woman—Crystal—isn't very sociable."

"Really." Eddie scratched his head, but didn't comment further. Crystal had seemed friendly enough; now that he thought about it, she'd acted oddly relieved. She'd certainly taken well enough to Lily and Ryan, who now sat with the woman and her husband around a small cooking fire, tending it carefully to keep the drizzling rain from putting it out. A small sheet of tin had been bent over and shoved into the ground to serve as a windbreak. Its overhang was enough to keep the worst of the rain off the wood; shoved amid the pile of wrist-sized branches was a battered cooking pot containing something that Eddie could smell from here—beans. Nothing fancy, but his mouth was watering.

A thought suddenly occurred to him. Naomi and her people over here, Frank and Crystal—and now Lily, him, and Ryan— over there. Out loud, he asked, "Don't you guys share food?"

Naomi gave him an enigmatic look. "No. We . . . get our own. I would've thought you knew that."

Eddie frowned. "What are you—" His mouth dropped open as he finally realized what she was talking about. "Jesus, Naomi. You're not . . ." He cast a furtive glance toward the fire and the people gathered around it and dropped his voice to a whisper. "Are you telling me you're drinking *blood*?"

Naomi chuckled. "Funny boy finally uses his brain," she said mockingly.

A gag started in his throat and Eddie swallowed hard to stop it. "Listen," he said, "don't you think you've carried this far enough? I mean, you're pregnant—"

"Yours, by the way. Just in case you were wondering."

"—and—and—" He stumbled over the words as a mixture of dismay and elation swept over him.

"And?"

"It can't possibly be healthy for the baby," he managed to finish. "An unborn child needs nourishment, vitamins—"

"The child lives or it dies," Naomi said flatly.

Eddie scowled. "Nice attitude, Naomi."

She shrugged. "Hey, I didn't ask to get pregnant. It just happened."

"That's not the point!"

"Then what *is*?" she shot back.

"The point," he said heatedly, "is that the baby inside you is a new life and you could give it a decent fucking chance, you know?"

"If you want it to have a chance at anything, then you'd better stick around until it's born." Naomi's voice was cold. "I have no intention of hauling some brat all over hell and back, and there's not exactly a day-care center anywhere to drop it into." Abruptly she grinned, showing abnormally elongated canines that made Eddie's skin crawl. What the hell had happened to her teeth? "On the other hand, maybe I should reconsider. After all, it'd be a fresh, portable source of sustenance, wouldn't it?"

Too shocked to speak, Eddie watched her stride away and felt his heart fill with black, bleak terror for his unborn child.

LITCHFIELD, ILLINOIS
AUGUST 18 . . .

"Didn't I tell you to go back to camp?" Joey's voice was more a low growl than words.

"I didn't want to stay there by myself," Alva whispered back. "I don't feel safe."

She knew it had been a mistake to say that by the way he looked at her in the darkness. His eyes, once nearly black, had taken on a hint of yellow moonshine over the last month, like the eyes of a wolf frozen in the oncoming glare of headlights. Now that predatory stare was directed at her and in it Alva saw impatience and derision for the weakness she had just admitted.

"Fine." Joey swung his gaze back toward the campfire beyond the line of trees. "Just be sure you don't make any noise."

She nodded resolutely and sat back to wait with him, thinking about the changes that had come over Joey since they'd left Chicago. Once he'd been chubby and spoiled, a street dealer with an easy life and a fuck-you attitude; now he was muscled, dark, and sleek—damned gorgeous—like a hard-to-spot tomcat prowling the countryside in search of a careless bird.

Alva sighed to herself and tried to get comfortable, her thoughts turning back to more immediate things. Crap—it'd been three days already. How long was he going to track this guy? She was hungry and tired, and the dried strips of meat from their last kill were almost gone. If they left now, she had enough to carry them both until they made it back to their own campsite, and game wasn't so hard to find in the woods around it that Joey had to make a fucking personal crusade out of getting this particular geek. Squirrel might be greasy, but at least they were easy to trap and they'd have a hot meal for a change.

"All right!" Joey said excitedly. "I think he's leaving them!" Despite his enthusiasm, his voice never climbed to where anyone other than the two of them could hear it; the trio of men a hundred feet away had never known they were there.

Alva looked up with interest, her thoughts of a fresh, hot meal taking a different turn. She had no qualms about what they did and what they ate—the last of her misgivings had faded away during the worst of the after-quake days, when game was scarce enough for them to think they were the only fucking things left alive in the world. A good portion of the others in the campground had died over the course of the impacts, crushed by the cars they'd stupidly hidden under, hit by the trees under which they'd cowered—Alva had never seen a more moronic bunch of people. A little too much marijuana or 'ludes or whatever the hell had been making the rounds had blotted out their common sense entirely. As for her and Joey—they'd laid off anything chemical long before The Big Day, planning in advance to have clear heads when they would need them the most. With only a few people left alive, they'd raided the tents of the dead but found little in the way of food and supplies—more indication that those idiots had possessed no clue about survival.

When the food ran out three weeks later and their empty bellies gifted them with hunger headaches and stomach cramps, Joey had stepped out of the tent one dark afternoon, walked across the field of rotting corpses, and shot the only other two people who'd survived the asteroids. He'd dragged the old man and his forty-year-old daughter back and gutted them twenty feet away from the tent while Alva sat retching inside. With nothing else to stop the screaming in the pit of her stomach, she'd spent two days immersed in the smell of smoking meat before finally giving in. Now there was no one to whom she had to answer for her actions and the world was a changed and brutal place; they—*she*—would do whatever was necessary to survive.

"Come on," he whispered at her side.

"How much longer do we have to follow him?" Alva hugged herself, then shadowed his stealthy moves past the campsite and the two men still crouched around the fire.

"Not much longer." He shot a glance behind them to make sure the other men hadn't decided to follow and Alva saw that same unearthly glow shine briefly across his eyes. "I'm pretty sure he doesn't have a gun, so we'll get just far enough away that his pals back there won't hear if he screams. He wouldn't have made it this far if he hadn't met up with those guys."

Mollified, Alva kept close behind Joey as he moved along the inside line of the brush, slowly closing the distance between themselves and the man he'd been hunting for the last three days. As the minutes crept by, Alva's movements were noisier than his, and more than once he glared at her and motioned for her to stop; this close, she could see that the guy carried something over his shoulder, a bag out of which poked several antennae and a coiled cord like the ones that had once hung from telephones—a radio of some kind. Alva blinked at the sight, nearly tripping over her own feet as an unexpected nostalgia filled her. *God,* she thought, *to be warm and dry inside a real house with a phone hanging on the wall and a fucking heater going beside the bed.*

"Watch it, you fool!" Joey's large hand closed cruelly over her upper arm and squeezed. Without thinking about it, she swiped at it with her other hand, gifting him with three bloody furrows across his skin. He yelped in surprise and they both dropped to the ground, scowling as the man with the radio setup spun in his tracks and stared back the way he'd come, his eyes searching the darkness and trying to pick out the source of the noise. She could feel Joey's rage vibrating through the leafless branches next to her, but he said nothing. Finally their prey moved on, though now he spent a good deal more time looking over his shoulder and in his left hand was a length of dirty silver—a hunting knife he'd pulled from a pocket in his vest.

"That's fucking great," Joey muttered. "This could've been easy and you fucked it up."

"You're the one with the big mouth," she hissed. "Don't ever manhandle me again!"

"Just shut up, would you?" He rose cautiously. "I've got other things to deal with right now than you." He gestured at the cracked expanse of I-55 to her left. "Cross the road and track him from the median ditch. Right before he gets to the underpass for Route 16, go for him. I'll hit him from the other side—and be careful of the fucking knife!"

Alva stifled a retort and nodded. Finally—she was starting to think Joey was going to make a career out of this. With Route 16 only a half mile up, she didn't have time to waste; she waited until their mark had checked behind him and faced forward again, then darted across the road, weaving between the lumpy concrete and three-foot-high clots of muddy soil in her way with a minimum of noise. Then she was in the clear and, finally, they had a prime position for taking him out.

She could see the overpass no more than an eighth of a mile

ahead, the tangle of its exposed metal supports spreading across the sky like a patch of spiky black against the thundercloud-filled horizon. Although she couldn't see him, Alva could sense Joey across the roadway, moving in perfect sync. As the gap between them and the man with the radio narrowed and the overpass loomed before them, she angled up the side of the ditch at the same time Joey did. Nearly even with the road, she tensed and prepared to spring—

A double flash of lightning filled the section of the interstate with a blue-white glow. Poised on the edge of the ditches, both she and Joey were washed with light, cruelly exposed. At the same time they saw the group of people at the far side of the underpass—at least a dozen men armed with rifles and shotguns—the others saw them. Shouts filled the night along with the ratcheting sounds of firearms being primed. The man between them froze in indecision, then spun backward and saw Joey only eight feet away, crouched and ready to leap like a wolf onto a paralyzed rabbit. He cried out in fear at the same time thunder rolled across the sky and blotted out his voice. Her eyes burning with the lightning's afterglow, Alva saw Joey dive for cover, barely a second before the first roar of a shotgun hammered through the darkness.

Fleeing swiftly down the length of the shattered highway, escaping easily into the night despite the volley of wild shots fired in their direction, Alva knew she and her mate would not be fed tonight.

GREENS FORK, INDIANA
AUGUST 23 . . .

"So you must be breast-feeding, huh?" Naomi tried to make her tone conversational, the voice of a mother-to-be asking the wiser woman who was already a mother. Crystal was not deceived.

"Why do you want to know?"

Naomi shrugged and gestured vaguely at her rounded stomach. "Oh, you know. Just . . . planning for the future."

The other woman stared at her. "I'm sure." They both looked up as an infant's cry echoed from inside the closed flap of the tent, sounding more like a mewling kitten than human. Crystal started toward the tent, but stopped when Naomi followed. "What do you want?"

"Well, Jesus," Naomi said. "I'd kind of like to see the baby. I mean, it's been weeks. Aren't you ever going to bring him out in the fresh air?"

"No," Crystal said tightly. "I'm not. He's small and I wouldn't exactly call this constant drizzle 'fresh air.' It's not healthy."

"Then can I go inside?"

The older woman's mouth stretched into a thin, hard line. "No. I don't want any chance of exposure to illness from anyone other than family right now."

"But—"

"Why don't you just mind your own damned business?" Crystal demanded. "Why is it so important for you to meddle in ours?" She balled her fists and took a step toward Naomi. "You stay away from my tent and my family, do you hear me?"

Naomi glowered at her. "Bitch," she finally spat. She spun and stalked away.

"Whatever," she heard Crystal call after her. *"Just don't come back!"*

"There's something weird about their kid or they'd bring him out and show everyone," Naomi told Eddie and Lily a few hours later. "Whoever heard of new parents not showing off their baby? It's not natural."

"Maybe the baby's sick," Lily said.

Naomi's mouth curled into a sneer. "If he was, she would've said so. That'd be the easiest excuse in the world." She rubbed her arms thoughtfully. "No, it's something else. And by God, I'm going to find out what."

"Naomi," Eddie said sharply, "maybe it'd be a better idea to do what she said and stay away."

Naomi flicked her hand at him. "I don't give a shit what she wants. I—"

"You could get killed."

Naomi stared at Lily, and wasn't this one something special? White hair tipped with dirty colors, thin as a rail but hard, too. Maybe dangerous. What was she, really? Eddie's girlfriend? Perhaps. Ryan's protector? Probably. Her gaze darted toward the boy; warm and healthy, he stood slightly behind Lily, as if reluctant to get within Naomi's reach. She grinned to herself, impressed with the boy's sense of self-preservation.

"I doubt it," Naomi said in response to Lily's statement. "Not by them."

Eddie frowned. "I wouldn't be so sure, Naomi. If Crystal thinks you're enough of a threat to straight out tell you to stay away, who's to say she won't strike out if you don't? A mother protecting her young can be a ferocious opponent. What do you need to know so badly for, anyway?"

Naomi didn't say anything for a moment. Eddie and his white-haired girlfriend, the boy—they would never understand. They just didn't know how it was . . . they didn't *hunger* like she did.

"It doesn't matter," Naomi said at last. She turned her back and stared across the field to where the lone tent waited; inside it, the couple's blurry shapes danced against the wet material, backlit by a glow of candlelight, or maybe a camping light kept low to conserve fuel. Her tongue flicked slowly across her cracked lips. "One way or another, I'm going to find out what the deal is in that tent."

AUGUST 23 . . .

What Crystal found most terrifying was that the woman nearly made it inside before she caught her.

She didn't know what made her decide to walk around to the back of the tent. Out front, Frank had found enough dry wood to build up the fire; now there was another pot of beans cooking, and this time it was a treat because it was flavored with packets of barbecue sauce that Eddie and Lily had found on the floorboard of a wrecked car on the interstate. There wasn't a noise or shadow, and the twins inside tended to go silent rather than cry out at sudden loud noises; it was just a . . . *feeling* she had, a flash of uneasiness. The others, Frank, Eddie, Lily, and little Ryan, were standing or sitting quietly around the fire, watching it carefully and occasionally extending their hands toward the bright warmth. They'd become a steady if not exactly close-knit group, and one that Crystal could feel comfortable with if she had to leave the entrance to the tent—Eddie and Lily would never think of violating their privacy. Despite their reassuring presence, Crystal stirred the beans one more time and, shooting an embarrassed glance at the others, got up and made her way around the mildewy-smelling canvas.

And a damned good thing, too.

Naomi was crouched at the rear, carefully slicing through the sodden fabric with a battered butcher knife. Like a cub whining in fear, one of the babies inside gave a faint whimper.

"Get away from there," Crystal said. Her voice was ludicrously calm as she covered the distance between her and Naomi in three long steps, dug her fingers into the younger woman's hair at the scalp, and hauled her backward.

Naomi screeched and flailed at her with the knife, but Crystal instinctively clawed at the scrawny, white-fleshed wrist. She cried out as she felt a brief sting when the blade skimmed her cheek, then she drove her knee up hard between Naomi's legs, feeling her kneecap bruise instantly as it connected with Naomi's pelvic bone. Naomi howled as her knife went flying, but Crystal couldn't tell if the sound was from pain or rage. From around the front of the tent she heard shouts of alarm as Frank and the others heard the commotion.

Thinking the smaller woman would stop now that her weapon was gone, Crystal shoved her away. Naomi stumbled back and Crystal wiped her face with the back of her arm; it came away stained with blood, a smear like black oil against the fabric of her dirty jacket in the murky, perpetual twilight. Crystal opened her mouth to swear at Naomi but got the breath knocked out of her instead. Suddenly she found herself looking up at the sky and its mass of constantly moving clouds, feeling the sting of gritty rain in her eyes and the drag of Naomi's dirty hair across her mouth. With a start, she realized that Naomi had leaped over and knocked her down; now she was lying on top of her and licking frantically at her face.

"What the—get *off* me, you disgusting pervert!" Crystal punched Naomi sharply in the back of the head and tried to throw her off, but the younger woman didn't seem to notice. Her hands, deceptively strong for such a skinny thing, gripped each side of Crystal's head as she sucked savagely at the wound on her face like some kind of leech. Saliva sprayed her mouth and filled her nose with the smell of bad meat; retching involuntarily, Crystal dug her feet into the mud and pushed backward, trying to wriggle away. It would have been useless if hands hadn't reached down and dragged her attacker away.

"Naomi, *stop it!*" Eddie yelled. Frank and Lily hauled Crystal upright and got her on her feet as Eddie brought his hand back and walloped Naomi a good one across the jaw. "Cut it out!"

"Did you see her?" Crystal gasped. She scrubbed at the slime on her cheek with the back of her hand and retched again. "Jesus—what *is* she? Some kind of vampire?"

Unexpectedly, Naomi laughed, high and loud, and not at all distressed, then curled her fingers into claws and swiped a final time at Crystal, who reflexively backstepped.

"Naomi, what the fuck is the matter with you?" Eddie demanded. He yanked on her arm and spun her to face him, his face white and shocked. "Are you out of your mind?"

"Let me *go,* Eddie." She jerked away from him. "You're not my keeper," she said scornfully. Naomi turned back and glared at Crystal, her gaze raking Frank and Lily, her elongated incisors tipped with fresh red. "What a waste," she said in a husky voice. "And all I *really* wanted was a visit with the little one."

"You want to see so bad, fine. Come on around front." Frank's voice was furious. "I've got something to show you." He whirled and strode away.

"Frank, no!" Terror rammed through Crystal at the thought of exposing her fragile children to this madwoman. As she scrambled after her husband, Crystal saw Naomi throw her a smug look as she pulled free of Eddie and stalked past. The others traipsed after them, but Naomi never made it through the opening at the front of the tent; instead, she nearly got slapped in the face by the wet canvas flap as Frank burst back out of the tent. Clutched in the crook of his arm was not one of their children, and Crystal sucked in a breath as he raised a rifle she'd never known he had—some kind of lever action thing like they'd used in the western reruns on old TV movies. He shoved it under Naomi's chin hard enough to make her teeth click together and she stopped short; the sound the gun made as he worked the lever and fed a round into the chamber seemed to go on and on and on in Crystal's ears.

Crystal saw Lily's hands come down on Ryan's shoulder and pull him aside at the same time as Eddie's eyes went wide. "Oh, hey," he said nervously. "Wait—"

"You're going to leave us, missy," Frank said grimly. "Tonight. And you'd damned well better not come back."

Naomi's jaw lifted under the pressure of the barrel but her eyes were unrelenting as she stared at Frank. "And if I don't?" she asked through clenched teeth. "What then—"

"I'll kill you," Frank said. "I was the one who invited you and your group to stay, and now I'm the one saying that you can't. You're dangerous and sick, and you're threatening my family, so just move it on out. You're not wanted here anymore." Crystal saw him push the gun harder into the soft underside of Naomi's jaw. "You think you're so special, let's see how you hold up against a .356 rifle round."

No one said anything for a moment, then Naomi closed her eyes and her nostrils flared as she breathed deep. "All right," she said at last. "We were getting tired of you people anyway."

"Frank," Crystal said later. "Where did that gun come from? I mean, I never—"

"I've had it for a while, just in case." His mouth was set, as though he were expecting her to protest. "I thought there might be times when we wouldn't always be able to hide or run. I wanted to be prepared."

"I . . . see." Crystal looked over at the babies, sleeping peacefully while somewhere outside roamed a new kind of predator. What would Naomi have done had she gotten inside the tent undetected? Involuntarily, Crystal's hand went to her cheek, the wound washed as clean as it could be and still stinging from a precious dose of alcohol; it was butterflied together and Lily had told her it would definitely leave a scar, but Crystal wasn't sure she'd ever have a mirror to see. The mental picture of one of her children writhing beneath the mouth of that . . . that *creature* would give her nightmares for years. Sweet Christ—the others that had been in her group were probably just like her. "Would you have used it?"

Frank's chin lifted defiantly and he met her gaze without flinching. "Yes. To protect you and my children, I wouldn't—and won't ever—hesitate."

In his voice, Crystal heard all the pride and devotion she'd wanted so badly on the night that Schuyler and Calypso had been born, and she smiled.

UNKNOWN BROADCAST
SEPTEMBER 1 . . .

"Pax Bailby here. I seem to be running on these three-week dates, despite intending to broadcast a lot more often. This time I feel lucky to be able to broadcast at all. Where am I? I'll be damned if I know. I lost my map about a week after my last broadcast and haven't been able to get my hands on another one.

"See, something started tracking me right about then. I'm not exactly sure when I picked up on it, or if I even knew right away. I never saw anyone or anything during the days—I guess it was about three—that I got followed. It was the strangest thing, like some sort of primal sense kicked in and told me to watch my ass, right up until I almost got hit. Not that it would've done much good when it came right down to it, but it kept me alive for a few more days.

"There were two of them. Although I only saw one at first, I had the sensation of something else being behind me, something just as big and dangerous as the man I glimpsed at the side of the road. When I spun, I saw the other one, climbing up the side of the embankment and not thirty feet away—did I mention this one was a woman? It sure was.

"It was raining—isn't it always?—but the thing that saved me was the lightning. No, no; there wasn't some big bolt sent down from God to strike down my enemies or any of that crap. I was almost beneath this underpass and what I didn't know was that there was one of those vigilante groups—I talked about them last time—camped out on the other side. They saw me at the same time I saw the guy who was almost on top of me. I screamed—I'm not at all ashamed to admit I was terrified—at the same time the men below the underpass started yelling and shooting.

"You ever hear gunfire underneath a concrete bridge? Even as cracked up as they are, it was like being inside a metal drum and having somebody beat on the sides. I didn't know what the hell was going on—if they were shooting at me, if they were with these two crazy people hunting me, what. It turns out I was lucky—they were aiming for the others. I got a good look at the man; he was big and muscular, lean like the rest of us. I think he might have been black, but who can tell in the middle of the night with the rain in your eyes? Shit—I was so scared I'm surprised I don't remember him being green. I won't ever forget his yellow eyes, though.

"When the shooting started, both he and the woman disappeared. They might as well have dissolved into rainwater, they were gone so fast, just darted back into the darkness. The men with the guns searched the ditches at the side and in the center of the road, but it didn't do any good. There wasn't a trace.

"Later, after I'd calmed down and got a good look at who'd saved my skinny butt, we sat around a fire and they told me about what had been following me. Called them 'human wolves' and said they hunted and ate people. I couldn't believe it—I mean, I knew that some of the military platoons had done this, but as time went by they'd seemed more and more to disband. These guys said that a lot of the army boys had been killed by bands of men just like themselves, who'd come together specifically to put an end to the killing going on around the countryside. Imagine that—a band of killers to end the killing! I didn't say that, of course.

"I guess I'm still pretty angry about this. I thought it would've faded by now—there are so many of the bad memories that have blurred because of the hardship of the last two months—but every time I think about it, I get pissed all over again. You have to go through it to know what it's like to be on the other side of the hunting party. These men, they had no idea. With their guns and their safety in numbers . . . to them it was just a game, open hunting season with the deer targets replaced by these so-called wolves. You could see in their eyes that they didn't do what they did so much as to protect anyone—hell, they were all nomads, just like me—as much as they did it for the thrill of it. Saving some pathetic would-be victim like me just lets them justify what they do. I don't think they'd bother with thinking they'd have to answer for their actions otherwise.

"I wish this were a real radio talk show, where folks could call in and give me their opinions. Which do you think is worse? The human wolves—men and women who hunt other humans for food and kill so they can eat—or the vigilante groups, pockets of men armed to the gills and who'll shoot anyone down at the slightest excuse? Oh, sure, I know—cannibals, you're thinking. What could be worse than that? Not much, I agree . . . but what if those two hadn't been human wolves? What if the bad guy there had been ME—maybe I'd taken something from these two, or maybe I was the human wolf who'd snuck into their campground and, I don't know, stolen their baby? So they come after me, either to get their kid back or revenge—and does it really matter in a situation like that?—but look who ends up shot. Them, because a half-dozen good old boys look up and decide, in the space of a half second and without ever asking a question, that THEY were the enemy, not me. And to hear them tell it, the countryside is filled with others just like themselves.

"Well, that's about it for me this time. In case you just found this broadcast on your ham setup, I'm Pax Bailby. Sooner or later I'll pick up another map and figure out where the hell I am and

*maybe where I'm going. I think—I hope—I'm still heading east.
I'm trying to follow the line of the sky where it seems lighter
because I'm tired of all this darkness and of all the crazy stuff that
seems to be thriving in it. Hell, if there's light left anywhere in the
world, I just want to get to it."*

LITCHFIELD, ILLINOIS
SEPTEMBER 6 . . .

Damn, Joey thought. Who would've thought she'd turn out to
be so *fragile*?

But there Alva was, lying on her side inside their shelter,
sleeping almost all the time now. She had pains, she said; her back
hurt and her stomach was upset all the time. So what did she want
from him—a hotel room with room service? His lip curled in contempt as he crawled outside and stood, stretching muscles
cramped far too long from staying by her side. She had, a lifetime
ago, seemed like such a strong, capable woman, a broad who
could look the worst of anything in the face and spit in its eye.
Joey could still remember the night she'd sat at the kitchen table
amid a fine, thoughtful display of weapons, giving him a hard lec-
ture on the facts of life the way they would be. And she had been
right—that was the kicker. All that foreknowledge and self-
assurance, and all she was in the end was a whining piece of flesh
with a swollen belly—and *that* was the only reason he hadn't
killed her weeks ago. He wanted that baby, damn it, his son or
daughter, and the child would need a mother to feed it and watch
over it. Alva's wide, well-padded hips were built for childbearing;
Joey was hoping for a quick, easy birth and then maybe she'd
regain some of her former vitality. Hell, the only thing strong
about Alva now was her mouth.

How much longer? Joey frowned and tried to think back, but
the past months were a blur. They *were* months, weren't they?
Sure—he could measure their progress by the size of Alva's
stomach, and it was by that same human "clock" that he could tell
the time wasn't yet ripe for his child to be born. She was still too
small to be near her time. He'd given his all to seeing that she was
kept well fed this last month, hunting by himself while she waited
in the tent with an uncharacteristically wan look on her face—
honest to Christ, if the world was still normal, he'd swear she'd be
sitting on her ass in front of a television somewhere, watching
daytime soaps and stuffing food into her face. Since the last run-in

with one of the growing number of watchman groups that patrolled the highway and the loss of the man with the radio, Joey had moved their camp to a more secluded spot deep in the overgrown woods that bordered an abandoned ranch. Despite their heavy firepower, the groups of men seldom ventured off the roadway, preferring to stick to the dryer spots beneath the underpasses that remained stable enough to offer cover. Joey still provided for he and Alva; mostly small game, a lot of field mice, and once he'd clubbed a porcupine to death. Meat was meat. It all translated to food in their guts and warmth in their blood.

A sound from the tent made him grimace, but he squared his shoulders and ducked back inside, wondering what the hell it was Alva could find to complain about this time.

VINCENNES, ILLINOIS
SEPTEMBER 10 ...

"Lily? Are you awake?"

Ryan's stage whisper might as well have been a foghorn; Lily had grown accustomed to sleeping lightly, just as her eyes had grown used to the limited amount of light available. She'd felt him crawl up next to her sleeping bag in the empty spot left by Eddie's body, had heard the soft intake of his breath as he prepared to speak. "Yes," she said. "What's the matter?"

The boy didn't answer for a moment and she could see his shadow beside her, a darker shade of black amid the vibration of her eyesight. Finally, he spoke. "Can we—I mean, do we have to . . . you know." He gulped air, then rushed on. "Do we have to stay here?"

Eyes widening, Lily lifted herself onto her elbows, then pulled out of the sleeping bag until she could sit up. "I thought you wanted to be with Eddie," she said quietly. Her hand found his thin shoulder. Beneath the heavy flannel shirt he wore to sleep in, she felt the resilient little-boy bones tremble against her callused palm.

"I do," Ryan admitted in a low voice. "But the others . . . they give me the willies. Especially Naomi." He turned his head as if he were looking for something she couldn't see. "She watches me all the time. I think she's some kind of monster."

Lily started to reply, but the words faded away. What could she say to something like that from a six-year-old? Besides, after what had happened back in Greens Fork, she'd be damned if she'd stick up for that crazy girl—Ryan was probably more right than he realized.

Ryan's voice pulled Lily back to the problem facing her now. "Can't we make Eddie go away with us?"

"Oh, Ryan," Lily said sadly. She tugged on his sleeve and the child came willingly, allowing her to hug him. "Remember when you said we couldn't make you stay behind with Mercy and Simon? Remember how you said you'd come after us if we did?"

Pain flitted across his face, but Ryan nodded. "Yeah. Is that . . . is that how it is now?"

"Yes, it is," Lily said truthfully. "If you really want to, we can leave—tomorrow, if you like. But I'm telling you now: there's no way Eddie will agree to go with us. Are you absolutely positive you want to go anyway?"

Ryan frowned in concentration, and she could imagine his young brain following a path of what-ifs that no child his age should ever have to face. Still, it only took a few seconds for his pinched expression to smooth out as he nodded. "Yes, I'm sure. Being here with Naomi and all the others . . . it just doesn't feel *good.* Not like it did when we were with Crystal and Frank."

Lily studied his small form, trying to read his shadowed eyes. "Is that where you want to go? Back to them?"

"Yeah!" For the first time, Lily heard eagerness in Ryan's voice. Suddenly his eyes sparkled, a glimmer that Lily nearly missed. "Can I tell you a secret?"

"Of course."

"No," he said hurriedly. The boy looked around, as though trying to be certain no one else was within earshot. "I mean, a *real* secret. Something not even Eddie knows."

Lily blinked. "Really?"

"You have to *promise* not to tell," Ryan rushed on. "Cross your heart and hope to die."

"I promise."

"Cross your heart—"

"—and hope to die," Lily finished for him. "Now 'fess up."

Ryan's face turned up to hers and his voice dropped even lower. "I saw Frank and Crystal's babies," he whispered.

Lily frowned. "Babies?"

"Shhhh!" Ryan looked around wildly, then sucked in a breath. "They're *twins,*" he continued. Excitement—or release—was making him quiver and Lily would have laughed had she not been so damned surprised. "And they're different colors."

Lily's frown deepened. "You mean like black and white?"

Ryan's head shook so fast she thought he'd fall over on the sleeping bag. "No! They have skin that . . . it . . ." For a moment the child was at a loss. "It matches the color of what's around them." Suddenly he tugged on her arm. "I know—like one of those lizards that hides in the bushes and you can't see 'em!"

"Ryan," Lily said firmly, "you aren't making this up, are you? Because it's not—"

"No—honest!"

"How did you get to see them?"

"It was Crystal. She needed to get something and didn't want to leave them in the tent all by themselves because she didn't like Naomi. But she made me promise not to tell *anyone* that it was twins or what they looked like, not even you or Eddie." Abruptly he looked ashamed. "Uh-oh, I guess I didn't do so good, did I?"

"It's okay," Lily said hastily. "I won't tell anyone else, I swear. And I won't even tell Crystal that you told me. She'll never know. I swear."

Ryan's hand, small and cold, found hers. "Can we go back, Lily? Please?"

It only took a moment for her to nod. "You bet we can, Ryan. We're out of here tomorrow."

Chameleon.

The word came to Lily just as she was about to drift off to sleep, and it made her eyes open wide in the darkness. Of course— she should have made the connection when Ryan had first told her about it. She'd gotten a glimpse of this, or something like it, in Savanna; despite everything that had happened since then, the memory was as fresh as if it had happened yesterday. Of course Crystal and Frank wouldn't want it known that their children were like this: how much easier it would be for them all to hide if Naomi and her troop of deviants had no clue what it was they searched for. And to keep it a secret that there were two babies— Lily had to grin at the couple's resourcefulness.

But . . . God. More road time, traipsing across the country like migrant farm workers following the harvest . . . except here there was nothing to reap. Then again, maybe there *was*. Eddie—such a sweet guy, but he was lost to her forever. It didn't take a college degree to know that the reason he shadowed Naomi was in her stomach: his child, conceived in another lifetime but doomed for birth into this one—unless Eddie saved it. In the meantime, Lily could fend for herself, but in the eyes of Naomi and her twisted group, Ryan was prey . . . *food*. They slavered after him like a pack of hyenas waiting for a lioness to leave her cub undefended for the smallest of instants. Lily would not sacrifice this child to soothe her own loneliness; if such a thing was meant to be, then somewhere out there was a person for her, a companion free of the shackles of some bloodsucking bitch who hid in the darkness like a bat. Other things loomed in the future, too, but the prospect brought a bittersweet joy that she didn't want to think about right now.

Almost asleep, for some reason Gena's words floated back to her, and Lily knew that *this* was what Gena had been prophesying; *this* was the time at which Ryan would have died if Lily had not been at his side.

Nothing like fulfilling the future.

SEPTEMBER 11 . . .

"My God," Eddie said. He knew his mouth was hanging open because he could taste the drops of dirty rain catching on his lower lip. "You can't be serious."

They were standing around a fire, a small one that lacked the warmth of the ones they had shared with Frank and Crystal back at Greens Fork. If that wasn't enough of a reason for Eddie to feel cold, Lily's words had just cut the rest of the warmth right out of his life. Right now she said nothing, just looked at him across the feeble orange glow; Ryan stood quietly at her side, his expression reflecting a stubborn side that Eddie hadn't known existed.

"W-when?" Eddie managed. He jammed his hands into his pockets to stifle the urge to cover his face.

"Now," Lily said quietly.

"We came to say good-bye," Ryan added seriously. "We didn't want to go away without telling you."

"Just like that?" He stared at them. "You couldn't even give me a day or two—"

Lily cut him off with a wave of her hand. "No. It wouldn't be safe, Eddie." Her gaze cut to the right, where Naomi sat with a couple of her cronies, seemingly staring at nothing but somehow seeing everything. Eddie knew exactly what Lily was wondering, and hadn't he had the same question run through his own mind a dozen times?

If she had half a chance, what exactly would Naomi do to little Ryan?

Lily had found a way to be sure the question would never be answered.

Eddie's shoulders slumped and he nodded. "Yeah. I see what you mean."

Ryan's earnest face peered up at him. "You could come with us?" he said in more of a question than statement. "You don't have to stay here with . . ." He shot a fearful look in Naomi's direction. *"Her."*

Eddie took a deep breath and let it out, wished briefly that it was hot and heavy with the smell of the sea and salt as it had been back in New Orleans. He bent his knees and lowered himself until he was even with Ryan, then tried to smile when his eyes met the child's. "I can't go, little buddy. There are other reasons I have to stay here. At least for now."

"Maybe you could come and meet us later," Ryan said hopefully.

Eddie glanced at Naomi, then couldn't meet Ryan's eyes again. Instead, he found a twig on the ground and poked at the mud with it. "That's a pretty big 'maybe,' " he said at last.

"Oh."

Oh. That single syllable said that Ryan understood it all. "It's a pretty big country," he said to try to offer an explanation. "We—"

"I think we'd better get going," Lily interrupted. "Before we end up . . . delayed."

Eddie realized that Lily's eyes had hardened and that she was watching Naomi closely out of the corner of her eye. "Yeah," he said. As heartsick as he was about losing them, he wanted more to see them safe. Lily was as strong as a she-bear, but she was still just one; what could she, even joined by Eddie, do if Naomi and her cohorts actually attacked? "You guys . . . finish getting your stuff together. I'm going to go talk to Naomi for a little while." He reached out and gave Ryan a companionable tweak on the nose. "Take care of Lily for me, Ryan."

Ryan's eyes filled with tears. "Please, Eddie—"

Eddie would have automatically backstepped if Lily's hand hadn't fallen on the child's shoulder and stopped him. "No,

Ryan," she said quietly. "You mustn't do anything to let the others know we're leaving, remember? Just say good-bye."

Ryan sniffled and looked down at his shoes, Batman sneakers so covered with mud that the dark knight wasn't visible anymore. "Bye," he mumbled. One small fist came up and rubbed at his cheek.

Looking as though nothing were different than yesterday, Eddie turned and started walking toward Naomi, reminding himself that the life of the unborn child he saved was surely worth the pieces of himself that would die today.

"Take care of yourself, Eddie," he heard Lily say softly. For some reason her soft tone brought back the times—precious few—that they had been together, and the way she had murmured in his ear as he held her. "And always watch your back."

He nodded without looking behind him. Damn Naomi for what she had done to his life, Eddie couldn't even hug the two people he loved most in the world as they walked out of his life forever.

LITCHFIELD, ILLINOIS
SEPTEMBER 12 . . .

The screaming was over at last.

Alva didn't know where the other had come from, only that she was there and her hands were rough but capable as they kneaded her convulsing belly and worked to turn the too small baby inside into a position to be born. Never, *ever* had Alva imagined such pain—it was like having your guts and back squeezed inside the world's biggest vise grip, and all she wanted was to shoot the fucker who was turning the handle. But this baby *would* be born, tonight, regardless of its tiny size in the face of a brutal world and whether or not its mother was ready. Not to mention sans sodium pentothal or something else that might've helped Alva get a grip on the monstrous agony rippling through the layers of muscle deep in her abdomen.

"Look," the woman said. She held up a dripping, twitching thing that rocked in and out of Alva's exhausted vision. "You have a son."

"Great," Alva croaked. "Let's have a fucking party." Her wisecrack was barely understandable. "Where—*shit!*" Another pain bloomed inside her and she bit down on the rag the woman had given her earlier to stifle her cries. When it passed, Alva glared at the other as though the whole thing were her fault. "Why isn't it over?" she demanded.

"You have to pass the afterbirth," the woman said calmly. To add to her words she crawled to a position at Alva's side and began to massage the loose skin of her stomach; it felt like the world's most painful massage. "This will help."

"Oh, *God.*" Alva moaned and her head fell back on the hard wad of a blanket that served as a pillow. "Isn't this ever going to be *over?*"

"Soon," the woman said cheerfully. "Very, very soon."

The woman's name, Alva learned, was Lishe. Now that she had her wits back, Alva could see that her benefactor was dark-skinned and Mediterranean, with a solid, heavy build much like Joey's. She also wasn't alone, and Alva caught glimpses of her two children—a boy of about ten and a pre-teenage girl—as she drifted back to sleep after breast-feeding her son every two hours. She wished she were as strong as this woman, but that would have to wait until later, when the bleeding that periodically soaked the rags the woman put underneath her finally slowed. Too, she wanted to know just where Joey had found this woman and her family, and what it would mean to them now that there were so many to feed.

"There," Lishe said. "See how strong he is, after not even two weeks' time. It is because you gave him mother's milk."

"Wonderful," Alva muttered. She pushed herself up on her elbows and felt immediately exhausted by the effort. *Damn it!* When was she going to be back to normal? To make matters worse, she jostled the baby and he began to wail.

"Have you chosen a name yet?"

Alva glared at Lishe, but the other woman's expression remained implacable, patient. Nothing got under this babe's skin, and Alva wished she could find her revolver and point it at Lishe's face—maybe that would wipe off her worldwise look. Thanks for the help and all that, but the more time the woman spent with her, the less Alva liked her. And trust? Forget it; the last person Alva had trusted had been her mother, and she'd died in 1988. What she needed was something to give Lishe and her two spooky brats a little motivation to take off for better hunting grounds. Where the fuck had that gun disappeared to?

"No, I haven't chosen a name yet," she said sarcastically. "I haven't really given it much thought."

"In my country a child must be named by its mother—or father, if the mother does not survive the birth—within a week or it can be claimed by another." Lishe studied her. "Do you not want this baby?"

"What I want is for you to leave me alone," Alva snapped. If only her body were as strong as her temper! "And this is not . . . wherever it is you come from. This is America, and I'll take as long as I like to name the boy. If I want to leave him as he is until he's ten, it's my decision."

"I see."

Alva stared at Lishe, her eyes narrowing. Something wasn't right here; this was the first day she'd felt well enough to do anything but sleep and the fog was trying to lift from her brain. Odd, how Lishe and her children had appeared just when they were needed the most, to help with the birth. What else were they . . . *helping* with? "Where do you come from, anyway?"

The other woman shrugged. Beneath a man's heavy shirt, the movement of her shoulders was muscular, like a pose by one of those steroid-pumped female bodybuilders. "It does not matter. As you say, we are all here now, in America."

Alva had never felt comfortable with the woman around, though being caught up in hard labor and the semi-hemorrhaging that came afterward had given her little choice. Now every mental alarm bell in her brain was screaming. Where was Joey? He wouldn't leave her with Lishe, not if he thought—"Sometimes people bring their customs with them." The words spilled from her mouth unwillingly.

Lishe looked up at her and beamed. Her teeth were very white and strong against lips a natural brownish-red. Like Joey's had once been, the woman's eyes were nearly black, darkened further by the oily spill of thick black hair that escaped its knot at the base of her neck. "Yes, yes!" The smile widened across her broad, dusky face. "You *do* understand—that is good."

Alva's heart skittered and resumed its beat, a slow thunder pulse of terror in her arteries. "Understand?"

Lishe nodded vigorously. From the back pocket of her denim

jeans, she produced a heavy, ridged hunting knife—Joey's. "It is good," Lishe repeated as she came toward Alva.

"My explaining . . . is sometimes not so clear."

Joey caught the rich smell of cooking meat not far from the camp. A stew of some kind instead of roasted or dried meat—it'd been a long time since he'd had something like that. Lishe was tending to an oversized cast-iron pot sitting directly on the wood, stirring it often to keep the contents from burning. In her arms, wrapped securely against the cold drizzle and out in the fresh air for the first time, was Joey's small son.

He stared at Lishe, then glanced back at the tent questioningly.

"She is gone," Lishe said simply. On the other side of the fire, her two children watched him warily, their lean faces waiting for his judgment.

Gone?

Lishe reached forward and stirred the food again, then lifted a battered spoon and offered him a taste. Joey took the spoon and brought it to his lips, hesitating.

Did he really want to know?

He slid the contents of the spoon into his mouth, savoring the rich, fatty taste of the meat before handing the spoon back and nodding his approval. Then he used his finger to prod at the baby's wrappings until he found a tiny, waving fist; the moment he touched the fingers, they curled securely around his. The woman before him was warm and willing and far, far stronger than Alva had been, much more capable in the survival matters at which Alva had only scratched. On this edge of the future, the years ahead with Lishe would be fertile and solid.

Joey smiled. "What do you think we should name my son?"

EAST ST. LOUIS, ILLINOIS
SEPTEMBER 22 . . .

"Naomi, are you out of your fucking mind? I can't believe you'd even consider staying *here*—of all the places we've been, this is the worst!"

"It's perfect."

"No, it's not 'perfect,' " Eddie yelled. "It's filthy and flooded and full of more rats than I've ever seen in one place. For Christ's sake, the river's so full of bodies we can't possibly drink the water. And it's *dark*, damn it. *All the time*. Do you want to spend the rest of your life feeling your way down the street?"

"I can see just fine," Naomi said calmly. "And we have fire— we're not exactly cavemen, Eddie. A decade from now somebody will figure out how to make an electric lamp work again. Maybe it'll even happen tomorrow." She folded her arms. "This is where I'm staying, funny man. Like it or not."

"I won't let you," he said hotly. "I will not have my baby born into this mess when there are plenty of places that are healthier and safer. Or maybe I just imagined the way you kept looking behind us earlier? You felt it, too—"

"Sure," she said. "Hunters. Like us. The place is full of them." She tossed her head. "And you don't have any choice. Your baby, my baby—what's the difference? It's inside *my* belly. No one asked you to come along, and no one's making you stay."

He opened his mouth, then closed it again, his fists balled uselessly at his side. Poor little Eddie, Naomi thought in amusement. Who would've thought that last kinky poke they'd had at Althaia would lead him here?

"The baby needs me," he finally said.

She laughed. "You're too much a white knight, always trying to rescue people. I would've thought you'd learned your lesson in New Orleans. The baby would never know the difference."

"Yeah," he sneered. "I'll just bet."

Naomi laughed again, unruffled. "What?" she said mockingly. "You think I'm going to cut the kid up and eat it?"

"Something like that."

"Don't be absurd," she said. She gave him a sardonic grin. "I'm not going to murder my own child. I am not a killer."

She had to hand it to him for bravery. "Maybe not, but things are different now," he snapped. "*You're* different. Some things are worse than—"

"Death?" Naomi rolled her eyes. "Oh, boy. Did you come up with that line all by yourself?"

Eddie grabbed at her arm. "Don't mock me, Naomi—I'm serious!"

"Fuck *off*," she snarled in response. Stronger than she looked, and he got a nasty surprise when her shove sent him stumbling backward. Suddenly furious, she stomped toward him, gratified to see him scuttle backward uncertainly. "This is where I want to be, and this is where I *stay*. This is a good place for me—I can feel it!

You complain about the rats?" In a move too fast for Eddie to follow, Naomi bent and snagged something amid a pile of rubble at their feet. When she held it up, he gasped at the squirming, squealing rodent in her hand, its head forced at an upper angle that kept it from biting. "This is *food,* whitebread boy. The *rats* are what you'll be eating when the canned goods run dry." She flung the creature into the darkness.

"I can sense and smell everything around here—the animals, the people . . . more than enough to take care of us. You want to know what's worse than death, Eddie? Well, I'll *tell* you." His agility was nowhere near the rat's and he simply wasn't quick enough to jerk out of her reach when she hauled him forward, pulled him right up close so she could scream straight into his pale, self-righteous face. "Being *hungry* all the time!" She pushed him away, watching without emotion as he fought for balance and finally found it, his mouth a grim, tight line when he glared at her.

"I will never, *ever* be like that again," she said in a low voice. "I swear it, no matter what."

Naomi left Eddie standing there, his eyes wide and fearful in the night.

9.
THE BIRTH OF THE LIGHTZONE

GREENS FORK, INDIANA
SEPTEMBER 23 . . .

"I haven't felt safe since that woman tried to get to the babies, Frank. I'll never feel safe unless we leave this place behind us."

"You're just experiencing paranoia," Frank said reasonably. "It's very common in times of extreme stress—"

"I don't need a psychology lesson!" Crystal glared at him. "Oh, I could just *shake* you—sometimes you're just too damned smart for anyone's good. Don't you ever think with your heart instead of your brain? Here—" She leaned over and scooped Calypso from her spot next to her brother atop the mound of blankets, then thrust the infant at her husband. "Hold your daughter and remember how it was to see the knife slit in the back of the tent. Then tell me again how it's nothing but paranoia."

For a while after the babies were born, Frank had found it . . . difficult to accept them. Although he'd never admitted it, she knew this as well as she knew the feel of her own heartbeat in the darkness or how to identify which child was crying without opening her eyes—Calypso always half hiccuped first. Holding the weight of his fragile daughter, Frank looked stricken, and for a moment

Crystal felt ashamed—but she'd be damned if she'd let a misplaced sense of guilt cost her the edge she had on this argument.

"Well?"

"But Naomi and the others are gone," Frank protested. In his arms, Calypso whimpered and he automatically shifted her upright and leaned her against his shoulder, rubbing her back soothingly. Whether he knew it or not, he'd slipped easily into the role of father and provider, protector—*if* she could just get past this final stumbling block. "For almost a month now," he added.

"To the day, as a matter of fact," Crystal said tightly. She gestured at their tent and the small, worn circle of ground surrounding it, the firepit charred black from constant use. "There's nothing so special about this place that we can't find the same somewhere else. The sky gets lighter every day, and this morning it even stopped raining for a couple of hours. You told me that you thought the light side of the Earth was to the east; I say let's go there."

"We'll cook," Frank said promptly. "With the same side locked toward the sun all the time, I can't even begin to guess how high the surface temperatures will climb. It'll be desert, unfit to live in."

An impish grin flicked over Crystal's face. "It's probably the closest we'll ever get to being back in Arizona."

"That's out of the question," he said impatiently. "Radiation, lack of water—"

"Oh, for crying out loud, I'm *joking*." She glared at her husband and at least he had the decency to look embarrassed. "We don't need to go all the way to the middle—I don't want to die of dehydration any more than you do." With Frank holding Calypso, Crystal bent and picked up Schuyler, cradling their son's body as though he were made of glass. Her eyes grazed Frank's, then lowered briefly. "Look, I know things have turned out . . . differently than we thought they would. But it's not just the babies—*we're* different, too. People like Naomi . . . I don't think they can survive as well in the same places that we can—I think that's why she didn't try to come back."

"Maybe Eddie and Lily wouldn't let her," Frank suggested.

"Maybe. Or maybe she killed them." Crystal turned her face toward the east and stared at the sky above the tree line. There was no question about it; it *did* look lighter. "I say we put as much distance between us and her as we can, Frank. If we move east and into the sun, maybe we can find a place where it's bright and dry and actually feels like home to all of us."

Crystal could read the answer in his eyes.

UNKNOWN BROADCAST
SEPTEMBER 26 . . .

"Pax Bailby, coming to you from the other side of Durbin, Indiana. I pulled out of there this morning; wasn't much to see, a bunch of ramshackle shelters thrown together, a small group of people who looked as worn out and used up as the stuff they were trying to nail up. It's kind of sad, really—seemed like a good location, fresh water, lots of farmland around, but I guess everyone there just kind of . . . gave up. Sure, there wasn't much sun this summer and it was cold, but the sky's a whole lot lighter now and the temperature isn't as chilly. We might not have the abundance of crops like we used to, but there are plenty of varieties—hell, I used to see them in the 'seasonal' aisle at the grocery stores—of vegetables that'll grow in partial sun or shade. Not as much, maybe . . . but there aren't as many people to feed now either.

"Anyway, Durbin's pretty much a ghost town, like a thousand others I've seen on my way east. For a while I had the idea I'd go right through Indianapolis, see what I could find in the way of supplies—figured in a city that size, there'd be plenty to go around. Hadn't been there since I was a child—and then only in the bus station—so I didn't know much about it except it was big and if there was anyplace in Indiana that there ought to be people left, I figured that was it. Big mistake—the place is a warzone. I could hear the gunfire a mile away. Hey, I'm no fool; I never got close enough to get a personal view, but I did talk to a family coming out of there. They said they'd gotten out because there were bands of people taking over and 'cleaning out' entire blocks of the city. The cleaning-out process included appropriating whatever supplies they wanted and leaving the bodies behind, and it was a toss-up as to whether or not they'd burn what they didn't take. The gunfire, I was told, could be either a clean-out crew or the watch groups that were springing up to fight back, or both. This man and woman had a couple of kids with them and seemed to have a lot of hope that the vigilante groups would make places livable again; I didn't have the heart to remind them that sometimes the cure is worse then the sickness. There was a big age difference between the kids, a boy and a girl, and I think they might've lost one of *their own along the way. I didn't feel right about asking such a personal question, though; it felt too much like I'd be reminding them of painful memories. I did warn them away from the west—we had a good long talk and they shared some beef jerky strips they had—and told them what I'd been through, even invited them to head east with me. They weren't taken with the idea of the east coast—if such a place exists anymore—and said they thought they'd go south if moving west was a bad route. I don't think they really believed me until I showed them my journal and they paged through it . . . hell, I couldn't make up a story as scary as that business back in Illinois. I hated to throw more bad news on their shoulders, but maybe it would help keep them alive a little longer. When we went our separate ways, they were headed in a south-west loop around the city. I never did get their names.*

"*Despite the reports about the clean-up crews and the roving bands of folks doing the same along the highways, I think America's on the mend—at least this little strip of it, anyway. Over all, it's a damned small section when you think about how huge this country was before Millennium hit us. I guess I've only come four, maybe five hundred miles, and in that time I've gone from total blackness to a steady light gray. I don't think I'm too far off in figuring that if I don't get a day and night where I am, no one else gets one either. As a little stupid humor, there used to be a daytime soap opera called* As The World Turns. *Well, if there's no day and night, I guess it just doesn't anymore.*

"*I feel a lot better about being in the open here in Indiana. The soldiers have all but disappeared, and I'm not afraid of getting my face shot off if I see someone else up the road and call out to them. It's good to let go of the impulse to hide just because there's another human being around. You still don't see many, but now when you do there's a good chance they'll talk instead of run or try to kill you. So I'm headed east, if for no other reason than to see if there's anywhere out there where the sun really shines through the cloud cover. Who would've thought I'd forget what that looked like, huh? Now it seems more like an impossible fantasy. I've gone from worrying about publisher's royalty checks and personal HMO insurance to hunting for a single beam of sunlight. Go figure.*

"*Okay, Pax Bailby signing off. If there's something interesting to report . . . well, you'll hear it. As I said, we seem to be on the mend, but every place still looks like any other. They're all blasted out and wrecked, so I might just save my air. But hey, if something really wonderful happens, well . . . whoever you are out there, you'll be the first to know . . ."*

GREENS FORK, INDIANA
SEPTEMBER 29 . . .

He tried really, really hard not to cry, but in the end, he couldn't help it.

"Hey, c'mon, short stuff." Lily knelt next to him and pulled him into a hug. "It's not the end of the world."

"Yes, it *is*!" Ryan cried. He tugged away from her embrace and when he was a few feet away, kicked savagely at a rock. "Why does everyone always have to *leave*?" he demanded.

Lily sighed and rubbed at her temple with one hand. "I can't answer that, Ryan." She peered around the field, but there was nothing to give them a clue as to where or when Frank and Crystal had taken their babies and gone. The only fresh footprints along the muddy, flattened ground were their own; all the others had long since been washed into indistinct depressions by the drizzle. She stood and cracked her knuckles. "But they didn't head west or we would have run right into them—provided they followed the interstate. I'd say there's a good chance they went east. Which would make sense, of course—Crystal would want to stay as far away from Naomi as possible."

"What if they're dead?"

She looked surprised at his question, as if the idea had never occurred to her. "I . . . well, then I guess there's nothing we can do about it," she said matter-of-factly. When Ryan stared at the ground and didn't say anything, she continued. "But we don't know that they are, so until I see some bodies, I'm going to keep thinking positive." Lily studied him carefully. "How about you?"

"I . . . dunno." Ryan walked along the tree line, his gaze reluctantly searching the line of broken branches and soggy brush, his gut knotted with the fear that he'd see something he didn't want to—the arm of the jacket Crystal had always worn, Frank's dumb purple flannel shirt, a diaper-sized rag covered in blood. Lily didn't say anything, just watched and waited to see what he'd do. That was one of the coolest things about her—for a grown-up, she wasn't pushy at all. When he'd made a full circle of the field and found nothing, he was back at her side with his hands shoved into his pockets and feeling no better than he'd been ten minutes earlier. "I just don't see how we'll ever find them," he said dejectedly.

"Oh, I don't know." Lily smiled. "People are pretty predictable, and sometimes the smarter they are, the more you can guess what they'll do."

Ryan frowned. "What?"

Lily began to head back toward the sloppy driveway that had once been the entrance into this pasture; now its dirt surface was soupy and pocked with treacherous, water-filled holes. Ryan followed her because he didn't have anything better to do. "Frank is a scientist type," she told him as they picked their way along the edge of the drive. "Didn't you ever notice how teachers at school always did things the same way? You and me—we're more . . . relaxed. We kind of wandered around on the way back here, going down one road or another because it looked interesting or just because we felt like it. Frank and Crystal won't travel like that." At the end of the drive, she was up and over the ditch and the remains of the barbed-wire fence in seconds, and Ryan had to admire how quick and smooth she was, especially for a girl. She held out her hand and he grabbed it—after all, she *was* bigger than he was—and let her swing him across. "They'll go whichever way is quickest, safest, most *logical*. Just like a teacher." She grinned. "They'll be easy to follow."

"I don't know," Ryan said again. He wanted to believe, but every time he did, the person he was counting on took off for some reason or another. The hows or whys didn't matter; it was like he *jinxed* them or something. He hadn't liked his dad much, but his mom, Aunt Erica, Eddie . . . What if he started to believe in Lily, or in Frank and Crystal, and something happened to them, too?

"Well," Lily said brightly. "Sometimes you just gotta run with it, whether you like it or not."

Ryan wondered if she'd read his mind.

HEBRON, OHIO
OCTOBER 4 . . .

"Frank, do you think I made a mistake?"

Years of familiarity made it easy for Crystal's voice to wake him, and Frank opened his eyes and saw, immediately, the dull grainy ceiling of their tent. After so many months of almost total darkness, he couldn't stop appreciating being able to see the simple things now: the interior surface of the canvas shelter,

Crystal's clear lapis eyes, the strangely changing facade of his children's skin. Yes, even that.

"What are you talking about?" he asked hoarsely. "Mistake in doing what?"

"Making you—*us*—leave Greens Fork."

He started to sigh out loud, stopped the sound only because he was afraid she would mistake it for something other than the plain weariness it was. He could tell her no, she hadn't; he could tell her yes, she had. Either would be a lie, because he didn't know. "Who's to say?" he finally said. "I think we're doing okay." He was silent for a moment. "I think you were right in that both of us feel safer. And while it's seemed like a long trip, it hasn't been hard."

"I'm ready to stop, I think."

Frank's eyebrows raised and he shifted inside his sleeping bag, fighting its confinement until he could turn and look at her. Her eyes were open and she was staring into space, looking at something he could only wonder about. "Really? It's only been two weeks."

"But it's been enough." She blinked, then pushed the hair out of her eyes and grimaced. "I'm ready to try and ... I don't know. Rebuild, I guess. Make some kind of a home for us and the babies." For a moment she was silent. "Do you think that's possible?"

"Oh, yeah." For some reason, Frank felt like grinning from ear to ear. "I won't say it'll be easy, but by God, it's possible."

"Here?"

Now it was Frank's turn to pause. "Maybe not exactly," he finally said. "But close. Very close." He reached over and squeezed her hand. "We're headed into an area where it's light, it's warm ... there seems to be a lot going for us finally. Not too populated or burned out ... in fact, I feel pretty good about the whole thing. I think by this time tomorrow we could be looking at our new homesite."

She flashed him a smile and he saw a little of the old Crystal in it, the laughter-filled girl he'd met in college. "I'd like a four-bedroom, please."

"Why four?"

"You and me, one for each of the kids, and one for Mom when she comes to visit."

He scowled at her for a second, then they both burst out laughing.

JACKSONTOWN, OHIO
OCTOBER 7 . . .

They were almost a month away from Eddie and Naomi when they walked into Jacksontown, Ohio.

Lily knew immediately that Frank and Crystal and the babies were somewhere in this town; it was an instinctive thing that blasted instantly through her senses, and the connection she made harkened all the way back to Savanna, Iowa, and the parked car full of people she'd only momentarily glimpsed. Now, in Jacksontown, Ohio, it was just a matter of finding the couple for whom they'd crossed three states.

If those folks wanted to be found.

What the hell am I looking for here? Lily asked herself four hours after they'd walked past the small green sign hanging from a metal post by one pathetic bolt that had announced the town limits.

A host of answers tried to jump to the forefront of her mind, and if it hadn't been for six-year-old—or was it seven by now?—Ryan, trudging gamely along at her side as she wandered the streets of this tiny Ohio town, she might have balled her fist and whacked herself on the head just to give her something else—like a headache—on which to focus.

In a way, she wanted as desperately as Ryan to find Frank and Crystal; after all, they were the closest thing besides Eddie that they'd had to sane human company since Mercy and Simon, Gena and Lamont. For Ryan it would be salvation—stability, a mom and dad figure, kids who would someday be playmates. But what would it gain *her*? There was a strange bitterness inside Lily when she thought of the couple and their babies, an achy reminder that she had come close, really *close*, to the concept of having a happy fucking little family of her own just like theirs. Her, Eddie and Ryan . . . all she'd needed was a house in the 'burbs and a station wagon. Oh—and another .5 child, just to support the statistic. Ha ha.

There was that urge to slap herself again, because it wasn't like she hadn't known how it was going to come out—Gena had certainly pulled all the mystery out of it. Lily could tell herself she'd gone with Eddie only to save Ryan's life, but was she any different from any other woman who'd driven down the "Maybe he'll change his mind and stay with me instead . . ." route? She'd seen for herself how easily the future could change—one small deviation, a last-minute change of heart, and everything Gena had predicted could've come out differently.

"Lily, do you think they left already?" Ryan piped.

Pushing aside the disturbing concept, Lily found enough wits to smile down at the boy. "Well, I suppose they could have," she said slowly. "But I don't think so. They're probably just being careful."

"Of us?"

"Of everything." They'd come in on the other side of Jacksontown and since then the signs of damage from the impacts had lessened, as though people—and it *had* to be more than one or two—were working through to clean it all up. She scanned the curb and the fronts of the trashed-out buildings, taking in the neat mounds of rubbish here and there and the noticeable lack of bodies—just like in Momence, where Howard Tanton and his townsfolk were turning it once again into a real place to live. A vicious sense of loneliness filled her, and suddenly she felt like bending over and throwing up.

"Lily?" Ryan's voice rose in alarm. "Lily, are you okay?"

"I'm fine," she managed. She wobbled a little and leaned forward, resting her palms on her knees. Her hands poked out the frayed sleeves of her jacket like pale, dusty starfish, trembling against the blotchy black leggings. "Just a little . . . tired, that's all."

"Then maybe you should rest."

Lily gasped and whirled in sync with Ryan to face the speaker. She almost lost her balance and someone else's hand, strong and warm, steadied her at the elbow. Her heart felt like it did a bungee-cord bounce in her chest, one deep loop—then abruptly calmed. At her side, Frank grinned easily, his face a little more weathered, his eyes no less welcoming. He nodded at her other side, and when she turned, Lily saw Crystal smiling at them, her arms loaded with two swaddled infants.

"Welcome to Jacksontown, Lily."

"So you guys have been here only a few days?" Lily asked, fascinated. "You can't have done all this cleanup work by yourselves."

"There are others here," Frank said. He glanced at his wife, who lifted one shoulder noncommittally. It was strange to see Crystal dressed in an oversized cotton shirt that kept sliding down one shoulder, unthinkable after this bizarre, freezing summer that she should be able to wear such a thing without a warmer outer covering. Nevertheless, the temperature in this area hovered at a steady seventy-five and Frank had speculated that it would eventually climb higher.

"Others," Lily said carefully, "who are . . . like you." Her mouth turned up in a wry grin. "That's very cool, you know. I could've used that kind of trick now and again."

Crystal looked at Frank nervously, but he didn't seem to know what to say in response. "I—"

Lily cut him off with a wave. "Oh, please—don't bullshit me. I saw a whole family like you in Iowa." Her grin got wider and she leaned forward. "You think you've got it made, huh? Wait'll you try to teach the babies not to move. That's what clued me into the people back in Iowa—the kids in the back seat couldn't sit still."

Frank looked embarrassed. "I'm sorry we never told you," he said. "We weren't sure we should."

Lily chuckled. "Hey, I wouldn't have told me, either."

"The others may take a while to warm up," Crystal said. "To them you're still a stranger. When you think about it, *we're* not much more than that."

"Is everyone here that . . . way?" Lily asked curiously. "I mean . . ." She shrugged self-consciously. "Isn't there anyone"— she stopped herself from saying "normal," but just barely—"plain, like me?"

Frank and Crystal glanced at each other, but couldn't meet her eyes. Finally, Frank shook his head. "No."

"Yet," Crystal added hastily. She reached forward and touched Lily's arm lightly—more strangeness, to feel human contact against her flesh, itself bared to the warmth of the sun. The sunlight felt good, heated and . . . *precious*. "Don't be in such a hurry to move on, Lily. Give it time. You found your way here, and so will other people." Crystal's fingers inched forward until they curled around Lily's wiry wrist and gave it a soft squeeze. The words she said next warmed Lily more than anything else in the world could have.

"There's no place on the face of this Earth that's better for you than right here with us."

Well, Lily thought, looking around. It sure wasn't her apartment back in Chicago. *That* had been filled with cockroaches, and this was a whole lot cleaner.

She snickered to herself, then tiptoed to the far end and checked on Ryan; he was as sound asleep as she'd ever seen him, actually *snoring,* for Chrissakes. If anything told her they were finally somewhere safe, this child's simple, deep sleep did it. She made her way back to her own cot, still marveling at the idea of actually having an *inside* to sleep in; this small, stand-alone bakery was one of several places that had been fixed up as temporary shelters. Sooner or later, she would have to stake a claim to something more permanent off the main drag of the town, but Frank had told her no one would expect her to think about that for at least a couple of weeks. The others, he'd added, would probably start introducing themselves tomorrow.

Sitting on the edge of her cot and pulling off her boots with a gasp of relief, Lily tried but couldn't recall the deep sense of loneliness that had hit her earlier in the day. Maybe thinking about Mercy, who was always in the back of her mind like a lost sister, had brought it on. But Mercy didn't need her anymore; she had Simon, and Gena and Lamont, and a life in Momence that would ultimately let her use her talents to help people while getting her "fix" of healing at the same time. Mercy's life had purpose, and Lily had to admit that if she'd stop wallowing in self-pity, she'd see that her own life was starting to shape up as well. Before Mercy, her existence had been nothing but a walking psychotic nightmare. Now she was okay; thin but incredibly strong, always a natural-born fighter. In a way she felt like a tamed mountain lioness walking amid these gentled people.

But her life wasn't quite reduced to monotony yet, oh no. More interesting times were yet to come. Damn it, Lily thought, but without any real anger. Nothing ever went the way a person expected, although there was very little she could predict nowadays. It was over a week now and there was no sign of the backache and cramps that had always signaled the onset of her time of the month. She might have been crazy-in-the-head Lily, but she'd always been regular as the sunrise when it came to that—

Uh-oh. Lily grinned, feeling panicky and a little exhilarated all at once; time to find a new comparison, something without clocks and sunrises.

It looked like she was going to get that .5 child after all.

10.
THE WORLD IN GENERAL

MOMENCE, ILLINOIS
OCTOBER 14 . . .

The babies woke her early, as they had every morning in the month since they'd been born. Neither had learned the fine art of sleeping through the night yet.

Mercy felt Simon stir beside her, heard him mumble something into his pillow. If she didn't get up now, he would, and while on more than one occasion she'd stayed where she was and pretended to be asleep just so she could watch him, it really wasn't fair to do it that often when she, more than Simon, tended to be the early riser. Smiling now, wide awake and thinking about how endearing it was to see Simon holding his son and daughter or changing their diapers with expert moves, Mercy climbed out of bed and tried not to jostle the mattress. Soft cries were coming from the single crib across the room, Disa and Thomas doing a fine job of waking each other up and *Hey, let's make sure Mom and Dad get up at five in the morning, too!* The not-very-strident wails fizzled out as she checked them for dryness, then hoisted them both into her arms for their first feeding of the day and went to sit in the beat-up rocking chair on the front porch. The climate here was pretty steady—mostly warm and damp—and Simon had scrounged up enough screening to make them a place to sit outside without getting ravaged by the mosquitoes. All in all, not a bad place to watch the empty morning street while she fed their children.

After all these years, Grandfather's tale had come back to haunt her, filling the nights before and after Disa and Thomas were born with perspiration-soaked sheets and bad dreams. The last time she'd thought about Shoi Lin had been when Erica had forced her out of medicine, and if nothing else had ever happened to her that reinforced that childhood warning, the destruction of her treasured medical career was the ultimate evidence that everything the old man had said was, sadly, true. So far, Mercy had been successful at playing doctor—and only that—in this small town. She'd slipped through the days with a mixture of satisfaction and dread; sooner or later, something would happen to reveal her secret—it always did, be it animals or hurt playmates in grammar school or suffering children in an emergency room.

Mercy's only solace in this was Gena, who seemed to have no inclination to give her insight about when and where; in some things, no news truly *was* good news, and Mercy had to believe that things would be okay. Otherwise, Gena would surely tell her ahead of time that . . . what? She shouldn't go in to the small medical clinic today? She shouldn't see so-and-so? Ridiculous; Mercy would no more listen to that than she had believed Gena's prediction of twins. *That* made Mercy feel guilty every time she thought about it; what must it be like to go through your life and have no one believe anything you said? Perhaps you got to the point where you simply stopped telling people things.

Tanton and his men carried the woman in at noon.

Lamont was with them when the door to the clinic burst open hard enough to slam against the wall behind it. Mercy had a single second to be grateful that there hadn't been glass in its window, then the small foyer was filled with the sounds of fear and confusion. The place was small, a converted cleaners chosen for its central location rather than size; half as many people would have made it seem crowded.

"Dr. Mercy!" Tanton bellowed. "We got us a real problem here!"

Mercy had been scrubbing down the counter that served as her examining table, savoring the rare smell of the pine-scented cleaner one of her patients had sent her. She dropped the rag in the bucket and hurried to the front. Four men clutched a corner of a stained sheet, and when Mercy's eyes focused on the figure balanced in the center, her stomach felt like it dropped three inches inside her.

"Bring him to the back and put him on the table," she heard herself say.

"It's a 'her,' " Tanton said miserably as they all shuffled forward, the sheet sagging in their grips.

"What happened?" Mercy demanded. She glanced at Lamont, but the look on his face was clear—he had no idea.

"We were trying to get a tow hook around one of the wrecked trucks down at the Beuchel dairy farm so we could pull it out of the drive," Tanton told her. "I don't know *what* happened. We got the chain on, we pulled, and the damned thing blew up. Must've been a pinhole leak in the gas tank and a spark or something. Vivian's job was to sit inside the truck and steer if it was needed." The big man's face was smudged with soot and dirt and he looked ready to cry. "The only reason she's here instead of in a million pieces is that she'd left the door open and the blast threw her clear. But everything on her was burning when she hit the ground. We smothered it as fast as we could, but . . ." He hung his head, and no one else in the room except Lamont could look her in the eye. "She's . . . we know she's probably not going to make it. But we had to bring her here, just in case."

Mercy's gaze ran down the figure on the table. It was easy to see how she would have assumed it was a man—all the scalp and facial hair was gone, as was most of the exposed skin. The woman had been wearing a shirt and blue jeans, but now it was impossible to tell where the charred material ended and the scorched flesh began; it all ran together in a soupy, black-and-red surface that stank of burned meat. Without turning her over, Mercy was betting she was burned over ninety-five percent of her body.

Tanton edged around the table until he was within earshot of only Mercy and Lamont. "I know you don't have the equipment to help her," he whispered. He shot a furtive glance at the others, but they were all staring at Vivian in horrified fascination. "I was hoping that you could give her something to help her not hurt so much. To make her a little more comfortable until . . . uh, in the meantime."

Mercy scowled; she had nothing strong enough to handle a case this severe. She looked at Lamont helplessly, knowing he was waiting. Dear God, he had been through this same thing—didn't he understand her fear? Her phobia about discovery? Yes, he did. She could see the answer in his eyes . . . and the solution. She cleared her throat. "Maybe everyone could just step out of the room," she began. "Then I could—"

"Vivian!" The wail came from the front of the office, and Mercy's breath caught. "Where is she? *Where's my wife?*" Less than a second later, another man, someone Mercy had seen around town but never spoken with, barged into the back room. He wasn't that big, but terror made him sound like he weighed a hundred pounds more than he did; judging from the number of men it took to slow him down, hysteria was a pretty good fuel. When he saw the still figure on the table, he started screaming and seemed unable to stop. *"Oh my God oh my God oh my God—"*

"Barney," Tanton pleaded, "you've got to try and calm down. Dr. Mercy will do everything she can to make Vivian comfortable—"

"Comfortable?" Barney cried. He tried to lunge free but Mercy guessed Lamont had a quiet hand in his being unable to do so. "That's not going to do any *good*! Look at her—"

"Barney," one of Tanton's men said desperately. "You don't want your wife to hear stuff like that. You—"

"Please," Mercy said sharply. "If you'll all calm down and step outside—"

The woman on the table choked and began to claw at her throat. An instant later everything about her began to jerk and the room erupted in shouts.

"She's having a seizure!" Tanton shouted. "Hold her down—"

"Don't touch her!" Mercy ordered. She shoved the nearest person aside, but before anyone could stop him, Barney wriggled out of the hands that were holding him and grabbed for his wife. It didn't matter to him what she looked or felt like as he tried to hoist her into a sitting position.

"She can't breathe!" he wailed.

Dimly, Mercy thought she heard Lamont yelling something to her, but the bedlam in the room overrode it. She'd thought the need to heal was gone, hadn't felt a thing vaguely resembling it since that last round with Eddie. If this was what her body had led her to believe, then it had lied; all of it, from the skull-splitting overload headache all the way to the sudden cold sweats and ferociously itching hands, returned in a single, time-stretched second.

No!

The drawn-out shriek filled Mercy's head but no one else heard it, and the fingers that felt like raw skin rubbed with liquid poison ivy *had* to belong to someone else because she had no control over them. Surely she was on the other side of the room and watching a shadow of herself step forward and take a precise, bare-handed hold on each of Vivian's blistered upper arms.

Then the small, chaos-filled room was washed in blue-white lightning.

"Damnedest thing I ever saw," someone was saying.

The voice faded away and Mercy squeezed her eyes tight, trying to quell the instinctive urge to open them. The longer she could keep them closed, the longer she could hide and not have to face what she had done, not have to answer to these people who had thought she was normal all this time. Seven decades separated today from what had happened to her grandmother before Mercy was born, but Mercy could've sworn she was nothing but a destiny-driven reincarnation of a woman she'd never known.

"Mercy, I know you're awake."

Simon . . . of course. They would have sent for him, told him to come and get this ungodly woman who was supposed to be his wife but could no longer masquerade as something so mundane and normal. Her grandmother, Shoi Lin—

"—died a long time ago. Stop beating up on yourself. Tanton's stepped out; you can sit up now." Mercy couldn't stop her eyelids from opening when strong hands pulled her upright and Simon's breath, warm and familiar, tickled the skin of her cheek as he spoke.

"Simon," she whispered. "Oh, God. What have I done?"

"Nothing you weren't supposed to," he said firmly.

"But now everyone *knows*—"

"But it's okay," Lamont said from her other side. Mercy turned her head and saw him smile. Of everyone in the world, this strong, tranquil man could understand how afraid she was, yet he seemed not at all concerned. Did that mean it really *was* okay, and that the townspeople could live with what they'd seen without singling her out as a monstrosity? And what about her loved ones—Simon, Gena . . . and especially Lamont? How would they be treated?

Suddenly Mercy sat up straight. "The babies—where are they?" Her voice filled with panic.

"In the other room with Vivian and Barney," Simon said soothingly. She tried to squirm out of his arms and he caught her chin between his thumb and forefinger. "Come on, Mercy. You're always telling everyone else to calm down. It's time to listen to your own advice."

She squinted at him, finally realizing why she couldn't bring his face into focus. Her fingers searched the area around her—her own examining table, how *embarrassing*—without results. "Where are my glasses?"

"You broke them again," he said, sounding amused. "I swear I don't know anyone else who had more tape on their frames."

"Howard thinks they might be able to come up with a new pair of frames," Lamont said hastily. "It's just a matter of finding some that fit your lenses."

"So Vivian's okay?" Mercy looked at the two men hopefully and they both nodded. "And all those people who were right there . . . no one freaked out because of it?"

"There were a few folks who were pretty surprised, but only *you* passed out." Simon smiled as her cheeks reddened and Mercy didn't need her glasses to see the happiness and tranquillity etched into her husband's expression. "The rest of our world is as right with us as we are with them." He squeezed her hand. "Chin up, sweetheart. There's a couple out there who're probably tired of listening to the twins' hollering. I think they also want to say thanks.

"Like it or not, I think your medical practice is about to *really* take off."

NOVEMBER 8 . . .

"Gena, why are you on your feet? You should be resting, not wandering around in the middle of the night."

She could hear Lamont's concern, and perhaps he was right to be worried. So many hours of labor, yet here she was, walking alone, feeling her way along the railing at the back of the small cabin Lamont had restored at the southeast end of the town. Hearing his words like that, deep and soft in the darkness, brought back old times, when his voice had rolled out a custom narration for some movie she couldn't see, helped to paint a picture in her mind that neither of them could know would someday be filled in. Before then, she had never felt so safe and cared-for, so valued. It was so odd that Lamont could do that for her; stranger still that he had no idea he did. What, Gena wondered, do I do for him in return?

Love him, yes. But even more, I accept him.

Always.

Lamont stepped up beside her and put his hand on her arm, feeling the warmth of her skin and the slight tremble of exhaustion. "Thank you," he said quietly.

Gena's face tilted toward him and she gave him a slight smile. "For what?"

"For being with me," he answered. "For . . . my son."

She laughed lightly. "Oh, I think you had a little to do with that."

He grinned and twined his fingers in her hair, grown long and thick over these last months. He still trimmed her bangs for her, but he preferred the rest of it like this. It made her look like some wild Indian maid. "Yeah, but I had the fun part. Yours was more on the strenuous side."

"I think I had fun a time or two."

Still smiling, Lamont turned and stared toward the east and the sun that never set. They couldn't see it in Momence—too many things blocking the way and now that ball of fire rode perpetually low on the horizon—but tonight, perhaps in honor of the new life that he and Gena had welcomed, the sky was remarkably clear. Doubtlessly that would change within only a couple of hours, but for now only a few of the constant rain clouds scudded along.

A wind rose, then died as quickly as it had been born, leaving a dry rash of grit on their arms. Glancing at Gena, Lamont got the feeling that she was staring into the distance without him, seeing things in a way he never could. There was no sunrise, not anymore, and he found himself missing the way the sun had come up and warmed the sky and air, welcoming the day. During rare clear times like now, they could see how it lightened farther to the east, how somewhere out there the star that brought light and warmth to their planet now burned the unmoving ground with relentless power. He wished desperately that Gena could still see. How could he describe the way that, lower in the sky and miles away, the air was so red it seemed to be on fire?

With her new set of dark glasses left somewhere inside, Gena flicked her hair out of her face. Her eyes, so seldom seen, looked soiled white, like mistreated antique pearls. Those sightless eyes, he knew, scanned the things he missed and saw it all, but differently—the sweetly brutal sun in the east, the darkness that now ruled eternal on the other side of the world.

The future.

"I suppose it's time to rebuild," Gena said quietly.

He found her hand and squeezed, felt bones that seemed so fragile beneath her skin and marveled that she could have survived all this, that *any* of them had. "The worst of it is over," he said.

Her face turned in his direction and a chill washed over him at her expression, intensified by the eerie way the reddish haze reflected on the pale surface of her eyes. "Over?" Gena whispered. "Oh no, Lamont, it's not at all over. It's different, *changing*. In ways we can't understand or control—especially on the darkside." She gripped his hand, her grasp suddenly fierce. Lamont was unnerved to see tears spill from her eyes, their paths leaving trails of glittering moisture down her cheeks. "There are things we know very little about being . . . born in the world," she continued in a soft, vaguely hypnotic voice. "The stuff that myths are made of—the way the world was before Millennium hit, no one noticed or believed these . . . creatures or whatever they are existed. They were always pushed to the background by man's technology and advancement. Now all that's changed. Civilization still exists, but it's fragmented and weak. We've managed to survive, but elsewhere men kill each other over scraps of food and trinkets. For every wonderful gift we have here—your strength, my sight, the talents that Mercy and Simon possess—there's something as equally *evil* somewhere else. Most of the world is gone, Lamont, inaccessible. Either it's cold and permanently dark, or scorched and uninhabitable. No one knows what's going on out there." She turned her head toward him again, with that same terrifying shine in her film-coated eyes. "I'm glad we don't live forever," Gena said in a low voice. "I don't think I'd have the courage to face what the world's going to be like in two hundred years."

"So what you're saying," Lamont asked slowly, "is that we've brought a child into a world that's doomed?" For a moment he felt as if the entire planet were sliding out from under his feet.

"Not at all." Gena's hand found his arm and stroked it. "All this"—she waved her hand at the landscape—"is still beautiful. I can feel the sunlight every time it breaks through the cloud cover and touches my skin, the wind on my face. We live on a world that we don't know anymore and struggle along beneath the promise of future sunshine on the edge of everything. But when you think about it, isn't that what mankind has always done?"

"But it's . . . so unfair," he said. "We try so hard but every time we gain something we just seem to lose it twice over—"

Unexpectedly, she smiled. "I don't have to be Simon to know what you're referring to, Lamont. You think that I should be more miserable than ever because I was blind, then I could see, and now I'm right back where I started. What you haven't considered is my memory—do you know how *full* it is now? Visual memories are something I never had before. Now when you tell me that flowers growing in a field are yellow, I'll know what they *really* look like, what a 'field' is, what it means to be told that an apple is round and red. And that's a wonderful, wonderful thing, a gift that can never be taken away." She reached up and unerringly ran her fingers across the smooth skin of his cheek.

"Most of all," Gena said very, very softly, "I remember the sight of your face."

EAST ST. LOUIS
DECEMBER 1. . .

When Eddie walked out of the tent with his son bundled against him, they were all waiting.

East St. Louis was a bitterly cold and dark place, like Chicago had been during that last frigid winter when Naomi had been with him at Althaia. Tonight his son was two days old: tiny and unnamed, with wrinkled red flesh and those squinty blue eyes with which all newborns take their first dim view of the world. He had snatched the child almost from under Naomi's nose, with her lying exhausted not so much from the pain of the labor as from the blood loss—did she truly have so little to spare that she could not survive what to Eddie seemed like an absurdly short and easy labor? It was that brevity he believed saved the infant—from first pain to delivery, the entire thing took less than twenty minutes.

Hardly enough time for Naomi to cry out, much less catch the attention of her cultists.

"Did you really think we'd just let you walk out?" Naomi sneered.

Standing semi-paralyzed outside the tent flap, his child's weight amid the other supplies Eddie had stuffed into his backpack was hardly worth mentioning. Yet it was that small burden that mattered the most. "You don't need the baby," he said in a hushed voice. "You don't even want the responsibility. Let me pass." He had used strips of a sheet to wrap the infant against his stomach and chest in a makeshift carrier and now Eddie could feel the boy's warmth against his shirt as he slept, unconcerned about the fight for his life being waged by his parents.

"No." Naomi glared at him. "He's mine, he's . . . all of ours." Abruptly her hungry expression turned slightly dreamy. "Don't you see, Eddie? I think that's why he was born—to show us how we could survive. How we could *keep* surviving in the worst of times."

"What are you saying?" Eddie felt bile rise in his throat and choked it back. "Did I hear you right? My God—you'd use your own son for *food*?"

"But we won't hurt him," she said. "We all have a purpose. Did you ever consider that maybe this is his?"

"To be passed around and sucked dry like a fucking ice cream bar?" Eddie demand furiously. "I don't think so!"

"What you think doesn't matter." Her face hardened again and Naomi stared at him coldly. "Give him to me."

"No," Eddie said grimly.

His former lover nodded at a thin man standing next to her, another flunky from the ranks of her followers for whom Eddie had never bothered to get a name. "Take the baby from him."

Eddie's hands were free, everything he owned—including his son—in some way strapped to his body. He had learned well from his time with Lily; although he'd never seen her fight, Eddie had never forgotten the value of having a weapon that an adversary didn't know about. He was not Lily and he didn't know any swift moves or how to fasten a switchblade to his arm so that he wouldn't cut his own hand off when it opened, but the buck knife his fingers closed around when he shoved his right hand into his jacket pocket was reassuring and would do just fine. "Get away from me," he said hoarsely. He backed away. "I don't want to hurt you or anyone—I just want to leave. And my son is going with me."

He might as well have been talking to a tree stump, for all the emotion or response the guy showed. Had it not been for the feeble light from the small fires here and there up and down the area where they'd settled, the night in this place would have been absolute; the only thing that Eddie could see of the man coming toward him was his face—despite the frigid temperatures his skin was pale and sweaty around deepset, dull eyes. Like Naomi and everyone else but Eddie, he was dressed in black; for Christ's sake, the guy looked like nothing but a disembodied head floating through the air. Everything about him was strangely neutral: his expression, his steps, the way his hands moved when he made the mistake of reaching for Eddie's son.

Eddie tried to backstep and felt his pulse triple when he bumped into someone, another hungry crony crowding up behind him, fish-white fingers trying to reach around the backpack to the tiny bundle in front. Something tugged at his arm on the left—a woman, trying gamely to find an end to the wrappings so she could start untying the baby.

Instinct took over. He pushed the woman as hard as he could and stepped into the space where she'd been to get away from the person behind him, then withdrew the buck knife with his right hand. A quick jab at the man coming toward him was enough to make the guy hesitate and look toward Naomi uncertainly.

"I'll use this," Eddie said hoarsely. He was hunched forward, his upper body curling protectively over his child. "If you want this baby, you'll have to kill me first."

"Go on, Jess," Naomi ordered. "He won't do anything."

"Try me."

Never would Eddie have thought that Jess—or anyone—would be foolish enough to face him down when he was clutching a hunting knife and fighting for the life of his only son, nor would he have thought himself capable of lashing out with the razored edge of the blade and slicing through the skin and muscle along his attacker's collarbone.

The most bizarre thing about it was that Jess didn't cry out. He stayed quiet as he looked down in amazement at the fourteen-inch line of crimson that appeared across his upper body, never uttered a sound as blood erupted from the wound like paint squeezing from a cracked tube and creating a shine like oil against the black fabric of his sweatshirt. He touched the gaping wound as though not believing it could actually be there, then turned toward Naomi and held out his hand. The fingers were coated in blood, and whether or not this was what Jess had intended, she and the others needed no further invitation.

Fleeing as fast as he could, Eddie hoped to God that he would never have to tell his boy that the last sight of his mother was with others of her kind, fighting like an animal over the bleeding body of one of her own dying people. By the time Naomi and her group finished their ghastly meal, Eddie Cuerlacroix was far away and headed steadily toward the Grayzone, the first of many miles already past on his search for a name for his small son and a future for the both of them.

EPILOGUE
ADAPTATION

JACKSONTOWN, OHIO
DECEMBER 31, 2000 . . .

"Pax Bailby here, broadcasting on the last day of the year 2000 from a wide spot off the highway in Ohio, a place called Jacksontown. This'll be my last broadcast because . . . well, let's face it. I've never gotten a word transmitted back and I'm just not convinced anyone's left who's got the setup to listen. Besides, I've got more important things to think about now, and playing with radio signals when I never get any answer just doesn't seem to be that much of a priority.

"Still, I can't resist a final report before I trash this beat-up transmitter. Since I started spouting off on the airwaves last summer, it occurred to me that almost everything I had to report was bad—all the destruction from the asteroid hits, people killing other people, cannibalism—hell, I started to sound like the ten o'clock news used to in the 'good old days!' With all that terrible information, I just couldn't fade away without letting anybody who's listening know that there's some good in the world, too.

"Now, I'll admit I haven't personally seen the things I'm reporting here. I have come across some pretty strange stuff, and some of it I can't tell you about because I've been asked not to.

There's a scientist here in Jacksontown who gave me a clear picture on what he thinks happened to the planet, and what we can expect. Where I am now, he says, is right on the fringe of what's become the Earth's lightside, and he doesn't recommend I go any farther east. The sun always shines there—no darkness, very little cloud cover, no escape from it. And like Mercury, the Earth now has a darkside—I've passed through it, so I know. It's filled with a lot of things most normal folk don't want to face, so I'd stay the hell away if I were you. Right in the middle is what Frank—that's the scientist's name—calls the Grayzone. He says it's the terminus, the place where the light- and darksides meet, and figures it to be about five hundred miles wide going from dark all the way to light. Lot of weather in there, thunderstorms and what all, because of the hot and cold air fronts from both sides that are always colliding in the atmosphere. The temperature's in the sixties or so, not too bad if you can stand the humidity. Jacksontown's pretty warm—low nineties all the time—but after my time in the Darkzone cold, I'm pretty happy with it.

"The people here are good and kind, and I've heard stories about others like them in towns in that Grayzone strip of the States that I passed through on the way here. One place in Indiana is supposed to have a woman who can heal anything just by touch, a man who reads minds, another who can lift a car as easily as tissue paper, plus a woman who sees the future. My first reaction was to scoff, but when I thought about it, I started thinking that if we could have and accept all that was evil and deadly in the world, why can't we do the same for something good? Maybe because goodness is such a rare thing—it always has been. Ten years ago I wouldn't have doubted for a minute that a guy stepping up to me on a dark street was going to rob me, yet I remember seeing a television show that did an experiment that was exactly the opposite. They sent a man out in broad daylight to try and give away five-dollar bills, no strings attached—and no one would take them! Nobody trusted that this guy just wanted to do something for them that was nice. Amazing, isn't it? There's someone here who's seen these people and swears by them, and that's good enough for me—hell, I can use something good to believe in for a change.

"As for me, I'm starting the new year out right. My wife Dora was a good woman and I miss her—we had a lot of good years together. But here we are at almost 2001, with no Space Odyssey

to look forward to or supercomputers left to figure anything out for us. But it's almost another new year, one I never thought I'd live long enough to see. What better way to start it? I've met the most amazing woman. She's got white hair, wears army boots, and looks like she walked out of a Harley-Davidson biker magazine, even at six months pregnant. I'm crazy about her!

"So, everyone, this is Pax Bailby, saying so long from Jacksontown, Ohio. It may not be utopia but maybe it's as close as it's going to get for the next millennium."

About the Author

YVONNE NAVARRO is a dark fantasy writer who lives in a western suburb of Chicago. Her first short story appeared in *The Horror Show* in 1984, and since then her short fiction has appeared in over forty anthologies and small press magazines. Since 1989, she has also had twenty-four dark fantasy illustrations published and reprinted in the small press, with the most recent being a reprinted piece on the cover of the 1996 World Fantasy Convention's Progress Report No. 1. *Final Impact* is her fifth published novel, and she has also authored a reference book called *The First Name Reverse Dictionary* for writers and parents-to-be. Two of her previous novels were nominated as finalists for the HWA's Bram Stoker award, the most recent of which was *deadrush* in the category of Best Novel. She is currently working on several more novels, and invites readers to visit her web site at the URL listed on the Acknowledgements page to learn more about past and current projects.